OPERATION HERKULES

The Axis Invasion of Malta

A Novel of Alternate History

June 1942: Nine Days that Changed
the World

By Scott Ward

# Contents

# PREFACE

This is a work of fiction. It began with a question. Might WWII have gone differently had

Hitler not made so many strategic blunders? Eventually I wondered what last, single blunder he

might have avoided and still had a chance to win the war? From Dunkirk to Stalingrad I read all I

could find on these mistakes and realized that of them all, the story of the siege of Malta and the

blunder of omission, that of NOT seizing the island, was perhaps the least well known of Hitler's

gaffes, at least in the United States, and that as late as the spring or summer of 1942 he still had

the chance to correct his error.

From this sprang the idea of this novel of alternate history. In it we'll meet many well-

known and some lesser known historical figures, but also purely fictional characters whose

experiences reflect those whose ordinary lives were interrupted by extraordinary times. Kenneth

Wiltshire, an American farm boy and volunteer pilot with the RAF, flies Spitfire fighters and

fights for his life from Malta's Ta Qali airfield. His English lover, the beautiful and mysterious

Maggie Reed, toils in anonymity from Malta on Britain's most vital wartime secret. Kuno

Schact, German Army officer is drafted as a last minute replacement for the invasion. His

 dreams are haunted by fear that his two young sons will someday fight and die for the Third

Reich. Roland Webster, Royal Navy gunnery officer; only combat gives him relief from remorse

of his lost love Althea, killed in the London Blitz. Through their eyes and many others we'll live

 the Axis invasion of Malta in June 1942 and follow their adventures in subsequent novels as

WWII is refought from a new point of reality.

    I have attempted to hew to a reasonable and plausible alteration of history. Neither side will

 come to possess alian technology, nor suddenly stumble on the secrets of high energy lasers. But

from June 21, 1942, the day Tobruk in North Africa fell to Rommel and his Afrika Korp a

single, simple change could have reshaped our history. Herewith, what might have come, had

Hitler decided to take Malta, rather than not.

# OPERATION HERKULES

## DAY 1.
June 21, 1942

The ululating wail of air-raid sirens sent a chill down his spine and set his heart pounding. Kenneth's boots crunched on gravel as he and his wingman dashed from the air-operations shelter to the runway. The roar of aero engines shattered the pre-dawn.

"Up you go, Sir," shouted the ground crew chief, boosting Kenneth onto the wing of his Spitfire.

Kenneth climbed into the cockpit and began a quick scan of his instruments as the crew chief snapped him into his seat harness. With a pat on Kenneth's head the crew chief finished with the harness and slid the fighter's canopy cover forward and closed. Abruptly the wail of the sirens was gone and now only the roar of the engine could be heard. Kenneth reached up and snapped the catches on either side to lock the canopy in place, then looked out to his right where his wingman Andy was also just locking his canopy down. Kenneth flashed a thumbs-up sign, then without waiting for an answer pushed the throttles of the Spitfire forward. It began to roll up the runway just as the crew chief leapt from the wing and ran for the safety of the air-ops shelter.

Kenneth revved the engine and let the Spitfire out onto the taxiway towards the runway, falling in behind other machines already waiting their turn to take-off. A pair of Spits roared down the runway and into the brightening sky. Other pairs followed at half-minute intervals until at last it was Kenneth's turn. He and Andy raced down the runway of Ta Qali airfield, into the sky over Malta. He felt the same exhilaration he always felt at being airborne.

He climbed for altitude with all the power the Spitfire possessed. In the dogfight he knew was coming altitude was life itself. Looking out and behind him he was pleased to see Andy's Spitfire tagging along close behind.

As he climbed he listened to the wireless chatter of the pilots who had taken off before him. He recognized the voice of Bull Whitworth of his own squadron: "Still no visual."

Another pilot answered: "Maybe the blighters have gone home." "HA-HA, wishful thinking lads!" Kenneth checked his altimeter. 14,000 feet. He needed more altitude! "Tally-ho!" Bull Whitworth's voice came over the short-range wireless, known as radio-telephone, or R/T. "Bandits at angels one-seven." Bull had spotted the enemy machines at 17,000 feet altitude.

Now Fighter Control ordered "Cut past the fighters, get the bombers, get the bombers!"

Heinz Sauckel licked his lips nervously. He checked his oil gauge for the hundredth time since taking off from Gerbini Airfield at the base of Mt. Etna on Sicily. Oil pressure was still normal. Sauckel was a replacement pilot to his squadron of the Luftwaffe's II Fliegerkorps. He had arrived by transport aircraft at Gerbini only two days before this, his first combat sortie. His squadron commander sat him down for a man to man talk the night before the mission, explaining that he would have preferred Heinz have his baptism of fire on another occasion, but the all out effort ordered against the Royal Air Force on Malta forced him to send every available pilot against the enemy. Sauckel swallowed hard, saluted smartly and returned to his quarters where he first signed his will then wrote a long letter to his mother in Munich. Heinz turned twenty years old that day, Saturday, June 21, 1942, also the day the Libyan port of Tobruk fell to Rommel's Afrika Korps.

Sauckel looked to port. His wingman, an experienced pilot named Stahl waved to him. Heinz waved back. He scanned the skies all about. Everywhere he looked were German fighter aircraft, seventy-two in the first wave alone according to his CO in the mission briefing the night before. Broken cloud filled the sky like fluffy puffs of pink candy, colored by the first rays of the morning sun now peeking over the eastern horizon. Heinz struggled to keep his aircraft on station at speeds just above stalling. "At this pace," he grumbled to himself, "it will take until Christmas to reach Malta."

In fact, the flight time to Malta was just 25 minutes, even at reduced speed and the British were determined that Heinz and his fellow Luftwaffe pilots be greeted well before they reached the island. Sauckel continued to struggle to hold his 'Emil' Messerschmitt Bf 109 in the air at low speed. In these conditions tight formation flying was impossible and soon the fighters of the II Fliegerkorps were all over the sky, diving periodically to pick up speed and regain control.

The squadron CO assured his pilots this type of hateful flying as decoys would last no more than fifteen minutes. The British fighters on Malta were sure to rise into the air as the first sign of the German attack appeared on the island's radar screens, lured by the slow speed of the attacking force into believing it was a large bomber formation.

Heinz looked again for Stahl to port. His wingman was drifting forty meters away. 'Not exactly the classic formation for going into aerial combat,' he thought sarcastically to himself. He checked his watch quickly. In the air now for almost fifteen minutes. The sun's orb rose over the rim of the world in the east, illuminating the dozens of nearby aircraft in Heinz' flight. The sea beneath them remained in darkness.

What was keeping the British? He checked his watch again. He frowned to himself. He had checked it only fifteen seconds earlier.

Suddenly a crackling sound came in his radio headset. Heinz moved his hand to his throttle in anticipation.

"Come on, come on", he said to himself impatiently.

The radio crackled again. "Valkyrie!" The signal! "Valkyrie! Valkyrie!" Heinz slammed the throttle to maximum speed. He was pushed back in his seat as his Bf 109e shot forward. He climbed for all the altitude he could gain before encountering the enemy pilots.

Heinz saw his squadron mates to left and right rising with him. He strained his eyes for a glimpse of the British he knew were ahead. There! Straight ahead of him and at the same altitude were the tiny flecks of the British craft, a dozen or more. He continued pushing the Messerschmitt for altitude as the British Spitfires rushed towards him.

Machine guns and cannon blazing, the top-cover Bf 109s

dove headlong into the rising Spitfires, breaking their formation and cutting off their climbs. One of the 'Spits' spiraled down slowly, trailing smoke from its engine cowling, but still under control until two Messerschmitts from the decoy 'bomber' formation jumped it. The Bf 109s poured machine gun and cannon fire into the Spitfire until the tail was blown off the British ship. It fell in a flat spin towards the sea below. "I got him!" cried one of the pilots who had hit the Spitfire.

The German pilots chattered excitedly to each other as the opposing forces crashed into one another. "Watch your tail!" "He's gotten below you!" "TURN, TURN!"

>>>>>>

Kenneth continued his climb as the lead Spitfire pilots reported visual contact with the enemy.

The Malta Fighter Controller broke in on the chatter. "It's a big group lads, Climb for angels, get above them!" 'Angels' was RAF slang for altitude.

"No bloody kidding," laughed Kenneth to himself. Nonetheless, he pushed the throttle all the way to the stops for more power. He could see the German formation now, tiny specks in the distance. A large, high-cover group of fighters still above him and an equally large group of planes at his own altitude partially obscured in a layer of morning haze, all south bound for Malta.

"I'm going in against the low group now," announced the lead Spitfire pilot over the R/T. "The top cover fighters don't seem to have seen us yet."

The lead Spits, already several thousand feet above Kenneth, nosed over and began a head-on dive into the lower formation of German aircraft. Immediately the top cover group of German fighters nosed over as well, as if they'd only been waiting for the British to make the first move. Kenneth felt a terrible sense of unease as he watched the two forces surge together on intersecting paths.

A frantic voice came over the R/T. "There are no bombers, they're all fighters!"

Another voice shouted. "It's an ambush!"

The top cover German fighters dove through the ranks of the lead Spitfires scattering the Spit's in all directions. One fell away from the main group and was quickly set upon by two Bf 109s who sent it plunging to the sea.

At the Malta air operations center burrowed deep underground in Malta's bedrock limestone beneath the fortress city of Valletta, wing commander Edwin Finch listened to the progress of the air battle over the R/T. He ordered the next eight Spitfires on the flight line into the air immediately, even though he knew they hadn't a prayer of reaching the dogfight in time to do any good.

Kenneth flipped over on his port wing and dove in behind one of the two Germans responsible for knocking down the lone Spitfire. The Messerschmitt pilot was busy congratulating himself and hadn't checked his tail. Kenneth slipped in behind him to within two hundreds yards before squeezing the trigger. His Spitfire's four .50 caliber machine guns and two 20mm cannon sprayed lead and tracer into the German's tail. The enemy pilot tried to twist away, but his control surfaces were already ruined. The Messerschmitt slid into a flat spin, trailing smoke and bits of metal down to the sea below.

Kenneth quickly checked over his right shoulder behind his own ship. A German was just coming into firing position. He yanked the Spit's stick back and went into a near vertical climb, then pushed the nose back over quickly. The German shot past him and was now below him to the right. Kenneth tipped over on the starboard wing and pursued.

The German knew what was in store once he overshot his attack on Kenneth's Spitfire. He twisted and turned in an effort to shake the British pursuer from his tail. Each time Kenneth got close enough to fire a burst from his guns the 109 danced out of the gun-sights at the last moment, leaving Kenneth to watch in frustration as his tracers plowed empty sky.

Finally, the German hesitated a split second too long and Kenneth saw three or four hits out on the port wing tip of the German fighter. Damaged, but not fatally the 109 danced on. Its pilot held one advantage; by bringing the dogfight back to the general melee he could get help from his squadron mates. Kenneth again had to check behind him to keep his tail clean and with his head turned the Messerschmitt jinked away and was lost.

Throughout the action he heard frantic chatter on the R/T. Pilots calling warnings to their friends, reports of their own kills and obscenities filled the airwaves. And the Malta fighter pilots were sending numerous "may-day" calls as their Spitfires were hit and knocked from the sky.

Kenneth looked for another target and singled out a Messerschmitt away from the main pack, circling over a plume of smoke trailing down to the sea. Whether the pilot was sporting over his own kill, or hovering over a fallen comrade checking for a parachute Kenneth could not tell. He turned to go after the lone German fighter.

>>>>>>

As Heinz drew near the battle he found the formations of British and German ships in a melee. Fighters slashed across the sky in all directions, climbing, diving and not a few falling in flames. Heinz focused his attention on a particular Spitfire. It came out of a tight turn on the tail of a Messerschmitt. The two machines were twisting and turning, but their general course would pass in front of him from left to right and below him by about a thousand feet. Heinz pushed the nose of his ship over and began to dive towards where he thought the Spitfire would be in a few seconds, picking up speed as the dive steepened. The other German fighter flashed through his gun sights and as it passed he squeezed the trigger. His four cannon spewed out a stream of 20mm shells. His heart skipped as he watched them slam into the Spitfire from nose to tail. The cockpit exploded in a shower of glass and metal. The Spit' rolled over on its back and plunged like a meteor, 15,000 feet to the sea.

Heinz' first kill was accomplished by one of the most difficult aerial maneuvers. Well over ninety percent of all aerial kills in World War II were recorded with the fighter directly behind its victim, but Heinz knocked the Spit' down with a pure deflection shot, hitting it from a right angle. Most fighter pilots, even the very good ones never mastered this technique.

A wave of exhilaration swept through him like a drug. He gave no thought to the pilot of the Spit'. He felt a detachment from the human element of the 'kill' he had scored. He knew only that he'd just destroyed one of the hated Spitfires which had bedeviled his squadron mates and killed so many of his fellow Luftwaffe airmen. Quickly he searched the sky around him, craning his neck to look behind him to left and right, then below and behind. His tail was clean.

The sky was a chaos of flashing aircraft. A Bf 109 trailing smoke was fleeing the action in a shallow dive, its nose turned back towards Sicily and safety. A Spitfire broke from the melee and dove on the German. Heinz snapped over and dove to intercept. He was above the other 109, but below the Spit and knew the British pilot would be unlikely to see him, concentrating, as he no doubt was on the crippled German fighter.

Heinz bored in on the intercept course. At the last second he drew the nose of his plane up in a sharp climb and snapped off a long burst of fire which caught the Spitfire in the engine.

The propeller of the Spit' sheared off, spinning away from the plane as the engine burst into flame, the fire immediately engulfing the cockpit. The Spitfire rolled over on its back and the cockpit canopy was thrown back. The pilot dropped from the upside down machine with smoke trailing from his body. The man's parachute opened but Heinz saw large open panels in it where flames had burned away the fabric. The 'chute opened only partially as the English pilot plunged after his plane into the sea.

Heinz turned to check on the other Bf 109. It was now clear of the melee, still trailing smoke, but the pilot had control of its dive and seemed safely on his way to Sicily. Heinz again checked his tail. Clean again. With two kills already to his credit in his first combat he turned back towards the battle.

>>>>>>

Kenneth stalked the circling German from slightly below, taking advantage of the thin layer of haze to mask his approach. Nearly in range now he took one last look over his shoulders to check his tail. All clear. He turned back to the enemy plane and quickly planned his attack. He shoved the throttle forward and went into a short shallow dive, then pulled out of it beneath the German. Climbing now his ship rose till the belly of the 109 filled his gun sights. He squeezed the trigger and held it down, pouring shells into the underside of the Messerschmitt. It exploded in a blinding flash.

Kenneth's Spitfire jolted and rocked as he flew through the flaming debris and smoke of the destroyed German machine. He took a deep breath then checked his instrument panel. All gauges showed normal conditions. He checked his flaps and ailerons. All

functioned normally. He seemed to have come through with no damage. He took another deep sigh before checking his tail again.
>>>>>>

Heinz checked his fuel gauge. Little more than enough remained to return safely to Sicily. Combat flying at maximum power sucked fuel from the tanks at a shocking rate. He was on the north side of the huge dogfight and so could turn for home without having to pass through or around the melee. He began his turn when he saw the Spitfire rising beneath the lone Emil on the northwestern periphery of the combat area.

Heinz shouted into the R/T, "Spitfire attacking below you! Break away!" But he knew it was too late. He shoved his own throttle forward to the stops and shot after his comrade, forgetting his own fuel situation in the process. As he raced towards the Spitfire and its unaware victim he saw the tracer shells fly from the wing mounts of the British fighter, slamming home in the belly of the 109. The Emil flew apart in thousands of pieces and a burst of flame and smoke. The Spitfire passed straight through the piece of hell that had been a German fighter a moment before. Heinz shouted in anger. No words but a deep, guttural howl of frustration echoed in his cockpit over the engine noise.

He bored in behind the Spitfire. Its pilot still hadn't noticed Sauckel's machine pressing the attack. The Spitfire loomed large in his gun sights now. Perfect position. FIRE! His guns barked streams of shells, hammering the fuselage of the Spitfire, breaking chunks of skin and airframe away, and then—NOTHING. He squeezed the trigger again and again, but no more shells flew out to finish the Spitfire off. His guns were out of ammunition.

Heinz nearly wept in frustration. The British fighter was clearly crippled, barely able to stay in the sky. Perhaps its pilot was even wounded. Just a few more rounds would finish it. Briefly he considered ramming the Spitfire to finish it off, but dismissed the idea as suicidal folly. The Englander would probably not even reach his home airfield on Malta and if he did ram the best he could hope for himself was a crash landing.

Heinz was suddenly overcome with curiosity about this English pilot. What was he like, was he young or old, tall or short, fat or thin. He watched the Spitfire for a few more seconds then made his decision.

He quickly scanned his tail for signs of any attackers. Nothing. He looked back towards the area of the melee. He saw that German and British survivors were now drawing away from each other, the few British back to Malta, the Germans to Sicily. He looked again at the crippled Spitfire slipping and jerking through the air. He eased his throttle forward and pulled in about thirty meters off the port wing of the enemy plane. He looked across to the cockpit and saw the British pilot there, clearly struggling with his ship's stick, fighting to keep control of the plane. He could tell little about the pilot behind his goggles and leather flight cap.

The Englander glanced up at Heinz briefly, then looked back at him again and held his gaze. Heinz felt all the hatred ease from his heart. He could fight this man, kill him even, but there was no hate for the enemy flyer, just regret that the two couldn't sit peacefully over a beer to discuss the joy of flying. Heinz gave a brief salute and saw the Englander nod his head in acknowledgement, unable to release either hand from the stick, however briefly to return the salute.

"Some other time, Englander," Heinz said then peeled away to join his comrades returning to Sicily.

>>>>>>

Kenneth watched the Messerschmitt pull away and leave him. Perhaps the German's guns were jammed or out of ammunition. It didn't matter, he'd been left with another chance at life and he was going to fight to keep it. He assessed his situation. Though unharmed himself he knew that his Spitfire was badly damaged. The controls were heavy and sluggish and turning to port was very difficult. He tested his flaps. Barely responsive, though looking out over the wings he could not see any damage directly to them.

"Must be a severed cable," he told himself. Flying and landing his badly damaged Spitfire would be a dicey proposition indeed. Better to bail out and be picked up by Malta's air-sea rescue service. He keyed his wireless. "May-day, may-day," he called. "I'm going into the drink about ten miles northwest of Mellieha Bay." He waited for the acknowledgement. When none came he repeated the may-day call, but still no response. His wireless was, literally, shot.

Unable to notify the air-sea rescue service he would be entirely dependant on a lucky sighting at this distance from the island if he were to be picked up. He would have to at least get close enough to Malta to be seen from the shore. Gently he nursed his wounded Spitfire round in a slow turn to starboard till his heading placed him squarely on course for Ta Qali airfield in the center of the island.

He checked his altimeter; 9,000 feet and falling. Kenneth quickly ran through the math in his head. He was two and half miles in the sky with ten miles to cover to reach a point near enough Malta's shores for a reasonable chance at being spotted and picked up. He needed at least 500 feet from which to bail out, one thousand was preferable. That left him a glide slope of five to one. Doable, so long as the Rolls-Royce Merlin power plant kept turning over. In any case not more than a few minutes of flight would put him in range of Malta.

The minutes ticked by and the engine kept an even roar driving the Spitfire closer to home. The rugged outline of the island came into view through the haze. Kenneth checked his altimeter again. His altitude was holding up well, still over 3,000 feet. Kenneth began to consider his chances of landing the plane safely. He fought with the damaged control surfaces of his Spitfire, struggling to keep the plane in the air and on course for home. Soon he was dripping with sweat from the exertion and nervous tension. He steadied the plane and momentarily took his left hand from the stick to wipe the sweat from his brow. The Spit yawed drunkenly to starboard. He grabbed the stick with both hands again and brought the plane back on level course.

The island of Malta grew before him till he was over the shoreline. He was north of the field at Ta Qali. He should turn to port now to line up for an approach to the strip, but he knew a turn to port was impossible with his damaged rudder. He would have to make a wide, sweeping turn to starboard, through 360 degrees to line up on the runway.

The Rolls-Royce Merlin engine continued its steady roar as he swept the Spitfire around in a gentle turn to the north then around to the east and finally back to the south. He checked his altimeter. Barely over 1,000 feet. If he was going to bail out it had to be soon, but he knew he'd passed on his last chance to abandon the plane and parachute down. To do so now meant the Spitfire would crash somewhere on the heavily populated island where its odds of killing civilians would be high. Now, it was Ta Qali or nothing.

He worried at his inability to signal Ta Qali by wireless of his approach. The Germans had tricked the defenders before, pretending to be a British plane in distress on approach for an emergency landing then roaring in at rooftop height to bomb and strafe the airfield. He prayed the anti-aircraft gunners would hold their fire long enough to recognize his Spitfire. The field came into view. He was lined up perfectly for his approach. To the left of the landing strip he could see a single plume of black smoke rising into the air. Most likely another Spitfire whose forced landing had gone badly. No time to think about the other chap's misfortune now though.

"Concentrate Kenneth!" he said to himself as the runway approached.

The airfield flags were blowing lightly, showing a slight crosswind from the southwest, not enough to worry about if it held steady. He crossed the runway threshold and began to ease down onto the strip. He was within ten feet of the ground when the crosswind died and the Spitfire yawed over to starboard. He kicked the rudder bar hard and the plane corrected slowly, so slowly, but on level flight again as the wheels touched down. The Spitfire bounded into the air and yawed again to starboard into a dangerous sideslip. He stood on the rudder bar and corrected his angle just enough to touch down. This time the wheels held the ground and he roared down the runway towards the taxi strips. He cut the throttle back and gently applied the brakes.

As the Spitfire came to a stop he released his iron grip on the control stick. His forearms screamed in protest, his fingers remained locked in position as though still on the stick.

>>>>>>

After Heinz left the wounded Spitfire and turned for home he scanned the sky around him. He was alone. The other 109s that had flown off to assault Malta's fighter defenses that morning were headed for home. He checked his fuel gage and felt his heart jump into his throat. He was well below the safety margin of returning to his airbase at Gerbini. He immediately throttled back to the optimum speed for fuel economy and set his Emil in a shallow glide angle towards Sicily. He estimated he was about 50 miles out from Gerbini, just at the edge of range on his remaining fuel.

Heinz cursed himself for losing track of his fuel consumption. It was an elementary mistake and he promised himself he would never repeat it. He hoped he would live to keep his promise.

He strained looking for the first glimpse of Sicily ahead in the distance. Slowly he discerned a white blur through the morning haze. Mount Etna's snow capped peak, rising over 10,000 feet above sea level resolved in his view. Heinz's veteran squadron mates had told him that on a clear day the island of Malta could be seen from Etna's summit, but on this morning the summer haze obscured the volcanic cinder cone of the mountain, leaving only the perpetually snow covered summit to stand out. For a moment the beauty of the mountain struck him. The early morning sunlight reflected a pale, pink hue from the mantle of snow that never left the mountain even now at high summer, reminding him of the snow-capped peaks in his native Bavaria.

The Emil's engine coughed. Quickly Heinz switched the feed back to his wing tanks. He'd switched from the wing tanks to the main tank in the fuselage before the dogfight began. The engine resumed its even purr as the Messerschmitt ate the miles towards home.

He checked his altimeter. 7,000 feet. Comiso airfield in the southeastern corner of Sicily was now within range, but his confidence was growing that he could reach Gerbini. Much better to land at his home airfield, saving himself the teasing he would take from his squadron mates for failing to keep track of his fuel.

At last Heinz could see the surf line below as he crossed the Sicilian coast. Eighteen miles now to Gerbini on the Catania plain at the foot of Mount Etna. He smiled.

The engine coughed then resumed its purr.

"DAMMIT!" he shouted. There was no choice now; he would have to set down at Comiso for fuel.

He keyed his wireless microphone. "Calling Comiso aerodrome, calling Comiso aerodrome, this is Messerschmitt four-one-three-six. I am declaring an emergency, over."

The reply was immediate. "Messerschmitt four-one-three-six, this is Comiso control. What is the nature of your emergency?"

Heinz keyed his microphone. "Messerschmitt four-one-three-six to Comiso control,

I have a fuel emergency. Request permission for an immediate landing."

"Four-one-three-six, you will be escorted to the airbase and are cleared for an immediate landing on the east runway."

"Acknowledged," Heinz replied. "Thank you, Comiso."

He looked out over his port wing. His "escort", another Bf 109 patrolling south of Comiso to spot any German aircraft in distress and to fly top cover over any downed pilots, joined him. He knew the patrol fighter was there also to guard against British aircraft that might try to sneak a raid onto the airfield by mingling among returning German machines. The other pilot waved to him, then pointed ahead, signaling for Heinz to proceed to his landing. Heinz waved back and nodded his head in acknowledgement, then focused his attention on the task of landing.

The field at Comiso was now in view about two miles ahead. He checked his altimeter and smiled. At 1,000 meters he had done well in preserving his altitude. He should have no trouble reaching the field now. His engine coughed and sputtered. The smile left Heinz' face. The prospect of a dead stick landing was not attractive. He pumped the manual squeeze for the fuel pump, but knew there were only a few cups of fuel left in the tanks. He had one shot only at the runway.

He centered the Emil on the runway and descended towards the field. Just as he crossed the landing strip threshold the engine coughed and died completely. He extended his flaps and glided down onto the dirt runway. The 109 bounced just once, lightly, then settled onto the strip. He did not apply his brakes. He had so little momentum he was fearful of not reaching the taxi strip at the end of the runway. He hoped to not have to be towed to the fuel bowser.

>>>>>>>>>>>>>>>>>>>>>>>>>>>>>>>>>>>>>>>>>>>>>>>>>>
>>>>>>>

Margaret Reed woke up hungry. She'd gone to bed early the afternoon of June 21 with no supper. Not the first time recently and probably not the last she realized. She checked her watch. Almost midnight. Time to get up, dress and make herself ready to report for duty.

She yawned, stretched her lean frame, and sat up. She dressed in the near dark of her dank sleeping cubicle. Deep underground it received no daylight and electricity was in short supply due to the chronic shortage of fuel oil for the generators. The only light crept under the door from the bare bulb hanging from the tunnel ceiling outside her room. Water from subterranean aquifers seeped through the porous limestone. Mold was a constant problem in the underground. Briefly she considered her own features in the small mirror hung on the wall above her washbasin.

"Still not bad," she thought, "though a bit of makeup would help." There'd been no makeup to be had on Malta for months. She was as thin as she had ever been since childhood. Initially, the weight loss she experienced was welcomed in a vain way. Not what men considered beautiful, she was cute in a clear-skinned English country girl fashion. When first posted to Malta she looked forward to the warm Mediterranean sun and to developing a tan, but months spent underground with only infrequent glimpses of the sun left her with the pale, almost translucent complexion she came to the island with. Short brunette hair, done in a wave when she had time, and pale, green eyes, looking back at her now from the mirror, completed the picture. She sighed, no longer welcoming the weight loss. She had become unmistakably gaunt.

Margaret, Maggie to her friends, left her room and turned towards the mess hall, also deep underground, delved in a complex of tunnels and shafts cut from the limestone foundations of the island beneath Lascaris Bastion, under the very ramparts of the fortress city of Valletta. Lascaris Bastion loomed over the aptly named Grand Harbor, one of the two great natural anchorages with which Malta is blessed and which give it its strategic significance. Modern flak batteries, 90mm hi-altitude guns and smaller, rapid-fire 40mm Bofors had replaced ancient, muzzle-loading cannon. The Knights of St. John had cut the oldest tunnels beneath Lascaris before the Ottoman siege of Malta in 1565. Through the years successive rulers of Malta had added to them and British engineers had been busy again, extending the tunnel complex in the years prior to the outbreak of World War II and now there was almost constant excavation as new caverns and tunnels were dug to house the various administrative and intelligence services of the British military presence on Malta.

In the mess hall she was served a thin soup of broth and a few vegetables, with a slice of bread, small pat of butter and a cup of weak tea. Slim rations, but more than many on Malta received, certainly more than the civilian population was getting in June 1942. Malta had been besieged since Italy joined Germany in the war against Britain on June 11, 1940. Initially the Italian air force, the Regia Aeronautcia, bombed Malta in a desultory and ineffective fashion, never daring to come to low altitudes where the accuracy of attack could be assured. But the arrival of the German Luftwaffe at the New Year 1941 changed the situation markedly. Since then air attacks were pressed with vigor and daring against the island and the shipping that kept its population fed and its British garrison supplied with the weapons and munitions of war. Malta had endured almost 18 months of determined air assault, often intense, occasionally more relaxed, but always the danger of attack hung over the island like a blanket of fear.

As spring turned to summer in 1942 the supply situation on Malta became desperate. Average daily rations fell to less than 1,000 calories, a third of that considered proper for an active adult. Everyone on Malta knew they had only a few months of effective resistance left before starvation made surrender inevitable. Only a major convoy delivering fuel, fighter aircraft and most importantly, food could save Malta.

"Hello, Maggie!" Margaret looked up and smiled at the cheerful voice of her friend,

Elizabeth Runyon. Elizabeth had come out from England with Margaret in February of 1941. They'd shipped out together, taking War Ministry passage in a freighter from the Clyde to Gibraltar then flown to Malta in a Sunderland flying boat, landing at Kalafrana, the Royal Navy's seaplane base on Marsaxlokk Bay on the island's south coast.

"Hello, Liz!" replied Maggie. "How're things overnight?"

Liz Runyon worked the mid-shift from 3pm to 1am while Margaret worked "grave yard", midnight to 10am. Their paths often crossed around this time in the mess hall.

"Not good I'm afraid," answered Liz with a shake of her

head. "The news is very bad."

"Why, what on earth has happened now?" asked Maggie, concerned and glancing about to see who might be listening.

"It's all over the island, not privileged stuff at all," Liz replied. "Tobruk has fallen to the Germans."

"NO! How? When?" cried Maggie.

"This morning," answered Liz. "It's a real shocker isn't it?"

"Good Lord!" said Maggie. "It certainly is! How's the Section Chief treating it?"

"Oh, it's a full blown flap as you might imagine," answered Liz. "You'd best finish your meal and get down to chamber right away. Chappie will want to see you."

Maggie nodded and said nothing. She gulped down her food and tea, hurried out of the mess and back down the tunnel, through pools of light cast by infrequently spaced bulbs hung from the ceiling. She passed many service men and a few other women in the course of their duties. After several turns she came to an area of the tunnels with much less traffic. One last turn and she came to a double steel door set in the solid rock. A heavy-set Royal Marine Sergeant sat at a small desk in front of the doors and two privates stood armed guard with fixed bayonets.

"Morning, Miss Reed," said the Sergeant. "Ready to start your day, are you?"

"Yes, Sergeant Harris, bright and early".

"Early anyway Miss. I don't know about bright at this hour, nor perhaps at all today with the news from North Africa."

"Dreadful news," Maggie agreed.

The sergeant pushed a paper on a clipboard across the desk to Maggie.

"Sign the duty roster please, Miss Reed," he requested, pointing to a line on the paper where he had entered her name and the current time.

"Thank you Sergeant," she replied. She signed and handed him back the roster.

Sgt. Harris tipped his head to the privates guarding the door. One of them swung the steel door open, admitting Maggie to "The Chamber".

Maggie stepped in and looked about, searching for Section Chief Chapman, "Chappie" as those who worked for him in the

Chamber knew him. The Chamber was a large room, over 40 feet in diameter with 12 feet high ceilings, roughly circular in shape and with rough-hewn limestone walls. Along these walls to the left and right of the entrance were a series of stout wooden tables reaching around the curves of the room towards the back. On each table rested a wireless set, with dials and lights and cathode tubes glowing through ventilator panels in the sides of their cases. The room was stuffy from the heat generated by the many radios. At each radio sat an operator with headset, listening. Occasionally one would adjust a dial or scribble notes on a pad of paper. The operators were about equally divided between men and women.

In the middle of The Chamber two massive steel beams stood from floor to ceiling, supporting the roof. Around these were more tables where operations manuals and maintenance logs for the wireless sets were stacked. A large copper teapot on a hotplate curled steam from its spout on one of the tables. The room was quiet; only the occasional murmured voice, the scratch of a pencil on paper and the low, background hum of ventilation fans disturbed a church-like silence.

Maggie began to walk to the rear of the room to a single steel door. As she approached the door it opened.

"Ah, there you are Maggie," said Section Chief Chapman as he stepped from the two room suite that was his combined office and living quarters.

"Hullo, Chappie," she said warmly. Chapman was popular among his subordinates, not the least for the easy informality with which he ran the Chamber.

"Heard the news I assume?" he asked her.

"Yes, everyone has. What does it mean Chappie?"

"For you and me it means we have work to do!" Chapman proclaimed. "Come along. I have a special task for you tonight." Chapman led her around the room past several of the wireless sets. Each table had tent cards on it, identifying a location or Axis command organization. They passed the tables labeled Regia Marina ( Italian Navy ); Regia Aeronautica ( Italian Air Force ); Luftwaffe/Sicily; Comando Supremo/Rome; OKH/Berlin, ( German Army High Command ).

Chapman stopped at a table where a thin, young, bespectacled man with bad skin sat, eyes closed, listening through the headphones. Maggie might have thought him asleep, except that the young man's right hand rested lightly on the direction finder dial, gently, slowly turning it back and forth searching for any sound. He was turning the antenna aerial of the wireless set between 125 and 135 degrees relative. The tent label on the table read DAK/Benghazi. "Benghazi" had been scratched out and written in pencil under it "Tobruk". DAK, the Deutsche Afrika Korp, Rommel's armored force assigned to North Africa.

"Simon here is listening for a peep out of our friend Rommel," said Chapman, laying his hand gently on the young man's shoulder.

Simon's eyes came slowly open and he turned his head to Maggie and Chappie.

"Hello, Maggie," he smiled at her, ignoring Chapman, "how are you?"

"I'm well, Simon," she smiled in return. "Have you heard anything yet?" she asked as he pulled one earphone away. She knew he was still half listening to the radio.

"Not since the evening hours, Maggie," Simon told her. "I picked up a signal to Comando Supremo from the DAK near Tobruk about six hours ago. I told Chappie right away," he told her with pride in his eyes.

"Of course it was encoded," said Chapman, "but I've no doubt it was to tell Rome and Berlin their good news. We got the news from our own people only shortly before Simon picked up the signal."

"Good work, Simon," she answered him, "you're the best at this!"

The young man blushed and turned away, back to the wireless dials, but Maggie and Chapman knew he wasn't listening to the radio any longer.

"Of course I had the signal forwarded to London immediately," concluded Chapman, making small talk, giving Simon time to recover his composure.

"Come along Simon, that's a good fellow," said Chapman finally. "Time for Maggie to have a go!"

"I can stay for a while Maggie, help you if you like," said Simon, handing her the headphones and standing from the chair.

"No, Simon," said Chapman. "We need you back here

tonight fresh as a new kitten!"

"That's right, Simon," Maggie agreed. "You'll want to be alert tonight. Run along and get your rest," she urged him. "And Simon!" she called to him as he turned to leave. "Thank you. We'd be lost here without you."

Simon blushed again and scurried from the chamber, unable to reply.

"That's the ticket, Maggie," said Chapman softly. "A word or two from you are worth a night's sleep to that lad."

Maggie busied herself recording in the log the condition and tuning of the wireless set as she took control of it, noting the time and date in her clear, fine print. She ensured the recording device used to capture intercepted signals was working properly.

"Anything particular to listen for this morning, Chappie," Maggie asked, "or just anything from DAK?"

"Of course anything from DAK right now could be critical to 8th Army," he answered, "but in particular anything addressed to Comando Supremo in Rome, or OKH in Berlin would be a red flag item".

Maggie simply nodded, already tuning her mind and ears closely to the set.

"I'll bring you a spot of tea in a bit," said Chapman and moved off to coordinate the turnover of another pair of wireless listeners. Maggie listened intently for any sign of a message from the direction of Tobruk on any of the several frequencies DAK headquarters was known to use in communicating with higher authorities in Rome and Berlin.

The Axis war in North Africa and the Mediterranean was officially considered an Italian campaign, notwithstanding the profound German force contribution, thus Rommel and the Afrika Korp reported to the Italian Supreme Command, Comando Supremo in Rome. Nonetheless, the British had learned through their 'Y' service, as their wireless intercept organization was known, that German forces often communicated directly with their own Army High Command, the OKH, in Berlin. Occasionally a transmission directly to OKW, Armed Forces High Command, was caught as well.

Maggie continued slowly walking her wireless aerial back and forth on the bearing of the Libyan port of Tobruk while also monitoring each of the several frequencies the DAK HQ used. High above her head, among the forest of aerials sprouted over Malta the mast for her set turned slowly in a short arc in response to her turning the control. It was painstaking work, requiring great patience and mental stamina. She had often sat at her console turning the dial, switching frequencies, listening and listening, and heard nothing at all for days.

The work could be singularly unrewarding even on the rare occasions when she did intercept a message. German and Italian signals were usually encoded. Margaret rarely had a clue to the content of the message, except in the rarest cases when circumstances made the nature of the Axis messages obvious, such as the evening before in the message Simon had intercepted. The job of the wireless intercept operators in the British 'Y' service was to find and capture the encrypted Axis signals, forward them to London and never wonder what was done there with them.

But Maggie could not help but wonder, and have her suspicions. Chapman's superiors in the 'Y' service had explained a process of "traffic analysis" in which trained intelligence analysts drew conclusions about enemy dispositions and movements based upon the locations from which transmissions originated. These analysts made predictions of future enemy actions based on changes in the volume of message traffic. If for instance a known enemy HQ suddenly showed a marked increase in message traffic this could be an indication that forces associated with that headquarters were gearing up for an offensive. Maggie settled in for a long morning of concentration on her monitoring tasks, recording in her logbook every fifteen minutes the sequence of frequencies and the relative bearings she scanned. For over three hours her log indicated no signals detected.

Then at 0436 hours the morning of 22 June she detected a telltale sound from a wireless transmission. She checked the recorder to assure its proper function in capturing the signal as she also tuned the direction dial. She found the bearing was identical to that recorded by Simon the night before when he caught the first DAK signal from Tobruk. She recorded time, bearing and frequency in her log, then raised her hand and waved it over her head.

Chapman hurried over to her station. "What have you got

Maggie?" he asked her.

"Same bearing and frequency as Simon picked up last night," she replied. "Sounds like DAK calling OKH in Berlin."

While all important enemy signals were encrypted, the trained intercept operators learned to recognize distinguishing features of the Axis transmissions that often gave away the identity of the sender and the intended recipient of the message. Every wireless operator has a distinctive style to the way he enters a keyed transmission. This style is known as the operator's "fist". Quite apart from the location the signal originates from, recognition of the known fist of an enemy wireless operator can identify the sending organization. Also, despite the fact the signals were encoded there was often a recognizable pattern at the beginning and end of the signals which were known or presumed to constitute the encoded address of the intended recipient and return address of the sender. When these patterns were repeated in enough different messages it was possible for the 'Y' service operators to identify both sender and recipient.

"This one is addressed to OKH in Berlin I think," Maggie said. OKH was the OberKommando Heer or Army High Command.

"Right on Tobruk's bearing I see," said Chappie softly so as not to break her concentration as Maggie worked to remain tuned to the signal.

"That's it then," she said, "message concluding now. Just waiting for an acknowledgement from the addressee."

It was customary for the recipient of most messages to acknowledge receipt, though this custom was ignored by ships at sea wishing to preserve the secrecy of their position by maintaining radio silence. Traffic analysis was understood by the Axis forces as well as by the Allies.

"There it is," said Maggie. Nodding in the direction of the operator manning the receiver tuned in the direction of Berlin.

"I'll get this off to London "pronto" as our Italian friends might say," Chapman said.

The signals intercepted by Simon and Maggie and by hundreds of other British 'Y' service operators during World War II were forwarded for analysis to an English country estate named Bletchley Park in a quiet, wooded area outside London. A forest of oak, birch and alder trees on the estate grounds concealed a forest of another kind. Hundreds of antennas sprouted about the 18th century manor house, taken over by the British government for the duration of the war and given the code name "Station X".

Signals from recording stations all around the periphery of Axis occupied Europe were sent there for analysis, an analysis that certainly did include the "traffic analysis" described to Maggie and the other 'Y service operators. But the work at Bletchley Park didn't end with traffic analysis. Unknown to anyone in the German or Italian commands the British had made great strides toward breaking the encryption keys of the Axis powers' military and diplomatic codes. Under the brilliant leadership of English mathematician Alan Turing the Bletchley Park analysts had broken the most important Axis codes, the German military and diplomatic ciphers. These German codes were predicated on a device known as "Enigma". Enigma was an ingenious mechanical apparatus that replaced characters in an original message text with seemingly random characters. These were then broadcast through the ether via wireless transmitter. The receiver, if equipped with the proper Enigma device could reverse the process, replacing the random characters with the correct message text. Every Enigma device was numbered and its whereabouts known at all times to the German Command and the Amtsgruppe Ausland or Abwehr, the German Military Intelligence service.

The system was further secured by use of cipher keys. The Enigma device used both the transmitted message and the current cipher key as input. The Cipher was changed from time to time at odd intervals to prevent any possibility of a captured or stolen key being used by the enemy in an effort to break into the code. Ingenious, and in theory, unbreakable. Or so it was believed in Germany. In fact, the Polish military intelligence service had discovered the existence of Enigma before the outbreak of hostilities on September 1, 1939. It had applied a mathematical analysis to intercepted German transmissions and had essentially built its own Enigma device through a process known today as "reverse engineering". As war with Germany drew near the Poles shared this work with their British allies who spirited away a number of the Polish Enigmas to England just prior to the start of war with Germany. These devices were installed at Bletchley Park where the Polish work was advanced and improved.

From early, hesitant beginnings when only an occasional phrase or fragment of a German message could be understood by the code breakers, round the clock, relentless effort at Station 'X' had brought the British an ongoing cornucopia of intelligence, often of the highest order and indisputable authenticity. The British controlled the distribution of this intelligence within their military and government under the code name "Ultra".

With great care the British military was sometimes able to act on Ultra information. Keeping the information at only the highest levels of British command and acting with discretion to never provide Germany a clue that its top codes were broken, the British affected the course of the war in subtle but important ways.

Notable among successes in using intercepted and decrypted German wireless messages was the sinking of the great German battleship *DKM Bismarck*. After a long sea chase in which the *Bismarck* almost escaped to the safety of French ports the British caught the *Bismarck* just outside of Luftwaffe air cover from the French coast and sank her on May 27, 1941. Publicly the British trumpeted the victory as a triumph of the overwhelming power of the Royal Navy, but in fact the *Bismarck* was located, and British warships concentrated upon it, through a combination of wireless intercept and intelligence techniques.

News of the fall of Tobruk came to Bletchley Park first through more conventional means. 8th Army HQ in Cairo, Egypt notified the British War Office in London's Whitehall of the fortress' fall on the evening of June 21st. Then the signal intercepted by Simon at Malta was Rommel's notification to Berlin, just as Section Chief Chapman speculated. Late that day the BBC broke the news to a dismayed and angry British public.

Bletchley Park was very busy that day, tracking and decrypting signals to and from a number of German U-boats operating in the Atlantic against Allied shipping. But the highest priority was put on decoding the message intercepted by Maggie Reed on Malta. The British urgently needed to know Rommel's next move in North Africa. Did he plan to attack immediately, to push through to the Nile Delta and the Suez Canal, or did he and his Afrika Korps need a respite to replenish depleted stocks of armor and munitions and for his soldiers to rest? The moment the

DAK signal forwarded from the Chamber beneath Malta was received cryptanalysts went to work on it. Within hours they had a complete translation of the message.

The message whose wording General Rommel and his senior staff had worked to perfect through the night began with a complete listing of the order of battle of Axis forces in North Africa, reporting to the German Army High Command the strength returns in men and equipment of every division and independent unit in the Axis armies. Next, it went on to a listing of the British forces defeated at Tobruk, totals of men and officers captured and held in captivity and of the substantial booty of war materials and provisions thoughtfully left for capture by the surrendered British garrison. Extremely useful information to the British all, even if much of it could be guessed or known in the absence of Rommel's message.

But the final paragraph of the message was a true intelligence gem, a diamond of clarity and brilliance worth a corps of troops, or a squadron of battleships to the British. It read:

*"The morale and condition of the troops, the quantity of stores captured*

*and the present weakness of the enemy makes it possible for us to thrust*

*onwards into the heart of Egypt. Therefore request that the Duce be*

*pressured to eliminate the restrictions currently placed upon my*

*movements and that all troops now under my command be placed at my*

*disposal to continue the offensive. Further request that Operation Herkules*

*be cancelled and that the paratroops, armor and aircraft apportioned to it*

*be redirected to my command for the capture of the Suez Canal."*

From prior intercepted messages the British knew "Operation Herkules" was the name given the Axis plan to invade and seize Malta, by air and sea assault. Bletchley Park forwarded the entire message text to Whitehall in London for the attention of the Imperial General Staff and to Washington, D.C. where Prime

Minister Winston Churchill and General Sir Alan Brooke, Chief of Staff of the British War Office were concluding a visit with American President Roosevelt and General George Marshall.

The Ultra information was also sent to several British Mediterranean commands. First among these was General Auchinleck as British Commander-in-Chief Middle East. On June 25, 1942 Auchinleck would fly to the front at Mersa Matruh, Egypt, sack General Neil Ritchie and assume personal command of the 8th Army. His task would be to stop Rommel from breaking through to the Nile Delta and Suez Canal.

Also informed was the British Governor-General of Malta, the sixth Viscount Gort. The holder of Britain's highest award for valor, the Victoria Cross, Lord Gort had taken command of Malta just six weeks earlier, on May 8, 1942, at a desperate time for its defenders. Thousands of Axis bombing sorties starting in January and through to the beginning of May had driven Malta's Royal Air Force fighter squadrons and attack groups of Swordfish and Blenheim Bombers to the very brink of extinction. The British evacuated the last surviving Wellington heavy bombers. The Royal Navy submarine base at Manoel Island adjacent to Grand Harbor was abandoned by the 10th Submarine Flotilla and the remaining warships of Force K, Malta's surface strike force were withdrawn, the heavily damaged cruiser *HMS Penelope*, nick-named *HMS Pepperpot* so riddled with holes was she, being the last to leave, sailing under cover of darkness on April 28.

On April 19 the American aircraft carrier *USS WASP* launched 47 Spitfire fighter aircraft from a position just southeast of the island of Majorca in the Spanish Ballearics. Intended to replenish the island's fighter defense force 46 of the fighters actually reached Malta, but a superbly delivered Luftwaffe raid caught most of these fighters on the ground shortly after landing. Within 72 hours every new Spitfire had been destroyed.

Malta's quartermaster estimated the island faced starvation by the end of August unless substantial supplies could be delivered. In April a convoy of four fast merchant vessels carrying fuels, food and munitions fought through to Malta with three of the four vessels arriving safely in Grand Harbor, but a daring Luftwaffe air raid sank all three merchantmen within the harbor itself, before they could be unloaded.

In early June the Royal Navy made another attempt to resupply Malta, launching two convoys simultaneously, one from Alexandria in Egypt to the east, and a larger convoy from Gibraltar in the west. Luftwaffe units on Crete and North Africa so harassed the convoy from Egypt that the escorting warships ran out of anti-aircraft ammunition and forced it to turn back with heavy losses. Not one gram of supplies was delivered to Malta. Two merchant ships of the Gibraltar convoy reached the island, delivering a desperately needed supply of food and ammunition, but thirteen merchant vessels and warships were sunk with eleven others damaged and forced to turn back, including all those carrying fuel. Malta had a reprieve, but was still in danger of falling to starvation. Against this backdrop of failure and loss was the expected invasion of Malta.

One bright spot for the British in this time was the return of the American carrier *Wasp* on two occasions in June. In company with the old Royal Navy carrier *HMS Eagle* she delivered over one hundred Spitfire aircraft with little hindrance from the Luftwaffe. A marked decrease in Axis air raids in late May and early June gave hope to the islanders that the worst was over. In fact, the Luftwaffe was busy assisting General Rommel's offensive, Operation Theseus, in North Africa and could not spare the sorties to maintain the killing pressure on Malta.

Then came the news to Lord Gort that General Rommel had requested Operation Herkules be cancelled and for permission to push directly for the Nile instead. It seemed to the British that, in Churchill's words, "…the pawn, Tobruk had been sacrificed to save the Queen, Malta."

>>>>>>>>>>>>>>>>>>>>>>>>>>>>>>>>>>>>>>>>>>>>>>>

Kenneth Wiltshire was born in the American farm town of Red Fern, South Dakota and he'd had a devil of a time getting into the war. As a boy he'd dreamed of flying since seeing his first 'barnstorming' exhibition. Canadian and American RAF veterans of the Great War with nothing better to do spent the 1920's and 30's flying from one rural county fair to another showing off their aerobatic skills in war surplus biplanes. Kenneth's parents took him to Pierre in the August of his tenth year to see such a show. He watched the aerial stunts performed by the pilots in their cloth and string biplanes and he *knew* he could out-fly any of them. That was in 1931.

From that summer on he poured through the local weekly newspaper, The Red Fern Gazetteer, tracking every traveling air show. Any time the barnstormers were anywhere in the region he pestered his parents relentlessly to go. Whether at Edmonton or Calgary in Canada, or in the United States at Bismarck, Des Moines or as far away as Spokane, Washington, by the time he was fifteen he was hitchhiking or riding a railcar to the site of every air show in the northern plains and Rockies of Canada and America.

At seventeen he took his first flying lesson. He dropped out the next day and never finished his senior year of high school. From that day he lived, worked, breathed and ate to fly. He left the family farm and took a job at a grain elevator in Pierre. Every penny he earned that didn't go to rent at the boarding house where he lived went to flying lessons. He soloed for the first time on his eighteenth birthday, August 20, 1939.

With the outbreak of hostilities he'd crossed the border and tried to enlist in the Royal Canadian Air Force, but quickly discovered the RCAF was an air force in name only. No training establishment and very few aircraft even existed. Worse, Canada's armed forces weren't interested in a high school dropout. Apparently only educated men could fight Germans. Disappointed, he hitched back to Pierre, but he hadn't given up.

Eventually in desperation he worked his way east on the rails, hopping a freight car out of Regina, Saskatchewan one morning in April 1940. He carried one clean shirt and his flying log. The war was almost seven months old and he'd missed enough of it already. Kenneth shivered his way across the Canadian Plains that frigid spring. When he got to Quebec he walked up the gangplank of the first steamship he came to at the docks and signed up to cross the Atlantic to England as an ordinary hand.

The SS Santiago sailed out the St. Lawrence estuary to join a convoy forming at St. John's, Newfoundland. Kenneth was put to work in the galley, washing dishes, scraping pots and pans and swabbing decks. The Santiago passed safely to England, though Kenneth witnessed the sinking of another ship in the convoy, torpedoed by a German U-Boat.

He arrived in Liverpool on June 5. He walked down the gangplank and sought out the nearest RAF recruiting station. The

Battle of France was well underway with German panzer formations slicing through the vaunted French Army, carving France like so much cheese or meat. The British Expeditionary Force in France had been knocked back on its heels and was reeling in retreat. The Luftwaffe was sweeping the skies clean of British and French aircraft.

The recruiting officer looked over Kenneth's flying log then asked about his formal education. Kenneth told the recruiter he had graduated high school. When challenged for his diploma he said it was lost in the Atlantic crossing. They both knew Kenneth was lying, but Britain was desperate for pilots. The recruiter bit his lip, and checked the box on the form that Kenneth had completed his primary education.

Unbelievably, Kenneth spent the entire Battle of Britain on the parade ground. As English and German pilots fought and died over England, Kenneth marched, marched and marched. It was four more months before he got into a cockpit for Elementary Flight Training, EFT. When finally sent to flight school for EFT in October, winter weather set in, severely limiting the flying that could be done by the rookie pilot cadets.

A long, dreary English winter under such frustrating conditions might have discouraged other young men, but Kenneth found the weather an improvement on the sub-zero winters at home in South Dakota. He flew at every opportunity, even riding as a passenger on transport hops between London and the airdrome at Fenwich Glen in Scotland where he trained. His instructors credited him with high marks on natural flying ability, but somewhat poorer grades on his written and theoretical studies.

Finally, in June 1941, almost a year to the day after arriving in England, Kenneth was awarded his RAF pilot wings and was assigned to a Fighter Command Spitfire squadron covering the east of England. RAF tactics of the time called for massive fighter sweeps, sometimes with as many as two hundred aircraft flying in waves over coastal France, trying to stir reaction from the Luftwaffe.

But by this time the Luftwaffe's pressure against England had eased, unknown to the English because the Luftwaffe was shifting its weight east for the upcoming attack on Russia. Kenneth saw few German aircraft. In eight months of flying he'd been shot at only twice, and had one "probable" to his credit, a Messerschmitt Bf 109 he'd tangled with over the channel off the mouth of the Thames River. He was far enough out to sea that no other RAF pilot saw the Messerschmitt go down.

Shortly after the Japanese attack at Pearl Harbor and America's entry into the war Kenneth applied for a transfer to the United States Army Air Corps. But the transfer hadn't been processed by the following spring and Kenneth was itching for action.

When the call came for volunteers for the North African Theater Kenneth jumped at the chance. He took ship to Gibraltar where he arrived at the beginning of March 1942. He boarded the British aircraft carrier *HMS EAGLE* which then dashed east from Gib' and the next day Kenneth flew his stripped down Spitfire from the deck of the *Eagle* at maximum range for a three hour flight of over 600 miles to Malta .

He and the other seventeen Spitfire pilots he'd flown in with received a warm welcome and a free drink from the Wing Commander at Ta Qali, an English pilot who'd become a legend on Malta at the ripe age of twenty-four,. The drink was delivered along with a stern lecture about the flying conditions and requirements they would be asked to meet. They would fly outnumbered and outgunned at all times. There was no room for personal glory, his new CO told them, no need on Malta for pilots looking to increase their individual 'score'. They must fly as a team whose purpose, more than destroying German and Italian aircraft was to force them off their bombing runs, protecting the airdromes and the harbors from devastation.

Their living conditions would be sub-standard. They were quartered in the Xaxa Palace in the old city of Mdina on the high ground less than a mile west of Ta Qali airfield, two pilots to a room. Each pair of pilots would have a Maltese batman to perform the menial cleaning chores for the pilots, but rations were thin, and after that first night the pilots would pay for their own liquor.

The new pilots were dismissed with twenty-four hours leave granted them to familiarize themselves with their new quarters, the lay of the land at the airdrome and with the island's limited entertainment opportunities. Several veteran Malta pilots were assigned to show the new men the ropes. Kenneth wound up traveling on borrowed bicycles with "Frenchy" Fuqua, another of the pilots who had flown in that morning and with Derrick Metcalfe, an Irishman who'd been on Malta since January. As such he was an 'old hand'.

"First, I want to show you around in the vicinity of the airfield itself," Metcalfe told them. "You'll want to be familiar with all the surrounding areas so you can find an air-raid shelter in a pinch or get back to the field in the dark."

"I did not come to Malta to hide in a shelter," protested Frenchy, who in spite of his nickname was a 'Geordie' who had never even been to France, nor in fact more than a few miles from his native Newcastle before the war. "If the Germans come over I want to be in the air!"

"Nice sentiment," said Metcalfe in his soft Belfast brogue, "but remember there are twice as many pilots as fighters on Malta right now. Add that to the fact that not every plane will scramble on every alert and you can see you won't be in the air every time the Germans come over." Derrick smiled, a wide, honest smile that lit his deep blue eyes.

Kenneth sized Metcalfe up. Black hair, with thick eyebrows and long lashes offset his pale, but clear complexion and those striking blue eyes. Near six feet and slim, with narrow waist, Kenneth decided Metcalfe would probably be very popular with women. He was someone Kenneth decided to stick to closely.

"All right," sighed Frenchy. "Point taken. Lead on to the nearest shelter. I suppose we shall have to tour them all."

Derrick laughed. "No, not all," he said. "Just a few of them in fact. We're going to Rabat first. It's the high ground on the central island. From there we'll be able to survey all the area around the airfield. I'll point out the shelters and the various paths and roadways, the dispersal pens and taxi strips. You'll get a good perspective of the whole island as well."

Derrick Metcalfe led the trio up the winding dirt road to Rabat past terraced farm fields, nearly all abandoned, cut into the slope of the rise. As they went he explained to them that the town was near Mdina, the ancient capital of the island. Ancient stone siege walls frowned down from Mdina upon the airfield. As they got closer Kenneth was impressed with the sheer proportions of the old fortress. Crenellated battlements stood twenty meters tall and looked to be about as thick.

When they reached the top of the hill at Rabat they dismounted their bikes and surveyed Ta Qali Airfield to the northeast. To Kenneth it seemed the field was set in the bottom of a large, shallow bowl. To the north and south of the field limestone ridges cut east to west across the island just beyond the ends of the runway, jagged strips of limestone poking through grass still green from the brief Malta winter. The southern ridge showed evidence of having been quarried and here and there shallow caverns were cut back into the white limestone bedrock. Across the field to the east lay the cities of Floriana, Sliema and Valletta clustered round the island's Grand Harbor.

Derrick explained that the airfield had been built by sacrificing the best farmland on the island and lay atop the long-dry bed of an ancient lake. The runway was laid out north to south, a 1200 yard long stripe of white limestone dust cut like a scar across the darker ground, with a huge circular taxiway a half-mile in diameter. The runway and taxiway together gave the impression of a huge gun sight drawn in white chalk on the ground. Inside the circle of the taxiway many thinner lines of white showed dispersal strips, paths by which aircraft were taken to and from their blast shelters. Throughout the area of the runway and taxi strips were innumerable bomb craters, many overlapping, blurred into massive white scars covering acres of ground. Not a single tree or blade of grass appeared to have survived within a half mile of the runway in any direction. But for human movement on the airfield it might have been a barren moonscape.

As they watched from the hill at Rabat a lorry trundled onto the runway, stopping at a fresh crater. A number of men leapt down from the lorry, ant like figures scurrying about. Fresh earth and stone were thrown from the lorry into the crater and the figures went to work with shovels to fill and smooth the crater. Within ten minutes the crater was gone and the truck moved on to another at the edge of the runway.

"Those are Army troops, detailed to the airfield to keep the runway clear," explained Metcalfe. "They do a tremendous job keeping the field in operation. Other troops serve as the aircraft armourers and mechanics." Next, he directed Kenneth and Frenchy to look to the southeast about three miles away.

"That's the airfield at Luqa," he explained. "Mainly bombers, Wellingtons and some Beaufighters too. The Beaufighters are the island's night fighter force," he said, "though there are also Spitfires there. You can't see it, but almost straight south of it is the Fleet Air Arm base at Hal Far on the southern shore. The Navy flies Swordfish torpedo bombers from there and it's also near the seaplane base at Kalafrana."

Metcalfe pointed north of Ta Qali. "You see that collection of buildings there?" he asked. "That's Mosta, one of the largest towns in the island's interior. Do you see the round topped building there in the-center? That's the dome of the Catholic Church. It's the third largest domed structure in the world, after only St. Peter's Basilica in Rome and St. Paul's Cathedral in London."

Kenneth turned back towards Ta Qali and saw two Spitfires taxiing into position for takeoff.

"Looks like a patrol going up," he said.

"No patrol," said Metcalfe. "We don't have enough fuel for patrolling. The radar must have detected a flight from Sicily. We'll hear the air raid sirens in a few moments."

The three pilots watched the Spitfires race down the runway, taking off to the north, climbing for altitude. Two more fighters took their places at the end of the runway, ready to takeoff at short notice. Just as Metcalfe predicted the island's air raid sirens soon began to wail.

"Ordinarily we should go to a shelter now," said Metcalfe, "but for this once you chaps may find it of interest to observe the party from above ground."

Within ten minutes a flight of eight Ju 88 bombers approached from the north at 8,000 feet. The two ready Spitfires raced into the air. As the Germans neared the runway the flak guns situated about the airfield opened up on the bombers. Undeterred the Germans flew on into the black puffs of exploding AA shells and dropped their bomb loads over the airfield at Ta Qali. Mushrooms of exploding earth leapt into the air, several directly on the runway. Secondary explosions, fire and a towering plume of thick, oily black smoke followed one bomb's explosion.

"Blighters scored a direct hit on one of the dispersal pens there," said Metcalfe. "Scratch one Spitfire."

The flak guns fell silent and the Germans peeled away to the north for their return to Sicily. One of the bombers however was trailing a thin stream of white smoke or vapor from its starboard engine.

"Watch now," said Metcalfe. "See the one the gunners have winged? Watch what happens to him."

As the bombers fled northward the wounded plane began to lag its fellows. The second pair of Spitfires pounced upon it like dogs on a bone. Without the supporting fire of the other ships in its flight the Ju 88 was soon riddled with cannon and machine gun fire and sent earthward like a flaming stone. Two parachutes opened behind it and floated slowly to earth.

The all-clear siren sounded as the other German bombers disappeared to the north. The three RAF pilots sat and chatted about their own flying experiences and watched for the return of the first Spitfires. After nearly an hour one of the fighters settled back to earth on the runway. It trundled to the taxiway then headed down one of the paths to its dispersal pen. The other fighter did not return.

It was late afternoon by then and the sun was sinking in the west. A stiff north wind blew the smell of snow down from Mount Etna whose peak on Sicily over sixty miles away was clearly visible over the northern horizon. The pilots pulled their collars up against the chill.

"Come on then," said Derrick. "The party's over, at least for now. Let's get down to Valletta before dark. I'll show you our night life."

The three mounted their borrowed bicycles and set off eastward across the waist of the island. To Kenneth the tiny sub-divided fields of Malta and the cut stone houses crowded one upon another in the towns and villages were as far from his home as he could imagine. The wide open spaces of the Great Plains, with its huge fields of grain stretching free and open to the horizon and the occasional lone farmhouse on the prairie had never seemed more remote.

Derrick Metcalfe, by rank an RAF Flying Officer, led them around the south of the airfield at Ta Qali, then east into the ancient city of Valletta.

"It's all down hill in this direction boys," he told them, "but if you get pissed in town be careful, it's a long climb back up the hill to the barracks."

They descended steadily as they pedaled east towards Valletta. The countryside became more built up, houses and stores replacing the little fields and stonewalls. Bomb craters and smashed buildings began to appear as they got to the outskirts of Valletta and its suburb Floriana. Soon every second or third house and store was a wreck.

"I thought we were going for a drink," said Frenchy. "If I wanted to tour bomb damage I could've done it in London."

"We're heading for a place called Maxime's," replied Metcalfe, laughing. "You'll get your drink there, dinner too if you're hungry. It also happens to be the best dance establishment on the island."

Kenneth's ears perked up. "Women?"

"Yes, women," laughed the Irishman again. "The local talent goes there as well as the few British girls on the island. Mostly English though," he finished with a sigh.

Frenchy and Kenneth exchanged looks and laughed.

"Lead on, oh fearless leader," said Kenneth.

"Yes, take us to your English girls," added Frenchy.

Maxime's was a big open hall with high ceilings. A second floor mezzanine looked down on the center of the dining room, which had been cleared as a large dance floor. About forty tables crowded the edges of the dance floor and diners were already seated. Waiters in black suits with white aprons tied at the waist scurried about taking orders and delivering meals. A long bar covered one of the side walls, a bandstand the rear wall. The *maitre d'* recognized Derrick immediately.

"Ah, Meez-ter Meet-caffe," he beamed. "Come right zis way wiz your frienz," he said, taking Derrick by the arm and leading them across the dance floor to a table near the bandstand. "Will zis table zuit you and your frienz, Meez-ter Meet-caffe?"

"Yes, Bay-al," said Derrick, smiling, "this table is magnificent, thank you."

Bay-al bowed and returned to the entrance.

"What about menus Meez-ter Meet-caffe?" Frenchy asked Derrick.

"No, menus here chum," smiled Derrick. "Only two things

left to eat on the whole island, Spam and bread."

"Spam!" exclaimed Kenneth. "We could have eaten that at the airfield!"

"Yes, but no one bakes bread like these Maltese. You'll eat more of it than anything else here on Malta," explained Derrick. "Besides, there are no girls at the airfield."

Kenneth looked around the dining room of the restaurant.

"There don't appear to be any here, either," commented Kenneth dryly.

"There will be," said Derrick, "there will be, once the band begins to play a little later."

A waiter appeared at the table, smiling expectantly, but said nothing.

"What will it be boys, gin or whiskey?" asked Derrick.

"Whiskey!" said Kenneth.

"Gin!" said Frenchy.

Derrick looked at Kenneth, ignoring Frenchy. "Scotch or Irish?" he asked.

"Irish!" said Kenneth.

"A man of good taste I see," said Derrick. To the waiter, "Three double Irish please."

The waiter nodded and turned for the bar. While he was away musicians began to occupy the bandstand, bringing a motley collection of instruments, more than a few apparently home made. Kenneth scanned the room. Still no women, but the dining room had filled and men in uniform were waiting near Bay-al at the door. The band began to tune their instruments.

The waiter returned bearing two trays, in one hand the drinks, in the other the food. He set their drinks down then set three bowls of thin soup and a basket with a round of bread wrapped in a grubby towel in front of the three pilots. The band began to play.

"Cheers!" said Frenchy.

"Cheers," his two companions replied.

Kenneth took a sip of his drink. He perked his ears up and began to hum along with the band, trying to sort out where he'd heard the tune before. In a moment his eyes went wide with recognition.

"Hey, I didn't think I was going to church tonight!" he said.

"What do you mean?" asked Frenchy.

"Listen to the tune," said Kenneth and hummed a few bars, then began to sing softly,

*"Wha-at a friend we have in Jee-sus."*

"You're right, Kenneth!" exclaimed Frenchy, "It's that hymn I used to sing in choir."

"Wait for the band to come back to the top of the first verse," said Derrick, nodding towards the crowd of uniformed servicemen gathered on the dance floor, drinks in hand. As the band came back to the top the crowd began to sing.

*"Whe-en this bleedin' war is oh-ver;*
*Oh! How happy I shall be.*
*Whe-en I get my civvy clothes on,*
*No more soldiering for me.*
*No more Church parades on Sun-days,*
*No more asking for a pass.*
*I can tell the Sergeant-Maa-jor,*
*To stick his passes up his ARSE!"*

Frenchy and Kenneth laughed till their sides hurt at the corrupted hymn. And so the early evening hours passed. The band played many popular favorites as well as other hymns whose words were even more fully perverted than the first selection. Several more double Irish whiskeys followed the first round and soon Kenneth found himself singing at the top of his voice along with the rest of the room.

He became dimly aware that Derrick, Frenchy and he had company at their table. Three young women joined them sometime during the singing of '*Hitler has only got one ball.*' Kenneth tried to focus on the women, but his eyes refused to co-operate. He tried to speak, but his tongue was like a rubber rope stuffed in his mouth that bounced in the way of his words. Frenchy and Derrick danced with two of the girls, but he could not stand up from his chair, even with help from the third girl. Somehow, Frenchy and Derrick got him home to the Xaxa palace.

In the over three months since arriving at Malta Kenneth saw a lot of action, particularly in April and early May when the Luftwaffe flew over 4,000 sorties against the island. Easter Sunday was especially busy and brutal. The Luftwaffe flew eight large raids that day. In the first of them, timed to coincide with High

Mass the domed Cathedral of Mosta was bombed. The sly old Priest of Mosta, an Italian who despised Mussolini as a lackey of Hitler's, anticipated the danger and held Easter Mass at 2am, then sent everyone home and to the shelters so their were no casualties in the church, but the famous dome was damaged by a bomb that crashed through it and landed in the front row of pews. It failed to explode. The islander's took this as proof of Divine Providence.

Kenneth flew as wingman to Derrick through the first two months of action at Malta and was with him that Easter Sunday, watching as Frenchy Fuqua's Spitfire fell to earth in flames near Mosta and exploded on impact.

There'd been little enough left to bury, but they'd attended Frenchy's memorial service the next day. Kenneth gathered Frenchy's belongings from their shared room, packed them in a duffel bag and delivered them to the Ta Qali quartermaster who placed the bag in a large warehouse several miles from the airfield, along with hundreds of other duffel bags belonging to soldiers from all over the British Commonwealth. It was hoped that someday the personal effects of the deceased could be returned to next of kin.

Flying as Derrick's wingman gave him few opportunities to add to his personal score, but he did his job well, keeping the Irishman's tail clean of German fighters as he attacked the bombers, and Kenneth managed to score twice. His first kill on Malta was an Italian Cant observation bomber he caught unawares coming out of broken clouds to the east of the island, the other a Ju 88 first crippled by AA fire over Ta Qali. He'd also seen over forty of his fellow Spitfire pilots killed in combat. When a pilot was killed it was said he had "Gone for a Burton" and many a Burton was gone for that spring at Malta.

All that spring mosquitoes and biting flies tormented him. Many Maltese and members of the British forces sickened from the bite of one or another of the island's insect pests. Skin infections like scabies were rife, especially among the army troops. They did backbreaking labor daily on the airfields and had very few chances to wash their sweat soaked uniforms. Salt sores and rashes in armpits and groins afflicted nearly every man. As a pilot Kenneth's lot was better than most. His batman saw to it that his uniform clothes were washed at least occasionally and his rations were a little better than the army troops'. Still, it seemed to Kenneth that he was constantly scratching one irritation or other.

During this time Kenneth also came down with the "Malta Dog" as the epidemic of amoebic dysentery was called. The whole island was infected as the incessant bombing severed sewer lines and forced the populace to rely on unfit water sources. Polio and tuberculosis struck Malta that spring of 1942, killing hundreds, disabling many more. A brief experiment using human feces to fertilize crops led to an outbreak of cholera that killed nearly a hundred people. The experiment was quietly discontinued.

As spring turned to summer on Malta the first cracks in the façade of invincible morale began to appear. Rations were slashed then slashed again for both native population and the garrison. By the end of May the fighting troops were down to one thousand calories a day, barely a third of what was considered adequate for a moderately active young man. All physical training was suspended. Instead, troops of the line were ordered to nap in the afternoons to conserve their energy. In their traditional stoic, deadpan humor the British soldiers called this "rest parade".

Civilians felt the pinch especially hard. They dragged themselves through their days, with barely the strength to feed themselves when food was available. Constant bombing forced them underground into crowded shelters almost everyday and made fertile fields for the spread of disease.

The British Overseas Air Corporation, better known as BOAC, increased its flights to Malta. Flying the enormous Short Sunderland seaplanes BOAC flew in twice a night, landing at the seaplane base at Kalafrana, carrying in critical medical supplies and aircraft spare parts, carrying out wounded. Malta formed the crucial intermediate stop in an airbridge stretching the width of the Mediterranean Sea, from Gibraltar to Alexandria by which critical personnel, mainly specialists in engineering, demolition or underwater salvage were flown back and forth the length of the sea.

In April the American aircraft Carrier *USS Wasp* delivered forty-six Spitfire fighters to Malta to bolster the air defenses. But disaster struck the British as the Luftwaffe attacked the airfields just as the new fighters were landing. Caught without fuel or ammunition the new fighters were like sheep in the fold to the

Luftwaffe wolves. Many were destroyed that first day. In less than seventy-two hours every new Spitfire was destroyed.

In May *Wasp* tried again, this time in company with *HMS Eagle*. Sixty-one Spitfires were successfully delivered on the 9th of the month. This time the ground crews were ready to immediately refuel the fighters and load their guns with ammunition. Pilots stood ready to relieve the men who'd flown from the carriers. Many of these new Spitfires were back in the air, armed and fueled in six minutes. They were a nasty surprise for that day's raiding Luftwaffe bomber pilots. By this time Kenneth was ready to lead a Spitfire flight and his new wingman, Andy White arrived with this second delivery of Spitfires.

Still, the situation for the defenders of Malta remained grave. The ammunition and food delivered in two destroyers in May only stretched the islands dwindling supplies a few weeks longer. By the beginning of June the flak guns were restricted to ten rounds a day, and the islander's daily bread was leavened with sawdust. Worse, no fuel was delivered. The island's population depended on kerosene for cooking and heating, and though the warm summer weather helped on that score, a two-week supply of cooking fuel was all that remained. The few scraps of lumber used in the construction of Maltese buildings were scavenged from wrecked homes and shops to stretch the supply of cooking fuel.

But aircraft can't fly on warm air and wood scraps, they require petrol and the Spitfire's Merlin engine gulped it in high-octane buckets. By the start of June Spitfire pilots were forced to take to the air with cold engines to save the fuel ordinarily used in warming up on the taxiway. A secret report prepared for Lord Gort and forwarded to the Admiralty in London showed that the island faced mass starvation by the end of July and that fuel stocks were down to a 30-day supply. Malta's spirit began to sputter like a candle before the wind. And the wind was rising.

But then, in early June came the start of a 'lull' in which the German and Italian air forces were drawn off to North Africa in support of the Afrika Korp offensive there. Two merchant ships of a convoy fought their way through to Grand Harbor delivering food and ammunition, staving off starvation for a few more weeks.

For the first time since his first night on Malta Kenneth was given a 24-hour leave. He and Derrick and the new man, Andy

White went into Valletta to Maxime's, the first time Kenneth had been back since the night of the drunken sing-along. It was Andy's first chance to sample the island's nightlife.

"Ah, Meez-ter Meet-caffe," Bay-al greeted them at the door. "Zo pleezed to zee you again."

"Thank you Bay-al," smiled Derrick. "I'm very pleased to see you as well."

"Will you and your frienz pleez come zis way?"

Bay-al led them to the same table near the bandstand. "I am afraid ze kishen iz clozed tonight Meez-ter Meet-caffe. We have no food to zerve, but we have plenty fine Irizh Whiz-key."

"Thanks, Bay-al," smiled Derrick. "Three doubles please."

"Of courz, Meez-ter Meet-caffe," answered Bay-al. "Right away." The *maitre d'* turned and snapped his fingers at a waiter. He held up three fingers and flashed them twice to the man who nodded and hurried to the bar.

Once again Maxime's was getting crowded though not with diners. Servicemen hungry for relief from the boredom and tension of their duties crowded into Valletta that night as the reprieve granted them by the Luftwaffe freed them from their duty stations. Other establishments in Valletta were filled as well, many of less repute than Maxime's. In Valletta's red light district, known as 'The Gut', skinny, mal-nourished whores turned tricks in a non-stop blur. Numerous bars and pubs in the city catered to the enlisted personnel of the garrison, many of whom were disappointed there was no beer. The brewery had been bombed a week before and the last stocks were gone.

Kenneth, Derrick and Andy took their seats. Andy smirked at Derrick.

"Meez-ter Meet-caffe?" he asked.

Derrick and Kenneth smiled thinly, remembering Frenchy Fuqua sitting in the same chair joking about Bay-al's pronunciation.

"I've invited a few birds I know to join us," said Derrick, steering the conversation.

"Local talent or home girls?" asked Andy who called London's West End home.

"Three English girls," said Derrick. "Not very many of them left on the island."

"I'll say," agreed Kenneth. "What are they still doing here?"

"Not sure, something hush-hush," said Derrick. "Best not to ask them either. A girl has to have some secrets ya know."

Kenneth and Andy laughed and looked at each other shyly. The thought of female attention was enough to catch Kenneth's breath. Growing up on a large farm he was certainly familiar with the basics of intercourse and had assisted in various ways with husbandry of the farm animals, but he had no practical experience of his own. That is to say, he was a virgin. With the number of pilots who had 'Gone for a Burton' over the past weeks he'd come to accept that he either had to pay a visit to 'The Gut' or die a mere boy. He was determined that one way or another tonight would be his night and he nursed his drink slowly to avoid getting drunk.

After a few sips Andy held his glass up to the light and eyed it suspiciously.

"Either I'm already pissed or this is the worst Irish whiskey I've ever had!" he complained.

"Sure, and you're tellin' an Irishman," said Derrick dryly. "There's not a drop o' real whiskey, or scotch or gin left on the whole island except maybe in their lordships' private cellars. Drink up and count your blessings."

"Well, all right," said Andy sulkily. "I don't really mind, but they oughtn't call it Irish whiskey if it's not."

"Straighten up now," snapped Derrick. "Here come the birds."

All three pilots stood and were joined at the table by three English women. Two were quite young and attractive, in their early to mid twenties Kenneth judged, but the third was a shock. Older, with hair graying at the temples and more than a bit dowdy she was close to fifty years old by his estimation and with a large, round mole above her right eye. Worse, the mole apart she bore an uncanny resemblance to his mother back home in Red Fern. Kenneth shuddered. 'Gut, here I come,' he thought to himself.

One of the younger women said to Derrick, "Hello, luv. I want you to meet my friends. This is Esther Woldridge," she said introducing the older woman, "and this is Margaret Reed."

Derrick introduced Andy and Kenneth.

"How d'ya do?" they both managed.

Kenneth held out a chair and to his relief Margaret sat down in it. Esther sat next to Andy who fired a look at Kenneth that boded ill for their next flight together. The other young woman sat next to Derrick who introduced her as Gabrielle Pearson. Derrick signaled the waiter to bring a fresh round of drinks for all six.

It became quickly apparent that Derrick and Gabrielle knew each other quite well. Gabrielle held Derrick in her gaze and virtually ignored the rest of the group for the remainder of the evening. Derrick played it just enough aloof to keep Gabrielle dancing to his whim. For the first time a flash of resentment towards Derrick hit Kenneth. Gabrielle was a pretty, petite brunette with deep, soulful brown eyes and it pained him to see how she fawned upon Derrick.

'Odd that English girls fall so for the Irish,' he thought.

Andy sat somewhat woodenly with Esther, finding little chance to strike up conversation until the drinks came. Esther took one sip and scowled at her drink.

"Neither Irish nor whiskey if you ask me," she opined sourly. "Still," she chuckled, "it's wet!" and with that she knocked back the better part of her double. Andy stared at her in amazement. "Come on lad," she said. "Bottom's up!" She waited till Andy took a big gulp of his drink. Soon the two were chattering away like long lost friends.

Kenneth smiled nervously at Margaret and struggled for words. After a few lame attempts at conversation he sighed and gave up, but he couldn't keep himself from looking at her. Her soft, clear skin and eyes drew his gaze and he fought to not stare. Soon the band began to play and he groaned as he heard the first notes of the opening number. He hid his head in his hands and stared at his shoes as the assembled service men joined in singing to the tune of *'Bless 'em All'*.

> *"Sod 'em all. Sod 'em all.*
> *The long and the short and the tall,*
> *Sod all the sergeants and WO ones,*
> *Sod all the corporals and their bastard sons,*
> *For we're saying goodbye to them all,*
> *As back to their billets they crawl,*
> *You'll get no promotion*
> *This side of the ocean,*
> *So cheer up, my lads, sod 'em all!*

Kenneth peeked from beneath his eyelids and was further amazed to find Esther and Andy arm-in-arm singing the song together at the tops of their voices. He looked at Margaret. She smiled at him and leaned over to speak in his ear over the din of the singers.

"It's OK," she said. "I've heard it before!" She leaned back in her chair, smiled again and hummed her way through the second chorus of the song.

Kenneth sat up and breathed a sigh of relief. He smiled and shook his head.

"I was worried you were a lady and would be shocked," he said then gasped as Margaret's eyebrow shot up. "Er, I mean, I know you are a lady," he stammered, "just not that kind of lady." She looked at him with a complete deadpan expression. "Oh, balls!" he said. He grabbed his drink and took a deep swallow.

Margaret was still looking at him quizzically, but a tiny smile curled the corners of her mouth. The band began to play a number popularized by Vera Lynn, *'The White Cliffs of Dover'*.

"Would you like to dance?" he asked hopefully.

"Yes," she replied after the briefest pause.

He stood, took her hand and led her to the dance floor. Before he could slip his left arm around her back she took it in her right hand. She looked him in the eyes and smiled. He sighed. They danced hand in hand, their bodies a foot apart.

Kenneth did not lose his virtue that night, nor the next time he saw Margaret, or 'Maggie' as she eventually asked him to call her, but he didn't care. He'd fallen in love with her that night, dancing and talking at Maxime's. He hadn't told her so yet, but he was sure of it and as June wore on quietly with the Luftwaffe otherwise engaged, he fell deeper and deeper for her. He never contemplated 'The Gut' again.

Maggie kept her own feelings to herself, but she never put him off when he got through to her on the telephone at her quarters under Lascaris Bastion. On a couple occasions in those three relatively carefree weeks in June she'd swapped shifts with other 'Y' Service operators to accommodate Kenneth's duty schedule. She knew he was just a boy, and an American at that, but he was sweet and kind, and more than a little handsome in a gangly sort of way. And he was oh, so lonely, and deep down she knew he was oh, so scared.

'There's no future in it, Mags,' she told herself. After all, fighter pilot lifecycles on Malta were measured in days and weeks. So, she contented herself with joining Kenneth for swimming excursions to St. Paul's Bay on the north shore and for picnic lunches to Kalafrana in the south, while the lull was on. They mainly talked about their lives before the war, his home in Red Fern and growing up on a large farm, and her suburban upbringing outside London and about their dreams for when the war was over. A little, they talked about his flying experience or the tom-foolery that went on at the airfield when things were quiet, but any time the conversation came round to her work, or of how she came to be on Malta, Maggie deftly deflected him, changing the subject, so that Kenneth never learned anything about wireless intercepts or the 'Y' Service. Eventually he learned to avoid the subject.

Then, came the news of Tobruk's fall on June 21. Kenneth and Maggie didn't know it yet, but their lull had ended.

>>>>>>>>>>>>>>>>>>>>>>>>>>>>>>>>>>>>>>>>>>>>>>>>>>
>>>>>>>>

"Your papers please." The SS Captain held his hand out to reinforce the demand.

The Army Major pulled out his orders and paybook, handing them to the SS guard.

"Danke," said the black uniformed SS captain as he took and unfolded the papers.

The Army Major turned and looked up into the clear blue, late afternoon sky above Berlin. It was a lovely day and the Major was again grateful that these daily conferences were scheduled so late in the afternoon. He looked down the street. It was crowded with pedestrians. Most were men in the uniform of one or other of the armed services with a fair sampling of women in uniform as well. They scurried back and forth on official business among the many government buildings on Wilhelmstrasse.

The SS guard studied the orders, then the paybook, scanning

the photo, comparing it to the features of the man standing before him. Satisfied, he folded both documents and handed them back to the Army officer.

"You may enter, Major," said the SS man, snapping rigidly to attention with a Nazi salute. "Heil Hitler!" he shouted.

"Heil Hitler!" replied the Major.

Tucking the papers back in his tunic he entered the Reich Chancellery building at 77 Wilhelmstrasse, passing through the rotunda and down the long central hall of the building that was the seat of the Nazi government. Party uniforms were more common inside the building. Most of the denizens of the Chancellery wore Swastika armbands.

He came to the side passage midway down the hall. Turning right he walked the short distance to the Chancellery's Garden Entrance. Passing back outside, he stepped out to the flowerbeds and shrubs of the garden and approached the above ground entrance to the Fuhrer Bunker. His identity papers were again examined before he was granted entrance.

As he stepped into the windowless interior the fetid air of the bunker struck him. The ventilation system was not up to cleansing the stale body odor and damp scent of mold and decay from the air in the underground complex. He paused briefly, letting his eyes adjust to the dim light then proceeded to a staircase and down four long flights of stairs to a landing at the bottom. Next he went down a wide hallway, his footsteps echoing loudly from the concrete walls and steel doors of the chamber. He knew that every step of his way was observed by several sets of unseen eyes, peering at him through secret slits in the passage. The Fuhrer's paranoia for his own safety could not be quelled.

He came to a small right hand opening, a short hallway leading to a single steel door. Two more SS stood guard and repeated the examination of his documents. They also required him to open his valise for inspection and confiscated his Walther pistol before admitting him.

At last the steel door swung shut behind him and he stood in the Fuhrer's conference room. The chamber was large, ten meters wide, twenty-five long. A covered map board stood at the far end, flanked by National Flags hung straight from the ceiling. A small inset to the left side of the far wall was another steel door, the only opening other than by which he had entered. He'd never been through that other door, but obviously it let onto an interior passageway to the Chancellery building.

An oval conference table filled the center of the room. High backed, ornately carved wooden chairs sat flanking the table. From painful experience the Major knew how uncomfortable the chairs were, by design he suspected, to keep officers and underlings awake during the endless forums held here. At the far end sat a single chair, raised on a small dais giving its occupant a perspective above all others in the room.

Over a dozen officers, ranking from Army Captain to Field Marshall and from all branches of service, Luftwaffe, Kriegsmarine, Heer or regular army and more black uniformed SS with Death's Head collar insignia, milled about the room. An Army captain served schnapps to Reichfurher and Luftwaffe head Hermann Goering at a massive oaken sideboard on the left wall. The Reichfuhrer helped himself to delicacies from silver bowls on the sideboard. A subdued chatter filled the room.

He scanned the room till he found the man he sought. Luftwaffe Lieutenant-General Lorzer, Commander of the Air Force's II Fliegerkorps. Lorzer had flown to Berlin for this conference, leaving his headquarters at the Hotel San Domenico in Taormino, Sicily with reluctance. His fighter and bomber squadrons were very busy, in close combat with Royal Air Force and occasionally Royal Navy Fleet Air Arm flyers in the skies over the central Mediterranean and North Africa. Lorzer was subordinate to Field Marshall Albert Kesselring, commander of the Lutfwaffe's II Luftflotte and overall commander of all German forces in the Mediterranean. Kesselring was himself in Rome at the moment. The Army Major maneuvered through the officers in the room and approached Lorzer.

"Herr General," he greeted Lorzer with a click of his heels and tip of his head.

"Major, do I know you?" asked Lorzer quizzically.

"No, Sir," he replied. "I am Major Kuno Schacht. I am to be the new Africa Corps liaison officer to your HQ."

Lorzer gave a thin smile as he studied the young officer before him, noting first the Iron Cross hung at the young Major's throat. With black hair and blue eyes on a lean, athletic frame just over six feet tall, Schacht cut an impressive figure in his Army uniform.

"I am pleased to meet you Major. We will have much to talk about after this," he said, gesturing to the conference room and assembled officers. "I wish to maintain the highest cooperation between 2nd Air Fleet and General Rommel's headquarters."

"Thank you, Sir," replied Schacht, a smile lighting his youthful face, touching the corners of his blue eyes. "I'm sure General Rommel is also most anxious for the highest cooperation between the two commands. As he drives closer to the British bases at Tobruk and Alexandria he will lean ever more on the assistance of the Luftwaffe."

"We shall see if General Rommel is permitted to continue his offensive," replied the airman, nodding his head to the smaller entrance that had just opened. Conversation died quickly as Adolph Hitler entered the room.

"Heil Hitler!" erupted from every man present and a forest of stiff armed salutes sprang up. Hitler responded with his characteristic half salute, arm bent at elbow.

"Be seated gentlemen," he said, "that is, if the Reichfuhrer can be dragged from the buffet!" This with a pointed, yet mirthful look at Goering. Polite, overloud laughter from his officers greeted the Fuhrer's humor, Goering himself louder than anyone else.

"Keitel, will you begin please? What is the situation in the East?" the Fuhrer asked.

Field Marshall Wilhelm Keitel rose from his chair at the head of the table nearest the map board. Keitel was Chief of Staff of the OKW, Ober Kommando Wehrmacht, the Armed Forces High Command. He gestured to an SS orderly who stepped forward and removed the covering from the board revealing a map of the entire Eastern Front from the Soviet Russian port of Arkhangel'sk north of Leningrad on the White Sea to Tehran, Iran in the south. Red ribbon ran in a ragged line from a point just to the east of Leningrad down to the city of Karkhov in the Ukraine, then over to a point east of the neck of the Crimean Peninsula. For a moment no one in the room spoke as they took in their first view of the East Front map.

Schacht was struck by the poles of the map, White Sea to the north, Black Sea in the south. "Our armies triumphant from white to black," he thought, but with more than a trace of private sarcasm. He personally knew full well how bitter was the fighting in the East, how dangerously underestimated had been the Soviet Bear.

The list of officers at the conference changed daily, most having attended many such briefings with a few relative new comers like Schacht himself who had been attending daily for just over three weeks. Each day there was usually an officer or two who'd never been privileged to attend before. These were easily spotted by the wide-eyed look of awestruck wonder they exhibited at the presence of the Fuhrer. Those who lasted more than a week generally adopted the more restrained demeanor of the veteran conference goers. Schacht glanced at Lorzer. The Luftwaffe General appeared at perfect ease, attentive yet not overwhelmed by the moment. He remembered his own first Fuhrer briefing. He had barely held his water through the afternoon. Since then he had carefully avoided beverages prior to the briefings.

"The situation around Kharkov in the south continues to stabilize," began Keitel. "Pockets of resistance to the south of the city are being liquidated and the panzer units of Army Group South are driving against light opposition through the Donets Basin towards the mouth of the river Don." Keitel pointed at each location on the map as he spoke, moving quickly through the past 24 hours' events. "Very shortly," he continued, "our forces will have removed the Ukraine from the Soviet Union." He turned to the Fuhrer with a broad smile. "The enemy will be deprived of his bread basket".

"And what of the Crimea?" asked Hitler. "Will the red dogs continue their stand? Remember Keitel, we can't afford to mount long sieges against pockets of holdouts!"

"Intelligence reports indicate the remnants of two Soviet Armies remain on the Crimean Peninsula my Fuhrer," admitted Keitel, "but they are worn out, greatly diminished in strength and are being attacked relentlessly by the Luftwaffe as they retreat." He tapped the map again, "Already our forces are across the Dnieper and have cut off the neck of the peninsula. We will be in position to destroy the remaining enemy forces piecemeal." He shrugged. "What few pitiful remnants have reached the port of Sevastopol will find their reprieve to be quite short."

Hitler nodded, warming now to the briefing and to the progress being reported. "Go on Keitel," he said, "what of the situation in the center?"

At that moment the door to the conference room opened. An Army General entered holding a sheet of paper. Schacht recognized General Franz Halder, Army Chief of Staff, head of the OKH. Halder paused as he came in the door then addressed Hitler.

"Your pardon Fuhrer," he said. "I have come from the Army signals room. I have a wireless transmission from General Rommel that you should see immediately." Halder was playing for dramatic effect. He had had the signal from Rommel for some hours before presenting it to Hitler at the conference that evening.

"Bring it to me Halder!" snapped Hitler.

Halder strode the length of the conference room around the table to the Fuhrer's chair, every eye in the room following him expectantly. He handed the sheet of paper to Hitler, then stepped back a pace as the Fuhrer held the sheet at arms length. Now the center of attention, Hitler took his time in reading the message. As his eyes scanned the page every other man in the room stared at him waiting for the news Rommel's message brought.

After some time, Hitler lowered the paper and scanned the length of the table, down one side and back up the other, making eye contact with each of the seated officers.

He began calmly. "Gentlemen," he said. "TOBRUK HAS FALLEN!" he shouted, his fist pumping the air.

The conference room erupted in wild applause. The conferees leapt to their feet with shouts of congratulations to the Fuhrer. Hitler beamed and accepted the praise of the officers, shaking hands with Halder, Keitel and several of the lesser nearby men. As the impromptu celebration wound down Field Marshall Keitel called the room to order.

"Attention, attention," he called above the din until he had quiet again, but there was an air of electric tension in the room. The officers gathered in the room knew they were among the very first in all Germany to hear of this latest triumph of German arms.

"Gentlemen," Keitel continued, "we have a full agenda today and I'm sure the Fuhrer will wish to make a public pronouncement regarding General Rommel's triumph at Tobruk, so let us continue please."

"Not now Keitel," Hitler interrupted.

"Of course, Fuhrer!" With a thin scowl Keitel bowed to Hitler and stepped back.

"Halder," Hitler addressed the OKH chief. "Prepare a signal to the Afrika Korps announcing the promotion of General Rommel to the rank of Field Marshall!"

Excited conversation rose again among the officers, followed by a spontaneous round of applause. Schacht felt a thrill of vicarious pride. He would now report directly to a Field Marshall! He turned to speak to General Lorzer on his left and was surprised to see a thoughtful expression on the General's face. After a second's hesitation Lorzer turned and looked down the table. Schacht saw that Lorzer's eyes met those of Admiral Raeder. The two exchanged a brief look, some shared thought understood by them both. The moment passed and Lorzer looked back to the head of the table where Hitler sat beaming. He saw Schacht and realized the Major had seen the look between himself and Raeder.

Lorzer smiled at him. "It's all right Schacht," he said. "Rommel has earned his red stripes. We shall see very soon what he is allowed to do with them." He nodded his head back up the table to where Halder and Keitel had drawn aside and were speaking quietly. The din in the room grew with the officers' excitement over the Afrika Korps victory.

Schacht watched Halder and Keitel as their conversation continued. They spoke too quietly for anyone but each other to hear, but it was obvious to Schacht that they were arguing. Finally Keitel cut off further discussion with a chop of his hands and pointed back to the conference table. Halder tipped his head as though in grudging acquiescence and moved down the table to the chair that had been held for him. Keitel resumed his role as conference chairman.

"Gentlemen," he called above the din of conversation. "GENTLEMEN," he shouted to be heard above the celebration. The room began to settle down as officers returned to their seats, concluding conversations with a few final words.

"Thank you gentlemen," Keitel said as the noise fell to scraping chairs, shuffling of papers and so forth. "The Fuhrer's generosity and wisdom in recognizing the leadership of General Rommel with promotion to Field Grade rank are an inspiration to all of us I am sure." With this Keitel turned and bowed to Hitler and a polite round of applause broke out. Keitel joined briefly then held his hands out for quiet.

"General Halder," he continued, "will prepare the signal as the Fuhrer directs and bring this joyous news to Field Marshall Rommel and the entire Afrika Korp upon conclusion of this conference. And now we must return to our schedule. We were discussing the day's events in the southern Ukraine." He turned to face the map and pointed to the region at the neck of the Crimean Peninsula when a voice from the room interrupted.

"Excuse me, Field Marshall Keitel!" Schacht looked down the table to see who had spoken. He saw that Grand Admiral Raeder had risen from his seat.

Keitel turned to him. "Yes, Admiral Raeder, what is it?" he asked with evident exasperation at being interrupted again.

Raeder tipped his head to Keitel in acknowledgment. "I beg your pardon and I certainly understand there is much to cover on the eastern front this afternoon, but I believe now is the time to determine the orders under which our newest Field Marshall will conduct his operations."

"Yes, Raeder," replied Keitel. "I see your point. The capture of Tobruk opens exciting new possibilities to Rommel doesn't it?"

"Indeed," Raeder said. "To an officer of Rommel's abilities and vision the allure of advancing deep into Egypt to threaten the British naval facility at Alexandria, the Nile River Delta and the Suez Canal itself will be very tempting."

"You do not feel, Raeder that these are appropriate goals for Rommel and the Afrika Korp?" asked Keitel.

"Oh, yes!" said the Admiral, "These are absolutely goals which the Mediterranean campaign should pursue, but notice that I say the 'Mediterranean' campaign. Alexandria, the Nile and Suez are targets, but for the combined naval, air and ground forces of Germany and Italy, not just for Field Marshall Rommel."

Raeder now strode to the end of the table where he pushed aside the eastern front map board, revealing a smaller board behind it. On it was a map of the Mediterranean Sea and surrounding land areas, from Syria in the East to Portugal in the west. Inset, covering an area of southern France on the larger map was a smaller one. Schacht saw the smaller map was of three islands surrounded by sea. Raeder turned the board to face Hitler.

"I know what you want Raeder!" interjected Hitler angrily. "You are going to bring up that damned Malta operation again aren't you?" He gestured at the airman at Schacht's side, "You think I don't know why Lorzer is here and Student down there with you?"

Schacht looked down the table and noted the other Luftwaffe General in the room. General Kurt Student commanded the Luftwaffe's elite paratrooper, or Falschirmjager formations. Schacht wondered at the Luftwaffe's heavy presence at the conference, Goering, Lorzer and Student. Goering was a frequent attendee, but Schacht had not seen the other two at the conference before, though admittedly his own attendance had begun just weeks prior.

The Fuhrer sat back, his anger subsiding slightly. "We have been through this before" he said wearily. "Malta in my judgment is impregnable by any of the means you have described till now. Paratroopers will suffer heavy casualties just as they did at Crete, there is no flat place on the island for a glider landing and our landing boats would not even get close to shore against Malta's guns. Even if a landing could be made on the island, by sea or air," he pounded his fist down on the table, "the Royal Navy would dispatch its fleets from Gibraltar and Alexandria and crush the assault force with heavy gun fire!" His voice rose again, "And don't tell me how the Italian Fleet will block them! The Eye-ties will run from the British, as they have every time they've been confronted by the Royal Navy." The Fuhrer leaned forward and stared down the table at Raeder. "I will waste no more of my time on this issue," he concluded as he looked back towards Keitel, but then as if to challenge the Admiral he looked back at him. "Unless, that is you have something new to try to sway me with?" Hitler's gaze was direct and menacing, a clear threat to the Admiral. For a moment history sat balanced on the edge of a knife, tipping first one way, then the other with the island of Malta the delicate fulcrum. Raeder took a deep breath and seemed about to slink back to his chair. But then, as though finding new resolve he went on.

"Yes, my Fuhrer," he began slowly, "I do have two new changes to the plan which I believe will address your concerns about Operation Herkules."

Schacht listened attentively to the Admiral. This was the first reference he had heard to an Operation codenamed 'Herkules', or any other planned assault on Malta. Hitler leaned back in his chair, waiting expectantly. Raeder hesitated again for just a moment, took another deep breath and went on.

"Two factors in the planned assault on Malta, Operation Herkules, have now been altered. First," he paused and bowed to the man at the head of the table, "the issue of flat landing zones for gliders." He turned back to the maps, pointing now to the smaller inset map and at the main island of Malta itself. "It is true that the countryside of the island is rocky and covered with low stone walls dividing farm fields, very dangerous for glider landings. Casualties just in landing would undoubtedly be high, BUT," he raised his voice to cut off the anticipated objection from Hitler, "we have until now ignored three completely flat landing zones, ideal for glider landings, right on the main island!" He looked back at the head of the table directly at Hitler. "These three sites provide General Student's Paratroopers and Gliders with perfect landing sites. They are large enough to land 7,000 men on the island at one time. The gliders that land with the first wave can deliver sufficient anti-tank weapons to keep the limited British armor on the island at bay until the follow-on waves have also landed and the air-head can be expanded."

Schacht turned his attention from Raeder to Hitler and saw that the Fuhrer was listening, but with a doubtful expression on his face.

"Come, come Admiral," he said. "We have studied the island for months. The only three sites with the topography you describe are the three British air bases on the island."

Raeder smiled and nodded his head, but said nothing.

"MEIN GOTT!" exclaimed Hitler. "Do you propose to drop Student's paratroops directly on the heads of the Tommies at the air bases? Our men will be slaughtered! Are you mad?"

"No, my Fuhrer," replied the Admiral. "I have complete command of my wits. General Student is prepared to discuss the details of this proposal." With a bow to Student he returned to his seat.

"If I may have your leave my Fuhrer I will explain the

revised plan." Student rose from his seat and walked to the map. "The night of June 25th, just four days from now, a nearly full moon will rise in the early evening hours over Malta and our air bases at Catania, Castelvetrano, Gerbini and Comiso on Sicily." Student tapped the island of Sicily on the map of the Mediterranean Sea. "It will remain bright until nearly dawn at 05:12; bright enough for our aircraft to make the short flight from Sicily, locate the landing zones and for the paras to drop and glider pilots to land their craft. The moon will wax until it reaches its fullest on June 28th then will wane. This gives us six nights of bright moonlight from the 25th to the 30th with which to augment daylight flying hours. The transport aircraft will be preceded to the target zones by waves of bomber and fighter aircraft of General Lorzer's II Fliegerkorps who will bomb the airfields and engage and destroy any enemy fighter opposition encountered. At the very least, the enemy fighter aircraft will be fully occupied, unable to interfere with the transports and gliders. Over the past several months and again in the days remaining before the assault the II Air Corps will work over the airfields to wear down British fighter strength ahead of the attack. On the morning of the attack the bomber and fighter sweeps will take place over the island's three airfields at 0010 hours. Constant fighter and bomber presence will be maintained by the II Air Corps throughout the invasion of the island, interrupted only by short intervals when neither sunlight nor moonlight is available. The longest such interval in the six days will be approximately one hour, fifteen minutes." Student surveyed the assembled officers then turned to the Fuhrer and continued.

"The paratroop force under the command of General Ramcke is exercising now at a location on the Italian coast which bears a strong similarity to Malta," Student told Hitler. "The force can be moved to its jump-off positions on Sicily within twenty-four hours of receiving its orders." Student turned and pointed to General Lorzer. All eyes in the room, including Hitler's focused on Lorzer. Schacht felt a very uncomfortable reflection of this attention.

The paratroop General went on. "Never before has the Luftwaffe concentrated such an intensive and long lasting presence over a single target. RAF and Royal Navy aircraft on the island will be destroyed on the ground and in the air and denied any opportunity to land safely to refuel or rearm. The British presence in the air will be swept aside! In addition, our aircraft will be in radio contact with the troops on the ground, ready to provide close air support, breaking up British counterattacks and bombing and strafing any concentration of troops or vehicles the enemy may attempt."

Schacht turned again to look at Hitler. The Fuhrer was very interested in the General's presentation. Student was held in high regard in the German Armed Forces for his ability to present a complex tactical situation in a clear way. It was Student who sold the German High Command on the paratroop assaults against Dutch and Belgian frontier forts at the start of the Nazi blitz into the Low Countries and France in May 1940. Schacht nodded approval. Raeder had been wise to defer to Student for this part of the appeal to Hitler. Student held the room.

"The timing of the paratroop drop and glider assault behind the initial air attacks is critical," he continued. "The glider troops will land directly on the runways and taxi strips of the British airfields even as the last bombs fall. The British will still be in their dugouts and shelters, except for the anti-aircraft gunners whose attention will be held by the bombers. The glider troops, over three thousand in all between the three airfields will seize the runways in a lightning 'coup de main' assault, extinguishing the fire of the surviving anti-aircraft guns and routing their crews."

Student surveyed the room. "Are there any questions to this point?" he asked.

An Army colonel of the panzer troops spoke. "Admiral Raeder indicated over seven thousand troops will land at one time. Where do the other four thousand come from?"

Student replied. "Because our airfields in Sicily lie less than thirty minutes flight from Malta our Junkers 52 transport aircraft will pull a heavy load on the first wave. Each Ju 52 will carry a compliment of thirteen paras rather than full capacity of eighteen, and on their first sortie the aircraft will carry only half their capacity of fuel. Fewer paratroopers and reduced fuel load will allow the Junkers to tow a glider with an average compliment of fourteen men. The aircraft can withstand this strain for flights of such short duration." He pointed back to the map gesturing with his hands to mimic the flight pattern of the transports. "After releasing the glider tow hooks the Junkers will veer off the airfield flight lines, odd numbered craft to port, even numbered to starboard and the paratroops in the first wave will drop just two hundred to five hundred meters off the runways. Four thousand paras and three thousand glider troops will reach the ground in the first fifteen minutes of the assault and the airfields will be in our hands." He smiled and tipped his head slightly to the Army Colonel.

Schacht wondered if Student and the Colonel had staged the question in anticipation of an objection from Hitler. In fact, Student had rehearsed his presentation for hours, with his staff asking every conceivable question until he was ready to answer anything.

Pointing back to the inset map of Malta General Student continued. "Our fighters will remain over the airfields to prevent any airborne British planes from attacking our troops. With the fields in our hands these British craft can remain in the air only until shot down by our fighters or they run out of fuel. From that moment forward we will have absolute command of the skies for the remainder of the operation."

Student now referred to the larger map. "The nearest British land bases are at Gibraltar to the west," tapping the British naval base at the Mediterranean's exit to the Atlantic Ocean, "almost one thousand miles distant, and to the east at Alexandria in Egypt," tapping the North African seaport, "also almost one thousand miles distant. The British have no aircraft capable of reaching Malta from any other land base to intervene."

Hitler interjected now, though with much less vehemence than earlier. "But Student, you have shown you can deliver seven thousand men to the island. The British garrison is three times that size. Your men will eventually be overwhelmed."

"In fact," replied Student, "intelligence estimates place the British garrison at over 25,000, though several thousands are administrative staff, not fighting troops."

"So," demanded Hitler, "how are your 7,000 to overcome 25,000 British?"

"Bear in mind once again the short flight time between Malta and our Sicilian air bases," answered Student. "The Ju 52 can make the round trip in less than one hour. From the moment the last troops of the first wave are dropped to the time the first troops of the second wave begin arriving over the airfields little more than one hour will elapse. The second wave will carry an additional four thousand paratroops. Also, nearly every paratrooper in the infantry squads will be armed with an automatic weapon, a MP 40 or Model 34 machine gun, thus greatly increasing firepower per man."

"Increasing ammunition consumption accordingly," snapped Hitler who waved Student off as he began to reply. "Never mind that Student, we can spare a few thousand extra rounds. Continue!"

Schacht could see that the Fuhrer was intrigued by the bold plan. Perhaps taking Malta would be feasible? Student went on, warming now to the presentation.

"Throughout the remainder of the morning hours and through the long daylight until 2130 hours in the evening the transports will continue to deliver troops to the island. By nightfall we will have landed over 25,000 German troops, including over 8,000 regular infantry who will fly in and land on the airfields once the runways are cleared. A force of some 5,000 Italian paratroops of the *Folgore* and *Superba* airborne divisions will also be landed that first day making a force of some 30,000 Axis troops. Along with our overwhelming air superiority these men are more than enough to defeat the British defenses. The next day 9,000 Italian infantry and our own 508th tank detachment, equipped with captured soviet armored vehicles will land from the sea to complete the occupation of the principal island and to squash any remaining pockets of British resistance."

"Yes, Student," began the Fuhrer, "I can see that the island might be taken, but can it be held?" he went on. "What of the Royal Navy? Do we expect it to sleep through your planned assault?"

Keitel now saw his moment to curry favor with Hitler. "Yes, Student you have failed to consider the consequences of the Royal Navy's' reaction to the assault."

Student bowed to both Keitel and Hitler. "Admiral Raeder is prepared now to describe the naval plan to prevent the Royal Navy from intervening at Malta." He returned to his seat as Raeder once again stood and strode to the map.

"The British will undoubtedly see this attack on Malta as the gravest possible threat to their position in the Mediterranean," he said. "From their air bases on the island and from the two superb harbors on the island's eastern shore they are able to dominate both sea and air travel lanes throughout the central basin of the Mediterranean. They won't give up such a base easily. Their response will be swift and with all the strength they can muster, with powerful surface and aircraft carrier forces both from Gibraltar," tapping the map, "and Alexandria. By the planned date of the assault eleven U-boats will be deployed to the Mediterranean from their bases at the French Atlantic ports of Brest and Bordeaux. They will join the nine U-Boats already operating there to form two Wolf Packs. Following the invasion they will be based at the Italian fleet bases at Naples," touching the west Italian port, "and at Taranto", moving down to the great port in the arch of the Italian boot. "Facilities are being prepared now for their arrival. They'll operate from these bases until threat of a British counter-invasion of Malta is eliminated." He shifted his finger on the map back to the west, resting it midway between Gibraltar and the Italian island of Sardinia.

"The first wolf pack will be responsible for attacking British fleet units from Gibraltar, striking here," tapping the map west of Sardinia, "outside Fleet Air Arm aircraft range of Malta. This Wolf Pack, code-named 'Tannenburg', will be composed of the eleven boats from France. Spotting and observation of the British fleet units will be performed by long range patrol aircraft of the Italian Air Force recently moved into Sardinia." Now, he shifted back to the eastern Mediterranean.

"The other wolf pack of nine boats will hit the British as they sail from Alexandria, again outside Fleet Air Arm range of Malta. This wolf pack is code-named 'Wagner'. It is the smaller of the two forces as it is known the British fleet at Alexandria has been reduced in the past months and is not as much a threat as the British fleet at Gibraltar. Both Wolf Pack's priority targets are airplane carriers, battleships and troop transports, though it's not expected the British will be able to quickly embark significant numbers of troops to relieve the island."

"Twenty U-boats against the whole of the Royal Navy's Mediterranean fleet?" shouted the Fuhrer. "It is preposterous! They will be swept aside. Oh, they may have some limited success, sinking a capital ship or two even, but they cannot stop the British alone!"

"Nor are they meant to my Fuhrer!" replied Raeder. "Combined with this U-boat force will be thirty Italian submarines and a force of our own Schnell Boats and Italian Torpedo Boats from the islands of Pantalleria and Lampedusa in the Sicilian Narrows. Heavy units of the Italian Navy based at Naples will also be available to counter the British threat. We are quite confident that until the Maltese airfields are in operation by the Luftwaffe we will be able to block the British from relieving the garrison or from delivering air or naval bombardments against our assault forces."

Hitler growled. "Even this force can't stop the British Raeder. The Italians will run when confronted by the Royal Navy, just like every other time they've faced the British."

"Quite so, Fuhrer," Raeder answered. "General Lorzer, will you describe the Luftwaffe element of the plan to turn back the British fleets please?"

Schacht turned to look at Lorzer, not surprised to find the Luftwaffe General in on the plan. Lorzer rose and walked around the conference table to the map. Schacht began to see that the senior officers involved in planning Operation Herkules had carefully orchestrated this day's conference.

"Thank you, Admiral Raeder," began Lorzer. He turned now to the Fuhrer. "There are two main premises of the Luftwaffe plan against the British fleets. First we must keep British airplane carriers out of flight range of Malta, or at least at such distance that any British aircraft that arrive at the island will be at the extreme limits of their fuel. With the airfields on the island in our possession the British will have to make the round trip flight to their carriers with no where else to land. Such few British as attempt this suicide mission will be prevented from attacking our ground troops by our fighter aircraft based nearby on Sicily." Lorzer scanned the room for questions. Seeing none he continued.

"Secondly, British surface units must be kept away from the island to prevent their shelling our paratroopers with heavy caliber shells from battleships and cruisers."

"In the west," he pointed to the island of Sardinia, "II Fliegerkorps has been reinforced with additional fighters, Stuka dive bombers and Junkers 88 bombers to attack the British fleet long before they are in range of Malta. In addition a number of the new He 111 Torpedo bombers have been stationed at Decimomanu airfield near Cagliari. As the British advance towards Malta the closer they must pass to our air forces, both on Sardinia and Sicily."

"Do you promise you can sink the British airplane carriers Lorzer?" asked Hitler doubtfully.

"We expect to make successful attacks against them Fuhrer," replied Lorzer, "though it is not strictly necessary that they be sunk for the success of the operation against Malta. Between shooting down their aircraft in aerial combat and attacking the ships themselves we are quite confident of preventing them launching effective air attacks against our Malta invasion force."

"And in the east you will launch similar attacks from Crete against the British that sail from Alexandria?" asked Hitler.

"Yes, Fuhrer," replied Lorzer, "that is correct. The VIII Fliegerkorps based on Crete has also been reinforced to carry out these attacks." Again, Lorzer paused and scanned the room for questions, then returned his attention to Hitler.

"All told we have assembled a force of some 800 fighter and bomber aircraft plus the Junkers transports to carry out the assault on Malta and to attack the British fleet as it tries to relieve their army garrison. The first attacks against the island defenses have already been carried out this morning, striking the three airfields and flak batteries on Malta."

Keitel, ever sensitive to Hitler's mood objected. "So, the island can be taken and perhaps even held, but at what cost and for what purpose? Any operation which detracts force or strength from the assault in the east is unacceptable!" Keitel's voice rose, but Schacht felt that the Field Marshall had for once mis-read the Fuhrers mood. Hitler was intrigued by the plan and was wavering in his opposition to it.

During the first conference session Major Schacht had attended the Fuhrer asked Keitel a question concerning coordination of air and ground attacks between the Air Force and Army. Keitel turned to Schacht as an army specialist on the subject and he had given a brief and satisfactory answer to the Fuhrer's question. Not until he had seen other officers cornered, unprepared to answer unexpected questions did he realize how close he'd come to a career-ending gaffe. Schacht came to despise the Field Marshal for the way he shifted blame and attention in this fashion. He'd also learned over the past weeks that many in the upper echelons of the Wehrmacht knew the Field Marshall by his nickname, 'Lakeitel', or 'nodding donkey', for his toadyism to the Fuhrer.

Admiral Raeder stood, placing the palms of his hands on the table and he addressed the Fuhrer directly, as though Hitler had asked the question, not Keitel.

"My Fuhrer," he began softly. "Field Marshall Keitel is quite right, anything which diminishes the strength of our forces on the eastern front is unacceptable."

Schacht turned to look at Keitel and found the Field Marshall's mouth agape at this unexpected statement from Admiral Raeder.

"Yes, Keitel," Raeder went on. "I do agree with you! We must focus all our energies in the east." Raeder scanned the assembled officers slowly now, looking each man in the eye as his gaze moved round the table. "But that is precisely the reason why Operation Herkules must proceed, why Malta MUST be taken!" Raeder shifted his eyes from one man to the next, passing Schacht, moving his gaze towards Hitler, speaking again as his eyes advanced to the head of the table.

"Currently, our war effort in the east is being drained by the commitment of forces we must make in the Mediterranean and North Africa to hold our southern flank secure and in the west to prepare for a possible Anglo-American landing anywhere from Norway to Spain. The Allies are effectively waging a second front against us!" He picked up a sheaf of papers from the table in front of him. "Here is a report on men, equipment and supplies embarked recently for Rommel's forces in North Africa from Italian and Greek ports. 400 tanks, 800 guns including 108 of the 88mm dual purpose guns in such desperate short supply in the east, 4,200 tons of fuel stocks, 22,000 tons of ammunition and food, 4,000 transport vehicles and 7,000 German troops." He dropped the papers on the table. "But worse than the quantity of men and supplies sent are the figures on arrival in Benghazi and Tripoli. British submarines and aircraft based on Malta have sunk over thirty percent of these supplies." He shrugged. "We've been fortunate so far that the British haven't torpedoed a troop transport. If they do there will be a huge loss of German lives." Raeder sighed and lifted his two hands, palms up to either side, raising and lowering them as though balancing a scale.

"Right now the British war effort teeters between two possible courses," he said. "On the one hand their effort depends upon supplies reaching their island by sea, including oil from the Middle East. In the month just ended our U-boats have sunk over 400 Allied merchant vessels totaling 600,000 tons of shipping. If this can be continued Britain will starve and freeze this coming winter, her aircraft grounded for lack of fuel, her ships confined to port or resting forever at the bottom of the sea. Britain can be forced to terms to save her civilian population the specter of starvation!" Raeder's gaze now fell upon the Fuhrer. Their eyes locked.

"All the resources we are devoting to fighting the British, in the air and on the seas, in the west and the Mediterranean can be thrown against the Reds in the east! We can crush the Soviet Union and end communism forever. But there is another possibility." Raeder stopped, his eyes again swept the room, his intensity holding, riveting the attention of every man present.

The Fuhrer breathed out, "Go on Raeder! What is the other possibility?"

The Admiral lifted his hands from the table and shrugged. "The other possibility," he said, "spells disaster for our forces. Every day the British gain new strength from their alliance with the Americans. Oh, it is true," he went on, holding his palms up before him, "that the Americans are woefully unprepared to counter our U-boat attacks, but this will change swiftly if we allow it!" He gestured to the map of Europe. "The Americans are delivering aircraft in the hundreds to Britain every month. Soon the figure may be in the thousands. American shipyards are producing cargo bottoms in unprecedented numbers. As their war effort builds they may be able to redress their imbalance in shipping production versus losses. American soldiers are crossing the Atlantic aboard the great pre-war luxury liners. These ships are fast enough to evade all attempts at U-boat attacks. Already over 70,000 men have been delivered to Britain. This figure is bound to grow." Raeder spoke more earnestly as he continued.

"The British and Americans don't even need to invade the continent to have a material effect upon our war effort. Just days ago a British bomber force delivered a devastating attack against Cologne in which some 4,000 German civilians were killed. Thousands more are without shelter. War production in the city, including vital U-boat components will be cut for months to come. These attacks can't be allowed to continue! The Air Force will be forced to devote more men and machines to the effort to stop them.

"But all of this can be prevented if we deprive the Allies of their Middle East oil. Rommel must drive the British, not just from Egypt and the Suez Canal, but also from Palestine, Syria, Iraq and Iran. The Persian Gulf must be closed to Britain and to do this our Mediterranean supply lines must be secured. Malta must be taken!" Raeder bounded back to the map of the Mediterranean. He punched his finger down on the tiny spot that was Malta.

"With Malta in our possession the British will be driven immediately from the Central Mediterranean. They cannot dare to venture through the range of all our airfields on Sicily, Sardinia, Malta, Crete and North Africa without land based air cover of their own. With Malta in our hands one hundred percent of the supplies we embark for Rommel will reach him. He can sweep the British from the Eastern Mediterranean. With the port of Alexandria in our hands," pointing to the British naval base in Egypt, "and the Suez Canal closed to the British we will hunt down and sink any units of her fleet Britain fails to withdraw from the Mediterranean in time."

Raeder turned back to Hitler. "And then the grand prize of this strategy; the oil fields of Iraq and Iran. By the depths of this winter we can deprive the British of their supply of oil. Their war effort will wither and die for lack of fuel. Our own can blossom from the possibilities presented by limitless reserves of oil."

Raeder moved now to Keitel's map of the eastern front. "Ultimately this strategy can also yield other enormous dividends." He pointed now to the borders of the Soviet Union with Iraq and Iran. "With Iraq in our hands the supply route the British have opened through the Caucasus region to the Soviets will be closed and an attack in the spring against the Soviets from the SOUTH becomes possible. We can force the Reds to fight a two front war. With success at Malta and Suez we can finally draw Spain into the war on our side and take Gibraltar from the British. Pressure on Turkey to choose sides will be overwhelming in our favor."

Raeder moved back to his seat. As he sat down he concluded. "The fulcrum upon which this balance rests is Malta. With it in our hands victory is possible. With Malta in British hands defeat is probable."

The room was completely silent. All the officers were impressed with the depth and passion of Raeder's appeal for Operation Herkules to proceed. But there was another reason for their silence. All waited now to follow the Fuhrers reaction. His was the only opinion in the room that really mattered.

For a moment history sat balanced on the edge of a knife, tipping first one way, then the other with the islands of Malta the delicate fulcrum. Then the Fuhrer spoke.

Luftwaffe General Lorzer, and Army Major Schacht left the conference together. After retrieving their side arms the officers emerged from the bunker to the warm Berlin evening. They re-entered the Chancellery building, retracing Schacht's route down the central hallway and out onto Wilhelmstrasse again. They paused outside the entrance.

"What are your travel plans, Schacht?" asked Lorzer. "How are you getting to Sicily?"

"I have a berth on the morning train to Munich, then on to Milan and Rome, General," replied the Major. "From there I am expected to find my way to Naples or Taranto to take the next available sea transport to North Africa. I must meet General, er uh, Field Marshall Rommel to assume my duties as liaison officer."

"A long trip you have in store for yourself. I leave at first light from Templehof," Lorzer said referring to Berlin's Military Transport airfield, "for Munich, Milan then on to Rome by this time tomorrow. I am to report to the Italians at Comando Supremo. Join me on my flight. I can save you many uncomfortable hours traveling by train."

"Thank you, Herr General!" said Schacht. "That is most kind of you".

"Not at all," said Lorzer. "We'll be seeing quite a lot of each other after you meet Rommel in Africa. As I said earlier, I am most anxious for close co-operation between the two commands. Besides, if you stop with me in Rome you may even get to meet Il Duce."

The two men laughed and joked as they walked until Schacht reached his turn.

"Until tomorrow then Schacht," said Lorzer. "Be at Tempelhof early."

"Yes, Herr General!" replied Schacht, snapping to attention with a military salute. Lorzer smiled and returned it.

Schacht hurried down the street to the streetcar station. He found a long queue of civilians waiting for the next coach. Presently the streetcar arrived and all piled on, though it was already crowded. Kuno squeezed aboard and rode in silence, letting his mind drift as he stood holding the leather strap suspended from the ceiling. He reflected on the day's events in the Fuhrer's underground conference room, but soon his thoughts turned to Hilda and their two boys, Rolf and Edmund. She would be disappointed to learn he must leave so early the next morning. He knew she was planning a big family breakfast before she and the boys accompanied him to the train station. His train was scheduled to leave mid-morning, but the change of plans to accompany Lorzer by air to Rome meant getting up long before the boys were awake and going to Tempelhof alone. He'd never considered declining the offer. To do so would have shown less than full eagerness to begin his new duty, unthinkable in the German Wehrmacht of the Second World War. In any case, he WAS eager to begin his new duty. The Mediterranean and North Africa promised to be full of action in the coming months. He'd be in the thick of it whether with Rommel or Lorzer at any given moment. Under the circumstances it seemed clear he would see a lot of both men.

As his stop approached Kuno worked his way to the rear of the car. He stepped off as the coach came to rest. He hurried down the block and ran up the steps to the door of his building, squeezing past the elderly couple that lived on the first floor and up the stairs to the third floor apartment he shared with Hilda and the boys.

Hilda was in the small kitchen washing vegetables as he entered and didn't hear him. He crept up behind her till he was close enough to place his hands on her hips. She spun to greet him and took his face in her two hands still wet from the sink. He pulled away.

"Is that how you greet a conquering hero?" he asked, laughing.

"No, just randy goats," she answered lightly. He looked at her lovingly and reached out to stroke her creamy smooth cheek with the back of his hand. She was beautiful, but he could see her eyes were puffy and red. She had been crying. He pulled her to him as she finished drying her hands and he kissed her. After a warm moment of response she pushed him away.

"The boys!" she said.

"Will take care of themselves," he finished, reaching for her again.

At that moment though the boys came into the kitchen from the small room they shared next to their parent's bedroom.

"PAPA!" they both shouted together and ran to him, each hugging him round one leg, holding him as tight as little arms and hands could grip. Six-year old Rolf looked up at his father with adoring eyes, while five-year old Edmund kept his face buried against Kuno's leg.

"'Take care of themselves', hhmm," murmured Hilda as she turned back to preparing their dinner.

"Come along now boys," said their father as he led them from the kitchen to the adjoining parlor. "Let's leave your mother to finish supper and you can tell me about your day. What about your school work, hm?"

"I am reading a new book in school!" proclaimed Rolf proudly. "Can I show it to you Papa?"

"Of course, Rolf!" Kuno exclaimed. "I should be delighted to see your book."

Rolf ran off down the short hall to the boys' bedroom and came back to the parlor waving a softbound book, little more than a magazine or comic. He handed it to Kuno who stood in front of his armchair staring at the book. The cover was a lurid, full color artists rendering of an army crew serving an 88mm gun. The men were stripped down to shirtsleeves and bare chests, all rippling muscles of Teutonic manhood, feeding shells to the gun. In the distance across a rolling landscape smoke rose from a burning farmhouse and tiny figures ran from German panzers; enemy soldiers fleeing in fear and discarding their weapons as they ran.

Kuno glanced down at Rolf, the boy's shining, expectant face beaming up at him. He looked back at the book and its title. It was from the collection of the War Library for German Children and was titled "Whole battery…FIRE!" with the subtitle "Heavy Artillery used against France".

"Well," said Kuno, not quite sure how to react. The boy's obvious interest in the topic worried him deeply. He wondered if German youths weren't being propagandized into a love of war.

"Well," he said again as he sat down in his chair, still holding the book. "There is still plenty of time before you must join the heavy artillery!"

"Oh, Papa," scoffed Rolf. "I'm not going into the artillery!"

"I'm glad to hear it!" said Kuno. "I see you as an educated man, a doctor or engineer, saving lives or building bridges!"

"I have decided to join the Luftwaffe," said Rolf as he sat on Kuno's right leg in the overstuffed chair. Edmund crawled up on his other knee.

"The Luftwaffe!" exclaimed Kuno. "Why on earth would you want to leave the Earth and fly?"

"Oh, I won't be a flyer," answered Rolf. "I'll be a paratrooper! I want to jump from the planes and be a hunter from the sky!"

Kuno swallowed hard. He was grateful the boy was only six. God willing this war would be over and Germany could live in peace long before Rolf was called upon to make such a decision.

"And what of you Edmund, what will you be when you grow up?" asked Kuno of the other boy.

"An Army officer," said the boy. "Just like you Papa".

Through their evening meal the boys chattered on with their father about their dreams of joining the German military service. Hilda was unusually quiet, speaking only when asked a question. When the dishes were cleared from the table she hurried the boys to bed over their fervent protests. Kuno joined her to tuck them into their bed. After Hilda kissed them goodnight and left the room Kuno sat on the edge of their bed and spoke with them.

"Boys, I must leave tomorrow for my next duty station."

"We know Papa," said Edmund as tears welled in his blue eyes. "Mother has told us."

"We're going to the train station with you and mother to see you off," added Rolf.

"There has been a change in my orders, Rolf," said Kuno. "I have not told your mother this yet, so you must be very quiet now. I will be leaving very early in the morning from Tempelhof airfield. I am flying, not taking the train."

"Oh, how exciting Papa!" breathed Rolf. "I love the airfield and all the airplanes."

"Yes, Rolf, I know," said Kuno. "But I must leave very early in the morning and you boys and your mother will not be able to come. You will still be asleep."

"Oh, Papa!" cried the boys together.

"Come now, you must be brave! No tears from Germany's young soldiers!" said the father sternly, fighting hard to swallow the lump in his own throat. "You will be the men of the home again, until I return. You must take good care of your mother for me."

Both boys lay there, blankets tucked up to their chins, sobbing and sniffling, fighting to be brave for their father.

"Remember that now your duty is at home with your mother. Do you promise to do your duty?" Kuno looked at them with a serious glare.

Rolf and Edmund nodded and wiped their eyes on their pajama sleeves. "Yes Papa," said Rolf. "Yes Papa," said Edmund.

"Very good then," Kuno said as he bent to kiss each forehead. "I salute you!" He snapped his right hand to his forehead. Rolf snapped his tiny fist up to his forehead in reply. Edmund reached his hand out in imitation of the Nazi salute. Kuno was grateful the boy was too choked with tears to say, "Heil Hitler!"

As Kuno left the room he looked back on the boys one last time, leaving their door ajar. He went to the parlor and found Hilda sitting in her chair wringing a handkerchief in her hands, tears welling in her eyes.

She looked up as he entered the room. "I'm sorry," she said with a weak smile. "I'm trying hard to be strong for you. I know it is enough that you go to risk your life without me to worry about as well."

"Nonsense," he said gently. "It is for you that I risk my life. For you and our boys and all German families."

"Oh, Kuno," she wailed, losing her composure completely now. "I would be poor, and Germany poor too, if you could be home with us!"

He pulled her to her feet and took her in his arms. "None of that defeatist talk," he said sternly to her, but with a smile as he lifted her chin to look into her eyes. "I may be home again sooner than you would believe."

He led her to their bedroom and shut the door behind them. Holding her from behind, he pulled her close and slipped her dress down off her shoulders. He deftly unsnapped her brassiere and cupped her breasts. She arched back against him and he leaned down to nuzzle her creamy white neck.

"Oh, Kuno," she breathed. "Take me."

>>>>>>>>>>>>>>>>>

## Day 2
June 22, 1942

Maggie Reed's shift the morning of June 22, 1942 proved quite eventful. Deep in the underground Chamber beneath Rinella Battery she'd intercepted the message from the Africa Korp to OKW in Berlin. Though she was unable to interpret its encoded message she was confident that under the circumstances of the fall of Tobruk in Libya to the Germans it was undoubtedly important. Now she went on adjusting the frequency and direction of her wireless aerial, scanning the atmosphere for any hint of other signals. She kept her aerial pointed between 125 and 135 degrees relative bearing, the direction of Tobruk and from which the earlier signal had been detected.

Chapman delivered a cup of tea about an hour after she intercepted the DAK message. She was sipping from the cup, slowly twisting the frequency dial when she heard the signal again. She jolted upright, spilling the hot liquid on her chin and lips.

"OW!" she yelped, then set the cup down quickly and raised her hand.

Chapman came at a trot. "Are you okay Maggie?" he asked. "What have you got?"

"An acknowledgement from DAK in Tobruk," Maggie replied. "Have you a napkin Chappie?" She mopped her chin and lap with the paper. "Someone else here should have something from Berlin or Rome".

Chappie looked around the room, but no other hands were up. He walked quickly first to the desk whose tent card label read "Comando Supremo/Rome".

"Have you got anything William?" he asked the operator.

"Nothing here Chappie," William answered as he spun the aerial through the bearings for Rome, 000 degrees, directly due north.

Chapman spun and moved down to the desk labeled "OKW/Berlin".

The operator there was rubbing his eyes and shaking his head.

"Wake up man!" growled Chapman. "Do you have a

signal?"

"Sorry Chappie," the man said as he adjusted the dials. "Yes, here it is. OKW in Berlin. Can't tell who it's for though."

"You missed the lead in Johnson!" said Chapman. "Stay on it now, make sure we get a clean recording."

"Right Chappie," answered Johnson. "I've got it now." He paused with one hand to his headset. "Short message Chappie, maybe not very important?" he said hopefully.

"They're all bloody well important Johnson, too important for you to sleep at your station."

"I'm sorry Chappie. I've been on eight hours now with no break."

"All right, all right," Chapman relented. "Give me five minutes and I'll have you relieved. Get yourself a cuppa and a smoke out in the tunnel."

"Thank you Chappie! Message concludes."

Chapman and Johnson worked together to remove the record and to replace it with a fresh one. Chapman took the recorded message to the transmitting station and helped the operator there to prepare the intercepted signals for transmission to London.

The latest signal captured by the 'Y' service on Malta from Berlin to the DAK was the message sent by Halder and Keitel following the Fuhrer's conference on the evening on June 22, 1942. The two senior generals worked into the morning hours to perfect the message. It carried a two edged sword for Rommel. The first part carried the Fuhrer's and indeed the whole German nation's congratulations to Rommel for the capture of Tobruk and announced his promotion to Field Marshall. The cryptanalysts at Bletchley Park thought this a bit too much 'cheek' of the Germans. Though unknown to the British till many years later Rommel, upon reading this segment of the message is reputed to have told his Chief-of-staff, Major-General Alfred Gause, "I would rather the Fuhrer had given me another division of German troops."

The second part provided the new Field Marshall with his operating orders for the next thirty days. He was to stand fast, consolidate his hold on the port of Tobruk and husband his armor and supplies. At the end of the thirty days he could expect major reinforcement and re supply by sea and a maximum effort on the part of the Luftwaffe to support a renewed Afrika Korp offensive whose aim would be the capture of the British naval base at Alexandria, the Nile River Delta and the Suez Canal. During this thirty-day interval Operation Herkules would be conducted.

Critical to the British however, and missing from the message, was the exact date of the invasion of Malta. Bletchley Park went all out, round the clock, putting highest priority on decrypting any message whose source and destination might have a chance of carrying the vital date of the assault. Every signal between Regia Aeronautica or Luftwaffe forces in Italy or North Africa was examined first. Teasingly, several of these messages referenced the Malta invasion, but without any indication of the scheduled date of the operation.

In London the service chiefs presumed the invasion was imminent, but that it could not be mounted in less than a week. In the prior several months, flights by reconnaissance aircraft based on Malta over the Sicilian airfields had shown activity in building new runways and extending existing ones, actions presumed to be in preparation for an air assault against Malta, but the large number of transport aircraft needed to launch such an assault had not yet made an appearance. Similar recce flights over Naples and Taranto showed slightly higher numbers of merchant vessels than normal, but no sign of a major sortie of the Italian Navy, the Regia Marina.

Putting together all available intelligence information, one last factor played into the British high command's estimation of German intentions. The moon would be full the night of June 27-28. The British service chiefs informed Prime Minister Winston Churchill and his war cabinet that they expected Malta to be assaulted on June 28th or at latest 29th. The Royal Navy and Royal Air Force would have to be ready by then to repel an invasion.

## Day 3
June 23, 1942

Oberleutnant Franz Popitz rose from his squatting position along with the hydraulic shaft.

"Stop periscope," he said.

The periscope shears were just at the surface, one moment a wave breaking over them, the next clear for a limited view of nearby waters. As was his custom he described to the crew in the conning station what he saw as he scanned the sea above them.

"Nothing on the surface nearby. Bring the scope up another meter." The tube glided silently up. Now Popitz was fully upright, the rubber eyepiece pressed to his forehead. He took the scope through a full sweep of 360 degrees.

"Still nothing," he said, "but it is black as pitch up there. No moon yet, just starlight."

He swung the scope round. "A faint glow to starboard. What is the bearing Merker?"

His executive officer checked the brass ring around the periscope shaft and found the bearing the scope was pointed at.

"One-six-five, Oberleutnant," he answered.

"Good," said Popitz. "Those would be the lights of Tangiers." He swung the periscope to port. "Lights also on the Spanish headlands. Good of the Spaniards to provide us a navigational fix." He swung the scope through another 360-degree sweep. "Still nothing on the surface," he said. "Sound?"

Petty Officer Grutzner answered, "Nothing sir, no sound detection on any bearing."

"Prepare to surface," the U-boat skipper said. "We'll make it a fast run on the surface, perhaps get lucky, slipping between British patrol grids. In any case we'll charge our batteries in the event we are driven under."

"The boat is ready, Sir," said Merker.

"Blow all tanks. Surface!" ordered Popitz.

"Blow all tanks. Surface!" acknowledged Merker.

The sound of high-pressure air flushing the tanks to the sea filled the boat. Grutzner climbed the bottom rungs of the conning tower ladder, waiting for the moment to crack the hatch and equalize pressure in the boat. The bridge watch crowded round the base of the ladder, ready to scramble onto the bridge to take their lookout posts.

"Equalize pressure," called Merker as the boat broached the surface.

A cascade of water poured down the conning tower hatch, drenching the bridge watch.

The petty officer heaved open the hatch and scrambled out onto the bridge, dogging the hatch open on its clips. The bridge watch hurried up the ladder after him, led by Popitz with his binoculars. Quickly he checked the bridge watch to assure they had taken proper position and were scanning their assigned sectors with their own binoculars.

Popitz opened the speaking tube to the control room. "Bring the main engines on, all ahead standard speed."

"Main engines on, all ahead standard speed," Merker acknowledged.

The thump of the diesel engines came to his feet through the deck as Popitz leaned on the forward binnacle, scanning the horizon to the front.

"Keep to your sectors," he said to the bridge watch. "The British are thick as flies here. We don't want to be surprised on the surface." He scratched at the black beard that was already starting to grow out after six days at sea. It always itched for the first few days without a shave on a war patrol.

The boat thumped on through six-foot swells. A brisk, warm breeze from the starboard quarter off the African continent blew spray up onto the bridge ensuring the watch stayed wet, but none minded. It was a warm evening and the cool spray was welcome.

Popitz leaned into the voice tube again. "Activate the Biscay Cross," he ordered.

"Activate Biscay Cross," Merker replied.

Out of a recessed well on the periscope shears a metal cross emerged and extended to above the top of the periscope. The Metox R 600 Search Receiver whose rather makeshift antenna was known to U-boat crews as the Biscay Cross had been developed by the U-boat service as a countermeasure to British Radar. It could detect the waves from a radar transmitter as they washed over the boat before a British aircraft or surface vessel was in range to pick up the reflected signal, allowing the boat time to dive before it was detected and attacked. Popitz watched it for a moment as it turned through its first circuits then returned to his own binoculars. As he scanned the horizon his mind drifted back to their last hours in port at Brest, on the Atlantic coast of France.

Popitz had wondered at the summons to the 'Castle'. His U-Boat, U-212 and its crew were ready for sea. Indeed, he had expected his sailing orders for several days. Normally though the sailing orders were delivered to him in a double envelope arrangement aboard his submarine at its berth in the massive concrete submarine pens under construction by the Kriegsmarine in the harbor. The outer envelope, to be opened immediately, would have the time and date he was to sail, usually less than eight hours from the time the orders were placed in his hands. Also inside the large outer envelope was a smaller one, wax sealed which he was not to open till out to sea. This inner envelope would contain his detailed operational orders; courses to steer, co-ordinates where he was expected to find Allied shipping and convoys, radio frequencies to use in reporting to base and in receiving further orders and so on. The seaport of Brest was known as a hotbed of allied spies and the French Resistance, or *Maquis* as they called themselves were also active. German sailors wandering the port alone at night seeking diversion in the manner of sailors everywhere had been found with their throats slit the next day. By double sealing the U-boat's orders some semblance of operational security could be preserved.

He looked out from the conference room window towards the massive concrete pens in the harbor below. Stretching across 330 meters of the Brest waterfront, with steel reinforced concrete six meters thick they had already proven all but impervious to British bombs. Still incomplete, there were fifteen operational bays or 'pens' into which a sub could seek shelter while refitting and repairing before going to sea for another patrol. Ten of the pens were also dry docks in which the most extensive repairs and maintenance were conducted. Steel blast doors rolled down over the entrance to the pens protecting the boats and personnel inside against bomb splinters. But here in the "Castle" as he and his fellow submariners referred to the building he did not feel as safe from British air attack. Formerly the French Naval Academy, the large, institutionally drab building overlooking the harbor now served the Kriegsmarine as headquarters of the I U-Boat Flotilla.

The conference room had been a classroom when used by the French Naval College. It was large, with rows of desk chairs to seat about 50 men. At the front of the room was a curtain, covering the entire wall from floor to ceiling and from side-to-side. Two doors on the right hand wall opened into the corridor beyond. Two large windows with half round transoms that opened to admit fresh air provided the room's light.

"Franz, tell us what you think of the news from Africa."

Popitz turned from the window back to the room. Over a dozen German navy officers were present, U-boat skippers and executive officers all. He replied to the other skipper who had spoken to him.

"I tell you Juergen I don't know quite what to make of it. It seems Rommel really has Tommy's number, but you know from your own experience the British still have plenty of fight left in them at sea. We'll know more if he is able to seize Tobruk this time round."

Juergen Peters commanded U-198 and with Franz Popitz had been at Brest since shortly after its occupation when France fell in June 1940, two years prior. Before Peters could answer, the door of the conference room opened and a Naval Commander entered followed by an Obersteuermann, or Warrant Officer.

"Attention!" shouted the Warrant Officer and the assembled U-boat skippers and their Executive Officers jumped to their feet.

The Commander, whom Franz had known for some months, ordered them to relax, and to smoke if they wished, then introduced himself.

"For those who do not know me, I am commander Stieff. You have been brought here to receive unusual orders which you will implement within the hour." He nodded to the Warrant Officer who moved to the drawstring of the wall curtain.

"Oberleutnant," he said to Franz, "will you close the window blinds please?" Franz obeyed, and for a moment the room was dim until an officer near the rear door pushed the light switch button. The overhead electric lamps came on.

The Warrant Officer now drew the wall curtain aside, revealing a map of an area that covered the French Atlantic ports, including Brest, south to the Canary Islands in the Atlantic Ocean, then east to encompass the whole of the Mediterranean Sea and southern Europe.

"Gentlemen," began Commander Stieff, "your boats will sortie within the hour to begin a major and important operation."

"Commander Stieff," Juergen Peters said, raising his hand. "My crew are scattered all about the port area. I can't round them all up in under an hour."

"Don't worry, Oberleutnant," Stieff replied. "Shore police are scouring the port now, returning all seamen to their boats. Your crew will be aboard before you are."

He turned and with a wooden pointer smacked the map. "Your mission is here, in the Mediterranean Sea."

A murmur went through the assembled officers. Discernible among the general noise was more than one groan.

"Yes, I know, I know," Stieff said. "The Mediterranean means you must transit Gibraltar and the British anti-submarine force there. You will see we have devised a plan to give you the maximum opportunity of passing Gibraltar safely. Seven boats from here at Brest and four more from the base at Bordeaux will transit to the Strait of Gibraltar, then through and into the Mediterranean."

Stieff first provided rough course outlines and timetables to bring the eleven U-Boats to the Atlantic side of the Strait of Gibraltar on the night of June 22. At 2200 hours they were to surface and await a wireless transmission that would direct them to one of two courses of action. If the word "osprey" was included in the transmission the boats were to turn about, proceed into the Atlantic and prey upon British shipping up and down the west coast of Africa. However, if the words "winter watch" were in the message text they were to continue with the plan to force the Straits and enter the Mediterranean Sea.

Stieff went on to outline how all eleven U-boats detailed for the operation were to force the Strait of Gibraltar together, on the night of June 22. They were to creep within range of the Strait submerged to avoid detection by long range British patrol aircraft operating from the airfield at the British base, then surface during the moonless period after 2300 hours and dash for the Strait at maximum speed. If detected they were to dive and avoid depth charging, continuing through the Strait submerged. It was felt the onslaught of so many boats passing the Strait at one time would overwhelm and confuse the British anti-submarine patrols. Stieff warned the officers about secrecy.

"As you all know, our boats have suffered a number of mysterious losses of late," he said. "It is imperative that you all go directly to your boats after leaving this building." He scanned the assembled officers sternly. "Speak to no one before sailing. You are to maintain absolute radio silence until after you have made contact with the enemy in the Mediterranean." Stieff briefly entertained questions, but refused to answer most of them, directing the officers to refer to the sealed, printed orders to be delivered to them at their boats in the next half hour. These envelopes would contain the detailed orders for the upcoming operation. Stieff then dismissed the officers to see to their boats.

Monique Covet worked as a secretary for the Kriegsmarine staff officers at the I U-

Boat Flotilla HQ in Brest. Twenty-two years old that spring of 1942 she'd known for

some years that she had a profound affect upon men. Just over five feet tall, slim and

lithe, her figure drew men's attention at any distance. Up close, her flawless pale skin,

raven-black, shoulder length hair and deep, dark eyes under long curled lashes left many

men speechless in her presence.

She came to the I U-boat Flotilla in answer to an advertisement placed by the Kriegsmarine in the local newspaper recruiting administrative staff from the local French population. She had no work experience, but once she presented herself at the personnel office she had no trouble at all in being granted an interview and in impressing the interviewing officers that she'd be a fast learner. She started work in February 1942, the day after her interview.

And she was a fast learner. Very quickly the pool of officers she was assigned to came to rely upon her for typing of letters, handling in-coming and out-going mail and phone calls and a hundred other routine administrative tasks. Always willing to work late when one of the officers had some last minute dictation or typing to be done she quickly set the standard against which all the other French administrative staff was measured.

It was inevitable given her beauty and her capable and willing handling of the officer's needs that the other French help who worked in the U-Boat HQ soon ostracized her. When passing any of them in the hall she was treated with a cold propriety that stopped just short of calling for action from the German superintendent of the French staff. Very soon she began taking her lunches with one or other of the German officers whom she supported, though always in a public place on the grounds of the HQ. Her demeanor with the officers was always strictly according to protocol. No one ever saw her flirt with any of the Germans. She also never accepted any of the many invitations she routinely received to dinner or other diversions after work. She was a model of decorum. In public.

Privately a number of the staff officers, and not a few officers of the U-boats had seen another side of Monique Covet. She had a way of holding a man's eyes with her own that made him feel as if no other man on earth had ever come to her attention. When alone with them she made the officers feel that her proper coolness in public was just a sham to protect the private feelings they shared for one another. Her shy behavior made them believe she had never known another man. She carefully and selectively began accepting the invitations for after hours *rendezvous'*. Every one of these officers believed his relationship with Monique must be kept a secret closer than any detail of military operations that might be of use to the enemy, and for a far more important reason. None of them would risk losing her attentions.

On June 15, 1942 Monique knew something big was afoot at the headquarters. More armed Germans than normal were at the entrance to the building and patrolling the halls. The senior officer in her group, Commander Stieff, had ordered her to remain in her office until his return. She had acquiesced immediately. Stieff was one of the very few officers able to resist her charms. She'd begun to think the man was a closet homosexual.

Still, something important was happening and she wanted to know what it was, so

Monique left the door to her office open as she busied herself with typing and mail. Shortly after Stieff left his office she began to see U-boat captains and other officers go past her door towards the large classroom/conference room at the end of the building's central hallway. They were gone for about a half hour before she heard voices and laughter returning down the hall.

Monique contrived to position herself near the door of her office with the top drawer of a three-drawer cabinet open and a sheaf of papers in her hands. Any casual observer would conclude she was filing reports or forms.

The voices drew nearer and she strained for snippets of conversation, but the officers restricted their talk to inconsequential matters that did not pertain to their duties. The officers began to pass her office door and she knew that each was appraising her none too subtly as he passed, but Monique carried on with her filing and did not acknowledge any of the looks that came her way.

Finally though a voice came to her that she recognized and she changed her stance to permit her to look out the door more easily. The voice came closer, alternating now with another voice that she also recognized.

"I was looking forward to leave at home next month," said Oberleutnant Franz Popitz, the commander of U-212, one of the boats based at Brest.

"I wish I could go too," replied Paul Merker, Popitz' executive officer aboard U-212. "It has been almost a year since I was home to Bremen."

"One of us must remain here to mind the show," replied Popitz, "otherwise the crew would all be in the brig when you and I returned."

The two men shared a quick laugh as they passed the door of Monique's office. She looked up in time to briefly catch Merker's eye, before demurely averting her gaze. The men's conversation continued as they went down the hall away from her office, talking about home and the pub Popitz planned to visit in his home of

Cologne and of the gifts he had for his parents there.

Monique continued her filing as the last of the U-boat officers passed her office door.

Commander Stieff brought up the tail end of the group. He came to her door and stopped, appraising the open door, then Monique as she finished her filing. He said nothing though before turning on his heel and crossing the hallway to his own office, shutting the door behind him.

Popitz and Merker meanwhile continued to the end of the hallway, busily engaged in conversation about their hometowns. They reached the end of the hallway and the staircase to the ground floor when Merker stopped suddenly.

"What is it Paul?" asked Popitz. "Have you forgotten something?"

"No, Captain," answered the XO, "but it occurs to me to check the mail office for any letters for our crew that have not been delivered yet. God alone knows how long we'll be in-" he stopped as Popitz quickly raised his hand. "Well, you know," he finished lamely.

Popitz looked at his watch. "All right Paul, but don't be long. We must prepare the boat for sea. I'll hold the car for you."

"No, Captain, go on ahead. I will catch up quickly. I'll get a ride with one of the other officers."

"All right Paul," said Popitz reluctantly as he started down the stairs. "Just don't make me send the shore patrol to fetch you!" he concluded with a laugh.

Merker laughed in return. "Of course, Captain, I won't be long!"

Paul Merker turned and hurried back down the hallway towards Monique's office. He wanted to break into a run, but dared not draw attention to himself. He came to her door and stood there with his two hands braced on either side of the open door jam, looking at her standing behind her desk by the window. She turned to him, but no sign of caring or recognition crossed her face. His heart fell into his stomach with disappointment. He ached for her beauty. She looked at him for a moment then signaled with her hand for him to come in and shut the door. He stepped in the office, closing the door behind him. She came from behind the desk and stood before him. She looked up into his eyes, but said nothing, waiting for him to speak.

"Monique," he stammered a beginning. "I – I have come to say good-bye", he said.

"Good-bye for now that is! I'll be back, I promise!"

She reached her hand up and placed it flat on his chest. She could feel his heart hammering beneath his uniform.

"Oh, Paul," she said. "The North Atlantic again?"

Merker glanced quickly around the office as if to assure they were alone.

"No, something different this time," he said. "I – I can't really talk about it."

She took her hand from his chest and turned back to her desk.

"Of course, darling," she said, but there was a subtle change in her voice, a hint of rejection.

"Anyway," said Merker, "I'll see you as soon as I return, but I'm not certain how long it will be." He was downcast again at the withdrawal of her affection.

"Perhaps you could visit my flat this evening?" Monique suggested.

"I can't," he replied, disappointment written like a book on his face. "We sail immediately. We've never had such short notice orders."

Her mood changed again and she came back to him, taking his hands in hers.

"Poor darling," she cooed. "Your duty is so demanding. And so dangerous?" The question in her voice led him to tell her more. He remained silent, looking into her eyes, so she lifted his hands to her lips and kissed them lightly.

"Your duty leaves you so little time for pleasure," she went on. "We have time, don't we Paul?"

"No, I told you I must sail immediately," he replied, but was unable to take his eyes off her or to pull away to leave. His breath began to come in short, sharp gasps.

"Leutnant Prost is away on leave," she told him. "His office is empty. We at least have time for your favorite".

"No! I don't know". He was near to tears of frustration and longing.

She lifted her face to his and kissed him, long and sweet, her tongue probing for his.

"Yes, darling," she said softly. "We have time for your favorite." She locked his eyes with hers. Through pursed lips she asked, "Which lipstick shall I wear for you darling?"

"Oohh, the red," he groaned as she knelt before him, undoing his fly. "Wear the red."

When he returned to his boat Popitz found his crew was indeed all aboard before him, several still hung over from their leave ashore. He began issuing orders to prepare the boat to castoff. Ordinarily this duty was handled by the XO, but Merker was taking his time with the mail. Finally, just as Popitz began considering placing a phone call up to the Castle to determine the XO's whereabouts, Merker raced up to the pier riding in the sidecar of a motorcycle combination driven by one of the guards from the HQ. He leapt from the machine before it stopped moving and ran to the boat. As U-212 eased away Merker hurtled from the dock to the gun deck where several waiting hands saved him from going over the other side of the boat into the harbor.

"Good of you to come aboard, XO," called Popitz from the bridge. "Join me please."

"Yes, Sir", said Merker as he climbed the ladder to the U-Boat bridge.

"Did you get any mail?" asked the Captain.

"Mail?" said Merker. "Oh. No, there is no mail. In fact," he said quickly "that was the cause of my delay. The mailroom clerk insisted our mail has already been forwarded to an unknown destination."

"Hhmmph!" answered the captain. "Confident aren't they?"

"Yes, so it seems," replied Merker quietly. "Would you like me to conn the boat out of harbor Captain?" he asked to change the subject.

"Yes, that would be fine, Paul," Popitz said. "I will go below to the control room. Call me immediately if there is any trouble or you have a question."

The Wolf Pack sortied *en masse* that afternoon under a heavy Luftwaffe umbrella to prevent their detection by nosy RAF patrol planes. U-212 took up station behind her sister boat U-198. Running safely on the surface through the remainder of the day and night, the boat did not submerge until first light the next morning. Remaining submerged during daylight hours, Popitz and his crew enjoyed an uneventful six days cruise passing within periscope sight of Cape Finnistre on the Spanish coast, then stayed close inshore for much of the south bound voyage. Neutral Spanish and Portuguese waters offered a convenient haven in the event they were forced to dive by a British warship. They reached their station on schedule the night of June 22.

For her part Monique marked time the rest of the afternoon of the conference at the U-boat HQ, impatiently waiting for the time to go home for the evening. Finally, the clock struck 6pm. She locked her desk and filing cabinet drawers, gathered her coat and left her office, locking the door behind her. She stepped across the hall and knocked on Commander Stieff's door.

"Enter," he called.

She opened the door and leaned her head in the office.

"I am ready to leave now Commander," she said to Stieff, seated at his desk. "Is there anything else I can do before going?"

"No, thank you, Mademoiselle Covet," he replied evenly. "Have a pleasant evening. I will see you tomorrow."

"Goodnight Commander," she said and closed the door behind her.

Monique walked quickly down the hall to the stairwell. As she did she heard a door open behind her, but she did not look back, not wishing to be detained at the last moment. She went down the stairs and signed out with the guard at the main entrance to the building and again at the guard shack at the gate in the barbed wire fence around the compound. She turned and walked down the hill toward the built-up area around the harbor. The town of Brest nestles around the waters of the harbor like a crescent of moon in an inky, night sky. The massive, unfinished bulk of the submarine pens loomed along the shore to her right. Construction cranes and derricks cast long shadows from the roof of the pens, but with the summer solstice just days away there were hours of daylight remaining. She came to the main street of the harbor district and turned down it.

The closer Monique came to the waterfront the more the damage done by Royal Air Force bombing came into evidence. Since the German U-boat Flotilla had moved in following the Armistice, Brest had become a frequent target of nighttime bombing raids. Most bombs fell miles from the wharves, piers and sub pens. Smashed storefronts and burnt out homes attested to the inaccuracy of the British bombing and contributed to a strong under current of anti-British feeling in the local French population, something the German's were careful to cultivate.

She walked along until she came to a street with rows of small shops and cafes on either side of the street. Presently she came to a small church, set back from the cobblestone sidewalk. A low stone wall edged the walkway and an iron gate hung open on rusty hinges, welcoming visitors. Monique walked past the gate, but then took a shuffling step and stopped. She turned, sat on the stone wall and bent down to remove her shoe. She shook the shoe as if trying to get a stray pebble out of it then ran her hand through the inside of the shoe. Satisfied, she bent to put the shoe back on, stood and continued on her way.

Across the street the keeper of a small bookstore was ready to close up for the evening. The owner completed his last sale of the day and escorted his customer to the door.

"Bon soir, Madame Duval," he said. "Good night."

"Bon soir, Monsieur Montagne," she replied.

Marcel Montagne closed and locked the door of his bookshop behind her and turned the "Closed" sign out in the window. Before turning to exit the rear of the shop he glanced out the window at the church across the street. On the iron-gate entrance to the church grounds he saw a small 'X' marked in chalk about half way up the post.

He unlocked and exited through the front door, relocking it with is key as he left and crossed the street passing through the iron-gate and entered the church. He paused at the alms box and dropped a few coins in for the poor, then walked down the narrow center aisle to the small altar.

He knelt in prayer a few minutes then lit a votive candle, leaving a few more coins and turned to leave. As he exited through the iron-gate he stopped, pulled his handkerchief from his pant pocket and blew his nose. When he moved on the chalk mark was gone.

Monique arrived at her small apartment building and went in the front door. She went up the stairs to her tiny, but neat three-room apartment. On the second floor of the three-story building, it was the only flat other than the landlady's with a private bath. A parlor, small kitchenette and bedroom completed the apartment. The bath was important. Without it she would have found it difficult to discretely entertain the German naval officers who sometimes visited her there.

Tonight however she had no plans for visitors. She hurried through a change of clothes and checked the small breadbox in the kitchenette. She frowned. There was half a loaf there. She wrapped the bread in some newspaper and put it in her shopping bag then hurried out the door and down the stairs to the street. She turned left out the front door and checked her watch. She must hurry to make the *rendezvous* on time.

As she went down the street she passed a vacant, weed grown lot. In peacetime as a teenage girl she had seen alcoholics and drunken sailors asleep there. But since the war there were no bums. The Germans didn't tolerate them. It was still daylight and she glanced up and down the street. There were people in each direction, but none seemed to be paying her any attention. She pulled the wrapped loaf of bread from her purse and as discreetly as possible pitched it behind a stand of weeds. She hurried on.

She came to a bakery that was open late, passing under the sign "Boulangerie" and entered the store. There was one other patron there, a man she didn't recognize in a black coat and fedora hat. He was browsing the limited supply of pastries in the display case.

"Bon soir, Monsieur," she said to the counter man. "May I have a fresh bagette please?"

"Oh, I am sorry, Mademoiselle," he answered, shooting a fast look of warning at the man examining the pastries. "I have no fresh baked bagettes remaining tonight."

"Oh, I see," she said. "Well, let me look to see what else I might take."

"Of course," the baker replied. "At your convenience." He moved down the counter to engage the stranger in conversation. As Monique browsed the shops limited supply of fresh baked goods she listened to the conversation between the baker and his other customer.

"Have you found a selection to your liking, Monsieur?" the baker asked the man.

"Yes, I would like the berry crumpet there in the front of the window," the man replied. Monique noted his perfect French, and strong Paris accent.

"Very good, Monsieur," the baker replied as he lifted the crumpet from the display in a tiny square of paper. "That will be two Francs please."

Monique selected a small lemon cake as the stranger concluded his transaction and left the store with a hearty "Merci!" from the baker. She waited a moment for the stranger to pass from view in the store's window before hurrying to the counter.

"Listen carefully Phillipe!" she said softly. "This is the most important information I've ever gathered." She glanced back out the shop door and windows. It was still clear. Phillipe the baker busied himself wrapping her cake. To any casual observer looking in the window it looked like any other commercial transaction taking place.

"You saw the U-boats leaving harbor today?" she asked.

"Yes," he replied. "Seven of them, one after another."

"Precisely," she said. "And four more from Bordeaux. They are all headed for the Strait of Gibraltar to attack the British in the Mediterranean."

Phillipe nodded. She was right; this was the most important information Monique had ever delivered to the Maquis, the French Underground.

"There's more," she went on. "They are to arrive at Gibraltar on the night of the 22nd.

After 2300 hours they are to surface and await a wireless signal. If the signal includes the word 'osprey' they are to turn away and attack shipping in the Atlantic, on the African coast. If the signal contains the words 'winter watch' they are to force the Strait, all together on the morning of the 23rd.

"Good work Monique," said Phillipe as he finished wrapping her cake. "This is top grade information. I'll see it is delivered to London immediately." He handed her the cake and stepped out from his counter to follow her out of the shop. He held the door open for her as she left.

"Bon soir, Mademoiselle," he said to her pleasantly as she left.

"Bon soir, Monsieur," she answered and turned back up the

street towards her apartment building. The afternoon sun was casting long shadows on the street as she turned for home.

She had gone only a few dozen paces when a voice from behind her called out.

"Mademoiselle Covet," the voice said.

She stopped and turned slowly. The stranger from the bakery was walking quietly up behind her.

"Do I know you Monsieur?" she asked.

"No, of course not," he smiled, replying in his perfect Paris accent. "We've never met. But I know you."

"How do you know me Monsieur?" Monique asked as she started to slowly back away from him.

The stranger did not answer her. Instead he pulled a newspaper wrapped package from inside his overcoat. Monique's heart leapt into her throat as she recognized the bundled half loaf of bread she had discarded on her way to the bakery.

"I believe you dropped this earlier?" he said.

"No, Monsieur, it is not my packet," she said. "And now I really must go." She turned to hurry on her way, but stopped short. At the corner stood two German Military Policemen, with the distinctive nickel-silver gorget hung round their necks on a chain. This chain and emblem of authority were known with respect and fear, by soldier and civilian alike, throughout German occupied Europe. It gave the MP's their nickname of 'Chaindogs'.

"You see," said the stranger pleasantly. "You have nothing to fear from me. Those two gendarmes are here to protect your virtue."

She turned back to face him. Her knees were weak and she struggled for control. A police whistle sounded from behind the man, from the direction of the bakery. The stranger didn't blink. A moment later another MP emerged from the store and approached the stranger from behind. He murmured something to the stranger, then stepped back and stood at ease waiting for further instructions.

"What do you want of me?" she asked in a small voice.

"Nothing," he said. "Almost nothing at all." He stepped close to her and she saw now that he was leering at her in the fading light. "Nothing at least that you have not already done today, Mademoiselle Covet."

He raised a hand over his head, never taking his eyes from Monique. A whistle blew and a car came round the corner and stopped at the curb. He took Monique by the elbow and led her to the car. He opened the rear door and bowed courteously to her.

"After you, Mademoiselle."

She started to say something, to object, but the words stuck in her throat. She fell mute. She looked back at the bakery and just then two more Chaindogs pulled Phillipe the baker through the door, supporting him at the elbows. He was handcuffed and sagged on his feet. He looked dazed and she saw that his nose was bloodied.

She turned again to the man in the overcoat. Her throat was dry as fireplace ashes. "What do you want of me?" she croaked.

"Oh, there's plenty of time for that," he smiled. "We'll be spending time together, you and I."

London never received her report.

<<<<<<<<<

Franz Popitz checked his watch. Forty minutes had passed and U-212 was now passing the lights of Tangier to starboard and approaching the Strait of Gibraltar. This was the most dangerous point in the passage, where the Strait is at its narrowest. British anti-submarine vessels out of the great naval base at Gibraltar operated around the clock in the Strait, seeking to deny transit to German and Italian submarines.

Popitz felt his nerves stretching taut as the Strait approached. They had been lucky so far, but could their luck hold through to the Mediterranean side of the Strait? Was he foolish to attempt this transit on the surface? He reviewed his options for the hundredth time. Passing the Strait on the surface could be accomplished in little more than two hours to reach 50 fathom water on the Mediterranean side. Submerged the transit would take five times as long. More important than the amount of time taken was that a submerged transit of the Strait would bring U-212 into the Mediterranean with no darkness remaining during which to run on the surface and recharge her batteries. Popitz would most likely be forced to remain below the surface, drifting with the four knot current to maintain his battery reserve, until night fell again late in the evening of the 23rd, a total of nearly twenty-four hours submerged.

A tingle ran up his spine. He made a snap decision.

"Prepare to dive!" he shouted down the speaking tube. "Clear the bridge!" he called to the sailors on watch. He pressed himself to the binnacle as the men of the bridge watch scrambled to the open hatch and tumbled down the ladder to the control room below.

"DIVE, DIVE!" he ordered through the speaking tube and dropped through the hatch himself. Popitz slid down the ladder with the instep of his shoes pressed to the outside rails, bending his knees at the bottom to absorb the shock of landing. Petty Officer Grutzner scrambled back up the ladder and dogged the hatch down as U-212 began to slide beneath the waves.

"Activate battle lanterns," ordered Popitz.

"Activate battle lanterns, Sir," answered the petty officer. The control lights dimmed and were replaced by the red light of the battle lanterns. The red light protected the captain's night vision in the event he chose to use the periscope.

"Captain," called Merker, "the Biscay Cross has detected enemy radar waves at extreme range. Unable to determine if they are from an aircraft or surface vessel." The dripping bridge watch and control room crew exchanged glances as the bridge watch exited the control room to change into dry clothing.

Popitz said nothing, but nodded his head as he turned away from his Executive Officer. He didn't really believe that a sixth sense had warned him of the approaching danger, but it would do nicely if Merker and the rest of the crew thought so. As they left the control room Popitz heard one of the bridge watch whisper to his mate, "How did he know?"

"He's a magician, that's how," came the whispered reply.

Lt. Commander Ian Mallory, commanding officer of *HMS Morning Glory*, a Flower Class corvette, stepped from the port wing of his ship's open bridge. He heard the whistle from the speaking tube.

"Bridge, Radar. Contact, bearing one-nine-zero degrees relative".

"Bridge, aye, bearing one-nine-zero degrees," he spoke into the tube. Then, "What range man?"

"Bridge, radar contact bearing now one-eight-nine degrees, range six thousands yards," came the reply. "Contact is disappearing. Gone now, Sir. From its size I'd say a submarine conning tower that has now dived, Sir."

"Bridge, aye," Mallory acknowledged. Then he blew into the tube and spoke again. "Bridge, ASDIC, do you have a contact bearing between one-eight-eight and one-nine-zero, range six thousand yards?"

"Bridge, ASDIC. Negative, Sir. No contact. A bit far for us yet."

"Bridge, Conn. Come to one-eight-six, increase speed to twelve knots," Mallory ordered, then, "Bridge, ASDIC. Go to active mode, see if you can get a bounce on our friend please."

"Conn, Bridge. Aye-aye, course one-eight-six, speed two-two."

"ASDIC, Bridge. Aye-aye, active mode pinging now. No contact yet."

"Bridge, Wireless," Mallory said into the tube. "Signal to base. 'Am pursuing radar contact bearing one-eight-six, range six thousand yards.' Add our position and copy the two motor launches also please, Sparks." Mallory was referring to the two type 'B' motor launches, ML184 and ML647. Together with *Morning Glory* the two launches formed one of six hunter-killer sub chasing teams patrolling the Strait of Gibraltar that night. Spaced at roughly one-mile intervals and staggered across the Strait each team was composed of a corvette or destroyer and two Motor Launches or Motor Torpedo Boats. The corvette or destroyer in each team was equipped with ASDIC to detect submerged U-boats and with search radar to find them on the surface. Tactically, the larger ship would establish and maintain ASDIC contact with the sub, while vectoring the smaller vessels onto the sub by wireless. The launches or torpedo boats would then alternate in delivering depth charge attacks. Each launch carried 12 to 16 depth charges. Some also had the new "hedgehog" anti-submarine weapon, a spigot mortar capable of firing a salvo of 24 light depth charges carrying a 32-pound charge that only exploded if it made direct contact with a submarine hull.

The six hunter-killer teams also worked with a radar-equipped Sunderland Flying Boat that stayed aloft through the hours of darkness each night. The Sunderland carried four depth charges as well. At the moment the Sunderland was away to the north of the Strait, helping to track another contact there. The time was 0014 hours, June 23.

"A busy night," Mallory said to himself.

As U-212 dived and the bridge watch moved out of the control room Popitz returned to his thoughts of the conference at I U-boat Flotilla HQ in Brest. After describing the plan to force the Strait of Gibraltar *en masse* on the night of June 22-23 Commander Stieff had gone on to describe the purpose of the boats going to the Mediterranean.

"We have reason to expect that a major British convoy, composed primarily of warships will attempt to transit the Mediterranean Sea from Gibraltar," tapping the map at the western entrance of the sea, "to Alexandria in the east," now tapping the British base in Egypt. Stieff had turned to the roomful of officers and smiled.

"You will have the opportunity to fulfill every submariners dream. Your priority targets will be airplane carriers, battleships and cruisers, though we expect that the convoy will have a large escort of destroyers and other light escort vessels and you have permission to attack these as well." At no point did Stieff mention Malta or the impending invasion. He did not in fact know of it himself.

Popitz' thoughts returned to the moment.

"Captain, sonar contact bearing zero-eight-zero," Petty Officer Grutzner said. "A surface ship has turned on its active sonar. Range four thousands yards."

"Has he located us?" Popitz snapped back to his duty in an instant.

"No, Sir," Grutzner replied. "He seems to be searching to his south. Perhaps he has another contact he is pursuing."

Popitz' mental calculator went into high speed. He immediately concluded that Grutzner was right, the British vessel had located one of the other boats in Wolf Pack Tannenburg and was now prosecuting the contact.

"Give me a bearing, course and speed," said Popitz.

"High speed propellers now coming through, Sir," replied Grutzner. "Estimate speed at over ten knots, course approximately one-eight-five degrees." Grutzner paused a moment, then, "Relative bearing zero-seven-five."

"Up periscope," said Popitz. He squatted to ride the eyepiece as the scope extended above the surface. "Stop periscope," he called as the optical lens broke the surface. He looked first quickly at bearing zero-seven-five seeing there the dim outline of a destroyer class escort vessel and a large launch or torpedo boat, describing these to the control room crew, then swung through a 360-degree circuit. Finding no other vessels he ordered, "Down periscope."

He turned to the helmsman. "Hold your course zero-nine-zero degrees."

"Course zero-nine-zero," the helmsman acknowledged.

"Make revolutions for five knots."

"Revolutions for five knots," came the reply.

"We're in a nearly perfect position to attack the British destroyer, Paul" Popitz said. "He is pursuing a sonar contact to his south and will cross our beam at a range of about 800 yards. I expect his sonar operators to be busy maintaining contact on the U-Boat he has already found. With any luck at all he will never know what hit him." Popitz chewed his lower lip in thought. Merker had seen Popitz prepare many attacks and knew the Captain's habit of talking through his attack plan aloud was a mechanism that helped him work out flaws in his approach. Merker said nothing.

"Contact the forward torpedo room," the Captain ordered. "Have them make ready tubes one and two. Set depth four meters."

"At once Captain," replied Merker. He relayed the orders to the torpedo room.

"Sonar, any change in the destroyer?" asked Popitz.

"No, Sir," replied Grutzner. "He is holding course one-eight-six, speed about 12 knots, range now down to 2,000 yards on the port quarter."

"I will take a fast look," said Popitz. "Up periscope."

The shaft rode up from its well. Once again Popitz located the contact first.

"It's a small destroyer or perhaps a corvette," he said. "The first launch is abeam on his starboard side. A second launch is just pulling ahead of him on the port side. They are beginning a depth charge run." He spun the scope round 360-degrees again. "No other contacts, down scope."

"Grutzner, keep the bearings coming!" barked Popitz.

"Contact corvette on course one-eight-six," said Grutzner. "Speed twelve knots, range twelve hundred yards, bearing now zero-eight-five on the bow."

"Merker, prepare to shoot on the next periscope bearing."

"Tubes one and two are ready, Captain," replied the XO.

"Up periscope!" Popitz ordered. "Final bearings. Angle on bow zero-nine-one, range, 750 yards."

"Zero-nine-one, 750 yards," repeated Merker.

"Fire one!" snapped Popitz.

"Tube one fired!" answered Merker.

"Fire two!" said Popitz.

"Tube two fired!"

"Helmsman, make course zero-four-five, speed 5 knots. We will pass behind him after the torpedoes have gone home."

The helmsman acknowledged the order.

"Time?" snapped Popitz.

"Torpedo one impact in 25 seconds," answered Merker.

A gentle, warm breeze from the south ruffled Mallory's hair on the bridge of *Morning Glory*.

"Bridge, ASDIC. Contact one-eight-one, Sir. Contact is diving. He's going deep."

"Wireless, Bridge. Have the launches set their charges for 300 feet," Ian Mallory called down the speaking tube.

"Bridge, Wireless. Set charges to 300 feet."

Mallory turned to his XO on the bridge. "Have our ash cans set for 250 feet. We may get a chance to get in a lick or two of our own."

"Yes, Sir," answered the exec, "Depth charges set for 250 feet." The exec spoke into the "Tannoy", the intra-ship speaker system aboard British vessels. His command echoed over the water, "set depth charges to 250 feet." He looked back over the bridge wing to the corvette's fantail where the crew at action stations hurried to adjust the pressure fuses on the depth bombs.

"ASDIC, Bridge. What is his range?"

"Bridge, ASDIC. Range down to 400 yards, Sir."

"Bridge, Conn. Slow to 8 knots."

Mallory turned to his XO. "Have the six-four-seven boat make the first pass then we'll bring one-eight-four over him from astern. We've got him!"

At that moment an ear splitting crash rent the night and a searing bright flame leapt from the starboard side of the *Morning Glory* just forward of the bridge. Mallory and the XO were thrown from their feet and slammed to the deck. The Captain struck his head on the binnacle as he went down.

As Ian Mallory lost consciousness he thought, "It can't be. The contact was for'ard. Must be a second sub. A busy night."

Merker counted down the seconds till their first torpedo was expected to strike.

"Four, three, two, one…" at that instant the sound of the explosion came to them clearly through the pressure hull of U-212. A cheer went up throughout the boat.

"Up periscope!" snapped Popitz. He looked briefly to starboard where he saw the corvette already sinking, then quickly scanned through 360-degrees before returning to watch the death throes of the British ship. He provided his usual running commentary for the benefit of the control room crew.

"His bows are blown off forward of the bridge and are already sunk out of sight. He's rolling onto his starboard side and burning as he goes down fast by the bow." He swiveled the periscope shears further to starboard. "One of the launches has broken off its attack and has put about to look for survivors. He's on the other side of the flame. I doubt very much if he could see us even if we were on the surface." He swiveled the shears again, this time to port. "The other launch is hidden from view behind the corvette, but he must have broken off his attack also. We have saved someone a nasty depth charging."

Popitz swung the shears through a full 360-degrees again.

"Still nothing else on the surface," he said.

He swung back to the corvette. "We're passing just 300 yards astern of him. Both launches are standing off him now, waiting for survivors." He swung the scope again lightly to port. "He is going to turn turtle as he goes down." Popitz began to snap the periscope handles up, but jerked the scope round to the stern of the corvette. "MEIN GOTT!" he cried. "Put your helm hard to port! All ahead flank speed!" He snapped the handles shut and the scope slid down its well. "Brace for depth charge!" he cried. "The Tommy's ash cans have broken loose from his fantail into the water. We're too close!"

The crew of U-212 gripped whatever support was close to hand as they waited for the explosions of the depth charges. Every second that passed took them farther from the scene of the sinking, closer to safety. The tension began to ease in the control room. Petty Officer Grutzner at the sonar station held the phones away from his head to protect his ears if the depth charges exploded.

Grutzner started to speak. "Perhaps the ash cans were not armed. Maybe they won't ex-" WHAM WHAM WHAM. Three explosions in quick succession hammered at U-212. The lights in the control room blinked, went out, and came back on. Dust and paint chips shaken loose from bulkheads, pipes and fittings filled the air throughout the boat. WHAM WHAM. Two more explosions, followed by a string of charges so close together they could not be told apart. WHAM-AM-AM WHAM-AM-AM-AM-AM-AM. The red battle lights went out in the U-boat, but in a moment the dim emergency lights came on.

Popitz looked about the control room. "Is everyone alright?" he asked.

Murmured replies indicated the crew was shaken, but unhurt.

"Merker," called the captain. "Get a damage report!"

"Yes, sir!" answered Merker.

"Make the boat at periscope depth," Popitz ordered next. "Up periscope!"

As the shaft came up out of its well, the captain once again swept the horizon through 360-degrees, then came back on the bearing of the corvette, now almost directly astern.

"Reduce speed to four knots," he said. "Make your course zero-nine-zero."

The battle lanterns came back on and the emergency lights went out. Popitz continued his sweep of the surface.

"There is nothing left, nothing but scraps and pieces," he said. "The corvette is gone, the two launches are gone. They were almost atop the depth charges when they exploded. There can be no survivors."

The control room crew was silent. No cheers greeted the captain's statement this time. Each of the crew of U-212 had faced the prospect of death from depth charging. Each could picture the crushed, pulped bodies that had been in the water when the high explosive ash cans detonated.

"Make your depth 50 meters," said Oberleutnant Popitz.

"Depth 50 meters, Sir," his order was acknowledged.

U-212 slipped silently through the inky waters, completing the remainder of its passage of the Strait of Gibraltar uneventfully.

In London, an emergency meeting convened late on the night of June 22-23, 1942 to work out Royal Navy strategy in the wake of the fall of Tobruk and the threatened German invasion of Malta. Prime Minister Churchill had not yet returned from his conference with President Roosevelt in the USA. Admiral Sir Dudley Pound, First Sea Lord of the Admiralty chaired the meeting.

A map of the eastern hemisphere adorned one wall of Pound's large office in the Admiralty building in Whitehall, London. Dark walnut panels covered the walls. Large leaded pane windows overlooked Horse Guards Parade; in peacetime the Parade Ground hosted the cavalry drills of the famous British regiments. In keeping with wartime blackout rules heavy red velvet curtains covered the windows at night. In front of the windows sat a massive walnut desk where Pound conducted his official duties during normal hours. Tonight however, Pound and his two guests sat in comfortable overstuffed chairs, situated across the room in front of the map. Pound turned from a great, hulking hunt chest beside his desk and walked to his chair. He was carrying a fresh gin.

"The question, gentlemen," began Pound, "is what forces can be sent immediately to Malta to repel an assault?"

"Devilish timing of the Jerries," replied Admiral Sir John Tovey, Commander-in-Chief of the British Home Fleet. "We're spread as thin as at any time in the whole bloody war, especially in capital ships."

"What are the big ship dispositions right now?" asked Admiral Sir Percy Noble, Commander in Chief of the Western Approaches. Noble's brief covered the sea-lanes to the west of the British Isles. As such he was primarily concerned with countering German U-boats and was not as familiar as the other two Admirals with the up to the minute deployment of the heavy ships of the

Royal Navy.

"Well, first there is Operation Ironclad," replied Pound, standing and moving to the map. He tapped the island of Madagascar in the Indian Ocean off the coast of southern Africa.

"Neville Syfret has the bulk of Force H off to the I.O. for the invasion of Madagascar," he continued. "He has two aircraft carriers, *HMS Indomitable* and *Illustrious* with him there and of course *Ramillies* will be out of action for months yet, dry docked in South Africa to repair the damage she suffered in the Japanese torpedo attack at Diego Suarez. Nearly two dozen destroyers and cruisers are with Syfret."

'Operation Ironclad' was the British amphibious invasion of Madagascar, launched by the Royal Navy to prevent German or Japanese submarines and aircraft from establishing a base there to attack allied shipping. The British had mounted the operation to seize the island from Vichy French troops.

The Battleship *HMS Ramillies* was at anchor in the port of Diego Suarez at the island's northern tip when a Japanese two-man submarine torpedoed her. Prompt damage control had saved the battleship from sinking, and it had made its way to Durban, South Africa where it would remain in dry dock for repairs for several more months.

"We could bring the carriers and a suitable screen of destroyers up Africa's east coast," offered Admiral Tovey. "They could come through Suez and approach Malta from the east."

"They'd be hard pressed to make the transit and reach Malta in time," answered Pound. "That's just six days till we expect Jerry to attack Malta. And they'd be exposed to Japanese submarine attack all the way to Aden." Pound traced his finger up the eastern shores of the African continent, around the Horn of Africa to the British port of Aden near the entrance to the Red Sea. "Then they must transit the Suez Canal," he continued, "within bomber range of the forward Luftwaffe bases around Tobruk."

"The Germans have only just taken those bases," Tovey replied. "With a bit of luck they won't be ready yet for long range operations."

"Perhaps so," replied Pound. "Still, it's a dicey proposition." He traced his finger through the Suez Canal to the Mediterranean Sea. "Even supposing they can transit Suez without incident they've still the whole of the Eastern Med to cross, within bomber range of the Luftwaffe both on Crete," tapping the Greek island, "and in Cyrenaica," tapping the bulge of Libya thrust northwards into the Mediterranean. The Royal Navy knew the sea of the Eastern Med between Crete and the North African coast as "Bomb Alley" due to the constant threat of Luftwaffe attack there.

"The carriers could form up with the fleet at Alex," said Noble. "Enough cruisers and destroyers and the carriers will have strong anti-aircraft as well as anti-submarine protection. What has Harwood got available there?" Admiral Sir Henry Harwood was Commander in Chief of the Royal Navy's Mediterranean Fleet. His HQ was at the British Naval base at Alexandria, Egypt, ubiquitously known as 'Alex' to British seamen.

"Not much, a few cruisers and destroyers, but no heavies at all," answered Pound. "Both carriers are off to Madagascar, and the battleships, *Queen Elizabeth* and *Valiant* are both still out of action." The other two admirals nodded their heads.

Italian Frogmen had penetrated Alexandria Harbor's anti-submarine nets the previous December, setting high explosive charges to the hulls of the two British battleships, sinking both at their moorings along with a tanker ship. The attack had been carried out with extreme daring and belied the popular opinion that the Italians had no courage. The British counter flooded the two battleships so that they settled on an even keel in shallow waters, giving the appearance to Luftwaffe reconnaissance that they were undamaged, but in fact neither was seaworthy, much less battle worthy.

"Still," Noble said, "with the carriers those cruisers and destroyers could make a formidable force to attack German or Italian aircraft and shipping. Surely the Germans can't plan to launch their attack and supply it entirely by air?"

"They did at Crete," answered Tovey, "and gave us a bloody nose doing it."

"What about the Home Fleet?" asked Noble of Tovey.

"We're over committed now as it is," replied the Home Fleet commander. "Most all my heavies are away to the north, in the Orkneys guarding against a sortie by *Tirpitz* against our convoys. The only carrier I have right now, *Victorious,* is with the American battleship *Washington* and our own *Duke of York.* They're all three at Scapa Flow ready to cover the next Arctic convoy to Murmansk, PQ17; thirty-five merchantmen with tanks, oil, ammunition and grain. I'm flying to Scapa myself in the morning to sail with *Duke of York.*"

Tovey referred to the convoy by its code designation. East bound convoys to the far north Russian ports of Archangel and Murmansk were designated "PQ", returning west bound convoys as "QP". PQ17 was therefore the 17th convoy of the war to or from the Russian ports.

"Not to mention *KG Five* is still dry docked," added Admiral Pound. The other Admirals again nodded their understanding. The modern battleship *HMS King George V* had been part of the covering force for the Arctic Convoy PQ14 the prior month. In a heavy fog east of Iceland she had rammed the Tribal Class destroyer *HMS Punjabi*, trampling the little ship under her mighty forefoot. The destroyer's depth charges, racked on her stern had broken free and exploded beneath the battleship, buckling her bottom plates. Miraculously, most of *Punjabi's* crew had been saved and *KG V* had made port, but was expected to remain at Liverpool for repairs for another three weeks.

"I can't spare anything more," Tovey went on. "Intelligence warnings indicate *Tirpitz* and several other German heavies are making ready to sail to attack the convoy."

"We could postpone the convoy," offered Noble, "delay it for a week or ten days."

"The Russians would have a fit," said Pound, "not to mention the Prime Minister. The Americans have valued the convoy's cargo at over 700 million dollars. It's enough weapons and supplies to equip an army of fifty thousand men. The Russians are desperate for the convoy to arrive and the PM is committed to helping our Russian allies, even to the extent of suffering heavy losses on these convoys. Besides, the convoy is already formed at Hvalfiord in Iceland.  Postponement now would throw all your escort schedules out the window for weeks to come."

In defending the decision to proceed with PQ 17 Pound was being a loyal subordinate to the Prime Minister. He was personally very much opposed to hazarding men and ships on the Russian convoys during high summer, when twenty-four hours of daylight and generally clear weather gave the Luftwaffe and German U-boats excellent hunting conditions in the latitudes above Norway's North Cape. On May 18, 1942 Pound had remarked to American Atlantic Fleet Commander Admiral Ernest J. King, "These Russian convoys are becoming a regular millstone around our necks...."

Tovey swirled his drink. "I've loaned both *Rodney* and *Nelson* out. They're away to the South Atlantic covering a troop convoy. They crossed the equator yesterday afternoon. The convoy is past any real danger from heavy German or Italian surface ships, but with their top speed of 24 knots *Nelson* and *Rodney* are six days out of Gibraltar. I've ordered them both to turn about for Gib' this morning, but chances of them getting there in time are practically nil." A smile crossed Tovey's face. He had a warm feeling for *Rodney*. He'd been her commanding officer from 1932 to 1934.

"Well, what of Force H?" asked Noble. "What has Syfret left behind at Gibraltar?"

Force H was the designation of the Royal Navy's heavy ships based at Gibraltar.

"That's about the only bright spot," answered Pound. "Force H has two carriers, *Eagle* and *Furious* available. The battlecruiser *Renown* is at Gib' now with the two battleships *Nelson* and *Rodney* on their way and about ten cruisers and over thirty destroyers in port. Right at the moment though, *Furious* is at sea west of Gibraltar."

"That's a powerful strike force," Noble perked up, "if *Furious* can be got back in time."

"Yes, but thin enough for all that," answered Tovey. "The two carriers between them can embark up to about fifty-five aircraft, but the Germans and Italians can throw two or three times that number of land based fighters and bombers against them from their airfields on Sardinia, long before our carriers are in range of Malta. It'll be very chancy counting on them being able to deliver Malta from an all out German assault. The battleships and cruisers have to pass within gun range of Malta to have any effect on the battle's outcome. The Germans will no doubt attack them from airbases on Sicily as well as those on Sardinia."

Noble nodded in agreement. "Yes, and lots of narrow seas to pass through too, and all likely with little or no air cover."

The three men swirled their drinks for a moment, racking

their brains for a solution to the problem.

"What about the Americans?" asked Noble, turning to Tovey. "They've loaned you their *Washington.* Don't they have a carrier at Gib as well? They've flown Spitfires out to Malta already this month."

"Yes," answered Pound. "The Americans loaned us the use of both the battleship *Washington* and the aircraft carrier *USS Wasp.* As we were planning the Madagascar operation we knew we'd be spread thin. The P.M. prevailed upon President Roosevelt to lend us the two heavies along with several other vessels to help us cover our obligations."

"Well, then," said Noble triumphantly. "Three carriers, the battlecruiser and the cruisers and destroyers at Gibraltar should be strong enough to fight through to relieve Malta!"

"Won't do, Percy," said Pound, shaking his head. "The Americans are hard pressed in the Pacific. They've recalled *Wasp.* She passed through the Panama Canal to the Pacific ten days ago." He paused. "They'll be wanting the battleship back by mid-July."

"A pity about the carrier," said Tovey. "She's larger, faster and more capable than any of ours. *Wasp* carries up to sixty-five aircraft, more than *Eagle* and *Furious* combined."

"Yes," said Pound, "and besides all that *Furious* is at sea right now," he repeated. On his map he pointed to the Atlantic Ocean in the area west of the Strait of Gibraltar. "She's providing anti-sub air cover to three convoys, one out-bound from Liverpool, around the cape and bound for Suez. Ten thousand troops for 8th Army." He tapped Cairo, Egypt on the map and arched his bushy, black eyebrows significantly. The other Admirals nodded. They understood the desperate need for reinforcements in the desert to stop Rommel and the Africa Korps.

"Convoy number two is in-bound from the far east," he continued. "Ten ships with rubber, tin and aluminum joined up with five large tankers from the Persian Gulf, all bound for Plymouth." Fuel and raw materials for the war industries in the south of England.

"Number three is also in-bound," Admiral Pound went on. "Six refrigerator ships from Argentina delivering beef and other food stuffs." He sighed and sank back in his chair. "*Furious* is covering over a thousand miles of the route for all three convoys.

We've timed their passage so she can cover them all at once. She can't leave station till at least the evening of the 25th. She'll have to put in to Gib for fuel and to exchange the patrol aircraft she's carrying for fighters. She can't approach Malta till the night of the 27th at the earliest."

"I say!" exclaimed Noble. "The ships are only the start of the problem aren't they?"

"Quite so, Percy," agreed Pound thoughtfully.

"What?" asked Tovey. "What have I missed?"

"Who's to command this fleet we're scratching together, John?" asked Noble. "Syfret is away to the I.O."

"It can only be Burrough," said Pound.

"Burrough?" asked Noble. "Harold Burrough? I thought he was commanding the cruisers on the Arctic run."

"He was," answered Tovey. "He's given his command over at Scapa Flow."

"Well, if Syfret is unavailable, Burrough is a great choice," opined Noble. "He ran the Malta thing last autumn didn't he?"

"Yes," said Pound. "September of last year. The most successful relief convoy to Malta we've ever had."

"Speaking of relief convoys," said Tovey, "we all know that gathering the warships for this thing is the easy part. Malta is on the brink of starvation as it is. Unless we also fight through with supplies, especially food and fuel Gort has already made clear the island will fall."

One of Lord Gort's first tasks on taking the Governorship of Malta just a month earlier had been to take a detailed inventory of all available supplies. He'd concluded that Malta must surrender if not re-supplied by mid-July. In early June, as part of Operation Harpoon two of a six ship convoy of merchant vessels had arrived at Grand Harbor, carrying between them 13,000 tons of flour and ammunition, staving off the immediate threat of starvation. Combined with a cut in the civilian food ration the date of capitulation had been pushed back to early September. But catastrophe befell the convoy when its only tanker ship, the *Kentucky*, owned by the American Texaco Oil Company and loaned to the British had suffered damage from a near miss. The damage was not severe, but *Kentucky* was in hostile waters and was disabled temporarily. She'd been sunk by a Royal Navy torpedo to prevent her capture by the enemy. Malta received no fuel.

"Well, the fast cargo ships are available at Gibraltar," said Pound. "But there are no tankers available with the kind of speed this job demands."

"Er," coughed Noble. "I hate to invoke the cousins again…?"

"Yes," said Pound dryly. "The Americans. I'm afraid 'that well is dry', as one of them might say. They loaned us *Kentucky,* which we promptly lost for them earlier this month. They've also loaned us her sister ship, the *Ohio*. She's at Greenock right now getting fitted out for another relief operation in August. She can't be ready in time for this lot though."

"Damned fine vessels, from all accounts," said Tovey.

"Yes, and exactly what's needed now," replied Pound with feeling. "We need to get fuel to Malta or all the battleships and aircraft carriers in the world will do us no good."

A discrete knock came at the door.

Pound answered it. "Enter!"

The door opened and a young Lieutenant Commander of Pound's staff came in with a message flimsy in his hand.

"Excuse me, Sir," he said. "This signal has just come in from Gibraltar. It's something you'll want to see immediately."

"Thank you Willoughby," said Pound as he took the message sheet. "That will be all."

"Yes, Sir," said Commander Willoughby. He turned and left the room, closing the door behind him.

Pound waited till Willoughby had left the room then pulled his reading glasses from his breast pocket. He scanned the message briefly, then read it carefully straight through.

"Well, gentlemen," he said. "This would seem to confirm the Malta intelligence estimates." His bushy black brows, so incongruous below his balding, gray-haired pate, creased in worry.

"What is it?" asked the other two admirals in unison.

"Anti-sub patrols at Gibraltar report German U-Boats have entered the Med in force," he said, handing the flimsy to Tovey. "Gibraltar estimates five to eight subs got through. They claim one probable kill on a U-Boat, but have also lost a corvette and two motor launches, apparently with all hands."

"The Germans are anticipating our response to their Malta invasion," replied Tovey as he handed the note on to Noble. "They're positioning U-Boats to try to stop our relief forces."

"So it would seem," said Pound. "Still, we may be able to dish up a surprise or two for

Jerry. I'll draft the orders immediately."

DAY 3

June 23, 1942

Kuno Schacht met General Lorzer at Tempelhof airfield early the morning of June 23. He boarded a Junkers 52 transport aircraft with the General and six officers of the General's staff as the dawn's first rays poked over the eastern horizon. There was little time for introductions, but Kuno quickly met Colonel Herrlitz, II Fliegerkorps intelligence officer and Major Bauer, Lorzer's logistics and maintenance chief. By the time the Ju 52 taxied into position on the runway the field was illuminated sufficiently for the pilot to get his bearings and to takeoff.

The first leg of the flight, from Berlin to Munich was uneventful and the officers all made an effort to doze during the trip of slightly over two hours. The constant droning roar of the engines made conversation almost impossible anyway, but also had a strange, soporific effect that never failed to amaze Kuno, no matter how often he flew. He fell into a light sleep in which he dreamed of his parting from Hilda that morning. She cried and clung to him and he wished so badly for one more day with her and the boys. He felt himself shaken gently and he smiled in his sleep at Hilda's waking him for love. His eyes came open and looked into the face of the Luftwaffe flight steward.

"We are approaching Munich, Herr Major," shouted the orderly. "Please prepare for landing."

"Thanks," mumbled Kuno as he rubbed the sleep from his eyes.

He looked about the cabin and saw the other officers straightening themselves as well. The roar of the engines dropped from ear splitting to merely deafening and Kuno felt the plane begin its descent. He turned and looked out the port side window at the mountains of Bavaria, their lower slopes carpeted in the green of spring, the peaks still mantled in winter's snowy white. He saw the flaps on the port wing extend and knew the Junkers was on its final approach.

When the transport taxied to a stop the orderly opened the fuselage door and extended the short, two-step platform to the ground. Lorzer stepped out first followed by the officers of his staff, with Kuno the last passenger from the plane. Lorzer walked towards a Luftwaffe Colonel waiting on the ramp with a staff car. Two Kubelwagens waited behind the limousine for the overflow of passengers. Ground crew swarmed out to the plane and a fuel bowser was wheeled up. The ground crew immediately set to work on refueling the plane. The flight crew emerged from the cockpit and began talking with the ground crew chief.

Kuno stretched his back and followed the more junior members of Lorzer's staff to the Kubelwagens. The general and the two officers Schacht had met in Berlin got into the limousine and drove off toward the terminal building. Kuno found himself in the front seat of one of the Kubelwagens next to the driver while two Captains of Lorzer's staff sat squeezed uncomfortably in the car's rear seat. Their driver spoke to them during the brief drive to the terminal.

"Gentlemen, you can expect to be on the ground for about one hour as your aircraft is fueled and serviced," he said. "Please don't stray far from the terminal building. You will find a small canteen in the terminal with refreshments and food. The convenience is in the rear of the canteen." He pulled the car to a stop outside the wide glass doors to the terminal. "I will come to the canteen to summon you when your flight is ready to resume," he concluded.

Schacht and the two Captains got out of the car and walked towards the building. As they entered through the doors Schacht turned to make introductions with them, but just as he did Lorzer called his name. The general was being served coffee and breakfast cakes at a table. With him were Colonel Herrlitz and Major Bauer whom Kuno had met on the tarmac at Berlin.

"Come over here Schacht," Lorzer called to him. "It is time I get to know you better."

Schacht nodded apologies to the Captains and hurried over to the General's table.

"Sit down, Schacht, sit down!" the general insisted.

"Thank you Herr General!" Kuno clicked his heels, bowed slightly to the general and took the fourth chair at the table.

"Coffee and cakes for the Major," Lorzer ordered the female Luftwaffe orderly on duty in the canteen.

As they began their breakfast Lorzer spoke with him.

"Tell me Schacht," he began, "what duty did you have before that little circus show at Berlin HQ, hmm?" The general chuckled, "Or have you spent the whole war attached to the general staff?" The other officers smiled and looked at each other. Kuno had the uncomfortable feeling he had been set up.

"No, Herr General," he replied. "I am a native of Berlin, but I have spent very little time there since the summer of 1939. I was a platoon leader in Poland and commanded an infantry company in France the following spring. After the French Armistice I attended a war college course at Leipzig where I learned the principles of close air support. I was assigned to the 12th Panzer Corps in General von Manstein's Army Group South last summer." The other officers and Lorzer were quiet now, listening to Kuno. He paused, breaking one of his cakes in half.

Lorzer spoke again. "It's a long way from Russia to the General Staff in Berlin?"

"One of our forward observers was killed in a local Russian counterattack just an hour before our division was to begin a major assault to cross the Desna River near Kiev." He paused again as he remembered that frigid December day. "There was no one else available who could take his place with the time of the assault so near, so I went forward with a replacement radio. The plan of assault called for a dive-bomber attack on the Russian positions on the other side of the river, followed by the infantry who were to cross on the frozen ice. The engineers would follow to bridge the river and get the Panzers across."

Kuno's lips curled up in mockery of a smile. "The Russians didn't subscribe to the plan however. The local counterattack turned out to be an entire infantry corps, backed up by their new T-34 tanks." He shrugged. "I had to call in the dive bombing attack on top of our own positions to stop the Russians. I was wounded by one of our own bombs."

Lorzer nodded at the Iron Cross hung at Kuno's neck. "You were awarded that for the action?"

Kuno only nodded in reply.

Lorzer said quietly, "Russia is not the walk-over we thought it would be".

"Anyway," Kuno concluded, "after recovering from my wounds I was assigned to Berlin for light duty and further recuperation. When I was chosen for the liaison job I was assigned to the General Staff for the past two weeks. I was told it was to give me an appreciation of the strategic situation."

Lorzer nodded his head, but said nothing before focusing his attention on the remains of his breakfast. After a moment Herrlitz and Bauer quietly began talking between themselves of their most recent leave at home.

Kuno's mind drifted back to the rest of the story on the banks of the Desna, the part of the story he hadn't told Lorzer and the others. He remembered the terror as the Russian infantry swept into the German positions, swamping the Panzer Grenadier's defense in brutal hand-to-hand combat, before the German tanks came up and swept the Russians back over the frozen river. In his minds eye he could still see the Russian infantrymen who fell through the bomb shattered ice as they tried to return to their own lines. Those few who managed to crawl back out of the water made only a few paces before collapsing. Within minutes they were dead, frozen nearly solid. He'd bandaged his own chest wound to slow the bleeding after the bombing attack blunted the Russian assault.

He thought back to the months spent in hospital recuperating from his wounds and of the thousands of injured German soldiers, limbless, blinded, emasculated who had passed through the hospital during his time there. And finally he thought of the few brief weeks he had spent with Hilda and the boys at home in Berlin.

"Attention please!" Kuno's mind snapped back to the moment. The Luftwaffe driver was standing in the door of the canteen. "Will General Lorzer's party please come to the tarmac? Your flight is ready to proceed."

Soon Schacht and the others were back in the air, bound now for Milan on the next leg of the trip to Rome. Kuno checked his watch. Just after 0900 hours. So far the journey was going well. He began to appreciate more the chance to fly with the General to

Rome. The journey would have taken him three days by train. Now it looked as if he would dine in Rome that very night.

The flight to Milan was smooth and uneventful. The Junkers passed over the Austrian and Italian Alps on a beautiful, clear summer day. The snow capped peaks of neutral Switzerland glittered in the distance to the west. The Alpine countryside was like a picture postcard to the travelers. Even Lorzer and his staff who had come this way just days before on their way to Berlin took their turns at the fuselage windows admiring the scenery.

After less than two hours in the air they landed at Milan where they once again had an hour wait before continuing. The final leg of their journey, from Milan to Rome was to be the longest of the trip, taking a little over three hours. Even so, their estimated time of arrival was now around 1600 hours. A mid-afternoon arrival would give Kuno an opportunity to see a little bit of Rome before continuing his journey next day.

Kuno spent the hour on the ground in Milan in exercise, stretching his cramped legs, walking around the tarmac surrounding the terminal and watching the take-offs and landings on the field. He climbed swiftly back aboard the transport when the time came to continue. They left Milan around 1245 hours on June 23.

About an hour south of Milan the port engine of the Junkers began to sputter and the pilot requested that General Lorzer come to the cockpit.

"Herr General," shouted the pilot to be heard above the engine noise. "If the engine holds up we can still reach Rome, however the engine temperature is rising and oil pressure is falling." He pointed to gauges in the cockpit instrument panel. "I believe it would be wise to choose an airfield to put down at for repairs rather than risk a forced landing if the engine packs up on us."

"Where are we?" shouted Lorzer in return.

"We have just passed La Spezia," yelled the pilot. "I could easily circle back there for a landing, or there is a strip at Pisa and another at Livorno about fifteen minutes ahead."

Lorzer thought very briefly then made his decision. "Carry on to Livorno," he shouted back. "I can make use of my time on a layover there at least!"

The pilot did not reply but nodded his head and pulled his chart case from the slot beside his seat. As Lorzer returned to his seat the pilot began contacting the field control at Livorno to alert them of his need to divert there for an emergency landing. Lorzer returned to the passenger cabin, shutting the cockpit door behind him. He gestured to the officers in the cabin to pay attention and they all leaned forward in their seats to catch his explanation of the problem.

"The port engine is packing up," he shouted. "We must divert to the military airfield at Livorno for repairs before continuing."

At that moment a burst of smoke issued from the port engine. Kuno spun to look at it and saw the propeller slowly windmill down in speed till it was turning only by force of the slipstream passing through it. The pilot had shut the engine down. The other officers peered over his shoulder out the window at the engine. In spite of being shut down smoke poured in greater volume from it. A burst of flame exploded from the exhaust manifolds and from around the engine cowling.

Lorzer shouted, "Strap in for landing! The pilot will have only one chance to land us safely!"

The Italian coastline passed by rapidly as the Junkers began to descend towards Livorno. Kuno gripped the edge of his hard bench seat near the door. He felt the sideslip of the plane as the pilot fought the drag of the dead port engine. He looked out the window and saw the ground racing up to meet them in a blur as the Ju 52 slammed onto the runway, bounced into the air again, and started to spin out of control. At the very last moment the pilot wrested the ship onto a straight course as it settled back to earth. The landing tires screeched at touching the runway, then the Ju 52 rolled down the strip, slowing as the pilot applied full brakes and flaps.

Looking back out the window Kuno saw the port engine was now fully enveloped in flames. With a start he realized they would all have to exit through the only door in the craft – behind the port wing.

But the pilot was an experienced flyer and knew what to do. As the Junkers rolled to a stop he spun the craft to put the port wing downwind of the fuselage. The orderly flung open the door and kicked down the steps even before the plane came to a stop. Lorzer dove through the door and hit the ground running, followed by his staff and Kuno, the orderly and finally the pilot and co-pilot scrambled clear of the plane.

A single fire engine roared up to the plane. Men jumped down and began spraying foam over the burning engine. Lorzer moved from man to man checking for injuries. He came to Kuno last.

"Well, Schacht!" he exclaimed, clapping Kuno on the back. "Aren't you glad you came with me now?"

"Oh, yes Herr General," Kuno replied. "I have not had this much fun since the Russian Front!"

"AH, HA!" proclaimed Lorzer. "That's the spirit Schacht! I remember my first crash well. You'll tell your grandchildren about this one, I assure you."

"If I survive Luftwaffe handling to meet my grandchildren I'll be happy General!" retorted Schacht. He realized both men were releasing the nervous energy generated by their close escape from death. A staff car raced up, skidding to a halt on the grass next to the runway. A Luftwaffe officer in paratrooper uniform jumped from the rear door and ran towards the plane.

Lorzer turned to Schacht and whispered urgently to him. "For God's sake, don't stare!" he hissed.

The paratrooper officer skidded to a stop in front of Lorzer.

"Herr General," he said anxiously, "are you injured, are you hurt? Let me take you to the hospital. The Doctors must examine you!"

"Take your hands off me Ramcke," replied Lorzer, brushing the paratrooper's hands away. "I'm fine. I am uninjured Ramcke!"

The Paratrooper glanced around at the other Luftwaffe officers and flight crew of the Junkers.

"Everyone is fine Ramcke," Lorzer told him. "We all got clear in plenty of time."

Ramcke's gaze now fell on the Army Major standing with the Luftwaffe General.

"Major Schacht, let me to introduce you to Brigade General Ramcke, commander of the 2nd Parachute Division," said Lorzer, seeing the question in Ramcke's eyes. "Schacht is on his way to Tobruk to meet the new Field Marshall. He's to be liaison officer between Rommel and me. I offered him transport in my aircraft, but I think now he regrets accepting!"

"I'm pleased to meet you Major," said General Ramcke, cordially shaking Kuno's hand.

"It is my pleasure, General," replied Kuno as he saw with a start that the paratrooper officer's teeth glinted like polished steel. He remembered Lorzer's admonition not to stare just in time.

Ramcke looked back at the plane. "Well," he said, "the fire is out, but this aircraft is going nowhere tonight. I can arrange another craft for you General, but it may take several hours. All the machines here on the field have been very active for the last few weeks. I have all available transport on stand down for maintenance. I wouldn't want to send you on your way in a plane that has not been thoroughly checked out."

"I agree, Ramcke," replied Lorzer.

Two more cars pulled up to the scene. More paratroopers piled out, carrying medical kits marked with red crosses. They quickly treated the few cuts and scrapes suffered as the Junkers was evacuated and the General and his staff piled into Ramcke's cars. This time Schacht was invited to ride with the two generals, all three in the rear seat. A glass barrier separated the rear passenger compartment from the driver. It was a warm day and the windows in the rear of the limousine were down, but Kuno found he was sweating anyway, wedged between two high-ranking Luftwaffe Generals as he was.

The airfield was a beehive of activity. To Kuno it seemed there were dozens of Junkers transports on the field, standing in rows off the runway. Many of them had cowlings stripped as teams of grimy mechanics overhauled their engines. Platoon-sized groups of men ran or marched in unison all about the field. They wore the distinctive jumpsuit and rimless helmets of the Fallschirmjaeger paratroopers.

"I have commandeered a spacious villa as my headquarters, General," explained Ramcke as they were driven from the site of the wreck. "Until we can arrange another craft for you we can relax there."

Lorzer said nothing as the car came up behind a platoon of paratroopers on a double time march along the edge of the road. As the car passed the men Kuno heard them singing the Song of the

Paratroopers, *"Red Shines the Sun"*. They sang with gusto and pride.

> *"Red shines the sun, ready made,*
> *Who knows of tomorrow and still we laugh?*
> *Start-up the motor, shove the throttles full forward,*
> *Start it up, today we fly to meet the enemy!*
>
> *In the aircraft, in the aircraft!*
> *Comrade, there's no going back.*
> *Far in the east stand shady clouds.*
> *Come along and be quiet, come along!*
>
> *Engines thundering-thoughts all alone,*
> *Then think fast of the love in your home.*
> *Then come, comrades, jump at the signal,*
> *And we'll float down upon the enemy.*
>
> *Quickly we land, quickly we land.*
> *Comrade, there's no going back.*
> *High in Heaven stand shady clouds.*
> *Come along and be quiet, come along!*
>
> *Small is our cadre, wild is our blood,*
> *We don't worry about the enemy, or about death,*
> *We know just one thing, Germany in red,*
> *To fight, to win, to pass into death.*
>
> *With the rifle, with the rifle.*
> *Comrade, there's no going back,*
> *Far in the west stand shady clouds.*
> *Come along and be quiet, come along!"*

Lorzer turned to Ramcke and smiled. "How is the training for Herkules going, Ramcke?" he asked as they drove. Ramcke started at mention of the top-secret operation. He looked pointedly at Schacht, then back to Lorzer.

Lorzer laughed. "Don't worry Ramcke. The Major is straight from the General Staff and the Fuhrer conference in which the invasion was authorized. He knows the whole plan."

"I see," said Ramcke, appraising Kuno again. "Well, things have gone very well, General. The coastline here and several areas in the nearby countryside bear a remarkable resemblance to the approaches and landing zones on the target. The training has gone well and as you've just seen the morale of the men is superb. They are ready to go when the order comes."

Kuno noted Ramcke avoided naming the target as Malta. Operational security for the invasion was an important prerequisite of success. He approved of Ramcke's caution.

"When do you move your force to Sicily?" asked Lorzer as the car left the airbase and turned down a dirt road that skirted the field. The other two cars followed close behind.

"The bulk of the force must go by train," answered the paratrooper officer. "The 6th Regiment leaves tonight, the 7th and 2nd Regiments in the morning. They'll arrive at Reggio di Calabria tomorrow night. They cross the Strait of Messina during the hours of darkness then go by lorry to the airfields."

"And your 23rd Regiment?" asked Lorzer.

"Most of the 23rd is already at Gerbini Airfield on Sicily. They are preparing the gliders now, packing the anti-tank guns and other heavy weapons. The remainder of the regiment will travel by air tomorrow morning. The transport aircraft must move to Sicily anyway, they may as well carry the remainder of the Regiment."

"How many Junkers do you have for the operation, General?" asked Kuno, speaking for the first time.

"Fewer than I would wish," answered Ramcke, "though all things considered, especially the situation in Russia I should be glad to have the 340 aircraft I've been allotted. We've arrived at my villa," said Ramcke pointing out the window to a sprawling, two story estate house.

The driver turned up a private lane to the house. White stucco with red tile roof in the Mediterranean style, a wide, screened veranda and climbing wisteria gave the impression of opulence and luxury. The driver swung the staff car up on the gravel circular driveway to the front doors. Kuno followed the senior officers out of the car. He looked out over the roof of the car down the lane they had just driven up. A rank of ancient, gnarled olive trees grew on either side, casting their shade on the lane. Rows of grape vines grew beside the wide lane, rolling over the undulating hills like waves upon the sea. Out past the end of the lane and beyond the main road another field of grapes grew, the vines marching in ranks down to the edge of a cliff overlooking the sea. Kuno gasped at the view from the villa.

It was a brilliant day on the Italian coast of the Ligurian Sea. The perfect blue of the sky contrasted beautifully with a handful of fluffy, white clouds. But it was the view of the sea that took Kuno's breath away. It was an amazing, deep turquoise, shimmering in the mid-day heat. Sunlight reflected from a million facets of water like diamonds on green velvet under a spot lamp. Two small islands lay offshore within his view. Each had substantial villas on them. Stone jetties projected into the sea from the rocky shores of the islands, so the wealthy owners could boat back and forth to the mainland at their ease.

General Ramcke broke Kuno's reverie as he stepped around the car.

"Magnificent, isn't?" he asked the Major. "I'll almost be sorry to leave."

"I can understand," answered General Lorzer as he too gaped at the scene before him.

"Come inside," said Ramcke. "We'll have a cool drink on the veranda and discuss your travel plans."

The three officers stepped into the two-story foyer of the villa. Kuno was amazed at the coolness of the interior. A cool breath of air washed over him as they crossed the tile entry to a side door leading to the veranda. He heard their staff car crunch away on the gravel drive and he wondered what had delayed the other officers. Ramcke ushered them to a large table with white linens on the veranda. It was placed to give an unobstructed view of the coastline.

"If you gentlemen will excuse me a moment I'll find my orderly and get us some refreshments." Ramcke bowed slightly and left Kuno and General Lorzer alone together.

"You noticed his teeth?" murmured Lorzer.

Kuno merely nodded his head.

"They are stainless steel dentures!" Lorzer went on earnestly. "Poor chap lost all his own teeth in a jump accident!"

"Please be seated gentlemen," requested Ramcke as he re-entered the room

The officers sat in silence, Schacht and Lorzer admiring the view, Ramcke enjoying his role as host. Presently the orderly entered the veranda. He carried a tray with glasses and a chilled bottle of white wine. The trooper poured for each of the officers, then left the veranda again, leaving behind the tray of extra glasses and the bottle.

Lorzer lifted his glass. "To Operation Herkules!" he toasted.

"Operation Herkules!" answered Schacht and Ramcke in unison, touching glasses.

As the officers enjoyed the refreshing light wine a car came up the lane towards the house at high speed. The driver spun the car into the circular roundabout in front of the house, the tires crunching gravel as the car skidded to a stop. Out of the back leapt a paratrooper in jump gear. He hurried through the front door into the house.

Ramcke, seeing this said, "This looks important. Pardon me please gentlemen," and started to stand up from the table.

He had not gotten fully to his feet when the entry to the veranda was flung open and the trooper from the car stormed in. He pulled up short when he saw Lorzer and Schacht sitting at the table. Schacht saw the wings of a Luftwaffe Colonel on the man's collar. Something was also vaguely familiar about him.

"Your pardon General," he said. "I was not aware you had guests."

"Not at all Colonel," answered Ramcke. "What is the flap for?"

"It's Captain Hartmann, sir," said the Colonel.

"Well, what of him," demanded Ramcke, quickly loosing patience. "Where is he?"

"Er, well, Sir," stammered the para Colonel.

"Out with it man!" shouted Ramcke.

"He's dead, Sir," answered the Colonel.

Ramcke's jaw hung slack for a moment, then recovering composure he asked simply, "Dead? How?"

"It seems he decided to have a last swim in the ocean this afternoon before embarking tonight," explained the Colonel. "The regimental surgeon believes he was stung by a jellyfish of some kind." The Colonel swallowed hard. "He's drowned sir."

"A jellyfish!" Ramcke exclaimed. "Drowned!" he shouted.

"My God!"

Kuno was revolted by the death of the man named Hartmann. He imagined himself enjoying a refreshing swim on a hot day; the sudden fiery sting of the jellyfish, followed by the rapid onset of paralysis as the poison worked into his bloodstream, the struggle to stay above the surface, sinking down, unable to breathe as the water closed over his head and through it all, fully conscious and aware of what was happening, utterly unable to do anything about it. Death in battle, swift and clean would be far preferable. Even the way he had almost died in Russia would be better than the fate suffered by the unfortunate Captain Hartmann.

Ramcke sat back down while the Colonel stood in the doorway. The paratrooper General sat staring at the table for a moment, then collecting himself he gestured to the Colonel to sit down. The man stepped to the table, pulled out a chair and plopped down in it. Without speaking Ramcke poured a glass of wine for the Colonel who downed it in one long swallow. Ramcke poured again for the Colonel, then poured for Lorzer, Schacht and himself.

He lifted his glass and said, "Captain Karl Hartmann."

The other officers repeated the toast, "Captain Karl Hartmann."

Ramcke stared at the table, reflecting on the dead officer. Then after a moment he turned to General Lorzer.

"I must attend to this matter immediately General," he said pushing back his chair. "Hartmann had an important role to play in the upcoming operation. I must see about his replacement promptly."

"Of course Ramcke," replied Lorzer, concern on his face. "What was the man's responsibility? Company or Battalion commander?"

"No, much more important than that," answered Ramcke. "He was the only man with any combat experience in the entire 6th Regiment as a forward controller for close air support." Ramcke and the Colonel left the room together.

Kuno stared after them with jaw open. He reached for the bottle of wine and filled his glass, downing it in one swallow, like the Colonel had done a moment before. He filled his glass again. He looked up from his glass and met General Lorzer's eye. Neither man spoke. Kuno drained his glass again then slammed the glass down on the table. He met Lorzer's eye again. This time the general smiled at him, a wide toothy grin, but still said nothing.

Schacht looked at Lorzer a moment then stood from his seat. "We'd best find General Ramcke," he said.

"Yes," agreed Lorzer as he too stood. "We'd best find him before he tears his hair out."

"Herr General, will you be so kind," said Kuno to Lorzer as they made their way out of the veranda, "as to inform Field Marshall Rommel that I shall be delayed joining him in Africa?"

"Of course, Schacht!" exclaimed the General, clapping Kuno about the shoulders as the two men followed Ramcke and the Colonel from the room. "I'm sure the Field Marshall will approve your taking a short Maltese vacation!"

"If you will come this way, Excellency I will introduce you in the amputee ward," said Dr. Buqa, pointing across the hall.

"Yes, of course," answered 'His Excellency'.

The two men stopped inside the door at the desk of the ward's head nurse. Dr. Buqa spoke quietly with the nurse as the great man surveyed the room. A row of beds ran down either side of the long ward, heads against the wall, feet to the central aisle. The great man quickly counted the beds down one side as Buqa finished speaking with the nurse. There were fifteen beds on a side, thirty on the ward. Every bed was occupied by a man, or at least by part of a man. The lucky ones were missing an arm or a hand. The less fortunate had lost two or more limbs. Sister nurses in long, gray and white habits moved about the room or sat at bedsides, spoon feeding men with no arms, cleaning the raw and bloody stump of a leg taken off above the knee, plumping a pillow.

Dr. Buqa stepped forward and spoke. All eyes in the room turned to him.

"Ladies and gentlemen," he began in cultured English with only a trace of a Maltese accent. "I have the very great pleasure of introducing to you our new Governor-General, Lord Gort." With a short bow the Dr. stepped aside.

"Thank you, Dr. Buqa," Lord Gort began in a clear, commanding voice that penetrated to the far end of the ward.

"Good morning to you lads!" he went on cheerily.

The poor, maimed wretches answered with a chorus of 'Good morning, Sir!'

"I'm in the process of touring the entire island," he went on, "visiting our lads wherever their duty may take them and here, at the Hospital of the Order of the Knights of Malta, I'm very pleased indeed to see the quality of care being delivered to our wounded by Dr. Buqa and his staff." As he spoke Gort made eye contact with each man in turn; several of them came to an attitude of attention in their beds. Gort paused before going on in a softer voice that forced the men to lean forward to hear.

"I know that many of you here have had it rougher than some others." He cocked his head to one side in a sympathetic gesture. "I know I needn't tell you that your service and sacrifice are valued, both here and at home," voice rising, "and have not been in vain! I guarantee you all that the Hun knows you're here and has come to regret it!"

A ripple of laughter and soft cheers ran through the room. Gort had them in the palm of his hand and knew now was the time for the icing on the cake.

"And now I have some good news for you. You've each earned a trip home and I can tell you today that you all have first-class chits for the first available transport!"

The news was greeted with shouts of "Good-O" and "Hurray!"

"Thank you all for your attention," Gort concluded.

"Thank you, Sir," the men answered in unison.

Gort moved to the bedside nearest him. "What is your name, son?" he asked the man there.

"Corporal Childers, Sir," the man answered.

"Liverpool, hmmm?" Gort guessed with a smile.

"Yes, Sir!" answered Childers proudly.

"You'll see home very soon, Childers," said Gort. "Carry on!"

"Thank you, Sir!" said Childers and snapped a salute, except that his right arm was gone below the elbow so that his bandaged stump rested against his forehead.

Gort returned a quick salute and moved across the aisle to another bed.

"What's your name, son?" he asked again. The man he spoke to had his sheets pulled up under his chin and was badly burned down the right side of his face.

"Bradford, Sir," the young man answered, "Flying Sgt. Bradford."

"Oh-ho!" said Gort. "A pilot, eh? What kite did you fly?"

"Spitfire, Sir!"

"Did you get any of them first, Bradford?" Gort asked with a sideways grin.

"Yes, Sir!" replied Bradford. "Two confirmed kills and a probable."

"Well done!" exclaimed Gort. "Well done! Carry on!"

Gort snapped a quick salute to the young pilot.

Bradford winced at the salute and only then did Gort realize there were no arms under the sheets. Gort nodded his head in understanding and patted Bradford on the leg through the sheets.

And so it went, down the aisle, speaking a few words of praise and encouragement to each man. When he'd spoken with the last wounded man on the ward Gort turned and strode purposefully from the room, Dr. Buqa at his side.

"That is the last ward, your excellency," said Dr. Buqa when they reached the hallway. "All told we have nearly six hundred patients here, including over one hundred men of the forces. That is an increase in both numbers of almost fifty percent since the start of the year. It's the same story at other hospitals on the island."

"Yes, I know," answered Gort. "I was at the 90th Field Hospital up at Mtarfa yesterday. The wards are full there too." He paused a moment, then asked, "Are you receiving all the supplies you need, Dr.? Anything you are short of."

"We're short of nearly everything but sick and wounded," snorted Dr. Buqa as the two walked slowly towards the exit. "The public health situation on Malta is extremely grave. Tuberculosis has become a serious problem since this past winter and almost everyone on the island has suffered amoebic dysentery to one degree or other." Dr. Buqa looked around to assure they were alone. "Worst yet," he said in a lowered voice, "we have documented nearly three hundred cases of infantile paralysis on Malta in the past month."

"Polio!" exclaimed Gort.

Buqa nodded his head.

"Yes. Polio. All of these diseases are caused, or are at least compounded by shattered sewage lines contaminating the drinking water supply." He shook his head. "I can't even recommend the population boil their drinking water. There is no fuel. On top of all that, add malnutrition." He shook his head. "The population of Malta is on the brink of a serious breakdown in health. If the situation isn't stabilized soon, we will have a major catastrophe on our hands."

"Thank you, Dr.," said Gort as they reached the hospital entrance. "I'll see what I can do to relieve your supply problem here, but you must expect that the overall situation will worsen before it improves."

"In that case, Lord Gort," said Buqa slowly, "the mortality rate will rise dramatically this summer."

Gort stepped out onto the street in front of the hospital. To his right, down the Triq il-Merkanti, Merchant Street, was the tip of the peninsula and Fort St. Elmo, guarding the entrances to Grand Harbor and Marsamxett Harbor. To his left, up the street was the Grandmaster's Palace, the ancient residence of the leaders of the Knights of Malta. In all directions the narrow streets were choked in rubble, with narrow serpentine paths cleared to permit travel.

Malta's capital city, Valletta is built on the northeastern tip of Sciberras Peninsula on the island's west coast and lies between the two magnificent ports that grace the island. Jean de la Valette, Grand Master of the Knights of Malta, designed the city as a fortress following the failed Turkish siege of the island in 1565. The old town's main streets run from southwest to northeast down the length of the peninsula. Valette laid them out to allow prevailing summer winds from the southwest to sweep down the streets in the afternoon, cooling the residents after the heat of the day.

The entire city is very compact, less than a square kilometer, and is completely surrounded by battlements and defense works. At the tip of the peninsula is Fort St. Elmo, commanding the approaches to Grand Harbor on the south side of the peninsula and to Marsamxett Harbor to the north. Down each side of the peninsula are a series of massive limestone battlements and gun batteries that dominate the two harbors and their approaches, looming over the docks and quays. Midway down the peninsula a dry moat, named the Great Ditch zigzags from Marsamxett to Grand Harbor, separating the old city of Valletta from its suburb of Floriana at the base of the peninsula. Behind the moat another series of battlements protect Valletta from the landward side. At King's Gate in the center of the peninsula the ditch is spanned and the bastion is breached with a single entrance to the city. When built in the 16th century Valletta was very nearly impregnable. Even the two allies of besiegers, hunger and thirst, were accounted for. Massive cisterns and granaries are dug into the limestone foundation of the peninsula beneath the city. When properly stocked in anticipation of a siege they were powerful weapons against starvation.

Yet the coming of the airplane in the 20th century rendered many of the island's conventional defenses obsolete and by the last week of June 1942 the old city lay mainly in ruins, its streets filled with rubble and its grand public structures cast down under the weight of bombs delivered by the Luftwaffe and the Regia Aeronautica. The granaries and cisterns were empty. Wreckage and flotsam filled both harbors and the Royal Navy submarine base on Manoel Island in Marsamxett Harbor lay abandoned. In the final weeks before the last of the 10th Submarine Flotilla's boats were withdrawn in May the subs were forced to lie submerged at the bottom of the harbor during daylight hours to avoid being bombed. The British hoped to resume submarine operations there if the lull in bombing continued.

Lord Gort retrieved his bicycle from the hospital portico and began pedaling up the street towards the Palace of the Grandmaster, navigating past heaps of rubble and around gaping bomb craters. He reached the Triq il-Arcisqot, but instead of turning right to the Palace he turned left toward Grand Harbor and the Lascaris Bastion. He had a meeting that afternoon with the island's senior military commanders.

Lord Gort's full name was John Standish Surtees Prendergast Vereker, Sixth Viscount Gort. The owner of this outlandish name was the British Governor-General of Malta and his name notwithstanding he was a remarkable chap, holding

Britain's highest award for military valor, the Victoria Cross, for heroism on the Western Front in the First World War. He'd commanded the British expeditionary force in France in 1940 and had disobeyed orders from the Imperial General Staff in London when he chose to withdraw his army from the battle and retreat to the channel port of Dunkirk. He managed the difficult withdrawal with skill and along with a measure of luck most of his army was saved.

But not Gort himself. Removed from field command with the stigma of the debacle in France he next served as Inspector-General of the Army, mainly because cashiering him would be bad for morale. Slowly, he earned his way back into more prominent service taking the job as Governor-General of the British Crown Colony, Gibraltar. He'd taken the posting to Malta just a few short weeks before, at the start of May when his predecessor, Sir William Dobbie was called home to England. The word put out for public consumption was that Dobbie was suffering from exhaustion and the strain of his office and this may well have been true enough, but in fact Dobbie was sacked by Churchill after reports reached London that Malta's Governor-General was losing his grip on the crisis and that infighting among the island's leadership was having an adverse effect on the military and political situation.

Gort was the perfect replacement. Stern and tough-minded with a lifetime of Military discipline behind him he was a no-nonsense kind of leader. He would not tolerate any squabbling or political factions among his underlings. Gort may also have seen his posting to Malta at this critical time as a chance to wipe out the stigma of France. There can be no doubt that he was fully aware of the depth of the crisis at Malta when he arrived in May.

Lord Gort, as he was known to all on Malta quickly established himself as the leader of civilian and soldier alike on the besieged island. Despite his exalted position he immediately adopted for himself the same rations as the common soldiers on Malta were held to, about 1,000 calories per day. As a further example to the garrison and populace Lord Gort rode a bicycle to all his duties to save precious fuel.

The side streets in Valletta, those running from southeast to northwest across the width of the peninsula descend from the spine of Sciberras to the battlements overlooking the two harbors. The last two or three city blocks descend steeply and are cut in steps from the limestone bedrock. The steps are wide, designed to permit a Knight in full armor to negotiate his way up and down without stumbling. Gort dismounted and pushed his bicycle the last yards to the gate of the Lascaris rampart.

The British built Lascaris in the 1850's as an addendum to the great stone fortifications built by the Knights of Malta in the 16th century. The massive stone battlement faced out to Grand Harbor and in the previous century the British mounted batteries of muzzle loading guns on the bastion to dominate the inner harbor in the event that an enemy fleet forced the harbor entrance. Nearly abandoned since the turn of the century, with the coming of war to the Mediterranean it was reoccupied. Along the rampart atop the bastion sat a battery of 40mm Bofors anti-aircraft guns. The RAF also manned an air observer spotting station connected by telephone to the island's Combined Operations Room.

Carved into the limestone beneath the fortress was a series of tunnels and chambers, used originally as magazines and storerooms for the batteries. Now, the Combined Operations Room from which the Army, Navy and Air Force planned and coordinated the defense of the island occupied the largest of these chambers. A massive three-dimensional mock-up of Malta and the surrounding sea covered over two hundred square feet. RAF staff used the mock-up to plot the approach of enemy aircraft as reported by telephone from Malta's radar sites and spotters located at strategic points about the island. Many of the smaller chambers were used as offices and one even by a pool of typists in addition to the 'Y' Service Chamber in which Maggie Reed worked on wireless intercepts.

The COR was also the Royal Navy HQ of Vice-Admiral Sir Ralph Leatham, commander of the Malta Naval Station. The Royal Navy moved into its subterranean quarters beneath Lascaris after a Luftwaffe air raid destroyed the peacetime RN HQ across the harbor at the naval barracks in Fort St. Angelo. By Royal Navy tradition a large naval barracks is classed a battleship and is referred to as *His Majesty's Ship,* thus Fort St. Angelo was known as *HMS St. Angelo.* The Luftwaffe claimed it as a Royal Navy battleship 'sunk' during the siege.

Lord Gort's appointment was to meet Admiral Leatham in the COR along with Air-Vice Marshall Lloyd, commander of the Royal Air Force on Malta. Gort parked his bicycle at the entrance to the underground caverns at Lascaris leaving it in the care of the Marine Guard there. He turned to look out over the harbor before entering the dungeon-like atmosphere.

In ordinary times the view of the harbor is beautiful and striking from the top of Lascaris Bastion, the deep blue of the harbor waters contrasting with the white limestone structures built all around it, but these were no ordinary times. The half submerged hulks of several large merchant ships littered the anchorage and the harbor's waters were coated with the rainbow sheen of oil leaked from sunken wrecks. Across the harbor from Lascaris in the ruined dry dock of Dockyard Creek Gort could just see the stern of the shattered wreck of one of His Majesty's destroyers. Considered too badly damaged to be saved it was stripped of guns and spare parts to keep other ships in action. To his left and across the harbor lay Ricasoli Fort on Ricasoli Point at the entrance to the harbor and adjacent to Fort St. Elmo. As Gort contemplated the scene air raid warning sirens began to wail over Valletta and Grand Harbor. It was the fifth warning of the day and followed seven raids the day before.

Lord Gort sighed and turned to enter beneath Lascaris Bastion. He saluted the Marine guard at the entrance and descended into the depths of the caverns, passing a mess hall and a Marine Barracks, then descending a flight of forty steps to an ante-room outside the COR. A Royal Navy Lt. Commander, the Admiral's Flag Secretary, met him. The officer bowed briefly to Lord Gort then escorted him to Admiral Leatham's office.

"Good afternoon, Lord Gort," the Admiral greeted him, and then dismissed his secretary. "That will be all Carruthers".

"Ralph, how are you?" asked Gort as the door closed behind the secretary.

"Just fine, John," answered the Admiral as they shook hands. "Just fine. Sit down, sit down. Our RAF friend will be along shortly. Have a drink?"

"Just water please Ralph," replied the Governor-General. "Haven't had a bite yet today, ya' know." Gort sat down in one of the plush armchairs offered him by his friend. He looked about the office. He marveled at the elegant furnishings of the room, here in a rough-hewn limestone chamber almost one hundred feet beneath ground.

"I say, John," answered Ralph as he handed Gort his soda water, "carrying this ration thing a bit far aren't you? We can't have you pack up on us so soon!"

"Don't worry about me," Gort answered, taking the drink from Leatham. "I'll be all right."

"Yes, I dare say."

Both men turned at a discrete knock on the door. "That should be Lloyd now," said Leatham. "Come in!" he commanded.

The door opened and Air-Vice Marshall Sir Hugh Lloyd entered, followed by Commander Carruthers.

"Signal for you, Sir," said Carruthers to Leatham. He handed Leatham an envelope and a clipboard and pen. The Admiral signed the acknowledgement and dismissed the secretary again.

Lloyd went straight to the Admiral's bar and mixed himself a drink. Just as he turned to take a seat the distant rumble of an exploding bomb was felt in the office. Limestone dust trailed down from minute cracks in the room's ceiling.

"Just in time, Hugh," said Gort, lifting his glass in toast.

"Bloody Germans," answered Lloyd, lifting his glass in return.

As the RAF commander made himself comfortable Leatham tore open the message envelope and scanned its contents. Vibrations from bomb explosions continued to rattle the room.

"Bloody Germans, indeed," he said, waving the message. "According to London the Germans and Italians have decided to proceed with their Operation Hercules. We should expect a German invasion within the week."

"I say," said Lloyd, mastering the famous English understatement, "that would explain the Luftwaffe's renewed interest in us, wouldn't it."

"It certainly would!" agreed Gort. "They're softening us up one last time before the assault."

"What details can London give us as to the date of the attack, its strength and composition and so forth?" asked Lloyd.

"Pretty thin on details I'm afraid," said Leatham reading the message. "Best estimate is for the 28th, that's just five days from now, but it's only a guess, nothing firm. Strong airborne forces expected to take part to be followed up by invasion from the sea." He handed the message sheet on to Gort.

"No surprises there!" snorted Gort as he read the flimsy. "How bloody else would they invade?" He read on. "Interesting details there about Rommel. Seems the Jerries don't all agree Malta should be next on their shopping list."

"The 28th begins the full moon," observed Leatham.

"Yes, good conditions for paratroop drops," agreed Lloyd.

"How is our fighter strength holding up?" asked Gort.

"We took a real beating yesterday," Lloyd answered. "We lost six Spitfires with five more heavily damaged. Four pilots lost and three injured as well." He took a swallow from his drink. "Of course Jerry lost twice as many, but he can afford the losses better than we can."

"At that pace what will be your strength on the 28th?" asked Leatham.

"Strength!" laughed Lloyd. "At that pace we won't have a fighter left on the island well before the 28th."

"We'd best see what can be done to fly in some fresh Spitfires before then, hadn't we," said Gort.

"Of course, that's the first order of business, yes," said Lloyd. "But that's not the end of it, is it? We're at absolutely low ebb on our fuel supplies right now. If the Germans force us to keep up this pace for the next five days a hundred fresh Spits won't do us a tinkers damn of good with no fuel to fly them."

"We certainly can't expect any tankers in port over the next few days," replied Admiral Leatham.

"So what's the answer?" asked Gort.

"I don't know," said Leatham. "I'll work on it."

"Meanwhile John," said Lloyd to Gort, "you'd best get with the Brigadiers, see that the regiments are prepared as best they can be."

Malta's army garrison was composed of some 25,000 troops, many of them in famous British regiments. These regiments were detailed as work battalions to the island's three airfields, the RAF stations at Ta Qali and Luqa on the high, flat ground in the middle of the island and the Fleet Air Arm base at Hal Far adjacent to Marsaxlokk Bay on the island's south coast. The soldiers toiled at repairing bomb cratered runways, at building revetments for the aircraft and in assisting the RAF "erks" in servicing and repairing the island's aircraft.

"Right!" said Gort. "Of course, we've got to keep them and everyone else on Malta in the dark on this for the time being."

"That's right John," said Sir Hugh. "No sense triggering a panic, especially since it may not come off. We've had these scares before."

"True," said Admiral Leatham. "Still, this time it feels right. With Tobruk in Rommel's hands the time is right for Jerry to clear up his supply lines before he pushes on to Suez and beyond. I think we should treat this as an accurate intelligence estimate."

"Agreed," said Lord Gort. "We must assume the Germans mean to invade Malta in five days time."

"All right," said Sir Hugh. "We'll see what we can do to scare up some extra fuel. I think we'd better have a look at the Italian Naval bases and the Luftwaffe airfields in Sicily as well. We'll be as ready for Jerry as we can be."

Squadron Leader Harry Bracewater was a Spitfire pilot on Malta. He'd been flying there since the start of 1942, once or twice a week, but in that time he'd never engaged in air-to-air combat with the Italians or Germans. He'd been shot at plenty, mainly by enemy flak, occasionally by an interceptor fighter, but he'd never shot back. In fact, his Spitfire didn't even carry any guns, so he couldn't have shot back had he wanted to.

Bracewater flew a special type of Spit, a Mark IV model AB300, equipped with high-speed cameras for photographic reconnaissance. Guns and ammunition were sacrificed, reducing the Spits weight, permitting higher speeds and ceilings. The AB300 Spitfire was reputed to attain speeds of 450 miles per hour and to have a ceiling of over 30,000 feet.

Six pilots shared the two AB300 Spits on Malta and one of them was in the air during daylight hours almost continuously that spring of 1942. Bracewater had written the flight rotation for the week several days earlier and had penciled his own name in for a daybreak recon flight over the North African ports of Tripoli and

Benghazi. One of the AB300's visited the area every second or third day, looking for Axis shipping in the harbors, a build-up of aircraft at the airdromes or of vehicles on the *Via Balbia,* the Italian engineered highway that ran the length of the Libyan coastline. Based on the recon photos a strike mission might be flown by the Malta bomber force, or details given to the Royal Navy to lay on a submarine or surface ship attack.

With extra fuel tanks installed the AB300 could over-fly axis territory within a 400 mile radius, reaching targets as far north as Rome, east to the Pelopennesus of Greece and west to Sardinia as well as south to the shores of North Africa as far east as Benghazi.

Bracewater walked into the tiny office he shared with the other five photo recon pilots at Luqa Airdrome on Malta. Not more than ten feet square it was built into the wall of the revetment belonging to one of the photo recon Spitfires and held a chair and small desk. On the desk was a telephone, connected to the Luqa operations center. Two clipboards hung on the wall. One held the flight schedule for the week with completed flights checked off, the other was used to keep the hand-written notes left by the pilots at the completion of each flight. The notes covered any observations the pilots made on the aircraft's performance or handling.

Bracewater read through the few notes on the fighter, Spitfire number 1892. The last pilot to fly it had noted it felt a little sluggish at high altitude. The maintenance crew chief however had noted no problem found in the air boost or supercharger that allowed the Merlin engine to breath at high altitude. He hung the clipboard back on the wall and stepped out of the office into the revetment.

The crew chief was just closing the cowling over the engine compartment. The phone in the office rang. Bracewater stepped back in the office and picked up the phone.

"Bracewater, Luqa," he answered it.

"Bracewater old chap, Ops here. You hadn't left yet had you old boy?"

Bracewater rolled his eyes and counted to five before answering. "No, Ops, I'm still here to answer the telly."

"Jolly good. Change of flight plan for you old boy. Frightfully sorry for the short notice, but it can't be helped. Need you to hop on up to Italy, take a look at the Eye-tie naval bases, then over to Sicily for a peek at the Luftwaffe airfields."

"Acknowledged Ops," Bracewater replied. "Naval bases and the Sicilian airfields. Anything else?"

"Do be careful old boy. That is all."

Bracewater laughed. "Of course. Out."

He sighed. Last minute changes in the photo recon schedule weren't all that unusual. This change wasn't as bad as some. The recon requested by ops that morning was for one of the standard routes the AB300 Spitfires flew routinely. It would not require him to work up a flight plan on the fly as it were. He went to the desk and pulled a sheaf of papers from the top drawer, thumbing through till he found the sheet he was looking for. The route over the south Italy naval bases and Sicilian airfields had been flown three days earlier by one of the other pilots. The written flight plan included all the course and altitude adjustments needed to over-fly each of the targets in turn at optimum altitude and angle of approach. Penciled in the margin would be any observations the pilot made during the flight about changes in the enemy air defenses, new ack-ack guns or a speedier intercept than was customarily seen. There were no such notes on the most recent flight sheet.

Bracewater folded the map and clipped it to the small clipboard sewn to the right thigh of his flight suit. He pulled on his flight cap as he walked to the aircraft. The crew chief presented him with the maintenance log, which he read as he went through a quick, pre-flight checklist. All was in order and he signed the log, returning it to the crew chief. Within minutes he was racing down the Luqa runway and on his way into the air.

To approach the Regia Marina bases in south Italy the Photo Recon Unit, or PRU Spitfires made a wide swing to the east when leaving Malta, rather than a more direct northeasterly course, this to avoid the chance of running into any Luftwaffe fighters coming down from Sicily, a distinctly undesirable prospect for the unarmed PRU flights. Bracewater flew east eighty miles as he gained altitude to 25,000 feet, then turned just slightly east of north to his first target, the naval base at Taranto. Just before landfall he swung in an arc so as to approach the base from the east, a course that gave the flak gunners the least time to find the range as he passed overhead. The sky was clear and calm as he activated the first camera with a switch on his instrument panel. A small metal port cover, which protected the camera lens from dirt and moisture slid back and exposed the lens. He squeezed off just twelve frames, as there did not appear to be any unusual activity in the harbor. The flak never came close enough to affect his flight. He closed the port over the camera as he completed his run.

Leaving Taranto on a westerly heading he changed course for Naples, slightly north of west and flew on for 150 miles. At Naples too, he approached from overland to limit the time the AA gunners had to find his altitude. Here he noted increased activity in both the naval and civilian harbors, with at least six more destroyers and cruisers than normal and an unusual number of small coastal type vessels at anchor or tied up to the wharves and quays. He also thought he could make out smoke drifting from the stacks of one of the two Italian battleships at anchor, though he couldn't be sure. He shot the remaining thirty-six frames of film in the first camera, covering the harbor in detail. Once again the flak was ineffective against him.

Turning south and east he now made for the Strait of Messina, between the island of Sicily and the Italian mainland. He passed over the beautiful island of Capri as he went, though at an altitude of 25,000 feet the famous resort's charms were hidden from him.

He'd been in the air just under two hours with about another hour and a half to go before touching down at Luqa. He settled in for the flight to Messina, forty minutes distant. The sky remained clear, both of clouds and of enemy aircraft.

His flight plan carried him southeast on a direct line from Naples to Messina on the Sicilian side of the strait and directly across it to Reggio di Calabria on the toe of the Italian boot. He would then turn southwest to the airfield at Catania south of Mt. Etna, then down the Sicilian coast, covering the small harbors of Augusta and Syracuse before turning west again for the last target on his itinerary, the airfield at Comiso. From there he had a short, twenty-minute flight home to Luqa.

The run from Messina to Comiso was the only tricky part of the trip, requiring five course changes in twenty minutes of flying, but he had flown the same route over a dozen times before and was confident he'd have no trouble at all in clear weather.

Once again, at Messina and Reggio di Calabria he found larger than normal numbers of small coasters and ferryboats assembled and he used thirty-six frames of his second camera between the two ports then swung quickly down towards Catania. As before the flak was ineffective. Mt. Etna loomed to starboard throughout this phase of his flight, its perpetually snowcapped peak glimmering white in the sunlight.

At Catania he hit the jackpot. Looking down on the airfield there he could see many more aircraft than normal spread across the entire dispersal area. He could not distinguish their types with the naked eye, but from their size and shape he deduced many were two or three engine bombers and transports while others were most likely gliders. He whistled softly to himself and shot the last twelve shots in his second camera and the first twelve in the third and last camera. Here was the explanation for the change in his recon flight. Clearly the Germans and Italians were planning to invade Malta from the air, most likely following it up with landings on the island's coastline using the small coasters he'd seen in the ports.

He considered breaking radio silence to alert Malta immediately of what he'd seen, but the time taken to manipulate both camera ports open and closed, to take the twenty-four photos and to wheel the aircraft to the southeast left him almost on top of Augusta. He noted more suspicious vessels in the harbor there and across the bay at Syracuse. He was only twenty minutes from home now and he elected to finish his reconnaissance without breaking radio silence. Once again the axis flak gunners tried, but failed to find his altitude and he swung west for the final photo run over Comiso airdrome.

Bracewater left the third camera's lens exposed for the short run from Syracuse to Comiso. As he came within range of the airfield he gasped. The field was literally a-buzz with activity. Seemingly hundreds of aircraft were either in landing and take-off patterns or dispersed over the field.

He toggled the switch on the camera and heard a tremendous bang in the rear of the Spitfire. The stick was nearly torn from his hands and the aircraft nosed over instantly in a near vertical dive. He hauled back on the stick, trying desperately to regain control.

The stick pulled back into his lap freely, but the Spitfire did not respond. Shrapnel from the flak near miss or the jolt as the fighter flipped over in its dive had snapped the control cables to the ailerons. He kicked the rudder bar, but got no response there either. The Spitfire rolled on its left wing, and began to spin.

Bracewater reached for the canopy lever, fighting the centrifugal force of the spin to grab the latch. The canopy popped open and was torn from the cockpit. He was instantly buffeted by wind as the Spitfire continued its death spin. He felt himself losing consciousness as the gravitational forces of the spin accelerated. He reached for the snap on his harness as dots swam before his eyes. Blackness descended and he knew no more.

Later that day Luqa flight ops listed PRU Spitfire number 1892 overdue and presumed lost.

## Day 4
June 24, 1942

Leading Stoker Harry Booth was engaged in the second favorite pastime of sailors ashore the world over. He was getting drunk, as the favorite pastime of sailors was difficult to find in World War II Gibraltar. The brothels in nearby Spanish La Linea, just across the neck of the peninsula connecting the Crown Colony of Gibraltar with the mainland were peacetime favorites of the world's sailors for generations. But even though Spain and Britain were not technically at war the Fascist government of Francisco Franco had no love lost for the British. While the border was not officially closed the British were very careful to watch who came and went, allowing only documented Spanish dockyard workers to enter by day, all to be gone every night, and placing Spanish soil off limits to any of His Majesty's 'Other Ranks' enlisted military personnel.

It was feared by the British that Axis agents operating freely in Spain would snatch Allied military men in an effort to gain information on ship sailings and cargos or on the port's operations and defenses. Quite apart from kidnap was the chance of desertion. The life of a Royal Navy seaman was hard in the Second World War. The attractions of a peaceful life in a neutral country proved hard to resist for many sailors.

So, late the night of June 23 - 24, 1942 Harry was getting drunk in one of Gibraltar's many bars when two toughs of the Royal Navy Shore Patrol came in. Harry wasn't worried. They had no reason to be looking for him in particular. He went on drinking at the bar.

After a moment he looked up into the mirror behind the bar and saw that the Shore Patrol men were standing behind him. One was a giant of a man with a barrel chest and a stupid looking face with heavy brows overhanging dim eyes. The other, obviously the leader of the pair was smaller and more intelligent looking, but with a mean smirk on his pinched face.

"*HMS EAGLE*?" the smaller one asked him.

"What if I am?" Harry replied. "It ain't no crime is it?"

"Now don't give us any trouble, mate," the smaller man smiled. A chill ran down Harry's spine at seeing that sadistic smirk in the mirror. "All *HMS Eagle* are ordered to report aboard immediately."

"Aw, sod it chum, I just got 'ere!" Harry said as he turned on his barstool to face the man. "Can't a bloke 'ave a spot of cheer in peace?"

The small man's face flushed with grim menace. "Not when 'bloke' has orders he can't!" he spat out. "Now move it before I have Mitchell here carry you aboard in a sack!"

Harry looked at Mitchell who took a menacing step towards him.

"All right, all right," he said, "no need to get nasty 'ere." Harry downed the last swallow of his rum and stood up. "I'm going."

Harry was put aboard *HMS Eagle* with a motley group of inebriated shipmates by the Shore Patrol harbor launch. Still half drunk he stumbled up the port side companionway to the hangar deck. He found the ship a beehive of activity. The fleet air arm complement of planes was struck down to the hangar deck where they were wedged in like parts to a puzzle with too many pieces. The biplanes, Swordfish torpedo bombers of the type that had wreaked havoc on the Italian battle fleet at Taranto in 1940, all had their wings folded up and were shoved together side by side and in rows with one plane's nose against the next plane's tail. The wing tips barely cleared the hangar deck's fire sprinkler plumbing, suspended from the deck above. The three Fairey Fulmar fighters aboard were similarly treated, stowed in the center of the forward hanger deck, surrounding the lift to the flight deck above, ready to be put on deck and launched on short notice. All about the hangar the ship's flight crew was active, stowing gear and lashing the planes down to stabilize them for sea.

Harry and his mates hustled through the hanger deck, ducking under and around the crowded aircraft to the central passage that led down into the machinery spaces and crew quarters of the ship. Before ducking down the ladder toward the engine room Harry glanced through the starboard wing of the hanger deck. There he saw a Spitfire fighter plane suspended by cables from the harbor's floating crane and being lifted onto the flight deck.

"Malta!" Harry said to himself aloud.

The boilers were well on their way to full steam by the time Harry reached the engine room. He was set right to work servicing the lubricating oil lines and pumps to the propeller shafts. *HMS Eagle* was an old ship, requiring almost constant preventive maintenance from her crew to remain in service. She'd first been laid down in 1913 under a contract to the Chilean government as a pre-*Dreadnaught* battleship, to be named *Almirante Cochrane.* At the outbreak of the Great War in August 1914 work on the ship was suspended until the Admiralty negotiated the purchase of the hulk from the Chileans. In 1917 work resumed and the ship was completed as an airplane carrier in June 1918. A famous idiosyncrasy of the ship was that her engine room instruments were all labeled in Spanish with metric measurements. Steam pressure for instance was measured in kilograms rather than pounds.

Within hours of his coming aboard *Eagle* was under way. The carrier eased around the mole that protected the naval harbor at Gibraltar from the open sea, turning first south then east. After clearing the harbor she ran up to her top speed of 24 knots, holding the pace for almost two hours before dropping back to a more easily maintained 18 knots.

Soon after cutting speed Captain Mackintosh addressed the crew from the bridge. The Captain's voice reached into every compartment of the great ship, into the crew berths and even the engine rooms, though there, Harry and his mates were forced to crowd round the Tannoy speakers to hear over the roar of the boilers and the crashing of gears.

"This is the Captain speaking." Captain Mackintosh's soft yet firm Scots brogue echoed through the hanger deck and the engineering spaces. As always, the sounds of his voice with its richly rolled 'r's reassured his crew.

"First, I want to apologize for the short notice with which many of you were brought aboard. The job we're on is a bit hasty, but important all the same. As many of you have no doubt guessed from our flight deck filled with Spitfires we're on another ferry mission to Malta. The Luftwaffe has been giving Malta a going-over again and the defenders there need those eighteen Spits to fight back. It's a quick trip, one day out, launch the Spits at first light tomorrow, then straight back for Gib'. Forty-eight hours there and back. In the meantime we can expect submarine alerts, though we shall endeavor to remain out of range of enemy aircraft. That's all then, stay alert, do your jobs and we shall be home in two days time. Carry on."

Captain Mackintosh left unsaid the Royal Navy's real plan for *Eagle* after launching the Spitfires to Malta. She was to loiter east of Gibraltar where the balance of her own Fleet Air Arm aircraft would fly out to meet her, then turn about to the east again as part of a larger fleet including another carrier and a battlecruiser. This fleet was to intervene in the axis invasion of Malta, expected on June 28th. For now though, *Eagle's* crew need not know of the next mission.

In the city of Ceuta across the Strait of Gibraltar in Africa a young man named Alejandro Hoyes Bilbao yawned and pulled his wrap more tightly about him. He shifted in his chair and stifled another yawn. He shivered. Even though it was late June the Atlantic breezes had brought a chill to the night air of Ceuta, the Spanish enclave on the Moroccan coastline directly opposite Gibraltar.

Five nights a week for the past eight months twenty-eight year old Alejandro sat atop the roof of the old El Jadida Hotel, one of the tallest buildings on Ceuta's waterfront, watching the Strait of Gibraltar for British ship movements. Others kept the watch before him from atop the Jabal Musa, the tallest of Ceuta's seven peaks and which with the Rock of Gibraltar formed the ancient Pillars of Hercules, but the climb to Jabal Musa was difficult and when British ships were sited it was a time consuming process to come down off the mountain to report the information, so the watch was moved to the El Jadida.

Most nights were dull and boring with no activity at all, other than the routine British anti-submarine patrol craft cruising back and forth in the Strait. Those nights were a struggle to stay warm and awake. Occasionally by the light of stars or moon Alejandro spotted British vessels coming or going at the British Naval base at Gibraltar. He dutifully noted these in his logbook with course and speed, doing his best to identify the ships by class and size as well. Each morning at dawn another observer took his place watching the Strait all day long. Before retiring to his room on the fourth floor of the once grand El Jadida he would take the elevator down to the tattered lobby and turn his logbook over to the Hotel's Concierge, an elderly Frenchmen known only as Rene'.

He thought back to the events a night earlier, the most action and excitement since Alejandro began his work as a naval observer. First, the vivid flash followed seconds later by the thunderous boom as the British corvette was torpedoed, then the series of explosions as the corvette's depth charges detonated one after another brought hundreds of people to the Ceuta waterfront for a glimpse of the action. But only Alejandro saw the events as they happened, through the powerful, German made binoculars he used.

Alejandro was a Spanish nationalist who burned in his heart at the English intrusion on Spanish soil at Gibraltar, though he gave no thought to the Spanish intrusion on Moroccan soil at Ceuta. As the Royal Navy's corvette went down his heart leapt for joy. He prayed for the safety of the crew and U-boat who had struck this blow again the hated English.

He brought the binoculars to his eyes for another sweep of the Strait and stifled another yawn. He could never grow accustomed to sleeping all day and always struggled to stay awake at night. He followed the watch pattern he had developed over the past months. Starting to the west of The Rock of Gibraltar he began his sweep pattern with the lights of the Spanish port of Algeciras, just across the harbor from Gibraltar, then slowly worked his gaze through the port area of Gibraltar itself, taking care not to look directly at any of the floodlights the British employed in an effort to prevent sabotage. Then he swept back west to the Atlantic approaches to the Strait. Nothing. He swept back to The Rock, then on into the Mediterranean approaches scanning in a wide, slow arc all the way down to the Moroccan coastline to the southeast. Still nothing but the routine anti-sub patrols. Each of these complete sweeps took him about five minutes to finish.

He held his watch up above his head to see its dial in the dim starlight. He picked up his logbook and the tiny pen light from his lap. Switching on the light he recorded the movements of the patrol vessels and the time. At the top of the page was the heading JUNE 23-24.

He switched off the light and waited as his eyes reacquired their night vision. He would wait about ten minutes before beginning the next sweep. No Royal Navy vessel could pass through his field of vision, either to or from Gibraltar in so short a time.

He stifled a yawn and stood, shrugging off the blanket. He

walked to the corner of the roof, careful to stay back from the edge far enough that his eyes were protected from the glare of the electric lamps in the street below. He quartered the roof before returning to his chair for the next sweep. He decided to pour a cup of hot coffee first.

Each evening as dusk faded to dark Alejandro met Rene' in the hotel foyer where Rene' gave him back his logbook, and an insulated flask of coffee. The night bellhop would deliver a fresh flask and a meal around 2AM.

The hot coffee burned his lips and warmed his insides as he settled back down in his chair, wrapping the blanket about him. He judged it about time to scan the Strait again, but he was comfortable and he decided to luxuriate over his hot coffee a little longer.

Finally, he picked up the Zeiss binoculars and began his sweep, as always with the lighted backdrop of Algeciras. Nothing moved there. He moved back over Gibraltar and on to the Atlantic approaches, stopping briefly to note the positions of the patrol craft, then east to the Mediterranean approaches starting in the dark waters to the east of The Rock. He paused to sip his coffee then lifted the glasses again to finish the sweep. Still nothing.

Wait! "Back up a moment Alejandro," he said to himself. He moved back over waters he had gone over too quickly a moment before. There! A white streak in the water. A ship's wake! Track it to the west first; catch it if it is about to enter the harbor. No, the wake diminishes to the west. Track it east instead. In a few more seconds he picked up the source of the wake, the low, sleek hull of a destroyer with 'a bone in its teeth', as Alejandro had heard it put by seamen. The destroyer was speeding through the water pushing a large bow wave before it.

He dropped the glasses from his eyes for a moment to think it through. He realized the cup of coffee was still in his other hand. He dropped the cup and stood, gripping the binoculars in both hands, picking the destroyer back up, but passing right over it, continuing to scan further eastward. Why would a lone destroyer be in such a hurry?

There! Another wake, dimmer, further to the north, but distinct nonetheless. Track its source. Another destroyer. Move east again. Nothing. Move to the south. There, again! A much heavier and broader wake this time. A cruiser or battleship perhaps? Follow it eastward. Pray it hasn't moved too far east to distinguish its type.

Alejandro followed the heavy wake further and further eastward into the gloom. The wake narrowed as he went, but it also got brighter and clearer until at last the broad stern of a great ship reared up above white water churning from its propellers.

Alejandro gasped. An airplane carrier! Quickly he scanned the waters around the carrier. After a few moments he'd found four destroyers forming most of a circle around the carrier. He felt sure there must be at least a fifth destroyer northeast of the carrier, screened from his view by the carrier's bulk.

He followed the fleet for several more minutes as it vanished into the eastern darkness. The time! He checked his watch. He logged his sightings in the book then sat back to think. If ever he'd made a sighting of importance this was it. He made up his mind. He gave one more fast scan with the binoculars over the waters from Gibraltar into the Mediterranean just to be sure there was no second group of ships following the airplane carrier. There was none.

Alejandro turned and raced across the roof for the stairwell. He tumbled down the stairs to the fifth floor below then across the short landing to the ancient elevator. He pushed the call button, but immediately gave up on it and ran back to the stairs. He flew down them to the first floor above the hotel lobby. He went to the last room on the first floor hallway and pounded on the door. He kept pounding until he heard Rene's voice from behind the door.

"I'm coming. I'm coming!" Rene' was pulling on his robe as he threw open the door. "This had best be good!" the Frenchmen growled. "Come in!"

Rene' closed the door as Alejandro stepped into the small apartment.

"Rene', the British have sailed in force," Alejandro cried excitedly. "I just tracked them out of Gibraltar!"

"Keep your voice down you young fool!" hissed Rene'. "You think the British have no agents in Ceuta?" Rene' pointed to his threadbare settee. "Sit down!" he commanded.

"I'm sorry, Rene'," said Alejandro. The two men spoke in Spanish with Rene' standing in front of Alejandro.

"Why have you left your post?" demanded Rene'.

"The British have sailed in force," repeated Alejandro, waving his logbook. "It's all here. I recorded it just as you have instructed."

"Let me see!" ordered Rene'. He studied the log entries on the last page of the book.

Finally he looked back to Alejandro. "You're sure of this, Alejandro? Not inventing this to try to get more pay?"

Alejandro jumped to his feet. "I don't do this for money!" he snarled at Rene'. "I hate the British! I do this for Spain!"

"All right," soothed Rene'. "Save your anger for Spain's enemies. Sit down Alejandro."

Rene' paced the room, smacking the logbook into his hand as he thought. At last he stopped pacing and faced Alejandro again.

"You were right to come directly to me, of course," he said. "This information is too important to wait for morning. Right now though you must return to your post. The British may send other warships to support those you've already observed."

"All right, Rene'," said Alejandro. "What are you going to do?"

"That's never to concern you, Alejandro," answered Rene' sternly. "The less you know about the way your information is handled the safer you will be." Rene' paused then added an afterthought. "Spain cannot afford to lose you Alejandro!"

The young Spaniards face lit up as he left the room to return to the roof.

Rene' waited until he heard the stairwell door close behind Alejandro before poking his head out the apartment door. The hall was empty. Still dressed in his robe, Rene' pulled the door closed behind him and went down the hall to the main staircase to the ground floor. In its day the El Jadida was a fine hotel, catering to the cream of European colonial society, its dining room hosting balls and banquets for visiting dignitaries.

But the El Jadida's day was long past. The cream of colonial society was skimmed in the first war. Such of it as survived The Great War went broke in the Great Depression of the thirties. The El Jadida hadn't hosted any balls or banquets in many years. Now, the carpet on the staircase was threadbare and worn and the tiles in the entry foyer were chipped and broken. Down on their luck seamen and pensioners were the only residents of the El Jadida.

Rene' looked for Abdullah, the night bellhop, but as usual the man was nowhere to be seen. Undoubtedly asleep Rene' concluded. He slipped quickly behind the reception desk, then through the door to the private offices behind the desk. Almost empty at this time of night, only one was occupied. In the tiny cubicle housing the hotel switchboard Rene' found the night manager, Lucas du Pin asleep in a chair. Lucas had been night manager at the El Jadida for over thirty years and Rene' marveled at how he'd been able to sleep his job away.

He shook the manager's shoulder. "Lucas, Lucas, wake up," he said softly.

Lucas awoke slowly, mumbling in French as his dreams of erotic glory were interrupted. "Rene'," he said. "It's you. What do you want?" Then coming fully awake he sat upright in his chair and began to straighten his suit and to smooth his gray hair. "Is there a guest to check in?"

Rene' smiled. "No, Lucas, there are no guests," he said. "I need to use the switchboard. Why don't you go to your office and catch up on your work?"

Lucas answered, "Yes, of course. I was – I was putting through a call for a guest and must have dozed off." He stood and squeezed past Rene' out of the switchboard cubicle.

"I understand," answered Rene' sympathetically. "Excuse me now won't you Lucas, I need to place my call."

"Yes, of course. I'll just go to my office and catch up on my work."

Rene' waited until he saw the office door close behind the sleepy night manager before sitting down to place his call. He started by ringing through to Ceuta's telephone exchange. He gave the operator a number on the Spanish mainland just across the Strait at Algeciras, then sat back to wait for the return ring when the connection was made. He did not have long to wait. At that hour there were very few conflicting calls. The Ceuta exchange routed the call to Algeciras over the undersea cable that passed beneath the Strait separating North Africa from Europe.

Briefly, in a simple code Rene' informed his contact in Algeciras of the course and speed of four or five destroyers and an aircraft carrier sailing east from Gibraltar at around 0020 that morning. He looked at the clock on the wall in the switchboard cubicle. Only 1 A.M. He could still get in a good night's sleep.

Franz Popitz and U-212 cruised the surface of the Mediterranean Sea transiting from Gibraltar to his assigned patrol zone midway between the Vichy French ports of Oran and Algiers. It was near dawn the morning of June 24th and U-212 had made good time to the east since surfacing at sunset the evening before. The bow dipped and crashed rhythmically through the wave tops of a following sea. His orders were to surface each night and to listen for fresh instructions via wireless especially in the hour before dawn. U-212 had raced east on the surface during the remaining hours of darkness after torpedoing the Royal Navy corvette at Gibraltar, then remained submerged through the daylight hours of the 23rd, letting a 3 knot current carry him to the east while avoiding British anti-submarine patrol aircraft and conserving battery power. He had surfaced just before dark to continue east at top speed to his assigned station athwart 3° east longitude, patrolling for British ships. He expected to arrive there during the evening hours that same day.

Popitz leaned on the conning tower rail surveying the sea through his binoculars. The moon had set and the sea was dark, but soon the first light of day would begin to brighten the eastern horizon. Franz wanted U-212 safely submerged before that happened. He paid special attention to the area of sea and sky to his west, as he knew the British were most likely to come from that direction, from their naval base at Gibraltar. He knew he should dive the boat now for the safety and concealment of deep water, but was reluctant to shut the boat up a moment earlier than absolutely necessary. Fifteen hours submerged and a submarine's air becomes fetid and thick. Nevertheless, he was about to issue the order to submerge when he heard the hail from the control room below.

"Control to bridge, Captain," he recognized Paul Merker's voice through the voice tube.

He leaned down to answer into the tube, "Control, Captain here."

"Captain, we are receiving a message from Flotilla HQ."

"All right, Paul." he answered. "Let me know when it is complete. It's time to dive the boat."

"Yes, Sir!"

Several nervous minutes passed for Popitz as the signal from

Brest was received and decoded to assure accuracy. The rising sun was lightening the eastern sky, back lighting the boat for any surface ship or aircraft to the west of them. Any British crew, afloat or aloft to the west would be blind not to see U-212. Finally, Merker's voice announced the message was complete and Popitz ordered the boat to dive.

Back in the control room Merker handed the Captain two message slips. The first informed him of the sailing of the Royal Navy's airplane carrier and destroyer escort that morning from Gibraltar with its estimated course and speed and directed all U-boats in the vicinity to intercept and attack the British force.

Popitz nodded his head and silently began the rough calculations to put U-212 on an intercept course. He looked at the second message sheet and frowned. It indicated a personal message addressed specifically to U-212 and its Captain had been received. This message was to be decoded only by the Captain himself.

"Now, what can that be?" he wondered to himself. "No time for it now." He decided to put it aside and return to it later. He joined Merker at the chart table.

"Paul," he asked, "have you charted the course of the British carrier?"

"Yes, Captain," answered the XO. "Assuming we continue on our course and the carrier holds its northeasterly course and speed of 25 knots it should pass just to the north of us about 1800 hours this evening."

"I think the British must hold their course," said Popitz. "After all, they have a limited set of possible objectives east of Gibraltar."

"They can launch air strikes against land targets on Sardinia or Sicily or against Italian shipping bound for North Africa," offered Merker "or they could be flying reinforcement fighter aircraft to Malta."

"Those are the likely choices," agreed Franz. "I suppose they may be trying to force a passage through to Alexandria, trying to bring aid to their 8th Army there as well."

"A desperate chance if that is their plan," answered Merker, shaking his head. "They would be under constant air attack all the way from Sardinia to Alexandria. They'd be unlikely to survive the passage."

"I agree," said Franz. "Their objective must be more limited, somewhere in the central sea, then turn around and return to Gibraltar."

"What could they gain for such a risk in attacking Sardinia right now?" asked Merker.

"Good, Paul," said Popitz. "You're right again. Sardinia isn't shaping events in the desert. For that fact, neither is Sicily directly." Popitz scratched his week old beard. "And if they plan to attack Italian shipping bound for Benghazi or Tobruk they'd have to pass through the Strait of Sicily to get within range. Almost as bad as passing through to Alexandria."

"So that leaves Malta," concluded Merker.

"Yes, perhaps," said Franz, "but that speed would place them within range of Malta well before first light tomorrow. They'd have to stooge around for hours waiting for sunrise." Popitz pointed to the chart just east of the mid-point of a line drawn between Algiers and Majorca and little more than two hundred miles from U-212's current position. "See, they need to be here, just to the east of us at first light tomorrow morning. That would permit them to launch fighters at maximum range, then turn and head for home. Within a few hours they would be back inside land based air cover from Gibraltar."

"But to do that they must slow down?" asked Merker.

"Yes," replied Popitz. "I'm betting that's just what they'll do. The high-speed dash out of Gibraltar was designed to get them clear of prying Spanish eyes as quickly as possible. Apparently it did not work," he concluded holding the message flimsy up.

"So we'll intercept them at first light as they are launching aircraft?" asked Merker.

"No," said Popitz. "We're going to catch them before they get there." He moved his finger back to the sub's current position then traced east along his own projected course. "If we find them here we'll have cover of darkness to make our attack. If we miss them on the way out we'll have a second chance at it when they turn around for Gibraltar."

Merker nodded his head. "Either way," he said, "we're already set to be in almost perfect position for the intercept."

"Take the conn, Paul," Popitz ordered. "Arrange it so the first watch comes on duty at 0200 tomorrow. I'll be in my cabin. I'll relieve you in a couple of hours."

Popitz ducked through the circular hatch in the control room's forward bulkhead. The first compartment forward of the control room was the wireless office with the Captain's quarters just beyond it on the port side. As he passed the radio compartment he remembered the message slip in his pocket. He stopped and ducked under the short curtain screening the radio operator and his equipment from the passageway. The radio operator stood as he recognized the Captain.

"Where is this message I must decode myself, Kruger?" asked Popitz.

"Yes, Sir, it's here," replied Kruger. He reached into a small tray on his tiny desk and handed Franz a sheet of paper.

"Leave me alone with it for a few minutes," commanded Franz. "Get some food."

"Yes, Sir," repeated Kruger, squeezing past the captain into the narrow passageway, then aft through the control room on his way to the galley.

Popitz pulled his set of keys from his pocket and sat down. Unlocking the bottom drawer of the desk he removed the leather bound codebook there. Next he unlocked the cabinet built flush in the forward bulkhead of the tiny space. He slid the Enigma machine, so like a typewriter, out on its rollers. Working steadily he entered the seemingly random strings of characters in the text of the message into the machine, then fed the key from the codebook in. He waited till the message was completely printed, then pushed the Enigma machine back into its cabinet and the code book back in the bottom drawer, locking both before picking up the message print to read.

*TO: Oberleutnant Franz Popitz, U-212.*

*FROM: 1st U-boat Flotilla.*

*DATE: 24-6-42*

*SUBJECT: IT IS WITH DEEP REGRET THAT THE CIVIL AUTHORITY OF THE CITY OF COLOGNE INFORMS OBERLEUTNANT POPITZ OF THE DEATH OF HIS PARENTS, HANS-GUNTHER AND LISL POPITZ STOP THEIR DEATHS ARE RECORDED AS A RESULT OF ENEMY AIR-RAID THE NIGHT OF JUNE 20-21 STOP*

*ADDENDUM: THE COMMAND OF THE I U-BOAT FLOTILLA ALSO EXTENDS ITS REGRETS TO OBERLEUTNANT POPITZ*

*END*

Franz stared at the message in disbelief. He thought of the gifts he'd bought in France for his parent's anniversary. They were stowed under his bunk in his tiny cabin in hopes of receiving leave to return home from Italy. He'd gone to considerable effort, not to mention expense to acquire the chocolate truffles, now so rare that no more chocolate was getting through from South America. He only found them in the end with the help of the French Secretary, Monique. His mother would never taste them now, nor his father the French wine Monique found for him..

After a few moments Franz realized his mind was racing in an uncontrolled orgy of free association, one memory from his childhood or adolescence leading to another. He stood up, straightening the tiny desk in the radio compartment and double-checking that the codebook was locked away before moving to his own little cabin next door. He pushed shut the thin metal door and stretched out on his bunk. He thought he should cry, but no tears would come.

He wondered how his parents could have been killed. Neither was a soldier. His father was a retired dentist, his mother a housewife. They did not even live near a war industry or factory. They lived in a quiet suburb of Cologne, well away from the town center and the industrial areas along the river. How could the British have targeted this suburb with its quiet, middle class streets and helpless civilians? What kind of monsters were the English? He drifted eventually into a fitful sleep, filled with dreams of his childhood and of his family home, now presumably gone.


>>>>>>>>>>>>


Harry and his engine room mates sweated over the engines and gears of *Eagle*, keeping the old ship running at high speed on her easterly course through the early evening hours of the 24th. Since sailing from Gib' early that morning the crew had stood watches four hours on, four hours off, a schedule that would be maintained so long as the ship was at sea. If action stations were sounded the entire off watch crew would turn out to man the guns or damage control stations. At 1820, shortly after returning to duty Harry was making a routine inspection of the propeller shafts when he noticed smoke curling from the bearing assembly housing of the port shaft. The propeller shafts ran back eighty feet to the three propellers through steel tunnels that stretched back and down from the engine room. A small steel hatch allowed access to each tunnel and in the hatch a heavy glass panel permitted the engine room crew to monitor the shaft without having to enter the tunnel. Naked light bulbs hung at intervals in the tunnel that was barely wide enough for a man to crawl on a small ledge to one side of the shaft. Mid-way down the shaft the tunnel bulged around a square box housing which held a bearing assembly and a small reservoir of lubricant for the bearings.

Harry pointed out the smoke to the Engineering Officer on watch. The officer peered down the shaft through the glass panel. He turned to Harry.

"Get a gallon tin of number forty oil," he shouted in Harry's ear over the din of the engines. "I'll request the bridge hold the ship steady while you crawl down there. You'll have to oil the bearings by hand."

Harry opened his mouth to object. Entering the propeller shaft while the ship was in motion was very dangerous and against regulations. With the propeller shaft spinning just inches away one false move would prove fatal. He shut his mouth and nodded his head. In enemy waters he knew there was no way the propeller could be stopped to permit repairs to the bearings. He went to get the oil.

"I'll have you relieved in an hour," promised the Chief Engineer, as Harry made ready to enter the shaft tunnel.

The propeller shaft access door was opened for Harry. Immediately the hi-pitched whine of the spinning shafts assaulted his ears and he paused to stuff them with balls of cotton of the sort used by the engine room crew for absorbing spilled fuel and oil. He climbed up into the hatch with the help of two of his mates. He'd crawled only a few feet down the tunnel when he felt more than heard the hatchway close behind him. A tremendous sense of isolation fell upon him and his stomach knotted up. He continued on all fours down the tunnel, pushing the gallon tin of oil in front of him. With twenty feet to the bearing housing still to go the ship lurched under him, throwing him off balance. He strained to lean against the wall of the tunnel, but he felt the spinning shaft plucking at his shirtsleeve. He lowered his center of gravity, down on his belly on the ledge and regained his balance. He paused for several deep breaths before continuing.

Finally he reached the bulge in the tunnel around the bearing assembly. Here the tunnel widened enough for him to turn around and to sit up, cross-legged Indian style. He pulled a spanner from his pocket and began opening the bearing assembly housing. He lifted the top plate off and a gust of smoke with the distinctive aroma of burnt oil and rubber came out of the housing. When he removed the side plate closest to him he could see where the problem must lie. The bearing assembly was fitted together with four massive bolts, one at each corner. The bolts pulled together the two halves of the assembly. Between them a thick rubber gasket sealed the assembly and contained the lubricating oils. Harry could see fresh oil streaking the sides of the lower half of the assembly. The gasket was failing and lubricant was leaking away.

Next he checked the oil reservoir. It was nearly dry, with just a trace of oil in the bottom. He uncorked the oil tin and topped off the reservoir. Almost immediately the smoke diminished as oil flowed again into the bearing assembly, but oil also started to flow down the sides of the assembly from the leak. After just a few minutes the reservoir level was dropping noticeably.

Replacing the gasket would be a two or three hour job in port. The top half of the bearing assembly would have to be lifted off and the old rubber gasket removed and the bearing assembly cleaned. Next, a new gasket would be cut and fitted on the spot from a sheet of thick, hard rubber.

But replacing the gasket at sea would be completely impossible. The propeller would have to be stopped, putting an unacceptable strain on the other shafts as well as slowing the ship and increasing her vulnerability to submarine attack. Somehow the propeller had to be kept turning and that meant the bearings had to be kept lubricated.

Harry glanced back down the tunnel to the engine room hatchway. The Chief Engineer was peering at him through the glass plate in the hatch. Harry gave the A-OK sign, which the engineer returned with a smile. Harry continued monitoring and filling the reservoir, and the oil leaked away at an accelerating pace.

The trip by train from Livorno, through Rome to Naples and on to the toe of the Italian boot at Reggio di Calabria is among the most beautiful journeys by rail in the world, especially in summer when the sky's azure blue is matched in beauty by the deep turquoise of the Ligurian and Tyrrhenian Seas. Today, wealthy tourists take the journey in peace and comfort, marveling at the quaint charm of the Italian fishing villages along the coast. Many take the journey in stages, debarking the train and spending the night in an inn or hostel where the local Italian peasantry serve wine and entertain the tourists with folk dance and song. Most also spend a day or more at both Rome and Naples, wondering at the relics of that bygone Roman Empire.

But on June 24, 1942 Major Kuno Schacht did not have the opportunity for sight seeing. The thirty hour journey was consumed in learning the plan for the invasion of Malta. The regimental staff rehearsed every detail with him over and over again. When he thought he had it down he drilled the other officers to test his own, and their knowledge. The schooling was non-stop with only brief breaks for meals and to sleep for a few hours.

He began by studying a thick intelligence report on the invasion's target, the principal island of Malta. Malta was quite small with an overall area of just 316 square kilometers and 197 kilometers of mostly rocky coastline. Its highest elevation was in the west central area of the island at 250 meters above sea level. Approximately 250,000 inhabitants were mainly clustered on the island's eastern shores around the two great natural harbors, Marsamxett and Grand Harbor. These two harbors provided the principal strategic asset of Malta along with its location athwart the shipping and supply routes from Italy to North Africa.

The island held three enemy airfields. In the center of the island was the main RAF fighter base named for the nearby village of Ta Qali. Built atop an ancient dry lakebed Ta Qali airbase had a single 1200-meter long north-south runway made of packed earth and gravel. Three kilometers to the south was the main RAF bomber base at Luqa. The airbase at Luqa included several hard-surfaced runways to facilitate operations under all weather conditions. Until recently Luqa harbored a force of twin engine Wellington bombers, but the Luftwaffe's spring offensive drove the last of these from the island. The latest Axis intelligence suggested that Luqa still harbored a mixed force of light bombers as well as some RAF Spitfire fighters. Finally, on the island's south shore was Hal Far, the Royal Navy's Fleet Air Arm base from which a variety of naval aircraft flew, including the Fairey Swordfish torpedo-bomber. Hal Far was adjacent to the Royal Navy seaplane base at Kalafrana on Marsaxlokk Bay. Short Sunderland flying boats were known to land at Kalafrana, especially at night, but none were believed based there permanently. The airfields at Luqa and Hal Far were connected by a taxiway named the Safi Strip in honor of another nearby village. Built by the manual labor of native Maltese and British soldiers it wound for over a kilometer, cutting through and around two limestone ridges that separated the two southernmost airfields.

Seizing the three airfields was the initial objective of the invasion plan. The airfields at Luqa and Hal Far would be attacked by a reinforced regiment each, the 7th and 23rd regiments respectively. Each Regiment had four Battalions. Ta Qali airfield was considered the most important objective. Centrally located and the closest of the three Maltese airfields to the Axis bases in Sicily it also afforded access to Malta's high ground near the town of Dingli just west of the field. The only two hard surfaced roads on the island crossed near the south end of the runway at Ta Qali. Seizing and holding the crossroads would hamstring the British defense of the island.

The 2nd and the 6th reinforced regiments would attack Ta Qali. Kuno Schacht would be attached to the latter, taking the place of the unfortunate Captain Hartmann. After seizing and consolidating the airfield itself these two units were to capture the high ground, first at Rabat and the island's ancient fortress-capital, Mdina and then on to Dingli if necessary. Once the heights were secured the Germans could dominate the surrounding areas with heavy weapons.

As Kuno studied the plan he found that the first wave of the assault was considered all-important. The Germans had to land safely on each of the three airfields and route the British defenders in the immediate vicinity to control the landing zones for subsequent drops. In the first wave each of the division's four regiments would deliver 1,750 men equally divided between paratroopers and glider assault troops. As the Gliders swooped down directly on runways and taxi strips the paratroopers would float to earth to either side of the airfields' main runways.

Traditionally armed with a mix of K98 rifles and other small arms the infantry companies were re-equipped with automatic weapons for almost every man, primarily the MP 40 machine pistol, deadly effective and accurate at ranges up to seventy-five meters. Each infantry company also had eighteen, two-man light machine gun teams, armed with the superb MG 34. Among the gliders would be several carrying mortars, anti-tank guns and machine gun squads to give each regiment extra punch with heavy firepower.

After the initial landing subsequent paratroop drops would take place at roughly hour and a half intervals through the morning until the balance of the division's 20,000 men were landed.     Italian airborne troops of the *Folgore* and *Superba* divisions were to follow after daybreak on the first day, flying from bases in the toe of the Italian boot. Once the airfields were secured and runways made serviceable reinforcements of regular German and Italian Infantry would be flown in and the airheads expanded. The Italian Navy would land some 9,000 men and a battalion of German tanks on the island's north shore. The airborne and amphibious forces would link up and crush pockets of British resistance. The plan envisaged that no more than 48 hours of fighting would be necessary to secure the island.

Kuno mastered the rudiments of the overall plan quickly then focused most of his effort on learning the details of his own role as leader of the 6th Regiment's HQ communications section. There were radio frequencies to learn, passwords, codes and recognition signals to commit to memory and of course he had to familiarize himself with the men of his staff, learning each man's background, training and experience and most importantly he had to take the measure of the man quickly, to get a feel for how he would react under pressure.

Kuno would command a fourteen-man communications section composed of himself and one other officer, four non-commissioned officers and eight enlisted men. The other officer,

Lt. Steup was fresh from the paratrooper training school at Stendahl and had no combat experience. Two of the non-coms, Sergeant Tondok and Corporal Weiss were veterans of Operation Mercury, the airborne invasion of Crete. Both had served with the drowned Captain Hartmann in the regimental communications section, but had limited experience in close air support coordination. A few of the enlisted men were also combat veterans, and were trained in close air support, but with no direct experience of it. Kuno would rely on the two veteran non-coms to provide solid leadership among the enlisted men, several of whom were little more than boys. Kuno approached General Ramcke soon after the train left Livorno with a question that was nagging him.

"Herr General," he began, "I wonder what opportunity I will have to learn even the rudiments of descending by parachute?"

"Not to worry Schacht," Answered Ramcke. "I wouldn't dream of having you make your first parachute drop directly into combat."

"So, I will make a practice drop on Sicily?"

"No, no, no," the general said with a steely grin. Once again Kuno forced himself not to stare at the General's metal dentures. "There's no time for that! Besides, almost one third of all first drops end with a broken leg or badly sprained ankle. We can't risk injury to you before you arrive on Malta." Kuno looked at the General with an expectant face.

"My dear Schacht, you don't think I'd ask you to jump from a perfectly good airplane do you?"

For a moment Kuno looked blankly at the General who merely smiled in return, teeth glinting, then a light of understanding came into Kuno's eyes.

"That's right, Schacht, you will land with the glider force."

"I see, Herr General," said Kuno. "Will you and the divisional staff also arrive via glider?"

"Good God Man!" Ramcke shouted, an expression of shock and horror on his face. "You won't catch me in one of those flying coffins! I have no desire to make any crash landings in a glider! I'll be jumping with a parachute in the first wave."

The two military trains that Kuno and the balance of the 2nd Paratroop Division boarded at Livorno the morning of the 23rd were given a clear track straight through to Reggio di Calabria. All other traffic on the road was forced onto sidings to wait for the troop trains to pass. The journey was marked by frequent, though brief stops as the tenders received fuel and water and food and water was delivered aboard for the officers and men, but the passengers were required to remain aboard during these stops. Only during two longer stops of about two hours each in Rome and Naples were the men allowed to disembark to stretch their legs and escape the stale, fetid air of the crowded troop cars.

In the 1930's the Italian railroads were among the best in Europe, but now, stretched beyond their capacity by the demands of war, they could not provide enough passenger cars for the two regiments. Most of the troops were transported in ordinary boxcars, noisy and devoid of comfort. Sanitary facilities were limited and crude. A bucket in each car served the needs of up to forty men. Often the bucket overflowed before it could be emptied.

Major Schacht and the other senior officers traveled in somewhat more comfort than the ordinary troopers, riding in a passenger car with cushioned seats and insulated to some degree against the noise of the tracks, but the out of repair rail beds made for a rough journey and sleep was hard to find.

Kuno made a quick discovery that delighted him. The Colonel whom he thought he had recognized at General Ramcke's villa in Livorno was none other than Colonel Friedrich August, the Baron von der Heydte, one of the heroes of the German airborne invasion of Crete the prior year. For some weeks after the invasion the Baron, at the time a Major, had his picture appear in all the weekly news publications. Kuno remembered seeing his picture in the *Berliner Illustrierte,* the paper delivered to one of the officers in Schacht's regiment on the Soviet border, just before the outbreak of war with Russia. Only the bigger news of the German invasion of Russia drove the victory at Crete and its heroes from the papers. Kuno wondered that he had not immediately recognized the aristocratic profile and Roman nose of the Baron when he first saw him.

In the few brief meal breaks the officers took from his tutoring Kuno had a chance to acquaint himself with Colonel August. The Baron was surprisingly unceremonious for an aristocrat and the two men quickly adopted an easy and familiar attitude with one another, though within the bounds of military decorum. Kuno discovered a man of complexity and depth. A devout Catholic and student of international law, the Baron had foregone his law degree to join the Army in the '30's, transferring to the fledgling paratroop corps of the Luftwaffe in 1940. Outwardly apolitical the Baron nevertheless revealed a subtle, guarded skepticism towards National Socialism that Kuno found refreshing, even if deadly dangerous. At mealtime on the evening of the 24th the conversation between the two turned away from the coming invasion.

"Are you familiar with *The Odyssey*, Schacht?" asked von der Heydte.

"*The Odyssey*?" answered Kuno. "Do you mean the Greek drama?"

"Yes," said the Baron, "precisely. Do you know the story?"

Kuno chewed his food and thought back to his school days. "*The Odyssey* is the sequel to *The Iliad,*" he said, "the mythical story of the Trojan War. The Greek hero, Odysseus encounters all sorts of challenges and obstacles as he attempts to return home to Greece after the conclusion of the war. It takes him years before he is able to reach home after a very round-about route."

"Excellent, Schacht!" exclaimed the Baron. "You didn't waste those years in school after all!"

Kuno adopted a stern visage. "We studied culture!" he growled. Both men laughed.

"Well," said von der Heydte, "one of his adventures is said to have involved Malta."

Kuno lifted his brows, encouraging the Baron to go on.

"Adrift on the sea, nearly dead of thirst Odysseus is rescued by Calypso, daughter of Atlas. She takes him to her island refuge of Ogygia where she nurses him back to health. She falls in love with him and holds him captive there for seven years."

"And Malta is supposed to be Ogygia?" asked Kuno.

"That's right, Schacht," said the Baron. "Of course, it is only one of several islands that claim to be Calypso's home, but it is considered the leading contender."

"But, all of this is just myth," said Kuno. "None of these events really happened did they?"

"That has been conventional wisdom for centuries," agreed the Baron, wiping his mouth on his napkin and pushing his plate away. "But there is considerable archeological evidence that there is some grain of truth behind it, at least the story of the Trojan War.

On Malta there is a cave, Calypso's Cave the Maltese call it, and it is said to be the place where she kept Odysseus for those seven years. It's in a grotto on the island's north coast."

"Perhaps we shall have the chance to visit it soon," said Kuno. "It strikes me I remember myths centering on Crete as well. You must have found it fascinating there," he went on, "at least once the fighting was over!"

"Yes," said the Baron, a strange expression coming over him. "Well, we'll see about the cave. Come, we must get back to your studies."

She slipped through the water silently, her wake so slight as to be unnoticeable more than a few yards away, her dull gray, rust-streaked hull sliding past the darkened buoys marking the mine-swept channel, her Captain shaping her course around the breakwater protecting the small port area from the choppy waves of the sea. The final glow of the sun faded in the west. For a few hours the sea would be dark until the moon rose. For the time being she was nearly invisible.

In the harbor a flotilla of lighters and other small craft awaited her arrival, Maltese seamen and British soldiers alike nervously marking the minutes as the ghostly shape materialized at the breakwater. On the bridge Captain Friedberger ordered engines all back one third; the engine room telegraph rang communicating the command. *HMS Welshman* eased to a stop 200 yards from the small wharves and single pier of the harbor. The waterfront looked much like any small Mediterranean port. Limestone buildings with peeling whitewash and tiled roofs fronted a narrow street overlooking the quay. Small boats bobbed along the stone sea wall, fishing nets hung to dry. Numerous buildings in the harbor area bore the scars of the Axis bombardment of the island. A rattle of chains was followed by splashes as the fore and aft anchors were let out and the crew of the ship was already busy shifting her cargo to the rails from the forepeak and mine stowage decks.

*Welshman* had already made two round trips between Gibraltar and Malta, carrying urgent supplies to the besieged island, delivering aviation spirits, spare aircraft parts and even the odd bag of mail, and taking away wounded and sick, Malta's only export during the time. On her first trip to Malta in May she'd been attacked by the Luftwaffe at her moorings in Grand Harbor. She'd delivered a desperately needed cargo of fuel and flour in the midst of an intense German air raid. *Welshman's* own guns combined with the harbor defenses shielded her and she escaped with slight damage, slipping out of the harbor between attacks and racing away at high speed. On her second trip she'd offloaded again at Grand Harbor on June 16, this time escaping the attention of the Luftwaffe.

*Welshman* was an Abdiel Class fast minelayer completed in August 1941 and on her time trials in the fall of that year achieved 39 ¾ knots on a measured course. She was designed to race into enemy waters under cover of darkness, drop a series of high-explosive contact or magnetic mines, and race away before daylight exposed her to aerial attack. With the fall of the French Channel ports into German hands in June 1940 the Abdiels seemed to be the right ships at the right time to help in the blockade of the German Kriegsmarine, but oddly the fast minelayers were rarely used for their designed purpose. Their extraordinary speed made them ideal for another purpose, as blockade-runners. And Malta was the ultimate blockade.

On her first two trips to Malta she wore false ventilator hoods and a sham mast, raked back to resemble the Vichy French destroyer *Leopard* active in the spring of 1942 in the Mediterranean between the Metropolitan ports of Toulon and Marseille and the French Colonial ports of Algiers and Oran. The plan was to remove the 'falsies' as her crew called the disguises on the advice of British Naval Intelligence who reported the Germans and Italians were on to the ruse, but the request from Admiral Leatham for *Welshman* to carry another emergency shipment to Malta came on just hours notice, so *Welshman* loaded her cargo at Gibraltar and rushed to sea still incognito.

Her crew was not told of the reason for their latest trip, nor even their destination till they were well out to sea, but when they saw the hundreds of tins of fuel coming aboard they knew it was to be Malta again. The harbor watch began loading the ship in the early morning hours of June 23 while the shore patrol set about rounding up the rest of the crew from the bars ashore. As they straggled aboard they were put to work, drunk or sober, until every nook and cranny aboard ship was stuffed with 5-gallon tins and 50-gallon drums of aviation spirit, diesel fuel and kerosene. The quartermaster was a most unhappy man as many of the tins were faulty and leaked the precious and volatile fuels. Before she ever left Gibraltar the mine stowage deck smelled like a petrol refinery.

*Welshman* transited from Gibraltar at high speed, timing her arrival to approach Malta at last light on the evening of the 24th. It was intended that she dock at Grand Harbor again, but German air raids during the day of the 24th left the main port and dockside facilities in no condition to offload supplies. In addition, the streets leading away from the docks were choked with rubble and debris, preventing any cargo being moved inland to the airfields until the roads were cleared, so *Welshman* was redirected to the tiny seaside village of Kalafrana on the south shore's Marsaxlokk Bay. In Maltese the letter 'x' is pronounced as a 'sh' sound. Marsaxlokk is Marsa Shlok, or Bay of the Sirocco, so named for the summer winds that blew ashore there from Africa.

Like the old town of Valletta the village of Kalafrana was evacuated at the beginning of the Luftwaffe air campaign against Malta, its inhabitants moving inland for safety. While it did not receive the same attention from the Germans as Grand Harbor or the island's three airfields, Kalafrana was still a dangerous place. It was adjacent to the seaside bluffs atop which sat Hal Far airfield, the Royal Navy Fleet Air Arm station. British flying boats, Short Sunderlands or American made Catalinas made Kalafrana an almost nightly stop on the air bridge route between Gibraltar and Alexandria. Bombs had hit many of the buildings in the village, and the wharf and numerous small piers all had suffered damage. Only a handful of fisherman still lived in the village itself. The burnt out skeleton of a Sunderland flying boat lay beached on the stone shingle several hundred yards from the village. An engine problem several weeks earlier prevented it from taking off before daylight. It was caught and destroyed by the Luftwaffe in a dawn raid.

As *Welshman* came to a stop the tiny port sprang to life. Using hooded lamps to guide them twenty-two small craft were brought alongside the minelayer. The Royal Navy crew used the ship's own derricks and boat davits to lower cargo nets filled with fuel tins and drums onto the decks of the small craft. At the stern the port and starboard mine doors were opened and the cargo was manhandled directly onto the decks of the harbor craft. The crew of the ship worked steadily, goaded by their Petty Officers to hurry. The Maltese fishermen transferred the cargo to the docks where British Army work crews loaded it aboard lorries and wagons to be delivered to storage sites inland near each of the island's three airfields.

Strangely, the men all worked very quietly. It was necessary to work with minimal lights in order to avoid drawing the attention of any enemy patrol aircraft in the area, but silence was not a requirement, yet the men barely spoke as they worked. Only an occasional muffled curse or murmured order relieved the sounds of the hoists and the bump and clatter of the tins and drums. Throughout the offloading operation the soft whine of the ship's radar aerial turning was loud enough to be heard over all the other noises.

The transfer of *Welshman's* cargo to shore proceeded smoothly and quickly. By 1220 hours slightly more than 160 tons of hi-octane aircraft fuel, about 46,000 gallons, was brought ashore and on the way to the three airfields. An additional 12 tons of diesel fuel, petrol and kerosene was delivered as well. Two dozen injured were transferred from shore to the ship and would be taken away to Gibraltar. As the last of the tins was handed out the mine doors *Welshman's* engines were rung up to all back one third. The mine doors were closed and she eased away from Kalafrana. By 1245, as the moon rose over Delimara Point and began to light the harbor waters she was racing west on the open sea at her top rated speed of 39 knots.

<<<<<<<<<<<<<<<<<<<<<<<<<<<<<<<<<<<<<<<<<

# DAY 5
June 25, 1942

At 0020 hours the morning of the 25<sup>th</sup> Harry looked forward to a few hours sleep before going back on watch aboard *HMS Eagle*. He'd been down the port propeller shaft tunnel twice to feed oil to the bearing assembly. By the end of his second trip he knew the rubber gasket was deteriorating. The reservoir needed more frequent filling to keep the bearings lubricated. He clambered up the companionway from the engineering spaces, then down the passageway to the aft starboard crew berth and his bunk. Along the way he squeezed past others of the carrier's company coming on or going off watch. Harry rolled into his hammock fully clothed. In peaceful, warm waters seamen would often strip to their skivvies, but in the war zone when action stations could be sounded at any moment no one had time to dress. He closed his eyes and almost immediately began to slip into blissful oblivion. But it was not to be.

On the bridge Captain Mackintosh dozed in his chair as the ship made its way eastward through the night. Lookouts posted to the bridge wings with powerful binoculars, specially designed to maximize night vision, scanned the sea to port and starboard, looking for the telltale of a submerged submarine, the white 'feather' of water rushing past periscope shears. The officer of the watch exchanged a murmur with the quartermaster at the helm, barely audible in the silence of the blacked out bridge.

"Signal from *Wolverine*, Sir," the young signalman on the port bridge wing sang out. Captain Mackintosh was on his feet moving to the bridge wing in an instant, awake and alert. He stood silently behind the boy looking across the water at the Aldis lamp flashing from the screen destroyer.

"*Wolverine* message reads 'radar contact, bearing 010, range 4900 yards. Am investigating,' the boy interpreted the message. "Signal ends, Sir."

"Acknowledge the message, son," commanded the Captain. "Signal the screen for a turn to starboard, course one-one-zero."

"Aye, aye, sir."

"Sound action stations," the Captain ordered.

"Action stations, aye, Sir," responded the Chief Petty Officer at the rear of the bridge. Immediately, the action stations alarm rang out through the great ship.

"Helm, make your course one-one-zero."

"Helm, aye, course one-one-zero."

Along with hundreds of others Harry was jolted awake by the strident action stations alarm.

"Do you hear there, do you hear there," the tin-voiced tannoy shouted. "Hands to action stations, hands to action stations!"

Harry was electrified, leaping from his hammock and hitting the deck running. He jostled his mates getting through the hatch from his crew berth to the passage beyond then ran for his action station, the port engine room fire station. Down one flight and over one bulkhead and he was there in a moment. He donned his fire resistant asbestos suit and gloves and laid the matching hood out to be put on instantly at need. Everywhere in the great aircraft carrier men settled into their action stations, manning the multitude of AA guns, the ammunition hoists and the damage control stations on every deck and in every major compartment.

>>>>>>>>>>>>

Franz Popitz let U-212 drift submerged through the daylight hours of the 24th, gently floating to the east with the current. Battery power barely turned the propellers enough to ease the task of maintaining the boat's trim and to keep its buoyancy neutral. The officers and crew of U-212 rested and slept as best they could through the day, conserving the boat's precious supply of breathable air by minimizing strenuous activity.

The Captain was as quiet as his crew. He relieved Merker in the mid-morning, having slept a little longer than he'd told the XO, but not so as to occasion notice. Such orders as he issued through the long day were given quietly, unemotionally, but in a purposeful manner.

The Captain's unusually somber demeanor reinforced the quiet attitude of the crew. Tools were handled more carefully; conversations were more muted than usual. A machinist working on torpedoes in the forward torpedo room dropped a wrench. It fell with a clatter that was amplified by the unusual silence of the boat.

He quietly endured the glares of his shipmates and handled the tool with two hands from that point.

At noon Popitz came to periscope depth and took a sun sight to establish his position precisely. Charting the coordinates placed U-212 eighty-five miles northwest of Algiers in 1500 fathoms of water.

As the evening hours approached the crew picked up its pace of activity. The diesel engines, silent all through the day, were oiled and serviced to ensure optimum performance when they were called upon again. The torpedoes in the tubes were drawn partially back on the loading racks and the pressure in their compressed air tanks was checked and topped off. The same was done for the number one reload torpedoes. The bilges and battery compartments were checked for problems. By the time darkness began to descend on the western Mediterranean the U-212 was ready in all respects to surface and go into action against Allied vessels.

At 2200 hours, as Harry Booth rested between trips down the propeller shaft in the engine room of *HMS Eagle*, Popitz ordered U-212 to surface. The bridge watch tumbled out of the conning tower hatch and assumed their positions. Each man made a quick scan of his assigned sector of sea and sky, then another more thorough check before singing out an all clear to the Captain. Popitz himself scanned the sea to the west of the U-boat. He had timed the surface to catch the last few moments of the sun's dieing light on the western horizon, hoping to catch a British ship in silhouette. Nothing was seen in any direction however and the watch settled into its normal, tense routine.

Popitz spoke into the voice tube to the control room.

"Conn, bridge," he called, "activate the Biscay Cross." The metal radar detector hummed up from its well in the periscope shears.

"Bring up the high frequency antenna," he ordered next. The antenna whirred into place. Popitz was eager for any intelligence on the movements of the British aircraft carrier task force that had sailed from Gibraltar early that morning. But at the moment the airwaves were silent.

Popitz laid out a search pattern to follow through the night. U-212 would follow an easterly course, zig-zaging north and south along a bearing of 080 degrees. Each leg of the zig-zag would cover twelve nautical miles along the course he expected the British fleet to take as it also moved east towards a position where the carrier would dispatch its fighter aircraft to Malta at first light in roughly seven hours. He guessed the British would launch the planes from a position along the line between Algiers on the North African coastline and the Spanish island of Majorca, roughly at three degrees east longitude, around 0500 hours, but he hoped to make contact with the British in the hours of darkness before the nearly three quarter moon set at 0430 hours. The moon would backlight any enemy air or surface craft to the west of the U-boat.

He believed it unlikely the British force was already to the east of him. They would have to have maintained close to the reported 25 knots they were making on leaving Gibraltar, but Popitz was sure they were still somewhere to the west, sailing eastward at between 18 and 20 knots.

His estimate of the speed was based on several factors. First, the British would prefer not to strain ships' engines to their limits until called for by a combat situation. An engineering casualty in the war zone could prove fatal. Second, at high speeds he knew the British underwater sound detection devices, ASDIC as the British called them, lost over half their efficiency. The Royal Navy depended on these devices for early warning of submarine attack. Finally, he reviewed his earlier estimate of where and when the British would wish to fly off aircraft for Malta and could find no holes in his logic.

The hours of the night slipped away with U-212 covering the Captain's course at ten knots on the surface. The boat plowed through four-foot seas pushed by a steady fifteen-knot wind directly from the south. A dry, dusty smell from the great Sahara Desert came with the wind to the men on the bridge. On the northeasterly leg of the search pattern this breeze followed U-212 and the boat rode the swells fairly smoothly. On the southeasterly leg the boat plowed nearly head-on into the seas. As the rollers broke over the bow of U-212 the wind blew the tops off the waves and hurled them in the faces of the forward bridge watch. All were soon thoroughly soaked despite the oilskin rain gear they wore.

By 0200 hours the boat was approaching the limit of its second northbound leg with still no sign of the enemy fleet. Franz went over in his mind his strategy for finding the British, and while he could find no flaws he was beginning to think the Royal Navy had outwitted him somehow, or that at best he'd make contact after moonset, vastly complicating an attack with the surface of the sea in near complete darkness. The first watch was coming on now in the control room, though Popitz himself and the XO, Merker had been on duty since the boat surfaced.

"Bridge, control room," Paul's voice came up the voice tube.

"Control, Captain here," Franz replied.

"We're at the limit of this leg Captain," said Paul. "It's time to turn southeast."

"Very good Paul, change course."

"Yes, Sir. Request permission to change the bridge watch."

"Granted Paul," said Popitz. "Bring them up two at a time and we'll cycle the whole watch."

"Yes, Sir," the XO acknowledged.

Franz felt U-212 heel to starboard as it swung into the southeast leg of its search pattern. At the same time he heard boots coming up the conning tower ladder as the first two replacement watch keepers came to the bridge. They took the places of the two aft lookouts, to port and starboard of the bridge, immediately scanning the sea and sky in their assigned sectors. The two men going off watch scrambled down the ladder and a moment later two more replacements were on the way up to take the for'ard lookout positions.

Popitz was scanning the sea to port, now to the northeast of U-212 as the boat completed its course change. The first of the for'ard replacement lookouts were just reaching the top of the ladder when one of the forward lookouts called out.

"A light on the sea to starboard, green twenty sector!"

Popitz spun about, turning his binoculars in the direction of the bearing, but saw nothing. He held his hand out to stop the replacement lookouts.

"Hold your positions," he said then came to stand beside the lookout, a young man barely eighteen years old, on his first war cruise.

"What did you see Eckhardt?" asked the Captain. "Tell me exactly."

"A light, Sir," answered the young sailor nervously. "There," lowering his binoculars and pointing off into the darkness.

"What color was the light, son?" asked Franz. "It's not there now."

"No, Sir. I mean, yellow, Sir. It's gone now, Sir," stammered Eckhardt.

"Was it flat on the horizon or did it appear to be in the sky?"

Gunther hesitated. "I –," he began. "I'm not sure, Sir. Flat on the horizon. I think."

"All right, Gunther," said Popitz. "Go below. Your watch is complete."

"Yes, Sir," answered the young man, then, "I did see it, Sir."

"Thank you, Gunther."

As Eckhardt left the bridge and his replacement took up his lookout position Popitz mulled the possibilities. The light could be a specter of a young, tired mind, even a manifestation of a subconscious desire to please the Captain. Or it could have been the flicker of an ALDIS lamp aboard a British vessel, or a scuttle briefly opened in violation of blackout regulations, even the flare of a match strike as a British sailor snuck a forbidden cigarette on deck. He made his decision. He stepped directly to the conning tower hatch and called down it to the XO in the control room below.

"Paul, come to due south, make speed for twelve knots. We'll investigate Eckhardt's sighting."

Merker came and stood at the bottom of the ladder, looking up at the Captain.

"Yes, Sir," he answered.

"I want to be ready to dive at a moments notice," the Captain continued. "If we make contact with the British I want to make a quick approach and attack before moonset." He checked his watch. "We'll have to move smartly!"

"Yes Sir!" answered Merker and issued the necessary orders in the control room.

Popitz resumed his scrutiny of the sea, in all directions, but primarily to the southwest in the direction of Eckhardt's light. With a course of due south he hoped to move to intercept a British vessel or fleet as it moved in an easterly direction, on or about course zero-nine-zero.

The minutes ticked by however with no further sightings. After nearly a half hour Popitz estimated U-212 had covered almost six miles in the direction of the light. He resolved to proceed for just a few more minutes before resuming his original search pattern.

"Ship silhouette on the starboard bow," shouted the starboard lookout. "Bearing…."

"I've got it," shouted the Captain, interrupting the lookouts report. Down the voice tube he shouted, "Come to course one-six-five, flank speed!"

"One-six-five, flank speed, acknowledged!" came the shouted reply.

"It's a destroyer, Paul," yelled Popitz down the tube. "Range about 7,000 meters. It looks to be on about course zero-eight-zero, speed, about twenty-two knots. We must be on the northern flank of a convoy or the fleet we've been looking for. This ship is part of its screen."

"Another ship silhouette, range 9,000 meters!" shouted the starboard for'ard lookout. "Looks like another destroyer!"

Popitz swung his glasses onto the new contact. "It's a destroyer all right, course zero-eight-zero, speed also about twenty-two knots."

"Heavy ship silhouette!" shouted the starboard lookout.

"What bearing man?" demanded Popitz angrily.

"Bearing two-two-zero," the man answered, "range, 10,000 meters!"

Popitz swung his glasses onto the bearing.

"Mein Gott!" he exclaimed. "He's a big one!"

He studied the silhouette as it resolved in his view, a black shape against a slightly less black background, barely highlighted by the moon. He leaned into the voice tube.

"It's the airplane carrier Paul! Come left to course one-four-zero. We're going to slip between the two destroyers in the screen and attack the carrier."

"YES, SIR!" The bridge watch all turned and grinned to each other, their ragged beards giving them the appearance of modern pirates on the high seas.

The range to the carrier closed as U-212 raced for the gap in the destroyer screen. Franz' brain worked at high speed on the complex geometry of the situation. The U-boat had to pass between the two destroyers on the aircraft carrier's port screen, ideally at a point slightly closer to the forward destroyer than the aft in order to approach the carrier on an angle perpendicular to its course, arriving at a range of about one thousand meters while also ahead of the great ship so that the torpedoes could lead it slightly. The angle was very difficult as the British carrier was already almost abreast of U-212 when it was spotted.

At a range of 6,000 meters to the carrier Merker called from the control room.

"Control to bridge, the Biscay Cross has detected radar waves," he said. "They are strengthening and are apparently from the aft destroyer. If they have not already detected us they will do so momentarily."

"If we dive now we'll never get close enough to the carrier for a shot Paul!" shouted the Captain into the voice tube.

"If we don't dive now the aft destroyer will have us for sure, Captain," answered Merker. "Already the signal is as strong as I've ever seen it."

Franz did not answer. He wanted that carrier!

"If we dive now we have a good shot on the aft destroyer," continued Merker "and we can try for the carrier on its return Captain."

"Dammit Paul," said Popitz. "Dive the boat!"

Merker was waiting for the order with his hand on the button. The klaxon sounded immediately. The main air induction vents, used to suck drafts of air into the boat to feed the diesel engines, clanged shut on the rear deck. The roar of the diesels was replaced by the quiet hum of the battery-operated electric motors.

The bridge watch scrambled for the conning tower hatch, tumbling one after the other down to the control room below. The hatch was dogged tight as Popitz reached the bottom of the ladder. Merker handed him a dry towel and he wiped his face and eyes clear of salt water. Franz threw the towel on the deck in the corner of the control room and turned his cap backwards on his head.

"Up periscope!" he commanded. He knelt as the 'scope came up from its well, pressing his forehead to the rubber eyepiece. He spun the 'scope round on the carriers bearing. "The carrier is well out of our reach now. He's showing us his stern." He spun the periscope back to the west. "The destroyer is still on course. I don't believe he has detected us. Range now down to 4500 meters. Down 'scope!"

The periscope sank down in its well. Popitz turned to Kruger, the radio operator. Kruger was in the passage just forward of the control room with his head poked through the hatchway. "Prepare a sighting report," he ordered. "'One carrier, several destroyers, am attacking,'" he dictated. "Add our position and be ready to transmit it as soon as we fire."

"Yes, Sir!" snapped Kruger and hurried to his radio compartment.

"Up scope!" Popitz rode the periscope up again, sweeping quickly forward of U-212, then to port and finally aft. "The destroyer is coming up on our starboard beam, she'll pass us at about 1000 meters. Down scope."

Popitz closed his eyes, visualizing the relative positions of the destroyer and his sub, counting off the seconds as the destroyer drew closer. The control room crew stood or sat silently at their stations. Those who could look away from their instruments watched the Captain, ready to instantly obey his next command.

"Come to course one-eight-zero," he ordered. "Open doors on tubes three and four."

"One-eight-zero," acknowledged the helmsman. The boat heeled almost imperceptibly to port as the rudder bit.

"Open tubes three and four!" snapped the XO into the microphone to the forward torpedo room.

"Up scope," the Captain ordered, once again riding the eyepiece as the periscope rose from its well. "Stop scope!" he said. The periscope was now at a height that brought it clear of the water in the trough of the waves, submerged at the crest. This minimized the 'feather', the line of white water caused by the disturbance of the sheers passing through the water's surface, making it less likely a sharp eyed lookout on the destroyer would spot the scope.

Popitz crouched at the eyepiece watching the destroyer. "Final bearing will be one-eight-zero, range 900 meters. Fire on my mark."

"One-eight-zero, range 900," Merker repeated.

The Captain raised his right arm in the air as he observed the destroyer.

"FIRE THREE!" he shouted, dropping his arm.

The XO depressed the firing circuit for torpedo tube three. The crew felt a jolt as the bullet of compressed air ejected the torpedo from its tube.

"Torpedo three fired!" cried Merker.

"FIRE FOUR!" shouted the Captain.

Again the jolt as the torpedo leapt from the boat, carrying its payload of high explosives towards the unsuspecting British warship.

"Torpedo four fired!" the XO cried.

"Extend the mast!" the captain shouted. "Kruger, send your signal quickly!" To the helmsman he said, "Come to course two-seven-zero, prepare to dive. I want to head right back down the destroyers bearing. If we miss we'll use his own wake to confuse his sound detection."

"Course, two-seven-zero," repeated the helmsman. The boat heeled again to starboard.

"Signal complete, Sir," came Kruger's call from the forward hatch.

"DIVE DEEP!" Popitz shouted. "Make your depth eighty meters!"

"Make depth eighty meters!" replied the planesman.

The boat tipped down forward as it dove deep. The control room crew gripped any available support to keep their feet as the deck inclined beneath them.

Popitz looked at Merker who was holding a stopwatch in one hand and gripped a pipe overhead with the other.

"Time?" the Captain demanded.

"Torpedo three, five seconds, four, three, two, one, zero. " BLAM! The XO's countdown was interrupted by the sound of a torpedo exploding.

A cheer erupted briefly in the control room. A hit!

"The second fish must be a miss," said Popitz. "Come to periscope depth. I want a quick sighting before the other destroyers can return to us."

Air hissed and rumbled from compressed air tanks as water was expelled from the boat's buoyancy tanks, allowing her to rise back to the surface. Popitz watched the depth gauge. When it reached twenty-two meters he called for the periscope again. He did a quick 360° circuit with the scope to assure no other vessel was approaching from an unexpected direction then he settled back on the destroyer's bearing.

"We've hit him square amidships," he told the crew. "He's fallen over to starboard and swerved off course. Paul, take a quick look." He surrendered the periscope to Merker who gripped the control handles eagerly and squinted through the scope.

"He's rolling over right before my eyes!" he exclaimed. "Range, about 500 meters. I can see crewmen diving into the water. No time for lifeboats or rafts."

Quickly, each of the control room crew was given a brief look through the scope, a reward for a smoothly executed attack. By the time the Captain took back the handles the destroyer was gone, rolled over and sunk, barely four minutes after being struck by the lone torpedo.

"Prepare a signal, Kruger," ordered Popitz. "Report that His Majesty has lost a destroyer."

*HMS Ashanti* staggered under the impact of U-212's torpedo. At the very last moment the lookout on the port bridge wing, a young seaman from Liverpool named Ernest Hawkins saw the telltale line of phosphorescent bubbles leading to the ship, but there was no time to shout a warning before the ear-shattering blast threw him off his feet.

By the time Ernest recovered his wits and struggled back to his feet *Ashanti* was already listing over to port. Ernest found it difficult to stand on the tilted deck. He staggered to the center of the bridge where the XO was trying to help the Captain to his feet. The Captain had a nasty gash in his forehead and was barely conscious.

"Help me with the Captain, Hawkins," said the Executive Officer.

"Yes, Sir," said Ernest.

He stooped and between them he and the XO lifted the Captain to his feet. Others of the bridge watch were struggling to their feet now as well. But the senior quartermaster who'd been at the helm would never move again. Ernest saw his body, thrown against the bridge's rear bulkhead. The quartermaster's head was crushed like an eggshell against the bulkhead.

"Help me get him into his chair," the XO urged, supporting the Captain's weight with an arm about the waist.

"Sir, don't you think we should get him to the side?" asked Ernest. "We're going down!"

"Nonsense!" shouted the exec. "*Ashanti* will not sink! The Captain will know what to do. Now help me get him to his chair!"

But in the short time it took to get the injured Captain to his bridge chair the ship's list became much more pronounced. The ship's electric service failed and the engines stopped. The torpedo had exploded in *HMS Ashanti's* engine room, killing the entire engine room crew instantly and opening the ship's bowels to the sea. As Ernest and the XO settled the Captain in his chair Ernest looked out the starboard bridge wing and was shocked to see waves lapping at the gunwales.

"Sir, we have to go!" he shouted to the Exec.

"You stand your watch Hawkins," the XO shouted back, "or you'll face a court, I swear it!"

Ernest caught the eye of the starboard wing lookout who shook his head and gestured over the side. The man slipped behind the XO and off the bridge. Ernest turned back to the XO and opened his mouth to plead with the officer, but saw that it was no use. The Exec was holding the Captain's hand now, bracing himself against the side of the Captain's chair.

Ernest turned and slipped off the bridge to port. Though no formal order to abandon ship was given many men were already in the water, swimming away from the ship before it should go under and take them down with it. For a moment he turned and looked back at the bridge, but he felt the deck begin to roll beneath his feet and he jumped to the rail then dove into the water, propelling himself as far from the ship's side as possible. He swam several strong strokes before coming up for air, rolling over on his back and turning to look back towards the ship. As he opened his eyes he gasped at the sight of the ship's lattice mast swinging down directly on him as *Ashanti* rolled over into the sea.

Ernest dove and kicked, desperately fighting to get clear of the mast. He heard the crash of the mast as it smacked the water. For a moment it slowed the roll of *Ashanti,* but nothing could stop it. After a pause she rolled over with her keel to the sky, then swiftly settled straight down in the water. As the last of her passed beneath the waves a great bubble of air burst from her ruptured hull, roiling the sea's surface like a pot on the boil.

Ernest looked around him in the water and was surprised at how few swimmers he saw. The sea surface was very dark and he could see only a few yards in any direction. He swam towards a group of men clustered together. Along the way Ernest grabbed hold of a small wooden crate bobbing in the water. When he got to the group he saw that only about half the men had life jackets. The others were treading water. He gripped his crate and backed away from the group. Already some of the swimmers were tiring, struggling to stay afloat.

"LOOK!" shouted one of the men, pointing back behind Ernest. He turned and saw out of the darkness the bow of a destroyer coming straight towards them at high speed, throwing a sharp bow wave off to either side.

"She's going to depth charge!" another of the men yelled. The group was electrified into frantic motion as the men in the water sought to escape the deadly range of the depth charge's concussion. Ernest abandoned his crate and swam for his life. With his youth and strength he quickly out-distanced the other men. He could hear the swish of the oncoming bow wave turn into a roar as the destroyer charged in on her deadly run.

*HMS Nubian,* Tribal Class sister ship to *Ashanti* bore down on the site of the sinking, her depth charges in her fantail racks armed and set to explode at a depth of 220 feet. Her Captain was prepared to deliver the attack against the German or Italian submarine, even in the midst of the swimming survivors in the water, but his ASDIC operators weren't able to establish a contact. The Captain ordered the depth charges to remain in their racks.

*Nubian* could not stay to rescue the swimmers though. To stop in these waters to pull swimmers aboard would be to invite upon herself the same fate as *Ashanti.* Also, the destroyer screen around the carrier was down to three ships; too thin to effectively protect *Eagle.* After throwing several dozen life preservers and two inflatable rafts into the water, *Nubian* turned about and at the maximum speed her twin Parsons geared turbines could deliver she raced back to reassume her position in the screen.

Of *Ashanti's* ships complement of 190 men it is estimated that some sixty of them went into the water though many fewer survived to see home again. Their story of survival is one of the epics of the Second World War at sea, but is not a part of this tale and must be told elsewhere.

U-212 surfaced again at 0430 after Popitz assured himself no

Royal Navy destroyer was lingering behind in hopes of catching him unawares. The three-quarter full moon had set in the west. He felt sure that the only threat to U-212 lay now to the east and the moon would not backlight the boat. He radioed Berlin with a more lengthy report on his attack and sinking of the destroyer and confirming the position, composition, course and speed of the British fleet as given in his earlier message.

He gave orders for tubes three and four to be reloaded immediately and made ready for action again later in the morning then he and the XO conferred over the chart table.

"I want another crack at that carrier, Paul," said Franz. "It's the most valuable ship we've ever had in our periscope sights."

"Yes, but the British will not return through this same position will they?" asked Merker. "They're more likely to go either north or south of here on their return."

"True enough," answered Franz. "The question is which way will they go, and how far?"

Harry Booth and his action station mates in the engine room firefighting team heard the sharp report of the torpedo detonating on *Ashanti* right through the hull and over the engine noise of *Eagle.* They knew a ship was dieing.

'Cor," said Harry in his Cockney accent, "there's one of them cockle-shell destroyers 'as caught 'erself a packet."

"Aye," said his mate, a Glasgow native named McTevish. "Ah wouldna' serrve aboarrd one o' them for all the haggis in Scotland."

On the bridge Captain Mackintosh and his staff reacted professionally to the loss of *Ashanti,* dispatching *Nubian* to try to find the U-boat, but on a very short leash. The screen would be thin enough with four destroyers, but with only three any U-boat skipper worth his salt could walk through the screen and attack the carrier during darkness. When *Nubian* wasn't able to make immediate ASDIC contact she was recalled to take her place in the defensive screen.

At 0530 *Eagle* commenced launching the Spitfires. For a half hour there had been enough light that any of the Fleet Air Arm pilots aboard could have safely launched from the heaving deck, but the RAF Spitfire pilots had never flown from a carrier deck before. They needed enough light to clearly judge the heave of the flight deck and to time their takeoff to benefit from the extra lift of the bow's rise on the sea. Captain Mackintosh ordered the ship turned south into the wind. *Eagle* swung starboard to course one-eight-zero into a dry wind blowing directly from the south at twenty-five knots.

Summer time winds follow a pattern over the central Mediterranean. Once the heat of summer has arrived a massive high-pressure ridge establishes itself over the huge Sahara Desert to the south. Hot, dry air is pressed down and out by this high-pressure system, flowing off the North African coastline over the cooler waters of the sea. There it picks up moisture and as the wind moves north humidity rises. A washed out haze, humid and sultry, replaces the clear blue skies that prevail in spring and again in autumn. The Arabs of the dessert know this hot, south wind as the *Sirocco*. The Spanish call this wind *Leveche*. On Malta it is sometimes called the *Khaimsin* and it comes every few weeks as the high-pressure system moves back and forth over the Sahara. It generally lasts one to three days at a time. On June 25th, the first *Sirocco* of 1942 began to blow. The stiff wind benefited the Spitfire pilots as they launched from the deck of *Eagle*. They lifted into the air without difficulty at half-minute intervals. As they took to the air they formed in groups of three then winged on their way to Malta for a three hour flight.

As soon as the last of the fighters was airborne Captain Mackintosh ordered the fleet turned for home on course two-two-five. Now the real work of the ship's flying crew began. First, the three Fairey Fulmar fighter aircraft down on the hangar deck were lifted to the flight deck. They were prepped for launch in the event radar should detect approaching aircraft. While out of range of land-based fighters and even most bombers, the Luftwaffe and Regia Aeronautica operated long-range maritime patrol aircraft from fields on the west coast of Sardinia. While incapable of mounting a serious attack against the ship these patrol planes could nonetheless radio her position to lurking subs.

Next, two Fairey Swordfish torpedo bombers were brought up from the hangar deck. Armed with a single 500-pound depth charge each they were to be launched in turns to fly ahead of the carrier and its escorts on anti-submarine patrol.

The Swordfish was a bi-plane of a design that any other navy would have considered obsolete, but Britain's aircraft industry was stretched to the breaking point by the demands of designing and building new aircraft for the RAF. The requirements of the RAF's Fighter Command, charged with the air defense of the Home Islands and of Bomber Command whose mission was to carry the war into the heart of German occupied Europe far out-weighed the Fleet Air Arm's priority for new aircraft designs. The Royal Navy contented itself reluctantly with the Fairey Swordfish and to their credit made virtues of the old plane's vices.

Its top speed was only 90 miles per hour and its construction was of fabric stretched over an aluminum and wood frame. It afforded little armor protection for its two or three man crew of pilot, observer and radio operator/navigator. Its open cockpit exposed the aircrew to the elements. The pilot enjoyed some advantage from the windscreen, but the observer and radio operator/navigator behind him had to huddle down in their seats for relief from the wind.

So much for its debits. On the credit side the Swordfish could lift a heavy load, typically a 2,000-pound torpedo. It was highly maneuverable and in the hands of an experienced pilot was surprisingly difficult to shoot down in aerial combat. Its slow speed also made it hard to hit with anti-aircraft fire from ship or shore. Flak gunners invariably led the Swordfish too much with their fire, finding it hard to believe the evidence of their own eyes that an airplane could fly so slowly. Finally, its low stalling speed of just 60 knots made it ideal for landing on a short carrier deck. Swordfish aircrew affectionately nicknamed the plane the 'Stringbag' and few would have traded it for the fastest fighter. As soon as the Swordfish were up on the flight deck Captain Mackintosh again turned the carrier south into the wind to launch one of the bi-planes on anti-submarine patrol. It was 0630 hours.

Lt. Commander Richard "Dickie" Whiting loved flying the Swordfish. Its maneuverability made it a joy to fly, its slow speed notwithstanding. In good weather with the sky to himself he could almost forget there was a war on. He took off from the flight deck of HMS Eagle at 0630 hours, after the last of the Spitfires was launched and the ship had turned back to the west. The early morning sky was free of cloud, but a damp haze limited visibility to about 3 miles. Several times as he ascended to his observation altitude of 4,000 feet the plane passed through a thick band of moisture that soaked the windscreen and beaded off the wings. A stiff crosswind from the south wanted to push the Swordfish its own way. In fighting the crosswind Whiting held the Stringbag in a steady sideslip.

At this time the bad bearing assembly finally forced Captain Mackintosh to cut *Eagle's* speed down to 18 knots and there was no guarantee she could maintain it. The destroyers were also forced to hold to this speed and maintain their position in the formation. With five destroyers, one of them was always free to speed about searching for random ASDIC contacts, but four destroyers was barely adequate to close the defensive ring about the carrier.

As Whiting began his patrol he noted the surface conditions. The south wind was driving the sea into six-foot swells, tearing the tops off the waves, throwing them as sheets of white spray. Combined with the haze, conditions for observing submarines from the air could only have been worse at night or in a driving rain. He turned and signaled to the observer behind him to keep his eyes on the water.

Harry Booth crawled back down the propeller shaft tunnel for his third shift oiling the bearing assembly at 0705 hours. The ship was still making maximum revolutions and the gasket inside the bearing assembly was not getting any better. Harry took two gallons of oil with him this time. The last man down the tunnel emerged with a very bad case of the shakes. Harry had to admit to himself that it was nerve wracking duty. Each time a man crawled the length of the tunnel the bridge was notified by telephone. Still, Harry knew that if a sub was detected at that moment *Eagle* might be forced to take evasive action. He hurried down the tunnel.

Harry was pumping oil directly into the bearing housing now. Even though *Eagle* had slowed to 18 knots the gasket in the bearing assembly continued to deteriorate. Two gallons of oil barely lasted an hour on the shift before his. He was reaching the end of the second gallon after just forty minutes in the tunnel. Despite pouring oil directly onto the bearings they were running hotter to the touch. He looked back down the tunnel and saw the engine room CPO looking at him through the open hatch. The whine of the shaft made speech pointless. Instead Harry tapped the empty oilcan and shook his head, then shook the can he was holding back and forth. Nearly empty. The Chief nodded his understanding and closed the hatch. A moment later he was back, signaling for Harry to return to the engine room.

On the bridge the increasingly frequent calls from the engine room asking for a stable course were received with mounting worry. Obviously the condition of the bearing assembly was worsening and already the plan for *Eagle* to take aboard the balance of her own aircraft and turn about again for Malta was in jeopardy. Worse yet, at least in the immediate term was the chance that the bearings might seize. A major engineering casualty could prove fatal in submarine infested waters. Captain Mackintosh ordered speed reduced again, to 16 knots.

In the engine room Harry and his mate McTevish were ordered up to the galley to get a spot of tea and a bite to eat to bring back to the engine room crew. Harry had been on watch or at action stations for twenty-seven hours.

>>>>>>>>>>>>>

Heinz Sauckel joined the stream of pilots crossing the field at Gerbini to the operations hut. The boisterous foolery of three days before was gone. The pilots of Sauckel's fighter squadron were somber as they walked to the daily mission briefing in the pre-dawn darkness of June 25th.

Somber and grim. They had sustained three days of maximum effort flying against Malta, facing the RAF Spitfires in the air, braving the flak put up by the British AA guns over the airfields. They had sustained their losses as well.

Over forty Luftwaffe aircraft were lost in three days of intense operations against Malta. As the combat was conducted over enemy territory almost every pilot and crewman of the destroyed aircraft was lost; if not dead, then at least in British captivity. Only the crew of those few damaged machines that managed to limp home to Sicily were still with the squadron.

An observer, just arriving at Gerbini and seeing the pilots headed towards the operations hut could well conclude their unnatural, somber quiet was a feature of broken morale. The observer would be wrong for these men were grim as well. There was a determination in their step and in their eyes that boded ill for their opponents.

After that first sortie on June 22$^{nd}$ when the German fighters ambushed the RAF Spitfires the battle settled into a more conventional pattern. Luftwaffe fighters escorted bombers to Malta, protecting them from the British Spitfires as the bombers plastered the three main airfields on the island with hundreds of tons of high explosives. Attacks on the airfields focused on striking planes on the ground and on targeting the many flak batteries that sprouted like weeds around the airbases. Sometimes, when the bombers were finished and if the British had not launched their own fighters to oppose the attack, Heinz and his squadron mates would linger over Malta as the bombers turned for home. Then they would dive to ground level and sweep over the airfields at 300 mph, strafing anything that moved. The Italian Air Force did not participate in these sorties, but maintained the bombing at night to deprive the defenders of their sleep.

Heinz and his fellows held the British pilots in high, professional regard. Nothing could diminish the respect that came from seeing the out-numbered RAF men scratch and claw at the attacking German forces, but a bitter, burning desire to rub out the annoying gadflies on Malta had taken hold. The Luftwaffe fighter pilots came to hate the RAF pilots of Malta. They wanted them dead.

And as they walked to the operations hut across the darkened airfield they knew they would be flying that morning to land the knockout punch. The weight of numbers was finally beginning to tell on behalf of the Luftwaffe. For three straight days they had flown against the RAF, as many as five sorties a day and always with a five-to-one or better numerical advantage. The Germans maintained a combat patrol above the three British airfields on Malta throughout daylight hours so that any RAF plane that attempted to land or takeoff had to do so under threat of strafing attack. In a battle of attrition the Luftwaffe was wearing the RAF on Malta down. With virtually no reserves left, the RAF had not opposed the final Luftwaffe bombing runs on the 24$^{th}$.

Heinz looked up into the eastern sky where the moon lit the heavens. Fat and gibbous, and just a few days from full, its orange light cast long, dark shadows from the hangars, barracks and under the parked aircraft. Across the dispersal area maintenance crews put the finishing touches on over one hundred fighters and bombers. Armorers were closing bomb bays on the bombers and the access ports on the wings of the fighters where long belts of cannon and machine gun ammunition were fed to the guns. Fuel bowsers pumped the last few liters of petrol, topping off fuel tanks.

Heinz had become a veteran quickly. Given credit for two confirmed kills and a probable on the first sortie of June 22nd he scored once again on each of the next two days. He caught a wounded Hudson twin-engine bomber on the 23rd as it flitted in and out of broken clouds near Luqa waiting for a chance to slip in to land between raids. Trailing smoke and with control surfaces already damaged the Hudson had no chance to evade. Heinz settled in two hundred meters behind and poured shells into its port wing root until the wing separated from the fuselage. The RAF bomber plunged into the sea just off the western shore of the island.

On the 24th he knocked down another Spitfire in the afternoon as it attempted to land at Ta Qali airdrome. He dived out of the sun as he saw the Spit sneaking back at rooftop level, probably out of fuel or ammunition or both, desperate to land. For once the flak gunners were late in taking aim and he squeezed a two second burst into the Spitfire's cockpit as he pulled out of his dive. The RAF fighter plowed into the runway and exploded in a ball of fire as Sauckel's Bf 109 raced away from the field.

He was one kill shy of being a fighter ace as he walked with his fellow pilots to the pre-flight briefing. He'd gained his squadron mates' respect over the past three days. The teasing he still took over his boyish good looks was more good-natured than when he'd first joined the squadron and he took it better as well, no longer resenting the questions about how many Hitler Youth merit points he had earned.

The pilots were still fifty yards from the operations shack when the air-raid klaxon began to sound. The pilots stopped and stared at each other in disbelief.

"Some damn fool has hit the panic button by mistake," said one of the other men.

"The Tommies wouldn't dare hit us now," said another. "Not after the last three days!"

The sound of aero engines rose above the klaxon.

"RUN!" shouted another of the pilots.

A mad scramble broke out all over the airfield as air and ground crew raced for slit trenches and shelters. Anti-aircraft guns began to bark as well, adding the popping of light machine guns and the harder crack of heavier guns to the din.

Heinz was running past the ops shack headed for a trench when he saw the first of the attacking planes. He almost stopped in his tracks. The attacker was a bi-plane, creeping across the field at rooftop height and incredibly slow speed, yet defying the flak whose streams of tracers rose from the ground like clawing fingers seeking to grasp the intruder and pull it to earth. Slung under the bi-plane's wings and fuselage he saw a series of mid-sized bombs, hundred-kilo size he guessed.

He dove headfirst into the trench just as he heard the click of the bomb release mechanism of the bi-plane. He burrowed down and covered his head with his arms. The bomb *whooshed* directly over him and slammed through the roof of the operations hut. A tremendous fireball leapt out from the building, over the top of his trench, singeing the hair from his forearms and the backs of his hands. A moment later a hail of stone and wood chips fell from the sky. A meter long splinter of board buried itself deep in the floor of the trench, inches from his abdomen.

A series of other explosions followed as the Royal Navy Swordfish and five others like it unleashed their loads across Gerbini airfield. Parked aircraft erupted in blinding flashes. Fuel, ammunition and bombs aboard the Luftwaffe planes cooked off, adding secondary explosions to the devastation. The rear seat observers in the bi-planes strafed the field as they passed, gunning anyone they caught in the open. Through it all the Swordfish bi-planes danced through and around the AA fire, escaping to the east apparently untouched.

The raid was over in minutes. In its wake sixteen fighters, bombers and Ju 52 transports were completely destroyed and eleven more temporarily out of commission. At the same time seven Blenheims struck Comiso airdrome to the south where they destroyed or damaged another twenty-one aircraft on the ground. The thirteen aircraft were the last bomber strike force on Malta and their crews carried out a desperate mission with skill and daring. For the loss of one Blenheim shot down by AA fire at Comiso they cut German strength on Sicily by nearly fifty aircraft.

Heinz crawled from his slit trench and stared in horror at the scene of devastation around him. Aircraft, buildings and vehicles burned all about the field. Dead and wounded lay where they had fallen. The air raid klaxon finally shut off and the cries of the wounded and the crackling of flames dominated. Ammunition in one of the burning aircraft began to crackle and pop as it cooked off in the flames.

For a moment Heinz was at a loss as to what to do next. He thought he should get his fighter into the air to pursue the enemy raiders, but one look at the main runway where a Ju 52 transport burned like a beacon told him it would be some time before any planes were launched from the field. He started off towards the transport but had gone only a few steps when a hand grabbed his shoulder. He recoiled in horror from the blood-streaked face of his wingman, Stahl.

"Never mind that now, Sauckel," the man shouted. "Come on with me. Some of our pilots are trapped in the ops shack. Help me get them out before they burn!"

Heinz nodded woodenly, but felt the shock begin to drain from him and a sense of purpose return. He followed the other pilot running for the ops shack where they began tearing away smoldering timbers and planks, working feverishly to clear the wreckage, responding to the cries of the men trapped in the ruined shack.

It was mid-day before the Luftwaffe could gather itself for a major effort from its two main Sicilian bases at Gerbini and Comiso. By that time sixteen of the eighteen Spitfires launched from *HMS Eagle* that morning of June 25th arrived safely at Ta Qali and Luqa airfields. The other two were lost with no explanation. Perhaps their pilots became disoriented in a fog to the south of the island. Untrained in long instrument flights over water they had either crashed at sea or made forced landings somewhere on Sicily or the North African coast. But the sixteen replacement Spitfires that did make it arrived just in time, joining only five Spitfires still in operation on the island.

British bomber crews returning to Malta from the raids against Comiso and Gerbini reported seeing large numbers of Junkers 52 transport aircraft on the fields. More ominous still was the presence of a fleet of glider aircraft.

To the military and government leaders of Malta it was quite obvious that invasion was imminent. Preparations to meet the expected airborne assault were accelerated. As a first measure rations were increased for the men of the infantry regiments specifically assigned to the defense of the airfields. Still below standard the extra food at least gave a fighting chance to the men of the old English County Regiments to stand their ground and make a fight of it.

At each of the airfields the work parties repairing the runways and taxiways and servicing the few remaining aircraft went on, but with a new assignment added. Soldiers were ordered on the 25th to begin extending the low piles of boulders and rock walls on the margins of the runways and taxi strips. It was hoped these rock barriers would wreck gliders as they landed, but these could not be placed across the runways and taxi strips proper as the small force of Spitfires needed unfettered access for takeoffs and landings. Spools of barbed wire were brought and stretched across any flat ground on or near the airfields and bombed or derelict vehicles and aircraft were pushed or towed onto the airfields as obstacles to glider landings.

At Ta Qali the reserve battalions of the Manchesters and the Inniskillings were ordered to join the balance of their regiments by the evening of the 26th. At Luqa, the Royal West Kents and the Buffs were to receive their reserve forces at the same time and at Hal Far the Devons would also be brought to full strength on the evening of June 26. The crowding would expose more men to bombing while waiting for the invasion, but it was deemed imprudent to wait till the last minute. Each man was issued fresh iron rations and a full day supply of ammunition.

The Royal Malta Artillery Regiment re-sited several of its batteries of guns, placing them to be able to bombard the airfields themselves should the Germans gain a toehold. At all costs it was vital to deny the Germans use of the fields until the Royal Navy could intervene.

On the afternoon of the 25th the Luftwaffe resumed its attacks against Malta and if the pre-dawn raids against their airfields on Sicily had cut the German strength they also served to increase their resolve. Bombing against the airfields was re-doubled. Hal

Far received special attention since the Germans believed the Swordfish bombers originated there.

Kenneth Wiltshire and his wingman Andy White were assigned the midday watch at Ta Qali. As the heat of the day built through the late morning they sat in the cockpits of two of the newly arrived Spitfires, suffering in their bulky flight suits on the sun-scorched runway, waiting for the Luftwaffe to return the favor. On such days the aluminum skins of the aircraft popped and crackled as they expanded in the heat. A careless pilot who rested bare skin against the cockpit frame could earn a painful burn.

Kenneth found the heat less a burden than the tension of waiting. Some pilots brought a book to read during their ready watches, others re-read old letters or wrote fresh ones, though no one knew when mail would next be taken off the island. That morning as he waited for an alert that would send him hurtling down the runway on a minute's notice Kenneth daydreamed about Maggie. He visualized her face and her eyes and imagined that she might love him as much as he loved her.

He'd made a date with her for that night and hoped the Germans wouldn't queer his special plans. He was in the middle of fantasizing about seducing her, and was just reaching the point of success in his dreams when the alert came. Within seconds the Rolls-Royce Merlin engine was turning over and the propeller was spinning. Kenneth pulled his goggles down over his eyes and pulled the cockpit canopy closed. He snapped the latches down and turned to look over at Andy. His wingman was ready, waiting for him to take the lead. Kenneth nodded to Andy and eased off the brake. The Spitfires gathered momentum and within seconds were rocketing off the runway and into the sky.

Once clear of the ridges to the north of the field Kenneth turned first east, then south to gain altitude before meeting the enemy attack. He tuned in the frequency of the Flight Controller, buried deep underground at Lascaris Bastion in Valletta. The calm, measured voice of the controller came through his earphones.

"Red Leader, Red Leader. Plus fifty flight," the controller intoned. "Ta Qali bound at Angels two-zero-zero."

"Roger that, Malta Control," Kenneth answered. An enemy flight of fifty or more aircraft was headed in the direction of Ta Qali airfield at an altitude of 20,000 feet. He pushed his throttles forward to gain more altitude as he and Andy swung back around to the north to meet the attack. As they flew over the airfield again they spotted the enemy aircraft in the distance.

"Talley-ho!" cried Kenneth. "Bandits at 2 o'clock!"

"Cut through to the bombers," ordered the controller. "Ignore the fighters!"

"Easy for you to say," grumbled Kenneth to himself, but he pushed the stick over and dove towards the bombers.

The enemy flight was over a mile away yet and the bombers were about a thousand feet below him when the top cover Messerschmitts reacted. A swarm of angry German fighters descended towards the two lone Spitfires and Kenneth knew there was no chance of fighting through to the bombers on this flight.

He keyed his throat mic button. "Stay with me Andy!" he shouted and then his hands were full with no more time to talk. A pair of Bf 109s came straight at him, head-on as though bent on ramming him. He squeezed the trigger. Cannon and machine gun shells arced out in front of him and the Spitfire bucked and jolted from the recoil of the guns. The Germans came on undeterred, returning his fire. Tracer shells flashed by his cockpit, so close he ducked in spite of himself.

He broke out in an instant sweat and his eyes were wide and unblinking behind his goggles. He steeled his nerve and held his course. He knew that if he flinched away now he would expose his fighter to the guns of the Bf 109s. The four aircraft sped together at combined speeds of over 600 knots, the Messerschmitts growing in his vision to impossible size. They would collide!

Kenneth screamed and yanked the stick over to his left just as the 109s were on him. His Spitfire was tossed about the sky in the slipstreams as the German fighters passed him; hurled upside down he struggled to regain control. Bringing his fighter back on an even keel he twisted round to check his tail.

"DAMN!" he swore. Just as he expected the Germans had taken advantage of his momentary loss of control and another pair of 109s had slipped in on his tail. He yanked the stick over to his left again and dove for the deck, but the 109s stayed on him. He flattened out and snapped back to the right, rolling the Spitfire over on its back and upright again then dove back to his left. The Bf 109 on his tail a moment before filled his gun sights briefly and he squeezed the trigger. Shells slammed into the German's port wing and a second later flame erupted from the ruptured fuel tank.

Before he had any chance to bore in and finish off the 109 he felt a shock in the rear of the plane and the stick was nearly torn from his grip. He hauled the stick over to the left again and dove for the deck. He stood the plane on its nose in a dive to escape the German on his tail. The Spitfire began to shake and buck as his speed increased past the design limits of the airframe. He held the dive for what seemed an eternity until he was sure no sane German would still be following him. He broke through a layer of haze and saw that he was out over the sea with the water rushing up to meet him. He hauled back on the stick, fighting to pull the Spitfire out of its dive. Individual waves resolved in his vision and still the fighter fell, plummeting like a meteor fallen from the heavens to Earth. He pulled the stick back into his stomach, trying to pull it back through his body. Finally, after a terrifying interval in which he doubted the fighter would recover it began to come out of the dive. He flattened out less than 500 feet above the sea. Quickly he checked behind him, but the 109s had given up the chase and he was alone.

He keyed his throat mic. "Andy, where are you?" he called.

He strained to hear an answer, any sign of an answer.

"Malta control, Malta control," he called. "This is Red Leader. Give me a vector, please."

Still no answer. He'd regained enough height now to see that the fight had taken him away to the west of the island about ten miles. As he climbed further he could see several towering plumes of smoke rising from the center of the island near Ta Qali. Black puffs hung in the sky over the airfield from the flak batteries fighting back against the German bombers. He powered his way back towards Malta. As he came back over land west of Mdina he tried his radio-telephone again.

"Malta control, this is Red Leader, Red Leader. Come in please."

"Red Leader, this is Malta Control. We read you." Kenneth breathed a sigh of relief. "Red Leader, return to station. Enemy withdrawing."

"Malta Control, this is Red Leader. Any word from my wingman?"

"Red Leader, your wingman is already on the ground, safe and sound."

Kenneth sat back but didn't dare relax for the last few minutes of his flight home. He settled back onto the runway at Ta Qali, passing through one of two plumes of black, oily smoke rising from aircraft revetments on the field; two aircraft hit on the ground.

When he taxied to a stop in a jerry can revetment he climbed stiffly out of the cockpit and examined the tail of his fighter. Four holes each as big as his fist were punched through the rudder. He peeled off his leather flight helmet and goggles and sagged to his knees, mentally and physically exhausted.

"Kenneth!"

He looked and saw Andy running towards him. His wingman skidded to a stop in front of him and knelt down beside him.

"Are you hurt, Kenneth?" Andy asked, worry in his eyes.

Kenneth shook his head. "No, I'm all right," he said. "Thought I'd gone for a Burton though. Are you okay Andy."

"I'm fine," Andy said with relief. "Kenneth!" he exclaimed. "We've both been credited with a confirmed kill. That's my second and your fourth! You're one away from being an ace!"

Kenneth hung his head and tried to control the shaking in his hands and knees. Finally he struggled to his feet and made his way back to the billet at Xaxa Palace.

Luftwaffe raids continued through the afternoon right up until last light. The RAF Spitfire pilots fought bravely to fend off the air assault but the weight of numbers told for the Germans. The British pilots gave a good account of themselves, shooting down two Germans for each of their own losses, but on each successive flight the RAF response weakened as the Germans knocked down one Spitfire after another. On the ground the gunners at the flak batteries suffered cruelly as the German bombers paid special attention to them. More than three quarters of the AA guns at the three airfields were out of commission at the end of the day. Those that remained were critically short of ammunition.

Late in the day, just before sunset a group of twenty Ju 88's hit Hal Far and the Kalafrana seaplane base adjacent to it at Marsaxlokk Bay. In this fourteenth raid of the day against Malta some forty thousand kilograms of bombs were dropped in one thousand and two thousand kilo canisters. Among these was a two thousand kilo delayed action bomb whose fuse was set to trigger the high explosive device twenty-four hours after impact. This bomb landed in the water, just yards from shore at Kalafrana. In the bedlam of the raid its landing went unnoticed by the British. It lay submerged, a literal ticking time bomb.

>>>>>>>>>>>>

Harry and his mate McTevish climbed out of the engine room and up to the mess deck, passing the NAAFI office, closed during Action Stations. They made the journey in silence. Both men were bone tired with drooping limbs and blood-shot eyes and the journey took much longer than it normally would. On the way they passed many other men in similar condition. They came to the mess and were just entering the main hatchway when the first of the torpedoes struck *HMS Eagle.* Harry was thrown from his feet by the explosion, landing hard on his backside. Crockery was thrown from tables and racks, smashing on the deck. Men screamed and the lights went out, but Harry kept his head and stayed on his rump, waiting for the emergency lights to come on.

Instead, a second torpedo struck *Eagle.* The din doubled as men around Harry came out of the shock from the first hit and started to panic. A dim shape lurched toward him in the dark. The man trod on Harry's hand as he staggered past, groping for the hatchway.

"Bleedin' sod!" Harry barked, but the man paid no heed.

"Get out!" another man screamed. "She's startin' to roll!"

Cries of "GANGWAY!" rang out as men stumbled to their feet and fought to get out of the mess.

Harry stayed on his rump. *Eagle* was a large target, worthy of more than two torpedoes in any U-boat skipper's book. The third torpedo struck like a hammer blow, hurling men off their feet throughout the ship. In the crew's mess they were thrown in a heap of broken limbs and cracked skulls near Harry and the hatchway. The deck started to tilt to port under him.

Harry groped about, looking for his friend, McTevish. He found a leg and then an arm. He gripped the arm tightly and the yelp that greeted his grip clearly belonged to the Scotsman. Harry chuckled in spite of himself.

"Come on, Mate," he said. "Time to get out of 'ere!"

Staying on his hands and knees Harry led McTevish to the mess exit. Men were starting to sort themselves out of the pile of bodies. McTevish groaned.

"Come on chum," Harry repeated. "Let's get out of 'ere."

McTevish screamed as Harry gripped his hand. As his eyes adjusted to the light Harry saw that his friend's right arm bent where it should not bend, between the elbow and shoulder.

"All right mate," he said, "all right. Give me yer other 'and."

He hauled McTevish to his feet by the left arm. Others were finding their feet as well. One man would clearly never move again, his head split against the bulkhead.

"All right, you lot," Harry shouted. "We've all got to get outa 'ere before she rolls over. Let's move."

Harry shepherded the group of men, about twelve in all, limping and groaning every step of the way out the mess exit and to the companionway ladder to the next deck up. As an engine room hand Harry was in tune with every sound and vibration of the great old ship, but it didn't need his special intimacy with *Eagle* for anyone to know that the ship's engines had stopped and that she was slowing, coming to a halt, dead in the water. Groaning noises from the decks below told him the ship was already starting to come apart.

Other men, in groups and singly were struggling up from the lower decks, screaming in fright, as they fought to keep their feet against the increasing list. The ladder was jammed with men fighting for their lives to escape the doomed carrier.

A shuddering vibration ran through the deck beneath their feet. The screaming and yelling increased as panic set in. Men were starting to push and pull others out of the way to get to the ladder. Harry looked about for an officer to restore order, but there were none present. Deep within the ship a groan of tortured metal plates sounded as *HMS Eagle* twisted on her steel frame.

"She's breaking up!" someone yelled.

The press at the ladder grew more intense. Harry gripped a fire main with his left hand to maintain his place. Suddenly *Eagle* lurched over to port. A bulkhead somewhere below decks had failed; tons of seawater poured into her every second. The lurch threw a group of men away from the base of the ladder and against the port bulkhead. Harry saw his chance.

"Come on laddie!" he said to McTevish, still held about the waist in Harry's right arm. Harry shoved him to the base of the ladder and heaved him up onto the first steps, pushing his shoulder into the man's bottom and lifting his legs up the ladder. A few steps to the top and they'd be clear on the hanger deck. *Eagle* lurched again as another bulkhead failed.

Dickie Whiting was on the port leg of his route around *HMS Eagle* and her escorts, struggling against the crosswind that wanted to push him to starboard. The Swordfish bi-plane was performing flawlessly in spite of the strong south wind.

He looked down at the sea below. A mixed and confused surface with increasing swells and the tops blown off the white caps by the southern *sirocco* wind made his prospects of sighting a submerged submarine very small. He twisted round and looked over his shoulder at his back seat observer. The man was gamely peering over the side at the sea below to port, goggles pulled down over his eyes, but Dickie knew there was little chance of spotting any sign of a submarine on the confused surface below.

Dickie started to turn back forward when the observer started out of his seat. The man shouted unintelligibly and pointed down to port. Dickie looked again at the sea's surface. He gasped and reached for the Aldis lamp to signal the carrier, but he knew it was already too late. Four torpedo tracks were streaking toward *Eagle's* port side. They passed under the Swordfish and he turned to starboard and watched in horror as the first torpedo passed under the bow of the carrier, but he knew the others couldn't miss. One after the other the three remaining torpedoes struck. Waterspouts rocketed hundreds of feet into the sky and hung there as though captured in a photograph before slowly falling back onto the flight deck, blown across the ship by the south wind. *Eagle* slewed round on her port beam and took on an immediate and pronounced list.

Whiting knew right away she was finished, and with her went the only safe place for him to land in four hundred miles. He turned back to port and traced the fading torpedo tracks back to the area from which they must have come. He turned and dove for the spot, his mind racing ahead of the plane. The torpedoes were launched two or more minutes ago. Where would the U-boat go after firing? Deep surely, but what else. Three choices only, since turning a U-boat 180 degrees underwater could not be done easily or quickly. No, the U-boat skipper could go to port or starboard in his dive, or straight ahead under the carrier itself. A turn to port would put the U-boat on course with the carrier and her escorts, not a good escape plan. To starboard or straight ahead? If the U-boat had dived under the carrier then he had no chance of a lucky hit with his lone depth bomb anyway. 'Starboard then,' he decided and swung the bi-plane back on a reciprocal heading to the carrier's original course, resuming his dive. He estimated the torpedoes had been fired from 1200 yards. Given the sub's momentum and turning radius it might have closed the gap to the carriers wake by 500 yards. It was all blind guess work and computed faster than it takes to tell. He pulled up out of his dive at 200 feet toggling the bomb release switch as the Stringbag leveled out.

The depth bomb fell away and the plane surged into the sky, relieved of the bomb's 500-pound weight. Dickie threw the Swordfish onto its starboard wing and circled to watch the bomb's flight and impact. The round canister hurtled into the sea with a mighty splash and immediately sank out of sight.

When an aircraft attacked a submarine in the Second World War it was usually when the sub was caught on the surface. While it would certainly dive as soon as its lookouts spotted the plane, the general expectation was that it would not have time to dive deep before bombs were dropped on it, thus the depth pressure fuse on the bomb was pre-set to detonate at just fifty feet. Dickie Whiting counted to five waiting for the explosion.

*HMS Wolverine* was about a half mile away on the port beam of *Eagle* when the torpedoes struck. It was immediately obvious to her skipper that the enemy submarine had slipped between *Wolverine* and *Eagle* and that it must still be somewhere between the two warships, diving deep.

"Aircraft diving, sir!" shouted *Wolverine's* starboard bridge lookout. "Green forty at two-thousand feet."

*Wolverine's* skipper looked up from the stricken carrier and followed the direction the young man pointed. Sure enough, the patrolling Swordfish was diving. It snap-rolled back to port, heading almost due east on a bearing reciprocal to the fleet's course. At two hundred feet above the sea and a quarter-mile astern the destroyer it pulled out of its dive and released its depth bomb.

"Hard about, starboard!" the skipper shouted. "All engines, full ahead!" The Swordfish must have seen the sub. *Wolverine's* mission was to sink it and avenge *Eagle*.

The depth bomb dropped by the bi-plane exploded in a boiling fountain of white-green water that collapsed back into the sea, leaving a white scar to mark the U-boat's suspected position. *Wolverine* heeled to starboard through her turn until the boiling remnants of the explosion were dead ahead.

"Steady your helm!" shouted the Captain. He turned to the XO. "Have the depth charges set to two-hundred-fifty feet," he said. Without waiting for acknowledgement he turned back to the fading signs of the explosion. He lifted the cover and spoke into the bridge voice tube.

"ASDIC, Bridge," he shouted.

"Bridge, ASDIC, aye," came the reply.

"Report! Do you have a submerged contact dead ahead?"

"Bridge, ASDIC, negative, no contact, repeat, no contact."

"ASDIC, Bridge, keep searching! Go to active mode!"

He snapped the cover closed and brought his binoculars to his eyes, scanning the waters in the area around where the depth bomb had exploded, looking for any sign, either that the sub was hit or was still making its escape. Nothing.

"Hold your course," he said to the helmsman.

He turned his binoculars toward *Eagle*. Just two minutes since she'd been hit, but already it was clear she was finished. She'd rolled off course to port and was listing heavily as she came dead in the water. No smoke or fire was evident, giving *Wolverine's* skipper a clear view of the stricken carrier. She was coming to a stop, beam on to the set of the waves that were slapping into the greatly reduced freeboard on her port side. The starboard side was lifting out of the water. He saw that any evacuation of the carrier would have to take place over her port side. The starboard freeboard was already too great for all but the fittest swimmers to dive clear of the ship. But with the set of the sea and the waves crashing against her port side many men would be smashed back against the side of the ship. Circumstances were contriving a catastrophe of the first order.

He dropped his binoculars back around his neck and looked

back at the spot he intended to depth charge. Three hundred yards more. He looked back at *Eagle.* Her freeboard was normally over forty feet, but as *Wolverine* charged down on the suspected position of the submarine the distance between the waterline and her flight deck had shrunk to only fifteen feet. She would surely roll over almost as soon as the freeboard was gone, leaving only minutes for her crew to abandon ship. Already men were leaping into the sea, struggling against the waves to clear the flight deck poised to crash down upon them.

Wells shouted down the voice tube, "ASDIC, Bridge. Anything?"

"Bridge, ASDIC. No contact, repeat, no contact. There's a lot of other noise in the water right now, Sir, from the carrier and the depth bomb both. In a few more minutes I may be able to isolate something, but not now."

*Wolverine's* skipper made the most difficult and controversial decision of his professional career. None of the other destroyers was in a position to reach the port side of *Eagle* in time to make a difference to the survivors. Only his ship could lie along the port side of the carrier, sheltering her crew from the crashing waves as they abandoned ship, pulling them from the water before they drowned. If he took the time to depth charge without a confirmed ASDIC contact hundreds of men might die needlessly.

"Helm, hard-a-port," he ordered. "Engines ahead one third!"

"Hard-a-port, aye," the helmsman acknowledged.

"Engines ahead one third," the quartermaster repeated. The enunciator rang as the engine room acknowledged the change of speed.

*Wolverine* heeled to port as she swung back on course beside the foundering carrier.

"Hang the boarding nets over the starboard side," the Captain ordered. "Starboard watch to the rails to assist swimmers." His commands were repeated over the tannoy.

He stepped to the starboard bridge wing. As the destroyer's speed fell off she glided in beside the carrier, a cable length away. The Captain slowed the ship till she was barely making steerageway. When *Wolverine* pulled even with *Eagle's* counter he hailed the men on the flight deck through a bullhorn speaker. Hundreds had gathered there already, though no order to abandon ship had been given. Electric service throughout *Eagle* was out from the first moments the torpedoes struck, leaving the Tannoy powerless.

"The flight deck *Eagle!*" he yelled. "Jump and swim for it as we pull abreast of you!"

Men waved and shouted to acknowledge they understood.

"Signal from *Nubian,* Sir," said the young man at the Aldis lamp.

"Read it to me," the Captain snapped, without taking his eyes away from the bulk of *Eagle,* looming above his cockleshell destroyer, a great weight ready to roll over on *Wolverine* to crush her.

"*Nubian* asks, 'What of the submarine?' Sir," the young man said, reluctantly.

"Tell *Nubian -,*" the Captain snapped then stopped himself. "Tell *Nubian,* 'No ASDIC contact'."

"Yes, sir."

*Wolverine* crept along the port side of the sinking aircraft carrier, the destroyer's hull sheltering the men in the water from the worst of the wind-driven waves from the south. Her starboard watch frantically hauled swimmers in from the cargo nets slung over the side. *Wolverine's* Chief Petty Officer tried to keep count as they came over the rail. He reached three hundred twelve by the time *Wolverine* pulled away from *Eagle.* Looking back from his bridge the Captain saw dozens of men still in the water with hundreds more still aboard the carrier on her flight deck. He knew many of these men were wounded, reluctant to enter the water until the last extremity forced them.

"Put about, helm to port," he called. "We'll go by for another pass. Both engines ahead full."

He looked back at *Eagle.* Waves were lapping onto the flight deck. Her starboard mounted 'island', the flight operations control tower of the carrier, hung like a great steel balcony over her flight deck. He knew there were no more than minutes left. He looked for the other escort destroyers. The last two escorts had joined *Nubian,* her Tribal Class sister ship *HMS Eskimo* and the 'I' class destroyer *HMS Ithuriel.* The three were searching for ASDIC contacts astern of the carrier and *Wolverine,* too distant to help with survivors.

Harry reached the flight deck with his wounded shipmate

McTevish, climbing a ladder tipped almost on its side and emerging in the open just aft of the island on the starboard side. The flight deck was canted away from him and his shipmate at a thirty-five degree angle. Looking over the port side the water was lapping at the flight deck. A destroyer was just pulling away, her decks filled with wet seamen, a cargo net hung over her starboard side.

"Let's go mate," he said. "It's all down 'ill from 'ere. Don't try to walk," he said, putting a restraining arm on the injured man. "Just slide on yer backside across the deck. Come on, follow me."

The two started to do as Harry said, sliding on their bottoms, side-by-side, feet first. McTevish had still not spoken since Harry first helped him up in the mess. He cradled his broken arm in the good one and slid beside Harry. They reached the port side as the water came up onto the flight deck. Harry looked astern and saw the destroyer returning.

"All right, mate," he said to the man. "Into the water, with you."

"But I canna swim with one arm," McTevish protested.

"Well you bleedin' well can't stay 'ere now can you?" asked Harry. "Come on now, I'll 'elp you time a wave."

Harry studied the set of waves approaching the ship. The fourth wave out looked likely, a roller that would reach up onto the flight deck. *Eagle* stood balanced on her beam, ready to roll over without a moments notice. Once she started to roll nothing would stop her but the bottom of the sea. The first three waves lapped the edge of the flight deck, then as the fourth wave approached a rumble deep within the ship portended her end. Those few left on the deck leapt into the sea, if they were able. Harry and his mate let the wave wash them from the deck and into the sea.

After firing the spread of four torpedoes from her bow tubes U-212 dived deep, following in the track of her shots to pass directly under the British airplane carrier. Oberleutnant Popitz buttoned the boat down in anticipation of a heavy depth charge counter-attack by the escort destroyers.

U-212 had found the British fleet exactly as Popitz hoped. After his successful attack against the escort destroyer in the early hours of the morning he was more convinced than ever that the carrier's mission was to launch a flight of reinforcement fighter aircraft to Malta. To do so she would continue on to the east then, at first light and maximum range from the island, turn into the south wind to launch the aircraft. She would, he reasoned turn back west immediately after launching and make her best speed for home on a course he estimated would be about twenty miles south of the track she had followed while east bound. He ordered U-212 to surface despite the danger posed by the bright moon rising in the east and raced south for the expected rendezvous.

For a little over two hours the boat crashed through the strengthening seas. Her bridge watch was drenched every few seconds by sheets of flying spray, but the aft blowers filled the boat with fresh air and the powerful diesels fully charged the electric batteries U-212 would depend on for power during the coming daylight hours. Popitz dived the boat shortly after first light.

The sun was well up in the morning sky when U-212 first detected the British. Through the periscope Popitz spotted a smudge of smoke on the eastern horizon. Within minutes the bow of a charging destroyer was in view, at a range of about two miles followed by the ponderous bulk of the carrier. The U-boat was in a perfect spot. All U-212 had to do was lay silent and wait as the destroyer passed over her. Soon the carrier presented her port side at a range of just 900 meters.

Popitz fired all four of his bow torpedoes. The first missed, probably just ahead of the carrier, but the other three all went home, striking in quick succession. U-212 dived directly under the stricken carrier, the German sonar operator reporting the crash of collapsing bulkheads and the rush of water as the great ship foundered. The carrier's engines went silent within seconds of the third torpedo hit.

Oberleutnant Popitz took U-212 a mile to the north or starboard side of the carrier, running on silent routine at a speed of three knots. His one bad moment came when sonar reported a splash as of an aerial bomb. A moment later the shock wave of a distant explosion rocked the boat gently from side to side, but it was too distant to cause damage to the boat. Franz took a deep breath. He had never seen the aircraft in his periscope looks during the attack. Franz ordered all engines stopped.

"Up periscope," he said. He swung through a very fast 360° sweep of the horizon before settling back on *Eagle's* bearing.

"The carrier is rolled over on her port beam, listing heavily," he reported to the control room watch. They hung on his description intently. "She's dead in the water and mortally wounded, I am sure," he said. He swung the periscope to the east. "Three destroyers are charging about a mile astern of the carrier. They are dropping depth charges. Obviously they are just guessing at our whereabouts!" he said. "Down 'scope," he ordered. The periscope hummed down in its well.

"We are well clear of the destroyers," he said, "but I don't want to give that aircraft a chance to locate us. We'll continue to move off to the north another mile or so. Our bow tubes are exhausted, but the stern tube is loaded. We'll see if we can get a shot at one of the destroyers. Perhaps they will linger for rescue operations." He turned to the XO.

"Paul, prepare a signal to Berlin," he said. "British carrier hit by three torpedoes, sinking. Give our current position. We'll wait for a chance to surface to send it."

"Yes, Sir!" answered Merker.

Aboard *Wolverine* rescue operations continued as *Eagle* entered her death throes.

"Captain, Chief Jones reports the sickbay is overflowed with wounded. We've over four hundred survivors aboard already."

Captain Wells turned to the young seaman sent by Chief Jones with the message.

"Thank Chief Jones," he said. "Tell him none of the other escorts are in position to assist the survivors. We'll have to take them all aboard ourselves, then transfer some to the others later."

"Yes, Sir," the young man answered. He turned and hurried from the bridge.

*HMS Wolverine* was on her second run down the port side of *Eagle*. The Captain kept his destroyer about 80 yards distant of the sinking carrier this time. *Eagle* looked to be completely abandoned now, but the water between the two ships was alive with men still struggling in the water trying to get clear before the carrier rolled over and sank. *Wolverine's* crew worked feverishly at the starboard rail dragging men up the cargo nets hung over her side. As soon as they were aboard they were rushed to the port side, out of the way, or below to wait for the attention of the destroyer's over-worked Doctor and pharmacists mate, her only trained medical staff.

The Captain's eyes shifted continually from the rescue operations on his ship's starboard side to the sinking carrier. He was risking his own ship, in so close to the carrier, but there were just too many men in the water to abandon them in the rough seas. He'd already watched helplessly as several exhausted or wounded swimmers slipped beneath the waves before they could be hauled aboard his destroyer. Suddenly a great groan of rending, tortured metal came from the hulk of *HMS Eagle*.

"Helm, hard to port, both engines ahead full!" he shouted.

*Wolverine* surged in the water, her two Brown-Curtis turbine engines generating their full 27,000 horsepower in an instant. The sea boiled as her twin screws beat the water; she moved off quickly even as more men were pulled from the sea at the last instant. The Captain watched as the carrier rolled over on her port beam, her flight deck rising to vertical, then past vertical. The carrier's hull rolled out of the water briefly, the great propellers and shafts that had powered her during life now still as she began her death plunge.

Over one hundred men still in the water screamed and thrashed trying to get away from the tremendous undertow as *Eagle* plunged into the depths. Trapped pockets of air were released to roil the surface. At the center of the sinking a great vortex of water spun, sucking the weakest swimmers down into the depths with the ship. The waters churned in torment for several moments, before one last great bubble of air burst to the surface. Then the sea resumed its natural demeanor, wind driven waves covering forever the final resting place of *HMS Eagle*. She'd sunk in just eighteen minutes.

The young seaman returned to the bridge of *Wolverine*.

"Chief Jones' compliments, Sir," he reported breathlessly, "and there's over six hundred survivors aboard, Sir."

"Thank Chief Jones," Captain Wells replied. "Tell him we'll have to clear the area before transferring any survivors to the other escorts."

"Yes, Sir."

Wells turned back to the site of the sinking. At long last the destroyer leader, *HMS Nubian* had dispatched one of the other destroyers from the fruitless search for the sub. *Ithuriel* cruised slowly over the sinking, picking the few remaining swimmers from the water. All told, *Wolverine* and *Ithuriel* rescued 857 men from

*HMS Eagle's* compliment of 1200, though some thirty-five would succumb to their injuries before reaching Gibraltar. Harry Booth and his mate McTevish were among the very last men pulled from the water by *HMS Ithuriel*.

The Swordfish on patrol when the carrier was struck was still in the air. The nearest friendly landing place was over 400 miles away and the bi-plane hadn't enough fuel to reach safety. By Aldis lamp *Nubian* signaled for the bi-plane to continue patrolling over the destroyers as they raced at maximum speed for home. When its fuel was nearly exhausted Dickie Whiting successfully executed a 'ditch' landing at sea near *HMS Eskimo.* He and his observer became the final members of the carrier's crew to be rescued.

>>>>>>>>>>>>

>>>>>>>>>>>>>>>>>>>

Kenneth Wiltshire kept his date with Maggie Reed the evening of the 25th. Maggie contrived to have her day off match with Kenneth's by trading a shift in the Chamber with her friend Elizabeth. He was fortunate to get the time. With the renewed Luftwaffe offensive against Malta the pilots were kept on a short leash, but his squadron leader was an understanding chap. Given that he had four pilots for every available Spitfire and that Kenneth had knocked down a Messerschmitt that afternoon while narrowly surviving a sortie for the second time in three days he gave Kenneth leave until noon the next day.

Maggie and Kenneth wanted to get away from Valletta and Kenneth arranged with his batman for the loan of a horse and a two-wheel buggy for the evening. He would take Maggie on a buggy ride to St. Paul's Bay on the island's north shore. St. Paul's Bay is reputed to be the landing place of the Apostle Paul after his shipwreck on Malta while on his way to Rome to appear before Caesar. Soaked and disheveled from fourteen days at sea in a fierce gale, Paul and his shipmates were treated kindly by the native Maltese who lit a fire on the beach to warm the castaways. According to the Bible Paul reached his hand into a bundle of sticks to feed the fire, but a viper was hiding among the sticks and it sank its fangs into his hand. The Maltese expected him to sicken and die, but Paul was under the protection of God and he simply shook the snake off as though nothing had happened. This miracle was the first step in the conversion of the Maltese to Catholicism.

The horse was little more than a pony compared to the great beasts Kenneth had managed on the family farm in Red Fern. Its ribs poked out from its malnourished frame, but this was a lucky horse. Many of his kind on Malta had been eaten by June 1942.

Kenneth picked Maggie up at 1900 hours, 7 P.M. to her, on the outskirts of Floriana, the suburb of Valletta, near the big telephone exchange building, one of the few prominent structures left above ground in Floriana or Valletta without major damage. Floriana was choked with soldiers on leave and it took some time for Kenneth to work the horse and cart clear of the old town. Once clear of the outskirts they were quickly trotting through the Maltese countryside, through the towns of Birkirkara and Mosta, past the ancient domed church, then on to St. Paul's Bay. The wind was behind them as they rode and it was a beautiful summer evening.

The seat of the cart was uncomfortable and quite narrow, a fact Kenneth noted with satisfaction when he'd picked up the cart. Maggie sat very close to his right side as they rode. When the cart hit a rut in the old dirt road and jolted hard Maggie threw her arm around Kenneth's waist and hung on for dear life.

"It's all right," he reassured her, "you're perfectly safe with me." But he put his right arm about her shoulders and pulled her close anyway. He slowed the cart. He enjoyed her smell and the soft feel of her skin under his hand.

They trotted slowly through the Maltese countryside, enjoying the picturesque fields, farmhouses and villages and the smiling and cheerful people they passed on the way. Every man, woman and child they passed had a smile and a friendly wave for them. Even so, reminders of the war were never far away. Bomb craters scarred the fields at random intervals and every village had suffered some damage. Between the New Year of 1941 and the spring of 1942 Malta endured frequent and heavy bombardment. Indeed, per square kilometer it was the most heavily bombed place on earth. A great many bombs, especially those dropped at night by the Italians went astray of their intended targets at the harbors or airfields, landing instead in the Maltese hinterland.

The RAF maintained a rest camp for aircrew at St. Paul's Bay. Nowhere on the island was truly safe during the spring and first days of summer of 1942, but at least the camp was far enough away from the airfields and harbors that stray bombs were rare and the airmen could enjoy a few days of relative peace and tranquility there. When Kenneth reached the rest camp he didn't pause, but kept right on past it down the shore of the bay, reveling in holding Maggie close to him. He happily clucked his tongue to the pony and wished the ride would never end. The road deteriorated the further they got from Valletta and Maggie clung tighter to him with every rut and pothole. He was sorry when the journey did end, they arrived at the little cottage he'd arranged for them and there was no more excuse to hold her.

They took turns changing into their swimsuits inside the cottage before walking down to the rocky beach to bathe. They swam out to an outcrop some yards from the shore where they rested on the rocks, soaking up the sun's last rays. Lying back on the rocks, his eyes closed, Kenneth felt Maggie slip her hand over his. He tentatively gripped her hand in return.

When the sun set they swam back to shore, splashing and playing. In the shallow water near the beach Maggie Reed kissed Kenneth Wiltshire, quickly on the lips, then swam away from him before he could hold her close. She reached the shore a few feet ahead of him just as a distant air raid siren sounded. She turned and waited for him to come out of the water.

"They won't let you forget there's a war on, will they?" she said.

"There's no war tonight, Maggie," he answered, holding her eyes with his. He moved towards her, but she backed away and turned.

"I'm cold, Kenneth," she said. "Let's get the towels." He followed her into the cottage. It was small, just two rooms, with a small kitchen with a stone washbasin and iron pump, and an "everything else" room with a table, two chairs and a throw rug. A fireplace opened on two sides for access from both rooms.

"I'll start a fire," he said, pulling the screen from the small fireplace, revealing sticks and wood chips, mainly bits and pieces of lumber salvaged from bombed buildings.

"We can't use their fire," objected Maggie. "That's a week's ration of firewood."

"It's okay," he replied, lighting the kindling. "I arranged it."

"Oh?" she said. "And what else have you arranged?"

"Just a little something to eat." He reached behind the fireplace into the kitchen and pulled a small wicker basket out. A red checker cloth held a bundle with bread, two small oranges and a small block of cheese. A sharp knife was in the bottom of the basket.

"Oh, I'm famished!" said Maggie.

"One more thing," said Kenneth. He stepped into the kitchen, returning with two glasses and a dripping bottle of Maltese wine. "It's been cooling in the basin," he said.

The flame in the fireplace caught and suffused the rooms of the tiny cottage with a warm, bright glow. Kenneth set the wine on the hearth and took Maggie's hands in his. He looked at her with a seriousness she'd never seen before, but she knew what it meant. She pulled her hands away and warmed them to the fire. She pulled an orange from the basket and began cutting it into pieces.

"I'm hungry," she said.

He looked at her for a moment then sat beside her. "Me too," he said.

They ate in silence. Maggie cut bread and cheese and orange slices, hand feeding Kenneth his.

"Kenneth," Maggie said at last. "You're not going to give me one of those speeches about how there's a war on, and how we need to live for today, because there's no tomorrow are you?"

He looked at her, eyes wide. She'd very nearly read his mind. "I've been practicing it all week," he admitted sheepishly.

She smiled. "That would insult my intelligence," she said.

"I wouldn't want to do that Maggie," he said. "I – I think I -," he paused and looked in her deep, green eyes under those incredibly long lashes.

"What is it Kenneth?" she asked.

He looked away, into the embers of their fire. He put another stick in the fireplace.

He turned back to her and stroked her soft, smooth cheek with the back of his hand.

"I think I'm in love with you Maggie," he said softly.

Another air raid siren sounded in the distance. They both laughed, but Kenneth felt the spell was broken. He held his watch up to the light of the fire. 2205 hours.

"Bloody Italians," he muttered. Maggie nodded her head. They both knew the Germans bombed in the day, the Italians at night.

She waited for him to return to his train of thought. They said nothing for long moments. Bombs exploded in the distance, away to the south.

"Ta Qali or Luqa," he said.

They sat in silence, staring into the fire together. Finally, he summoned the courage to try again. It took much more bravery to speak at that moment than he'd ever needed in facing combat in the air.

"Maggie," he said, staring back into the fire. "I meant what I said."

"Yes," she said. "I know. The Italians are real bastards."

He laughed and looked back into her eyes. She was smiling; a bright, warm smile and it lit her face and his heart. He ached for her suddenly and it showed in his face. She reached up a hand behind his head and pulled his face down to hers. She kissed him, sweet and full on the mouth. He reached for her and pulled her tight against him. He passed his hand over her hip, up her side to her breast, finding her nipple through the swimsuit. He slipped the strap off her shoulder exposing her breast. They fell back on the rug and made love to the light of the dieing embers of the fire and to the wail of an all-clear siren. Kenneth thought he might die of pleasure.

>>>>>>>>>>>>>

As Kenneth and Maggie trotted through the Maltese countryside towards St. Paul's Bay The Second Parachute Division, *Der Zweit Fallschirmjager Division* began its final preparations for the assault on Malta. During the day Luftwaffe fighter and bomber squadrons on Sicily flew the final pre-assault sorties against the British, hammering at the flak batteries on and near the airfields and making it nearly impossible for the British troops to extend their defensive works and glider obstacles. After the first raid of the day German fighters maintained a continuous fighter patrol over the three British airfields both to prevent a repetition of the prior night's British air raids and to afford fighter protection to the German bomber forces that were never far away through the afternoon. Any RAF bombers that remained undamaged kept a low profile, staying grounded through the day.

At Gerbini and Comiso airfields the paratroopers began to stir in the late afternoon. Those that had traveled by train from Livorno were allowed to sleep late before being rousted out of bed. They then set to work preparing the jump gear.

First and foremost to every paratrooper of any nationality is always the parachute itself. In the German Luftwaffe the parachute pack was nicknamed 'The Bone Bag'. Each man packed his own Bone Bag with the assistance of another man in his 'stick', the group of men who would jump together from a single aircraft. Long, narrow tables were erected where the men laid their 'chutes out flat and began the time consuming and painstaking task of carefully folding them into their bags. As on all such occasions black humor was evident. Men making their first combat jump were assured by the veterans that they would receive a complete refund on the purchase price should the 'chute fail to open.

Next came the weapons. The combat drop onto Malta for Operation Herkules was a departure from prior German airborne landings, into Norway in April 1940, at the frontier forts of Holland and Belgium in May 1940 and especially the drops on Crete in June 1941. On those occasions the paratrooper's weapons were dropped by parachute in specially constructed bags designed to cushion the impact of landing. The 'troopers had to shed their own parachute harnesses, then find the weapons canisters, unpack them and sort out the weapons and ammunition supplies, a time consuming process. This delay had proved costly at Crete where a number of Fallschirmjager were killed before they could even get to their weapons.

For the drop on Malta a new system was devised. The 'troopers would jump while carrying their own weapons. As they approached the ground they would lower the weapon to the ground ahead of them on an eight-meter rope. This freed the 'troopers hands to help him brace against impact and made his weapon immediately available to him upon landing. This was a vital feature of the plan to drop directly upon the British defenders of the three airfields. Each trooper would also carry from one hundred to two hundred rounds of small caliber ammunition. Ten stick grenades or an 81mm mortar round were in special pouches sewn into his jumpsuit. Other weapons and additional ammunition would be dropped in canisters starting with the second wave.

Gliders were also given their final pre-assault packing and inspection. In the first wave of the assault the gliders would deliver 3,500 men, half the initial assault force. Two basic glider designs were available for the attack.

The DFS 230 glider held a payload of ten men seated in a single row down the center of the fuselage in a compartment separated from the pilot by a thin wooden bulkhead. Simple turnkey handles allowed wide exit hatches to drop from the sides of the craft so that the troopers could exit quickly after landing. Infantry and machine gun squads would use the DFS 230.

The GO 242 model glider was a very much larger craft than the DFS 230, and was equipped with a rear loading hatch and ramp. The GO 242 carried a payload of up to twenty-five men or 4,000 kilograms of cargo and would be used to deliver heavy weapons and supplies to Malta in the first wave, including each regiment's two heavy weapons companies and one of its four machine gun companies. GO 242's would deliver Kubelwagen staff cars, PAK 36 and PAK 38 anti-tank guns and an assortment of motorcycle and motorcycle/sidecar combinations. Kuno Schacht and his radio team would land in a Go 242.

Hundreds of men attended religious services that day, specially conducted by the Division's Chaplains and the local Italian Catholic Clergy. Many letters home were mailed to wives, parents, sweethearts and siblings and each man was given the chance to finalize a will. Every man in the division knew that Malta would be a difficult and hard fought battle. They were under no illusions as to their own personal odds of surviving. The men expected casualties up to fifty percent killed and wounded. But if they held no illusions, neither did they have any doubts. They were going to seize Malta and make it a German base. Now, all that remained was to do it.

>>>>>>>>>>>>>

Arthur Arbottle was born and raised in Manchester, England and until going into the army had never been more than ten miles from his birthplace. At age fourteen he took part-time work in one of Manchester's many cotton mills and in the depths of the depression he and his family were glad of the tiny wages it paid. His father was an out of work ship fitter who took to drink as the depression deepened, his mother a part-time scullery maid at one of the city's fine homes. Between Arthur and his Mum they barely managed to keep a roof over their heads in Manchester's teeming slum and to feed themselves and Arthur's four younger siblings.

When war broke out between Germany and Britain in September 1939 the family's employment prospects brightened. The old man found work again in the shipyards and forsook the bottle. Arthur and his Mum were steadily employed for the first time in years.

It didn't take long though for the situation to change. In May 1940 the French collapse and British withdrawal at Dunkirk suddenly left the Home Islands vulnerable as they had not been since threatened by Napoleon. Pressure mounted for Arthur to join the service. About this time the Old Man began drinking again. Soon it became apparent he resented Arthur, resented having another Man 'o the House, especially one earning more money than he was. It was a mean, poor existence Arthur led, from beating to beating at his father's drunken hands. Nearly anything would be better.

One summer day in 1940 Arthur walked down to the recruiting office near his factory and, at eighteen years of age, joined the local county regiment, The Manchesters, a unit with a long and colorful history. Arthur wasn't interested in the past though; he only wanted to escape Manchester and his father.

He got his wish. Shortly after his training ended he shipped off from Liverpool with the regiment, destination unknown. He was thoroughly seasick from the moment his transport weighed anchor and sailed. He arrived on Malta two weeks later in condition for hospital, not service, but with his feet on dry land he recovered quickly. He settled in to garrison duty on Malta easily and did his work quietly, without coming to the attention of anyone.

A skinny, homely lad Arthur was completely unremarkable, with only one real friend in his platoon, a young lad from Stockport, just outside Manchester. His name was Gordon Lanks and he came from a middle-class family of merchants. Fair and handsome where Arthur was dark and plain, of modest education where Arthur was very nearly illiterate, glib where Arthur was shy, Gordon took a shine to Arthur for some reason no one could fathom, especially Arthur himself. Yet, soon the two were very nearly inseparable. Arthur began to come out of his shell under Gordon's guidance.

The Manchesters were based on Ta Qali Airfield and for months the men worked as ditch diggers, filling bomb craters on the runways and taxi strips, building revetments for the RAF fighters on the field and even assisting the RAF 'Erks in their service and maintenance of the planes. When not repairing the runways or assisting with the aircraft the Manchesters worked preparing defensive positions about the airfield. The work was steady and hard and Arthur filled out and strengthened under the Mediterranean sun.

As the siege tightened in the spring of 1942 the rumor mill ran rampant through the Regiment. Nearly every week an invasion scare ran through the 'other ranks'. When word came down to put the garrison on half rations the men were certain the invasion was imminent. The brief lull at the start of June raised hopes that the siege was lifted, but then Tobruk fell and the Luftwaffe renewed its attention to Malta. The Manchesters worked harder than ever keeping the airfield clear. At the start of the last week of June came the order to prepare landing obstacles on the clear ground around the runways. This was as sure a sign as any that the crisis was at hand.

The afternoon of June 25th Arthur and the men of his platoon were given a twelve-hour leave. Over a hundred men of the regiment were given the evening off, and though no one told the men that invasion was considered likely in as little as three days, they all expected that this would be the last leave many of them would ever take.

On Malta in the summer of 1942 there were many fewer recreational opportunities for the 'other ranks' than there were for the officers and specialists like pilot Kenneth Wiltshire. Clubs like Maxime's were too expensive and anyway, the few English girls on the island who frequented Maxime's and the other clubs like it weren't interested in enlisted soldiers; the officers and pilots were their 'game'.

It was not always so on Malta. Before the war a lively social scene existed for all classes of the island's inhabitants, Maltese, British and visitors alike. Maltese social life centered on the hamlet, village or neighborhood, often revolving around the church. Even the tiniest of villages had its own Catholic Church, often constructed in grandeur out of all proportion to the community it served. Throughout the year a series of religious festivals marked the turn of the seasons for the Maltese. Brightly colored floats built under the direction of the town Priest paraded through the narrow streets, villagers danced in costume and fireworks lit the night sky.

The ruling class of English on the island established the social clubs that characterized the English wherever they colonized. Chief amongst these was the Marsa Race Course and Club near the base of Grand Harbor where the English attended the pony races, played golf and polo and gulped gin. At the Imtarfa club near the ancient citadel of Mdina they played tennis on courts swept clean by Maltese batmen and football on lawns kept manicured by the local Maltese grounds crew. And they still drank their gin. The Opera House in Valletta attracted world-class musical talent.

For the island's elite, the Governor and other titled English as well as the top tier of Colonial bureaucrats the highlights of the social season were the frequent cocktail parties and receptions thrown aboard His Majesty's warships in Grand Harbor. Before the war the Royal Navy's Mediterranean Fleet was based at Malta and there was almost always a battleship or aircraft carrier in port. Royal Navy bands entertained into the wee hours and in keeping with the Royal Navy's "wet" tradition the gin, whiskey and scotch flowed freely.

There was entertainment aplenty for the commoner as well. Cabarets like the Morning Star Club employed pretty young English girls with long, shapely legs to entertain the men of the fleet who came to visit. Alcohol was cheap and abundant with beer and hard liquor just pennies a drink. At the Morning Star and several of the more reputable clubs the entertainment was largely legitimate, but there were other establishments of a seedier nature, where the men could satisfy their most prurient desires.

But by the summer of 1942 the siege had taken its toll on the island's nightlife. The Marsa Race course was taken over by a battalion of the Kents with flak guns dug in around the remains of the stables and trenches crisscrossing the race course. Bombs cratered the courts and playing fields at Imtarfa and the clubhouses were taken over for a military hospital. Rationing of food and liquor forced most of the legitimate clubs out of business. During the spring blitz the lone surviving brewery was bombed and the last stocks of beer were exhausted.

Most of the pre-war population of English girls had long since gone home, though interestingly a small cadre of them found employment with the RAF Operations Center in Valletta or with the Military Intelligence section beneath Lascaris Bastion. These women also maintained a sort of roving dance revue informally known as the 'Whizz-Bangs', comparable on a small scale to the American USO. Many a homesick British soldier found the sight and sound of a girl from home, albeit attired in the most outlandish and bare oriental costumes, a tremendous relief during the siege of Malta. Still, there were others unsatisfied with sights and sounds.

So, Arthur Arbottle and his mates headed for the seediest part of Malta, Straight Street in Valletta, but more popularly known as 'The Gut'. For decades The Gut was Malta's very own Den of Inequity. Innumerable bars, restaurants and nightclubs lined the street, with wild music, cheap liquor and cheaper girls the watchword. For all the devotion to Catholicism among the island's natives, prostitution flourished in The Gut. It was nurtured by a non-stop supply of nubile females who came from nearly every Mediterranean country and was watered every fortnight by the paymasters of the Royal Navy and Army. Some of the women had left their native lands seeking adventure, others to escape the smothering restrictions of traditional cultures. Few intended turning to prostitution, but when they ran out of whatever meager funds they'd set out with they were left with little choice.

This wasn't Arthur's first trip to The Gut. He'd been there as a sort of initiation shortly after arriving on Malta. Once he'd discovered the pleasures of the whores in the red light district he went back as often as he could get leave, spending all his pay there. He didn't care that he was always broke. He didn't expect to live through the war, and anyway he had nothing to go home to. He took pride in being called 'tiger' by the men in the platoon.

Arthur had a favorite house in The Gut. Near the waterfront overlooking Grand harbor it hadn't escaped damage from the bombings, but it was built atop a substantial basement with two subterranean floors and the house's work was conducted underground, both literally and figuratively. The British authorities on Malta may have found prostitution morally repugnant, but aside from monthly lectures to the troops from service doctors and chaplains, whose alternate themes of "clean bodies" and "clean souls" did little for either, the authorities did nothing to discourage the world's oldest profession. They recognized the men needed some release from the monotony, tension and the backbreaking labor they performed at the airfields.

Arthur and the men of his squad crowded into the ancient, coal-burning bus for the ride to Valletta, choking on its fumes as they jolted down the pockmarked gravel road. They'd done their level best to clean themselves up, but hygiene was one of the daily features of life that suffered that spring and summer on Malta and they all smelled. Fortunately, the windows in the bus were blown out by the concussion of a bomb that landed near it in April, so there was adequate ventilation. The men joined in lewd and bawdy songs as they rode down to Valletta. One of the cleanest:

*Kiss me goodnight, Sergeant Major.*
*Tuck me in my little wooden bed.*
*We all love you, Sergeant Major,*
*When we hear you calling - 'Show a leg!'*
*Don't forget to wake me in the morning,*
*And bring me a nice hot cup of tea.*
*Kiss me goodnight Sergeant Major.*
*Sergeant Major, be a mother to me.*

Laughing, Arthur and his friend Gordon piled out of the bus on the outskirts of Floriana, the suburb of Valletta. The streets were so choked with rubble the buses could no longer enter the city itself. Arthur paused as he stepped off the bus. He turned to the west to the sunset, ending the day in a blaze of orange and red. He turned to the east and saw the rising moon, its rim just over the horizon out on the sea. Nearing its full phase, but pale at that moment it would shine its light on the evening's fun in The Gut. The wind gusted, blowing the smell of the sea over Valletta. Most Englishmen have some sense of the sea and the wind and Arthur thought, somewhat absently, that it would be a damp dawn.

Arthur, Gordon and the other men of their platoon moved off, around and over the rubble, through Floriana towards King's Gate, the only landward entrance to Valletta. After entering the old city itself some chose to stop at one or another of the many bars, to drink bathtub whiskey served from empty old bottles of expensive brands.

The Gut was crowded that night. Men from all over the island were there for a few hours leave, looking for a night of release and relief. So intent on the pursuit of pleasure were they that when the inevitable air raid siren sounded shortly before dark they ignored it completely. Even when the crash of bombs and the flak batteries delivered the news of an especially heavy raid against the airfields the men showed a grim determination to drink or make sport with the ladies of the night.

Arthur was determined to be laid that night. Gordon suggested they stop for a drink, but

Arthur shook his head and pressed on in single-minded pursuit of his goal. His favorite house

was called Dolly's and he had in mind his favorite girl, a voluptuous, raven-haired Maltese

named Zita. She had a way of grinding her full hips onto his skinny frame that made him short of

breath every time he thought of her.

Arthur, Gordon and two other men of the platoon came around the corner on the block where

Dolly plied her trade. They stopped short. A queue of at least fifty men waited outside the

entrance to Dolly's and they were in a near riotous mood. Several bottles were passing up and

down the line. Worse than their drunken state, Arthur noticed that the men were from almost every regiment on the island. Inniskillings and Buffs, Devons and Manchesters mingled with

Royal West Kents. Only the King's Own Malta Artillery regiment, composed mainly of native

Maltese, was not represented. The mix was a prescription for a brawl.

A burst of laughter came from the next block as a crowd of soldiers spilled out onto the street

from a bar. A Maltese man followed them out, shouting and waving his arms.

"Doan you boyz come back 'ere tonight," he called after them. "You boyz all wild tonight!"

"All right, chum," one of the troops laughed and called out to the Maltese, "all right. Don't get your pecker up! We'll be back some other time to show you what!" The men laughed and stumbled down the street.

"Ah, come on chums," said one of the men Arthur was with. "I'm not waiting on queue for these whores tonight. We'll be an hour waitin' for one of these sloppy bints."

The other man laughed. "Yeah," he said. "We've no need o' this. Let's have a drink!"

"Right-o!" said the other man. "It'll be a royal piss-up tonight!"

With a laugh and a cheer the men moved off looking for a bar. Gordon lingered for a moment.

"Come on Arthur," he urged. "Look at that queue. You'll wait all night for sloppy seconds."

Arthur shook his head. "No," he said. "I have Zita in mind."

As Gordon ran off to catch up to the other men Arthur moved alone towards Dolly's. He approached the queue slowly and settled in quietly at its end. He had no interest in fighting with the other regiments that night; he only wanted Zita. The thought of the number of men she would have been with that night before he could get to her forced its way into his mind. He closed his eyes and pushed the image away, replacing it with the vision of Zita's enormous breasts bouncing above his face. He lost himself in the vision, letting the fantasy arouse him. He lost track of himself for a few minutes, standing there in line at Dolly's with his eyes closed, thinking of Zita. The queue ahead of him moved as a fresh batch of paying customers was admitted to the underground whorehouse. Behind him a group of five Devons had gotten on queue. They were passing a bottle of cheap liquor and it wasn't the first of the evening for them. They were pretty well pissed already. When Arthur didn't move forward promptly with the queue the Devons began to slip past him. He awakened from his reverie just in time to object.

"Here now, no queue jumping!" he shouted. "You lot can wait your turn just like anyone else."

"All right mate, all right," said one of the Devons, the leader, a big, blond country boy from the southwest of England. "Don't get your pecker up with us, now. You're a might slight to pick a row with the five o' us."

"Well, all right," Arthur said, grudgingly. "Just wait your turn."

The sun's last rays disappeared over the bombed and blasted rooftops of Valletta and darkness descended. Arthur waited on queue, growing more and more impatient with the pace. Finally another group of men left the basement whorehouse. The queue advanced again. Arthur hopped from one foot to the other. He counted the queue. At least thirty to go. He sighed.

>>>>>>>>>>>>

Major Kuno Schacht walked to his glider at 2145 hours. All over the airfield men were marching to their assigned machines, the transports or gliders. A curious silence hung over the men. Their conversations were muted when they spoke at all. The tramp of boots and the clank of weapons and equipment were the only sounds heard on the field as thousands of men prepared to launch the greatest airborne assault in history.

Kuno approached his command, the fourteen-man regimental communications squad. They were lounging on the ground around the GO 242 glider that would carry them to Malta. Sgt. Rudel, the glider's pilot was making his last inspection of the tow-hook and cable connecting the Go 242 to the Ju 52 transport that would tow it. He came to attention as Kuno walked up.

"Everything is in order, Herr Major," he said. "The machine is ready for you and your men to board." Kuno nodded and turned back to his command. They looked at him expectantly.

"We will wait for the signal," he said. He turned and looked over the field. Everywhere in the gloom men were reaching their aircraft. The sounds of movement slowly died to be replaced by an eerie quiet. At Gerbini and Comiso, 7,000 men waited in silence for the signal to board the aircraft. The minutes ticked by with the rising moon in the east casting the field in an eerie two-tone tableau of orange and black. Trees at the field's edge and the aircraft themselves cast deep, black pools of shadow.

Kuno sat. He was fitted with paratrooper jump gear, though not with a 'chute. He wore the rimless paratrooper helmet, straps dangling loose under his chin. He pulled a cigarette from a box in his tunic then offered the box to his second in command, Lt. Steup, gesturing for the cigarettes to be shared out among the men. The box moved down the line of men seated against the sides of the glider. One by one the men lit up. A soft chuckle ran through the group as a young private named Schuenemann who didn't smoke coughed on his first drag on a cigarette. A figure approached out of the gloom. Kuno stood and saluted as the Baron Von der Heydte came to the Go 242 glider on his final rounds before boarding began.

"At ease, Major," said the Baron. "Are you and your men ready in all respects?"

"Yes, Colonel," replied Kuno. "We await the signal."

"Good, good," answered the Baron, absently. "Um, have you double checked the crystals in your radios? We can't have any foul-ups on frequencies, you know."

"Yes, Colonel. All is in order."

"Good, good."

The Baron turned to the men on the ground by the glider. They began to rise to attention, but he waved them down.

"Is everyone ready?" he asked. "All last minute preparations are complete?"

"Yes, Sir," and "Yes, Colonel," the men answered softly.

"Good, good," he replied. "You must take good care of Major

Schacht," he told them. "As you know he has never ridden a glider. I'm relying on you experienced men to bring him safely home." More murmured assurances from the men.

"Good, good," the Baron said. "Good luck to you all."

"Good luck to you, Colonel," the men answered in unison, softly.

As he turned to move on to the next craft the Baron took Kuno by the arm.

"Remember Schacht," he said. "We have a date to visit Calypso's cave on Malta."

Kuno smiled. "I plan to keep it, Colonel," he said.

The Baron smiled and moved on. Kuno turned to the east and looked at the rising moon. It was finally getting bright enough for the aircraft to take-off. He looked at his watch. 2205 hours. The signal to board would come soon.

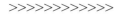

Another group of soldiers staggered out of Dolly's and a moment later the queue moved again. Arthur now stood four places from the entrance. He smiled. He would be in the next group to enter. He looked at his watch. 2205 hours. Another fifteen minutes and he'd be with Zita.

Raucous laughter burst out down the street. He looked towards the sound and saw that a fight had broken out between two soldiers. Shouts of encouragement came from a crowd that gathered as the two drunks circled each other warily then crashed together, more wrestling than boxing. The men waiting in Dolly's queue hooted and whistled as the two combatants fell to the ground in a heap, with little harm done to either of them. Willing hands reached out from the crowd, helping each man to his feet and propelling them together again. Half blind punches were thrown till one of the men landed a lucky punch. His opponent sagged on rubbery knees and collapsed to the ground. A derisive cheer greeted the end of the match.

"Boy-o," said the big Devon behind Arthur. "The lad's have all got their peckers up, haven't they?"

"God help Jerry if he comes tonight!" said another. They all laughed, even Arthur.

The queue moved again and Arthur was in the door.

"What's your pleasure tonight, Dearie?" asked Dolly when his turn came to speak to the Madame. Dolly stood in the rubble filled stairwell to the basement, collecting payment from the customers as they entered. Dolly was an aged English whore with enormous, sagging breasts revealed by a low cut, dirty, white silk negligee. Pancake makeup and a platinum blond wig done in an enormous bun atop her head completed a vision to scare many a patron away, but Dolly treated each man like a king for his crowns and shillings. At least on most nights, but the evening of June 25th was a landmark in the history of prostitution on Malta. Men in the hundreds visited every house in The Gut and the whores were very busy. There was no time for pleasantries.

"I want Zita," said Arthur. "Straight."

"Oh, Zita," said Dolly, nodding and smiling. "She's very busy tonight, Love. Ten shillings, please."

"Ten shillings!" exclaimed Arthur. "I've never paid that before!"

"Ah, Dearie," Dolly chuckled, "if you're here to waste my time then I can have Charlie here show you some fun for free." She put her hand on the arm of an enormous, swarthy Maltese with a livid knife scar across his cheek. Charlie stood impassively, his arms folded, staring at Arthur.

"No," said Arthur hurriedly. "I can pay. I'll pay." He dug in his pockets until he'd counted out enough coins to pay the Madame.

"Thank you, Dearie," Dolly cooed as the coins disappeared somewhere in her negligee. "Zita'll be ready in just a few minutes. She wants to make herself all pretty for you!" she laughed.

Arthur stood in the stone stairwell waiting his turn. He checked his watch. 2250. An air raid siren began to wail in the streets outside Dolly's but no one left. They were as safe in the basement of the whorehouse as in any shelter they could get to. A door opened at the bottom of the stairs and a soldier, buttoning his pants came up towards Arthur.

"There you are, Dearie," said Dolly. "Zita's ready for you now."

Watching the man come up the stairs the thought of following so closely behind another suddenly hit Arthur hard. He turned to look at Dolly. He briefly considered demanding his money back, but one look at Charlie told him that would be no good. He swallowed hard and went down the stairs. The air raid sirens continued to wail as he entered Zita's tiny bedchamber.

>>>>>>>>>>>>>

At 2315 hours yellow flares went up over Gerbini and Comiso. Pilots began the process of starting the engines of the transports. Ground crew stood by with fire extinguishers, prepared in the not uncommon event of an engine bursting into flames at ignition. The paratroops would not enter any transport or its tethered glider until its engines were safely started. The roar of engines echoed across the field at Gerbini, rising to deafening levels. Kuno and the men in his squad covered their ears against the roar as the engines of their own transport came to life. When the pilots were satisfied the engines were up and running smoothly they signaled out the cockpit windows to the crew chiefs. They in turn waved white flags to the paratroopers, their signal to begin boarding the aircraft. Such was the attention to the maintenance of the aircraft that not one engine fire was reported in the launching of the first wave that night at either Gerbini or Comiso airdromes.

By the time Kuno and his men received their signal, transports and gliders all over the field were taxiing to takeoff positions. The men boarded hurriedly once the signal was given. They strapped themselves into their crash positions, each man double-checking the snaps of the men nearest him.

At the fields' control towers teams of officers used hooded signal lamps to guide aircraft into position, bare meters separating the whirling propeller blades of each Ju 52 tri-motor from the tail rudder of the plane or glider ahead. When all was ready with all planes lined up for the fastest possible take-offs, a green flare was fired from the tower. The time was 2340.

From the moment the first transport-glider combination left the ground the pace was furious. On each of the field's four runways a Ju 52 and its towed charge took off every fifteen to twenty seconds, thirteen a minute over all. The first craft in the air circled the field waiting to form the first 'V' shaped wings on their way to Malta. In an amazing piece of well-rehearsed coordination the entire transport force was off the ground from the two fields in just eighteen minutes.

From Catania airfield, near Gerbini the bombers and transports and the fighter escorts for both were launched. Heinz Sauckel and his Bf 109 were among those flying on the first sortie. A fleet of Ju 88 and Ju 87 bombers raced ahead of the first wave of transports. A hundred fighters escorted over one hundred bombers in total. Ahead of the main bomber strike six JU 87 Stukas and four Bf 109 fighters flew low over the water to avoid radar detection until the last possible moment.

Kenneth and Maggie lay in each other's arms, naked on the rug in front of the fireplace in the old stone cottage at St, Paul's Bay. The last red spark from their fire was dead, but they both still felt its glow.

He ran his fingertips down her spine, from the nap of her neck to the top of her cheeks, then traced the smooth, round outline there. She shuddered at his touch. After a moment of this torture she reached behind her, pulled his hand up to her shoulders and held it there.

He looked down at her face, snuggled in the crook of his arm. Her eyelash brushed his chest when she blinked. He began drifting into the dreamy state between wake and sleep.

"Kenneth?" she said softly.

"Hhmm?" he murmured. His hand began to stray again. She let it wander, closing her eyes, letting goose bumps creep onto her flesh.

"Kenneth?" she said again.

He opened his eyes and rolled onto his side, facing her.

"Yes, love?" he said.

"When this all ends, where will you go? What will you do?"

He propped his head up on his elbow and looked at her.

"I don't know Maggie, not for sure at any rate." He thought a moment. "Only things I know how to do are raise wheat and fly. I expect I'll want to stay in aviation, one way or another. Not much interest in wheat anymore."

He caressed her breast. She took his hand again, but this time she held it in place, guiding it, teaching him. She closed her eyes and sighed, as her nipple grew erect.

"Wherever I am," he went on, "I want you there."

She looked back into his face and saw her love reflected there. She smiled and moved his hand slowly down her belly.

"I'll be there Kenneth," she said. "I swear it."

On Straight Street Arthur finally made his way down Dolly's cellar steps. He entered Zita's chamber full of reticence and when he first saw her he almost turned and ran. She was tired and it showed. Dark circles under her eyes and the lethargic way she greeted him were a great disappointment. She was clothed in a simple, short robe, dirty white, tied about her waist and open at the neck, revealing her great plunging cleavage. Her full, smooth thighs were bare.

The room held a bed, little more than a cot, a tiny nightstand with mirror and a chair sized to fit. They looked like a child's furniture. All but the bed. Rumpled and soiled it looked used and was not very inviting to Arthur. Zita stood, facing the wall, her back to Arthur as he sat on the edge of the bed.

Zita turned and stared, deadpan, at him. Then, never taking her eyes from his she began slowly to untie the knot in her robe. As she loosened the strings the robe worked open at her neck, revealing more and more of those magnificent breasts. The robe fell open, but still covered her nipples and she demurely kept her hands over her pubic area. Arthur sat back and stared at her hands. He was becoming warm and felt the surge of blood in his loins. He looked back at her face. She had a little smile and was looking out from under her eyelashes. She averted her gaze, looking down at her hands. She began to move her hands up her body, slowly reaching under the robe to pinch her own nipples. She rolled her head back and closed her eyes, leaving just a slit open to keep an eye on Arthur. The boy was starting to sweat and not just from the warm, stuffy atmosphere in the bedchamber. His eyes were wide and wondering. He'd not seen this performance yet, from Zita or any of the others.

Zita let out a small cry and began to breathe heavily, to pant. Her mouth hung open and she began to sway, bending at the knees and rocking back against the wall. She looked at him, snapping her head forward with such force that Arthur fell back on the bed with a cry. He pushed himself back on the bed against the wall, in awe and fear. Zita plunged her hand into her groin and began to rub herself. Wild-eyed, she stared at Arthur and moaned. She rolled her head and her long, jet-black hair tossed about her head.

Arthur's blood pounded in his ears. He was already on the verge and didn't know how much more he could take. He hadn't touched Zita yet, but he knew already he was having the sexual experience of his young life. With a cry Zita tore away her robe, revealing her glorious, full body. Gasping, she jumped at Arthur. He cringed away, trying to press himself through the wall behind him. She planted her knees on either side of him and grabbed him by the belt, nearly lifting his skinny frame off the bed as she tore at his fly. She yanked his trousers down to his knees and grabbed his cock, stroking him as she moved to mount him.

Arthur could hold himself no longer. He shouted, "God help me!" and arched his back, thrusting his pelvis to meet her. But he never made it. He came before he entered her. She settled back on her haunches, sitting on his knees and fondled him, stroking him till he was spent. She leaned down and kissed him quickly on the cheek. Just as quickly she'd rolled off him and was back in her robe.

He lay on the bed gasping for breath.

"Come on sweetie," Zita said. "Pull your nappies up."

Arthur collected himself slowly. He stood up, buttoning his fly, still shaky, but already re-living the experience in his mind's eye. He looked at Zita. She'd sat down in the tiny chair, her legs crossed, the robe tied smartly about her waist again.

He smiled at her. "Next time," he said, "you'll not get off so easy."

She smiled back, sweetly. "Promise?"

At St. Paul's Bay Kenneth gently eased away from Maggie. He

looked down at her nude, sleeping body and felt himself stir again. He closed his eyes and turned away. He knew she needed sleep. He covered her with his flying jacket and stepped into the little kitchen for a smoke. As he lit up an air raid siren began to sound. He shook his head and held his watch up to the burning match. 2345.

"Bloody Eye-ties," he muttered.

He stepped to the kitchen window and pushed open the wooden shutters. There'd never been any glass in the cottage's windows. He looked out over the moonlit shore.

"Bright enough to fly tonight," he murmured aloud to himself. He went on smoking, leaning on the window frame and staring out into the bright moonlit night.

At 2350 six Stuka dive-bombers rose from the sea and flattened out at 6,000 feet above Valletta. Certainly the defenders on the ground knew the bombers were there, but anti-aircraft ammunition was too precious to waste on the nuisance bombing Italians, the only attackers that came to Malta at night. No flak greeted the Stukas.

The leader tipped over in his dive and the other planes in the flight followed. Within seconds the gull-winged bombers that had inspired such terror across Europe were hurtling earthward, each plane carrying a 1,800-kilogram bomb under the fuselage and a 500-kilo bomb under each wing.

The flight leader had studied his target carefully for days. Aerial reconnaissance photos were taken every day for a week, from all possible angles to assure the target could be easily identified. Grimly he centered his bombsite. He knew the other five handpicked pilots of his flight were right behind him. At 800 meters a single flak gun on the ground opened up. Too late. The lone alert gunner had no time to range and find the Stuka's altitude. At 350 meters the flight leader toggled his bomb release and pulled back on the stick, coming out of the dive. In quick succession the five planes behind him dropped their deadly loads and peeled out of their dives.   The eighteen high-explosive bombs hurtled to earth, slamming into a city block on the outskirts of Valletta.

Kenneth stood in the little kitchen, smoking his cigarette, tapping the ash out the windowsill and staring at the moon dappled waters of St. Paul's Bay. The air raid siren continued to sound.

From the south a string of short, sharp cracks indicated a flak gun had opened fire, but he'd heard that a thousand times and he went on staring at the peaceful waters of the bay. A series of quick, heavy explosions from behind him, to the south broke his reverie. He frowned. The pattern of explosions was wrong. The night bombing Italians dropped their bombs randomly and at wide intervals. These blasts were tightly grouped, so close together he couldn't count them, but he was sure that over a dozen heavy bombs had landed in quick succession in a small area. Precision bombing. German bombing.

He stood smoking his cigarette in the dark mulling over the sounds just heard. After about five minutes he stubbed his cigarette out on the sill and started to turn to go back in the cabin to sleep. He stopped and cocked an ear. Aero engines, distant, but getting closer. Quietly he stepped through the tiny front room, past the sleeping form of his lover. For a moment he paused and looked at Maggie. Her hair was spilled across her cheek and the flight jacket he'd covered her with left her creamy white legs bare.

The sound of the engines brought him back again. Still nude he stepped through the front door into the yard and looked up into the sky. The sound of the engines was increasing with every second, but still no aircraft could be seen. Kenneth looked up and down the shore. Deserted. The other cottages nearby were all dark. The pony was tethered to the post at the corner of the house, stomping and shifting nervously at the rising sound. The beast knew from months of experience that the sound of aero engines meant danger. Kenneth looked back into the sky, searching in all directions, but still could see nothing. There was plenty of moonlight. Anything within his line of sight should have been visible. The sound of the engines grew louder.

"Kenneth?"

He turned around to the cottage door. Maggie was there, clutching his flight jacket tightly about her shoulders.

"Get dressed, Maggie," he said. "Quick!"

"What is it, Kenneth?" she asked. Her voice sounded her fear.

"I don't know," he answered, "but it's big. Now go get dressed!" He had to raise his voice to be heard over the approaching roar.

He turned and looked again into the sky. The roar was

approaching from the north, he was sure, but still no aircraft could be seen. He went back into the cottage, grabbing his trousers and shirt. Maggie was buttoning her blouse.

"Come on," he said. "Finish dressing in the cart."

He hopped out into the yard, pulling his pants on as he went.

"Bring our shoes!" he shouted. He put his arms in the sleeves of his shirt, but didn't bother to button it.

The occupants of the other cottages on the bay-shore were beginning to come out of their homes, awakened by the noise. Kenneth began harnessing the pony to the cart, glancing at the sky as he worked on the traces. His fingers fumbled with the snaps.

He closed his eyes. "Calm down, Kenneth. Get a grip!" he said to himself.

"KENNETH!" Maggie screamed at him.

He turned. She was pointing into the night, to the north. He looked up where she was pointing and gasped. The sky was filling with aircraft, twin and single engine bombers and fighters. The bombers were in V shaped wing formations of from five to eight craft. Kenneth counted twelve wings before losing his place.

He looked back at Maggie. She was shouting something to him, but the roar of the engines was now deafening and he couldn't hear. He pointed to the cart and yelled for her to get in. He was almost done with the harness, but now the pony was badly spooked. He fought to control it, hauling the bridle back as he clambered onto the seat.

The first waves of planes were passing overhead. He estimated their altitude at just 3,000 feet and he recognized the bombers as Ju 88s and Ju 87s, the fighters as Bf 109s. He gave the pony its head and they raced onto the road. Maggie sat on his right, clutching her arms about his waist while still trying to keep their shoes aboard with them.

"Where are we going?" shouted Maggie.

"Get you back to your billet at Rinella," he shouted. "Me to Ta Qali."

A series of quick flashes lit the horizon to his south, in the direction of Ta Qali. Seconds later Kenneth felt as much as heard the dull rumble of exploding bombs. He struggled to keep the cart on the road as the roar of the airplane engines continued, wave after thundering wave directly over their heads. The flashes from the south intensified till they ran together as one flickering light rather than distinct flashes. Streams of glowing red and white flak shells lifted from the ground to the south in long, graceful arcs. Searchlight beams snapped on and probed the night sky, picking out targets for the gunners on the ground to aim at.

He snatched glances at the sky whenever a straight stretch let him dare take his eyes from the road. As they approached the turn to skirt around Mosta and the shattered dome of its ruined cathedral he looked up and his heart fell to the pit of his stomach. Ju 52 transports towing gliders roared overhead. The German invasion of Malta was beginning.

Maggie screamed in his ear and tugged on his bare arm. He shot her a quick glance. She was pointing back behind them and he suddenly became aware of the sound of an aircraft engine in a dive. He hauled back hard on the traces. The pony reared and skidded sideways, its feet scrabbling for purchase on the loose dirt road as the cart careened along behind it. It was on the verge of regaining it's footing when it hit a stretch of broken, limestone gravel, poured on the road to fill a bomb crater. The pony folded at the knees and went down, dragging the cart into the ditch behind it.

Kenneth and Maggie were thrown from the cart in a tumbling heap, fetching up against a stonewall separating a farm field from the road. The cart tipped over and hit the wall with a splintering crash just feet away from them. Machine gun and cannon fire raked the road where just seconds before the cart and its passengers had been. The BF 109 thundered away to more important errands.

Kenneth shook his head. He was on his back, pressed up against the stone of the wall. He put a hand to his right temple and found blood running down his cheek to his neck. There was a gash and a nasty knot rising already, but his head began to clear, slowly. The thunder of engines continued without letup. He realized the Germans were throwing hundreds of aircraft against Malta. Over the roar he heard the pony whinny, a long, frightened cry of pain.

He took a mental inventory, wiggling toes and fingers, flexing knees and elbows. Many sore and tender spots told of bruises, cuts and abrasions, but so far as he could tell nothing was broken. In the back of his mind though was the nagging feeling that he was forgetting something, something very important. He tried to sit up, but felt a weight pressing him down.

Only then did he realize his eyes were still closed. He made a conscious effort to open them and his right eye stung with blood when he did. He tried to focus with just his left eye, but became dizzy and closed it again. He pushed against the weight; it was soft and yielding and rolled away from him. He sat up carefully and tried opening his left eye again. For a moment the world spun about him, but he concentrated fiercely and his vision began to settle down. He wiped his right eye as best he could and found he could see from it as well, though blurred. He used the sleeve of his shirt to wipe it out more and to clear the blood from his face. He looked up into the sky. Transports and gliders still roared over his head. He looked down at his hands, then at the pony. It lay in the road, struggling to get to its feet, but its front right leg was useless, clearly broken.

The cart! He'd been thrown from it. They'd been thrown from it. MAGGIE! He nearly swooned when he realized she had been with him when the cart went off the road. He cast about for her and was shocked to find her right at his side. He realized she was the weight that had held him down.

She lay completely still on her back next to him. There were no evident injuries, yet there was no motion at all. He held his breath and stared at her motionless body. He looked for signs of breathing, but her body appeared perfectly still and lifeless. He reached out his hand and patted her shoulder.

"Maggie?" he asked.

Even without the roaring engines over his head his voice would have sounded small and weak. The terrible thought that she was dead tried to crowd into his head, but he crushed it back, unwilling to think such a thing.

"Maggie?" He reached out tentatively to touch her again. He laid his hand on her forehead. It felt cold to his touch. He leaned down and put his ear to her mouth, but his hearing was numb from the constant thunder in the sky. He felt at her throat for a pulse, but the very ground was vibrating beneath them from the waves of planes passing directly overhead and he could feel nothing through the shaking.

He smoothed the hair back from her face. He wondered what to do. He looked at the horse. It staggered to its feet, but was holding its right leg off the ground, curled under it. It looked back at him miserably and nickered. There was no way the animal could carry either of them, or pull the cart. He looked at the cart. It had fetched up against the wall, but it appeared intact.

He looked at the girl. "I'll be right back, Maggie," he said.

He climbed unsteadily to his feet and stumbled over to the cart. It was upside down, its wheels in the air. He pulled it away from the wall and heaved it over upright. The axle was sound and the wheels unbroken. He looked up in the sky where the transports and gliders were still streaming over his head. He followed their course to the south. In the distance he could see streams of tracers and the flash of exploding flak shells over the airfield. Ta Qali was still fighting back. The bigger flashes of heavy bombs exploding had stopped as the bombers cleared the field for the following transports. As he watched the AA fire sputtered and began to die. Puffs of white suddenly blossomed over the field. Parachutes opening. He turned back to Maggie.

"I have to move you, Maggie," he said. "I'll try not to hurt." He knew she wasn't hearing him; couldn't have heard him even without the planes overhead. It didn't matter. He wanted to talk to her, even if she couldn't hear or answer.

"I'm going to put you on the cart, Maggie."

He worked his arms under her knees and her shoulders and hefted her off the ground. She was so light. He felt the soft flesh of her body through her clothes as he set her on the cart seat. He started to sob as he used the buggy's traces to tie her securely to the seat. He put his hand on her cheek. He bent to kiss her, but couldn't bring himself to touch her lips. Instead he brushed her cheek.

He turned around and took the cart's harness arms under his armpits. He began to pull. As he did he realized the roar was diminishing. He looked up again and saw the last wave of transports passing overhead. To the north the sky was clear. He looked at his watch. 0011. Just a short while earlier Maggie was asleep in his arms. Now he was pulling her lifeless body down a dirt road and he did not know where he was going or why.

When Arthur left Dolly's after his encounter with Zita he resolved to not share all the details with the men of his platoon. They'd laugh at him for letting Zita work him for a 'quickie' and an expensive one at that. Air raid sirens were still wailing when he exited Dolly's stairwell. The line of men waiting for their turn with the whores was just as long as before and they appeared just as unconcerned by the sirens.

Arthur began to walk slowly up the hill to the bus stop. He was in no particular hurry to get back to the regiment, but he had only a few pennies left; not enough for further entertainment. He picked his way through the rubble-strewn streets, working his way up the hill towards King's Gate and the bus stop beyond. Soldiers of all the island's regiments were on the streets, moving from bars to brothels and back to the bars again. More than a few fights had erupted and the MP's were busy locking men up for the night.

Arthur was re-living his experience with Zita when he heard a shout.

"Oy! Arthur!" He turned and saw his friend Gordon coming up the hill towards him. Gordon was alone and weaving as he walked.

"Hello, Gord-o," he greeted his friend. "It's a piss-up is it?" Arthur observed.

"And wot of it?" smiled Gordon, bleary-eyed. "I s'pose you had more fun with the whores?"

"Come on, Gord-o. Let's get you back to camp."

"Not before we form a relief party," Gordon slurred drunkenly.

"All right Gord-o," Arthur said. "Here, behind this wall chum."

Arthur stood by as Gordon urinated behind the front door of a bomb-shattered house. The two friends continued up the hill, passing through King's Gate, leaving Valletta, crossing the Great Ditch and entering Floriana. Several times Arthur had to catch Gordon as his drunken friend stumbled and nearly fell. Lost in thought about Zita, Arthur steered Gordon round the corner near the Telephone Exchange building and bumped right into a man turning the corner the other way.

"'ere now," the man said. "Be careful, mate."

The man had a low forehead and small, close set eyes and was built like a hay baler.

"It was you, you big lummox," snapped Arthur.

Immediately, he regretted his mouth, for the man was not only a big lummox, but had three friends with him. Arthur tried to slide around the man, but his friends quickly blocked his path, growling and muttering angrily.

"Oh, a big lummox, am I?" asked the man, in a deep, slow voice. "Well, then, you must be a small fry!"

Arthur knew he should bite his tongue, but something about the big, stupid face leering at him made it impossible to keep his mouth shut.

"A brilliant lummox at that!" said Arthur. "Then you must be a small fry," he mimicked the man, sticking his lower jaw out and hunching his shoulders.

"Is that so?" growled the lummox. "Well, let's just see 'ow smart you are when you're in 'ospital!"

Gordon chose this moment to intervene on Arthur's behalf.

"My good man," he began drunkenly, slurring his words badly. "Kindly remove your lummox hands from this poor boy."

The lummox peered at Gordon in the gloom a moment, then turned to his friends and said, "Oy, look wot we 'as 'ere, chums. A member of the bleedin' peerage 'e is!"

The other three men, all brutes like their friend, closed the ring about Arthur and Gordon, pressing them back into the entry doorway of a bombed out building. Arthur stepped back, casting about for some way out of his dilemma. Across the street two MP's guarded the entrance to the Telephone Exchange, but they showed no sign or inclination to intervene on his behalf. He started to cry for help, but the lummox clapped a meaty hand across his mouth, stifling any sound. Two of the other brutes did the same with Gordon. Arthur felt himself taken under each armpit and hauled backwards into the dark recess of the door.

The lummox leaned in close to Arthur's face examining him closely. Arthur was wide-eyed with fright. He broke into an instant sweat. The Lummox said nothing, but moved his face about Arthur's as if sniffing him. A flak gun somewhere nearby opened up. The lummox paused for a moment and his friends looked back over their shoulders, but the hand stayed clamped over Arthur's mouth and the grip under his arms didn't relax at all. Arthur stared past the Lummox at the MP's across the street. They stepped down from the portico and gazed skyward.

With a sudden shout the MP's ran from the telephone exchange and for one second Arthur thought they were going to help them after all, but they passed his doorway on the dead run without so much as a glance at him. Then he heard the airplane engines. It was a sound he'd heard many times before at the airfield; Stukas in a dive.

The brutes didn't know what to do. Arthur squirmed and tried to speak, but the grips tightened on his arms and over his mouth. He closed his eyes and thrashed in the hands of the brutes, but they didn't let go. The bombs struck.

Arthur was hammered back against the door and a great, black cloud of dust and dirt and stone was hurled into his face. The sound followed the blast wave, but Arthur heard nothing. The bodies of his four assailants absorbed most of the blast, but they in turn were hurled against him, crushing him under their weight, smothering him in a heap under their lifeless bodies. The rain of heavy debris began as stone and timbers from the Telephone Exchange and surrounding buildings fell back to earth. The overhang of the recessed doorway collapsed; the remaining shell of the upper stories of the gutted building followed with a crash. Arthur swam into unconsciousness.

When rescue teams arrived at the telephone exchange minutes later, there was nothing to tell them that a doorway across the street concealed four brutes and two boys from Manchester. They ignored the heap of rubble there.

## Day 6
June 26, 1942

The flight was smoother and quieter than he'd expected. From the moment they'd lifted off the runway at Gerbini the GO 242 glider settled into the slipstream of its Ju 52 tug and performed beautifully. Kuno might almost have thought he was riding in the rear seat of the finest automobile. The drone of their tow craft's engines seemed distant, though still loud enough to make conversation impossible.

Not that any of the men wanted conversation at this point anyway. Each was lost in his own thoughts. Some men dreamed of home and family, others prayed, for their lives or for their souls. A few looked forward to the coming fight. Each knew that odds were good he'd soon be a casualty, dead or wounded.

The great air fleet thundered on through the moonlit night. By the time the last of the transport/glider combinations of the first wave was off the ground the lead elements, carrying the lead troops bound for Hal Far were already halfway to Malta. Behind them came the 7th Regiment whose target was Luqa airfield. Kuno with the 6th Paratroop Regiment along with the 2nd Regiment brought up the rear. Their target was the most important of the three airfields, Ta Qali.

At first Kuno looked out through the large windows in the GO 242's sides, but there was little to see, save for other nearby aircraft. Soldiers in general and paratroopers in particular are famous for their ability to sleep at will, but with such a short flight Kuno didn't expect anyone to doze off. Yet, incredibly several men in his glider seemed to do just that, mouths open, heads lolled to one side or other. Faint snatches of snoring could be heard over the transport's engines.

Kuno checked his watch. 2359. They should be crossing the Malta coastline within minutes. He looked to the front of the fuselage. Three small light bulbs in a row, colored green, yellow and red were at the top of the bulkhead separating the pilot and the cockpit from the passenger and cargo area. The green light came on shortly after takeoff and indicated ten minutes or less to landing. The yellow light would come on inside two minutes of landing, the red indicating the pilot was about to set down. The passengers would brace for impact when they saw the red light. As he watched, the green light flickered off and the yellow came on. He looked again at his watch. 0000. Midnight.

Other sounds came to him. Deep, rumbling thumps and sharp, short cracks; bombs exploding on the ground, flak shells in the air. A shift in the gliders center of balance threw Kuno forward against his straps. He'd been told this signified the glider had released its tow cable and was free sailing. The sensation of speed increased as the glider nosed over in a shallow dive. The red light lit up on the bulkhead. In the passenger compartment the men were all awake now and they braced themselves against one another. They tucked their knees in tight together and crossed their arms at the wrists over their chests, gripping the straps of their shoulder restraints.

Kuno stole a glance out the window beside him. Images flashed past, almost too fast for him to see. Stone walled structures, gutted by bombs, white parachutes opened like moon flowers in the sky, bomb craters on a road, a crashed and burning glider, blazing men tumbling through its escape hatches and about it on the ground.

Kuno was thrown forward again, harder this time as the pilot deployed the drogue parachute behind the craft just before touch down. The drogue slowed the glider marginally, but its purpose was to stabilize the glider on impact, preventing it from fish tailing as it bounced across uneven ground.

A heavy THUMP from under his feet told Kuno the glider had touched down and bounced back into the air. The two heavy tires under the fuselage near the wing roots absorbed the initial impact. The Go 242 settled back to ground and bounced again. The pilot held its nose in the air as long as possible, then it dropped down and the heavy skid plate under the cockpit slid across the ground.

The glider had slowed noticeably when suddenly it pin-wheeled on its left wing and was thrown sideways. The skid plate caught and tipped the right wing down where its tip dug into the ground. The wing was torn from the craft with a great, tearing, crunch. Several men on the left of the cabin were torn free of their restraints and were thrown across the cabin, flying into the men on the other side. Wind came in through the torn fuselage as the glider continued to spin. It came to rest having spun all around, its nose pointed back in the direction from which it had come. Stars flew in

Kuno's eyes. He was dazed from the shock of the landing. He rubbed and slapped his face briskly to restore his wits. The familiar sound of small arms fire came to his ears. He fumbled with his snaps for a moment before collecting his wits sufficiently to undo them. Other men were stirring as well.

"Come on!" he yelled. "Get out before the Tommies find our range!" He twisted the handle on the starboard side exit hatch and shoved. It was jammed shut, twisted in its frame. He jumped across to the port side exit. It dropped open instantly. He unsnapped and hauled out the heavy pack of radio batteries from under his own seat and leapt out into the night. A rifle bullet smacked into the fuselage right behind him.

Crouching low he looked around for a likely spot away from the glider to set up his post and establish first radio contact. Numerous small fires burned nearby; together with the bright moonlight they illuminated the airfield. Low rock walls and cairns lay all about with barbed wire entanglements in between. Bombs had blasted breaches in both the rock walls and the barbed wire and in many places gliders had done further damage to these barriers.

In front of his own glider's nose, back along the glider's path on the ground about thirty meters lay a low wall, about one meter high, composed of loosely set stones. He saw that this wall explained the glider's gyrations at the end of its landing. The rock wall had caught the left side undercarriage, spinning the glider 180 degrees. Stones were torn from the wall and scattered along the gliders path.

In the sky the last of the Junkers transports were peeling away from the airfield, the final sticks of paratroopers floating to earth. Parachutes on the ground billowed in the wind; mostly discarded they blew away toward the north end of the field until they snagged a rock or a glider. A few were anchored in place, still attached to their dead owners.

Others of Kuno's team were jumping out of the glider now, carrying weapons and communication gear; radios, batteries, field telephones and spools of cable, the glider was loaded. It would take several trips to unload everything. The crackle of small arms fire was increasing steadily. They would have to hurry to get everything out of the glider safely.

His second-in-command, Lt. Steup tumbled through the

hatchway, landing with a thud and a great "Woomph!" on his back, dropping the ammunition case he was carrying.

A machine gun chattered somewhere nearby, the heavy, throaty bark of a British Vickers. Schacht jumped to help Steup to his feet. The man had the wind knocked out of him, but there was no time for him to recover.

"Get up, Steup!" shouted Kuno. "Get on your feet!" He planted a kick on the man's hip. "Move the men to those rocks over there. NOW!"

Steup, gasping for breath, responded. He rolled over and grabbed up the ammo box. He ran with it stooped over, staggering really, to the rock wall. He dropped himself down on the far side of the wall.

Kuno re-entered the glider. One man only remained behind, the young private named Schuenemann seeing his first combat. The boy was terrified, his mouth hung open slack and spittle dripped from his chin. Tears streamed down his face. He sat in his seat, still strapped in. He started as Kuno came in the hatch.

"Mutti!" he cried. Mommy.

Kuno took two quick steps to the lad. "I'm not your mother!" he shouted and slapped the boy hard, once, twice across each cheek. He unsnapped the boy's restraint harness and hauled him to his feet by the pockets of his jump suit.

"Get your ass out Schuenemann!" he shouted at the boy and flung him through the hatch.

A grenade exploded close at hand and the Vickers started up again. Kuno grabbed a satchel filled with stick grenades and dove through the hatch. The Vickers had found the range and a stream of bullets peppered the fuselage over the exit door. The young private was on his hands and knees, the shock he'd experienced overcome by the shame of being slapped by his commanding officer. He was gathering loose gear on the ground. Still sobbing, he was nevertheless, back under control.

Kuno crawled on his hands and knees to the nose of the glider. The cockpit canopy was thrown back and the pilot was scrambling to get out. The Vickers barked and .303 caliber shells shattered the canopy glass. The pilot dove away as the bullets thumped into his seat and smashed the cockpit's instrument panel.

Kuno crawled to the pilot. "Are you all right, Rudel?" he

shouted.

Rudel turned to him, wild-eyed. "FUCK ME!" he shouted.

For all the danger of their situation, Kuno couldn't help but laugh.

"You're fine!" he shouted back, grabbing the man by the shoulders. "Help me with the battery cases." The two crawled back to the hatchway. The young private was there, hauling gear through the hatch. He was in complete control, doing the duty he'd been trained to do.

In relays of twos and threes the men were racing for the shelter offered by the rock wall. Each time one moved the Vickers barked again forcing him to dive to earth after just a few steps. Another man would move out and the Vickers would shift its fire to him.

Kuno finally took a moment to look beyond the immediate area of the crashed glider. All about the landing zone German troops were pouring from gliders. Many had hit obstacles like his rock wall and others were struggling to free themselves of the barbed wire entanglements they'd landed in. The British had obviously placed the rock walls deliberately across any long, flat piece of ground. They'd wrecked dozens of gliders including his own. Some were completely smashed, a few tipped over on their tops.

The Vickers fired again and this time he saw where it was, about two hundred meters away behind a low sandbagged bunker with a ring of barbed wire about it. The machine gun was dug in, probably connected to a trench line that would soon be swarming with British infantry. The Vickers would have to be dealt with swiftly.

Kuno and the pilot grabbed up two of the sets of heavy batteries for the radios and moved off for the rock wall. The Vickers' attention was drawn to a squad of paratrooper infantry running across the field. It fired at them, dropping the last two in line in heaps on the ground. The others dove into a bomb crater. The distraction allowed the last of Kuno's men to reach the safety of the wall.

The sharp crack of an MG 34 drifted across the field, mingling with the intensifying sounds of rifle fire. Another Vickers opened up, more distant. Harsh shouts, in German and English rang out over the field. A man screamed somewhere nearby, German or English could not be said. A Schmeisser machine pistol added its notes to the symphony of death at Ta Qali.

Kuno lay behind the wall, peering over the rim assessing the situation. Small arms fire was increasing every second. The British were reacting with unbelievable speed, as if they'd been warned of the drop in advance. A light mortar round landed near his glider. More than half their equipment and supplies were still aboard. Given time the machine gun and the mortar would destroy the glider. He estimated the mortar was in the trench near the Vickers. A bullet spanged off the rock near his face. He fell back below the lip of rocks.

"SHIT!" he said.

Slowly he raised himself back up, careful not to expose himself again for so long. A quick glance about showed several groups of German troops nearby, leaderless and ineffective.

"Steup!" he shouted.

"Here, Major," the Lieutenant responded from down the wall.

"Get down this side of the wall to that group of men there," he said pointing. "Do you see them? In the bomb crater?"

"Yes, Major!"

"Take command!" he ordered. "Get them moving to the right. Get on the flank of the machine gun. We'll go left from here. When you draw his fire we'll advance until he switches, then you advance. You understand?"

"Yes, Major! I understand," nodded Steup.

"We've got to clean out that trench before they get their riflemen into it or we're in trouble. Now move!"

Steup scrambled along the wall, bullets smacking into it with more and more frequency. Another mortar round exploded, this time just meters away from the glider.

Kuno turned to the team. "Leave all the radio gear," he ordered. "Machine pistols and grenades only. Follow me!"

The squad followed him down the wall, scrambling on hands and knees across the broken rock. Already they all had torn pants and bloody knees. Kuno moved them left till they were about a hundred meters to the right of the British machine gun. Here a glider had smashed through the wall. The gliders nose was smashed in, telescoped back to the cargo compartment, two meters of aircraft compressed into a few centimeters. Blood trickled from the machine's smashed cockpit into the dirt.

Beyond the glider there was a gap of about ten meters in the wall where a bomb had struck. Sheltering in the crater they found five German privates, one of whom was badly injured and unconscious. Kuno and his squad rolled into the crater.

Rifle fire crackled all about them now, a sure sign the British were deploying their infantry, faster than Kuno would have thought possible. He looked at his watch. They'd been on the ground only seven minutes. Even with twenty minutes radar warning the British were responding with lightning speed.

"Where is the rest of your squad?" he asked the men. "Where are your non-coms?"

One of the privates, the oldest looking answered. "They are dead, Major," he said. "Killed on landing." He pointed to the wrecked glider with smashed cockpit.

"You're with us now!" said Kuno.

Just then another mortar round landed, this time right under the nose of their glider.

The craft jumped in the air and settled back to the ground, the cockpit completely shredded, a tiny flame beginning. The passenger and cargo compartment would be next. Kuno knew they had to get that mortar before it fired again.

"Sergeant Tondok," he said to his senior NCO. "You stay here with the new men. Lay down a covering fire whenever the machine gun fires on us."

"Right!" Tondok replied. Quickly he deployed the four new men around the rim of the crater.

Kuno turned to the glider pilot, Rudel. "You stay here too."

The Vickers fired at something off to Kuno's right.

"NOW!" he shouted. He and the six remaining men of the team scrambled out of the crater and to their feet. Their training took hold and they spread out as though on an exercise, racing to get around the flank of the Vickers gun. They'd covered more than half the ground before the machine gun crew swung around and drove them to cover. Kuno watched on the Vickers' other flank as Steup and his group of ten men scrambled to get behind the British. A heavy explosion rocked the night a thousands meters or more behind the British gun, a ball of flame roaring into the sky, briefly illuminating the field like noontime. Secondary explosions quickly followed. An ammunition supply had been hit.

The Vickers shifted its fire, but Steup and his men reacted perfectly, hitting the ground before the gun could find them. Schacht and his team leapt up and made the last dash for the enemy lines. As they got close Kuno confirmed his suspicion. A freshly dug trench with sandbagged rim ran laterally across the airfield, perpendicular to the runway. Shouts in English and the sound of many running feet came from further down the trench.

Kuno was several meters ahead of his men and reached the trench before them. He hurdled the meter wide trench at the dead run, just as the Vickers spit fire at them again. His men hit the ground, leaving him alone on the far side of the trench.

Sergeant Tondok and his men cut loose with a burst of automatic weapons fire, temporarily silencing the Vickers. Kuno signaled his men to stay down, cupping a hand over an ear and pointing down the trench. They nodded their understanding. Stick grenades were produced from the capacious pockets of their jump suits; bolts were drawn back on their machine pistols. Voices were drawing nearer, but Kuno could still see nothing. The moon cast its light only across the top foot or so of the trench and did not penetrate its depths.

It seemed an eternity, but only seconds passed before the tops of helmets began to appear in the trench, thirty meters away. The British were running through the trench, trying to reach their strongpoint where the Vickers and trench mortar were positioned near a small bomb shelter.

From behind him Kuno heard the chatter of MP 40 automatic machine pistols, the crack of German assault grenades and the cries of men as they were shot. Steup! The Lieutenant had done it. He'd taken the Vickers. Hopefully he would silence the mortar as well.

The sound of the firing so near made the Tommies in the trench cautious. They advanced slowly then stopped. The sound of every kind of small arms now came from all directions. The flat "whack" of exploding grenades and the "thump" of mortar rounds filled the air. The Tommies came on again, the tops of their helmets the only thing visible. Kuno knew that they only needed to pop their heads above the trench line and he and his men would be seen. He pressed himself flat, keeping one eye on the tops of those helmets. The British advanced to within ten meters of his position before he pulled the fuse rings on his grenades. His men on the other side of the trench saw this action and followed suit. Kuno counted four, then sprang to a kneeling position and threw the two grenades, one at the front of the British infantry group, the other to the rear. His men threw five more grenades. They dropped flat on their faces.

Cries of alarm and warning erupted in the trench, but before the Tommies could reject any of the grenades they began to explode. The British had nowhere to run; the trench confined them and amplified the concussion from the blasts. The grenades went off in a quick series of explosions, muffled by the trench walls and the bodies of the soldiers packed in tight. Men screamed in agony as they were seared and torn.

"NOW!" shouted Kuno. He leapt to his feet and began spraying the trench with his MP 40, running down its length, hosing down the survivors of the grenade attack. His men did the same from the other side of the trench so that there was nowhere to hide, even in the bottom of the trench for any of the enemy. Kuno exhausted a magazine. He stepped back from the trench a few feet, replaced the magazine then continued the slaughter. Finally, he and his men found no more targets in the trench. He waved his arms over his head, signaling the men to cease-fire. Smoke and dust drifted up from the trench, mingled with an occasional moan or sob.

Kuno knelt at the trench side and peered down into the carnage. In the dim light he could see bodies heaped atop one another in a tangle, arms and legs all askew. No motion could be seen. He was about to stand and leave when he realized there was something wrong with the picture. He pulled his map light torch from his tunic. Careful to shield its light from being seen above ground he leaned down into the trench and switched it on. He played its beam across the bodies in the trench. To a man, the Tommies were in full combat kit. Belts held full pouches of extra ammunition, a canteen hung at every hip. Helmet chinstraps were all done up tight, every boot was properly laced and tied. Not one feature of uniform or kit appeared out of place or hurriedly set. These men were prepared for combat long before the 2nd Parachute Division had left Sicily.

He scanned the trench. Over a span of forty meters at least a hundred men lay dead. Here and there in the trench some movement could be seen or a groan heard. He ignored these signs of life. He had no time for prisoners or even to treat his own wounded.

Sgt. Tondok appeared out of the dark, running. The four survivors of the crashed glider and Rudel, the pilot, followed him.

"Major!" Tondok shouted.

Kuno shut off the torch and stood.

What is it Tondok?"

"I've gathered another twenty men at the rock wall, Major," reported Tondok. "There are small groups of men scattered all about. There's little or no organization. I can't find any sign or evidence that the battalion or regiment command staffs are established yet. It's a mess."

"Yes, I know," replied Kuno. "It's even worse. Look here, Tondok." He knelt again at the trench and shined his light down on the bodies there.

"Fully equipped," nodded Tondok. "It's the same on the other bodies I've seen. These men were ready for us."

Kuno switched off the torch again and looked at his watch. "There's only fifty minutes till the second wave begins arriving. We've got to get the field cleared of the flak guns and machine gun pits or the second wave will be wiped out as they hang from their 'chutes."

Malta's ancient capital of Mdina lay just west of the airfield at Ta Qali and overlooked the airfield from the high ground surrounding Rabat. The pre-historic ruin there was the chosen spot for the regimental HQ of the The Royal Inniskilling Fusiliers, known more simply as The Inniskillings. The North Irish regiment first suffered at the hands of the Germans in May and June 1940. In position on The Dyle during the 'phony war' period the German Blitzkrieg threw them back, in succession to Amiens, Arras, Boulogne, Calais and finally to Dunkirk. They'd been withdrawn on June 3rd, 1940 during the famous British evacuation of the seaport.

Later that same month they were delivered to Malta to strengthen the garrison there. Since then they had been laborers more than soldiers, digging and building on the airfield at Ta Qali, suffering under the Axis air bombardment with little chance to hit back. In the two years since their arrival on Malta they'd received replacements to bring the regiment back to its full complement of 3,200 men. Until the last week of June their efforts were directly on the airfield itself, constructing revetments to protect the aircraft, digging bomb shelters and underground ammunition and fuel bunkers, and repairing bomb damage to the runways.

On June 23rd the daily routine changed. The work was still backbreaking, but with a difference. From the 23rd on they dug slit trenches and other infantry defense works. The reserve battalion was brought up into position to the west of the high ground at Rabat, ready to reinforce the regiment's defense of the airfield. The significance was not lost on the men. Though not told, it was clear to the men that the high command expected a German attack soon.

On the night of the 25th however, the expected date of the assault was still three days away. Enlisted men in the Inniskillings that hadn't had leave in the past month were given the night off to carouse in Valletta. Nearly 300 men were on leave as the German drop began.

When the radar report of the large enemy air raid came in, the Air Operations Center forwarded the report to the other airfields and to the HQ's of the Inniskilling and Manchester regiments. Luqa and Hal Far airfields forwarded the report to the HQ's of the Buffs and Kents respectively. The Flak batteries at all three fields were warned as well. These calls went through just before the Telephone Exchange in Malta was bombed. They would be the last calls placed on the island's main phone network for nearly a month.

At Luqa the warning triggered the take-off of the island's entire surviving night fighter force; three twin-engine Beaufighters roared off the runway to oppose the massive German force bearing down on Malta.

In the ruins of Mdina the Inniskilling regimental staff set to work. They ordered the regiment's ready battalion to occupy the forward bomb shelters on the airfield's perimeter. The duty battalion was already stationed at strong points on the field itself. They would withdraw to small local shelters during the expected bombing raid, emerging from the shelters when the all clear sounded to form the first line of defense against the invaders.

The British plan of defense was to hit the first wave of air assault troops hard as they hit the ground, not giving them the time to organize their force and to secure the field itself. If the first drop could be defeated the enemy wouldn't dare to follow with another.

In the event the Germans did seize the field the British would fall back on the high ground at Rabat, shelling the exposed Germans on the flat airfield with mortars and artillery from the heights. After pounding the Germans the Inniskillings and Manchesters would join in an assault to eliminate the airhead. It was a sound plan and the defenders had the men and weapons available to implement it.

Two things went wrong with the defense plan right away. First, nearly ten percent of the two regiments were on leave, one platoon from most companies. Both the duty and ready battalions were under strength. Second, phone lines all over the island were knocked out by the destruction of the telephone exchange. There was no way to coordinate the defense with Lord Gort in Valletta or with the other regiments at Luqa and Hal Far fields.

Soon after the assault began it became evident to the hundreds of troops in Valletta what was happening. The entire island of Malta is barely seventeen miles long, Valletta is only four miles from Ta Qali and the white parachutes of the German attackers were seen by many in Valletta and to their everlasting credit hundreds responded on their own initiative, returning as best they could to their units.

Here, a problem presented itself to the British in their defense of Ta Qali. The regiments were based on the high ground to the west of the field, but the men on leave were east of it in Valletta. They were separated from their regiments by the Germans who'd landed on the field like a bolt of lightning in the night.

Major Schacht and his men returned to their glider and with the help of paratroopers they'd rounded up on the field they cleared out the remaining supplies and equipment and established their communications post in the Vickers machine gun bunker, heaving the bodies of the dead British defenders out into the night. They were situated at the north end of the airfield, about 300 meters east of the runway. The highest-ranking German officer Kuno had found by this time was a captain. There was still no sign of the battalion or regimental commanders.

Nonetheless, a sizable force of paratroopers was coalescing around Schacht's radio team. He became the de facto commander of the paratroopers at the northern end of the field; a situation he hoped and expected would be temporary. Rifle and automatic weapons fire crackled all around, but primarily to the south and east. A tremendous firefight seemed to be underway at the south end of the field, but Kuno and the men under his command had not yet made contact in that direction.

"Tondok!" shouted Kuno.

"Yes, Major!" Tondok had stayed glued to the Major since the massacre at the trench. He'd become a combination of the Major's *Aide de Camp* and Chief of Staff.

"Report!" snapped Kuno. "How many men have we brought together. Tell me their dispositions."

"I estimate 450 to 500 men inside our lines, Major," Tondok replied smartly. "We hold the northeast corner of the airfield, from the northern end of the runway south for about 500 meters. Our western perimeter is the runway itself; on the east we hold the field to the furthest aircraft revetments, approximately 1000 meters east to west." Tondok paused and looked at Kuno before going on. Kuno nodded. He approved the direction of the report.

"The bulk of the force is disposed to the west and south," Tondok continued, "along the runway and on the trench line near where our glider landed. Lt. Steup is in command on the southern line. A reinforced platoon is here with the communications team as a reserve force. We're in the process of stringing field phone lines to the perimeter."

"What about the weapons and machine gun companies?" Kuno asked. "Have any of them reported?"

"I have one 37mm PAK gun on the runway. No other anti-tank guns, or heavy mortars have been located yet. The machine gun companies are well represented however. We have about fifty MG's deployed. There are a number of wrecked gliders inside our lines or just outside them in which I suspect we will find some of the heavy weapons."

Kuno nodded. Tondok had done a professional job of organizing and deploying the available forces.

"Put these men together as a provisional platoon," Kuno ordered him, pointing at the most recent paratroopers to straggle in. "Get them over on the south-west flank. They're to route out any British holding positions on the runway itself, then dig in."

"Yes, Major!" snapped Tondok.

Kuno looked at his watch. 0035 hours. Thirty-five minutes

since the landing began, about thirty till the second wave was due to begin its drop. By now both battalion and regiment should have their HQ's up and operating. No sign of either was evident.

Signs of heavy combat however were in abundance. Rifle and machine gun fire crackled continuously, intermingled with the explosion of grenades and mortars. Twice, Kuno and his radio team were forced to snatch up weapons and join in defending against attacks by platoon strength British infantry. On both occasions the assaults were driven back, Kuno's only consolation being that the British defense of the airfields seemed as unfocused as the German attack.

From the reports of the stragglers who came under his command it became clear that the piles and walls of rocks the British had placed on the field had done heavy damage to the glider force. Whole gliders of troops were killed on landing, while other gliders had delivered only a few of their passengers alive. It was clear also that he and his team were extraordinarily lucky. Only those gliders that landed directly on the runways or taxi strips had escaped serious damage and safely delivered all their passengers.

"Major Schacht!" It was the young private, Schuenemann. He was kneeling with one of the wireless sets, its black aerial raised above the lip of the trench, a headset clamped over his ears. "I have contact with a bomber crew orbiting the field! They're the lead of a flight of Stukas."

Kuno knelt beside the young man. A bullet thumped into the soft earth piled at the rim of the trench. A Schmeisser chattered.

"First rate, Schuenemann," Kuno praised the lad, clapping him on the shoulder. "Ask what other contact they have established with our forces on the ground."

The young man nodded his acknowledgement of the order and relayed the question to the bomber crew. He listened intently a moment, one hand clapped to the headset, the other making fine adjustments to the radio's frequency dial. He looked back at Kuno.

"We are the first contact, Major."

"What about the other airfields, Schuenemann? Ask about Luqa and Hal Far!"

"The bomber crew reports there has been no other contact with any of our forces on the island," replied Schuenemann.

"Find out if the second wave is on schedule," ordered Kuno. "Ask the crew to relay to the second wave that the field at Ta Qali is not secure, repeat, Ta Qali not secure."

After a moment Schuenemann reported the transport aircraft were landing on Sicily at that moment. The second wave was expected to be on schedule.

Kuno paused a moment to think. A Vickers spit lead nearby. A sudden flurry of rifle fire signaled another British counterattack.

"Schuenemann," he said, "stay in contact with that crew. Right now they are our only link to air support and to division. Don't loose that connection!" He rushed off to the sound of the firing, racing down the trench, over the bodies of dead Englanders. He reached a turn four hundred meters down the trench where a platoon of forty or so paratroopers were manning the positions they'd only just taken from the British. A wrecked 40mm Bofors gun lay burnt and broken against the side of the trench. He found Lt. Steup in command.

"What is happening Steup?" he demanded, gasping for air from his dash down the trench.

Steup turned and pointed out over the rim of the trench.

"The British have massed infantry to the south on the left in that set of craters at two hundred meters and behind those rocks," indicating a wall two hundred meters to the right. "Each group is at least company strength and growing. I am amazed at how quickly they have organized a force for a counter-attack."

"They are going to try a squeeze play," said Kuno. "They'll hit you with light mortars first, then keep your heads down with machine guns from directly in front as the infantry attacks from the sides."

Steup looked at him. "It's a good plan," he said. "It will probably work."

"They're not ready yet," said Kuno. "If they were the mortars would be dropping right now." He looked at his watch. "Give me four minutes, then fire a red flare over the heads of the infantry behind the rocks to the right. Put a green flare over the ones to the left. Tell your men to keep their heads down."

Steup smiled as he checked his watch.

"I'm sure they won't need to be told twice, Major!"

Kuno retraced his steps down the trench at a dead run, reaching

Schuenemann in just under two minutes. Breathless from running the trench twice he gasped out his orders, kneeling beside the young man. Quickly Schuenemann relayed the instructions. Kuno checked his watch. One minute to go.

"Request acknowledged, Major!" cried Schuenemann.

Kuno stood and turned towards the section of trench sheltering Steup and his men. He pulled his binoculars from his tunic and swept them over the area. The bright moonlight put the bare, rocky ground in sharp relief, a world of black and white, with no color. No movement. He dropped the glasses and checked his watch. Any second.

The red flare lifted out of the trench and arched over in the direction of the rock wall to the right of Steup and his men. Seconds later a green flare was launched to Steup's left, lighting the craters where the British infantry hid, waiting for their signal to attack.

Cries of alarm erupted from the British positions. Kuno took his binoculars back up and quickly scanned the rock wall and the craters. Nothing to be seen. Faintly at first the sound of aero engines came to him, rising in volume as the Stukas roared down on their targets. Kuno raised his glasses to the sky, finally spotting the Stukas in their dives. A pair of flak guns from the south end of the field and one gun straight west of his position opened fire. Kuno carefully noted their positions. A string of 500-kilo bombs whistled down from the wings of the leading three dive-bombers.

Kuno shouted, "Take cover!" and dropped into the bottom of the trench, covering his head with his arms, drawing his knees up under his chin.

The six bombs went home directly in line with the rock wall, crossing it at a slight angle. The earth erupted over a two hundred meter front hurling rocks the size of footballs from the wall. Dirt and rock rained down on Steup's position, but his men remained safe, huddled in the trench against the blast and falling debris. Choking clouds of dust billowed from the impact site, completely obscuring the area from view from all directions. The first string of bombs landed right amongst the British infantry, men of the Manchester Regiment, as they prepared to rush the German held trenches.

A second string of six bombs from the remaining three Stukas of the flight hammered the British infantry, also Manchesters, at the craters. The explosions were so close behind the first set as to be barely distinguishable. The thunder of the explosions died away as the gusting south wind drove the choking cloud of dust north over the German occupied corner of the field.

Kuno uncoiled from his fetal position in the bottom of the trench. He looked at Schuenemann. The boy shielded his radio set from the blast with his body. As the dust cloud rolled over them he turned to Kuno and smiled.

"The Stuka leader asks if the attack was satisfactory Major!"

"Tell him he gets a top score from the professor," replied Kuno. "Now, get to work with him identifying the aircraft that are in the pattern about the airfield. Find out what ordinance they have available. Develop a schedule based on the bomber's fuel as to when each flight will be forced to leave. Do you understand so far?"

"Yes, Major!" replied Schuenemann. Everything the Major had covered were basics in the training of close air support radio personnel.

"Good," said Kuno. "You've got the training, now put it to work. Two things you must do as top priorities." Kuno ticked off a finger. "First, establish contact with other aircraft so that when these must leave to refuel we are still in communication. Second," he said, raising another finger, "arrange for all aircraft departing for fuel to drop their remaining bombs on the high ground to the east in the absence of a specific target from you." He pointed towards Rabat and Mdina.

He turned away and looked at his watch. 0045. Only twenty minutes till the second wave was scheduled to begin its drop. Unless more of the airfield could be brought under German control the second drop would be met by British infantry firing from protected positions at the paratroopers.

The sound of firing from the south of the field had not abated. Kuno heard the sharp crack of a 50mm PAK gun lending its voice to the growing symphony of battle.

"Tondok!" Kuno shouted.

The Sergeant appeared as if from nowhere.

"Yes, Major?"

"Gather the reserve platoon. I'm taking them with me to the

south," Kuno told him. "We're going to join Steup and his men, there. We've got to extend our lines before the second wave comes in."

"Understood, Major!" said Sgt. Tondok.

"Your top priority is to extend a field telephone behind Steup and I," said Kuno. "Get it strung right behind us Tondok!"

"Yes, Major!" exclaimed the Sergeant. "Good luck, Sir!"

"Thank you, Sergeant." Kuno turned to the young radio operator.

"Schuenemann!"

"Yes, Sir?" the boy answered.

"Have your bomber crew relay a message for the second wave," he said. "The entire drop at Ta Qali must be made to the *EAST* of the runway, repeat, the *EAST* of the runway. Do you understand?"

"Yes, Sir!"

Tondok had formed the reserve platoon in the trench, waiting for the Major. The men were quiet, shifting about uneasily, or smoking. A soft murmur as a pack of cigarettes was passed from hand to hand was the only conversation. The cloud of dust and dirt from the bomb explosions drifted over the top of the trench, settling slowly as it drifted to the north. Moonlight shining through the dust cast an eerie orange hue over the group.

The sound of small arms fire had diminished in the immediate vicinity, but to the south it was rising steadily. It was clear to all the paratroopers that the south end of Ta Qali Airfield was being hotly contested. A growing chorus of exploding mortar shells joined the regular crack of the German 50mm PAK anti-tank gun. The paratroopers could not tell whose mortars they were.

"Men!" Kuno shouted. "Follow me at the double!"

Kuno and the scratch platoon trotted down the trench, the third time Kuno had made the trek in just minutes. The trench was only wide enough for the platoon to proceed in single file. Soon they were spread over nearly a hundred meters of trench. Kuno was well aware that he was placing the group in the same position the company of British had been in just a short time earlier, racing blindly down the trench. A small group of enemy firing down on them from the trench lip could wipe the paratroopers out easily. He was counting on the shock of the Stuka attack to keep the British from acting for several more minutes.

He slowed down as he approached the turn in the trench just before the positions of Steup and his men. Holding his hand up to stop the men behind him Kuno stopped just short of the turn.

"Viking?" he called, providing the pre-arranged password.

Scuffling noises and voices too low to be understood were his only response. He gripped his Schmeisser and thumbed the safety.

"VIKING!" he shouted. Men behind him in the trench were crouching now, getting ready to arm grenades and to shoot it out.

"Major Schacht," came Steup's plaintive voice. "I've- I've forgotten the countersign."

"Steup, you fool!" said Kuno. "Show yourself immediately!"

A pair of empty hands with fingers splayed open appeared from around the turn in the trench. The remainder of the Lieutenant followed, the man's face bearing a sheepish expression.

Kuno and the men behind him relaxed and stood. The angry Major approached the downcast Lieutenant.

"DACHSHUND!" said Kuno. "Don't forget it again!"

Steup kept his eyes down.

"Yes, Major," he said. "Dachshund."

"Now, listen Steup!" said Kuno, his anger not abated. "We've got to extend our lines to the south, try to link-up with the troops fighting at the south end of the field. The second drop is only minutes away and we've got to secure the landing ground or they'll be wiped out as they dangle from their harnesses."

Steup snapped to attention.

"What are your orders, Major?"

"You're to take your men south on the left through the craters," Kuno explained. "I'll go right with the reserve platoon over the rock wall. We keep moving till we meet opposition, then either attack or dig in, depending on enemy strength. Use your whistle to get my attention. I'll do the same. Then follow my hand signals, but at all times use your initiative, Steup!"

"Yes, Sir!" said Steup. "May I ask a question, Major?"

"Quickly, Steup!"

"What about the west side of the field? So far we have made no progress there. What will the men do that land on that side of the runway?"

"Schuenemann has established radio contact," Kuno replied. "I've directed that the entire drop be conducted to the east of the runway. Now move Steup! This dust cloud is good cover, but it won't last long. It's already dissipating. If we wait much longer the British on the high ground will be able to target us here with mortars."

"Yes, Sir!"

Quickly Schacht and Steup moved their men into position. The wind was blowing the dust from the bomb strikes clear. In another few minutes they would be exposed to any watchers on the high ground to the west. Kuno checked his watch. 0050. The second wave was on its way to Malta.

"LET'S GO STEUP!" he shouted.

About two hundred meters separated the two groups of paratroopers as they scrambled from their trenches. The dust cloud had almost cleared and the troopers ran stooped over, zigzagging across the open ground. They conducted a classic infantry maneuver, just as if on exercise at the Stendahl training grounds, the paratrooper jump school 160 kilometers west of Berlin. The troopers raced forward in shifts, one group covering twenty to thirty meters and then dropping to the ground to cover the advance of the next group. In this fashion they leapfrogged across the open ground between their start point in the trench and the craters freshly dug by the Stuka bombs, a distance of some 200 meters. They encountered no opposition.

As they came nearer the site of the bombing Kuno and his men began to see its results. Large rocks from the wall and bits of kit and weapons lay about, mingled with human flesh, blood and bone. Kuno kept the men moving, hustling them past the macabre scene, giving them no time to dwell on the horror.

Past the grisly scene of the bombing they came to an abandoned trench, only half dug, still strewn with shovels, picks and wheelbarrows. The trench ran from east to west and ended about forty meters from the runway on its west end. To the east it ran off into the dim moonlight, beyond Kuno's vision. Nearly a dozen gliders lay on the runway and just off its margins in this area, among the very few Kuno had seen that appeared to have made smooth landings. He scanned the area around the gliders, looking for their passengers. He found them in two places. A number of men had taken shelter in a drainage ditch running parallel to the runway. They had disposed themselves well, in position to make the British pay very heavily for any attempt to cross the runway from the west side. Other paras lay dead on the runway itself, mingled with the bodies of their enemies. From all indications there'd been a fierce fight on the runway around the gliders a short time earlier. He signaled for Steup and his men to take cover in the trench and to hold position. Kuno and the reserve platoon settled in to the shallow trench to Steup's right, at the western end of the trench, about 70 meters from the runway. The sound of firing from the south was now very near, the occasional stray bullet thumping into the earth or ricocheting off one of the many stones piled at the trench rims.

Kuno first turned his attention to the south, scanning the area with his binoculars. A pitched battle was building 600 meters to the south. British infantry were advancing against paratroopers defending a box shaped area bounded on the west by the runway and on the north by a taxi strip leading from the runway to a set of five aircraft revetments to the east of the field. The British attack was developing from the west, with groups of infantry crossing the runway, swinging round the north and south sides of the Germans to envelope and flank them. He estimated the attackers' strength at close to a thousand.

Kuno pulled his binoculars from his tunic and quickly surveyed the field starting on his right. Over the runway on the flats below the high ground to the west he could dimly see movement among the crashed gliders, moving shapes darker than the shadows cast by the wrecked machines. A MG 34 coughed from beneath the wing of one of the gliders, its muzzle flash briefly illuminating the area around the craft. In a series of quick flashes he saw a small group of paras, sheltering under the glider's wing, behind the rock pile that had wrecked their craft. He moved on quickly, scanning the area east of the runway. Everywhere he looked he found small groups of Germans fending off much larger bodies of British infantry. Parachutes billowed across the field, rippling in the wind, snagged by rocks or wrecked gliders. Others were held in place by their owner's bodies. He concluded the landing on the west side of the runway was a disaster with hundreds of paratroopers killed on landing or even before they set foot on the ground. He turned to the reserve platoon's Corporal.

"What is your name?" he demanded.

"I am Kleditzsch, Major."

"All right Kleditzsch," said Kuno. "Here's what I want you to do. Pick another man and scurry down the trench here to the runway. Make contact with the men there. Tell them they must hold the runway at all costs. The second wave will drop any minute on the east side. They must hold the runway."

"I understand Major."

"Do you remember the sign and countersign?"

"Yes, Sir," answered Kleditzsch, smiling. "Viking and dachshund."

"Get moving then!"

Kleditzsch scrambled down the trench towards the runway, slapping a private on the shoulder along the way. The two men moved off on their mission.

At that moment the sound of aircraft engines came to his ears, softly at first, but strengthening fast. He checked his watch. 0052. The second wave was early by at least eight minutes! He turned to the north scanning the sky with his binoculars. Nothing. The sound of the engines grew, though not to the thunderous roar the great fleet of transports should generate.

"There they are!" shouted one of the men in the trench. The man was pointing into the southern sky.

Kuno turned and located the aircraft. As he watched them the flight of five Ju 88 bombers swung over the center of the field, then turned west at 1000 meters altitude. Flak guns from the west side of the field and from the high ground around Rabat and Mdina opened up on the bombers, but they held their tight formation in a shallow dive. Glowing tracer shells rocketed into the night, flashes exploded all around them yet the Junkers bombers continued on their impossible run, flattening out as their bomb doors swung open. Their combined 10,000 kilograms of bombs tipped nose down and sailed like darts thrown by a master into the eastern slope of the high ground.

Bulls-eye! The slope erupted in flame and smoke. The terraced farm fields on the slope overlooking the airfield, so often the victim of stray bombs meant for Ta Qali, now suffered the shock of a concentrated attack. The shock wave of the blast was visible briefly to Kuno over a mile away in his trench. Seconds later the sound of the blast reached his ears.

Kuno admired the skill and nerve displayed by the bomber crews. The attack was pressed home at low altitude against determined flak and was placed perfectly to separate the airfield from the high ground, where the British were undoubtedly holding their reserve infantry.

The Ju 88's peeled away to the north, but did not escape scot-free. One of the bombers was hit in its starboard engine as it banked over to turn north. It staggered, smoke trailing from the engine, then straightened as its pilot fought to control it. Just as it appeared he might regain control the damaged engine shattered in a bright, fuel fed explosion, severing the wing from the fuselage. The bomber plunged to the ground trailing burning fuel and chunks of metal skin. It slammed into the ground, disintegrating in a ball of flame into tiny pieces.

A mighty cheer went up from British troops all over the battlefield. Kuno felt anger for the first time, though he knew he'd have cheered too if he were in the Englander's shoes. He realized suddenly that the crackle of small arms fire had died down all over the battlefield as men of both sides paused in their life and death struggle to witness the drama of the bombers.

Now the fire picked up again, growing to a crescendo as the British moved to complete the destruction of the paras in the box. A red flare launched from the British center arched into the night sky, passing over the moon.

The British rose from trenches, craters and stonewalls with a cry and rushed at the German box, firing as they ran. Heavy mortar fire began landing in the box, fired from the heights to the west.

Kuno assessed the situation. If ever an infantry force was vulnerable to air attack, then these British were. He turned to the north, scanning the ground he'd covered with the reserve platoon. Tondok was as good as his word! Two paratroopers were making their way across the cratered, rocky ground, carrying a spool of phone cable between them. A field phone case was slung over one man's back; the other carried a second spool of cable. Kuno recognized Corporal Benckner and Private Tscheuschner as members of his team.

The troopers had come within one hundred meters of Schacht and his men when they stopped. They knelt on the ground with the spool and began to detach the end of the cable.

"DAMN!" Kuno cursed. The cable on the first spool was exhausted. The troopers would need to splice the two cables before continuing. A minute or more would be lost before the phone cable could be extended to him and put in operation. There was no time. He jumped to his feet and ran towards the men, pulling his whistle out as he went. He put it to his lips and blew on it furiously as he ran, trying to be heard over the din of battle. He'd covered nearly half the ground to the men before he got their attention. Gasping for air he held one hand to his ear and made a cranking motion with the other. The field phones were powered by a hand-crank. His signal to the men told them he needed the phone in operation immediately.

The man carrying the field phone dropped it from his shoulder and unpacked the phone from its case. The other man was stripping the leads on the cable to connect to the phone when Kuno skidded to a halt on his knees beside them, the three men all kneeling in a circle about the spool and field phone.

"Connect the phone," he gasped. "Hurry!"

The two communications ratings went to work without a word, Corporal Benckner stripping the leads on the cable, while the Private unpacked the phone and exposed the cable posts for the connection to be made. Kuno pulled a small map case from his tunic as he watched the Corporal use his knife to cut back the soft insulation over the wires, then twist the copper leads and wrap them round the posts on the phone. He drew a paper from the case and unfolded it to reveal a map of the airfield marked off in a grid.

The other man waited for the Corporal to finish. His hand was poised on the phone crank, ready to power the device as soon as it was ready. The Corporal finished the posts and threaded them down, twisting them by their large wing nuts. He lifted his hands clear to indicate he was finished.

The Private began to crank vigorously, generating the electric current from the coil in the phone box. He'd spun the crank a half dozen times and the phone was nearly charged when his hand slipped from the crank and he pitched forward on his face.

"Tscheuschner, you clumsy fool!" Kuno raged. He grabbed the phone and cranked it himself, desperate to make contact quickly. He looked down at the Private, still flat on his face in the dirt as Kuno pulled the handset from its cradle. He looked at his watch.

0055.

"Tondok!" he shouted. A brief pause. "Tondok! It's Schacht. We need an immediate bombing mission. Get Schueneman on the line!"

Corporal Benckner chided Tscheusner. "Get up man! You can't lie on your face all night!"

Benckner shook the private, then with dawning realization he lifted the man by the shoulder, rolling him over on his back. A spreading black stain in the center of Tscheuschner's chest told the whole story. Benckner and Schacht both rolled lower to the ground, Kuno watching Benckner grimly, but he said nothing, waiting for Schuenemann to come on the line.

A sudden flurry of rifle fire broke out nearby. A bullet plucked at Kuno's left sleeve.

"Schuenemann!" Schacht shouted to be heard over the din of the battle. "Call in a mission, the first available bombers. Have them strike co-ordinates TQ SW twelve through twenty."

He paused, listening to Schuenemann repeat the co-ordinates back to him.

"That's correct, Schuenemann," he shouted. "I don't care which aircraft or bombs are used, but they must deliver a heavy attack! Now get on it! This attack must take place before the second wave drop begins!"

Kuno turned to Benckner. The Corporal had pulled Tscheuschner's body clear of the phone and its cable and had relieved him of the extra spool.

"Finish running that line, Benckner," he ordered, pointing south to the position held by Lt. Steup and his men. "Alert Steup of the bomb attack about to begin. They will hit from the runway west for about 500 meters."

"Yes, Sir!" snapped Benckner as he unwound the cable from the phones posts. Kneeling beside the dead Tscheuschner he began splicing the ends of the two spools of cable together.

Kuno put his hand down to brace himself as he stood up. He felt a curious wet, squish in the cuffs of his sleeve. He looked down at his left hand and saw it covered with blood running through his fingers into the dirt. That curious feeling of detachment he'd experienced the previous winter in Russia came to him again. It was as if some other man was wounded, someone else's blood was trickling into the ground. Benckner stopped his work on the phone and started to reach for Kuno's arm.

"Finish the telephone, Benckner!" Kuno snapped. "I'm all right."

He got to his feet, clapping his right hand over the wound in his left arm. He set out to rejoin the reserve platoon in the half dug trench.

Malta was a densely populated place, almost two thousand persons to the square mile, with the far western reaches of the island being the only sparsely inhabited area. There, the island drops straight into the sea; in many places four hundred foot sheer cliffs plunge directly into the waves crashing against Malta's very foundations.

To the east, north and south and through the center of the island Malta is highly developed with only narrow corridors of farmland separating the cities and towns from one another. Even these narrow strips are not lonely, rural stretches. The farm fields are small and crowded, the largest no bigger than a few acres. Stones and boulders work themselves slowly to the surface where every spring Malta's farmers painstakingly remove them from the fields and heap them in walls at the edges of their tiny plots.

The farm plots and orchards of Malta are intensively cultivated to maximize yields of grain, fruit, vegetables and potatoes, this last a surprising staple of the Maltese diet. Even so, under the best conditions Malta grows only about half its own food supply.

In daylight hours the fields are beehives of activity with farmers and their beasts busily engaged in the nearly year round production of the island's food supply. Often whole families work the farm plot. The farmers live in the smaller towns and villages or on the outskirts of the island's cities, traveling to their fields at each dawn for their day's labor.

In the pre-war years of peace the Maltese farmers often spent their summer evenings in the cool fields, gathered in small groups around glowing braziers or kerosene lanterns, playing guitars and singing their songs. On the warmest nights they occasionally slept in the fields, in small huts or lean-tos, watching the stars wheel over their heads through the clear, windswept skies of the central Mediterranean as they drifted off to sleep.

These are the same stars that sparked imaginations and birthed the myths of the ancients at the dawn of man's civilization. Malta has a share of the myths. The Maltese believe the island is held above the sea by the Pillars of Hercules, placed there during the Greek hero's seven-year captivity in the arms of the bewitching Calypso.

World War II changed many of these customs. Many of the island's orchards were destroyed in the two years of bombing prior to the German invasion at the end of June 1942 and the island's overall production of food was down by nearly half from its pre-war levels.

The cities, Valletta and its suburbs of Floriana, Sliema and Vittoriosa, were evacuated once right at the outbreak of war. When nothing but haphazard night bombings by the Italians happened for months most of the evacuees returned to their homes, only to flee again when the German bombing assault began in earnest at the start of 1941. The towns and villages became crowded with refugees with two or three families pressed into accommodations barely large enough for one Maltese clan.

Despite its small size most of Malta's people had never been more than a few miles from home before the war. There were only two good roads on the island, one running down the eastern coast, connecting St Paul's Bay in the north to Marsaxlokk Bay in the south, with Valletta in between. The other road ran from Valletta to Mdina and Rabat in the island's center near Ta Qali Airfield. All other roads were dirt and stone tracks whose width depended entirely on how many feet traversed it to keep vegetation at bay on the shoulders.

With the evacuations due to Axis bombing residents of small communities suddenly found themselves hosting shopkeepers, artisans and ( GASP! ) dockyard workers from the cities. These somewhat more cosmopolitan and worldly refugees had lived in close proximity to sailors of the Royal Navy and the world's merchant fleets for generations and brought with them certain outlooks at first at odds with the conservative rural residents, but to the surprise of some and the relief of all they quickly came together, sharing a common bond of hardship and hatred for the enemy. Hatred, that is for the Germans. The Maltese, who saw Mussolini as The Fuhrer's lap dog viewed the Italians with simple contempt.

During the spring of 1942 many Maltese slept in simple huts in the fields as a means to escape the claustrophobic conditions in their crowded dwellings and to avoid spending their nights in air raid shelters. There were no musical parties. There was no fuel to spare on lamps or fires, even if light wouldn't have attracted bombers.

On the night of June 25-26, as the German Luftwaffe launched Operation Herkules thousands of Maltese awoke in the fields to the roar of the hundreds of fighters, bombers and glider towing transports hurled against the island. They'd never seen such a tremendous spectacle of power in the air. They stared at the night sky, not at the stars of the Greeks and Romans, but at the war birds of the Third Reich.

Antony "Tony" Mostok was the Mayor of the small village of Grieppa. It was mainly an honorary title with no pay attached, but one which permitted him to preside each year over Grieppa's Festival of St. Peter and St. Paul. Held on June 29th the Festival was the high point of the summer season in Grieppa. Tony was looking forward to the festival. It would be blessed by a full moon in 1942, and promised to be lively and high-spirited with the party lasting well into the night, in spite of tight rations on both food and fuel. The people of Grieppa needed the lift in spirits the festival would bring after so many months of siege.

Tony owned a two-acre plot on the outskirts of Grieppa, about a half-mile from his home in the village. In the Mostok family for many generations the farm was handed down from father to eldest son so many times the count was lost. The Mostok farm grew vegetables and melons and on the roof of the house in Grieppa a chicken coop kept the family in eggs before the war, but now grain to feed the chickens was too scarce and the birds had gone into the pot, one-by-one until there were only four hens and an old rooster left. Two of the hen's days were numbered. They were marked for the festival.

On the night of the German assault Tony, his wife and five children, aged six to fourteen were sleeping under the stars at the Mostok farm. First, Tony then his wife Marie was awakened by the sound of approaching airplane engines. The air raid sirens sounded belatedly, long after the roar of the engines could be heard.

With so many people awakened nearby it is small wonder that Kenneth Wiltshire hadn't gotten more than a few hundred feet down the dusty trek from Mosta toward Birkirkara and Valletta when he was surrounded by farmers and villagers offering help. Soon after the last of the transports passed overhead they began to emerge from the fields. At first he resisted them in a kind of shock, trudging along with his burden behind him, staring straight ahead and saying nothing. The Maltese quickly recognized his glassy stare and gently restrained him until he gave up and just stood, holding the cart's traces in an iron grip.

They tried to speak to him in that charming pigeon English developed over a century and a half of close association with the British Empire, but he ignored them, lost in his own world of dead dreams. Presently several of the women approached the cart and the still form huddled on its narrow bench. They whispered among themselves as they examined the woman on the seat, unconscious, barely breathing. They found a nasty lump and a thin trickle of blood seeping from behind her right ear. In their own language they told the men that the woman was alive, but in desperate need of a Doctor's care.

Several men separated Kenneth from the cart, gently, but firmly and led him to a seat on the rock wall separating the dirt road from a field. Two other men took over the handling of the cart. Slowly and carefully they moved off with it in the direction of Mosta and the small hospital there. Two women from the group accompanied them, walking beside the cart on either side to do what they could for the injured girl. Tony and Marie stayed with Kenneth. They alternated trying to speak to him in English and to each other in Maltese.

"Hey, Een-glizh?" Tony said gently. "Wha'z your name?"

Kenneth sat on his rock, staring straight ahead.

"You're a zoljer, right?" Tony prodded. "What unit you from Een-glizh?"

"Maybe he's hurt too," suggested Marie in Maltese. "Do you think you could check him over?"

"I dunno," said Tony. "He's apt to hit me or something."

"Naw!" scoffed Marie. "I'll hold his hands nice and soft." She knelt in front of Kenneth. Looking in his eyes she took his hands in hers. She switched to English.

"'e won't 'it you. You zheck 'im out Tony."

"O-K, Marie," Tony said in Maltese. He reached up slowly and touched Kenneth's forehead with his fingertips.

"Go on Tony!" snapped Marie. Tony jerked his hand back.

"You do it Marie!"

"Oh, fine!" she said.

Switching back to English she raised her hand to Kenneth's cheek and said "Are you 'urt, Een-glizh?" Slowly she worked her fingers up around his ears, to the crown of his head and down the back to his neck. She kneaded his scalp while watching his eyes. There was no reaction or sign of pain and she felt only the one bump and no blood except from the gash in his scalp above his forehead.

"I don't find anything much wrong with him," said Marie. "I don't think he's hurt bad. It's some kind of shock or something."

"We'd better get him to the Doctor too," said Tony, glancing up at the sky. The last of the German aircraft had passed overhead, but the roar of their engines had not faded.

"The Doctors will be busy tonight I think," said Marie.

>>>>>>>>>>>>>

Dieter Jänsch thought Ta Qali looked like some vision from Dante; a sub-level of the lowest pit where demons practiced rites of special pain for the suffering of the damned. Tiny pinpoints of flame flickered like scattered candles guttering in the draft from an open window. Smoke rose from the airfield. The south wind, the *Khaimsin* as the Maltese called it, lifted the smoke in ghostly, moonlit tendrils that joined in an oily, black column at the north end of the field.

Dieter banked his Ju 87 Stuka over on its right wing and began the southbound leg of his bomber's circuit around the Maltese airfields. He and the other bomber pilots were circling the three airfields at 4,000 meters, above the effective range of British flak, waiting for a call from the forward air control teams on the ground. So far, an hour into the assault only the paratroopers on Ta Qali had established radio contact. Silence greeted every effort to reach the assault troops at Hal Far and Luqa.

Indeed the fields at Hal Far and Luqa were dark. Fires started by the first waves of bombers on the two southern fields had died down. Only a few smoldering hot spots sent thin wisps of smoke into the night sky. It seemed likely that the defenders at all but Ta Qali had quickly overcome the landing forces.

He checked his fuel gage. Fuel for one more circuit before leaving for Sicily. He checked his watch. The second drop would begin in less than five minutes anyway. His radio headset crackled in his ears.

"Dieter!" the voice of his rear seat crewmate called to him.

"Yes, Walter," Dieter replied. "What is it?"

"We have been assigned an attack mission," Walter replied. "We're to strike the southwest corner of Ta Qali. The British are massing their infantry for a counter-attack against our troops."

"Give me the coordinates quickly, Walter!" shouted Dieter. "The second wave is due any minute. We have to be clear of the field before the drop begins."

Kuno raced back to his position in the trench with the reserve platoon. The men there were in position and ready to provide fire support for the paratroopers to the south. The British attack was developing along classic lines. Heavy mortar rounds fired from the heights to the west continued to hammer the German positions as the British infantry moved quickly to envelope the Germans from west, south and north. The paratroopers were unable to respond effectively while under fire from the mortars.

Kuno looked up and down the trench. His reserve platoon was deployed in two groups, Steup's men to the east, his own small unit to the west, close to the runway. The north arm of the British infantry attack was already to the east of the runway, about two hundred meters south of Kuno and his men, somewhat beyond the effective range of the MP 40 machine pistols most of his men were armed with. Only the five MG 34 machine guns deployed with the reserve platoon could hit the British accurately at that range.

Kuno's arm began to throb. He clutched the wound and found that his lower sleeve was completely soaked with blood. No time to deal with it now though. He put the pain aside and moved a few meters to the west to the first of the paratroopers in that direction. He clapped the man on the shoulder, leaving a bloody handprint on the para's tunic.

"There is a bomb strike coming to the west of the runway," he told the man. "Pass the word. When the bombs fall, open up on the British to our front."

"Yes, Major!" the man snapped and scrambled off towards the runway to spread the word in that direction.

Kuno moved east and repeated his instructions to the first troopers he found there.

He poked his head above the trench rim and checked the progress of the British infantry. Their envelopment of the German position in the southeast corner of the field was almost complete. They would begin their assault within minutes. As he watched, the pace of the British mortar bombardment intensified, a sure sign the British were about to attack. He checked his watch. Barely two minutes since he had called for an air attack against the main British infantry to the west of the runway. If the bombers were not prompt, they might be too late.

A thin whine came to his ears through the thunder and crash of mortar shells and the non-stop chatter of small arms. Kuno smiled as he recognized the sound of a Stuka Dive bomber's siren. The whine strengthened into a powerful wail as men about the field, British and German alike, looked to the sky. The roar of aero engines and the bark of 20mm cannon joined the scream of the sirens as the Stukas bored in to attack. Flak guns added their crack to the medley.

"There they are!" shouted a paratrooper in the trench. Kuno turned and followed the man's pointing finger into the sky. The Stukas were diving one after the other on the field, the lead bomber spitting fire from its cannon and machine guns as it dove. Angry flashes of fire burst about the bomber as the flak gunners began to find the range. At less than 500 meters altitude the bomber pulled out of its steep dive and released its bomb load. 2800 kilos of high explosives plunged to the ground 300 meters west of the runway, right in the heart of the massed British infantry, waiting in trenches and craters for the signal to attack.

Earth and stone erupted in fountains of fire from the British positions as the bombs exploded. In quick succession two more Stukas struck the concentration of British infantry to the west of the runway. Huge clouds of dust and smoke towered into the air.

As the clouds drifted north on the wind they obscured all of Ta Qali airfield from direct observation from the heights to the west.

Kuno raised his whistle to his lips and blew furiously, signaling to his paratroopers to open fire on the British now caught between the German forces on the east side of the runway. The five MG 34 machine guns barked out and instantly British troops began to drop. The mortar fire slackened as the British found they could no longer observe the fall of their shells through the clouds of dust and smoke. The German troops at the south of the field now emerged from cover and poured a deadly crossfire into the British.

The attack of the Tommies dissolved in a hail of lead. In less than a minute the survivors took to their heels and were fleeing back to the west. They were cut down as they tried to cross the wide, flat runway. As the last of them scrambled on hands and knees over the runway the sound of aero engines once more came to Ta Qali. The sound rose steadily in volume to a roar until it drowned all other sounds on the field and still it grew louder.

Kuno lifted his left arm to check the time. Pain stabbed up his arm to his shoulder. A wave of blackness threatened to overcome him. He dropped his arm and put his head back against the trench wall, forcing himself to concentrate, to retain consciousness. Slowly his vision began to return to normal. He looked up into the sky. Through the smoke and haze white blossoms sprang open as the paratroops of the second wave jumped from the Junkers 52 transport aircraft. The Germans on the ground broke out in a hearty cheer at the sight.

Fire from several flak guns on the west side of the field rose into the sky to challenge the transports. As the second echelon of Auntie Ju's flew over the field the gunners found the range, hammering the starboard engine of the westernmost transport. Kuno cringed as the Ju 52 swerved out of line, losing altitude rapidly. Men tumbled from its exit door and the first few managed to get their 'chutes open, but as the plane tipped over in its death dive the last paratroopers to escape the transport were already too close the ground. Kuno watched in horror as the last three men out the door hurtled to the ground, their parachutes unopened.

Dozens of German machine guns opened up from the east side of the field targeting the British flak guns to the west. The sheer volume of fire was incredible as red-hot tracer shells ricocheted off the mountings and barrels of the flak guns. The anti-aircraft fire sputtered and all but went out as the British crews were unable to stand to their guns under the murderous fire. The remainder of the second drop on Ta Qali proceeded against very limited and sporadic flak fire.

Kuno looked back down at his left arm. His lower sleeve was well soaked with blood that trickled down his wrist and dripped from his fingertips into the rocky soil. He pulled his bayonet from his belt and cut the sleeve from the wrist to above his elbow, exposing the wound on the outside of his bicep. The bullet had cut a furrow through his flesh, but had passed through cleanly and not struck bone. A corporal in the trench saw his wound and came to assist, first cleaning the wound, then packing gauze into it and finally wrapping the arm tightly. In a few moments the bleeding was controlled.

>>>>>>>>>>>>>

At Whitehall the message announcing the Axis invasion of Malta was immediately distributed to the three service leaders and the intelligence and operations sections, including Room 39 where the Royal Navy's Naval Intelligence Directorate maintained its staff around-the-clock.

The NID performed traditional naval intelligence duties such as tracking Axis ship movements and its submarine tracking room had built a truly astonishing level of operational intelligence about the German U-boat fleet. It contributed regular, timely and highly accurate advice to Allied convoy commanders. This advice was already in the early summer of 1942 starting to shift the balance of the Battle of the Atlantic towards the Allies.

Rear-Admiral Sir John Godfrey commanded the NID. He had assumed the role of Director of Naval Intelligence shortly before the outbreak of war, finding at that time a sorely neglected service. By summer of 1942 he'd built a highly competent and professional, though very much overworked staff which had already provided notable input for the Royal Navy's operational commands. It was the NID which had put all the intelligence pieces together and correctly forecast that the *DKM Bismarck* would head for safety in the French Channel ports, allowing the

Home Fleet to intercept and sink her, avenging the loss of *HMS Hood.*

When word of the invasion of Malta reached NID at 0230 hours London time the morning of 26 June, the staff set to work immediately putting together the latest known details on the movements and condition of individual surface units of the Italian Navy, the *Regia Marina,* and of the whereabouts of over thirty German and Italian Submarines believed to be in the Mediterranean. Their work was complicated because they were already putting a comparable effort into tracking main German fleet units and submarines in the Norwegian Sea as convoy PQ17 prepared to make its dash for the Russian ports of Arkhangel'sk and Murmansk.

News of the invasion was also forwarded to several important Royal Navy fleet commands. Admiral Harwood at Alexandria and Admiral Burrough at Gibraltar were alerted as was Admiral Syfret, in command of the aircraft carriers *HMS Illustrious* and *Indomitable.* The two great carriers, capable of launching over 100 modern aircraft between them, turned the corner of the Horn of Africa early on the 25th, entering the Red Sea and beginning the run to Suez. They'd been ordered north days earlier when the British first learned of the planned invasion. Narrow, shallow waters and numerous shoals and reefs in the Red Sea forced the carriers and their escorts to slow down, just as the need for speed became most critical.

In the United States Prime Minister Winston Churchill was concluding a visit with the American President Roosevelt. Churchill motored from the White House in Washington, D.C. to the harbor at nearby Baltimore to board his Boeing flying boat for the return flight to Britain.

Churchill came away from his meetings with the President without the strategic agreement he sought. The British position was that a direct assault on German occupied Europe could not be mounted during 1942, but that a more peripheral attack in North Africa or the Balkans was possible. The Americans were still determined to press for an early decision in Europe, with an amphibious assault against the French Channel coast in the autumn. The two allies had agreed to study the issue further before coming to a decision.

The Prime Minister and his party were on the quay saying their farewells to their American security staff when a member of the American team drew General Sir Alan Brooke, Chief of the Imperial General Staff aside for an urgent phone call in the Navy command shack. When he returned to the quay his face was grave. He leaned in to speak softly in the Prime Minister's ear. Those who witnessed the tableau knew that General Brooke had delivered very bad news indeed, for Churchill's face drained of its color and he passed his hand over his eyes.

In the Atlantic *HMS Furious* forced her way eastwards, leaving her station west of Gibraltar where she had provided anti-submarine air patrols for three allied convoys. Wind driven spray was flung back across the deserted flight deck as the bow plunged into the oncoming seas. Admiralty signals first received on the morning of June 23, ordered *Furious* to be prepared to turn about for Gibraltar immediately as soon as the convoys had cleared the area. At Gib' she was to take on a complement of Spitfire fighters and receive fuel and an exchange of escort destroyers, then after a few short hours proceed on her way into the Mediterranean.

Shortly before sunset on the evening of the 25th *Furious* had recovered the last of her aircraft, a Fairey Swordfish that had flown anti-submarine patrol over two convoys in-bound to the British Isles, carrying food stuffs, raw materials and fuels for the British people and industries to carry on the war effort. The convoys passed into the care of long-range RAF Coastal Command aircraft flying from the extreme south of England.

The moment the flight deck arresting gear trapped the tail hook of the bi-plane *Furious* and her escorts turned east and at maximum speed began the 300-mile dash for Gibraltar. Initial speeds approached thirty knots, the top speed of the four escort destroyers, but a freshening sea forced the fleet to slow down, first to twenty-five knots, then later again to twenty-two as the evening wore into the early morning hours.

Well before dawn on June 26th *Furious* received the signal from Admiralty that the Axis invasion of Malta had begun. She was still almost one hundred miles from Gibraltar.

>>>>>>>>>>>>>>

The drop of the 23rd Fallschirmjager regiment at Hal Far airfield on Malta's south coast went badly from the start. The Luftwaffe's final bombing assault against Malta was strongest at Ta Qali and Luqa Airfields in the center of the island. Hal Far was not totally neglected, but the force that attacked it was less than half that which struck Ta Qali. As a result the flak defenses on Hal Far were in better repair when the assault began. Also, Hal Far, as the furthest south of the three Maltese airfields, received a precious minute more warning of the approaching assault than the defenders at Ta Qali and Luqa. The flak gun crews were better prepared and quicker to find the range and altitude. They held their fire through the final bombing attack, then let loose with a furious barrage as the transports and gliders came within range.

From the cockpit of the lead JU 52 transport the field at Hal Far came into view just as the last of the bombers broke off their attacks and turned for home. Flame and smoke roiled into the sky from several places on the field.

"No flak!" shouted the co-pilot to the pilot over the roar of the engines.

At that very moment the ground on the field erupted in fire. The flak gunners sheltering in the sand bag bunkers built for their guns leapt to their 40mm Bofors and 90mm hi-angle guns and poured streams of high explosive flak into the sky.

"Someone forgot to tell the British!" the pilot shouted back.

One of the very first shells hit squarely in the starboard engine of that lead Junkers. The engine erupted in a fountain of flaming fuel and a shower of red-hot debris.

"SHIT!" shouted the pilot.

He and the co-pilot both jumped on the rudder to compensate for the drag from the flaming engine.

"It's no good!" shouted the pilot. "We can't hold it! Turn on the jump light!"

Behind the transport the pilot of its towed glider saw the engine explode from the flak hit. Though well short of the intended drop point he didn't hesitate for a second, but reached down beside his seat and pulled the tow-cable release lever. The GO 242 glider dropped free and the pilot nosed it over immediately to clear the curtain of flaming fuel trailing the Junkers. As he flew the glider, searching frantically for a spot on the ground to put her down, out of the corner of his eye he saw paratroopers jumping from the transport plane. Several of the chutes caught fire as flaming fuel blew back in the slipstream. The Junkers staggered out of formation, losing altitude as it crossed the airfield and disappeared over the sea south of Malta.

Other glider pilots took their cue from the lead craft and began releasing their own tow-cables, over a kilometer too soon. Many crash-landed short of the airfield where they fetched up against centuries old stonewalls in the nearby fields. A few lucky glider pilots were able to set down on the Safi Strip, the taxiway connecting Hal Far and Luqa airfields, but on the whole casualties among the troops in the gliders were very high and the survivors found themselves short of the target zone. Among these gliders were those carrying the regimental commander and his staff and the regimental communications section.

The flak guns surrounding the field continued their barrage. Before they were able to land their paratrooper cargo nine transports and six gliders of the eighty-five Luftwaffe tandem combinations sent against Hal Far were shot down.

The first wave of the 23rd regiment, decimated before it ever reached the ground, leaderless and without communications, scattered and off target was unable to gain a foothold on Hal Far. The old English county regiment, the Devons, moved quickly to isolate small groups of paratroopers before they could coalesce into more cohesive units. In just over an hour the fighting at Hal Far was a mopping up operation, with British medical teams moving about the field, saving wounded of both sides. The German force suffered over 600 killed and wounded and almost all the remainder of the force of 1,750 men fell into British captivity. Only a small force of just over one hundred men who slipped away to the west of the field remained free.

The Devons set to work clearing the runway of crashed gliders and transports and filling in bomb craters. As dawn approached five of the remaining Spitfires in service on Malta were carefully wheeled from their revetments to shelters nearer the runway. Camouflage nets covered them and their pilots were kept on close stand-by.

>>>>>>>>>>>>

Kuno lay back in his trench east of the runway and watched the spectacle of a mass paratroop drop from the ground. His message had gotten through to divisional HQ on Sicily. Hundreds of parachutes drifted down on the field, all well east of the runway. A handful of flak guns still fired from the western heights, but their fire was disrupted by German troops on the ground that kept the flak positions under constant machine gun fire. Small arms fire continued to crackle over the field, but the punch was knocked out of the British counter-attack by the direct bomb attacks they'd been subjected to. But for the continued mortar fire directed from the high ground against the field the second drop on Ta Qali might almost have been an exercise.

As he watched, it seemed to Kuno that parachutes were coming down like flakes in a snowstorm. Each paratrooper drew his knees up to cushion the impact, but most of them still met the Earth with a heavy thud, rolling over several times before regaining control. Troopers already on the field quickly met the new arrivals, forming them into squads, platoons and companies and the process of moving them into position began. Captivated by the skyscape it was several moments before Kuno realized someone was looking down at him from the lip of the trench. He made a conscious effort to focus on the figure.

"Baron!" he exclaimed at last. "So good to see you, Sir!" he had to shout to be heard over the roar of the Ju 52 transports thundering overhead.

"My dear, Schacht," replied the Baron von der Heydte, "it is I that am pleased to see you. For a moment I thought I was looking at your corpse. Are you injured?"

"It's minor, Sir," answered Kuno as he struggled to his feet. "I'm fine. I was just admiring the drop and I'm afraid I let myself start wool gathering." He slung his machine pistol over his shoulder and using his right arm he started to pull himself up out of the trench, but the Colonel waved him back and jumped down into the trench instead. The two men smiled at each other with genuine warmth.

As the two officers appraised each other a stick of paratroopers drifted to the ground across the trench line, landing with a series of thuds, rolling with the impact, then bouncing up to control their parachute shrouds.

"I want to thank you for the bombing attacks, Major," said the Baron. "I assume it was you that ordered them?"

"Yes, Colonel," replied Kuno. "We were able to establish contact just in time, though. It was a very closely run thing."

"Indeed!" snorted Colonel August. "This whole operation seems to have been closely run. It's obvious to me that the British were forewarned of our coming. Their response to the landing was much too quick." A heavy mortar round landed nearby with a crash. Both men ducked instinctively, but continued their conversation.

"I agree, Colonel," said Schacht, "and yet they have not hit us with any armor yet. If they knew we were coming wouldn't they have had just a handful of panzers nearby? They could overrun us yet with a half dozen. We have not retrieved more than a couple of the PAK guns from all these wrecked gliders."

"Yes," mused the Baron. "Perhaps they kept their tanks a little too far from the field in order to avoid having them bombed before the attack."

Dirt kicked up at the trench rim as a stream of machine gun bullets ploughed into the ground. The two Germans dropped to their knees.

"Well, whatever the explanation," said Kuno, "we'd best get ourselves sorted out quickly. We need to clear the west side of the field and to do that we must get those mortars silenced."

"Precisely, Schacht," agreed the Baron. "I'll leave that to you. I will organize the attack to clear the field of opposition."

"Yes, Colonel!"

The Baron moved off down the trench and Kuno turned back to the field telephone. He briefly contemplated the crank. He did not want to have to crank it himself. He knew he was still weak from his wound and loss of blood. He stepped up on a dirt ledge and poked his head above the trench. Two paratroopers were a few yards away gathering in their parachute shrouds. Junkers transports continued overhead in a seemingly unending stream. Fresh sticks of paratroopers drifted to earth all over the eastern half of the field.

"YOU TWO!" shouted Kuno. "Come here!"

The two men dragged their chutes into the trench with them and reported to Schacht.

"Yes, Major!"

"What regiment are you in?" Kuno demanded of them.

"We are of the 23rd regiment, Major," one of the two men, a Corporal, replied.

"The 23rd!" exclaimed Kuno. "But you are on the wrong drop zone! You should be at Hal Far!"

The two men looked at each other, then back at Kuno.

"I'm sorry, Major," answered the Corporal, "we jumped when we were told to jump. We know nothing of why we are on the wrong drop zone."

"It's all right, Corporal," said Kuno. "I'm glad to see you regardless. I want you to find your platoon or company commander and bring him to me here. Now go!"

The Corporal scurried off to find his Officer. Kuno turned to the other man, a private.

"You're to assist me in operating the field telephone," he told the man. "Have you any experience with the device?"

"No, sir!" the man answered.

"Don't worry," said Kuno. "It is very simple and I will direct you."

Under Kuno's direction the man quickly cranked the set. Kuno took the phone from its cradle.

"Tondok!" shouted Kuno into the mouthpiece. "Give me Schuenemann!"

A flurry of mortar rounds slammed down on the field. The British were recovering their wits and were trying to interfere with the landing. Still, the Ju 52's poured over the field with hundreds more parachutes descending. Desultory flak fire from the west side of the field continued, but every time one of the guns seemed to find the range a flurry of German small arms fire would drive the British crew off.

Schuenemann came on the line. "Yes, Major?"

"Are any dive bombers orbiting the field right now, Schuenemann?" Kuno demanded.

"Yes, Major, I have two flights of three each in the pattern."

"They must locate and attack the British heavy mortars. They must be positioned on the reverse slope of the high ground to the west." Kuno turned and looked to the west. The moon was well toward the western horizon, but from its position in the sky he could see that the western slope of the hills should be bathed in bright moonlight.

"Right away, Major!" shouted Schuenemann.

"Do you have any contact with the other drop zones?"

"No, Sir," answered the radioman, "but I established direct contact with Division, Major."

"Excellent Schuenemann!" exclaimed Kuno. "What news have they?"

"Not good, Major," said Schuenemann. "They report no contact with our troops at either of the other airfields. They have re-directed the entire second drop here to Ta Qali. It is feared that our attack at the other fields has failed."

"Thank you, Schuenemann," replied Kuno. "Now call in that strike against the mortars!"

Kuno hung up the phone without waiting for a reply. He looked at the private from the 23rd Regiment.

"Now I know why you are here," he said.

"Sir?" the man asked.

"Never mind," Kuno said.

He checked his watch and looked into the sky. 0128 hours. By concentrating the drop on Ta Qali he estimated a further 3,500 paratroopers would be delivered in this drop and in each of two more by just after dawn. By sunrise about twelve thousand paratroopers would occupy Ta Qali, over half the division.

"Come with me," he told the trooper. "We'll find your officers ourselves."

He looked again at the sky, watching the transports stream away from the field to the south then peel away to west and east for the return flight to Sicily. He turned to go seek out nearby officers of the fresh troops, but he stopped and looked again to the south. He frowned and lifted his binoculars to his eyes. He struggled to focus them on the thin white line drawn across the sky above the ridgeline south of Ta Qali.

At the Regimental HQ of the Inniskillings at Mdina confusion reigned. The Brigadier in command of the Regiment was caught in Valletta by the assault. He and several of his Regimental Staff were spending the night as guests of Lord Gort following an evening of meetings concerning the disposition of ammunition and deployment of troops and artillery on the island. The destruction of the telephone exchange severed his communications with his regiment. He resolved to set out by car for Rabat and was on his way by 0030 hours for a trip that should normally have taken him little more than twenty minutes.

In fact, the trip took him the rest of his life. As his driver careened the staff car around a bend in the road near the south end of Ta Qali airfield a Messerschmitt BF 109 dove on the car in a strafing run. The nearby sounds of battle covered the noise of the plane's engine until it was too late. The Brigadier and his driver were both killed instantly by 20mm cannon fire and two of his aides were critically wounded when the car went off the road at high speed into a stonewall.

The Regiment's second in command was unaware of the Brigadier's fate and was unwilling to take decisive action without approval of higher authority. As the Germans worked frantically to consolidate their grip on Ta Qali airfield command of the British defenders descended into chaos.

Even before the second drop was complete the German assault against the west side of Ta Qali airfield was underway. Sgt. Tondok and the 6th Regiment's Communication team succeeded in connecting field phones from the north to the south end of the field. The Baron used the phones to coordinate a frontal assault to sweep west along the entire length of the runway. German paratroopers hunkered down in the drainage ditch on the east margin of the 1200-meter long strip, waiting for the signal to attack.

The intensity of the British mortar bombardment however was growing. Up to ten heavy rounds a minute struck the east side of the field. Heavy caliber artillery shells were beginning to fall also, though the British artillery was inaccurate. The British had not restored their own telephone communications and the artillery wasn't in contact with forward observers.

Kuno rejoined Tondok, Schuenemann and the others of his communications team in the small bunker where they had knocked out the British Vickers machine gun right after landing. Kuno knelt beside the young paratrooper and listened to Schuenemann command the bombers orbiting the field. Gone was the terrified boy Kuno had slapped back to his senses just over an hour earlier. Schuenemann was professional and confident, sure of himself and his skills.

There were eight bombers and four fighters orbiting the field to provide cover for the German force. The twelve aircraft were in flights of two or three aircraft at a range and altitude both of 4,000 meters in a clockwise orbit of the airfield, essentially a ten-kilometer circle. As each group of aircraft reached the southwestern corner of the field in their circuit they swerved out to the west to encompass the high ground surrounding Rabat in an effort to identify the locations from which the British mortar barrage was being fired.

The British however were very coy. They held their fire until the German aircraft passed on then cut loose a flurry of mortar shells against the paratroopers on the airfield. They went silent again as the next flight of aircraft came close. In this way they kept their exact position from the Germans and maintained an intermittent fire against the airfield. Their fire was obviously still directed by forward observers, as it was quite accurate. Any group of paratroopers that exposed their positions for more than a few moments could expect to be targeted. Frustration and casualties among the Germans on the field grew.

Kuno sat, timing the barrage and counting the shells. The net effect was that about every two and a half minutes a barrage of twenty-four rounds landed on the field. From this, Kuno deduced there were twelve tubes in the British mortar battery positioned on the reverse slope of the high ground to the west around Rabat and Dingli.

"Green Four, Green Four," Schuenemann called into the radio's microphone.

Green Four, the flight leader of one the Stuka groups responded. "This is Green Four, Ta Qali. Go ahead."

"As you break off the pattern to the west please continue to orbit west of the high ground," Schuenemann commanded. "Spread your pattern so that the west side of the hill is under constant observation by at least one aircraft. We must identify the source of this barrage!"

"Acknowledged, Ta Qali," came the reply from Green four.

The three Stukas broke their formation and peeled off one by one to the west of the field, spreading themselves out in an oval circuit of some six kilometers, two kilomcters between each aircraft. In this way one of the three was always just over the western slopes, while the other two craft circled back. The British were faced with the choice of holding their mortar fire or of revealing their positions.

"SCHACHT?" a voice called his name. Kuno stood and looked about. "SCHACHT?" the voice came again. This time he located its owner.

"Over here, Colonel!" Kuno replied. He waved his good arm over his head to draw the Baron's attention.

"There you are, Schacht!" huffed the Baron von der Heydte. "What are we doing about these mortars?" he demanded. "We can't launch the assault under these conditions!"

Kuno lifted his left wrist with his right hand and held the watch face up to the moonlight.

"Actually, Colonel, I believe young Schuenemann here has silenced the mortars, at least temporarily."

"EH?" The Baron looked quizzically at the young radioman. "I have not seen a bombing attack take place."

"No, Sir," replied Kuno, "but it has now been four minutes since a mortar round fell on the field. Schuenemann has reconfigured the flight pattern of the bombers over the field to keep the high ground under constant observation. The British don't dare to fire lest they reveal their positions."

"Good, good," murmured the Baron. "And yet, Schacht," he said, "as soon as we begin our attack they will fire even though it gives away their position."

"The Stukas have been warned to attack immediately if the British reveal themselves," replied Kuno. "Anyway, we can't wait. The bombers will be forced to leave for fuel soon. Once they're gone the British will be free to fire upon us at will."

"You're right, of course," answered the Colonel. "Besides, the artillery fire is starting to pick up. We are fortunate it has been inaccurate, but that won't last. I wish we had our own mortars in operation. We could at least lay a smoke screen." He paused and thought a moment. "All right," he said. "I'll order the attack to begin in five minutes. A red flare will signal the first wave to attack. Warn your bombers, Schacht. Everything now depends on them being alert."

"Yes, Sir!" answered Kuno.

Through the continued chatter of small arms Kuno heard

whistles blowing to the north and south of him along the east side of the runway. German non-coms were shepherding the paratroopers to the start line for the attack. He used his binoculars to scan the east side of the runway. From north end to south end the drainage ditch on the runway margin was crowded with paratroopers and more were being fed in as he watched. They ran bent over, keeping as low to the ground as possible. Even so, men were falling here and there as they were hit. The British still had fight in them.

Kuno checked his watch. 0150. The second drop had begun thirty minutes earlier. Just under an hour to the start of the third drop. Just then a red flare arched skyward over the runway, signaling the commencement of the attack.

Dozens of machine guns all along the German line began to bark, spitting streams of shells and red-hot glowing tracer across the runway. One minute of heavy fire and a second red flare burst over the runway. With a roar the drainage ditch came alive as the first wave of paratroopers leapt to their feet and began to race across the runway.

The raised bare ground of the runway, one hundred fifty meters wide and still brightly lit by the setting moon was a perfect place for the British to catch the massed German paratroopers and the Germans knew it. They dashed across the runway at top speed, firing their Schmeisser MP 40 machine pistols from the hip as they ran.

Small arms fire erupted from the British side of the field. A Vickers gun directly opposite Kuno barked out a stream of deadly lead cutting down a dozen paratroopers in their tracks as they crossed the runway. Several of them thrashed about in the agony of their wounds, the others lay still where they had fallen. But the British were hampered by the small groups of Germans from the first drop still holding out on the west side of the field. It was impossible for the British to bring concentrated small arms fire against the paras as they crossed the runway.

Then the mortar rounds began to crash down. The British had the entire field, including the runway pre-registered for fire from their mortars. A dozen rounds crashed down squarely on the runway at hundred meter intervals, just as the first of the paras began to reach the west side. The effect was appalling as men were cut down in droves by shrapnel and deadly bits of rock and stone hurled with the speed of bullets. Shouts of fury and pain echoed across the field and clouds of dust filled the air.

A second round of shells crashed down thirty seconds later. In his trench Kuno felt the concussion of the shells in his feet over one hundred meters from the nearest blast.

"SCHUENEMANN!" he yelled.

"The Stukas are attacking now, Major!" the private yelled back. "They have determined the positions of the British mortars!"

Kuno gripped his binoculars, instinctively using both hands, grimacing in pain as his wounded left arm protested. He held the glasses to his eyes with his right hand and tried to pierce the dust and debris to see the high ground. It was useless; he could see nothing.

Then, over the sounds of battle and the cries of the wounded he heard the wail of sirens as Stukas dove on a target. The sirens were there for just a brief snatch of a second before they were drowned again, first by the rapid fire of British flak guns, then by the crash of a third round of mortars.

A wave of choking limestone dust rushed over the bunker and trench where the comms section was sheltered. Kuno ducked below the trench rim and pulled his tunic up over his mouth and nose. And in the distance he heard the crash of bombs as the Stuka attack went home.

Through the dust he checked his watch, marking the instant of the explosions, counting the seconds following them. The dust began to thin as he reached the one-minute mark. He poked his head above the trench line, peering through the swirling cloud towards the runway. The mortars were silent.

"TONDOK!" he shouted.

"Yes, Sir!" Tondok appeared at Kuno's elbow as though he'd been waiting for the summons.

"Find the Baron, Tondok!" said Kuno. "Tell him the British mortars have been silenced. It is time to send the balance of the attack!"

Moments later whistles blew up and down the runway. Hundreds more paratroopers leapt to their feet and dashed onto the landing strip. Here, paradoxically the British mortars served the German cause. A thick dust cloud lingered over the strip, masking the assault force from view from the enemy infantry. Random fire, especially from heavy Vickers and light Bren machine guns still caused casualties, but the paras were able to cross the landing strip to the west side of the field, hurdling the drainage ditch on that side of the runway and emerging from the dust cloud with machine pistols blazing.

Kuno watched the assault from the trench outside his radio team's bunker. He strained to see through the swirling dust and clouds of smoke as the German troopers poured across the runway, firing their MP40 machine pistols from the hip, screaming like devils. Here, the decision to equip the entire assault force with automatic weapons paid huge dividends to Germany. The MP 40 is a deadly, close range infantry weapon. In the confused, face-to-face fight that ensued the German sub-machine gun was the decisive factor.

The British infantry were snowed under in a hail of lead. Anywhere they attempted to make a stand the German paratroopers surrounded them, and then charged from all sides to wipe them out. Cornered, with nowhere to run the English infantry of the Manchesters and the Irish infantry of the Inniskillings fought for their lives in defense of Ta Qali, but they fought in vain. The Germans paras, rested, well fed and fit, routed the malnourished, dysentery weakened British defenders from their trenches and bunkers with grenades and machine gun fire.

Kuno struggled to hold his binoculars, but the wound in his left arm forced him to use only his right hand and the glasses refused to hold steady. Finally he knelt in the trench and rested the glasses on a stone at the rim. Bringing the lenses into focus he watched as a group of paras stormed a large, sandbagged bunker on the west side of the field.

A furious barrage of fire from inside the bunker felled men right and left, but the paras came on, firing their Schmeisser machine pistols from the hip, spraying lead along the top of the British trench line and at the embrasures of the bunker. At the last instant the Tommies poured out of the bunker with fixed bayonets to meet the Germans. A vicious hand-to-hand battle ensued with men skewered by bayonets, clubbed to the ground with gunstocks or strangled with bare hands. The ghastly scene played itself out in the fading moonlight and swirling clouds of limestone dust as men of both sides were knifed and bludgeoned to death in the bottom of lonely trenches and bomb craters.

As the dust slowly cleared Kuno was better able to watch the progress of the assault as it swept westwards across Ta Qali field. As the paratroopers advanced and doubt of the outcome of the assault disappeared the British infantry began to break and run.

"TONDOK!" shouted Kuno.

Once again the Sergeant appeared as if from nowhere.

"Here, Major!"

"Get ready to run field phones to the west of the airstrip," Kuno ordered. "For the time being your wire can cross the runway. We'll reroute it round the ends later. Right now we must be able to communicate with the troops there. Draft as many men from the infantry companies as you need to do the job quickly!"

"Right away, Major!" Tondok acknowledged.

The Sergeant hurried off, smacking troopers on the shoulder as he went. Kuno checked his watch; nearly a half hour to the third drop.

A tearing, ripping sound that changed to a high-pitched screech came to his ears. Instinctively he ducked as the shell passed almost directly over his head and exploded a hundred meters away to the southeast. Paratroopers nearby threw themselves on the ground, covering up in fetal positions.

Kuno checked his watch again. If the British had forward artillery observers in communication with the gun crews it would take about three minutes for the gunners to adjust their aim and begin plastering the center of the field and the runway.

"Schuenemann!" he shouted, setting off back down the trench line towards the comms bunker. He broke into a trot as he approached the sand bag emplacement. He skidded to a stop beside the radio operator and listened to the conversation the young man was having over the airwaves.

"That's right Green One," he said, "the next target is to be heavy artillery to the northwest of the field, over."

Schuenemann paused and listened. Kuno checked his watch. Over two minutes since the ranging shell was fired.

"I don't know exactly where the guns are Green One," said Schuenemann in exasperation. "They are somewhere northwest of the field. The shell was at least a one-oh-five, so they must be at least five kilometers out, over."

Another pause as Schuenemann listened again to the aircrew aboard Green One.

"Watch for the gun flash, Green One," he went on. "The British will fire again, over."

Kuno looked again at his watch. He leaned over and tapped Schuenemann on the shoulder. When the young man looked at him Kuno tapped his watch face then pointed skyward with arched eyebrows. Schuenemann picked up his meaning immediately.

"Green One, they will fire any second now, over."

The ripping, tearing screech rose from the northwest, rising in pitch then flattening.

"GET DOWN, SCHUENEMANN!" Kuno screamed and threw himself bodily atop the young private, knocking him flat, wrenching the headset from his ears, tearing the microphone from his hands.

The first shell slammed into the trench thirty meters away, erupting in a fountain of earth and rock. A set of five others followed, all grouped within fifty meters of the command post, heaving the earth, bouncing Schacht and Schuenemann about on top one another. The wall of the trench began to collapse, then caved in completely, burying them in earth. Kuno struggled to fight his way clear, pushing himself up on his knees, but the weight of the earth pushed him back down, crushing him against Schuenemann's body. The earth closed over him and he fought for air. His mouth and nose filled with dirt and blackness closed over him.

>>>>>>>>>>>>>

A cup of tea was pressed to his lips. At first he paid it no attention and did not drink, but the nurse was patient and she held the cup under his nose until the aroma started to have its affect. Finally, he looked down at the cup and pursed his lips to drink. He looked at the nurse and gave her a thin, wan smile. He did not speak. He heard the dull rumble of an explosion and became aware for the first time of the distant crackle of small arms fire. The nurse took his hand and lifted it to the cup. He held it and felt the warmth in the palm of his hand. He sipped slowly from it as the nurse watched.

"Tha'z better," she said gently. "Won' you tell me you name now, Een-glizh?"

He smiled at her again and tried to speak, but his heart was still in his throat and his eyes began to water. He shook his head and set the cup down, covering his face with his hands.

The nurse tried a different tack.

"Who's the girl you was wit', Een-glizh?" she asked. "Wat was happened to you two tonight?"

"Her name was Maggie," he whispered.

The nurse leaned over to catch his words.

"Mac-gee?" she asked. "Zhe an Irizh girl?"

He shook his head.

"No," he said, "she was English."

"You both Een-glizh," the nurse said. "You know each other before you come Malta?"

"No," he answered. "We met here."

"Wa's your name Een-glizh?" she asked again.

"My name is Kenneth," he said. "Kenneth Wiltshire, and I'm not English, I'm American."

"Oh, a Yank!" said the nurse. "We seen plenty you fellas here. Say," she went on, a quizzical look coming over her features, "how come you got Yanks don't like being called Yanks?" she asked.

He laughed, short and sharp and smiled at the nurse. He shook his head and shrugged his shoulders. He looked at her and saw her for the first time. She was a middle-aged woman, thin and wiry in the Maltese way, black hair just starting to gray, eyes so brown they seemed black.

"Wat abou' the girl was wit you, Kennett?' she asked. "Was you on a date?"

The smile disappeared from his face. He nodded his head, but said nothing.

"Well," she said. "You finish you tea and I zee if Doctor will let you zee her yet."

The nurse got up from her stool and walked out of the room, through a doorframe with no door. Kenneth looked about the room for the first time. A very typical Maltese abode with thick, white limestone walls and a tiny window set in a deep recess in the wall. He was sitting on a narrow cot. A candle burned on a small table next to the bed. He picked up his teacup and drank the lukewarm tea down.

He set the cup back down and stood. He realized he had gone into a form of shock from which he was only just beginning to recover. His mind backed up to the events on the road. His heart plunged in pain every time he thought of Maggie. He tried to steer his thoughts away, but everything brought him back to her. He hung his head and started to cry, deep and sobbing, but softly, quietly. After a few moments he heard Maltese voices in the hallway outside the room. Quickly he wiped his eyes and turned his back to the door, fighting to control himself.

"Hey, Yank!" the nurse said, poking her head through the door. "You come now. Doctor say it's o.k."

Turning to face her misery was written on his face and lines of tears still coursed down his cheek.

"Oh," she said. "You won' do like dat!" she pulled a rag from her apron and daubed at his cheeks. "You doan wanna see dat pretty Een-glizh girl looking like dat. You scare her!" she scolded him. "Now come on, put youzel' toget-her."

Kenneth felt his heart skip. He grabbed the nurse by the shoulders.

"What did you say?" he asked, barely daring to hope, his voice the thinnest whisper.

"Tha's right!" she said. "Zhe's worried abou' you. Zhe wan to know where you iz. Now come on!"

She broke free of his grip and left the room. He closed his eyes and paused a moment before following her. "Please God," he said a silent prayer then hurried after the nurse. She was waiting for him at a door down the hall. She put her finger to her lips.

"Now you don' exzite dis girl," she said sternly. "Zhe took a nassy bump on de head and zhe don' need no more excitement. You be calm an' quiet!"

"Yes, Ma'am," he said. "Can I see her now please?"

The nurse opened the door a crack and poked her head in.

"Okey-dokey," she said, looking back at him. "Doctor is wit her now. You come in for a few minutes."

She stepped through the door and Kenneth pressed after her. His heart leapt at what he saw. Maggie lay on a hospital bed, covered in a blanket up to her neck. A thick pad of bandage was wrapped about her head, coming low on her forehead and down around her jaw, covering her hair completely and leaving just her beautiful face unbound. Her skin was very pale, but two spots of color showed high on her cheeks. Her eyes were closed and the long, brown lashes were still, but through the blanket he could see her chest rise and fall in a slow, even pattern as she breathed. She was alive!

The Doctor, a swarthy Maltese stood to one side of her, holding her wrist and looking at his watch. After a moment he nodded his head and put her hand down gently. He looked at Kenneth and saw the worry on his face. He smiled.

"I am Doctor Mieza. Don't worry," he said in educated English. "She has received a very nasty bump on the head, but should make a full recovery if she can have rest and quiet."

"Has she been awake," Kenneth asked in a whisper.

The Doctor smiled again.

"Yes," he said, "but very briefly. She'll sleep a lot over the next few days. We'll be moving her to a private home nearby in the next few hours. We, uh, we expect other clients will be arriving in larger numbers soon." He arched his eyebrows meaningfully.

Kenneth nodded his head in understanding. The crash of explosions and the drone of aero engines came faintly in snatches through the thick walls every few minutes. The Doctor knew the score and that his tiny hospital would soon be overwhelmed by battle casualties.

"Can I sit with her?" asked Kenneth. "Hold her hand?"

"Yes," replied the Doctor, "but you must be quiet. If she wakens you mustn't tax her strength."

"I promise, Doctor." Kenneth pulled a small stool beside the bed and sat. He hesitated a moment, then gingerly took Maggie's hand in his.

Hilda was beckoning to him to follow her into the boy's bedroom. He tried to ask her what she wanted to show him, but she turned away and walked down the short hall to the bedroom. She reached the bedroom door and turned to wait for him. She was smiling and she beckoned to him again to hurry up. She turned and opened the door, stepping through into the darkened room beyond. He followed, more curious than ever.

He stepped through the door, but as he did so the light from the hallway began to fade to blackness. Hilda was there, but very dim. Yet she was so near he felt he could reach out and touch her. He tried, but his arms remained immobile at his sides. He tried to speak, but his tongue was thick and dull.

The room descended into near total darkness and his curiosity began to slip away. How peaceful just to sleep right here in this warm, dark room. In the last glimmer of light he saw Hilda come to him. She reached out and shook him with one hand and gestured with the other. The light in the room slowly brightened again, and he looked down at the bed.

The two boys Rolf and Edmund were there on their bed, sleeping peacefully side by side. Kuno smiled, but the smile quickly turned to a frown. The boys were in uniform, Rolf as a Luftwaffe pilot, Edmund as a paratrooper. Their arms were crossed over their chests, a rose stem in the hands of each boy. The Iron Cross hung on a red, black and gold ribbon around each young neck.

Hilda continued to shake him, more and more violently. He looked at her and tried to speak, but still couldn't. At last she spoke and he heard her calling his name.

"SCHACHT!" she shouted. "SCHACHT!"

He shook his head. Her voice was unnaturally harsh and low. "SCHACHT!"

The image of Hilda slowly faded. He blinked and reached for her, trying to bring her back, but she faded away like a night mist burning off in a summer morning's sunshine. He called her name.

"Hilda!" he choked on her name and coughed, deep and retching.

"Good, good," Hilda said in that harsh, low voice. "That's better, Schacht. Much better."

Kuno blinked his eyes, but screwed them closed again immediately. They were both filled with dirt and sand.

"Careful, Schacht!" said the voice. "Can you sit up?"

"Yes, I think so, Baron," he replied before a coughing fit took hold of him.

Kuno sat up with the assistance of several sets of willing hands.

He rubbed his eyes, slowly working out the dirt and grit until he was finally able to open them carefully. The Baron's face came into focus in front of him.

"We must get you to your feet, Kuno," the Baron told him. "Can you stand?"

"Yes, I think so," Kuno repeated.

He started to brace himself with his left hand, then remembered his wound and shifted his weight to his right arm, his hand resting on something soft and yielding. He looked down and saw a paratrooper tunic. For the first time he began to realize where he was and how he had come to be there. He looked at the Baron, then back at the figure beside him, searching for the face. He looked back at the Baron.

"Schuenemann?" he asked.

"Yes, Schacht," the Baron replied. "He is dead. We only just got you unearthed in time, but now we must get you out of here. There is still a danger."

The Baron and several paratroopers helped Kuno to his feet and started to guide him away from the collapsed trench. Kuno stopped and looked back.

"Must we leave his body there?" he asked.

"Schacht," the Baron said, "look there at his feet." He pointed into the loose earth near the dead radioman's feet. There lay a smoking 105mm shell, unexploded. Kuno looked at the Baron and nodded his head. He recovered his wits quickly as they moved down the trench.

"We must recover the radio equipment," he said, stopping and looking back.

"The radio is dead, Schacht," answered the Baron. "It's smashed beyond all repair."
He smiled and went on. "It was the first thing we dug out."

"What of the British guns?" Kuno asked.

"A flight of Stukas dropped on the British artillery," answered the Baron. "They have been silenced."

"But we are out of communication," said Kuno. "We no longer have the means to direct a bombing attack."

"For the time being that is so, Schacht," said the Baron, "but after I found the radio smashed I had you dug out so you can fix the situation."

Kuno had recovered sufficiently to appreciate the Baron's humor and he smiled. "Thank you, Baron," he answered.

"Besides," the Baron went on, "we still have a date with Calypso's Cave." At last they reached a point in the trench far enough from the unexploded shell to satisfy the Baron.

"Sit down here, Schacht," he said. "I've sent for Sgt. Tondok. He should be here shortly. You and your team must see to restoring our communications with air support."

"Where will you be, Baron?" asked Kuno.

"I'll be driving the assault onto the high ground," the Colonel answered. "So long as the Tommies hold the high ground they'll be able to pound us with accurate artillery."

Kuno sat and collected his wits as the Baron moved off to coordinate the assault. He checked his watch for the thousandth time that night, wincing in pain again as he forgot his wound and started to lift his left arm. 0245 hours. The third drop was just minutes away. He took the watch off his left wrist and transferred it to his right. He struggled to his feet.

"TONDOK!" he shouted and promptly collapsed in a paroxysm of coughing. His mouth and nose tasted of dirt. He fought down the coughing and took a drink from his canteen, rinsing his mouth and spitting it back on the ground.

A squad of paratroopers passed him in the trench, headed for the west side of the field. He fell in behind them. He reached for his machine pistol and was shocked to find he had lost it. He was armed only with his Walther pistol.

The squad he was following turned a corner in the trench and came to a large sandbagged bunker about thirty meters off the runway. After the assault across the runway it was taken over as an aid station for the wounded. Two medical corpsmen and the 23rd Regiment's surgeon worked frantically on the wounded, even as more were brought in. The injured overflowed the bunker and spilled out into the trench on either side of the entrance. The squad of men stepped carefully around and over their wounded comrades. Kuno looked in the entrance to the bunker as he walked by. The surgeon in blood-splattered apron was operating on a crude table of planks set up across sandbag stacks. Orderlies were lifting one paratrooper onto the table as another was lifted off. He turned away. The scene was all too familiar to him.

They passed the aid station and reached the end of the trench. Ahead lay the runway. The men scrambled out and, keeping their heads low began to move across the runway at a quick trot. Several shots rang out, kicking up dirt around the men's feet. They doubled their pace into a dead run and crossed the runway safely.

He looked up and down the landing strip. Small groups of Germans were crossing on the run, mostly from east to west, but here and there a lone man crossed on the run in the other direction, messengers and runners, or two or three men crossed together, assisting a wounded comrade.

Another group of men came up behind him in the trench. On their shoulders they wore the blue shooting star emblem of the 23rd Regiment. Members of one of the machine gun companies, there were eight men in two-man teams. One member of each team carried the MG 34 machine gun and a box of ammunition while the other man carried two boxes. Each man had two bandoliers of belted ammunition slung in an 'x' across his chest. They paused a moment to rest before crossing the runway, acknowledging Kuno with respectful nods.

Kuno turned again to watch the runway. He focused on a lone man crossing the strip from west to east at a dead run, Schmeisser slung and carried in the crook of one arm.

"TONDOK!" he shouted and once again found his lungs not yet up to the task. Through his coughing he watched the Sergeant running across the open ground. He would miss him if he did not get his attention quickly.

Kuno turned and gripped one of the machine gunners by the arm. He pointed out on the runway at the running man and managed to splutter out a command.

"Call that man! Tondok!" he ordered before the coughing took him over again.

The machine gunner stepped up to the trench rim, shouting the Sergeant's name and waving his arms. To his relief Kuno saw that Tondok heard and adjusted his course towards the trench. In the last few meters bullets were kicking up dust at his heels. Tondok dove headfirst for the trench, sliding over the side and landing on his back in the bottom. Kuno knelt at his side.

"Are you hurt, Sergeant?" he asked.

Gasping, Tondok shook his head and sat up.

"What of the phone lines?" Kuno went on.

"The field lines are strung in two places across the runway," Tondok gasped, fighting for breath. "One to the north of here about 400 meters, the other just to the south about 100 meters. Both are in operation and connected back to the Regimental HQ."

"Good work, Tondok," Kuno replied.

The two men got to their feet. Tondok appraised Kuno's disheveled and dirty features.

"You've had some trouble, Major?"

"Schuenemann is dead, the radio destroyed," Kuno explained. "British artillery. We've got to retrieve the backup equipment from the cache and get back into contact. Without air support this thing can still turn very badly against us."

Kuno turned and looked back over the runway.

"What is happening over there?" he asked.

"We've broken the British main line of resistance," the Sergeant replied, "but there are dozens of small bunkers and air-raid shelters the British still hold. The sniping you see to our front is coming from one of them."

The Corporal leading the machine gun squad was listening intently.

"Where is the bunker, Sergeant?" he asked.

"Quickly, Tondok," Kuno interjected, "then we must be about our own business."

Tondok took the Corporal by the arm to the trench rim and hurriedly pointed out the British positions across the runway. Kuno and Tondok watched the squad as they broke from cover and raced across the runway. Ducking and zigzagging the team reached the far side safely, despite being fired upon.

"You are unarmed, Major," observed Tondok.

"We'll pick something up along the way," answered Kuno. "There are discarded weapons all over the field, I am sure."

The two men set out to return to the rock wall where their glider had crashed. The bulk of their equipment, including the spare wireless set was still there. Kuno checked his watch, now on his right wrist. 0254 hours. For the first time it occurred to him that his watch might have been damaged in the trench collapse.

"Tondok," he gasped, still spitting up dirt and grit.

Tondok stopped and reached to support the Major, but Kuno

shook him off.

"Check your watch, Tondok," he said. "Mine may have been damaged."

The two men compared their watches and found them in agreement. Only five minutes remained till the next drop was scheduled to begin. They hurried on towards their glider. As they went they passed other groups of paratroopers who were working to empty the contents of some of the many crashed gliders.

The drone of aero engines was rising in the north as Kuno and Tondok arrived back at their own glider. A quick glance around its interior confirmed they had cleaned it out shortly after landing. They rushed on to the rock wall and the stash of the remainder of their equipment. The backup radio gear was there, just as they'd left it. Tondok pointed to a small sandbagged enclosure about forty meters away.

"There?" he asked.

"It's as good as any," Kuno replied.

Tondok took two heavy battery cases while Kuno lifted the lighter radio itself and they moved off to the sand bags. The two men set to work unpacking the radio, but they knew they were out of time. There was no hope of getting the radio in operation before the drop began.

"Will they make the drop if they don't have contact with the ground?" asked Tondok.

"I think so," said Kuno. "I hope so. Yes, I think they will."

Kuno looked up from his work on the set and saw the first of the transports come into view north of the field. Tondok followed his gaze, but said nothing. They continued with the task of attaching the power cables from the batteries to the set and of powering it on. It would take several minutes to warm up before they could attempt to make contact.

Flak guns began to fire, but the guns on the field itself were all silent now. Only those on the heights at Rabat to the west and the more distant heavy guns around the harbors to the east took up the challenge against the German transports. Bright flashes erupted near the edges of the stream of transports and Bf 109 fighters dove against the flak guns, strafing their positions and disrupting their fire. But the British served their guns in spite of the harassment they received from the fighters. A Ju 52 in the second echelon was struck in its starboard engine. It broke formation and dove away to the southwest even as paratroopers continued to jump from it. It disappeared behind the high ground, trailing smoke and flame.

Several other aircraft were damaged, but none seriously and all disgorged their passengers safely. Though diminished by combat casualties and operational failures a wave of over two hundred Junkers transports, each carrying eighteen passengers delivered 3,600 fresh paratroopers in the third drop at Ta Qali.

Both on the field at Ta Qali and on the high ground at Rabat to the west the third drop was seen by the interested parties as swinging the tide of battle in favor of the Germans, but the British had not lost hope of denying the field to the Germans and of turning events back in their own favor. The British possessed powerful artillery forces on the island. Many of the heaviest guns were permanently sited to fire only out to sea, but there were a number of batteries of mobile artillery that could be moved into position to fire on the airfields.

In the days prior to the assault, with the forewarning given them by the Ultra intelligence system the British began to move these mobile batteries into position. They were hampered by a shortage of heavy transport lorries, but more critically by a lack of fuel. They were literally scraping the very bottom of the barrel for all purposes and the highest priority was to keep the Spitfires in the air. Only eight of the island's sixteen batteries of heavy mobile artillery had been moved by the early morning of June 26th. Of these, three were sited to fire on Hal Far or Luqa and five against Ta Qali. One battery of 25-pounder guns had fired the shells that killed Schuenemann and nearly Kuno Schacht. This battery was wiped out in the Stuka attack called in by Schuenemann just before his death. The other four batteries remained intact.

But the gunners were not in direct contact with forward observers near the field. The destruction of the island's telephone exchange had severed phone communications. They were unable to observe the fall of their shells and to adjust their aim until new field phone line connections were made, a task given the highest priority by the British command. The first battery connected to forward observers was destroyed almost immediately by Stuka attack after delivering the brief barrage that buried Major Schacht. The British worked feverishly to connect by field phone the other four batteries capable of firing against Ta Qali.

In Valletta Lord Gort and his senior staff launched into feverish activity from the moments after the telephone exchange was bombed. It was quickly apparent that the expected invasion was under way, three days earlier than expected. By 0040 hours Lord Gort had drafted his signal to London. Within minutes it was encoded and being transmitted.

*Axis invasion of Malta underway stop Powerful*
*airborne landings at all three airfields supported*
*by overwhelming air forces stop Further landings*
*are expected stop Immediate relief and resupply*
*most urgent stop Critical shortage of fighter aircraft*
*and aviation fuel crippling to defense stop Soldier*
*and Civilian inhabitants of Malta prepared for*
*battle stop God Save the King*

>>>>>>>>>>>>

Kuno and Sgt. Tondok worked frantically to bring the radio into operation even as the third drop began. In the absence of instructions from the ground to the contrary the transport force operated on the same premise as for the second drop. The entire third drop was made to the east side of the field. Kuno and Tondok watched the first parachutes opening as their radio was warming up. The roar of the transports was once again nearly deafening.

Tondok leaned close to Kuno. "It should be ready, Major!" he shouted.

Kuno nodded and gestured for Tondok to take the microphone and headset. "Try to make contact!" he shouted back. "I'm going to find Steup and the rest of the team! We've got to get fresh field phone connections made from here to the Regimental HQ." Tondok nodded in acknowledgement and set to his task.

Kuno set out to find Steup just as the first of the paratroopers began to reach the ground. He was moving back to the west and south in the direction he'd last seen Steup. Now that the landing zone was secure he needed to bring the communications section back together to do the job they had trained for, to coordinate the close air support so critical to the success of the invasion. He was moving across open ground and had covered about fifty meters when he came to a dead paratrooper. He knelt and quickly took the trooper's machine pistol. He ransacked the man's tunic for spare magazines and in twenty seconds was on his way again.

Looking towards the runway he saw two men carrying coils of phone cable. They were carrying one of the spools between them, running out the cable. Kuno veered towards them. He focused on the two men, trying to discern their features, to recognize them as members of his team. A shout broke his concentration. He stopped running and looked around. The shout came again louder, closer. He spun about, but saw no one.

"LOOK OUT!"

He looked up, just in time to dive aside as a paratrooper hurtled to earth, landing with an explosive "OOMPH!" rolling several times awkwardly before he gained control. He stood with his back to Kuno as he gathered up the shrouds of his chute. The trooper looked back over his shoulder.

"Are you trying to be killed?" he shouted at Kuno.

"Sorry," Kuno said to the man over the roar of the aircraft engines before hurrying on.

As the third landing of German paratroopers at Ta Qali began at 0300 hours on the morning of June 26th 1942 the British assessed their situation. On the one hand, the Germans were in possession of Ta Qali airfield with a powerful force already on the ground and more arriving every minute. It would take a major effort to dislodge them and retake the field.

But the situation was not all grim. Word from Hal Far was that the German assault there was a failure. The field was in British hands with hundreds of German prisoners under guard. At Luqa the situation was almost as favorable, though it hadn't started out that way. The initial German assault caught the field's defenders off guard as at Ta Qali and had it been followed up by a second drop the paratroopers would probably have taken the airfield there as well, but as at Hal Far for some reason the Germans had chosen to forego a follow-up drop. The Germans at Luqa were surrounded on the east side of the field and being pounded with a steady diet of mortar and machine gun fire. It was only a matter of time till they were forced to capitulate. When Luqa was secured reinforcements from the British regiments at both Hal Far and Luqa could be sent to the fight for Ta Qali. Meantime, the British decided to sit back on the high ground and continue to pound the Germans on Ta Qali with artillery.

Kuno carried on towards the runway, taking care now not to be killed by a falling paratrooper. They were coming down like a winter blizzard again, through the thunderous roar of the transports. Discarded 'chutes littered the field, clumping in snowdrifts where the wind drove them to snag against rock walls and gliders. Canisters containing weapons, ammunition, food and medical supplies were scattered all about. British flak was almost completely silent, with just two guns to the west of the field still in action. With the German drop taking place again to the east of the runway their fire was ineffective. The Germans lost just one aircraft to British fire during the third drop and the landing was not disrupted at all.

Kuno reached the men laying the phone cables. They were Corporal Weiss and one of his enlisted men, Private Hauser.

"Major, Schacht!" exclaimed Weiss on seeing Kuno's filthy appearance. He had to shout to be heard above the roar of the transports overhead. "Are you all right, Sir?"

"I'm fine, Weiss," Kuno dismissed the man's concerns. "Now listen to me. Artillery has struck our original command post. The field phone net has been interrupted by the artillery strike. Get back to the original command post. Splice the lines back in operation. Sgt. Tondok is re-establishing communication using the backup radio apparatus. He is set-up near our glider. You must connect his location to the field phone net. Do you understand your orders, Weiss?"

"Yes, Major!"

"Then let's move, Weiss!"

Kuno took one of the spools of cable from Private Hauser. Weiss and Hauser worked to unwind the cable from the spool as they hurried towards the old command post through sticks of freshly arrived paratroopers. The field was a blanket of white with discarded parachutes rippling in the breeze everywhere Kuno looked.

They arrived near the area of the first command post, all churned earth and stone. Weiss and Hauser set out to find the severed ends of the field phone cables and to repair them. Kuno knelt and took a moment to wipe some of the grime from his face. He flexed his left hand. Numbness was setting in to the wound and his arm was stiffening. He massaged his upper arm with his other hand.

The roar of engines began to diminish as the last of the Ju 52's dropped their human cargoes over the field and turned again for Sicily. He checked his watch. 0330 hours. Remarkably the third drop was finished only fifteen minutes behind schedule despite the change of plan in which all reinforcements were delivered to Ta Qali. He knew the next drop would not occur until after dawn and the field was sunlit. He lifted his binoculars and scanned the drop zone. Paratroopers were organizing into squads, platoons, and companies and moving out. Some went to the east and north sides of the field to secure the invasion's flanks, but the majority were directed to the west and south where they would join the assault on Rabat or prepare to move south against Luqa.

He scanned to the west. In the fading light of the setting moon he could just make out dim forms and figures of paratroopers moving forward into position. Here and there the muzzle flash of Schmeisser sub-machine guns lit small areas in a brief and eerie strobe light.

Kuno stood and just as suddenly knelt back down. The ripping, tearing screech of a heavy shell passing overhead preceded the explosion of the shell just east of the runway and about five hundred meters south of his own position. One hundred meters further south of the explosion a company of Germans forming up to move out threw themselves to the ground.

"No, you fools!" Kuno shouted, but knew they were too far away to hear his warning.

He breathed a sigh of relief as he saw officers of the company hustling the men back to their feet and out of the immediate area. The first shell was a ranging shot. British forward observers would be in contact with the gunners by field phone. The next shot would be a barrage from all six guns of the battery and would annihilate the infantry if they remained in place. He watched as the infantry got away at double speed.

The last of them were clearing the immediate vicinity when the sound of shells racing overhead drowned everything else out. The British forward observers were well trained. They had anticipated the movement of the paratroopers and adjusted the fire of the guns to account for it. The trailing platoon of troopers was caught in the barrage. Kuno clenched his fists in fury and frustration. He jumped to his feet and ran for the new communication team command post.

Kuno was forced to seek cover three times in traveling the 300 meters to Tondok and the new communications post. The British artillery was intensifying till he now estimated four batteries of six guns each were pouring fire on the field at a rate of forty rounds per minute. If sustained this rate of fire would cripple the invasion. The fourth drop scheduled at dawn would be impossible in the face of such fire on the ground. When at last he reached Tondok he found the entire team had rejoined and were finally focusing on the task they'd been trained for. Enough paratroopers were now on the field to deal with all the infantry needs, unlike in the first minutes when only Kuno's personal intervention saved the German force at Ta Qali from disaster.

Kuno quickly counted heads. Aside from the unfortunate Schuenemann and Tscheuschner all were accounted for. Lt. Steup worked with Sgt. Tondok to establish radio contact with the bombers while Weiss and Hauser completed the final connections in the field phone net. A row of phones lined a wall of the bunker, on two wooden planks set up as shelves. Other men had set up a table in the corner of the bunker and laid out charts, maps and artillery fire tables. Using calipers and a slide rule they were feverishly working on the formulas to determine the trajectories of the enemy shells in order to locate the guns. The rest of the team was in the trenches outside the bunker, using binoculars to try to determine from which directions the shells were coming and at what angle of descent. Their observations were used as input to the calculations being done inside the bunker. Sgt. Tondok was hunched over the radio set, one hand clamping the headset to his ears the other holding the microphone to his mouth.

"Blue One, Blue One!" he shouted into the microphone. "Do you read me, Blue One?"

Lt. Steup made an adjustment to the frequency dial and signaled Tondok to try again.

The sound of heavy shells passing over their heads made every man in the section duck. The explosions were less than one hundred meters distant and tightly grouped. The sound of small arms fire had almost completely died away, replaced by the freight train-like sound of the shells. Kuno guessed that the Baron had postponed the assault on Rabat while the barrage lasted.

"Blue One, do you read me?" shouted Tondok again.

The Sergeant's face broke out in a relieved smile. He turned to Kuno and Weiss and flashed a thumbs up signal. He had made contact!

"Blue One, this is Ta Qali control! The situation is urgent," he continued. "We are under heavy and accurate bombardment by at least four batteries of heavy artillery. You must locate and attack these guns!"

Tondok paused and listened.

"We have an estimated position of only one of the batteries, Blue One," he shouted. "They are approximately three kilometers northeast of the field." Tondok read the co-ordinates of the British battery's estimated position.

Another pause. "Acknowledged, Blue One. Out!" shouted Tondok. He turned to Kuno. "Major," he said, "I have re-established contact with our bombers. Blue One is the flight leader of five Ju 88's. He is conducting a surveillance of the area to the northeast of the field, trying to establish the position of the British guns."

The impact of the shells' landing sent rivulets of dirt and stones rolling down the sides of the bunker. Clouds of dust filtered between the planks in the roof and drifted to the floor. Kuno was about to step out into the trench when one of the field phones rang. He reached for it and answered it himself.

"Communications!" he shouted. "Major Schacht."

"This is regimental HQ," came the reply. "Please hold for the Colonel." After a moment the unmistakable aristocratic voice of the Baron von der Heydte came over the line.

"SCHACHT!" he shouted. "What are you doing about this shelling? If it keeps up we won't be able to assault the high ground before daylight as I planned!"

"We've re-established communication with the bombers," Kuno replied. "We've given them the estimated position of the first battery and we expect them to attack it within minutes. We're working on the coordinates for the other batteries now!"

"Good, good," answered the Baron. "SCHACHT! Tell them to

hurry!" The line went dead.

Kuno replaced the handset and walked out of the bunker. He leaned against the trench wall and peered into the gloom to the northeast. Shells were exploding all about the field. Everywhere he looked all German activity had been driven to ground. If the British were ever to counter-attack this was the moment.

"Ta Qali control, this is Blue One."

"Blue One, this is Ta Qali, go ahead."

"We've located two of the batteries that have been harassing you, Ta Qali," answered the navigator of Blue One, flight leader of the Ju 88's orbiting the field. "They are located atop the ridge line northeast of the field. We'll be paying them a visit shortly. Stand by."

"Acknowledged, Blue One!" shouted Sgt. Tondok.

Kuno threw himself on the floor of the trench as a series of shells slammed to earth near the command post. He covered his head with his hands as chunks of smoking earth and rock rained down around the trench and command bunker. He waited several moments before tentatively lifting his head. Favoring his wounded arm he struggled to his feet and assessed the damage. The communications bunker was not seriously damaged, but the trench had taken a direct hit forty meters to the east. Paratroopers were already working to dig out their buried comrades. Kuno spun on his heel and ducked through the entrance to the command bunker. Tondok was still at the wireless transmitter.

"Acknowledged, Blue One," he said into the microphone. "Thank you."

"Tondok," snapped Kuno. "Report!"

"Blue One reports they have attacked two of the batteries of guns firing on the field, Sir," Sgt. Tondok replied. "They believe both batteries have been silenced."

"Tell that to the men outside," Kuno snarled, jerking his head at the entrance door.

He listened intently though, and after a moment he realized the intensity of the barrage had lifted considerably. He checked his watch and counted eighteen explosions in one minute, down from over forty a minute a short time earlier.

"Very good, Tondok," he admitted with a nod of his head. "Keep them looking for the other guns. Their fire is still heavy enough to prevent us moving on the high ground to the west."

"Yes, Major!" Tondok said and turned back to the wireless.

Kuno left the bunker again. As he stepped out in the trench he shouted, "STEUP!"

"Here Major!" the lieutenant answered.

Kuno craned his head to see him. Steup was atop the bunker, kneeling above the door.

"Steup, what the hell are you doing up there? Come down before you are killed!"

"Major," replied Steup. "From here I can see the muzzle flashes of the enemy guns as they fire. I have almost isolated their positions, or at least their bearing." He pointed with the flat of his hand held vertically. "One battery is just a few degrees west of straight north of us, probably about 5 kilometers out. It is beyond the short ridge line at the north edge of the field."

Another salvo of shells passed overhead and Steup threw himself flat on the roof. Kuno pressed himself into the door frame as the shells exploded a hundred meters or more beyond the bunker. He stepped back into the trench and looked up at Steup again.

"Well?" he said crossly. "Where is the other battery?"

"It is harder to isolate because of the intervening high ground," Steup replied as he sat up. He turned and pointed towards Mdina. "But it looks to be almost straight west of us, maybe a little south as well."

"All right, Steup," Kuno relented. "Good work. Come down here now and give Tondok the bearings so he can get the bombers on target. The moonlight is fading and we may be left without air support until dawn!"

"Right away, Major!" said Steup. He leapt from the roof down into the soft earth at the bottom of the trench, straightened and ducked through the entrance door.

Kuno looked about furtively for a moment to see who might be watching, then carefully clambered part way up the sloped, sandbag wall of the bunker till his head was just above the roof. He watched first to the north. It took almost a minute before the British fired, but the quick, faint flash of the guns was unmistakable, even through the haze of dust in the air. He noted the British fire had slackened considerably. No doubt the gunners were tiring. He turned to the west. This time he waited only a few seconds before confirming Steup's finding. He turned and looked south over the airfield. A number of the gliders were burning. The British knew the Germans had not had time yet to retrieve all of their heavy weapons and they had targeted the intact gliders to destroy the equipment they still held.

There was now enough of a gap between shell bursts for the sounds of small arms to be heard again. He strained to see or hear where the main fighting was, but in the fading moonlight he could not make out much at ground level beyond his immediate vicinity. Kuno was about to climb down when he glanced up in the sky to the south. He stopped and lifted the binoculars to his eyes. The cause of the white line he'd seen earlier was now apparent. He glanced at his watch. 0420 hours. Official moonset was not until 0530, but the high ground to the west would begin to block the moon much sooner.

>>>>>>>>>>>>

Lt. Commander Giuseppe Gianaclis scanned the southern horizon with his binoculars. The seas were rising from the south; ten foot rollers with the tops torn off by the wind. The 7,000 ton cruiser *RM Muzio Attendolo* was pounding directly into the seas, with great sheets of spray bursting across her bows each time she plunged into the troughs between waves. The clear view screen wipes on the cruiser's bridge were spinning at high speed. They were barely keeping up with the seawater thrown over the breakwater and against the bridge.

He turned and looked out the starboard wing of the cruiser's bridge at the *RM Raimondo Montecuccoli,* sister ship of *Muzio.* Sailing 500 meters apart the two cruisers were just an hour north of the Strait of Messina, with the Lipari Islands in their wake. The two cruisers were in company with nine destroyers and the battleship *Vittorio Venetto.* The massive bulk of the battleship was behind and between the two cruisers about a half-mile. Close enough to keep station in the thickening weather, not so close as to risk collision. The destroyers formed a screen around the three heavier ships protecting against submarine attack.

Giussepe turned and went back to the small charthouse at the rear of the bridge. As the *Muzio's* navigator he would soon be called upon to steer the task force into the narrows at Messina. There the ships would alter formation to line astern in passing down the shipping channel. He checked his watch. 0505 hours. Twenty minutes to course change and speed reduction. Twenty-four hours to Malta.

>>>>>>>>>>>>

"SCHACHT!"

"Here, Baron!" answered Kuno, waving his right arm above his head.

The Colonel trotted down the trench to where Kuno leaned against a heap of sandbags. The trench was deep in shadow. The moon had fallen behind the high ground to the west and the sun had just begun to lighten the eastern sky. Thin wisps of fog floated over the airfield, blown in from the sea on the southerly wind. Further south and to the east and west Kuno could see the fog was more solid, lying like a fleecy blanket low over the land. It seemed that only the center and northern parts of the island were mostly clear of fog.

"Well done, Major," said the Colonel. "With the enemy batteries all but silenced we can finally move against the high ground."

Based on Steup's directions the Luftwaffe had located and bombed the last two enemy batteries firing on the airfield. There'd been no shelling for almost twenty minutes now.

"Thank you, Baron," answered Kuno. But he didn't smile. His expression remained pensive.

"What is wrong, Schacht?" asked the Baron.

"I still cannot fathom the British," replied Kuno. "They obviously had forewarning of the attack, but they still have not counter-attacked in strength, nor with tanks. Why?"

The Baron von der Heydte nodded his head.

"The same questions have been haunting me," he answered, "but what can we do about it but proceed with the plan? Perhaps we'll find the answers on the high ground."

"Yes, perhaps," said Kuno. "Still. With the extra men on the field now would it be wise to detail some of them to retrieve whatever they can of the anti-tanks guns from the intact gliders?"

"I see your point, Schacht," said the Baron, rubbing his chin. "All right," he said. "I'll give the orders detailing men of the 23rd Regiment to scour the gliders for anti-tank weapons."

"And have you noted the fog, Baron?" asked Kuno.

"Yes," replied the Colonel. "Perhaps it is for the best that further landings on Luqa and Hal Far have been cancelled. The transport crews would have a difficult time locating the landing zones. What news do you have of the next drop?"

"According to Division it will be delayed until 0600," replied Kuno. "They are reconfiguring the flight stream to avoid bunching so many transports together. They're worried about mid-air collision."

"Yes," said the Baron. "I've seen it happen. There were several such incidents at Crete. Very tragic."

"They also want to know if we've had any luck locating General Ramcke and his staff and when we will move against Luqa airfield," Kuno told him. "At the moment command of the entire division has devolved to you. Neither the General nor any of the other regimental commanders have reported in yet."

"I don't believe it is safe to move against Luqa until the high ground is secured," said the Baron, nodding his head towards the fortress of Mdina, clearly visible now on the heights to the west, silhouetted by the setting moon. "I believe General Ramcke would agree if he were here. So long as the British are in control there we will remain at the mercy of any heavy guns they can bring to bear."

"Yes, Sir," said Kuno. "I agree entirely. But the move against the high ground will probably take all day and will be a difficult assault as well. It will be at least tonight before we are ready to move south against Luqa and Hal Far. Any of our troops there will have to hold on another twelve, perhaps even eighteen hours."

"Still no contact with the other drop zones, eh?" questioned the Baron, stroking his chin.

"No, Sir," Kuno shook his head. "But reports from the south side of the field indicate there is still considerable small arms fire to be heard during the lulls here. Without reinforcement our troops at Luqa will be hard pressed."

"Five kilometers away and across terrain made for defense," observed the Baron. He closed his eyes in thought for a moment.

"No, Schacht," he said at last, looking up at Kuno. "We've got to secure the high ground before moving against Luqa."

"Yes, Sir," answered Kuno.

"Anything else, Schacht?"

"Yes, Sir," replied Kuno. "My team was designed to provide communications at the regimental level. I haven't the staff or equipment to manage the communications for the entire division. My senior NCO has drafted a number of men from the infantry companies to help with laying cable and so forth, but I haven't enough field phones or cable to stretch much beyond the current network. I've requested the next drop include more of everything, including a back-up wireless, but until it is delivered and put in operation our communications are very fragile."

"Understood, Schacht," the Baron nodded his head. "We'll keep all our communications as simple and terse as possible until your equipment situation sorts itself out. Meantime you are authorized to help yourself to all the manpower you need."

"Thank you, Baron," Kuno replied.

"One last thing, Schacht," said the Baron. "If you have any aircraft low on fuel in your pattern have them strike the stone fortifications on the high ground before leaving. Otherwise they are to hold their munitions until we give them the signal. I plan to co-ordinate the assault with the next drop at 0600."

>>>>>>>>>>>>

Kenneth rotated his stiff neck and stretched his back. The rising sun was chasing away the lingering shadows of the night. In a few moments it would lift its rim above the eastern horizon, signaling the start of another bloody day. Not that the bloodletting needed a fresh start. The Luftwaffe had bombed the area around Ta Qali at least seven times since the first drop and attacked the docks and harbor areas around Valletta during each of the paratrooper drops, effectively suppressing the heavy flak guns there, preventing them from interfering with the landings. Through the night the sound of small arms, mortars and artillery didn't let up at all, they were merely interrupted, overridden by the thunderous roar each time the transports returned for another drop. The brief sound of British guns firing against Ta Qali before they were silenced by the

Luftwaffe seemed pitiful next to the might the Germans were bringing to bear.

He turned away from the tiny window and looked back at the girl. She'd slept peacefully through the night, her breathing even and full. She might have been the only person on the island to sleep through that eventful night. Dr Mieza checked on her twice during the early morning, checking her pulse and heart rates, nodding in satisfaction and assuring Kenneth that Maggie was out of serious danger. Now she was stirring, stretching. Her eyelids fluttered open then squeezed shut again at the light from the window. He turned back to the window and leaned out to pull the shutters closed, but she stopped him.

"No, don't," she said softly.

He left the shutters open and moved to her bedside, tentatively taking her hand in his. Her eyes were barely open, just dark slits. Her face, pale to begin with, was ashen, but for two bright spots burning high on her cheeks.

"Maggie?" he asked.

"I like the light," she said, her voice barely a murmur. "There's no light where I've been."

"Maggie," he said again. "How-how do you feel?"

She sniffed and smiled, her eyes coming open a little more.

"Like bloody hell," she said, but laughed quietly. "All things considered I suppose I'm alright. Where are we?"

"You're in hospital," he said. "A country Doctor's clinic just outside Mosta."

She closed her eyes and settled back on her pillow.

"Maggie?" he said. "How much – how much do you remember?"

A smile came to her, faint but genuine, crinkling the corners of her eyes, in a way that always caught his heart in a vice. She squeezed his hand.

"I remember enough, Kenneth," she said, opening her eyes and looking up at him. "Everything that matters. But how did I end up here?"

"We were heading for Valletta in the cart," he answered. "The bloody Luftwaffe forced us off the road."

"Bloody Germans," she said softly, closing her eyes again. After a moment she went on, her eyes still closed. "I remember they were so loud, louder than I'd ever heard them before." She paused again. "They filled the sky," she said dreamily.

Kenneth watched her face and the slow, even rise and fall of her breasts. He concluded she was asleep again and was about to gently disengage his hands when her eyes snapped open. They were wide with fear.

"Kenneth!" She hissed his name. An instant bead of sweat popped up on her forehead. Color flooded back into her face.

"It's alright, Love," Kenneth soothed her, stroking her cheek. "They're not here. You're safe. It's alright."

"It's an invasion isn't, Kenneth?" she asked.

He hesitated.

"Kenneth!" she hissed again. "Don't lie to me! It's an invasion, isn't it?"

He nodded his head. "Yes, Maggie," he said. "It is. They've been dropping paratroops at Ta Qali all night. I expect at the other airfields as well."

"Oh, God!" she gasped. "Ta Qali. How far away Kenneth?"

He hesitated again.

"Not much more than a mile," he said finally. "But don't worry," he rushed on as her eyes widened again. "They have no reason to come here now. We're safe, at least for the moment."

Maggie started to push back the blankets and to struggle upright.

"Whoa, Maggie!" he exclaimed. "Steady on. You can't sit up now."

"Kenneth, we've got to get out of here, back to Rinella."

"Rinella!" he exclaimed, confused. "You can't be moved across the room, Maggie. Why would you go to Rinella, anyway?"

She sagged back on the bed, exhausted and dizzy from the brief effort to sit up.

"My work, Kenneth," she said softly. "My work." She pressed her hand to her forehead, fighting to not pass out.

"Your work can wait, Maggie!" he said softly, but firmly. "You're in no condition!"

She opened her eyes again and gripped his hand with all her feeble strength.

"Kenneth, you don't understand," she said. "I have to get to Rinella. I can't be taken."

"Taken where, Maggie?" he asked, completely baffled.

"By the Germans, Kenneth," she said. "My work. I can't be taken by the Germans. Not alive."

As the dawn broke over Ta Qali black smoke swirled skyward from more than a dozen fires burning on or near the field. The wind dropped to a gentle breeze as dawn approached, so the smoke drifted slowly to the north, hanging in a pall over the field. Small arms fire and the crump of light mortars continued to the south and west.

Kuno lifted his glasses and focused on the flight of bombers circling the field. Five Ju 88's carrying heavy bombs orbited, their wings catching the first rays of the rising sun, ready to pound the ancient fortifications on the heights to the west. He sighed. Yet another antiquity to be destroyed in this war.

He lowered the glasses and examined Mdina's stonewalls. Solid limestone, fifteen meters tall and topped by crenellated battlements, they brooded over the terraced slope before them and the airfield beyond. Imposing fortifications when built, they defied the might of the Turkish Emperor Suleiman in 1565. His dreams of a Muslim Mediterranean Empire were dashed upon their redoubts. But Mdina's builders never dreamed of the kind of attack they would be subjected to that summer morning in 1942.

Here and there on the battlements a figure could be seen moving. Light glinted back at him as a British soldier atop the wall surveyed the airfield through binoculars. Kuno chuckled at the idea the man might be staring right back at him at that very moment. Very little else could be seen of the British dispositions.

He surveyed the paratrooper positions in the first light of day. The German perimeter around the airfield was a thousand meters to the south and east of the main runway. At the northeast corner of the field this placed the Germans within small arms fire of the outskirts of Mosta. On the southern flank they occupied a ragged line, zigzagging through farm fields and bomb-shattered orchards. In places the Germans here were within grenade toss of the British lines. To the north the German outposts had only advanced three hundred meters to the Wied tal-Isperanza, the dry bed of a seasonal stream running perpendicular to the main strip. On the west side of the field the Germans had worked their way to the crest of a short ridge mid-way between the strip and Mdina five hundred meters from the fortress.

Kuno watched as a group of Germans in company strength moved out to the west, skirting the northern flank of Mdina, using a spur of the heights as cover. They were moving towards a complex of buildings with large Red Cross emblems and banners painted on the roofs. Obviously a hospital, the buildings would be in the midst of the attack. Other paratroopers were moving on the southern flank, enveloping the fortress from three sides. By 0545 they were to be in position for the attack. When all was in place Kuno would order an air attack against the battlements. Every available bomber would strike Mdina in a concentrated blitz. Even as the bombs were falling the paratroopers would move up for a frontal assault. The air attack must breach the fortress walls in several places for the ground attack to succeed.

Behind him in the HQ bunker his communications squad was busy distributing the final orders to the troops on the field. Kuno stepped down from the rim of the trench and ducked into the bunker. Most of the team was present. Tondok and Steup were manning the wireless apparatus against the back wall of the bunker, maintaining communications with the flight leaders of the bombers circling the field. Corporal Benckner and the other enlisted men were all on the field phones arrayed on shelves down each side of the bunker, passing orders from the Baron's command staff on to the infantry companies or receiving information from them. A number of privates drafted from the infantry stood by as runners and to assist with cranking the field phone batteries. A paratrooper sat perched atop a stationary bicycle apparatus, happily pedaling at a steady clip. The bicycle was a simple generator providing electricity to the radios and telephones. The minutes before a major attack were always near chaos in any command center and Kuno observed his men closely, noting with satisfaction that they were handling the situation smoothly and professionally. One of the field phones rang, but there was no one on the team available to answer it. One of the infantrymen-turned-orderly reached tentatively to answer it. Kuno stepped forward putting his hand on the man's arm.

"I'll do it," he said. "Stand-by."

"Yes, Sir," the man said with evident relief, stepping back and standing at ease.

Kuno lifted the handset from its cradle.

"Command!" he barked into the phone. "Major Schacht."

The response electrified him.

"**PANZERS!**" was the single word he heard.

For an instant his breath caught in his throat as he reacted to the dreaded word.

"Issue a proper report!" he shouted down the line. "First, who are you and where are you located?"

"Sorry, Sir," the man replied, abashed by Kuno's stern order. "I am Corporal Hartz. We are south of the airstrip five hundred meters south of the road."

As Kuno listened to Hartz he reached out and grabbed the orderly by the arm and pulled him close. "Bring the Colonel, NOW!" he said softly into the man's ear. The trooper hurried from the bunker.

"How many tanks do you see?" demanded Kuno of Hartz.

"We are not sure," Hartz replied. "That is, we don't SEE any, but we can hear them moving up from the southeast."

"Do you have any anti-tank guns deployed?" pressed Kuno.

"We have just one 37mm gun here," the man said. "If they hit us with Panzers they will go through us like butter."

Kuno checked his watch. 0541. Just nineteen minutes till the planned assault on Mdina and to the start of the next drop.

The pilot stood beneath the camouflage net, listening to the sound of aircraft engines circling over the field. Twenty minutes after dawn and the low cloud and fog was still streaming in from the ocean on the southern breeze, wisps and clumps drifting along the runway at ground level, a solid ceiling of cloud at about 800 feet. The German combat patrol was above the clouds, screened from view themselves, but also unable to see the ground and the runway.

"Not much for flying weather is it, Sir," his crew chief quietly came up beside him. He offered a mug of steaming tea to the pilot.

The pilot took the mug gratefully and smiled before sipping, but said nothing. The buzz of the circling aircraft came closer and louder before fading again, but never quite went away completely.

"The Germans don't seem to mind it much, do they, Sir?" the crew chief pressed.

"No, they don't mind it much," he finally answered. "I should think we'll have the word soon," he went on. He took a sip of the tea. "Make sure the kite's set will you, please?"

"Yes, Sir." The crew chief turned back to the Spitfire resting beneath the canopy netting. On either side of the runway a similar scene was set as three of the last Spitfires on Malta were made ready to take-off and oppose the German landings.

Derrick Metcalfe sipped his tea slowly, savoring each warm swallow, enjoying these few golden moments of relative peace. Relative, but far from complete peace. To the north the distant crackle of small arms fire had continued unabated throughout the night. On Hal Far itself wrecked gliders littered the field and medical teams moved among the bodies scattered about, seeking anyone still alive after the fierce fight in the early morning hours. Work parties had cleared the runway of wreckage and debris and filled in several bomb craters on the strip itself.

It was still unclear why the Germans had not followed up the first drop and glider landings with more troops. Certainly the paratroopers of the first assault had fought fiercely and had they received more support might have prevailed. As it was there was fear that some had escaped to the north and west where they were hiding among the gullies and steep canyons of the coastal range of hills. Hundreds more were taken prisoner and were herded into a set of disused caverns at the southeast corner of the field, near the Station Infirmary.

A tern winged across the runway, flitting and dipping, in pursuit of an insect perhaps. The soft crunch of boots on gravel broke into his reverie. Derrick turned and watched his wingman, Andy White duck under the canopy and walk towards him, hands in pocket, lips pursed, whistling soundlessly.

"Time for a cuppa?" asked Andy.

Derrick laughed softly. "All the time in the world, laddie," he said, his blue Irish eyes dancing.

Derrick waved to his crew chief and held up his own mug. In a moment the man was there with a fresh steaming cup for Andy.

"Ta," said Andy.

"My pleasure," the crew chief said then turned back to Derrick's Spitfire.

Derrick checked his watch. 0543 hours. The air raid sirens began to wail.

>>>>>>>>>>>>>

"Come right, now," he coaxed. "A little more, a little more. That's it. Steady now."

The Mark I Cruiser, the number 11 painted in large white numerals on the turret lurched and rattled round another tight corner in the road, its right side treads rolling up and over the threshold stone at the door of a Maltese house, the left side skirt scraping down the low limestone wall separating the gnarled and blasted stumps of an olive grove from the road. He leaned out of his turret hatch first to one side, then the other and guided his driver, Corporal Walsh as the tank crept down the narrow lane.

Captain Martin "Marty" Chadwick of the King's Royal Tank Regiment shook his head for the thousandth time. He'd opposed posting the tanks to Hal Muxi in the first place, insisting they needed to be kept together in a single force and laagered near open ground, to give them room to maneuver and fight. But the brigadiers and Lord Gort overruled him. They felt it necessary to spread Malta's thirty tanks about the island where they could be better hidden from German air attack and be in position to oppose the enemy at each of the possible landing sites. In Chadwick's mind Gort was simply repeating the mistakes of France.

Fourteen tanks, the largest body, were at Bur Marrad near St. Paul's Bay in the north. They were positioned to oppose an amphibious landing on the island, either in the bay itself or at any of the beaches on the northeast coast. Six more tanks were at Ghaxaq in the south ready to move against Hal Far airfield or Marsaxlokk Bay and the quay at Kalafrana.

Chadwick and his troop of ten Mark I Cruisers was posted outside Hal Muxi, a small village midway between Ta Qali and Luqa. The tanks were housed in shallow caves, dug out of a limestone bluff to the west of the town. They were about equidistant to Ta Qali and Luqa and in theory could move quickly against either field, but in practice narrow roads and rough terrain hemmed them in. Now Chadwick and his troop were struggling to break out onto the more open ground to the south of Ta Qali.

They'd set out at 0430, before first light and just minutes after a phone call from HQ at Mdina. Chadwick had been waiting for the orders since the first of the German airborne troops landed and his tanks and their crews were prepared to move on just a minute's notice. They'd worked through Hal Muxi itself under cover of darkness and as the sun rose Chadwick said a quick prayer of thanks for the blanket of fog that had moved inland over the island's southern half.

His orders had them in position for an attack against the German's southern perimeter at 0600. They would be supported by infantry of the Inniskilling Regiment and were to sweep down the middle of the field on the runway itself, breaking the German lines and allowing the infantry to route the invaders from trenches and craters to the east and west of the strip.

Above his head he could hear the German air patrol buzzing about from time to time, but the fog held and blanketed his movements as they approached the Wied Incita, one of Malta's many streams run dry in the heat of June. As they came closer to the southern boundaries of Ta Qali airfield he began to hear the sound of small arms fire in snatches over the clank and rattle of treads and the roar of tank engines. At last his tank negotiated the final narrow point in the road and could begin to pick up speed. He turned and watched the 12 tank ease its way between the house and the wall, then lurch forward once clear. It took almost twenty minutes for the ten tanks of his troop to slip past the choke point. He checked his watch. 0544. Overhead patches of deep blue sky started to poke through the mist.

>>>>>>>>>>>>>

Above the island Heinz Sauckel yawned and stretched. He'd flown twice during the night and now at dawn he was flying his third sortie of Operation Herkules. So far he'd had no chance to engage in aerial combat. Heinz was guarding the western flank of the transport fleet on the first flight of the night when the British threw a token force of twin-engine night fighters against the German air armada, but the three Bristol Beaufighters were swept aside by the massive fighter escort of Messerschmitts long before they ever got close to the Junkers transports. He'd never even seen them, much less had a chance to take a shot.

He'd had only one chance at anything resembling action. After covering the initial drop on Ta Qali he lingered over the field, spotting movement on the ground, a vehicle of some sort on the road at the south side of the airfield. He swept down to investigate and strafed an automobile, forcing it off the road. Even the flak was subdued for him, holding fire for the transports.

He repeated the now familiar pattern of the earlier sorties, taking off from Comiso and orbiting to the west of the field as the ungainly transports lumbered into the air and formed up in their echelons for the short flight to Malta. He was a little sleepy, but that wore off quickly, as it always did when he flew. His squadron leader warned him that both Hal Far and Luqa fields remained in British hands. The British were expected to put every available Spitfire into the air to oppose the first daylight drop.

Originally scheduled for just minutes after dawn the drop was delayed in order to reconfigure the transport echelons for a drop on one location, rather than three as first planned. The orb of the sun was well above the eastern horizon by the time Heinz fell in on the flank of the transports and began winging towards Malta. The now familiar island came into view after just minutes in the air, looking like a dried and crinkled brown leaf floating on the deep blue of the ocean.

Heinz scowled to himself as his Bf 109 approached the north shore. Fog lay across much of the sea and extended well inland over the southern half of the island as well. He chewed his lip nervously, waiting to see if the drop zone itself would be clear. Not until he'd flown over the two smaller islands of Gozo and Comino did he feel confident that Ta Qali was not shrouded in mist. He focused on watching his sector as the transports approached, but he couldn't help himself from stealing a look as five Ju 88's winged across the field ahead of the transports.

>>>>>>>>>>>>

"Give it full power right from the go," Derrick told Andy as they listened to the air raid sirens blaring over Hal Far field. "The runway here is much shorter than you're used to at Ta Qali. When we get in the air stay right under the ceiling, don't climb for altitude and keep right with me. I'm going to circle back to the west to get out over the water."

Andy White nodded his head as Derrick explained his plan. Both men were now very serious. They each knew they might have only minutes to live.

"We'll sweep up the west coast under cover of the fog," Derrick continued, "then cut inland north of Rabat. We'll avoid the high ground there if you please," he said archly.

Andy cracked a thin smile. Neither man wanted to fly into a hilltop in the fog.

"We'll stay in the fog as long as possible then pop out to hit the transports at low altitude. Ignore the fighters and listen to my commands. We'll dive back into the fog over land when the 109's get on to us. We know the terrain better than they do. They won't be able to follow us down onto the deck." He paused and looked Andy in the eye. "Any questions?"

Andy looked down at his toes and shook his head.

"Right-o!" said Derrick. "Let's go give these Huns a nasty surprise, eh?"

Andy looked up and smiled. "Let's do!" he said.

A rimless paratrooper helmet poked cautiously above the trench rim, its owner stealing a quick look across the road and through the stumps of the shattered olive grove before dropping back down again. It wouldn't do to take too long a look. British snipers were very accurate since first light. Nothing to be seen, but the danger was very real. The paratrooper officer could hear the rattle of tank tracks clearer than ever now. He turned and stooping low trotted down the trench to the sandbag bunker where he'd established his company HQ.

"Hartz!" he hissed.

"Yes, Captain!" Hartz answered.

"What the hell are they telling you about these damned tanks?"

the Captain demanded. "Do they expect us to fight them with bare hands, hmm?"

"Headquarters says they will attempt to direct an air attack against the armor, Sir," replied Hartz. "They have also retrieved a pair of anti-tank guns and are rushing them to us."

"Too damned late," snarled the Captain. He looked up in the sky. "At least this damn fog is thinning a little. Give H.Q. our best coordinates for the tanks. Tell them to bring in the bombers immediately!"

But to the north Kuno watched the flight of bombers strike the fortress at Mdina in frustration. He'd been unable to change the target of the bombing in time and the Ju 88s delivered a beautiful attack through light flak against the fortress just ahead of the arrival of the fleet of transports. Fifteen heavy bombs exploded with a roar that briefly drowned the sound of the approaching transports. Enormous stones from the ramparts hurtled high in the air on the force of the blasts. Huge clouds of dust erupted over the high ground, obscuring the results of the attack while the five bombers winged their way west, clearing the scene and beginning their return to Sicily.

Kuno lowered the glasses to the slopes in front of Mdina. Tiny figures were scrambling uphill all over the slope, flitting from one piece of cover to another. The high ground was obscured in a two hundred meter radius around the fortress itself, but the lower reaches of the slope were still in the clear. He focused on a group of paratroopers moving up the hill directly in front of the main battlements. They were conducting a textbook infantry assault. Half the men took up covering fire positions while the other half rushed forward forty or so meters before dropping to the ground themselves to provide cover for their comrades. In this way the men leapfrogged their way up the hill. So far Kuno saw no evidence of resistance or that any of the paratroopers had fired their own weapons. Kuno sensed a presence at his side.

"The assault is off to a good start, Colonel," said Kuno without lowering the glasses. He raised his voice to be heard over the thunder of approaching transports. The start of the fourth drop was less than a minute away.

"Good, good," said the Baron von der Heydte. "But the panzers are my chief concern now."

Kuno lowered the glasses and leaned closer to his commanding officer. He said, "Two 50mm PAK guns are on their way now to the south end of the field." He was nearly shouting as the first of the transports roared directly over his head. "I believe the British may have missed their chance to hit us while we are at our weakest."

"Let us hope so, Schacht. Let us hope so," the Baron replied. "But I was unable to dispatch an experienced officer to site them properly."

Kuno smiled and shook his head. He said, "The situation is in hand here, Baron. Would you like me to get down there and supervise the placement of the guns?"

The Colonel slapped Kuno on the shoulder and smiled. "Good, Schacht, good!" he exclaimed. "Report back here after the guns are sited."

>>>>>>>>>>>>>

Heinz had the throttle pulled right back. The Bf 109 was barely above stall speed. He'd watched the flight of Ju 88's deliver their bombs against the high ground to the east of the runway, just clear of the fog that blanketed the south side of the island. An enormous cloud of dust obscured the ancient fortifications. So far at least the British flak guns on the heights were silent. Maybe the guns were knocked out in the bombing, or perhaps the clouds of dust blinded the gunners.

The first echelons of transports dropped their human cargo over Ta Qali and peeled off to east and west for the return to Sicily. The second rank of Junkers was just reaching the drop zone in a great 'V' formation. A sudden urge gripped him and he pushed the throttles forward several notches. The 'Emil' leapt forward. Following the urge he pushed the nose over and went into a shallow dive. The ragged edge of the fog bank rushed towards him.

"SAUCKEL!" His flight leader's voice rang in his ears. "What the devil are you doing? Get back up here!"

Berating himself for his impulsiveness Heinz reached to throttle back and began to ease the stick up. At that instant a lone Spitfire burst from the fog bank below and in front of him moving at a right angle to his course from his right to his left. He hesitated for a split second then shoved the nose over and kicked the rudder a touch. He was in a nearly perfect position. As the Spitfire broke clear of the fog it filled his gun sights and he squeezed the trigger. Cannon and machine gun shells hosed the enemy fighter from nose to tail, breaking away chunks of the engine cowling and shattering the canopy. Glass and flame erupted from the cockpit and the Spit' slid quickly into a flat spin. The stress was too much for the airframe and it flew apart before his very eyes. Heinz pulled back on the stick and zoomed over the cloud of black smoke left in the wake of the fighter's destruction.

>>>>>>>>>>>>>

A cloud of blue smoke trailed behind them as Kenneth and Maggie crept down the Mosta road. The old jalopy shook and rattled as it bounced from rut to rut, coughed and spluttered and nearly died each time Kenneth shifted gears. Dr. Mieza had refused at first even to consider allowing Maggie to be moved further than a house down the street, patiently pointing out the girl's injuries as though Kenneth wasn't already aware of them. Finally Kenneth was forced to tell the Dr. of Maggie's fear of capture by the Germans. He avoided particulars, mainly because he didn't know any, but Mieza accepted that Maggie was involved in secret work that would subject her to harsh treatment, perhaps even torture at the hands of the Germans if taken prisoner. The Dr. agreed to help arrange transportation for the couple.

Kenneth expected a wheelbarrow and hoped for a horse and cart, but when the old Ford Model T pickup appeared in the courtyard behind Dr. Mieza's Hospital he was dumbfounded. It was identical to the one he'd driven on the farm in South Dakota.

"I used it to visit the sick in the countryside who couldn't come to the hospital," Mieza explained, "but since the war began fuel is impossible to obtain and I've kept the auto in a shed nearby." He put his hand on the driver's side door and smiled. "I've managed to preserve a few gallons, for some sort of emergency I suppose."

Kenneth smiled, but said nothing. The Dr. was obviously very fond of his car.

"Anyway," Mieza went on, "there should be more than enough for you to reach Floriana or Valletta."

Kenneth replied, softly. "Thank you Dr.," he said. "Is there anyone there I can leave it with to see that it gets back to you?"

Mieza laughed. "There is only one Model T on all of Malta," he said. "Many people know it. If the car survives it will be returned to me. Don't worry."

Mieza and the nurse Kenneth spoke to in the middle of the night helped him load Maggie into the passenger side seat of the Model T, cushioning her against the door with a mound of blankets and pillows. They placed a small basket of food behind the seat. As Kenneth eased the Ford out of the courtyard at 0540 and pulled away from the hospital the first combat casualties began to trickle in. Three British walking wounded from the fighting at the northeast corner of Ta Qali field were limping up the street and four Maltese civilians carried a badly wounded soldier on a stretcher. Dr. Mieza and his nurse rushed to help with not another word to Kenneth.

Now he drove slowly through the narrow streets and lanes on the eastern outskirts of Mosta, staying close to buildings when he could to hide the car from the air, hurrying across short stretches of open ground. The girl was awake, but still very weak. She kept her eyes closed and said nothing as Kenneth steered the car down narrow, twisting lanes. His plan was to avoid the main road south from Mosta as long as possible staying to smaller side roads and hoping to avoid further attention from the Luftwaffe. The Ford was of American make and the steering wheel was on the left side, but of course this was just as he had grown up accustomed to in Red Fern. Anyway, he really wasn't concerned about meeting any traffic on the road that morning. If he met a German patrol he'd be happy to use either side of the road to escape.

The morning air was chill, but he drove with the window rolled down, the better to listen for danger. The streets were almost completely deserted of Maltese civilians, though more than once he caught a flash of movement out of the corner of his eye when a door or shutter swung closed as they passed. As he left the last buildings of Mosta behind him he heard the chatter of small arms again drifting to him on the wind. An occasional heavier explosion denoted a mortar or artillery shell exploding.

The Model T was capable of only about ten or twelve miles an hour on flat ground, a little faster downhill; even so, if they could avoid trouble they could reach Rinella and Maggie's billet there in less than two hours, even with all the winding and indirect routes he planned to take. He checked his watch. 0556.

He shifted into the Ford's highest gear and pressed the accelerator to the floor. The car jolted forward, bouncing on its leaf springs, incredibly making the car hard to control at just twelve miles an hour. Kenneth stole a quick glance at the girl. Her eyes were closed and she was leaned back amongst the cushions and blankets, but her arms were outstretched as though to brace herself against an impact.

"It's alright, Maggie," he assured her. "The car is safe."

She nodded her head almost imperceptibly and lowered her arms to her lap, but Kenneth could tell she was still tense. They were on a long stretch of road with very little cover and he tried to push the accelerator through the floor, but not an ounce more power could he squeeze from the old car's laboring engine. Scanning down the road the next chance for cover was a small copse of trees clustered round a crossroad a half-mile away. To either side of the road were a series of small fields. All were fallow and several bore the scars of bomb craters. The night-bombing Italians regularly missed their intended targets on the airfields, making it nearly impossible to grow a crop anywhere within two miles of any of the airstrips.

Small arms fire crackled and popped, the distant bark of a heavy machine gun briefly drowning out the sound of other weapons. Suddenly he heard it; the muted, throaty roar of aircraft engines in the distance. He shot a quick glance at Maggie, but her window was rolled up and she hadn't heard it yet. He cranked his window closed, but it barely muted the sound which grew in intensity every second.

"Kenneth?" she asked, struggling to sit upright.

"Stay down, love," he told her. "Stay down. We're going to stop under some trees until they've passed."

The first of the transports flew into sight before he reached the trees. Kenneth slammed on the brake pedal as soon as the overhanging limbs sheltered the Ford from the sky.

Kenneth hopped from the driver's seat and ran to one of the trees on the south side of the road; grabbing a low hanging limb he hoisted himself into the tree. He reached a sturdy limb about twelve feet off the ground with a view to the south. He shielded his eyes from the morning sun and squinted in the direction of Ta Qali. He couldn't see the field itself. The low ridge running across the north end of the field blocked his view, but what he could see told him plenty. Smoke rose from a number of fires burning where he knew the field lay. A bank of fog seemed to lie across the southern half of the island, ending somewhere south of the southern end of Ta Qali's runway. A flight of Ju 88 bombers was hurtling across the field from east to west and as he watched them their bomb bay doors swung open. He immediately realized their target was Mdina, the ancient fortress on the high ground overlooking Ta Qali. Flak guns on the heights opened up, peppering the sky with black puffs of high explosive, but Kenneth knew the bombers stood a very good chance of delivering their attack. The bombers swept into their final approach when they were most vulnerable to fighter attack, but no fighters appeared and the bombers released their deadly cargoes into the fortifications. There was a flash followed seconds later by the rumble of the explosions. For a moment the explosions were louder than the transports. The bombers continued on to the west, passing in front of a flight of Messerschmitt fighters flying escort to the transports.

Looking up through the leaves of his tree he saw a great 'V' of Ju 52's passing over. They continued on to Ta Qali and a moment later parachutes started opening behind them, drifting down on the field. The Junkers peeled off to left and right to clear the air space above the field.

Instinctively Kenneth's right hand closed in a grip as though on a Spitfire's control column. His finger tightened on the trigger and he gritted his teeth, imagining himself sweeping down the line of transports, gunning one after another. But the transports flew on unmolested. He pounded his fist against the trunk of the tree in frustration.

"You BASTARDS!" he screamed at the top of his voice. The roar of aircraft engines was so loud he didn't even hear himself. The second echelon of transports approached the field.

He was about to climb down to check on Maggie when he noticed one of the German fighters west of the field swooping down in a dive. It passed over the enormous clouds of dust rising from Mdina and seemed bent on a strafing run against some ground target, but Kenneth couldn't see what it was. Suddenly a lone Spitfire burst out of the fog at full power. The German swooped down, gunning the Spitfire into a ball of flame. Kenneth slammed his fist into the trunk of the tree. Tears of rage welled up in his eyes.

Heinz pulled out of his dive, kicking the rudder bar over to the right, away from the path of the Ju 52's, craning his neck to watch the flaming wreckage plunge to earth. Just as the fuselage slammed into the ground two more British fighters rocketed out of the fog below and behind him at full speed, clawing for altitude, aimed directly at the bellies of the defenseless transports.

A flurry of shouted warnings filled Heinz' wireless headset, but he knew it was impossible to prevent the Spitfires from bursting in amongst the helpless 'Auntie Ju's'. The enemy planes timed their emergence from the fog perfectly, flashing behind him as he shoved his throttles to full power and kicked his 'Emil' round in a tight climbing turn that brought him in behind the British at a distance of over one kilometer. He was much too far away for a shot. Other German fighters were diving to try to intercept the enemy, but Heinz could see no hope of them being stopped from attacking the transports.

The Spitfires bored in relentlessly, angling for the underside of the lead transport in the second echelon. Finally the Junkers' pilots became aware of their peril and the orderly 'V' began to break up. Too late, the transports veered away or dove out of formation, but the two Spitfires were already on them. Smoke appeared from the fighters' wings as 20mm and .50 caliber shells poured into two of the Junkers. The starboard engine of one of the transports erupted in fire as shells hammered into it; burning fuel streamed away from the wing as paratroopers began tumbling from the exit door. The other transport took a beating in the fuselage with chunks of its corrugated skin breaking away in the plane's own slipstream. Somehow it remained in the air as the Spitfires roared past on their way to attack another Junkers that had dived away.

Briefly Heinz pictured the carnage inside the passenger cabin as the paratroopers waiting the order to jump were torn apart by the enemy attack. He forced the dreadful image from his mind and focused on his immediate task, cutting off the Spitfires' escape. Instinctively he understood they would attack the Junkers already in their gun sites then dive for cover at the ragged edge of the fog bank south of the airfield to evade the swarm of Messerschmitts diving towards them. He had no chance of preventing the Auntie Ju from being attacked. Instead he snapped his fighter over to starboard, putting himself in position to cut ahead and intercept the Spitfires when they turned away to escape. His engine roared at full power as he fought to gain as much altitude as possible. Confused chatter filled his headset as the transport pilots screamed for protection and the Messerschmitt squadron leaders issued desperate, hopeless orders. Heinz ignored all these distractions, calmly lining up his attack.

The Spitfires delivered a devastating double blow to the Junkers they had singled out, hammering its cockpit to shattered pieces. As the Junkers nosed over Heinz saw the starboard side exit door thrown open and men begin to tumble from the hatch, desperate to get out of the death trap. Only three escaped before the plane tipped over on its port wing. Inside the cabin gravity threw the other troopers away from the exit, dashing their only hope of escape. The Junkers slammed into a low ridge just off the northeast perimeter of Ta Qali airfield, a great, billowing ball of flame marking its destruction. The British pilots threw their own craft into a headlong dive to starboard, to the south, heading for the fog. Heinz slammed the nose of his Emil over and angled to intercept.

Sure the third Junkers was finished Derrick keyed his throat mic. "Break right for the fog!" he shouted and shoved the stick forward and hard right. The Spitfire responded in a tight, diving turn, still at maximum throttle. Derrick looked at the ground below him. He was directly over the runway now, southbound over Ta Qali field. He adjusted his course slightly to the east. He knew there was a gap in the range of low hills to the south of the field and just east of the runway's southern end. He planned to drop down low and pass through that gap. Ahead of him the fog was already thinning, the heat of the sun melting it back at its edges like ice on the sidewalk on a hot summer's day.

He craned his head about, looking behind himself, first to the left – NOTHING! – then to the right. His heart froze. A Bf 109 was plunging towards him and his wingman on a course to intercept them before they reached the fog.

"Break left!" he shouted, yanking his own stick to the right, hoping that by splitting up they could confuse the German and evade him.

The Bf 109 held its course steady, flashing over Derrick, ignoring him to focus on Andy's Spitfire. The wall of fog enveloped him and Derrick could see no more. His last minute turn to starboard had put him off his estimated course for the gap in the hills and he eased the stick up slightly to gain some altitude, but still stay within the fog. He eased the throttle back and the scream of his engine died down to its customary roar. He pushed his goggles up on his forehead and rubbed his eyes, somewhat surprised to be alive. He pressed his throat 'mic'.

"Andy, where are you?" he called.

Heinz squeezed the trigger and held it, adjusting his aim as the tracer shells arced out in front of the British plane. He'd led the Spitfire perfectly. It flew right into the stream of 20mm cannon shells. They shredded the fighter's starboard wing, rupturing and igniting the wing fuel tank. An explosion tore the wing root from the fuselage and the Spitfire cart wheeled, enveloped by flame and breaking apart as it slammed to earth inside the German perimeter on the south edge of the airfield.

"Well done, Sauckel!" His squadron leader's voice shouted in his ears. "Rejoin the flight. The one that got away may be back."

Heinz ignored the order, snapped over to starboard and dove into the fog.

>>>>>>>>>>>>

On the ground to the south of Ta Qali the roar of aero engines came louder and louder. At first Corporal Hartz thought they were the engines of Luftwaffe bombers come to deliver an attack against the British tanks to his south, but quickly the noise grew beyond anything any handful of aircraft could generate. He knew the chance to hit the tanks from the air had been missed. The transports were delivering the next drop and the bombers couldn't attack in the flight path of the transports.

Marty Chadwick waved his arms furiously trying to hurry his troop of tanks forward. They were behind schedule and wouldn't be on time for the planned attack at 0600. They still had half a mile to cover before they could disperse to either side of the road. He estimated they would be ten minutes late.

Faintly at first, then more clearly another sound began to drown the rattle and clank of his tanks. He'd heard the sound three times already the night just passed and he recognized it instantly. Another paratroop drop was about to begin. He lifted his binoculars to the northern sky, picking up the leading transports almost immediately. Still distant dots even with the glasses, they grew in size till he could see the glint of sunlight sparkling off windshields and wing edges, shining like stars against the orange sky of morning. Directly above him the sky cleared as the morning sun's warmth dispersed the mist. He was about to lower the glasses when he spotted several of the dots that seemed much closer and were moving on a different course than most of the enemy aircraft. Focusing the glasses on them he counted five aircraft that grew quickly until they resolved in his sight as twin-engine bombers. They streaked across Ta Qali from east to west in a shallow dive, flattening out as they approached the fortress of Mdina. Flak guns on the heights let loose a barrage peppering the sky with black puffs of smoke that hung in the air as though suspended from some monstrous string. The bombers pressed on. He watched as the bomb bay doors of the bombers swung open and their deadly cargoes hurtled earthward.

Chadwick recognized them as Ju 88's and the bombs they dropped that morning were among the heaviest in the Luftwaffe's arsenal. Each bomber let fly three bombs, one 2,000-kilogram bomb from the internal bomb bay and a 500-kilo bomb from under each wing. 15,000 kilo's of high explosive plunged down on the ancient ramparts of Mdina.

Chadwick gritted his teeth and twisted round in his tank turret hatch. He gestured angrily for the tanks behind him to hurry it up. At long last they were nearly in position. He snatched up his binoculars and scanned the area to his front as the tank eased to a stop. On either side of him the other tanks of his troop spread out. A platoon of five tanks moved to the west on his left, with his own tank and four others stopped at the edge of a small olive grove, the trees all shattered and leafless.

A red flare arced into the early morning sky followed immediately by shrill blasts from whistles all up and down the British lines. Men scrambled to their feet and began to move forward, crouching low, moving tentatively at first. They sought cover from a stone wall here, a tree trunk there, anything that could shield them, however briefly from the German fire they expected at any moment.

Chadwick shouted to his driver, "Let's move, Walsh!" and the Mark I Cruiser tank lurched forward as Walsh engaged the transmission. They moved forward between rows of olive tree stumps in the ancient orchard. Many of the olive trees on the island were hundreds of years old and had been tended by generations of Maltese, but by the summer of 1942 most of the groves near the airfields held only shattered, gnarled stumps, burnt and blackened by the blast of bombs that had missed their intended targets around the runways. Only a handful of the trees held any spring leaves at all.

Ahead in the distance over Ta Qali field he could see the falling white flower petals of parachutes as the German drop continued. Already three echelons of transports had passed over the field, though many in the British lines cheered as two Spitfires set upon the second rank, shooting down three Junkers and scattering the others, a cheer that died as one of the Spits was brought down by a German fighter. The surviving Spit roared almost directly over his head less than a hundred feet off the ground.

Chadwick looked to his right, checking on the other tanks of the first platoon. The 12 tank was on his flank, two rows of trees over and the 13 tank was two rows beyond that. On his left the 14 and 15 tanks advanced as well, moving up at a uniform four miles per hour. The second platoon's five tanks moved up three hundred yards to his left. Infantry accompanied the first platoon tanks through the orchard, including a group of five men who'd decided to stay behind his tank for shelter.

A series of sharp explosions to his front signaled the beginning of the planned mortar barrage. 81mm shells began to rain down on the German front lines. Heartened, the British infantry picked up their pace. Chadwick wasn't entirely clear on exactly where the German lines were and he watched the smoke and dust erupt several hundred yards away with interest, trying to discern some feature of the terrain for a clue where the Germans were, but nothing was revealed. He slouched down lower in the commander's cupola of his tank, ready to drop in and slam the lid closed at a moment's notice. The mortar barrage ended and the sound of tank engines was once again the loudest thing to be heard.

A machine gun chattered to his right, the sharp, rapid cracking of a German weapon, sounding like some monstrous zipper being ripped open rather than the slow, throaty bark of a British Vickers or the popping of a Bren gun. The infantry paused for a moment, then continued their advance once they were sure they weren't immediately threatened, shouts of officers and non-coms prodding them along.

"Time to button-up!" Chadwick shouted to his crew.

He dropped down through the cupola into the cramped interior of the tank, slamming the hatch down and latching it. He pushed the control bar and the turret swung slowly to the right, the 40mm main gun tracking across the tops of the tree stumps as if smelling for a target. He watched through the slits in his cupola but saw nothing worth shooting at. He tracked the turret back to the left, but could see little but dust and smoke ahead. The leading elements of the infantry were just entering the fringes of the dust cloud, but still the Germans had not responded.

The soft south wind was slowly clearing the dust, pushing it away to the north as Chadwick's platoon edged out of the olive grove and up onto the shoulder of the road at the edge of the orchard. Infantry crossed the road as well, dashing from one side to the other. He watched through his commander's slit carefully as this was a moment of maximum exposure.

His lead tank clanked and rattled onto the road, crossing the crown and dipping down the other side. Just as the tank tipped forward into the next field beyond the road a tremendous clang sounded against the hull and the Cruiser rocked on its suspension. The hull reverberated like a church bell struck by its clapper. Cries of panic came to him from the crew.

"We're hit!" shouted Walsh from his driver's seat.

"My God! Get out!" screamed the loader.

"Hold your positions!" shouted Chadwick. "We're all right! We're all right! The shell has bounced off us. Did anyone see where it came from?"

Walsh gunned the engine and the Cruiser lurched forward again, off the north margin of the road and into the field there. As the ringing in his ears started to subside Chadwick heard a great clatter of small arms fire and shouting from outside the tank. He peered out his viewing slits, looking first to his front where little but the dust clouds could be seen, then to the sides. On his right the 12 tank was right with him, twenty yards over, its turret nosing back and forth looking for a target. Further over the 13 tank was also apparently all right, slipping down off the road and into the field. Infantry were racing across the field pausing occasionally to fire their rifles then race forward again.

He squirmed around and looked out to his left. The 14 tank was still on the road, its hatches blown open with flames and smoke pouring out like some great pot boiled over. Its commander hung out of his hatch, his upper body stretched backward across the turret, his legs still inside the tank being consumed by fire. Beyond it the 15 tank lurched safely into the field. As he watched, its 40mm gun fired, but he could not see if it had a specific target.

"Move us out, Walsh!" he shouted. "If we stop here we're dead for sure!"

As the tank lurched across the field he kept his eyes glued to his observation slits, sweeping the turret back and forth looking for any threat or target worth firing at. Small arms fire increased dramatically and the infantry were beginning to suffer, dropping in their tracks dead or wounded. Bullets ricocheted harmlessly off the steel armor plate. Suddenly the hull mounted machine gun barked out. A stream of tracers arced out ahead of the tank, hammering into a low stonewall seventy-five yards ahead and just becoming visible through the murk. There was a line of small trees and bushes behind the wall. The Vickers gun was mounted in the hull in a small ball turret in such a way that the driver Walsh could aim and fire it with one hand. Walsh must have seen some movement on the other side of the wall.

Chadwick strained to pierce through the dust and see what was ahead, but was frustrated by how slowly the dust was settling or blowing away on the wind. A streak of flame lanced out from behind the wall forty meters to his left and the bell clanged again. The 15 tank flashed in a shower of flaming fuel and exploding ammunition, its turret dislodged from the hull ring and slewed over, the barrel of the main gun pointing at the sky.

He shoved the turret bar over and his gun swung round to the left. He'd gotten a rough picture of where the German gun was this time and was determined to not give the enemy gunners time to reload and shift target. He fired his co-axially mounted .303 caliber machine gun, spraying the area around the enemy gun. Chips and flakes of stone spit up from the wall. Still, he was unable to spot the gun itself. He let up on the machine gun, but kept the turret trained as the tank advanced across the field.

For the first time he saw enemy soldiers. They were popping up here and there from behind the wall firing machine guns and machine pistols at the advancing British infantry. He fired his machine gun again, using the turret to walk his fire along the wall from left to right. Several German paratroopers spun away or slumped down as they were hit.

They were within thirty yards of the wall now and through the lingering dust and smoke he could see Germans with their backs to him as they ran from the assault. Both he and Walsh fired, gunning the fleeing Germans in the back mercilessly.

"Rev it up Walsh!" he shouted. "Breach the wall!"

The tank's engine roared to full power once again all but drowning the sounds of battle from outside. They surged forward at top speed and slammed into the limestone wall with a crash. Walsh had his hands full now steering the tank and guiding it up and over the rubble of the wall, but Chadwick kept his machine gun fire up, replacing the drum when he ran out of ammunition.

Germans were fleeing all across the front now. He looked out to his left and could see the trails and breech of the anti-tank gun, abandoned by its crew as British infantry swarmed over the wall in pursuit of the paratroopers. With a cheer the British infantry broke into a run as the routed Germans fled before them. Beyond the trees the ground sloped gently down to a dry streambed filled with gravel and small stones. The Germans hit the streambed, stumbling and slipping among the loose stones. The men of the Inniskilling Regiment cut loose with a furious volley of rifle fire, dropping many of the paratroopers in the streambed before they could get clear. The survivors scrambled up the steeper slope on the north side, diving for cover behind yet another low stonewall.

Chadwick slapped his thigh in frustration. He shouted, "Walsh, get us clear of these bloody trees! Jerry is getting away!" On cue the tank surged forward again, getting clear of the last of the rubble of the wall and crashing through the brush line, bowling over a substantial tree stump in the process. Chadwick tracked the turret round and squeezed the trigger on the main gun. The 40mm belched out a solid shot that smacked into the second wall, tossing stones and men about. Next he tracked the co-axial machine gun across the wall, cutting down several more paratroopers. By the time the tank was half way across the 100 yard wide field the Germans were in flight again.

"We've got them on the run," shouted Chadwick. "Move it Walsh, move it!"

Once more the tank surged forward, catching up to the infantry who'd gotten past them while they were hung up on the first wall and trees, smashing over the next stonewall as it had the first. The three surviving tanks of his platoon pushed on, the Inniskilling Irish infantry racing headlong, driving the Germans from one possible line of defense after another. Each rock wall, line of brush or trees and streambed was cleared ruthlessly though Chadwick began to see that the Germans seemed to have little stomach for holding their ground. The British troop's urgency was driven by the sight of wave after wave of Junkers transports, peeling away to east and west after dropping their paratrooper cargo over the airfield.

Twenty minutes after launching the attack the British forces came to the top of a low ridge, not much more than fifty feet above the flat ground of the island's central plain. Known as Mt. Carmel it was the site of a Carmelite convent and hospital. The Germans had surrounded the grounds of the convent and hospital just hours before and after a quick search determined there were none but wounded and sick in residence, leaving the nuns and their patients unmolested.

As they crested the ridge the British infantrymen paused and surveyed their goal, Ta Qali airfield. The southern edge of the great wide runway lay just 400 yards in front of them. Hundreds of parachutes were drifting down as yet another phalanx of transports approached the field from the north. German troops fled away from the ridge towards the field, even as the new arrivals scrambled to gather in their 'chutes and make their weapons serviceable.

Chadwick unlatched his hatch and popped up through the cupola. He looked to his left, the west, scanning the top of the ridge for the tanks of his second platoon. Hundreds of British troops were reaching the top of the ridge, even as the Germans abandoned it. He turned and looked behind him, in the tracks his tank left as it climbed to the top of the ridge. His heart leapt at the sight there. Hundreds more British troops were surging up the hill; men of the Manchester regiment come to reinforce the attack of the Inniskillings.

As he turned back to the west a tank surged onto the ridgeline over three hundred yards away. He snatched up his binoculars and scanned the tank's hull. It was the 23 tank, the white numerals clearly visible. A moment later two more popped up together, followed by a fourth. Scanning the hulls he found only the 22 tank was missing. Seven of his ten tanks had survived the preliminary assault and were now poised to sweep down on the runway. He lifted his red signal flag and waved it over his head, giving the signal to attack forward. A moment later he saw the acknowledgment signal waved from the turret of the 21 tank.

"Let's go, Walsh!" he shouted and once more the Cruiser surged ahead, plunging down the slope of the hill. Over the din of battle and the roar of aero engines he heard the shrill blasts of whistles as the officers and non-coms pushed the men forward, but the infantry needed little encouragement. Flush with victory, hearts racing with battle lust they charged down the hill with a cheer heard over all the other sounds filling the air. Chadwick and his tanks followed.

>>>>>>>>>>>>

At the south end of the airfield Kuno peered over open sites down the length of the gun barrel, assessing the field of fire for the 50mm PAK 38 anti-tank gun. The gun had been professionally prepared, its trail spades properly dug in to absorb recoil, the gun barrel well clear of any obstacles and well oriented to fire on the runway 350 meters away. He turned to the paratrooper in command of the gun.

"Did you arrive in the same glider as this weapon?" he asked the man. Even though they were inside a sandbag bunker he had to shout to be heard over the thunderous din of the Junkers transports above their heads.

"No, Sir," the Sgt. shook his head, shouting back. "My glider flipped on landing and our gun was wrecked. We retrieved this gun from a different glider."

"What is your name," Kuno asked the Sergeant.

"I am Koll, Sir," the Sgt. answered.

"You are familiar with the PAK 38, Koll?" pressed Kuno.

"Oh, yes, Sir," the man assured him. "I am fully trained on this gun."

"Demonstrate the range of traverse," Kuno commanded. He stepped back and watched, right hand on his hip, left arm still in its sling.

"Yes, Major!" the man snapped. He stepped over the left side trail leg and knelt behind the splinter shield. He gripped the small wheel mounted on the leg and spun it clockwise. The gun and carriage tracked to the left until it came to a stop at its limit bar. Next the Sgt. spun the wheel counter-clockwise, traversing the gun to the right side limit bar then spun the wheel back until the gun was centered again. He looked at Kuno expectantly.

"Very good," said Kuno. "Who are your loaders?"

The Sgt. sprang to his feet and snapped his fingers twice at the other men in the bunker. He said, "Loaders, forward!"

Kuno eyed the two paratroopers who stepped forward to attention. Both just boys, they looked barely old enough to shave.

Kuno looked at the boys. He said, "What are your names?"

"Kiesslich," said one.

"Lintz," said the other.

"Kiesslich and Lintz, hm?" Kuno appraised the two skeptically. "You pups can load this gun?" he demanded.

"Yes, Sir!" the two answered in unison.

"Show me!"

The two boys jumped to the gun. One spun open the breech while the other pulled a 50mm round out of an ammunition case on the ground behind him. He rammed the shell home with confidence, lifting his hands clear as the first boy slammed the breechblock closed.

"Very good," said Kuno. "Who is the aimer?"

The three paratroopers hesitated and looked at each other for a moment. Finally the Sgt. answered. "Lt. Gross was wounded shortly after landing, Sir. He was our gun commander and aimer."

"Are any of you trained to aim the gun?"

"Lt. Gross has begun my training, Sir," the Sgt. replied. "I can aim the gun."

"Never mind that," said Kuno. "I will remain with you to aim the gun."

A phalanx of transports was peeling away to west and east after completing the drop. The next group of twelve Junkers was just coming into sight to the north of the field. For a moment there was relative quiet. He only needed to raise his voice slightly to be heard.

He asked the Sgt., "How much ammunition have you retrieved?"

"So far there are only five cases of three rounds each," the Sgt replied, pointing to the rear of the bunker. Four metal cases were stacked there. The end caps were removed, revealing the blunt noses of three shells side-by-side in each case. The fifth case was right behind the gun. One shell was in the breech with two more remaining in the case.

Kuno frowned. Fifteen rounds only.

"Are any of these high explosive?" he asked.

"No, Sir," replied the Sgt. "All of this ammunition is armor piercing."

Kuno knelt beside the gun and lifted his binoculars to survey the field through the bunker's embrasure. The gun was sited 350 meters to the east of the runway and about 200 meters from its southern end. The bunker provided a clear flanking shot across any point on the southern 500 meters of the strip. He looked across the field and found what he was looking for. The second gun was being dug into a low mound of earth almost directly across the runway from the first gun and between 300 to 350 meters off the runway. Paratroopers were stacking sandbags around it and he could see dirt flying from behind the sand bags. The second gun's cover was not as good as his position's, but it did seem well sited to fire across the runway.

A stick of paratroopers drifted down on the field in front of his bunker. To the west he saw six Junkers transports wheeling away for the return trip to Sicily. They veered south of the high ground to avoid any flak guns that might still be operating there. For a moment there was another lull between waves of transports. He lowered the glasses and listened. The sound of small arms fire came to him, carried on the soft, south wind. A Vickers machine gun coughed and he heard the sharper crack of a tank gun. He leaned out through the embrasure, but couldn't see around the sand bagged rim of the bunker to the south end of the field. He closed his eyes and listened. Just above the rising notes of the next wave of transports he heard whistles and a mighty cheer.

>>>>>>>>>>>>

Heinz plunged headlong into the fog bank in pursuit of the fleeing British Spitfire, ignoring repeated orders from his flight leader to return. From the moment he entered the fog he was flying entirely on instinct, with no visual references, not even a horizon to help him maintain level flight. He gripped the control column, eased back on the throttle and strained his eyes to pierce the mist, but he could see nothing. He forced from his mind thoughts of slamming into a hillside or clipping a tree or building and tried to focus on keeping straight and level in the fog. He was determined to hunt down and destroy the third British fighter.

He tried to think like the Englander. What would he do next if he were flying the Spitfire? He could return to Hal Far or perhaps even Luqa. With his no doubt intimate knowledge of the terrain the Englander could find his way down safely through the murk. He discarded this option quickly. The enemy pilot wouldn't be content with the one brief attack he'd already made. The British would be desperate to interfere with further reinforcement of the German landings. The Spitfire could attack the stream of transports flying back to Sicily. They had minimal protection on the return flight and the Junkers would be relatively easy picking, but Heinz felt sure the Englander would not choose this option either. No, the Spitfire pilot needed to attack the transports before they dropped their troops on the field, not only destroying the aircraft, but killing their passengers as well if his own sacrifice were not to be in vain.

To attack in this way against the overwhelming fighter escort the Germans provided he would have to circle back to the north, jumping out of the fog bank again for another quick attack just as the transports approached the drop zone, then back into the fog to repeat the process until his ammunition or his luck was exhausted. Heinz shoved his throttles forward and snapped his Emil over to port in a climbing turn to the east. He had no way of knowing which direction the enemy would turn, so he guessed.

In a moment he had climbed up out of the fog into clear sky. Only then did he realize he was holding his breath. He exhaled and relaxed his grip on the control column, flexing his fingers and the muscles of his forearm. He leveled off, but continued his turn till he'd come about 180 degrees and was now flying due north. He eased back further on the throttle until the Emil was once again just above stall speed. As he approached the northern fringe of the fog he turned east again, this time to starboard and held the turn, orbiting slowly to counterclockwise 500 hundred meters above the fog.

Another echelon of transports had disgorged their passengers over the field, leaving the beautiful white parachutes to float to the ground in their wakes. Six of the Junkers peeled off in his direction and he watched them bank away in a wide circle to avoid passing over Valletta and the anti-aircraft guns around the harbors.

He was glad he had guessed the Englander would go to the east. From his current position somewhere to the north of Grand Harbor and the city of Valletta he could look west across the whole island and out to sea beyond. Had he been on the west side looking east he would have been staring into the early morning sun.

He completed his third orbit and was beginning to wonder if the Englander had decided to land safely after all. The Spitfires had destroyed three transports and most of their passengers. Not a bad morning's work to survive. Heinz checked his fuel gauge. Down to two thirds. Plenty of time to orbit slowly and give the Spitfire pilot time to gather his courage.

He was on the southern leg of his short loop when the Spitfire rocketed out of the fog towards the next wave of transports approaching the field. Heinz' heart leaped and he slammed the throttle forward, juicing the engine to full power in an instant and he hauled the stick over hard to port. The engine whined in protest of this rough treatment, but the Bf 109 responded beautifully and brought him 1000 meters behind the Spitfire in just seconds.

Again he saw there was nothing he could do to prevent the Spitfire from making an attack against the approaching transport planes. The two fighters were at full speed and very evenly matched. The Englander bored in towards the outboard Junkers in the echelon, eating the distance between them in just seconds in a nearly head on attack. The Junkers pilot saw his danger and heaved the control column over, but the ungainly tri-motor wasn't nearly as agile as the Spitfire.

Puffs of smoke blew back from the Spitfire's wings as the Englander fired at a range of 800 meters, holding the trigger as he walked his tracers into the undercarriage of the Junkers, hammering up through the floor of the passenger compartment. At the last moment possible to avoid collision he threw the fighter over to port, holding the trigger for a sweeping shot at the next Junkers in line. Chunks of tail plane and rudder flew away from the second transport and it veered drunkenly to port as its pilot fought for control.

Heinz gritted his teeth and squeezed the control column in a death grip, but for all the temptation to cut loose a long-range shot at the Spitfire he kept his composure. He turned to port also, cutting inside the Spitfire's arc, reducing the range to 700 meters.

For all his anger he couldn't help but admire the Englander's flying skill and courage. Against overwhelming odds the enemy pilot had destroyed or forced off course five Junkers transports in just minutes, reducing the reinforcements to the German airhead by nearly a hundred men. Heinz was determined to not allow another transport to be attacked.

The two fighters shot beneath the rest of the 'V' formation and hurtled on to the west in a high-speed turn. Other German fighters were angling for position, but Heinz knew none could intercept the Spitfire before it dodged back into the fog. Heinz eased back on the throttle a little to give his Emil a tighter turning radius, sacrificing a little speed to cut inside the Spitfire's turn. So far as he could tell the Englander still had no idea Heinz was behind him.

With the range down to 500 meters he realized the Spitfire would reach the fog bank before he had a clean shot. He had to divert it back into open sky. He aimed a pure deflection shot ahead of the British fighter, squeezing off a long, three-second burst, sending red tracer arcing out before him. It worked! The Spitfire snapped back to starboard, parallel to the fog bank and still a kilometer short of it as the Englander reacted in surprise to the tracer shells that suddenly flashed by his nose from some unknown source. Heinz slammed the throttles forward to full speed again and engaged the boost, squirting raw gas into the fuel ports of the engine, squeezing every ounce of power from the Emil to close on the enemy.

"Come on, come on," he urged the Messerschmitt forward.

He lined up the Spitfire as the range fell towards 400 meters. As the Spitfire filled his gun sites he squeezed the trigger. The Emil bucked and jolted as cannon and machine gun shells flew from wings and nose, but in a flash the enemy was gone. Where just seconds before there had been a Spitfire now there was empty sky! He craned around to look behind him, first to his left, then to his right. Nothing! Where had the Englander gone? His mind raced and for a split second he was indecisive, then he hurled the Emil over on its starboard wing, diving and turning, still at full power. Red tracer flashed past his canopy and several ragged pieces were torn in the tip of his port wing as 20mm cannon shells punched through the thin aluminum frame and skin. He held the dive and turn at full power, sliding down in his seat as gravity pushed the air from his lungs. Black spots swam before his eyes as the g-force pulled his blood away from his brain and into his legs.

Finally, he eased the stick back and allowed the fighter to assume level flight. He gasped for air and shook his head, praying that his desperate turn had shaken the Spitfire. When his vision cleared he craned around to look behind him. The enemy fighter was still behind him, but well beyond effective gun range. He understood the Englander's maneuver now. The enemy pilot had applied his flaps as an airbrake, slashing the Spitfire's speed and diving, causing Heinz to hurtle past above him. As soon as the Bf 109 passed him the Englander went to full speed again, closing on Heinz from below and coming within an instant of ending his life.

Cold sweat beaded his forehead and his breath came in choking gasps. He checked behind him again. The Spitfire remained behind him as their course took the two fighters out over the sea to the northeast of the island at an altitude of 3000 meters. Heinz looked around for help, but his squadron mates were obeying their orders and were staying with the transports. For the moment at least he was on his own. He veered to the east in a sharp, diving turn; craning his head around to watch the Spitfire he saw the Englander match his turn, cutting inside it and shortening the range perceptibly. When he'd come back around to a southerly heading Heinz straightened out and slammed the throttles forward again at 800 meters above the sea as he crossed back over land. If he could draw the Spitfire back over the airfield Heinz would have the help of the German fighter escort there.

The final echelon of transports was just splitting to east and west for the return to Sicily. Parachutes drifted down on the field. Tracer shells flashed past his canopy again as the Spitfire continued its pursuit. He veered right, away from the shells, then yanked the stick back to the left and threw the Emil into a tight roll as the two machines crossed back over the airfield.

Kenneth stood on the tree limb, transfixed by the spectacle of the massive paratroop drop. He'd cheered as if at a high school football game at home in South Dakota when the Spitfires attacked the transports. He'd cursed and clenched his fists in rage as two Spitfires were destroyed and cheered again when the surviving Spit re-emerged from the fog to strike two more transports. Now he craned his neck to watch the duel that was developing between the sole remaining Spitfire and the Messerschmitt that had already shot down the other two RAF fighters.

Both machines were clearly piloted by men of extraordinary flying skill. The Spit' pilot had dodged a near fatal attack by applying his airbrakes, turning the tables on the German and but for the brilliant anticipation of the German in turning away at the last second would have downed the 109. The Spit pursued the Emil away to the northeast and nearly out of sight over the sea before they turned and made their way back over the island, bobbing, weaving and diving as the German sought to shake the Brit.

The two fighters roared directly over his head at under 1000 feet altitude, passing back over Ta Qali as the last of the German transports turned for home. Once again the Spitfire closed the range to attack and again, just as the tracer shells had zeroed in on the German the 109 spun away in a tight barrel roll that brought it up right behind the Spitfire.

"WATCH IT! WATCH IT!" Kenneth screamed, pounding his fist against the tree trunk.

The Spitfire weaved and dodged across the field, the 109 clinging tenaciously to its tail. The two banked over the high ground at Rabat and the Spitfire tried to break for the lingering fog, but the other German fighters were free now of their responsibilities to the transports and they forced the Brit back over the field.

Kenneth hung his jaw in incredulity. Once the Spitfire was over open ground the other Germans backed off. It was to be a dogfight between the lone German and his British counterpart, a duel to the death in the skies over Ta Qali. He tore his eyes off the air battle and turned to look back at the car. He knew he and Maggie should be moving again, but his eyes were drawn back to the sky.

Derrick's hands were clammy and sweat stung his eyes. He twisted and turned frantically, looking for a way out, but at every turn another Messerschmitt blocked his escape. But every time he thought he was a goner the Germans backed off. It finally dawned on him that he had only one way out. He had to down the 109 on his tail to live.

He rammed the throttle forward and yanked back on the stick, pulling it into his lap, holding it there, bringing the Spit' up, up, up and over in an inside loop, back down and up behind the 109. He squeezed the trigger, but the German was gone just as fast, rolling away to his right. Derrick dragged his forearm across his eyes, wiping away the sweat. He craned around looking for the German, finding him right where he'd come to expect him to be, on his tail again. Smoke erupted from the German's wings and Derrick snapped over to his left. Too late! Shells hammered into the side of his Spit, passing through the canopy above his head. Glass showered down on him, cutting his cheek and forehead. He held the Spit' over in his turn and dove.

All over the airfield men of both sides paused in the Battle of Ta Qali and stole glances at the sky, watching what has become one of the most famous individual dogfights of the Second World War. The Irishman from Belfast, Derrick Metcalfe and the German from Munich, Heinz Sauckel twisted and turned over Ta Qali, first one, then the other seizing a momentary advantage before suddenly finding himself in the sites of his enemy.

On the ground British infantry poured down the slope at the south end of the field, German paratroopers in full flight before them. Anywhere the Germans turned and tried to make a stand thcy were swamped and overrun by the tidal wave of cheering madmen pouring over Mt. Carmel and down towards the airfield. Chadwick drew his seven tanks together across a 300-yard wide front, headed straight for the southern edge of the airfield, firing their machine guns and occasionally the 40mm main gun in support of the infantry. His 11 tank lurched and rumbled onto the flat ground at the base of the ridge about 100 yards from the southern edge of the runway. Parachutes still drifted down on the field though the last wave of transports was winging away for the return to their Sicilian bases.

"Come left!" shouted Chadwick. "Make for the center of the runway!"

The Mark I Cruiser lurched and turned left as Corporal Walsh disengaged the left hand tracks for a second until the right track turned them in the correct direction.

Chadwick peered through the slits in his commander's cupola. The attack was headlong now as the Inniskillings and Manchesters pursued the fleeing Germans. A squad of infantry ran past his tank on the right, their Sergeant urging them on. To his left the 25 tank fired its main gun at a line of sandbagged trenches near the runway. A cloud of dirt and dust erupted. Several German troops staggered away clutching their wounds. Others remained, motionless.

A stream of bullets ricocheted against the tank turret, making the crew duck in spite of knowing the armor would protect them from MG fire. When Chadwick looked again the infantry squad on his right had been cut down. Several were still thrashing in the agony of their wounds.

"LEFT! LEFT!" he shouted. Too late. Even as Walsh brought the tank left the treads ground over the legs of one of the wounded. Chadwick closed his eyes and fought down his gorge.

More bullets spattered against the hull of the tank. Chadwick opened his eyes and forced himself to look out again. German resistance was stiffening the closer they got to the runway. British troops were dropping more frequently; many were taking cover to return fire. He spun the turret a few degrees to the right and fired his machine gun at a trench line, hammering away at it as the cruiser drew abreast of it, cutting down German troops, heaping their bodies like obscene cordwood cut for the fire.

He stole a look at his watch. 0640. He looked through the slits just in time to see a pair of fighter aircraft flash across the field, one chasing the other. Infantrymen nearby shouted and pointed into the sky. He had no time to watch the dogfight. The Cruiser rumbled onto the southern threshold of the airstrip, jolting up onto the crown of the runway. Right away the bumping and jolting eased as the tank tracks road over the smooth- compacted crushed gravel surface of the runway.

"Move it Walsh!" he shouted.

The tank sped up and fairly raced up the runway. Chadwick turned the turret, gunning German paratroopers with his machine gun, searching for a target for the main gun. He smiled to himself.

"We'll have this lot washed up in an hour or so," he said, slapping his loader on the shoulder.

First light at Gibraltar the morning of June 26th revealed a scene in the anchorage of intense, though not to say frantic, activity. Still in the morning shadow cast by The Rock, Ships were tied up at every pier. Destroyers and cruisers received supplies of food, fuel, ammunition and every requirement of warships in expectation of imminent action. Dockside cranes and hoists clanked and clattered and hummed, men shouted and steam whistles hooted as the assembled fleet was provisioned.

At the south end of the anchorage the heavy cruiser *HMS Liverpool* rested in the harbor's Prince of Wales Dry Dock undergoing repairs. She'd been torpedoed less than two weeks earlier by an Italian aircraft while covering Operation Harpoon, the most recent Malta relief convoy. Repairs would take at least another month before *Liverpool* was fit for sea.

Away from the docks the other heavy ships rested, moored to the anchor buoys of the outer harbor. Barges and lighters were tied up alongside each, pumping fuel and fresh water into the great storage tanks of the ships.

*HMS Renown* towered above the others. *Renown* was the survivor of a two-ship class of battlecruisers laid down in the First World War and designed with a hard punch and strong legs. Her six 15-inch guns could pummel any smaller ship and her speed of

29 knots let her run from anything bigger. But her sister ship, *HMS Repulse* found she could not run from aircraft. *Repulse* was sunk along with the battleship *HMS Prince of Wales* by Japanese aircraft the prior December off the Malay Peninsula.

*Renown* was connected in an odd way to *HMS Eagle,* the British carrier sunk by U-212. Following the loss of three British battlecruisers at the Battle of Jutland in the First World War the Royal Navy recognized their design was faulty, providing too little armored protection to critical areas of the ships, most especially the magazines. *Renown* was given an extensive refit to remedy the deficiency and the armor plates used in the upgrade were those originally made for the construction of *Almirante Cochrane,* the Chilean battleship converted to aircraft carrier at the end of the first war.

*Renown* had had a busy second war. Her speed made her a valuable asset as the Royal Navy hunted down the numerous German commerce raiders that preyed on Commonwealth shipping at the start of the war and she'd spent a good deal of time in the first months of conflict chasing the *Graf Spee* around the South Atlantic. She'd engaged the German battlecruisers *Scharnhorst* and *Gneisnau* in April 1940, shortly after the German ships had sunk the carrier *HMS Glorious* with gunfire off the coast of Norway. All three ships were hit, but *Renown* got the better of the exchange and the Germans ran for the safety of their own air cover. Now *Renown* readied herself for more action. In the Atlantic Ocean the battleships *Rodney* and *Nelson* had turned around after crossing the equator, leaving the troop convoy they were escorting and racing north at their top speed of 24 knots, but were still three days sailing from Gibraltar when the Axis invasion of Malta began. For the relief operation to Malta the Royal Navy would have to rely on *Renown's* heavy guns alone.

An area to the north of the naval anchorage was conspicuously vacant. The final element of the fleet was still at sea. *HMS Furious* was due to arrive within the hour. Most of her Swordfish bi-planes had flown ahead to land at Gibraltar's airfield at the very northern edge of the Crown Colony. The Harbor's two largest barges lay waiting for her to begin loading Spitfires onto her decks.

"Damnable luck, *Eagle.*"

Admiral Sir Harold Burrough turned from the port in his flag quarters aboard *HMS Renown*. He sighed and strode to the chart table in the center of the room.

"Damnable luck or not, she's gone," he replied to his Flag Officer, Lt. James Harris.

The deck hummed under their feet, the vibration of the engines transmitted through the hull as they geared up to ease *Renown* away from her berth. She would sail within the hour. Just at the edge of hearing a low pitched hum told the Admiral and his secretary that the ship's radar aerial was already turning through its search. A shout came through the open port as a Petty Officer on deck berated a work party. Admiral Burrough ignored the distraction and focused on the chart spread across the table in his suite. Now he pondered the expanse of the Mediterranean Sea with a frown.

Studying the chart with him was an assemblage of senior officers, commanders of the ships of Force H and the Admiral's Flag Staff. Captain Sir Charles Saumerez Daniel, C.O. of the *Renown* hosted the conference.

Burrough was a big man, over six feet, built like a wrestler and with enormous hands. With a roman nose and craggy features weathered by decades at sea keeping watch on the bridge of one or another of His Majesty's Ships, Burrough was handsome in a rough hewn way. To those who knew him he was highly intelligent and completely devoted to the Service. He had only recently arrived to Gibraltar, having just relinquished his command of the Arctic Cruiser Squadron.

The Captains of several of the cruisers in harbor were in attendance. The Commanding Officers of three Dido class cruisers were present. Captain Brooking of *HMS Sirius* was there as were Captains Frend and Voelcker of *HMS Phoebe* and *HMS Charybdis* respectively. The latter had only just taken command that month of his anti-aircraft cruiser. Captain Paton, Flag Captain Cruisers and Chief Staff officer to Admiral Burrough commanded *HMS Nigeria*. Rounding out the cruiser commanders was Captain Russell of *HMS Kenya.* Also present was Captain (D) R.M.J. Hutton, commander of the nineteenth Destroyer Flotilla, escort to the capital ships. He would command his destroyers from the bridge of *HMS Laforey*, first ship and namesake of her class, specially configured with special signals gear for communications and accommodations for the Flotilla leader's staff. At 1,920 tons she was the largest destroyer in the escort. Rounding out the conference attendees was Lt. Commander Geoffrey Oats, Staff Intelligence Officer, Gibraltar. The officers from HMS *Furious* were not present, having not yet arrived at Gibraltar.

"Somehow we've got to do with just the one carrier," Admiral Burrough went on, "and it must provide air cover for the fleet and also deliver the Spitfires to Malta."

"What is the one-way range of the Spitfires," asked Captain (D) Hutton.

Admiral Burrough looked at each of the officers in turn waiting for the answer. Finally, a throat was cleared at the back of the room. The Admiral peered over the heads of the more senior officers in the front rank.

"Did you, uh, say something Commander?" he asked with a gesture that showed he couldn't name the officer.

"Lt. Commander Oats, Sir," the Intelligence Officer replied, "and, yes, I believe the one-way radius of the Spitfire is approaching 700 miles, based upon what was said in advance of the convoy operations earlier in the month. But that was using Spitfires that were stripped of armament, ammunition and all other unnecessary weight. The Spits for this operation have to fly into Malta fully armed as they may arrive in the midst of a dogfight. Under these conditions the range is between 500 to 550 miles. Best to figure on no more than 500."

"Thank you, Commander," said Admiral Burrough who now looked at his Staff Navigator, Captain Lloyd with a raised eyebrow. Lloyd read the question in the Admiral's face and leaned down onto the chart.

"That would put us east of 6° east longitude," he said, placing his finger on the chart north of the Algerian coastline. "But that is as the crow flies. Our pilots are forced to avoid flying over Vichy territory in North Africa."

He traced a route over water that skirted the Algerian and Tunisian shorelines before turning south over the Strait of Sicily to Malta.

"With the course they must fly they must be as far as 6° 30' east longitude before they fly off. Of course, weather conditions can affect this as well. A strong headwind can shave many miles off the flying radius of a Spitfire."

Burrough pondered the chart.

"6° east longitude places us within range of the Sardinian airfields does it not?" he asked.

Once again Commander Oats responded.

"Yes, Sir," he said. "At 6° east longitude you'll be well within range of Ju 88's from Decimomanu Airfield on Sardinia's southwest tip, but somewhat outside round trip range of enemy fighters."

"Of course we'll have to launch the Spitfires at first light," mused Burrough. He turned again to his navigator. "Lloyd, calculate course and speed to bring us to 6° 30' East Longitude at first light day after tomorrow please," he ordered.

"Now," he said, "let's turn our attention to what we can expect east of there," he tapped the chart. "Here between the Tunisian headlands and Sardinia and again, if and when we transit the Strait of Sicily. What has the enemy in store for us there?"

Oats cleared his throat and spoke again. "Everywhere from first light at 6° East Longitude through nightfall on the 27th you can expect air attack from Italian Regia Aeronautica and German Luftwaffe bombers on Sardinia," he said. "The latest word from those parts is that both enemy air forces on the island have been strengthened considerably in the past two weeks. Now we know why." Oats paused sheepishly as if he'd spoken out of turn in school.

"Go on, Oats," the Admiral prompted him.

Oats took a deep breath then wedged himself up to the table. He smoothed his hair down, self consciously flattening the cow lick that always seemed to stand on end on the back of his head.

"Still, that's not the worst of it," he went on. "After nightfall, say east of 9°," he leaned over and tapped the chart in the area north of the Tunisian port of Bizerte, "you can expect concentrated submarine attack and as you enter the Sicilian Narrows you'll be subject to attack by Motor Torpedo Boats based at Trapani on Sicily and the island of Pantelleria in the Strait itself. Both the Italians and Germans are there in some strength, again with recent reinforcement."

Oats looked around the table. Every officer's eyes were riveted upon him.

"In addition we know there are minefields in the Narrows." He tapped the chart between Sicily and the Tunisian mainland. "We don't have all of them charted. The Italians have a flotilla of minelayers working between Trapani and Pantelleria and undoubtedly they are laying more right now." He drew his finger across the chart in an arc between the two island ports. "After transiting the Narrows, in daylight on the 28th you'll find yourself about here," he said, pointing to an area to the west of Malta, between the island and Tunisia's eastern shoreline. "You'll be within range of land based bombers from Sicily at that point, though with luck the Spitfires you deliver will keep the Luftwaffe busy and away from you." He shook his head. "Then there's the Italian Navy to consider. We don't know what their intentions are, but they have powerful surface units based on Naples as well as lighter escort type vessels in Sicilian waters." Oats paused, conscious of having run off at the mouth.

Admiral Burrough looked at Commander Oats, sizing him up. He saw a young reserve officer with a clear eye and confident demeanor, one of the new breed of naval officers, at home with all the scientific and technical aspects of war.

"But the Italians always avoid night action situations don't they?" asked the Admiral.

"That's true, Sir," replied Oats. "Our latest intelligence indicates the Germans still have not shared their radar technology with their allies. The Italians are mostly blind at night. Even so, we're entering a period of full moon. The Italians are at less of a disadvantage under clear, moonlit skies."

Oats looked about the cabin.

"I'm afraid you'll be confronted by constant danger from all quarters on this voyage, Sir," he said. "Especially past 6° East Longitude."

"Don't worry, Oats," Burrough said, smiling. "I'm taking you along to keep me out of trouble."

Oats swallowed hard amidst the chuckling of the other officers.

Across the harbor from Admiral Burrough's conference aboard *Renown* Sergeant Pilot Bryan Treadway and over thirty other RAF pilots waited aboard barges for the arrival of *HMS Furious*. The pilots were to observe the handling of their Spitfire fighters as derricks on the barges lifted them onto the flight deck of the carrier. Bryan checked his watch. 0525 hours. He scratched his scalp through his sandy-blond hair. *Furious* and her escorts were expected by 0600. The pilots, along with nearly everyone else in Gibraltar had been kept in the dark as to their ultimate destination and speculation ran rampant among them. The smart money was indeed on Malta, but a minority was convinced they were destined for Egypt to confront Rommel's Africa Corp and a few had bets on Dakar in French West Africa. All would know for sure soon enough.

Treadway was a Londoner, and like most fighter pilots was very young, but as a married man he was something of a rarity. Few British fighter pilots in 1942 had lived long enough to marry, but Bryan had secretly wed his girl. The Royal Air Force was still unaware of his change in marital status.

Everything that could be made ready for *Furious'* arrival was done. The first two Spitfires to be loaded were already slung in their lifting lines, waiting to be hoisted from the barges. Other barges were ready to pump fuel oil, aviation petrol and fresh water. Crates of ammunition and fresh food stood ready to be ported aboard.

"THERE SHE IS!"

The shout carried across the harbor from the lookout atop the mainmast of *Renown* as he spotted the first tell tale of smoke from the approaching carrier. Bryan peered out to the south, but could see nothing from his position on the deck of the barge just five feet above the water. He turned and for the tenth time went over the couplings and lines by which his Spitfire would be hoisted. Everything remained in order, but the exercise helped him to kill ten minutes. By the time he finished and looked back out to sea again he could clearly see the great carrier and several of its escorts pushing on towards The Rock, as Gibraltar was known to its British owners.    The sun was well up in the sky, though not yet clear of the imposing granite monolith that formed the spine of the peninsula and gave the colony its nickname. A warm breeze blew off the Spanish mainland to the north. It would be a fine, hot and glorious summer day.

Bryan watched as *Furious* slowed, making her way round the breakwater that protected the naval anchorage from sea waves. Harbor tugs met her and she took aboard the pilot to guide her to her place. When at last the carrier came to rest the anchors were let out, fore and aft and she was ready to be provisioned. The barge crew scrambled about as it was brought alongside ship. Bryan's barge remained on the starboard side, well forward, just aft of the island, the superstructure that projected above the carrier's flight deck. The other barge carrying Spitfires was tied up on the port side near the stern.

With much shouting, mainly unnecessary in Bryan's view the first Spitfire was hoisted from the barge into the sky. The derrick aboard the barge was just tall enough to lift the aircraft to the level of the flight deck 60 feet above the water then to swing it aboard with a scant three feet clearance. As each plane was lifted aboard the crane operator slowed the load till deck hands could reach the handling lines trailing from the aircraft. They then guided the plane round till it hung completely over the flight deck where it was eased down softly. The coupling hooks were quickly released and the derrick lowered to the barge to pick up another plane, while the craft just placed aboard was manhandled clear by deck hands. Each aircraft took about five minutes to load.

Finally Bryan's turn came. He watched the Spitfire lifted from the deck of the barge, then raced up the gangway of the carrier to its hanger deck and up a stairwell to the flight deck. He arrived breathless, in time to see his plane lowered smoothly to the deck and to supervise its being wheeled into position aft.

It took almost two hours to complete the loading and to see the carrier on her way, but by mid-morning thirty-six Spitfire fighters were crowded on to the aft flight deck of *Furious*. Her remaining Swordfish bi-planes remained below decks as well as five Fairey Fulmar fighters. These were to be used as anti-submarine and combat air patrol after the Spitfires flew off for Malta.

A shortcoming of the carrier's design and construction was revealed here. Her lifts to bring planes from the hangar deck to the flight deck were too small to accommodate the Spitfires or any other aircraft not equipped with folding wings. All the Spitfires had to be carried on her flight deck, leaving enough room for the lead planes to take off. There could be no question of landing again on the shortened flight deck. The Spitfires were headed on a one-way flight to Malta.

*HMS Furious* was built during the First World War as a

battlecruiser, armed with two enormous 18-inch rifles mounted one each fore and aft. Initial gunnery trials had revealed the performance of the experimental guns to be unsatisfactory and within four months of her commissioning *Furious* was back in the dockyard being re-fitted with a 'flying-off' deck for aircraft, replacing the forward gun mount. As the name implies this deck was suitable for take-offs only. It was not considered practical for landings to be attempted, but in 1918 *Furious* became the first vessel to launch an offensive air strike when a flight of seven Sopwith Camels took off from her deck and attacked the Zeppelin base at Tondern at the mouth of the Elbe river near the Danish-German border. Surprise was complete and the British aircraft successfully bombed the Zeppelin hangars at the German base, destroying two. Strategic effects of the raid were negligible, but a new era in naval warfare was born, even if few at the time recognized it.

In the early 1920's the ship was modified again, this time into a true aircraft carrier capable of launching and recovering aircraft from a single long flight deck, her remaining 18-inch gun removed. Finally, in 1939 with war brewing the tiny 'island' control structure was added to the starboard side of the flight deck.

While the loading of the aircraft went on other barges and lighters delivered supplies, mainly fuel for the ship's engines and her aircraft along with fresh water for her boilers and for the crews' consumption. Shortly after the carrier's arrival the first escort vessels began easing away from their berths, slipping past the breakwater and out to sea. Soon after, the battlecruiser *Renown* swung round on its moorings and left port, first going directly south to clear the headland, then sharply east. For all her age *Furious* was a fast ship, capable of 31 knots. She and her close escorts would leave port nearly two hours after *Renown* , planning to catch them up later in the day. After seeing to their machines Bryan and the other pilots stayed on the flight deck as the ship left port.

"Last time any of us will see the old Rock," said a voice behind Bryan.

Bryan laughed. "You're a morbid sod, Billy!" he exclaimed. "Why can't you keep your cheerful opinions to yourself?" He looked with fondness on Gibraltar.

The ten days he and Billy and the other pilots in their group spent there were like a holiday. They hadn't realized how bad it had gotten at home, but by the spring of 1942 England had been at war for two and a half years and it showed in the shabbiness of the cities and in the thin rations of soldier and civilian alike. The people had shivered through the winter just passed, clutching their worn, threadbare clothes about them. Shortages of coal and gas kept their homes and workplaces cold and dank.

But in Gibraltar the spring sun and sparkling sea warmed the pilots to their bones. The shortages and hardships of home could almost be forgotten. The restaurants served wonderful, un-rationed, full course meals, Spanish-style with onion soup, baked chicken and rice or Moorish-style lamb roasted over an open fire on a spit with figs and dates. Madeira, Sangria and Algerian wine were plentiful and any kind of citrus fruit could be had from the numerous curbside vendors. The shops were filled with all manner of goods not seen in Britain since shortly after the outbreak of war. Troops of all services and every nation of the Commonwealth and Empire swarmed the shops, buying silk stockings, watches, cameras, dainties and delicacies like perfume, cosmetics and lacy female underthings, most delivered to Gibraltar in hard fought convoys from America.

In the afternoons the pilots strolled down from their billets among the tunnels delved by the Royal Engineers in 'The Rock', past the three great dry docks at the south end of the naval harbor and on to Rosia Bay where they swam and sunned themselves like beached seals. Once Bryan and his friend Billy walked all the way to Europa Point, the southern tip of the peninsula where they'd watched the Royal Navy's anti-submarine patrols bobbing about in the Straits.

After dark the pilots caroused in the many bars on Main Street from the Imperiale Café to the Grand Hotel. Bar hopping was their preferred sport and the favorite establishments were those where the patrons were led in sing-alongs and amateur talent contests. Many an aspiring crooner found his dreams of stardom dashed by good-natured hoots of derision before stumbling off to his cot in disappointment.

One evening just a few nights earlier Bryan and Billy were on the move between bars when the rumble of a distant explosion carried up from the south. Moments later a series of dull blasts followed. They scrambled onto a wall and peered out to sea, but could see no indication of the source. Not till next morning did they learn that a corvette and two sub-hunter launches had been lost to an enemy submarine, bringing the reality of the war back with a shock.

Gazing back at the port Sergeant Pilot Billy Wilson shook his head. "All right," he said, "but mark my words, we'll never see it again."

"I'm glad you managed to keep that to yourself," Bryan said, speaking through the side of his mouth. "Gwen would not have appreciated your conviction that I'm a walking dead man."

Billy laughed and clapped Bryan on the shoulder. "She knew it already old son, I didn't need to tell her. Why else would she have married you besides pity?" Bryan stood at the edge of the flight deck lost in memories of home as Billy turned and walked away.

*Furious* cleared the headland and turned to the east, she and her escorts running their engines to full speed to catch *Renown* and the other ships already forty miles ahead. Bryan remained on the flight deck as *HMS Furious* raced eastward from Gibraltar at the carrier's top speed of 31 knots. She was in company with the cruiser *Nigeria* and three destroyers, *Eskimo, Tartar* and *Sikh,* Tribal Class sisters of *Ashanti* and *Nubian,* escorts to the ill-fated *Eagle.* It was a brilliant day and he enjoyed the morning sun and the brisk wind the carrier's speed created. He took off his cap and brushed his rather longish blond hair back over his head. His pant legs whipped in the wind as he strolled along the flight deck above the port catwalk. Behind the ship a broad, foaming wake attracted squadrons of gulls who wheeled and dove, snatching at morsels swirled to the surface by the mighty propellers. Far behind *Furious* the great concrete rain catchments on the eastern slope of The Rock stood out like livid white scars against the darker gray of the monolith. To the north the peaks of the Sierra Nevada mountain range in Spain glimmered in the morning sunshine. The sun and sparkling sea were dazzling, beautiful beyond his belief. He breathed deep, filling his lungs with salt air, and saw himself a part of the long tradition of English sea dogs like Sir Francis Drake and Admiral Horatio Nelson.

Gazing astern of *Furious* in her wake he saw *HMS Nigeria,*

8,000 ton Fiji Class cruiser with twelve 6-inch guns and bristling
with smaller caliber anti-aircraft armament. *Nigeria* was the only
ship available at Gibraltar with the specialized staff and Very High
Frequency VHF wireless apparatus to serve as control ship for the
Spitfire fighters. Bryan turned to port where the 1,870-ton
destroyer *HMS Sikh* kept station 500 yards abeam the carrier. She
knifed through the calm seas, throwing a towering bow wave to
either side. Crewmen moved about on her weather decks in
shirtsleeves. Bryan started to wave, but checked himself, not
wanting to appear the amateur. He resumed his walk, coming to
the rounded end of the flight deck. He stopped and looked down on
the long, narrow bow section of the carrier. Bryan was unfamiliar
with the carrier's history, of her first incarnation as a battlecruiser
and subsequent conversion to aircraft carrier and he could make
little sense of why the flight deck ended so far short of the bow.

    To his left was the Port Flying Control Position, an open
platform recessed below the flight deck level and projecting out
over the side of the ship. The Commander (Flying) controlled
flying off and landing operations from this position. To his right
was the Starboard Navigating Position from which the Captain
conned the ship while at sea. Directly below Bryan's feet was the
Central Navigating position. It was generally used to conn the ship
while in harbor and could be raised and retracted by a lift set below
the flight deck. Passageways below the flight deck connected all
three positions. The crew of *Furious* had given nicknames to these
three positions. The Port Flying Control Position was known as
'Pip', the Starboard Navigating as 'Squeak' and the Central
Navigating Position was known as 'Wilfred'. The origins of these
nicknames are lost to history. Bryan briefly watched the ship's
officers in 'Pip' as they conned the ship before turning his
attention forward.

    The bow of the ship projected 140 feet beyond the end of the
flight deck at Bryan's feet. A twin 5.5-inch anti-aircraft gun was
mounted another deck down and forward of the bridge in the
center of the bow with two multiple two-pounder pom-poms to
port and starboard behind it. To his right stood the island, the small
tower above the flight deck. In other navies and indeed aboard
other carriers of the Royal Navy the island was the seat of
navigation and air operations control, but aboard *Furious* the island

served as a platform for flak guns and gunnery control. Even here, within sight of The Rock both the guns and the island were fully manned in anticipation of action.

Beyond the island, 500 yards to starboard sailed *HMS Eskimo* and a half mile dead ahead of the carrier steamed *HMS Tartar,* both Tribal Class sister ships of *Sikh.* The three destroyers formed the anti-submarine screen for the carrier and the cruiser.

Bryan remained on deck for more than an hour, imagining himself the Admiral in command of these warships. He'd show the Hun what for! The Eye-ties too, for that matter. Eventually though his restless nature left him bored with the calm seas and perfect skies and he went below decks, seeking his flying mates, and his friend Billy Wilson in particular. He found Billy in the aircrew quarters just below the hangar deck. As usual Billy had beaten him to an upper bunk. Billy was a cribbage player of considerable ability and was busily engaged in fleecing a Fleet Air Arm pilot of a pence a point.

"Fifteen two, fifteen four, a pair for six and a three card run makes nine," Billy called his hand. He pegged off his points on the board. "Whatcha' have chum?" he asked his opponent.

The other man scowled and laid his cards down.

"Fifteen two and a pair makes four," the man said, pegging his own points.

Bryan looked at the board and laughed. Billy was well on his way to winning by a hundred points. "Billy," he said, "you oughtn't to take advantage of the Royal Navy this way. We're their guests!"

"Just a friendly game, Bryan," Billy answered, looking up at Bryan while the Navy man dealt the next hand. "You can have next game if you like."

"Oh, no," laughed Bryan. "Not me! I've been on that road before!"

Billy picked up his hand and quickly ordered the cards. The Navy pilot was rather slower in making sense of his hand. Billy was about to speak again when the metallic scratch of the Tannoy speakers stopped him.

"Do you hear there, do you hear there," the speaker squawked in its barely intelligible imitation of a human voice. "The Captain will address the ship's company."

The three pilots looked at each other and waited. After a moment the clipped tones of Captain T.O. Bulteel came over the Tannoy. Bulteel was the first actual aviator given command of a Royal Navy carrier.

"I've to begin," he said, "with some unsettling news. A short time ago we received a report that *HMS Eagle* has been torpedoed and sunk northeast of Algiers while homeward bound." In fact, Bulteel was aware of *Eagle's* loss even before *Furious* arrived at Gibraltar. "We all have many friends in her ship's company. At this time preliminary word is that hundreds of survivors have been rescued. I'll inform you further as I receive more information.

"Meanwhile," he continued, "I'm afraid that's not all. Word from Malta this morning is that the Germans have affected an airborne landing on the island. Our Army forces are resisting and so far they are holding their own.

"That brings me to our mission. We'll be joining up with *Renown* and her escorts around mid-day then on for Malta to relieve the garrison there. We'll be flying off the RAF Spitfires for Malta then covering the fleet with our own aircraft. Meanwhile, these are dangerous waters and we've all got to do our jobs. I know I can count on every man. That is all."

Bryan, Billy and the Navy pilot looked at one another, jaws open, eyes wide.

"Well!" exclaimed Bryan. "Malta!"

The Navy pilot shook his head. "Poor old *Eagle*," he muttered.

"We'd better find the airfields still held," commented Billy. "If Jerry holds the fields there'll be no place for us to land."

"Let's get down to the wardroom," said Bryan. "If there's any news it will be there."

The Fleet Air Arm pilot looked at the cribbage board and shrugged his shoulders, happy to leave this game unfinished. The game was abandoned as Bryan and Billy hustled out down to the wardroom.

The pilot's wardroom aboard an aircraft carrier resembles nothing so much as a university lecture hall, but much smaller and tighter, with a low ceiling festooned with pipes, conduits and ducts. A raised dais with a large map board at the front of the room provides the stage from which squadron leaders deliver briefings to air crew. Rows of chairs bolted to the floor face the dais. Each chair has a small writing surface so the pilots and navigators can make notes during mission briefings. As Billy and Bryan entered the room they found almost every one of the pilots in their squadron already there, crowded about the dais, demanding answers of each other.

"What will we do if the airfields are lost to the Germans?" one man demanded of no one in particular.

"We can't return to the carrier," another pilot answered. "None of us are trained for deck landings!"

"Maybe the FAA pilots will fly our Spits," another suggested.

"No, no," yet another answered. "They're no better trained to fly Spits than we are for deck landings."

"But what do we do then if the airfields are held by the Jerries?" asked the first pilot and the whole conversation started again. Pandemonium reigned. Bryan and Billy looked at each other and shook their heads.

A side door to the wardroom opened and their squadron leader, Commander Nesbith entered. Nesbith was a short, slim officer whose most striking physical feature was the magnificent handlebar moustache he wore in the grand tradition of the Royal Air Force. He was a cracker of a pilot, having flown Hurricanes during the Battle of Britain in the summer of 1940 and was well respected by his men. He bounded onto the dais and waived his arms above his head.

"All right, all right!" he shouted. "Quiet down!"

But rather than quiet down the excited pilots all started shouting their questions at their commanding officer instead of each other. Nesbith looked disgusted, then folded his arms across his chest and studiously ignored the chaos before him, pretending a profound interest instead in the maze of pipes and electrical conduits crisscrossing the room's ceiling. The pilots broke into a laugh at Nesbith's studied indifference and quickly settled down to silence.

"Right then," said Nesbith. "Thank you. Here's what we know at the moment. The Germans have landed on Malta in considerable strength at all three principal airfields, Ta Qali, Luqa and Hal Far."

The pilots were silent now, hanging on every word.

"The situation at Ta Qali and Luqa is not yet clear, but at Hal Far we know the German landing has failed~"

A mighty cheer erupted from the pilots at the news.

"~ and the field remains in our hands," Nesbith finished, shouting over the din.

He let the pilots carry on an impromptu celebration, shouting and pounding each other on the back. After a moment Nesbith held his hands in the air again until the pilots settled back down.

"The situation is very dicey, though," Nesbith went on, "and we're still a long way from our takeoff point, so there's no need everyone staying here in the wardroom. The ship's FAA Commander has been kind enough to loan several of his men. They'll maintain a sort of information office here in the wardroom. You can stop in when your curiosity gets the better of you and they'll pass along any new information. Meanwhile I want every man to get his rest and feed and be ready to give Jerry a bloody nose!" The pilots broke into another cheer as Nesbith hopped down from the dais and left the room.

>>>>>>>>>>>>>

"That's right, Steup," Kuno said into the field phone. "I've found the gun on the east side of the strip. I can see the position of the second gun, but I have no contact with it and won't be able to get to it before the British attack is upon us. Get me some bombers, Steup. Immediately!"

He returned to the gun, leaning around the splinter shield and out the embrasure of the bunker. Small arms fire and even shouting were coming to him clearly now, but the sandbags still blocked his view.

"DAMN!"

He ran from the bunker out into the trench. He jumped up on the firing step and looked out over the rim of the trench. British infantry was swarming up from the south end of the field. He counted seven panzers nearing the southern threshold of the runway itself, moving quickly to the north in a 'V' that looked much like the just departed Junkers transports. The tanks' machine guns spit a constant stream of death. Occasionally their main guns fired also, helping the British infantry to subdue the numerous German strong points to either side of the runway.

Kuno looked up and down the trench. Hundreds of men were sheltered in it, ready to spring onto the firing step to pour hot fire into the British infantry. He caught the eye of the young paratrooper Captain in command of these men of the 23rd Regiment. They nodded grimly to one another, the unspoken understanding between them that they would soon be fighting for their lives. He scanned the field to his north. Hundreds of the new arrivals still milled about, freeing themselves of their parachute shrouds and making their weapons serviceable. Within ten minutes they would begin to come together as a cohesive combat force. But ten minutes might be too late.

The high-pitched buzz of an aero engine in a dive caught his attention. The sound grew rapidly as Kuno spun about, scanning the sky. Streaking across the field were two fighters, one behind the other, twisting and turning, diving and looping; as one fought to shake its pursuer, the other strove to get in a shot. The two fighters were in a seemingly headlong dive straight for him. Other men in the trench were on their feet and watching the fighters as well. At the last possible moment the two planes pulled out of their dives and screamed over the bunker. Men up and down the trench threw themselves to the ground in fear the planes would crash upon them, but they roared past, low enough for their passing to kick up dust and small pebbles on the ground. As they flashed past Kuno he glimpsed the German cross on the front plane and the RAF rondel on the pursuer.

He ran back in the bunker, grabbing the Sergeant by the arm and dragging him to the gun.

"Get ready!" he snarled. "The panzers will be in range momentarily."

The two young privates knelt to the gun breech, ready to reload on command. Kuno's mind raced ahead, trying to anticipate every possible situation and to prepare for it. He found his chief concern was with the chance the British tanks would not keep to the runway. He doubted they would veer off the hard, compacted surface of the strip, at least until they came under fire from the PAK guns, but if they chose to spread out they could easily flank the gun.

He turned to his loaders and said, "Be ready now. Once we start firing I will expect instant obedience!"

"Yes, Sir," the boys answered together.

Kuno stared at them, seeing them for a moment as his boys,

Rolf and Edmund bent over a gun, preparing to kill or be killed. He shook his head to clear the image and looked back out the embrasure. The first tank came into view to his left, centered on the runway. He knew there were three more to either side of it.

"Traverse right!" he commanded the Sergeant. "I want the lead tank just past our center line when we fire."

The Sgt. cranked the traverse wheel; the gun tracked slowly to the right.

"Stop!" ordered Kuno. The gun froze.

He let the tanks come on until all seven were in his field of view and the lead was approaching the spot the gun was aimed at. British infantry trotted along beside the tanks, firing to left and right and spreading out from the runway to either side. Kuno lifted his hand slowly in the air, sighting down the barrel.

"Ready now," Kuno warned, holding his hand up. One of the loaders held the lanyard in his hand, staring nervously at Kuno. "And FIRE!" he shouted.

The boy yanked the lanyard and the gun roared, bucking back against its trail spades. Dirt and dust from the bunker roof rained down upon them.

Kuno shouted, "Reload!" and jumped to the embrasure to assess the first shot. He heard the breech open and the empty shell case eject then the sound of the next round banging home and the breech slamming closed. Squinting, he at first couldn't see beyond the dust in front of his face, but leaning out further and waving his good hand to clear the air he quickly found what he was looking for. The lead tank was stopped on the runway, smoke pouring from its rear engine deck. Hatches flew open and the crew began to bail out. The man climbing from the turret hatch, probably the commander, slumped over backwards with his legs still inside the tank, hit by small arms fire from a German position on the edge of the runway. Kuno jumped back behind the gun, sighting once more down the barrel.

"Traverse left slowly," he said, softer this time to calm the gun crew. "Stop!"

Once more the gun froze. He lifted his hand in the air.

"FIRE!" he shouted.

Again the gun bucked and heaved as the trail spades deadened the recoil. Dirt and dust rained down again, though not as much as the first time the gun was fired. The two boys jumped to reload without his command. Kuno strained to see through the dust. After a few seconds he saw his target. The shell had hit the tank in the right side tracks, snapping the treads. The mechanical beast had rolled on for a few meters till the tread was all run out, then slewed round to the right on its dead road wheels. This crew was also struggling to get out, though no smoke was evident.

"Traverse left!" The other five tanks began to turn towards him, the turrets swung round first then the tanks themselves as the drivers put the thick armor at the front of the tank towards the anti-tank gun. "Stop!" He raised his arm. As he did a stream of machine gun bullets peppered the mouth of the embrasure, several of them ricocheting from the gun's angled steel splinter shield, thudding into the sand bags of the roof over their heads. All four of them ducked until the bullets had passed. Kuno peeked up over the splinter shield again. The tank he had intended to target had slipped past his line of fire, but another was easing into it.

"Steady," he said, holding his hand in the air again, watching the tanks as they completed their turn. Now all five were nearly head on to him. His target was the lead tank in the center of the five. He crouched down behind the gun shield as he waited for the tank to come into his line of fire. The British would surely spot the bunker as the source of his next shot and begin returning fire from their main guns.

The second tank from the left suddenly erupted in flames, burning fuel rocketing into the sky as if pumped from a hi-pressure hose. Almost immediately ammunition in the tank began to explode and the hatches were blown off their hinges, flying dozens of meters away. The tank had been hit by the other PAK gun on the west side of the runway.

"Fire!" shouted Kuno, jumping to the front of the gun even as it settled back down from the recoil. He took a quick look to confirm his shot and then shouted at the others, "Get down."

He hurled himself under the ledge of the embrasure, curling into fetal posture and covering his head with his arms, wincing in pain from his wounded left arm. Machine gun rounds hammered into the opening of the bunker, banging off the gun's splinter shield in a hail of lead. Dirt and sand poured down on him from ruptured sandbags. The bunker rocked from a direct hit from a heavier shell fired by the main gun of one of the surviving tanks. In his brief glimpse before taking cover Kuno was unable to tell if he had hit his target again, but he was certain that the gun sited across the runway had finally taken a hand in the fight. The exploding tank had been hit in its most vulnerable spot, directly from behind and its fuel and ammunition 'cooked off' almost immediately.

But the British still had three or four effective tanks on the runway and the hail of lead on his bunker did not let up. Another main round smacked into the bunker, shattering one of the main beams in the roof, caving in a corner of the bunker.

"Get out!" screamed one of the boys. Sobbing in fear he scrambled for the door, but the Sergeant was faster, diving against the back of the boy's legs, bringing him down as another main round came straight through the embrasure, splintering the beam holding the door frame. The door caved in, completely sealing the entrance in a heap of sandbags and splinters. Grabbing the boy by the collar the Sergeant dragged him back behind the splinter shield of the gun.

Kuno kept his own head down, but reached out to the other boy, putting his hand on the back of the boy's neck, gently holding him down, calming him. After a moment the din subsided and he dared to lift his head. The bunker was choked with dust and very dark. The only light came from the narrow embrasure at the front. Kuno listened for a moment, but the bunker was no longer under direct fire.

Choking and spluttering he raised his head till his eyes were just over the lip of the embrasure. Five of the seven tanks were stopped, disabled or burning. The two remaining tanks had turned their attention to the west side of the field, banging away at a target there. Kuno assumed it must be the other PAK gun. British infantry had taken cover in the ditches on either side of the runway and around the tanks and were trading fire with paratroopers in trenches and bunkers. Kuno reached down and grabbed the Sergeant by the collar.

"On your feet!" he barked. "See to the gun."

Kuno jumped to the rear of the bunker and starting clawing at the collapsed sandbags, but it was hopeless with one hand. He turned back to the embrasure, tripping on the debris on the dark floor of the bunker. He quickly scanned the terrain outside. No

British were within earshot, but there were plenty within rifle range. To scramble out through the embrasure would be suicidal.

"In the trench!" he shouted. "In the trench! Clear the bunker door!" He kept shouting until he heard an acknowledgement.

To the Sergeant he said, "What is the condition of the PAK?"

"The barrel has been damaged," the man replied. "If we fire it again it is likely to explode in our faces."

Kuno nodded his understanding. He pulled on his earlobe for a moment. He turned and started digging out the collapsed sandbags at the side of the bunker. After a moment he turned to Koll and the two young Privates.

"Don't just stand there!" he roared. "Help me dig out the field phone!"

Kuno stepped back and let the three men dig the phone out. Small arms fire suddenly broke out somewhere very nearby. The phone emerged with its connection wires severed.

"Keep digging," Kuno ordered. "Find the other ends to the wires." He pulled his knife from his belt. Quickly and expertly he cut and spliced the wires and reconnected the phone box.

"Kiesslich," he said. "Crank the device."

Kiesslich tentatively took the handle and began to turn the crank. Kuno lifted the handle and waited an infuriating time for a reply. Finally he spoke.

"Steup, is that you?" Kuno barked. He listened a moment. "What the hell took so long to answer?" he demanded. Koll and the Privates, Kiesslich and Lintz listened to Kuno's half of the conversation.

"I did see two fighters pass over this end of the field some minutes ago," Kuno went on. "You don't have time to watch dogfights, Steup!" he growled angrily. "I need a bombing attack on the south end of the runway. There are two tanks still giving us trouble down here. I need them knocked out."

He paused and listened for a long moment. Light spilled in the rear of the bunker as the troops in the trench broke through the collapsed doorway. The Captain in command of the paratroopers led the way in, shoving aside the last of the sandbags and splintered timbers. Kuno held his hand up to stop the Captain.

"What about fighters, Steup? Are there any fighters available."

Kuno nodded to the Captain. He mouthed the word, "Thanks,"

to the Captain and shooed him away. The Captain saluted, turned and left the bunker. Koll and the two privates set about clearing the rest of the doorway.

"Yes, Steup," Kuno answered. "Order the fighters to strafe the panzers on the runway." Another short pause. "I know how close our positions are. Do it Steup before the British wake up and move their tanks off the runway! If they get in among our positions we really will be in trouble."

Kuno turned to Koll and the boys.

"Come with me," he said. Grabbing up his machine pistol he led the way from the bunker into the bright morning sunshine. The others snatched up their own weapons and followed, blinking and shielding their eyes as they grew accustomed to the bright morning sunshine.

Rifle and machine gun fire were getting louder again. Several of the officers and non-coms in the trench were on their feet, peeking south over the edge to assess the British progress. The men stayed down, hiding their presence from the enemy. Kuno found the paratrooper Captain several meters away peering through binoculars at the tanks on the runway. They'd begun to move again, just two remaining of the original seven tanks, nosing cautiously now to the north, infantry in close company. Kuno leapt up on the firing step next to the Captain.

"Are the panzers staying on the runway?" he asked.

"For the moment they appear to be, Major," the Captain replied. "Though God alone knows why. If they got out amongst our positions it would make it impossible to attack them from the air."

Before Kuno could answer he heard the buzz of aircraft engines. Shielding his eyes he scanned the sky for the planes, finding them to the north, at low altitude and coming towards him over the runway. Just two planes were coming. He had expected a whole flight to attack the tanks.

"Where are the bombers?" asked the Captain. "Why aren't they attacking with bombers?"

"The runways on Sicily are all overcrowded with transports," Kuno repeated what Steup had told him. "The bombers can't get off the ground until the Junkers' have all gotten down safely."

"Someone didn't think of that, did they?" the Captain replied. "Anyway, now that this dogfight is over, the fighters can take a hand."

"It's over?" Kuno exclaimed. "Who won?"

Kenneth stayed in his tree throughout the first daylight drop at Ta Qali, watching in awe as wave after wave of three-engine transports deposited thousands more troops on the field. He tried to count the transports, but lost count when the dogfight between Heinz Sauckel and Derrick Metcalfe distracted him. He made a pretty good estimate however that over 200 Ju 52 transports carrying between fifteen and eighteen paratroopers each had delivered another 3,500 Germans to Ta Qali. Aside from the four transports shot down with one more damaged by the Spitfires there was little opposition to the airdrop. Only two flak guns west of the field fired against the German air fleet.

As the final transports winged away from the field Kenneth remained, even though he knew Maggie had to be gotten to safety. He couldn't leave his vantage point while the Spitfire and the Messerschmitt continued their personal dance. He'd recognized from the outset that the two pilots were among the very best he'd ever seen, the British pilot's flying more refined and schooled, the German's raw and rough by comparison, but more inspired. The German was obviously a gifted natural flyer, while the RAF pilot was better trained.

The dogfight went on for what seemed an incredible time. From his own experience Kenneth knew how difficult it was to maintain concentration for a few minutes in a dogfight. From the moment the German first got on the Spitfire's tail through the paratroop drop the two fighters danced and weaved through the sky, advantage shifting first one way then the other, for almost twenty minutes. Every time the Spit tried to break away to escape in the fog bank the other German fighters in the area herded him back to open sky. Once, the two fighters weaved their way across the airfield itself, dancing between two echelons of transports before diving for the deck, screaming along just a few feet off the ground, out of Kenneth's sight briefly behind the ridge in front of him.

The roar of the transports faded as the two fighters cavorted to the east of the field. Kenneth shielded his eyes against the morning sun to keep them in sight. Unconsciously his right hand was in a fist as though gripping the control stick of his fighter. The German was on the tail of the Spitfire at this point and the Spit led the pair back towards the airfield, diving and turning to the west.

"Full power! Full power!" Kenneth shouted encouragement to his comrade. "Break right!"

Heinz was drenched in sweat. It ran into his eyes and stung, but he barely dared take his hand off the throttle long enough to wipe it away. The Englander tried every trick Heinz had ever heard of and several that were completely new to him. Twice the tables turned and Heinz found himself the hunted, the Spitfire on his tail. On both occasions his Messerschmitt was hit before he could shake the Spitfire, but so far his luck held and none of the wounds was fatal to the aircraft. The Spitfire dove away to the right and Heinz snapped the stick over to follow, back towards the airfield, speed increasing as the dive went on, the Messerschmitt slowly coming into range for a shot.

A thousand calculations ran through his mind as he passed through 4,000 meters altitude. He knew that as soon as he reached a range to attempt a shot the Spitfire would twist or turn away, leaving him frustrated again. Worse, his fuel situation was critical. Already he was below the fuel needed to return safely to Sicily, the high speed flying slurping fuel at an alarming rate. He knew he was going to have to end this dogfight soon, one way or another and try a desperation landing on the airfield or abandon his plane and parachute to the ground.

At 2,000 meters altitude he was almost close enough to fire. Once again his natural instincts took over and he snapped the Bf 109 over to the left, exactly anticipating the RAF pilot's evasive maneuver by a split second. His move allowed him to cut inside the arc of the Spitfire's turn, shortening the range and giving him a clear view for a snap shot at the enemy fighter's engine. He squeezed the trigger just before the Spitfire filled his sites and a flurry of shells slammed home even as the Englander realized the danger and snapped back to the right. Flame erupted, first from the exhaust nacelles, then from around the engine cowling. Smoke filled the cockpit as the flames grew in intensity.

Heinz came out of his dive and leveled out, keeping one eye on the Spitfire. His grip on the stick slackened, then relaxed completely. He took the time to wipe his eyes and forehead. As his hand returned to the stick he noted it was shaking, a tremor running from his fingertips, up his forearm to his elbow. He gripped the stick with both hands and concentrated until the shaking stopped.

The Spitfire circled away from him a half kilometer or so, still burning, its cockpit filled with smoke, yet the aircraft remained under control. Heinz' heart ran cold. He realized the RAF pilot was trapped in the burning fighter, the canopy jammed as the pilot fought to release the snaps. He checked his own fuel gauge. There was no question of trying to return to Sicily at this point. He would have to land on Ta Qali somehow or bail out over the German held airfield and abandon the Emil to its fate.

The Spitfire turned and headed south, trailing smoke and losing altitude slowly. Suddenly the cockpit canopy banged open; a ball of flame burst from it, fanned by the wind. The fighter rolled over on its back and a smoldering object dropped straight down from the open cockpit. The fighter, fully involved in flame continued its roll; its dive steepened until it nosed over and plunged like a meteor through the thinning fog. A bright flash like dry lightening signified its end as it crashed into the ground south of the airfield.

The pilot fell hundreds of meters tumbling out of control and Heinz had concluded he was either already dead or unable to pull the cord for his parachute, but at around 300 meters the chute began to open and the RAF man was pulled up with a jerk that left him dangling in his harness. Still smoldering he drifted slowly towards the ground until he too disappeared in the fog.

Heinz leaned back in his seat, completely spent. He allowed his mind to wander and his muscles to sag. The shakes returned and this time he didn't try to stop them. After several minutes of aimless flying his senses began to return. He heard a voice in his ear.

"Sauckel? Do you hear me?" For a moment he looked around to find the source of the voice. "Sauckel! If you can hear me, respond."

Heinz took a deep breath and pressed the throat mic switch.

"I am here," he said.

"Are you injured Sauckel?" his squadron commander asked. "What is your condition?"

"I am unharmed," Heinz replied. "But I am low on fuel. Not enough to reach Sicily."

"I suspected as much," came the reply. "The rest of us are also near our fuel limit. We must turn back for Sicily now. I recommend you abandon your ship. Bail out over the airfield while you still have power and control."

"What about the runway?" Heinz asked. "Is there any chance of a short landing?"

"None whatever Heinz," his commander replied. "The runway is completely obstructed with gliders and other wreckage. It would take a miracle to set down on it safely."

"Understood," he answered. His mind was still groggy and he suspected he was suffering a form of shock.

"We must leave now Sauckel. Two fighters from the three-twenty-third squadron are going to stay with you until you are on the ground. For the moment they are the only aircraft we have over the field and they cannot stay long so don't delay! Get out while you can."

"Understood," he answered again. He looked down at the ground. From an altitude of 2,000 meters he could see the runway was indeed choked with gliders and all manner of other gear and wreckage. At the south end of the strip were several fires. What appeared to be vehicles, perhaps even tanks were burning. As he watched one of the tanks moved and puffs of smoke from small explosions popped up all round the south end of the field. Not a good sign. Heinz knew the Germans had no tanks on the field. They must be British machines. He turned and looked towards the north end of the strip. No fires and it seemed more peaceful than the southern end. He turned and banked for the north.

Kenneth bunched his fists in rage and sorrow as he watched the Spitfire plummet to earth in flames. The pilot managed to get his chute open, but he wouldn't allow himself to even think about the injuries and burns the RAF man had probably suffered. The worst fear of every combat pilot was to be trapped in a burning cockpit, unable to escape, listening to his own flesh sizzle, smelling himself cook. A few minutes later the German pilot drifted down over the north end of the field, not much more than three-quarters of a mile from Kenneth's perch in the tree. For a moment he fantasized about following the German, pouncing on him as he landed and killing him with his bare hands, but Maggie was never far from his mind and he knew he couldn't leave her now on a suicide mission of vengeance.

He scanned the sky again, but in contrast to the last half hour there was relative peace in the air. He could only discern two small fighters circling high over the field. He swung down out of the tree and trotted back to the car. The girl remained bundled in her bandages and blankets, leaned into the corner of the Model T's passenger seat, her face hidden from him.

"Maggie?" he whispered.

"Oh, Kenneth," she cried weakly. "Where have you been? I've been so frightened!" Her voice was wracked with sobs and his heart skipped a beat with guilt at leaving her for so long. He reached over and pulling aside the blankets he stroked her cheek and hair gently. Her red-rimmed eyes remained closed and her tear-stained cheeks were ashen.

"I'm sorry, Maggie," he said, his own voice choking up. "I'm sorry. I'll never leave you again." She reached her hand out and he took it. Lifting it to his lips he kissed it softly then put her hand back in her lap.

"We've got to move again, Maggie," he said softly. He moved the car out from under the trees and back onto the Mosta-Floriana road at top speed.

"Off the runway!" shouted Chadwick. "To the right! To the right!"

Bullets bounced off the hull of the Mark I Cruiser, ricocheting away across the runway. He peeked out through the observation slits in his commander's cupola, checking on each of the six other tanks that had come onto the runway with him. The 12 and 13 tanks were burning on the east side of the runway, hit in their flanks by the anti-tank gun hidden in the bunker on that side of the field. So far as he could tell, none of the crews had escaped. To his left the 21 tank was disabled, its right side drive sprocket smashed by an anti-tank shell from the same gun. Its crew was out and working feverishly to remove the stub of the drive sprocket, but German small arms fire was making the task impossible. The 23 and 24 tanks also blazed. Ammunition in the 24 tank started exploding, sending the crew of the 21 tank scurrying for cover. Only his own tank, numbered 11 and the 25 tank of the second platoon remained in action.

The tanks had moved almost 200 yards onto the runway, leading infantry of the Inniskilling and Manchester regiments against the German airhead on Ta Qali field. Chadwick smacked the turret with the ball of his fist. Things were going very well before the A.T. guns hit them. German troopers were running headlong before the combined assault of British armor and infantry. Chadwick saw himself leading the charge right up the runway and sweeping the field clear, crushing the German invasion with a steel-mailed fist. He'd pictured the Victoria Cross hung round his neck by a grateful Sovereign at Westminster and maybe even a Knighthood. His daydreams were abruptly shattered by the crossfire of anti-tank rounds they'd met. He'd reacted quickly, turning to the right, locating the source of the fire and burying the bunker the first gun was hidden in after it had gotten off just three shots. But all three shots had been on the money, brewing up the 12 and 13 tanks and hitting the 21 tank, the second platoon leader, disabling it.

Now Chadwick was leading his two remaining tanks off the runway to the east. He no longer had the punch to force his way up the runway, but by setting his sights a little lower he still hoped to break the German perimeter and regain control of part of the airfield.

Despite the number of paratroopers that had apparently reached Ta Qali, Chadwick knew the German situation was still precarious. Their landing at Hal Far had failed completely, the first wave landing force overrun and destroyed. They hadn't fared much better at Luqa either. The first wave there had surprised the British garrison defending the field and had there been a second landing it might well have carried the airbase, but the Germans had not made a second drop at Luqa and the paratroopers there were surrounded and being hammered from all sides. It was only a matter of time until the tiny airhead at Luqa was eliminated.

The German advantage was at Ta Qali. By British estimates the Germans had already landed over ten thousand men at Ta Qali during the night and in the drop he'd just witnessed he knew thousands more had arrived. No doubt further drops were planned in the coming hours. Unless the field could be brought under direct fire there was nothing to prevent the Germans pouring thousands more troops onto the island. The RAF, weak to begin with, had shot its bolt already that morning all but exhausting its small reserve of fighters to attack the transports in the first daylight drop.

Only by recapturing a part of the airfield could the British interfere with the German plans.

The Cruiser jolted down off the berm of the runway, smashed across the drainage ditch at the edge of the strip and continued on. He stole a glance to his right. The 25 tank was right with him thirty yards away. He scanned the field in front of him, finding the bunker he'd fired at to silence the AT gun.

"Make for the bunker!" he shouted at Walsh. He reached out the toe of his boot and tapped Walsh on the right shoulder, signaling him to steer to the right. The tank lurched round to the right until it was pointed at the bunker.

Chadwick could see helmets to the left and right of the bunker, popping up and down in the trench line to either side. He swung the turret and sprayed machine gun bullets along the top of the trench to the left of the bunker. A moment later he heard the 25 tank do the same to the right.

"I want to pass to the left of the bunker, Walsh!" he shouted, stretching his toe out again. The tank lurched a little to the left and ground through a large clump of barbed wire, flattening a path for the infantry to pass through.

He stole another look out the side observation slits. Infantry were keeping pace with his tank, running forward, stopping to fire at the trench, racing forward again. As he was about to turn back to the front he took one last quick glance to the north, up the runway. Hurtling towards him at very low altitude were two aircraft.

"Air attack!" he shouted. Almost against his will he drew his knees up and hunched over in the turret as machine gun and cannon shells tore through the ground towards him. Shells rocked the tank, ringing against the hull and turret in a cacophony of demonic church bells before passing over and on. The cruiser came to a stop.

Chadwick collected his wits, doing a quick mental inventory, first of his own body and finding himself apparently unhurt, of the tank as well. The motor was still running and when he hit the turret lever it swung smoothly round in both directions. His loader stared at him, a look of near hysteria on his face. Chadwick leaned down and patted him on the shoulder.

"Are you hurt?" he demanded.

The man simply shook his head, still unable to speak.

"Walsh!" he shouted. "Are you hurt?"

"No, Sir!" Walsh answered.

"Then get us moving, dammit!"

Chadwick peered back out the slits as the tank lurched forward again. The strafing run had raised a lot of dust, obscuring his view in all directions. Near the tank he could see infantry still on the ground, including many that would never move again. To his right he could just make out the shape of the 25 tank as the dust slowly cleared. Its turret was skewed round and tilted at a crazy angle. The force of 20mm cannon shells hammering against it had dismounted the turret. The drivers hatch was flung open and the driver spilled out onto the ground, rolling away from the tank before scrambling to his feet and running to the rear. He saw no other sign of life before the tank disappeared again behind him.

"Move it Walsh!" he screamed. "Top speed straight ahead. We have to get in among the Huns before the fighters come back!"

The ground on this part of the field was strewn with boulders and half filled bomb craters. At top speed the tank bumped and jolted forward, throwing its crew against the hard, knobby surfaces of the interior, leaving them all bruised and battered, but they all understood the alternative. As they approached the trench line Chadwick fired his machine gun again. Walsh had his hands full driving and his gun remained silent. As they closed the trench Chadwick fired the main gun as well, mainly for the terror effect of the weapon as it could not be depressed enough to actually fire into the trench. Fifty yards from the trench he heard whistles as the infantry leaders urged their men forward. With a cheer the men of Ulster and of Manchester surged forward, at the dead run now with bayonets fixed.

Kuno peeked between two sandbags at the lone remaining tank as it bore down on his position. He had a feeling of utter helplessness. There were no more anti-tank weapons to bring to bear and the tank was already too close for the fighters to strafe again for fear of killing Germans instead. The main gun in the turret fired occasionally, but the worst damage was being down by the co-axially mounted .303 Vickers, spraying lead up and down the trench line, keeping the paratroopers from firing effectively against the charging infantry. For a moment, over the din of small arms fire and of men fighting and dieing he heard whistles and then a cheer and he knew the moment was at hand.

"On the step!" he cried at the top of his voice. Men up and down the line clambered onto the firing step, but still they kept their heads down, avoiding the hail of lead the infantry and the tank were firing along the trench lip.

He peeked again through the sandbags. Barely forty meters away now. He raised his good arm over his head. "FIRE!" he shouted.

Hundreds of paratroopers rose up above the rim of the trench and began to fire their automatic weapons. At such close range the Schmeisser MP 40 is a deadly weapon. British infantrymen were cut down in their tracks by the score as they charged the trench line. Seconds later the heavier rattle of MG 34s joined the din, adding to the toll among the British. Others came on behind the Tommies and were cut down too, until the dead and wounded began to stack up in grisly piles. The tank's turret machine gun barked again, this time joined by the gun in the hull. Paratroopers fell or were hurled back off the firing step as the tank ground inexorably towards the trench. Dirt and grit kicked into Kuno's face as the tank's machine guns sprayed lead up and down the trench line. British infantry again rose and followed the tank firing their rifles and Sten guns from the hip as they charged the final meters to the trench.

Kuno unclipped a grenade from his belt, armed the fuse and threw it over the lip of the trench, landing it just five meters in front of his own position. It went off and he heard clearly the cries of the British through the explosion. He held his machine pistol between his legs and pulled the bolt back with his right hand, then leapt onto the firing step. He rose up above the rim and fired at point blank range, holding the Schmeisser like a pistol in one hand before him. Enemy troops were mowed down as he swept the MP 40 back and forth, emptying a whole clip.

The tank crashed into the row of sandbags at the rim of the trench to his right, then lurched up and over the trench and beyond. His last glimpse of it was of two paratroopers climbing onto its rear deck as it crossed the trench. One was shot and fell backward immediately; the other carried a rucksack that he knelt over as the tank passed out of Kuno's view. Frantically the young paratrooper struggled with the fuse of the satchel charge, fighting to keep his balance on the lurching rear deck of the tank. At last the fuse sputtered and caught and he jammed the satchel down against the steel mesh screen above the engine deck. He turned to leap from the tank, but a stream of bullets from a British Sten gun ripped into him. He collapsed atop the explosive charge just as it detonated. Marty Chadwick's dreams of a Knighthood died with him as his tank's fuel and ammunition caught fire and exploded.

In the next instant British infantry flung themselves into the trench, lunging with their bayonets at the paratroopers who fell back against the opposite wall. Kuno tripped and fell heavily on his back to the trench floor, knocking the breath from his body. His MP 40 spun away, disappearing among the tangled feet and bodies at the bottom of the trench. He gasped for air, but was momentarily paralyzed and couldn't get his breath. An English Tommy jumped down in the trench and aimed to plant his bayonet in Kuno's belly. Kuno watched the rifle rise and plunge down towards him. His eyes bulged in their sockets as he saw his death approach.

The Englander's head exploded as a Schmeisser was shoved in his face and fired. His rescuer reached down and hauled Kuno to his feet. Kuno had no sooner gotten his balance than his rescuer was shot in the back and fell against him. Kuno pulled his Walther automatic pistol from his belt as the young man slid down to the ground. He fired the pistol and dropped the Englander who'd killed the trooper.

The trench was in chaos as the battle went from close-range to hand-to-hand. Men screamed, cursed and cried. One huge Englishman towered above his friends and foes alike. He moved down the trench bashing Germans over the head with his rifle in one hand or slashing them with his knife in the other. Kuno took deliberate aim and fired, hitting the giant in the chest with one-two-three quick shots, felling him like a mighty oak tree cut down with an axe.

More British were pouring over the trench lip and by sheer weight of numbers began to overwhelm the paratroopers. Kuno heard an explosion behind him, but had no time to look to see what had happened. He was standing atop the bodies of the dead and wounded, piled two and three deep on the floor of the trench. He slipped and struggled to keep his feet.

A paratrooper fought against an Englander a few feet away.

Both men had lost their weapons and were fighting with bare hands, desperately clawing at each other. The Englishmen had his right hand on the German's throat while the paratrooper clawed at the eyes of his foe. Kuno took a step forward, pushed the Walther into the small of the Englander's back and pulled the trigger. He didn't wait to see the man fall, but turned around, barely in time to dodge a wicked thrust from a bayonet. Falling against the wall of the trench he shot the man in the chest. A look of stunned surprise came to the young Tommy and he stared at Kuno as he slowly sank to the ground.

A burst of machine gun fire arced over the top of the trench, followed by the shorter, sharper fire of MP 40's. More Englishmen tumbled into the trench. He fired the Walther repeatedly, dropping an enemy with each shot until the magazine was empty.

Another Englander lunged at him with his bayonet. Kuno threw the Walther in the man's face and dodged away from the thrust, but the man turned and came at him again. At the last moment the man slipped in a pool of blood on the trench floor. Kuno deflected the thrust away from his belly, but the blade slashed across his left breast and went past where it sank in the wall of the trench. Kuno brought his right fist down in a crushing blow on the back of the man's neck, driving him flat. He felt bones smash under the blow, but wasn't immediately certain whose bones they were. He sank to his knees beside the Englander and pushed his face into a soft, wet pile of bowels spilled open from a paratrooper's belly, holding the man down until he was sure he was dead.

Kuno tried to rise, but a white-hot lightning bolt of pain shot through his chest. He cried out and sagged back against the trench wall, pressing the palm of his hand against the wound to stop the blood. He stared down at the man he'd just killed, drowned in a puddle of blood and feces. He was suddenly surprised when he realized tears were streaming down his cheeks.

Looking up he saw British troops climbing out of the trench, fleeing back the way they had come. Automatic weapons fire intensified and several of the fleeing British were cut down, shot in the back. They fell back in the trench and on its rim, sprawled in the rag doll postures achieved only by those who die violently. A paratrooper appeared at the rim, firing his MP 40 in short, directed bursts down on the British who remained in the trench. Other

Germans hurdled the trench in pursuit of the fleeing enemy.

Kuno leaned his head back against the trench wall. He took his hand away from his breast and wiped the tears from his cheek, replacing them with smears of blood. The trench began to spin. He closed his eyes against the dizziness and let darkness descend.

The closer they got to Floriana and Rinella the more signs of life began to appear on the road. Small, mixed units of soldiers from the Island's regiments were moving west armed with an odd assortment of weapons or in some cases without arms at all. Twice Kenneth and Maggie had been stopped at Military Police roadblocks. He presented his identity papers and explained that the wounded girl belonged to a Headquarters in the Rinella area and that he needed to get her back to her billet and then travel on to Luqa or Hal Far to see about getting back in the air. They passed him on with a warning to avoid open stretches of road and to watch out for aircraft. Maggie remained mostly quiet, but as the journey progressed she strengthened and was more alert. The distant crackle of small arms fire was their constant companion.

By 0805 they passed the neck of the peninsula and left the road to Valletta behind. They were making the turn on the south side of Grand Harbor at Cospicua to the road for Rinella when they came to another checkpoint manned by Royal Marines. A beefy Sergeant stepped from behind the barricade and strode towards the car. Kenneth brought the Model T to a stop with the uncomfortable feeling that came from having a number of rifles pointed straight at his head.

"What's your business here, son?" he asked. "Trying to get away from your unit, are you?"

"No, Sergeant," Kenneth replied dryly. "I'm not a deserter. I'm a pilot. I was away from the field on leave when the Jerries hit and I'm trying to get back to an airfield."

"Really?" said the Sergeant. "Bit far from the airfields aren't you lad? Going the wrong way, hmm?" The Sergeant leaned in the window and growled in Kenneth's face. "Get out of the car!"

"Sergeant," Kenneth pleaded. "I've got to get this woman to Rinella. She works there."

"The road to Rinella is closed. Now get out of the car!"

"Sergeant?" Maggie's voice was weak and tremulous, muffled by the blankets and bandages.

"It's all right, Maggie," Kenneth soothed her. "I'll get this straightened out and we'll be off again."

Maggie reached up and pulled the blankets from around her face, squinting in the morning light. She ignored Kenneth and peered blearily at the Marine.

"Sergeant Harris?" she asked, her voice soft and low.

"Aye, miss," the Sergeant answered, curiosity and suspicion playing equally across his face. He stared at the girl. "Do I know you miss?"

"It's me," she said, her voice so soft the Sergeant had to lean in the window to hear. "It's me. Maggie Reed."

"Miss Reed?" Sergeant Harris asked. "You're injured? What are you doing with this boy?"

Maggie smiled, faint and wan.

"He's who he says he is, Sergeant Harris," she replied. "He's a Spitfire pilot. He was with me when the Germans attacked. We were forced off the road and I got a nasty bump on the head. He's trying to get me back to my billet." She paused and passed her hand across her forehead. "I can't be taken, Sergeant," she said. "You understand why."

Harris turned and peered in Kenneth's face, sizing him up. He squinted at Kenneth in a way that made clear he didn't like pilots who were 'with' young women like Maggie Reed. Finally he sighed and looked back at Maggie.

"All right, Miss Reed," he said. "But the road to Rinella is still closed. You won't find your unit there anyway, Miss. They've been evacuated to Hal Far just about three hours ago in a great rush." He looked back at Kenneth. "If this pollywog really is a pilot that's where he ought to be going anyway."

As Kenneth turned the car and headed back through Cospicua the distant sound of aero engines returned to his ears.

>>>>>>>>>>>>>

The day was dank and drear, an overcast winter day, and he shivered. The two flower-bedecked caissons rolled slowly up the cobblestone street, each pulled by a riderless black stallion. A single mounted honor guard with a kettledrum followed behind. The thousands of drab, shapeless figures and faces lining the street were silent. Only the slow thump-thump-thump of the drum beating out its dirge broke the late afternoon peace. Even the horses' hooves were strangely muffled.

The caissons turned a corner and approached a heavy, wrought-iron gate let into a tall stonewall. Marble eagles with outstretched wings perched atop the gateposts. The gate was open and the cobble stone street continued through it, up a low hill. Two soldiers stood at attention on either side of the gate, their rifles resting on their shoulders, gleaming and sparkling with polish. Green lawns and stately trees lay on either side of the road. At the top of the hill stood a group of twenty or so silent people, but he couldn't make out who they were or what they were doing. The caissons passed through the gate and started up the hill. He followed behind, even though no one else on the street had moved. He wasn't sure whose funeral it was, but somehow he felt he should attend, that his duty demanded it. He hurried to catch up. He arrived at the top of the hill just after the second caisson rolled to a stop. The mounted guard came to a stop too, but kept up the relentless, tuneless thump-thump-thump on the drum. He walked up past the caissons towards the group on the hill. They all had their backs to him now and he still couldn't see any faces. He turned back to look again at the caissons and was amazed he hadn't seen the flags draped over the coffins before. The red, white and black Swastikas were the only splash of bright color in the cemetery. Pallbearers came from the trees and shouldered the coffins from the caissons. Six Luftwaffe airmen and six soldiers of the Army, resplendent in their finest uniforms, trudged solemnly onto the lawn. The crowd of people parted and the coffins were borne to wooden platforms beside open graves. He wanted to ask who was being buried, but the silence other than the drum was so complete and profound as to be like a spell he didn't dare break. In the front ranks of the group before the graves was a woman, tall and slim, dressed all in black, with a hat and veil. Black nylons covered shapely legs and Kuno jerked his gaze away. He couldn't bring himself to admire the bereaved widow.

An officer he didn't know stepped forward, and he realized the funeral was for some important persons. The officer wore the gold braid and red trouser stripes of a Field Marshall. A cry came from the group, at last shattering the silence. He turned to the source and saw the woman holding a handkerchief up under her veil, sobbing piteously.

"No!" she wailed. "No! No! No! No!" She kept it up non-stop.

"Germany has known too many such days," he thought to himself, but knew better than to speak this thought aloud. Defeatism was punishable by death.

The Field Marshall made as if to speak, but choked by emotion he couldn't go on. He gestured to the pallbearers who stepped forward to the coffins and began to unsnap the seals. Kuno pushed forward through the crowd around the graves until he was in the front row, directly across from the widow. Others in the crowd were crying now as well. He stopped and listened. Not really crying. Some were moaning, or shouting. One man somewhere in the group was cursing, slowly and rhythmically.

"Jesus Christ! Jesus Christ! Jesus Christ!"

The beat of the kettledrum got louder until he felt it reverberating in his chest. He felt his breath catch and he struggled to breathe, gasping for air. But he couldn't take his eyes off the coffins. As the lid of the first coffin swung open he stepped forward and stared down in horror at the body. It was Rolf, the Iron Cross hung on a beautiful ribbon round his neck. Kuno staggered to the other coffin, knowing what he would find before he looked. It was Edmund, also bemedaled. Kuno tried to reach out for Edmund, but his arms wouldn't move for him. He tried to speak, but his voice was caught in his throat. He looked across at the widow, but by now he knew who she was too and he turned away, not wanting to see Hilda in her grief. One of the other mourners grabbed his arm and shook him.

"Major Schacht!" he said. "Major Schacht!" He kept repeating Kuno's name more and more insistently. "Major Schacht!"

Kuno slowly opened his eyes, fighting to open them though they seemed glued closed with molasses. Wooden planks swam into view. He turned his head to the sound of the voice. A man loomed over him, looking down into his face with concern. He held up his hand.

"How many fingers do you count?" he asked.

Kuno said, "Three. Let me up."

The man put his hand on Kuno's right shoulder, gently holding him down.

"I am Dr. Mueller. You're not going anywhere so fast."

"What is the situation in the battle?" demanded Kuno.

The Doctor ignored him completely.

"Follow my finger without turning your head," he commanded and passed his index finger slowly back and forth. Kuno rolled his eyes, but then did as he was told and followed the finger.

"No apparent brain or neurological damage," the man commented. "Do you want to try to sit up?"

Kuno nodded. "Yes, please." He took the man's outstretched hand and pulled himself up. "DAMMIT!" he yelped as pain seared through his right hand.

The Doctor chuckled. "Good news!" he said. "You have no nerve damage!" Dr. Mueller took Kuno's hand in his and felt the bones between the wrist and knuckles, probing until Kuno winced. "Probably broken," he said, letting the hand go. "Nothing to be done about it here. You'll need a proper set in hospital when we get out of here."

Kuno looked around him. He was on a low table in a sandbag bunker with a wooden roof. All around lay wounded and dieing men. In the corner was a young paratrooper who'd lost his right arm. The boy stared at the bandaged stump saying, "No! No! No!" over and over again. Orderlies moved among the wounded dispensing shots for pain and checking bandages. The bunker was jammed with wounded and the orderlies had to step carefully around and over them. A gut shot trooper lay on an adjacent table as another surgeon prepared to operate on him. The trooper was groaning in pain and shouting, "Jesus Christ!" over and over. The bunker shook from the concussion of distant explosions.

He turned and looked at the Doctor. He wore an apron over his jump tunic and a surgical mask dangled from his neck. The apron and mask were almost completely covered in blood.

"How long have I been here?" Kuno asked.

The Doctor looked at his watch. "About six hours," he replied. "You came in at 1130 hours. I'm not sure how long you were out there before you were found." He hooked his head at the entrance door.

"It's 1530 now?" Kuno asked.

"Yes, that's right."

"I have to get back to my command."

"Yes, of course." The Doctor nodded his head. "The Baron said you would be in a hurry when you woke up. Your wounds are not life threatening unless you rip open your stitches and bleed to death."

For the first time Kuno assessed himself. His tunic was unbuttoned and cut back, exposing a thick wad of bandages taped to his breast over his heart. He looked up at the Doctor.

"Forty stitches," the Dr. said, "but nothing serious. It's not too deep, and it missed all arteries; maybe a nicked rib. I didn't have time to poke about to know for sure. You should recover fully, though you'll be left with a nasty scar."

"Another badge," said Kuno.

"Yes, I saw the signatures of other surgeons."

"What is the current situation?" asked Kuno again.

The Dr. looked around the bunker and shook his head.

"There are more wounded than I can get to," he said sadly. "Men are dieing that could have been saved." He looked down at Kuno. "Forgive me, Major," he said with a wry smile. "You meant with the battle didn't you?"

Kuno nodded, but kept silent.

"I really don't know, Major. I've been too busy for current events."

"Can I leave?" Kuno asked.

"Yes, of course," the Dr. said. He looked over to the door of the bunker and snapped his fingers. A paratrooper there came to attention. "The trooper at the door is to escort you to HQ. Now if you will excuse me, Major," he said, "I have many wounded to attend."

"Thank you, Doctor," said Kuno. He swung his legs off the table and onto the floor and buttoned his tunic over the bandages. Picking his way over the wounded he made his way to the door. He picked up a Schmeisser from the stack of spare weapons there and set off to find his men.

>>>>>>>>>>>>

As he drove from Cospicua towards Hal Far Kenneth encountered even more British forces. Men on the move from Valletta and Floriana trying to rejoin their units trudged along the roads. There were few weapons and fewer officers. They moved slowly in small groups of ten or twenty and kept a constant eye on the sky. German fighters prowled above the island and after the morning fog burned back the Germans pounced on movement on the ground. North of the small city of Tarxien he came upon a group that had been strafed. Two men were dead and six wounded, two seriously as four other men tended them. Kenneth stopped and agreed to take the two seriously wounded with him to Tarxien to find a Doctor. The two were loaded into the back of the pickup with one other man to care for them and Kenneth drove on. In Tarxien he stopped and asked a Maltese policeman for directions to a Doctor or hospital. The city streets were nearly deserted of Maltese civilians as he made his way through the narrow, cobblestone paved lanes and alleys, finally finding the hospital by following a British Army ambulance. Wounded from the night's battles were already streaming into the hospital, as to every hospital and Doctor's office on the island. Kenneth delivered his charges and moved on quickly.

Twice they were forced to hide beneath trees just off the road as roving German fighters swooped down looking for game, but his luck held and the Model T went undetected. The girl strengthened as they traveled, eventually pulling the blankets from around her face, alert and aware. The waxy, ashen hue in her face was replaced by her natural clear-skinned pale glow and her eyes showed some sparkle and life, though she remained mostly silent, speaking only on the occasions they encountered armed patrols or checkpoints on the road and she was asked to identify herself. In all cases she made no reference to her work, just that they were trying to reach Hal Far where she could rejoin her unit and Kenneth might find a fighter to fly.

As they got closer to the airfield they began to see more action in the air. German fighters and bombers were maintaining a constant presence over the airfield, no doubt to prevent any British aircraft getting into the air, and the defenders on the ground did their best to keep the enemy at a distance. Fluffy black puffs of smoke would suddenly appear in the sky in the direction of Hal

Far, followed seconds later by the crack of the exploding shells. German aircraft buzzed about, but rarely ventured directly over the field, contenting themselves with keeping a close enough watch that no British aircraft could get off the ground unmolested.

It was early-afternoon when they reached the end of the paved road in the sleepy little seaside village of Birzebugga overlooking Marsaxlokk Bay on the island's south coast. The gravel road from Birzebugga to Hal Far bore due south hugging the shore of the bay for a quarter mile before veering west towards the airfield. The view across Marsaxlokk Bay is strikingly beautiful and Kenneth stopped the car for a moment under a rocky outcrop. To the east, across the sparkling blue waters of the bay stood the Delimara Lighthouse on Delimara Point, dark now for over two years since the Italian entry into the war. Just ahead on the western side of the bay lay Kalafrana and the manmade slipways and piers of the harbor there and the Royal Navy seaplane station with its concrete ramp used to pull the amphibious aircraft out of the water and up into the hangar on shore. The port was unusually silent. No fishermen sat on the quays, mending nets or swapping fish stories. The few boats and harbor launches were tied up and seemingly abandoned. Beyond Kalafrana was the great stone breakwater, stretched out across the mouth of the bay from Point Benghisa and protecting the port area at Kalafrana from the open sea. Fountains of white spray spouted from the ocean side of the breakwater as waves rolling up from the south smacked against it. Gulls wheeled and dived over the waters of the bay, as if they didn't know there was a war.

"It's beautiful, isn't it?" asked Maggie softly.

"Yes," said Kenneth, turning to look at her. "I'm glad you're feeling well enough to enjoy it."

"I'm feeling well enough to be famished," she replied with a wan smile. "I don't suppose you have another of your picnic baskets up your sleeve?"

With a startled cry he reached behind the seat and pulled out the basket Dr. Mieza's nurse had put there when they left the clinic that morning. He found it contained two small loaves of the famous Maltese bread, a handful of dried dates and a small glass bottle of water. As they ate, Maggie slipped her hand into Kenneth's and squeezed. He thrilled at her touch and his eyes welled up with tears at the love he felt for her. They finished their meal all too quickly for Kenneth, devouring every morsel and sharing the water. Kenneth carefully replaced the empty bottle and basket behind the seat, silently giving thanks again for Dr. Mieza and his nurse.

The road swung inland just above Kalafrana and now they were less than a mile from the gates of Hal Far. Kenneth watched the sky constantly, keeping watch on the German aircraft circling like vultures over a kill, waiting till the enemy planes were on the westward part of their orbit, then dashing from one point of cover to another.

At 1410 hours on June 26th he finally approached the gates of the airfield where he was stopped at a checkpoint by Royal Marine guards. A red and white striped pole barred the road. Kenneth kept his hands in plain sight as the Marine Sergeant in charge at the gate approached the car. A dozen or more rifles were pointed squarely at his forehead and he had the distinct feeling that one wrong move would be his last.

"What's your story?" demanded the Marine.

From repeated practice Kenneth had his story down pat.

"I'm an RAF pilot," he answered. "Sgt. Pilot Wiltshire. This is Miss Reed," he went on gesturing to Maggie who smiled from beneath her bandages. The food had done much to bring her further round. "She's an English girl attached to the Headquarters at Rinella. She was away from her billet on leave when the attack came. By the time I could get her back to Rinella the HQ had been evacuated. We're told it was sent here. Miss Reed has been injured as you can see and needs to see a Dr."

"You're a Yank?" asked the Sergeant with evident distaste.

"Yep," said Kenneth, bridling.

"You both have your papers?" asked the Sgt.

Kenneth and Maggie produced their pay books. The Sgt. inspected the photos on the inside cover, comparing them to the faces before him.

"All right," he said finally, satisfied. "Report to the Officer in Charge at the mess on the east side of the field. You know where it is?" Kenneth nodded and the Marine went on. "Park the car out of sight for pity sake, Sergeant or you'll draw the bleeding Luftwaffe – your pardon Miss -- down on yourselves. Carry on."

"Thanks Sarge!" Kenneth put the car in gear and pulled forward as the barrier was lifted clear. Within minutes he was parking the car in a sandbag revetment behind the Hal Far Mess. Men milled about the old girl's school dormitory, requisitioned by the RN as a barracks and mess hall. The building had suffered serious bomb damage, but was made of solid limestone blocks quarried from a hill at the south end of Luqa airfield and had withstood numerous near misses in the past two years.

"Stay with the car, love," he said to Maggie. "I'll find out what's what."

He ran into the building, stopping briefly when challenged by sentries at the door. He was gone for almost fifteen minutes before returning to find a party of Royal Navy 'erks' examining the car with an eye to requisitioning it for their own use. As he shooed them away Kenneth realized the only reason the car was still there was that Maggie was in it.

"I've located your crew I think," he told Maggie as he started off again. "The duty officer says there is a HQ unit from Rinella holed up in an air raid shelter back the way we came, towards Kalafrana. He's going to ring ahead and have someone there to meet you."

Maggie nodded thoughtfully, but said nothing for a moment, then, "What are you to do, Kenneth? What did he tell you?"

"All pilots, regardless of service branch, are on stand-by here on the field," he replied. "Right now there are more pilots than aircraft, but the duty officer hinted that situation might just change soon."

They passed back out through the airfield gate on the Kalafrana road. The Sgt. waved them through without a question; the Duty Officer had phoned the gatehouse. A short distance beyond the gate Kenneth came to a fork in the road and he turned right, to the south and went down a narrow dirt track that wound its way through a field of enormous boulders and rocky outcrops. As he came round a particularly large rock he was confronted by a party of Royal Marines, standing watch on the road. The Duty Officer was as good as his word and the Marines were expecting them. After a brief stop to present their identity papers they were waved through again. Around the next corner they found the shelter. Built of sandbags it stood in the flat ground between two large outcroppings of rock. Scrub brush growing in crags and ledges overhung the bunker, sheltering it from sight from the air. A sentry directed Kenneth to park the car beneath a camouflage net fifty yards from the shelter. Tucked away under the net Kenneth spied a number of fuel drums and stacks of fuel tins. Numerous signs warned in bold, red lettering against smoking in the area. Kenneth didn't know it, but this was one of the caches where the fuel recently delivered by *HMS Welshman* was stored.

Kenneth got out and moved round to Maggie's passenger side door, holding her hand as she gingerly swung her feet out onto the ground. She paused and closed her eyes before easing herself out of the car and onto her feet. She swayed unsteadily for a moment then took a tentative step. With Kenneth supporting her with an arm around her waist she put one foot in front of the other towards the bunker. About halfway to the door two men and two women in khakis came out of the bunker and trotted to them.

"Maggie!" one of the men exclaimed. "Good God, we'd about written you off!"

"Hello, Chappie," Maggie responded, her voice barely audible over the distant drone of an aero engine. Chapman had to bend close to hear her. "Hello, Liz, hello, Pam," she greeted the other women. "Hello, Simon," she smiled at the other man. "I'm glad you're safe."

Kenneth appraised Chappie and Simon. Chappie was the older of the two and obviously in command. Simon was a gangly, pimply youth and it was immediately obvious from the way he fawned over her that he had a crush on Maggie. The women, Liz and Pam took Maggie from Kenneth and began walking her to the bunker, Simon close behind. Chappie turned to Kenneth.

"You're young Wiltshire I take it," he said extending his hand. "I'm Section Chief Chapman, Maggie's C. O."

Kenneth shook his hand and said, "I'm pleased to meet you, Sir."

"You must tell me your whole story of course, but first fill me in on Maggie's injuries. Does she require further treatment?"

Kenneth told Chapman how Maggie had gotten injured, that she'd been cared for by Dr. Mieza in Mosta and that the Dr. had only consented to let her travel when Kenneth impressed upon him the danger she would face if captured by the Germans.

"What are your orders," Chapman asked.

"I'm to return to Hal Far after delivering Maggie. All Pilots are on alert."

"I see," Chapman answered noncommittally.

"What are your plans, Sir?" asked Kenneth. "Er, you know, if the Germans…." He left the thought unfinished.

"It's all up in the air right now," said Chapman. "There's been a lot of talk and rumor of being evacuated by flying boat or surface ship tonight, but so far there's nothing for sure."

"I'll leave the car with you, Sir," Kenneth said. "It's a short walk back to Hal Far, but you may need it to get Maggie down to the docks tonight."

Maggie reached the door to the bunker and stopped. She turned and looked at Kenneth, then murmured something to her friends. They led her to a seat on a sandbag ledge on the wall of the bunker and stepped discretely through the door.

"Thank you, Wiltshire," Chapman said.

Kenneth nodded his head, but couldn't speak. A hard lump formed in his throat and his eyes began to well up.

"I'll give you a few minutes," said Chapman, once again shaking Kenneth's hand. "And thank you for bringing Maggie back safely."

Kenneth moved to the bunker and sat beside the girl, quietly taking her hands in his. The day had turned fine and sunny with only a light haze hanging over the island. Maggie squinted against the sunlight and smiled at Kenneth, but said nothing.

"I don't know when I'll see you again, Maggie," he began, finally squeezing the words past the lump in his throat, "but I promise you I will." In the distance a series of heavy, but muffled explosions sent a tremor through the ground at their feet.

"Oh, Kenneth," Maggie cried and flung her arms around his neck. "Why this bloody war?" She began to sob. Though he felt his heart would break he kept his tears in check and hugged her back, squeezing her gently.

"Without this war," he spoke gently in her ear, "we'd have never met. I'd be at home on the farm in Red Fern and you'd be getting ready to marry some safe stock broker or insurance salesman or something."

She snickered and pulled away from him, wiping her eyes.

"Do you think you'll be able to call?" she asked.

"I'll try," he promised.

Chapman appeared at the door. "Maggie," he said. "The Doctor wants to see you now." Chapman ducked back in the bunker.

"I love you, Maggie," Kenneth whispered. He waited a moment then leaned to her and kissed her softly on the lips. He stood and without looking back he strode away, back up the road towards the airfield. Maggie sat on the sandbags, watching him walk away through the tears streaming down her face.

"I love you too, Kenneth," she whispered.

Kuno left the aid station in the company of his paratrooper guide, Private Zobrist. They made their way across the runway to the west side of the field. As they walked Kuno tried to get a picture of the situation from the Private, but Zobrist was not well informed. Kuno sighed and contented himself with observing all that could be seen as they crossed the field.

Paratroopers moved about openly and while small arms fire could be heard in the distance to the south there was no sign of fighting currently under way on the field. On the runway parties were at work dragging wrecked gliders to the sides of the strip, clearing the way for aircraft to begin landing. Kuno noted Italians among the work parties. A BMW motorcycle raced down the runway on some errand or messenger service. In the air several flights of German aircraft circled the field, out of effective flak range, ready to attack ground targets or to protect the airhead from British air attack. As Kuno and Zobrist reached the western margin of the airfield and began to climb the slope towards Mdina a flight of three Stuka dive bombers stooped over the ground south of Ta Qali, delivering their bombs on the crest of the low ridge there. The field reverberated with the explosions, but the work continued uninterrupted.

Halfway up the slope Kuno paused to rest and to survey the battlefield. Ahead of him lay the ancient fortress of Mdina, or at least the ruins of it. Smoke still rose from the keep itself and huge holes were torn in the ramparts. Blackened, broken blocks of stone had been thrown down the slope from the walls. Bodies lay scattered near the base of the battlements and paratroopers moved among them searching for any wounded among the dead. The attack on the high ground appeared to have been successful if costly.

Turning to look out over the airfield he confirmed the impression he'd gotten on the runway. The field was firmly in German hands and was a beehive of activity. Thousands of men were in evidence, manning positions on the perimeter and working on the airstrip, but the bulk of the force was on the move. Streams of men were formed up and moving south, towards Luqa airfield.

Kuno turned to Zobrist and signaled they should continue. They climbed through a breach in the ramparts of Mdina, stepping aside for a pair of troopers rushing by with a wounded British soldier on a stretcher. Zobrist led Kuno to the southern ramparts where a flight of broad stone steps rose to the crenellated battlement above. At the foot of the steps was a heap of dead bodies, all British and piled six deep and over twenty wide. Making their way along the top of the wall they came to a stone guardhouse above the wooden gate let into the southern face of the fortress. The wooden door was blasted to splinters and the stone around the doorway was burnt and blackened. Zobrist pointed inside.

"The command post is here, Major," he said.

"Thank you Zobrist," said Kuno, saluting. "Return to your duties."

Entering the guardhouse he paused to adjust his eyes to the dim light. Shapes and shadows moved about the room. He recognized Sgt. Tondok after a moment and moved over to him.

"What is the situation, Sergeant?" he asked.

"Major Schacht!" Tondok cried. "We had feared the worst for you. Are you all right, Sir?"

Steup and others of the communications team came towards him, but he waved them back to their work.

"My injuries are not serious, Tondok," said Kuno, but he smiled this once to show his appreciation. "Where is the Baron?"

"SCHACHT!"

"Never mind, Tondok," said Kuno. "The Baron has found me."

"How are you, Schacht?" demanded Colonel August reaching to shake Kuno's hand.

Kuno winced and cried out as pressure was put on his broken

hand.

"I am well, Baron," Kuno replied, gingerly withdrawing his hand, "though I'm not much good as a soldier. Shot in one arm and this hand is broken, I'm afraid."

"I'm sorry, Schacht," said the Colonel. "Come into my office, I need to speak with you."

Colonel August led the way into a small antechamber of the guardroom. A small table and two wooden chairs were the only furnishings. A map of Malta was spread upon the table. Light came into the room through three narrow, angled embrasures in the meter thick stonewall. In ancient times archers firing down at attackers at the fortress gates used the embrasures as firing slits. For a moment Kuno envisioned Christian archers firing down on Muslim hordes below. Shutting the door behind them the Baron gestured for Kuno to sit.

"How much have you learned about the current situation?" asked August.

Kuno snorted. "The guide you left me was ignorant of all important facts, but from what I have observed since leaving the aid station I conclude the attack against our southern flank was repulsed and we have driven the British back to their original positions or perhaps even further. The perimeter of the field appears secure and obviously our assault here on the high ground has been a success. The airfield is covered by our troops and I saw some Italians as well, so I assume the subsequent drops went forward as planned. The strip at Ta Qali is being cleared. It looks like we might actually start landing planes there by morning."

"Good, good," agreed the Baron. "You've got the picture up to that point. The entire division has now arrived on Malta and the Italians have delivered the first of their two airborne regiments. I've been informed of your role in repulsing the British tanks. Well done, Kuno!" He glanced at his watch. "The second set of Italians should begin to arrive in about twenty minutes. Each of the drops has been delayed and higher than expected operational losses among the transports has slowed deliveries, but the force on the island is more or less what we planned for at this moment."

"So far, so good," said Kuno.

"Perhaps, perhaps not," replied the Colonel. "General Ramcke has been found. He was seriously injured upon landing. He and his entire staff came down off the airstrip to the north in a field of boulders. Several were killed and others injured, broken ankles, sprained knees and the like. The surgeon fears the General has cracked his spine. In any case he is out of commission. None of the other regimental commanders has turned up to this point."

"So command of the entire invasion still rests with you," Kuno concluded.

"Not quite," the Colonel replied. "The Italians have landed some General or other who thinks he should command."

"What, because they have three thousand men on the island to our twenty thousand?"

"Exactly," agreed August. "It's a sticky problem and has required considerable effort at diplomacy. To make matters worse, combat casualties among our officers have been very high. The 23rd Regiment is now commanded by its junior battalion leader. One bright spot has been your team. Steup and the others have stepped up to the challenge of handling communications for the entire division and have maintained excellent contact with the fly-boys." He gestured out the window where the drone of an engine was just coming into hearing. "But communications on the ground are still thin, most especially to the 23rd. The only contact I have with them south of the field is by messenger." Kuno frowned. With the 23rd Regiment commanded by an inexperienced officer communication was more vital than ever.

"Look here," said the Baron, pointing to the map. "We do indeed have a firm hold on Ta Qali airfield." He stabbed his finger down on the map. Kuno leaned close to see in the dim light. "We hold the high ground here at Mdina," said the Colonel, tapping the map, "and on the east and north side of the field we have established defensive lines along various natural features, ridge lines, stream beds and the likes. What forces the enemy have to the north and east appear to be concentrated near the landing beaches on St. Paul's Bay. Our lines are thin at points, but the British seem to be concentrated to the south, in front of the 23rd on the right, and my 6th on the left."

Kuno nodded his head in understanding of the briefing.

The Baron went on. "This is where we have our greatest challenge and our greatest opportunity. If we can hit the British tonight, before they have had time to muster their strength we can seize Luqa by dawn. If we dawdle, the British will have time to strengthen the defense and make our assault much more costly, perhaps even blunt it. We must attack tonight."

Colonel August looked at Kuno. "You understand don't you?" he asked.

"Yes, I'm afraid so," replied Kuno, smiling.

"Good, good," said the Colonel. "I can't wait to attack, but I can't attack with a junior officer in the lead at 23rd Regiment and no communications to boot. I want you to select men from your team and as many troopers as you need to carry equipment and supplies. It is 1810 now. Get down to the 23rd Regiment before dark and take command there and along the way establish communication between your new HQ and this room."

Kenneth walked back up to the gate at Hal Far. The Marine Sgt. watched him trudge up the road along with a group of infantry of the Devons, returning from a patrol.

"What's become of the car, Sergeant?" he asked.

"Ran out of petrol at the air raid shelter," Kenneth lied. He didn't want to explain why he had left the vehicle behind.

"Best get on up to the mess, 'toot-sweet' then," said the Marine. "There's a pilots briefing at 1830."

Kenneth checked his watch. 1821. He sighed. He had hoped for time for a bite to eat, but if the briefing led to his getting into a fighter and hitting back at the Germans he'd forget his hunger swiftly. He hurried through the gate and up the road to the mess, arriving in time to fall in at the tail end of a group of pilots, mostly Royal Navy flyers, but some RAF men he knew from Luqa as well. He scanned the group looking for any of his own squadron mates from Ta Qali and especially for his friends Derrick Metcalfe or Andy White. There were over eighty pilots there ahead of him and while he saw many familiar faces none were his squadron mates from Ta Qali. For pilots the men were all uncharacteristically quiet, shuffling to their seats in the auditorium without any of the usual banter and high spirits common among young warriors.

Kenneth found a chair near the rear of the room and had just sat down when men in the front of the room jumped to their feet at attention, boots stomping and chairs scraping as the hush was broken. A Naval officer in flying kit strode onto the stage from the wings and approached the rostrum.

"As you were," the officer said and leaned his arms on the dais. "Smoke if you have 'em." Kenneth and the other pilots settled back in their chairs, waiting expectantly.

"For those of you in the RAF that don't know me, I am Commander Pring-Wesley of the Royal Navy. First, let me update you on the current situation. The Germans are in control at Ta Qali. They have landed fresh troops throughout the day to follow-up the initial paratroop drop in the wee hours. They have repulsed the Army's first counterattack at mid-day today and are gathering strength for a push south, to Luqa and then here, to Hal Far. We got three Spitfires off the ground this morning with the heavy fog cover and they were able to do some damage against one of the German transport flights. We believe they may have gotten as many as ten or twelve of the German Junkers, and that's a costly loss for Jerry, I assure you."

Murmurs of approval ran through the pilots, but among them, only Kenneth knew the real tally for the morning's combat was four Ju 52s and three Spitfires.

"We have more trouble planned for Jerry this evening," Pring-Wesley went on. "After the sun sets this evening there will be a brief period of about forty minutes during which time the moonlight will be sufficient for our aircraft to get off the ground, but not so bright as to give Jerry a clear view of the field from the air. During that time we're going to launch every aircraft we have, saving only two Spitfires for tomorrow morning. Our bombers are to attack the German airhead at Ta Qali and our fighters will hit the Luftwaffe in the air." Pring-Wesley's voice rose and he smacked his fist in the palm of his hand on this phrase, bringing his Royal Navy pilots out of their seats with a cheer. He held his hands out, palm down to calm the room.

"Right now we have many more crew than aircraft," he said. "From among the Royal Navy flyers I've selected the crews to fly tonight's mission. I'm not familiar with the RAF Spitfire pilots, so we're going to draw lots to select the pilots for tonight. A sort of 'winner take all raffle' if you will," he added with a smile. A chuckle ran through the men in the room.

"Right then! RN get your flight assignments on your way out of the hall. RAF Spitfire pilots come to the front please." Pring-Wesley strode off stage to the wings.

Kenneth rose and made his way to the dais, struggling against the tide of Fleet Air Arm pilots making their way to the exit at the back of the room. When he got to the rostrum he found himself in a group of about twenty RAF pilots waiting for Pring-Wesley to come down from the stage. Several of the men smoked nervously. He knew several of them from Luqa, but there were no other Ta Qali fighter pilots present. He introduced himself quickly to those he didn't know.

"Have any of you seen any of the other Ta Qali pilots?" he asked. "There are over forty of us on the station." The men shook their heads, no, avoiding his gaze.

"Shouldn't think many were able to get away from the field with as fast as the Germans hit," one of the pilots said. "I nearly copped it myself at Luqa. How did you escape?"

"I was away on a night's leave," said Kenneth. "Up at St. Paul's Bay. Took me all day to get here. I've only just arrived within the past half hour."

"Ask the Commander about your chaps," the man suggested, leaning down and crushing his cigarette out against his heel. "He may have some word or other."

Pring-Wesley came back out on stage and jumped down to greet the RAF pilots on the auditorium floor. A Navy Chief carrying an old tin waste bucket followed him.

"Right then," he began. "I have three Spitfires available for this evening. They were rolled down from Luqa on the Safi strip this morning under cover of the fog and we've hidden them away safely under camo nets all day today. I've put all your names in a hat and will draw three names for tonight's mission. The men whose names are drawn will fly tonight. Right?" he asked.

Kenneth spoke up. "Sir, I've just arrived in the past few minutes. I'd like my name included too."

Pring-Wesley looked at him. "Wiltshire, is it?" he asked.

"Yes, Sir," Kenneth answered. "Sgt. Pilot Wiltshire, Sir."

"Duty Officer told me about you. Didn't say you flew Spit's. All right Wiltshire, give me a moment to add your name to the hat and then we'll draw."

The Commander turned to the stage and with his back to the group pulled a piece of paper from his pocket. He leaned on the stage and wrote on the paper, then carefully folded it and dropped it in the waste bucket. He turned back to face the pilots.

"As I don't know any of you personally it seems fairest if I draw the names. Any objections?" He scanned the solemn faces. Each man nodded his acceptance. Pring-Wesley shook the bucket about for a moment then set it on the stage. He reached into the bucket and pulled out the first slip of paper.

"Williams," he said. Kenneth's heart skipped a beat on the first syllable. He closed his eyes and took a deep breath. Williams stepped forward and took the slip from Pring-Wesley's hand. He stared at his name before crumpling the paper and tossing it on the floor.

"Caruthers," was the next name drawn. Caruthers didn't bother to take the paper, but pulled a cigarette out and calmly lit it.

"Priestly," said Pring-Wesley. Priestly smiled and shaking his head let out a little chuckle.

"Right then," said the Commander. "Williams, Caruthers and Priestly are to go with the Chief. He'll get you in your gear. The rest of you remain here with me for a moment."

He waited for the select three to go and then addressed the remaining group.

"As I said earlier, there are two Spitfires in reserve for tomorrow morning. If we get a fog cover again overnight those two Spits are to be flown off at first light to harass the Germans to the fullest extent. The Duty Officer will draw lots among you tomorrow morning to see who flies. That is all." He turned to walk away.

Kenneth trotted after him. "Commander?" he asked.

Pring-Wesley turned back to him.

"Yes, Wiltshire, quickly," he said.

"Yes, Sir, thank you, Sir," Kenneth said. "The other men said you might have some word on other pilots from Ta Qali?"

"Besides yourself there have been only two others from Ta Qali get to us here. They flew this morning's mission along with a chap from Luqa."

"I see," said Kenneth. "I watched that mission from the north side of Ta Qali this morning, Sir. I saw all three Spitfires go down. One pilot bailed out. Who were the Ta Qali pilots please, Sir?"

Pring-Wesley thought for a moment but said, "I can't recall their names son." Seeing the crestfallen look on Kenneth's face he hastened to add. "The leader was a good looking Irish chap with his wingman."

"Metcalfe, Sir?" Kenneth asked. "Derrick Metcalfe?"

"Yes, I believe that's his name."

"And his wingman would be Andy White?" pressed Kenneth.

"Yes, that's right, Wiltshire. Metcalfe and White were the two Ta Qali pilots on that flight. White never got out of his kite I'm told, but Metcalfe bailed out over Luqa."

"Did he survive the fall, Sir?" Kenneth asked, dreading the answer.

Pring-Wesley put his hand on Kenneth's shoulder. "He was alive when they found him Wiltshire, but I'm sorry to tell you he was badly burned and didn't last long. Merciful really. He'd have only suffered had he lingered. Now you must excuse me."

Pring-Wesley started to walk away, but Kenneth stopped him.

"One more thing, Sir," said Kenneth. "I came in today with an injured English girl from the headquarters at Rinella. I've dropped her back with her unit at an air-raid shelter towards Kalafrana. May I have permission to call to see how she is? I feel rather responsible for her injuries."

Pring-Wesley sized Kenneth up for a moment.

"The phone circuits are overloaded," he said, "but tell the Duty Officer I authorized you a pass to walk down there and see for yourself. Just be back before midnight. And now I really must go." He turned again to walk away, but stopped and turned around. "You saw our Spits this morning, eh Wiltshire?"

"Yes, Sir," said Kenneth. "Four Junkers destroyed, one other damaged."

"Keep that under your hat, Wiltshire," said the Commander. He turned and strode purposefully from the room.

Kenneth's head spun with the news that Derrick and Andy were both dead. All the friends he'd come to Malta with and now so far as he knew all the ones he'd made since getting there were gone, save for Maggie and he'd near enough been responsible for her death too. Slowly he made his way in a daze out of the mess and surveyed the airfield. Hal Far was the smallest of the British airbases on Malta and its runways the shortest. The main north-south runway was just 800 yards in length and ended on the bluffs overlooking the sea on the island's south coast. German aircraft still circled overhead in the fading daylight and he was careful to remain within sight of a trench or air raid shelter in case the Luftwaffe chose to attack. As at the other airfields almost all the pre-war buildings on the surface at Hal Far were destroyed or badly damaged. Wrecked gliders littered the field with fires still smoldering at several places and the flak batteries were all fully manned. Across the field he could see a line of men walking toward the caverns delved in the limestone rock to the west of the runway. He knew the station infirmary was located there and he suspected it was very busy with wounded from the fighting. An air raid siren began to wail. He sighed and walked slowly to the nearest shelter.

>>>>>>>>>>>>>

Kuno found the 23rd Regiment's HQ just before sunset. The HQ was situated in an olive grove, its trees torn and shattered and devoid of leaves. The convent and hospital at Mt. Carmel was on the peak of the large hill behind the HQ. Wounded of both sides were still arriving there and the overwhelmed nuns worked side by side with both German and British corpsmen. A large white sheet with a hastily painted red cross hung across the third floor dormer windows of the convent.

Kuno selected Sgt. Tondok and two enlisted men from his own team and drafted a squad of paratroopers to carry equipment and cable from Colonel August's divisional HQ at Mdina. They'd strung a single field phone line as they went, exhausting their thin supply of cable to cover the two and a half kilometers. As the Baron had told him the 23rd Regiment was under the command of its junior battalion leader, a Captain named Thaler. The two officers hunched over a map spread across the top of a stonewall separating the olive grove from a gravel road.

"Describe your dispositions, please," Kuno ordered the Captain once introductions and change of command was effected. The Captain seemed grateful to be relieved of his short-lived responsibility. Captain Thaler lifted the map to the dieing sun and pointed as he described the Regiment's positions.

"The second battalion is on our far left," he began. "They have contact with the 6th Regiment further east and are strung out along a dry streambed with a half-kilometer of front. The second battalion arrived in the second drop in the morning and has seen the heaviest action so far. Strength is estimated at about 800 men of the original 1100." He looked up to see if he was satisfying the Major. Kuno nodded his approval to continue. "Third battalion is directly to our front and continuing on to our right, the west, also along the same stream bed and covering a little more than a kilometer. They arrived later in the morning and are nearer full strength; about 1050 men." Captain Thaler looked up from the map. "The first battalion was dropped at Hal Far in the first wave and we have no contact with them. The Regiment's entire anti-tank, heavy machine gun and mortar companies went in with the first battalion at Hal Far, so we're very thin on heavy weapons. A handful of light mortars and one 50mm PAK gun rolled down from the airstrip a short time ago. I have them in the center, supporting the area between the two regiments."

Kuno nodded his head thoughtfully. "Well, done, Captain," he said. "The summation is that with the first battalion and all the heavy weapons lost the regiment is at little more than fifty percent strength?"

"That is correct Major."

"What contact do you have with the 6th Regiment on your left?"

"Our flanks are within earshot of each other, but between the two Headquarters the only contact is by runner."

"What do you know of the 6ths strength and dispositions?"

"They are much closer to full strength, though their first battalion which came into Ta Qali in the first wave suffered heavy casualties in the early hours. Command of the regiment has passed down to one of the battalion leaders with Colonel August taking command of the division."

"Very well," Kuno said. "You will remain here as my chief of staff. Summon the battalion commanders. We attack tonight."

>>>>>>>>>>>>

Maggie dozed fitfully in the dim shelter through the afternoon and into the evening. She was vaguely aware of comings and goings around her; hustle-bustle seen through dreamy eyes as she drifted in and out of sleep. For the most part she was left alone. When at last she stirred it was hunger that brought her fully awake. The shelter was lit by a lone battle lantern hung on a post in the center of the single large room. A soft breeze blew through the room, moving the lantern gently. Its red glass globe cast an otherworldly glow on the walls and ceiling. Its light seemed to flicker like the reflection of distant flames.

Elizabeth sat by Maggie's bedside tipped back in a chair. Her eyes were closed, but she was humming softly to herself. Maggie listened quietly to the peaceful tune, an old hymn she'd sung hundreds of times in chapel.

"Hello, Liz," said Maggie when the tune was finished.

Elizabeth opened her eyes and smiled at Maggie. "How are you feeling?" she asked.

"Hungry!" Maggie replied with feeling.

"It's good you're awake," Elizabeth said. "We're to be moved again soon. Evacuated again, to Kalafrana this time. I'll get you a fast bite to eat."

Maggie sat up slowly, swinging her feet down onto the floor one at a time. Her dizziness was mild and didn't last long so she stood, holding to the edge of her cot. She was still weak, but it felt good to stretch her stiff limbs. Her head still ached, but it was tolerable and her eyes focused easily.

She looked about the shelter. Others of her 'Y' Service section slept or played cards or chatted quietly. Chapman stood near the door with his hand on Simon's shoulder, speaking earnestly with the boy. Maggie thought it looked like a father-son chat and smiled. It never occurred to her that she was the subject of the talk. A blackout curtain hung across the door and as she watched Chappie and Simon the curtain parted and an army officer stepped through. He spoke a few words in Chappie's ear then went back out. Chapman clapped Simon on the shoulder and left the boy at the door staring at his shoes. After a moment Simon stepped out through the blackout curtain.

Elizabeth returned to her side with a mug of steaming tea and an English biscuit.

"Afraid it's all I can find," she said as Maggie sat back down.

"God bless you, Liz," said Maggie gratefully. She wrapped her hands round the mug and sipped the scalding tea. Her thoughts turned to Kenneth. "What's the hour, Liz?" she asked.

"It's about nine o'clock," Liz replied. "Er, ahem. 2100 hours," she corrected herself, looking down her nose at Maggie. They both laughed.

"Is everyone else in the Section accounted for and safe?" asked Maggie.

"Yes, dear," said Liz. "You're the only one had Mum worried."

Chapman spoke from the center of the room. He'd stepped up on a box to be seen.

"Can I have your attention, please?" he called over the slap of cards and the murmur of conversation. The background noise settled down and the forty-person team waited expectantly.

"Thank you," Chappie said. "I've just been informed that we've to move to Kalafrana within the hour. We're to be evacuated by flying boat tonight before midnight. We haven't much time to get our kit together, so turn to everyone!" He stepped down from his box and came straight to Maggie as the rest of the team busied themselves getting their gear gathered up and ready for the move.

"How are you feeling Maggie?" he asked.

"Much better Chappie," she said. "How can I help?"

"By resting," Chapman said firmly. "We've a very trying time ahead of us Maggie. You're going to need all your strength later. Let Elizabeth take care of you. The rest of us will get packed."

"All right, Chappie," she agreed.

For the next twenty minutes the shelter was a buzz of activity as the 'Y' Service section gathered their personal belongings and made ready to travel, but in truth none of the unit had more than a small bag of personal items and soon they were sitting about again with nothing to do. Maggie remained awake and alert during this time, sipping her tea and nibbling her biscuit.

Finally the Army officer she'd seen earlier returned and spoke to Chapman. The Section Chief addressed his unit again from his stage on the crate.

"It's time for us to leave for Kalafrana," he began, "where we're to be evacuated from Malta by seaplane. The army has kindly provided us with two lorries, but I'm afraid it's going to be a bit of an uncomfortable squeeze. I know you all won't mind getting chummy for a few minutes." Polite laughter. "I want the 'A' team to the door now. They'll take the first lorry. As soon as the 'A' team is out the door the 'B' team will assemble and load the second lorry. Maggie, Elizabeth and I will bring up the rear in the automobile Maggie arrived in this afternoon. Now let's get cracking!"

Maggie hurriedly finished her tea as the members of the 'A' team gathered their pitiful few possessions and made their way to the door. Simon was in the 'A' team and he contrived to come past Maggie on his way out.

"See you at Kalafrana, Maggie," he said.

She smiled in return. "Yes, Simon," she said. "See you there."

The boy smiled shyly and floated to the door.

"Not a word for me, has he!" harrumphed Elizabeth in mock fury after Simon left.

Chapman approached as the 'B' team made its way out.

"Come along ladies," he said with a bow. "Your chariot awaits."

Elizabeth held Maggie under the arm, but Maggie was feeling much stronger than she had at any point that day and was embarrassed by the fuss being made over her.

"Not at all!" Chapman insisted. "The lorries are overcrowded and we need to make use of the car anyway. I'm familiar with American automobiles, so you see there's really no fuss at all."

Elizabeth stayed with Maggie and assisted her to the car while Chapman supervised the loading of the two lorries. It was almost dark; just the faintest smudge of the day's light lingered in the west and the just risen moon was still too low in the east to cast more than a pale glow that did nothing but deepen the long shadows. Malta's 'Y' Service section groped their way to the lorries in the dim light and began to climb aboard over the rear lift gates. A fair number of stepped on fingers and a bit of cursing accompanied the operation, and as they loaded aboard the two lorries they found they were indeed quite cramped. But after just a few minutes all were settled as comfortably as possible for the short drive to Kalafrana.

When he was satisfied all were accounted for and safely loaded Chapman gave a few brief words of encouragement to each group then hurried to the Model T as the lorries moved out. He squeezed into the driver's seat with Maggie in the middle and Elizabeth on the other side. The drivers didn't dare turn on the headlamps, the sound of aero engines buzzing overhead was never long gone, so they crept up the darkened dirt road at barely more than walking speed, the two lorries followed by the American made car.

Maggie felt herself begin to cry as she realized she was leaving Malta without the chance even to say good-bye to Kenneth and she wondered if she would ever see him again or even learn his fate. Tears rolled silently down her cheeks and a dull pain grew in her chest as she thought of him, of their few brief weeks together and of their one night of love.

The lorries came to the main road from Hal Far to Kalafrana and turned right, down the hill towards Kalafrana on Marsaxlokk Bay. As the Model T made the turn Maggie heard a shout from up the road.

"Chappie, wait," she sobbed. "Oh, wait, please."

Chapman stopped the car and stared at the girl, trying to make out her features in the dark. "What is it, Maggie?" he demanded. "We can't stop here!"

Already the two lorries were disappearing in front of them in the gloom. The shout came again.

"It's Kenneth, Chappie!" she sobbed. "I thought I'd never see him again and now he's here. Oh, please stop," she begged.

"We can only stop for a few minutes," Chapman relented reluctantly. "And you're not to get out of the car," he added sternly.

Chapman left the motor running as he and Elizabeth got out. Kenneth came running up, skidding to a stop on the loose gravel road, panting, out of breath. He leaned in the driver's door. Maggie threw her arms about him and kissed him with all her feeble strength.

"Oh Kenneth," she gasped at last. "When you didn't call I thought I'd never..." her voice trailed off into a sob as she began to cry again.

"I know, love," he told her. "I just barely was able to get away."

Chapman spoke from the road. "Young man," he said. "We've got to get to Kalafrana to be evacuated tonight. I know you won't want to be the cause of Maggie being left behind."

Kenneth turned to him. "No, Sir!" he exclaimed. "She's got to be gotten away. May I ride to Kalafrana with you, Sir? I'll ride in the rear."

"What about your own unit?" Chapman asked.

"I've been given leave till midnight, Sir," answered Kenneth. "After you're away I can return with the car to Hal Far."

Chapman glared at Kenneth in the dark for a moment. "All right," he finally decided. "You drive." He signaled to Elizabeth and the two of them climbed in the bed of the pickup where that afternoon Kenneth had carried wounded.

Kenneth put the car in gear and began moving slowly down the road, hurrying a little to catch up the lorries. It was difficult in the dark and he and Maggie were silent as they proceeded down the hill towards Kalafrana, but whenever he could take his hand off the gearshift they held hands. They were nearly to the gates of the Navy Yard before the rear of the second lorry loomed up before them. Chapman hopped down from the Model T and ran forward to the Royal Marine checkpoint where he established his credentials. The three vehicles were waved forward with Chapman standing on the running board of the lead lorry. They made their way through the built up area of the port facility, past machine shops and warehouses, mostly in ruins from the persistent bombing in the months leading up to the invasion. They crept through narrow tracks cleared in the rubble of the streets and alleys.

Kenneth and Maggie were silent as they inched their way toward the Kalafrana waterfront. About halfway through the town they heard the long familiar sound of bombs exploding. Looking back over his left shoulder Kenneth could see the flashes of explosions lighting the sky to the northwest. Maggie put her hand on his in a gesture he understood as a question.

"Its Luqa," he said. "They're bombing Luqa before they attack on the ground."

At last they came to the great stone wharf. The lorries pulled to a stop in front of a large stonewalled building whose front was wide open and whose roof was made of heavy steel girders covered with corrugated tin sheets. Here and there a star glimmered through holes in the roof where bomb damage opened the roof to the sky. The inside of the building was completely dark and the shadows were impenetrable, but Kenneth knew the building was the hangar where the seaplanes at Kalafrana were serviced and repaired. In front of the building a wide concrete apron sloped down into the water, extending into the surf. Pale moonlight from the east dappled the gentle waters of Marsaxlokk Bay as the moon rose behind Delimara Lighthouse on the bay's eastern shore. Heavier surf crashed into the breakwater with a roar, casting sheets of spray that reflected the moon's early light like sparkling gems cast against the black velvet background of the open sea. Kenneth looked out over the waters of the bay and discerned the shadowy shape of a seaplane bobbing gently about a hundred yards out.

Navy seamen from the hangar unlatched and dropped open the rear gates of the two lorries and began to assist the passengers as they unloaded. The 'Y' Service teams jumped down from the truck quietly as if fearing the Germans might hear them if they spoke too loud. Overhead a plane's motor droned into earshot and Maggie's comrades froze in their tracks, barely daring to breathe until the sound passed.

Kenneth and Maggie got out of the car and stood on the ramp, staring out over the water. Neither was able to speak for fear of losing control and breaking down in tears. Finally Kenneth swallowed the lump in his throat and turned to her.

"In a few hours you'll be safe at Alex' or Gib'," he said.

"I don't want to leave you darling," she whispered, her eyes misting up in spite of her efforts.

"I know, Love," he said and held her close, gently smoothing her hair around the bandages, whispering in her ear. "But if I'm to ever get out of here myself I have to know you're safe somewhere. Anywhere. But I have to know you're safe." She buried her head in his chest and sobbed.

A small harbor launch puttered up to the side of the ramp at a set of stone steps leading down to the water. A sailor jumped out and held the boat away from the stone quay. A man sitting in the stern sheets at the tiller spoke out.

"We'll carry five at a time out to the seaplane. Please board carefully. The quay is slick."

Chapman began herding the first small group of his people to the boat. He and the sailor on the quay assisted each passenger until all five were seated on the thin plank benches. The sailor cast off and the boat puttered away from shore towards the seaplane.

Kenneth held onto Maggie with increasing nervousness. The light of the moon was increasing every minute. Already he could make out more of the shape of the seaplane. It was a Short Sunderland Flying Boat, a four-engine behemoth capable of a three thousand mile non-stop flight carrying depth charges or bombs. For this mission it had flown from Gibraltar carrying a payload of small arms ammunition for the island's garrison, skirting the North African shoreline just outside Vichy French Colonial airspace, timing its arrival at Malta with sunset. The Royal Navy erks at Kalafrana had just finished unloading the ammunition from the Sunderland; it would be taken to Hal Far on the lorries.

Chapman approached and spoke quietly to Kenneth.

"I'll take Maggie on the last trip out, but there must be no delay when the time comes," he warned.

Kenneth nodded his head without taking his arms from around the girl. "Thank you, Sir," he answered softly.

The launch returned and another group of five boarded to ride out to the seaplane. Once more an aircraft droned overhead. They all waited nervously for a sign that they were discovered, but the plane passed on uneventfully.

Kenneth looked across the water at Delimara Lighthouse as the third boatload approached the Sunderland. The moon had risen above the headland on the opposite shore and was casting its light across the bay. If they didn't hurry he realized the flying boat would have to take off bathed in moonlight. Its wake especially would be clearly visible from the air. Kenneth's mind went through the calculations; four minutes round trip for each boatload, five people per trip, twenty-five remaining people, five more trips, twenty minutes before the Sunderland would be able to taxi out to the center of the bay, say twenty-five minutes minimum until it was airborne. He turned to Chapman.

"You need to overload the launch," he said. "It's taking too long. The moon."

In the shallow waters off the launching ramp at Kalafrana a tiny mechanism wound down the final few seconds of its twenty-four hour clock and clicked to zero as Chapman turned to answer. 2,000 kilograms of high explosive in the time-delay bomb dropped there the night before detonated with an ear-shattering roar twenty feet beneath the keel of the flying boat, lifting the seaplane out of the water and splitting its frame aft of the wing roots. The blast hurled the front half of the seaplane forward, plunging its nose down beneath the surface. The rear half of the fuselage shattered and the fuel tanks there and in the wings ruptured. A geyser of water and fuel rocketed skyward, the fuel flashing into flame as the harbor launch and its passengers disintegrated in the blast.

On shore the concussion knocked everyone on the ramp flat. Seconds later they were drenched as the plume of water thrown into the air by the explosion came cascading back down upon them. Kenneth landed heavily on his right shoulder; Maggie's weight knocked the breath from him and he lay on the cement ramp in agony, unable to breathe. Stars flew before his eyes and he floated on the verge of consciousness. Only the feel of the girl in his arms kept him from letting go completely. The deluge of water combined with his struggle to breathe gave Kenneth the horrible sensation of drowning.

Though nearly paralyzed for lack of air he managed to roll onto his left side, gently cradling Maggie to the concrete ramp. Finally he managed a strangled gasp that brought the first sweet taste of oxygen back to his lungs. He rolled over again to his hands and knees; keeping his head down he gulped air until his breathing returned to a semblance of normal and the spots before his eyes started to fade.

Staying down on the ground he looked about. Chapman was standing near him at the moment of the explosion and he too was struggling to recover, up on one elbow and gasping for air. Others on the ramp twitched from injuries or lay motionless. The whole scene was lit by ghastly pools of fuel burning on the surface of the water in front of the ramp. The airframe of the seaplane could barely be seen through the smoke and flames. Only a small section of fuselage forward of the wing roots and aft of the submerged cockpit could be seen clearly. Bits and pieces of debris were scattered all about the ramp or bobbed about on the water in a radius of over a hundred yards. A foot long splinter of wood, probably from the launch stood vertical, impaled in the body of one of the lorry drivers, prone on the ramp.

Kenneth turned his attention to the girl lying beside him on the ramp. Maggie's eyes were closed, but she was breathing, her chest rising and falling steadily.

"Maggie?" he said. "Maggie?" He realized he couldn't hear his own voice and wondered if he still wasn't breathing properly. Chapman was struggling to his feet, looking at Kenneth. His lips were moving, but Kenneth couldn't make out what he said.

Chapman stumbled over to Kenneth. "Are you all right?" he shouted. Kenneth as much read Chapman's lips as heard him, but he nodded his head, yes. The two men knelt beside Maggie and between them they lifted her into the bed of the Model T pick-up. Kenneth's right shoulder howled in pain at the effort. He stayed with her a moment before turning back to the ramp to try to help others. Most were starting to come round and were struggling back to their feet. Several had nasty cuts or gashes and Kenneth's was not the only injured limb in the group. Sailors raced out from the hangar to assist, bringing stretchers and medical supplies with them.

Kenneth turned to look at the burning Sunderland. Flames had consumed the fuselage and

wings down to the aluminum ribbed frame. Twisted and glowing, steam hissed from it as it sank

into the water. Kenneth watched it go down and he saw Maggie's chance of evacuation go down

with it. As the Sunderland sank from view and the flames were extinguished Kenneth's hearing

began to return. The cries and moans of the injured mingled with the sounds of intensifying

bombardment at Luqa Airfield.

Through the day and into the evening of June 26th *HMS Furious* plowed on through the calm Mediterranean Sea towards Malta. At 1530 hours the masts of the ships that had sailed before her hove into view and by 1730 the carrier joined the battlecruiser *Renown* to form a single fleet. *Renown* had sailed from 'The Rock' with a powerful escort of her own, including the Dido class anti-aircraft cruisers *HMS Phoebe, HMS Charybdis* and *HMS Sirius*. The sixteen ship Dido class, each named for a figure from Greek mythology, was designed with a main armament of ten 5.25-inch dual-purpose guns coupled to radar fire direction and equally effective against air or surface targets. In addition each ship of the class fairly bristled with over two-dozen 40mm and 20mm flak guns. Completed from 1939 to early 1942 the three Dido Class sisters with *Renown* were fast and modern and very formidable fighting ships, though one of the trio differed in her main armament from the standard Dido design. *Charybdis* had the misfortune, along with her sister *HMS Scylla* then serving on the arctic run, of completing her construction at the same time as the battleship *King George V*. The battleship required sixteen of the 5.25-inch dual-purpose guns and production problems led to a shortage. *Scylla* and *Charybdis* were completed with four twin turrets of 4.5-inch guns and 'Q' turret forward of the bridge was replaced with a twin pom-pom flak gun. For their lighter armament the two ships were known in the Royal Navy as "The Toothless Terrors," though in fact opinion within the Navy was divided, with many officers believing the 4.5-inch guns were more effective against aircraft than the larger 5.25-inch guns.

Rounding out the cruiser force accompanying the battlecruiser was *HMS Kenya,* Fiji Class sister to *HMS Nigeria,* also completed in 1939 and mounting twelve 6-inch guns and twenty-four lighter flak guns. Each of the five cruisers in the now combined fleet possessed six launchers for 21-inch torpedoes, in keeping with pre-war Royal Navy doctrine that enemy warships were to be battered by the heavy guns of the fleet and then sunk by torpedoes fired by cruisers and destroyers.

Eight destroyers accompanied *Renown* as well. In addition to the Flotilla Leader, *HMS Laforey*, were seven destroyers of vintage construction, most having been completed in the final year of the First World War. Of the so-called 'Modified V and W' classes they were *HMS Wishart, HMS Vansittart, HMS Wrestler, HMS Westcott, HMS Wanderer, HMS Wolsey* and *HMS Venomous*. All were fitted with ASDIC underwater detection apparatus and carried up to forty-five depth charges each. Despite their age these ships were fast, with top speeds approaching thirty knots and they were deadly sub-hunters. At their normal cruising speed of fifteen knots their range was over 3,000 nautical miles. They had one very serious shortcoming however.

The main armament of the V and W class destroyers escorting *Renown* were from an era when air attack at sea was hardly imagined. The destroyers were each equipped with four 4.7-inch guns, but these were mounted such that they could not be elevated above a thirty-degree angle, rendering them useless against most air attacks. This feeble main armament had been supplemented by several mountings of light machine guns. The Royal Navy knew these ships as 'Western Approaches' destroyers as they'd been designed to patrol the shipping lanes to the west of the British Isles and they were singularly well suited as anti-submarine escorts, but virtually defenseless against aircraft. The Royal Navy's fleet of Western Approaches destroyers was being slowly refitted with high angle guns, but a shortage of the guns coupled with the demands on dockyard space and of keeping ships at sea prevented the destroyers at Gibraltar from being upgraded by the summer of 1942.

The commanding officers of all Force H's fighting ships were experienced, professional sailors of the Royal Navy, though every ship's company was leavened with a large number of reservist officers and among the other ranks were many 'hostilities only' ratings, men who would have been rejected for peacetime service. Still, most of these men were veterans of two to three years at war and were inheritors of the British tradition of seamanship.

Rear-Admiral Sir Harold Burrough took command of the cruiser squadron at Gibraltar earlier that month of June 1942 after commanding a squadron of cruisers with the Home Fleet. His Home Fleet cruisers had covered the Arctic convoys to Russia through the winter and spring just passed and his posting to the Mediterranean and the warmer climate was a welcome change to him. In taking over the cruiser squadron at Gibraltar his orders were to make preparations for Operation Pedestal, the Malta relief convoy planned for mid-August during the dark phase of the moon. Pedestal had to wait until August for the aircraft carriers *HMS Illustrious* and *HMS Indomitable* to return from Madagascar and their participation in Operation Ironclad. Pedestal's plan called for the two fleet carriers to join with *Furious* and *Eagle* for the convoy, but now Burrough found himself in command of Force H in the most dangerous of circumstances. He was forced to rely on a single carrier for air cover during the Malta relief operation.

A Sunderland flying boat from Gibraltar maintained a submarine watch over the fleet all day on June 26th. Under its watchful eye there were a number of submarine scares and the destroyers in the screen were kept busy, racing to and fro, dropping charges on suspected ASDIC contacts, but the battlecruiser, five cruisers and the carrier sailed on peacefully in the center of the formation in two columns. *Phoebe* led *Renown, Charybdis* and *Kenya* in the port column. *Furious* and *Nigeria* followed *Sirius* in the starboard column. The entire force zigzagged at irregular intervals on command by signal flag from the flagship. At sunset the Sunderland was relieved by another equipped with rudimentary surface search radar in an effort to provide coverage against surfaced submarines after dark.

The RAF Spitfire pilots aboard *HMS Furious* paid regular visits to the wardroom through the day, dropping by in ones and twos to check for any new information, but there was precious little they could be told. The news from Malta remained the same; heavy fighting at Ta Qali and Luqa, while Hal Far remained in British hands. Between visits to the wardroom the pilots walked the flight deck, wrote letters home hoping they would someday be delivered and played cards, though they all knew to stay away from Billy Wilson and his cribbage board.

In the late afternoon the RAF squadron pilots gathered on the flight deck to watch the sunset. Bryan and Billy knew nearly every man in the squadron. They'd gone through training with most of them and had sailed to Gibraltar with them. The pilots were drawn from the United Kingdom and every corner of the British Empire, with a heavy dose of Australians and New Zealanders. There were no Americans in the squadron. Earlier in the war this would have been unusual, so many Yanks having volunteered for the Royal Air Force since the outbreak of war in 1939, and indeed a number of Americans like Kenneth Wiltshire had served on Malta, but after the United States was brought into the war by the Japanese attack at Pearl Harbor and subsequent German Declaration of War the two Allies agreed that American pilots with the RAF would be transferred to comparable flying duties in their own services if they so chose. Most Americans in the RAF opted to return to their own air force for the chance to serve with their fellow countrymen, not to mention the much higher pay. Now as the fleet steamed steadily eastward Bryan and Billy leaned against the tail plane of a Spitfire, watching the sun sink to the horizon.

"I tell you Bryan," said Billy, "you've got to tell Nesbith before we fly off. It's not the kind of thing you can keep a secret forever anyway, and at this point he can't cashier you. He doesn't have a pilot to replace you if he locks you up."

"I know you're right, Billy," answered Bryan, "but Nesbith has got his plate full right now. I can't just waltz in on him and announce I've gotten married without permission of the service."

"Don't you see, Bryan," Billy argued, "it's actually the perfect time. There's nothing he can do about it now, and anyway the two of you may well be dead in two days time regardless. If you do survive it will be a big joke between the two of you."

"Ever the optimist, aren't you Billy!" exclaimed Bryan. "What would I do without you to cheer me up?"

During the night of the 26th Force H met with *HMS Evening Dale*. The fleet oiler had sailed from Gibraltar the morning before in company with two destroyer escorts, *HMS Verdun* and *HMS Vanquisher,* two more of the antiquated WWI vessels. The oiler's top speed was just 19 knots so she'd been given time to make seaway to the east before joining Force H south of Majorca. The oiler slipped between the two columns of heavy ships and took up station behind *Sirius* in the starboard column. In pairs the fleet's escort destroyers slid alongside the *Evening Dale* and began their refueling program. It was a delicate and dangerous operation with a destroyer on either side, refueling at sea at night, but British seamanship was equal to this challenge and before dawn the *Evening Dale* had refueled all the destroyers in Force H. Straining at its maximum speed of 19 knots the *Evening Dale* nonetheless held the fleet to a reduced pace. And as events on Malta were soon to demonstrate, speed was of the essence.

>>>>>>>>>>>>>>>>>>>>>>>>>>>>>>>

# Day 7
June 27, 1942

"The moment of decision is fast approaching, Gentlemen."

Lord Gort placed the palms of his hands flat on the map table. Leaning forward he gazed at his two friends. The three senior leaders of Malta were alone in the war room of Lascaris Bastion in Valletta. It was early in the morning, June 27, 1942 and the eastern sky was just lightening with the new day, but high above their heads they heard the staccato chatter of anti-aircraft guns firing at yet another wave of attacking bombers. In their feet they felt the dull rumble of bombs exploding in the city and harbor area, targeting the remaining flak batteries there.

Air Marshall Lloyd spoke up. "There are up to thirty-six fighters arriving to Hal Far later this morning," he said. "If we can land the bulk of them safely and get them back in the air we can still turn the tide."

"Yes, and by tomorrow morning the Fleet should be here to shell the German landing zones," added Admiral Leatham.

"By tomorrow morning the Germans may be in command of all three airfields," retorted Gort. "We can't wait till then to make our decision. Do we call for an evacuation or not?"

"Certainly we have to try again to get the 'Y' Service and other high priority personnel out," answered the Admiral. "We can't risk them being taken by the Germans."

"No, of course not," said Gort. "But that's little more than a hundred all told."

"And difficult enough for all that to get them away," added Lloyd. "Seventeen dead, twelve hurt and a Sunderland destroyed last night at Kalafrana. I'm afraid further evacuation by air is out of the question during this full moon."

"It won't be any easier by sea," countered Leatham. "No surface ship can dare make its way into any of the harbors. They'd be bombed to the bottom before they'd dropped anchor! We were damned lucky to get *Welshman* in to Kalafrana with a cargo of fuel."

"So that leaves us evacuation by submarine," said Gort.

"Yes," agreed the Admiral. "And no large scale evacuation is possible that way," he said. "At best a sub can carry away forty passengers and a very dicey thing it is too. With that many extra aboard the time submerged must be very limited to avoid suffocation."

Gort straightened and a look of resolve, or resignation came to his face. "Make the signal," Gort directed the Admiral. "Ask for all available submarines to commence taking off critical personnel. You have the priority list?"

Leatham pulled a folded sheet of paper from his pocket.

"Yes, right here," he said unfolding the paper. "The 'Y' Service and other HQ are at the top, followed by the intelligence sections of the service branches, government ministers and English women and children, what few of them are still here at any rate, pilots and aircrew, nurses, engineers." He paused. "We'll never get that far down the list. Lucky to get any of them away."

The three men stared down at the map of the island on the table for a moment. Air-Marshall Lloyd broke the silence.

"Of course," he said at last, "the three of us are on that list as well."

Gort straightened, a scowl crossing his face. "I've left by boat once," he said. "Not again." He shrugged. "Of course the Germans won't take me alive."

The Admiral and the Air-Marshall exchanged quick glances.

"Agreed," said Lloyd.

A deep, rolling rumble passed beneath their feet, lasting many seconds, shaking dust down from the ceiling.

"Good God!" exclaimed Lloyd. "What was that?"

The Admiral answered. "Naval artillery."

Lt. Commander Giussepe Gianaclis lowered his binoculars and nodded his head in

satisfaction. He turned and gazed over the side of the *Muzio Attendolo. Raimondo Montecuccoli* crashed through the waves to port, her bows lifting and falling with the set of the ten-foot swells. Behind the two cruisers was the battleship, *Vittorio Venetto,* her 39,000-ton bulk barely noticing the seas, shouldering her way through with ease. He checked his watch. 0530. In just minutes the great guns of the battleship would swing out and fire, signaling the start of the seaborne invasion of Malta.

Gianaclis had done his job well, navigating the *Muzio Attendolo* and the rest of the battle fleet into position and on time off Malta's northern shore, making his landfall exactly as planned, nine miles northeast of Qawra Point on St. Paul's Bay then threading his way carefully through the charted gap in the minefields laid off Malta's northeast coast by speedboats of the Italian Navy. Now as the final minutes ticked down he watched in pride as the three heavy ships turned in towards shore in a single column. Dawn's first glow had strengthened, bringing the contours of the shoreline into view. He lifted his glasses again and examined the Maltese coast. Rocky and forbidding through most of its length, here in the northeast was one of the few good landing sites.

He couldn't see the shore defenses, the miles of strung barbed wire, the trenches, mine fields, bunkers or the sandbagged machine gun nests. He couldn't even see the heavy guns along the shore, but he knew they were there; indeed he knew exactly where they were down to the last meter. Two years of aerial reconnaissance led up to this day and before that many years of peace afforded the Italian navy the chance to make detailed charts of the island's defenses. Many an Italian naval officer enjoyed his 'holiday' on Malta before the war, disguised as an ordinary tourist. Gianaclis had spent a month on the island in the spring of 1938 with his wife Maria and their two young daughters, all expenses courtesy of the Regia Marina.

A command was spoken over *Raimondo's* loudspeakers, and it carried across the intervening quarter mile of water. A moment later the command was repeated aboard the *Muzio* and the cruiser's main armament, her eight 6-inch guns, swung out, the electric motors of her four main turrets humming as they trained the guns out to starboard. Within the ship the hoists below the guns lifted powder charges and shells up to the guns. From the bridge he heard the relayed word from each of the main turrets that all was in readiness to fire. He leaned out and looked aft at the *Raimondo Montecuccoli* and behind her at the battleship *Vittorio Venetto*. Both had their guns trained out as well. He waited expectantly, a thin smile on his face.

*Vittorio Venetto* fired first, her nine 15-inch guns belching out a salvo of half-ton high explosive shells. The report of her great rifles rent the air and rings of smoke as from some monstrous cigar billowed away from the muzzle flashes. Her first targets were inland. The two cruisers followed suit, their combined sixteen guns hurling 6-inch projectiles against targets on or near the shoreline. Gianaclis lifted his binoculars to observe the fall of shot. He frowned. The first salvo from the cruisers was short, landing offshore in the surf. Before the shells even landed the guns were being reloaded and readied to fire again.

*Muzio's* second salvo pounded down on target, obliterating the observation post on Qawra Point and chewing the trench lines and barbed wire entanglements there to pulp. Two more salvoes finished the job at Qawra, knocking out concrete pillboxes and machine gun nests before *Muzio's* gunnery officer shifted target, raining steel and high explosive down on a shore battery guarding the entrance to St. Paul's Bay, then on to an army barracks and training area down the neck of the peninsula.

Meanwhile, the heavier guns of the battleship probed inland, hammering at the stone breastworks of the Victoria Lines, the string of defense works from the prior century that stretched east to west across the island south of St. Paul's bay and north of Mosta. Four feet thick and loop-holed to permit riflemen to fire down upon invading troops, the stone breastworks plugged gaps in the rocky ridgeline that ran across the island. But they'd been designed in an era when the very thought of naval artillery reaching miles inland didn't occur to its engineers. 15-inch shells hammered holes in the breastworks like they were made of cardboard.

For over an hour the three ships prowled up and down off the northeast coast of Malta, always remaining outside the range of the shore batteries on the island. For their part the Royal Malta Artillery Regiment gunners held their fire, refusing to be provoked into any futile demonstrations. They hunkered down in their underground shelters, protected by meters of limestone and concrete and they bided their time, praying against a direct hit and hoping they'd emerge to find their guns intact when the barrage lifted.

One of the last targets attacked was the tank park outside Naxxar north of Mosta. *Vittorio Venetto* fired her final four salvoes there then the three ships paused their bombardment and allowed the south wind to sweep the dust and smoke from the air over the island while the gun crews rested and cleaned the guns.

>>>>>>>>>>>>

At Luqa Kuno knelt in a bomb crater and gingerly lifted his binoculars to his eyes. He found he could only grip them without pain using thumb and forefinger of his right hand. He surveyed Luqa airfield from the north end of the field in the elbow of the main north-south and east-west runways. Smoke drifted over the field from a dozen fires, obscuring his view. Behind him stood the remnants of the airfield's hangars and control tower, reduced to little more than piles of rubble atop cracked and broken foundations. In between pockets of smoke he could see German and Italian paratroopers moving cautiously about in small groups, scouting bunkers or sections of trench. Bursts of automatic weapons fire rang out at frequent intervals and from the west side of the field came a steady crackle of rifle fire as a large but disorganized force of British troops continued resistance.

At the south end of the field fighting continued also as the British fell back towards Hal Far, the Royal Navy Air Station on the island's south coast, now less than five kilometers away. Resistance was centered on a series of limestone bluffs and quarries at the south end of Luqa field. With difficulty he focused the binoculars on the bluffs, wincing in pain as he forced his middle finger to adjust the focus. The bluffs stood out very plainly, the white limestone of the cliffs in sharp contrast to the browns and grays of the hills and the deep blue of the morning sky. He scanned from east to west across the bluffs, noting the many natural defensive positions they afforded the British. He stopped at a spot at the far right of the bluffs where the cliffs receded in shadow, even with the morning sun shining directly upon them from the east. His eyes slowly adjusted to the darker area and he discerned the outline of a cave or tunnel opening with a large steel or wooden door closed at the entrance.

He paused and let the glasses hang around his neck. He glanced behind him. German and Italian troops continued to pour onto the field from the north following the success of the Axis early morning attack against Luqa. Stiffened on their right flank by Italian paratroopers of the Folgore and Superba airborne divisions the German 23rd and 6th airborne regiments launched their attack before midnight, at the height of the full moon. The attack was preceded with concentrated bombing by Stuka Ju 87 dive-bombers. The Stukas stooped upon the forward British positions like owls upon mice, hammering the rock walls, trenches and bunkers of the British and breaching their defensive lines. The Stukas suffered heavily from flak fire, losing six of their own with damage to twice as many more, but the Axis paratroopers flowed through the breaches and flanked the surviving British from their positions, forcing them into the open where they were cut down in droves by heavy machine gun fire.

At dawn the Germans were on the northern fringes of Luqa when the British counterattacked. An odd mix of over a dozen British aircraft appeared from the south, obviously from Hal Far airfield and managed to make several passes over the German and Italian lines, strafing and dropping light bombs. Over a hundred Axis casualties were suffered as result of the air attack, but it lasted only a few minutes as Luftwaffe fighter pilots, surprised at first, recovered their wits and drove off the British attack in an air battle fought in the eerie first light cast by the rising sun. Several RAF or RN planes were seen to crash in the vicinity of the airfield, shot down by the Messerschmitts. A disorganized counterattack by British infantry was beaten back as well.

Kuno quickly reorganized his force and resumed the attack, driving the British over the east-west runway at the north end of the airbase. The crews of several British flak guns on the field depressed their weapons to fire flat across the exposed runway and temporarily stalled the attack again, but small groups of Germans flanked the guns and routed their crews making the runway safe to cross. As he renewed the attack shortly after sunrise the sound of heavy guns and explosions came from the north, but a call from Colonel August assured Kuno that the fire came from Italian Navy ships offshore, preparing for phase two of the invasion plan, the amphibious landings on the island's north coast.

Boots crunched on gravel behind him and Kuno turned around as Captain Thaler jumped down into the crater to join him. Thaler stepped carefully around a pair of British bodies near the rim and crouched down beside Kuno.

"The field is almost cleared," the Captain reported, "but it can't be called secure until we've routed the Tommies out of the rocky ground to the west and south."

"Agreed," said Kuno, "but I won't order that until I have secure communications with the Air Force. Air support is crucial for digging out entrenched infantry."

"It would take hours and many casualties to go through there stone by stone," Thaler agreed. "But there is no more cable to extend the field phone lines. It may be hours before we are in contact with HQ. Right now I have runners going back and forth from here to the end of the line at last night's HQ."

Kuno chewed his lower lip.

"Tondok!" he shouted.

"Here Major!" the Sergeant shouted, materializing at the crater rim as if by magic.

Kuno chuckled. "What took you so long Sergeant?"

Tondok merely smiled.

"Draft a team of men, Germans, NOT Italians," he stressed. "Go through the British bunkers and trenches. See if you can scavenge any useable cable for the field phones. We MUST get back in direct contact with Colonel August at HQ."

"Immediately, Major," Tondok snapped and jumped to his feet to carry out his orders.

Kuno turned his attention back to the field to the south. He gestured towards the limestone bluffs he'd been studying before Thaler joined him.

"You see those cliffs, Thaler?" he asked.

"Yes, Major."

"Use your field glasses. Find the area hidden in shadow. Do you see it?"

It took Thaler a moment, but he found the spot. "I see it Major."

"You see the door set into the recess in the cliff face?"

"Yes, Sir. Four meters high and just about as broad. Seems to be made of steel."

"That will be the airfield munitions depot entrance. There will be caverns delved into the solid rock behind it. Probably also a rear entrance, perhaps on the other side of the hill. We need to seal this entrance to prevent the Englanders from using it to attack our flank as we move south. You understand?"

Thaler nodded and said, "Yes, Sir."

"Good," Kuno answered, "but we must be careful. If we get a lot of troops too close to the cavern the Tommies will choose that moment to destroy the ammunition supply."

"Yes, Sir," said the Captain.

"Thaler, give the job to the Italians."

By first light of June 27th Force H had progressed eastward to a point one hundred-eighty miles northeast of Algiers, about fifty miles from where *Eagle* had been sunk two days prior. At 0530 hours they were joined by a fresh Sunderland flying boat from Gibraltar.

Bryan and Billy and the other pilots slept soundly through the night just passed, all things considered. They thought they were a day away yet from the prospect of flying from the carrier to their uncertain fates. The pilots weren't in the know, but Commander Nesbith was aware that the British were improvising. The plan originally worked out in London on the night of the 22nd was based on the German invasion of Malta coming on the 28th, or at least no earlier than the 27th. It called for *HMS Eagle* to make a quick delivery of eighteen fighters to Malta on the 25th, then to turn back to the west just far enough that the balance of her own aircraft could fly out to her the afternoon of the 26th. *Furious* and *Renown* would join her during the night along with the cruisers and destroyers and the whole force would sail for Malta, *Furious* delivering another thirty-six Spitfires to Malta and *Eagle* providing air cover for the fleet. Depending on circumstances *Renown* and the cruisers might attempt to fight their way through to Malta, demonstrate to the west of Sardinia as a distraction to the Italian fleet or turn back to Gibraltar.

Under no circumstances did the British contemplate *Renown* venturing within range of German and Italian land based bombers without benefit of British air cover. The Royal Navy had learned a costly lesson in January 1941 when Force Z, the battleship *HMS Prince of Wales* and *Renown's* sister ship *HMS Repulse* were caught and sunk by Japanese land based bombers off the Malay

Peninsula. From that time forward the British were careful not to expose their capital ships to unopposed land based air attack.

Now the loss of *Eagle* and the German landings on Malta earlier than expected forced Burrough to change this already hastily made plan. *Furious* would not proceed as far east as originally planned before launching the Spitfires. She would wait until either radar contact with enemy aircraft was made or to 6 degrees, 30 minutes east longitude, well within range of enemy aircraft based on Sardinia, whichever came first. Meanwhile, the battlecruiser, cruisers and the tribal class destroyers with them would sail eastward to a point south of Sardinia's Capo Spartivento, at 8° east longitude. There they were to expect a signal from the Admiralty ordering them either to turn back or proceed to Malta.

Bryan and Billy ate breakfast in the pilot's mess shortly after dawn. They ate reconstituted eggs with bacon, toast and coffee; a very American style breakfast. Their conversation turned to the same old topic; when would Bryan tell Commander Nesbith of his marriage to his sweetheart, Gwen? They spoke in intense undertones to avoid being overheard in the crowded mess.

"Billy, I just haven't the nerve," said Bryan. "He has so much on his plate right now, I can't add to it."

"You may never have another chance to set it right, Bryan," Billy argued. "You wouldn't want Gwen widowed without even a service pension would you?"

"Damn you and your optimism," Bryan growled in return. "I'm getting sick and tired of you putting me in an early grave!"

"Not just you, Bryan," hissed Billy. "All of us, you sodding idiot! Lots of pilots go to Malta. None come back!"

"Bollocks!" Bryan hissed softly.

"Name one!" insisted Billy.

Bryan's only answer was silence.

"Exactly," Billy said softly. Then, "Ah look, Bryan, I'm not saying you haven't a chance. Any of us could make it. Christ!" He snorted a short laugh, "maybe you'll come home wounded."

Bryan's face twisted in a sardonic smile. "That's better, Billy. Look on the bright side."

"Come on," said Billy. "Let's get down to the wardroom. Maybe the Germans have taken Malta and the whole show is cancelled." The two pilots carried their trays away and were leaving the mess when the Tannoy speaker system came to life.

"Do ya hear there, do ya hear there?"

Bryan and Billy paused for the announcement.

"R. A. F. pilots to the wardroom immediately, R. A. F. pilots report to the wardroom."

"Come on, Billy!" exclaimed Bryan. "Let's go!"

The two friends broke into a run, dashing through passageways and up ladders to the wardroom. Most of the pilots were already there, laughing and joking with one another, a little too loud, Bryan thought to cover their nervousness. Commander Nesbith was just bounding up on the dais as they entered the room.

"All right, settle down, please," Nesbith shouted. "Settle down." The pilots came quickly to order.

"Right then," began Nesbith. "We have news from Malta. The Germans have begun their assault on Luqa airfield."

The pilots broke their silence with a collective groan at this news. Nesbith let them chatter on for a moment then called them back to order.

"The good news," he went on, "is that Hal Far Airfield remains in our hands, and it's more urgent than ever that we get our Spitfires to the island and start knocking down the transports and German bombers that are making it so rough for our lads. Therefore, we'll be flying off for Malta sometime this morning rather than wait for tomorrow." Again the pilots broke into excited conversation.

"This morning, Billy!" Bryan said, his eyes alight with excitement.

"Yes," replied Billy. "This morning." He looked at Bryan with such sadness that Bryan was taken aback.

"Billy," he said, "this is what we've trained for, waited for. You don't have cold feet now?"

Billy smiled. "No, of course not," he said. "But you're out of time Bryan. You're right of course. You can't hit Nesbith with your news now. It'll have to wait till we get to Malta and things, er, things settle down a little."

Nesbith again called the room to order.

"We've a lot to cover so get out your pads and make notes. We'll start with your flight path, then cover wireless frequencies and procedures."

Lt. Arturo Toscano scanned the sea and sighed. His Savoia Marchetti S.79 Sparviero or "Sparrowhawk" was performing flawlessly, the tri-motor bomber's engines all purring along like the motor of the sports car Arturo drove before the war. The Toscano family was old aristocracy and through family connections arranged for Arturo's appointment to the Regia Aeronautica, the Italian Air Force. Unlike so many such cases of nepotism throughout the Italian Armed Forces in Arturo's case this resulted in a competent young man being placed in a position of responsibility. Toscano became a skilled pilot, finding flying to be an even greater thrill than the auto racing he had so loved before the war and unlike so many Italian aristocrats he was able to form a bond with the common men under his command. They respected and liked him.

The Savoia was a bomber, but the morning of June 27th Toscano was ordered to fly it southwest from Decimomanu airfield on Sardinia on a maritime search mission. He was told to look for a task force of British warships, to report their position by wireless and to shadow them to the limits of his fuel if he found them.

He'd been airborne for almost three hours and was sipping ersatz coffee from a flask as he approached 7 degrees, east longitude, thirty-five miles from the North African coast and at 2,500 meters altitude. A heavy haze lay over the sea, limiting visibility to between five to eight miles. A twenty-five knot south wind was whipping the sea's surface into sets of rollers with tops blown off as white spray. He was screwing the top back on his flask when his co-pilot started upright in his seat.

"Arturo!" he exclaimed.

Toscano sat up and looked out the cockpit windscreen. The Sparrowhawk had an elongated nose and the number one engine's propellers spun directly in front of the pilot. It was a less than ideal patrol aircraft, but was pressed into service for the Malta invasion. For a moment he saw nothing but the spinning propeller and the haze covered sea. Then, squinting he saw the first wake. Within a minute one wake had turned into over a dozen, with eight large ships in two columns at the center of the formation.

His signal reporting the ships was received at Decimomanu and was passed to the Italian High Command, the Commando Supremo in Rome.

Lt. Erik West, officer of the watch aboard *HMS Sikh* stepped to the voice pipe.

"Radar, bridge."

"Bridge, radar. We've got an aircraft bearing zero-four-five, range nineteen miles, estimated course two-two-five. He's headed straight for us, Sir."

"Radar, bridge, aye. Keep the bearings and ranges coming."

Lt. West stepped out on the starboard wing of the bridge, checking his watch as he went. 0944.

"Make a signal to the Flagship," he said to the signalman there. "One aircraft detected, range nineteen miles, bearing zero-four-five, course two-two-five."

West returned to the bridge. He turned to the quartermaster of the watch.

"Summon the Captain, please."

Admiral Burrough was sipping tea in the flag plot of *HMS Renown* when his Flag Secretary delivered *Sikh's* signal to him.

"Has *Furious* received this message?" he asked.

"Yes, Sir," answered the officer.

"Signal *Furious* to begin launching the Spitfires immediately," the Admiral ordered. "We're out of time."

The Spitfires were arranged in twelve rows of three planes each on the flight deck of the carrier, the middle plane in each row spotted slightly forward of the other two so that its wings overlapped theirs. The aircraft in the final row had their tail wheels within inches of the flight deck's aft edge. This arrangement packed the planes into the least possible space on the rear half of the flight deck.

Nonetheless, twelve rows of Spitfires took up over 250 feet of the 560 feet long flight deck, leaving a mere 310 feet for the first three Spitfires to get airborne. The available flight deck would lengthen by about twenty feet as each row of three planes left the deck, until the last three Spitfires had the full 560 feet.

Nesbith chose the most experienced pilots for the first rows, working back to the least experienced pilots in the last. Bryan and

Billy found themselves in the middle of the pack, in row seven. Bryan was in the starboard plane, Billy in the middle aircraft, the leader of his three-plane flight. Commander Nesbith would be first off the flight deck of *Furious*.

At 1010 hours the pilots ran up the ladders from the wardroom to the flight deck and raced to their planes, Nesbith in the lead. The pilots' feet pounded across the flight deck as Captain Bulteel turned the carrier into the wind. Four of the destroyers followed to provide her escort, but the oiler, *Renown* and the cruisers maintained course and speed, steadily plowing on to the east. The carrier was to catch them up with her superior speed after launching the Spitfires. The pilots could smell land in the sand and grit borne up from the south on the hot *Sirocco* wind. *Furious* swung through her turn until the smoke from smudge pots at the for'ard edge of the deck was blowing straight down the flight line. The bows plunged up and down with ten-foot swells. The ship went to maximum speed into the wind, effectively generating a fifty-five knot wind down the deck to assist in lifting the Spitfires into the air.

The ship's flying crew was already on deck, stripping off the tarpaulins covering the engine cowlings of the fighters and manhandling Commander Nesbith's Spitfire into position for takeoff on the centerline of the flight deck. Deck crewmen were hand rotating its propeller to build compression in the engine.

Nesbith ran around the starboard side of his plane and leapt up onto the wing. He turned briefly and watched the other flyers run past. A few of them stopped briefly, looking up at him standing on the wing. He threw them a quick salute before he climbed into his cockpit and allowed the deck crew to snap him into his parachute harness. He ran through his pre-flight routine, checking the ailerons, flaps and tail planes. The deck crewmen were nearly finished with the propeller when the compression build-up caused a backfire. The propeller snapped back on the man pushing the blade, striking him in the chest and throwing him back from the plane. Blood sprayed into the air and was blown back against Nesbith's cockpit canopy by the wind.

Bryan watched, appalled as other crewmen ran to the aid of the injured man. They hauled him off the deck without any hesitation. A moment later the signal was given and Nesbith started his engine. It coughed a cloud of gray-black smoke as it caught. Nesbith ran his engine up to full speed, standing on the ship's brakes to hold her on the deck till he was ready to take-off. Bryan's breakfast sat like a brick in his stomach. He wished for time to visit the head, but there was no time. He started to sweat in his bulky flight suit, but knew that soon, as he climbed to altitude the sweltering heat of the day would give way to frigid cold.

Commander Nesbith released the brakes and his Spitfire jumped like a steed finally given its head, gathering momentum as it sped down the shortened flight deck. Bryan's heart fell to his stomach as Nesbith approached the for'ard edge of the deck and the ship's bow plunged into an especially steep trough. A little cry escaped Bryan's lips. Nesbith had mis-timed his take-off! He would reach the end of the flight deck while the bow stood down in the trough of the wave. He'd be flung off the deck and into the face of the next wave! Bryan felt his knees weaken with fear for Nesbith.

But *Furious'* bows reared into the air as she climbed the wall of the next wave. Nesbith fired from the deck on the upswing, timing his take-off perfectly. With the added lift he struggled into the air, holding his fighter just above the wave tops as he built his speed until at last he roared into the sky.

Bryan felt his stomach heave. He turned from the scene and dropped to his knees on the deck as the next Spitfire was rolled into position for take-off. His breakfast came up in a rush, flying across the deck in the wind, splattering reconstituted eggs and half digested bacon in a nauseating smear to the tail wheel of his plane. He heaved again and again until his stomach was emptied. He sat back on his haunches; his eyes welled up with tears for a moment until he regained his equilibrium. A pair of boots swam into sight as his vision cleared.

"Come along, Sir," a voice from above the boots shouted over the wind.

He looked up at the owner of the boots.

"Come along now, Sir," the deck crewman repeated, shouting to be heard over the roar of fighter engines. "You're not the first RAF pilot to lose his tummy before his first flight from an aircraft carrier. You'll be all right once we get you on your feet."

The crewman reached down and helped Bryan back up. Bryan

turned back to watch the next aircraft take-off and was surprised to see the first three planes were all in the air already, the last of them clearing the wave tops and winging its way into the sky.

"Get on with you now, Sir," said the crewman. "Your turn will come up quickly."

Bryan nodded his head and mumbled a thank-you, but the words were snatched away in the wind. He wiped his mouth on his sleeve and took a deep breath, closing his eyes and gathering his nerve. A Spitfire engine roared to a crescendo before receding down the flight deck to take-off.

He turned and looked behind him on the deck. Billy was standing on the wing of his own plane, about to climb into the cockpit, but he'd stopped and was staring at Bryan.

Bryan smiled at him and waved weakly. Billy gave him a worried, questioning look and started to climb down from his wing, but Bryan held his hand up to stop him. Billy paused and Bryan gave him a thumbs-up signal.

"I'm O-K," he mouthed to Billy. Another thunderous roar as another Spitfire rolled down the deck.

Bryan turned and climbed onto the wing of his plane, the acid taste of vomit in his mouth. He stepped up and threw his leg over the edge of the cockpit, climbing into the seat, closing his eyes and allowing the deck crewmen to snap him into his harness. He took deep, regular breaths to steady his nerves.

Another roar, another Spitfire launched into the air. Bryan opened his eyes and looked out over the port side of the cockpit, craning his neck to see beyond the nose of his plane. One more row to launch then he and Billy would be up. His stomach started to tighten again.

"Here you are, Sir!" Bryan looked back to his right. The same crewman that had helped him to his feet was on the starboard wing holding a clear glass bottle filled with water. He held it out to Bryan. The lead plane in the last row ahead of Bryan's sped down the flight deck and into the air.

"Rinse your mouth out and spit it over the side!" the crewman shouted over the wind and the roar of Spitfire engines. Bryan took the bottle and did as he was told. The wind carried the spit back over the tail of his plane. He started to hand the bottle back, but the man held up his hand.

"Keep it!" he yelled. "Now get ready! We need to start your engine now. As soon as your leader moves up into take-off we'll be pushing you to the center! The plane to port will go first, then you. Do you understand?"

Bryan nodded and pulled his goggles down over his eyes.

The crewman on the wing used hand signals to clear the other men from around the propeller.

"Go!" shouted the crewman.

Bryan depressed the starter button. The engine coughed and spluttered, ejecting a black cloud then catching and settling down to a steady purr. Bryan brought the engine up to speed quickly, but smoothly. The engine temperature rose quickly into normal flight range. It took only moments in the Mediterranean heat for the engine to warm up for take-off.

He looked over the side of the cockpit again. Billy's Spitfire was taxiing forward a few feet to clear the wingtips of the other two Spitfires in the row. He thundered down the deck and into the air, catching the rise of the bow perfectly, though at that point with five rows of fighters airborne there was more than one hundred more feet to take-off in than Nesbith and the others in the first row had. The other pilot in the trio followed quickly behind Billy.

"Now your turn, Sir!" shouted the crewman. "Watch your hands!"

The crewman slid the canopy forward and Bryan locked it in place. The man smacked the canopy with the flat of his palm, waved to Bryan and leapt off the wing. Bryan's mouth was dry as ashes, but he pushed the throttles forward as he stood the Spitfire on its brake.

RPMs came to full power. He checked his flaps and other control surfaces and found them all moving freely. He looked out on the flight deck. The deck crew signalman was frantically waving his flag, ordering him to take-off. He swallowed hard and realized he was delaying the launching operations. He eased off the brake and was thrust back in his seat as the Spitfire surged down the deck.

Too late he realized he had not timed his start to catch the bows of the ship on the upswing! Briefly he considered aborting the take-off, but it was already too late to stop before he reached the end of the deck. He rammed the throttles forward to the stops and gripped the stick with both hands. The bows plunged sickeningly as he came to the end of the deck. Straight ahead he was looking down into a wall of sea green water, rising from the ocean to swallow him and his fighter. He hauled back frantically on the stick at the very end of the flight deck and punched the button to retract his landing gear. His fighter and the white-capped wave raced towards each other, the wave seeming to tower above him. He wasn't going to clear!

Bryan screamed and closed his eyes. The propeller blades of his Spitfire spun through the top of the wave, hurling water back against the canopy. The stick was nearly torn from his hands. The undercarriage on the nose of the fuselage dug through the wave top and seemed to observers aboard *Furious* to fairly skip from the water into the sky. Bryan opened his eyes. But the water thrown back against the engine cowling snuffed the air intakes for a brief second. The engine lost power and the Spitfire nosed over before the engine caught again and surged back to full speed. He was clear of the wave and climbing. But another wave was on top of him in a flash. He hauled the stick back into his stomach, urging the fighter into the air by sheer will power. He was going to clear!

But he didn't. The propellers caught the wave top again and this time the stress was too much. One of the blades sheered off. The suddenly unbalanced propeller hub gyrated and wrenched at the engine and its mountings. Thrust fell off and the Spitfire nosed over again and this time did not recover. The plane plowed into the ocean two hundred yards ahead of the carrier. Within seconds the massive forefoot of *Furious'* bows reached the sight of the crash, trampling Bryan and his plane beneath it.

Billy Wilson orbited to port of the carrier, as the number two man of his flight got airborne. He watched as Bryan's Spitfire sat on the deck longer than it should to get airborne. He looked at his instrument gauges and quickly verified his plane was performing flawlessly then looked back to watch Bryan's take-off.

"NO!" he shouted. Bryan had mis-timed his take-off. It would probably not have mattered if Bryan was launching from the last row, near the fantail. With the full 560 feet of deck to gather speed he would have had enough lift to clear the first wave and live to laugh about his mistake.

Billy watched in horror as Bryan died. He knew it was hopeless, but he lingered for a moment, waiting until the carrier cleared the spot of the crash. He scanned the waters in the wake of the ship, praying for some sight of Bryan, but aside from some floating bits and pieces torn from the Spitfire there was nothing.

The next Spitfire on deck raced into the air and Billy knew he had to go. There was still another pilot to lead to Malta.

"Good-bye, Bryan," he said softly, tears trickling down his cheeks. "I'll see Gwen for you chum. If I can."

Arturo Toscano reported the launching of what he assumed to be a flight of Spitfire fighter aircraft, over thirty of them and most likely destined for Malta. He provided course and speed and stayed well clear of them. He knew they had a more important mission than chasing him; still it wouldn't pay to tempt them by getting in their way.

In a second signal sent moments later Arturo remembered to report that the carrier had separated from the main force and was escorted by four destroyers. He provided course and speed for both groups of ships.

The launching of the Spitfires from *Furious* took thirty minutes, during which time the carrier steamed south into the wind at thirty knots. This took her within thirty miles of the North African coast, just north and east of the Gulf of Bejaia, midway between Algiers and the Tunisian border. Meanwhile *Renown*, the cruisers and their escorts continued on their easterly course at the oiler *Evening Dale's* top speed of 19 knots. When the carrier was finished launching the Spitfires she turned northeast at her top speed planning to overtake the main force within an hour.

The uncoded signals sent by Lt. Toscano aboard the Italian patrol bomber were received by the Regia Aeronautica at Decimomanu, but were also read by the Luftwaffe command there. The Luftwaffe in turn forwarded the details of the messages to the headquarters of Field Marshall Albert Kesselring in Rome. Kesselring was the senior German commander in the Mediterranean theater and he exercised a cross-service command unique to that point in the German war effort. No other senior German commander had exercised complete operational command of air, ground and naval forces. Kesselring forwarded the sighting report to both Italian and German naval HQ's at Naples. They in turn broadcast the reports to Axis naval forces at sea. The German and Italian Motor Torpedo Boat Flotillas on the island of Pantelleria in the Strait of Sicily were among those that received these signals.

Most Axis submarines west of 6 degrees east longitude remained submerged during daylight hours, fearing air attack from prowling British long-range patrol bombers, but within range of Axis air support from Sardinia and Sicily the subs sometimes surfaced for short periods during the day to recharge batteries and freshen air in the boat.

The Italian submarine *Perla,* commanded by Lt. Renaldo Cosani picked up the message from Naples at 1205 hours. Cosani and his Executive Officer, Luigi Mortobello plotted the reported course of the British fleet on the tiny chart table in the *Perla's* control room.

"What do you think, Luigi?" asked Cosani.

"They're headed for the Skerki Bank, Captain," replied Mortobello, putting his finger on the chart on the shallow water northeast of Bizerte, Tunisia. The Skerki Bank is a rise in the sea floor that extends sixty miles into the Mediterranean from the North African coast between ten and eleven degrees east longitude. There are many shallow points and uncharted rocks making the area hazardous for any deep draft vessel.

"I agree," said Cosani. "The battleship and the carrier will have to pass around it to the north to transit the Sicilian Narrows."

"You believe they are destined for Malta then?" asked Mortobello.

"Yes," answered the Captain, "I do."

"Their heavy ships have always turned about at Skerki before," Mortobello prompted.

"With the German invasion of the island the British must try to intervene or concede the whole central sea to us," Cosani answered confidently. "The battleship and escorts will attempt to win through to the island. They will intervene with any amphibious assault our navy mounts or shell the German lodgement on the airfields."

"These heavy ships make the most attractive target," commented the XO with a smile.

Cosani laughed.

"Indeed they do Liugi," he answered. "Indeed they do. Tell me.

Where would you attack them?"

Mortobello put his finger on the map again.

"We are here," he said, tapping a spot northwest of Sicily's Capo San Vito on the island's northwest coast. He traced his finger 120 miles to the southwest of their current position and tapped the map north of the Skerki Bank.

"I would move to here," he said, "and attack them as they try to slip around the Bank at dusk. The setting sun will back light their fleet while we will be in the shadows to the east. They will want to stay as far from the airfields on Sicily as possible, yet they must still give themselves sea room to maneuver at the bank."

"Yes?" said the Captain. "And what would be your plan?"

"I'd be to the northwest of the bank about ten miles," the XO answered. "Stay on the surface to pick up any additional sighting reports and move on them. Ideally I would attack from the northeast, from the port side of their fleet, on the surface, prepared to dive if detected by the escorts. Anything they do to avoid attack would drive them into the shallows."

"We should expect others to have come to the same conclusions you know," said Lt. Cosani. "Those waters could be thick with submarines; ours and the Germans, not to mention the patrol boats out of Pantelleria."

"Potentially, we could benefit from some confusion in the British force," Mortobello affirmed.

"Set course, Luigi," ordered Cosani. "I want to take up station well ahead of any aerial patrols the British may make."

*Furious* and her destroyer escorts changed course to the northeast as soon as the last of the Spitfires was airborne, the carrier maintaining her top speed to rejoin Force H. The flight operations crew also maintained their pace. They rushed to bring Swordfish bi-planes and Fairey Fulmar fighters from the hangar deck to the flight deck. With wings folded the planes rose one at a time on the ship's two mechanical lifts. The flying crew worked to unfold and lock the wings into position. The aircraft were already armed and fueled below deck. The Fairey Swordfish bombers carried 500-pound depth charges. As a precaution the fuses were not set until the planes were on the flight deck.

Through all this activity aboard the carrier her faithful shepherds, the escort destroyers, raced along at her side, laboring to keep up. At their top speed, the destroyers gulped fuel from their tiny bunkers, cutting down on their range till next refueling. Worse, the high speed drastically reduced the efficiency of their ASDIC underwater detection apparatus. The water rushing over the dome suspended below the bows of the destroyers created a great deal of noise that masked the subtler sounds made by submarines. Even the active ASDIC that transmitted a pulse of sound, a "ping", through the water and then detected its echo when it bounced off the metal hull of a submarine was rendered nearly useless. Only when directly above a submarine could any of the destroyers detect the undersea menace.

HMS *Wrestler* was an old veteran of the Mediterranean Sea. She'd been with Somerville off Oran when the Royal Navy bombarded the French Fleet at Mers-el-Kebir in 1940 barely escaping destruction when the French battlecruiser *Strasbourg* slipped away from the harbor under cover of the dense clouds of smoke from burning ships and shore installations. The French ship fired over forty heavy caliber rounds at *Wrestler*, the final salvo straddling her, drenching her decks and riddling the hull with shell splinters before the British ship made good her own escape. *Wrestler* had been on the Malta run many times in the two years since and had cheated fate more than once. She'd taken a 500-kilo bomb from a Stuka close aboard her starboard quarter the prior winter and had required two months in dock at Gibraltar to repair the damage. But despite the dangerous waters in which she sailed and the narrow escapes, *Wrestler* was considered a lucky ship, and a happy one. For all her narrow escapes she'd suffered remarkably few casualties. That changed just after 1020 on June 27th 1942.

The Italian submarine *Uarsciek,* sister ship to the *RM Perla,* was patrolling to the northwest of Cap Bougar'oun on the Algerian coast. Little is known of the details of her actions that afternoon as she was certainly sunk by the depth charging delivered by *HMS Westcott, HMS Wanderer* and *HMS Wolsey.*

It can never be known for certain how she found herself in position to strike *Wrestler* with a torpedo. Most likely *Uarsciek* received the signal from Naval HQ in Naples providing the position and course of the British fleet and attempted an attack against the carrier, but range and angle of approach defeated this effort, leaving *Uarsciek* with a shot at the destroyer instead. In any case, with a single torpedo she left *Wrestler* dead in the water, her stern blown off behind her aft 4.7-inch gun and with twenty-eight dead or missing.

In friendlier waters *Wrestler* would probably have been saved, towed into port and rebuilt, but within air range of Sardinia there was no hope for her. After the other British destroyers dropped over thirty depth charges they confirmed the kill on the axis sub. *Wolsey* took off *Wrestler*'s crew and sank her with two torpedoes.

Meanwhile, the first Italian air attack against the fleet came at 1025 hours. Seven Macchi 202 and three Reggiane RE-2002 fighters escorted a strike force of twenty-two high-level bombers, dive-bombers and torpedo-bombers. They were meant to deliver a coordinated attack against the British, but the three flights of bombers became separated during the flight from Decimomanu due to the hazy visibility and they arrived at different times. The high level bombers, seven Caproni CA-135 twin-engine bombers, attacked first, finding *Renown*, the oiler and the cruisers in two columns and surrounded by destroyers on anti-submarine patrol. A blizzard of flak forced the bombers off target and their bombs fell in empty sea. Two of the bombers trailed smoke behind them as they fled back to Sardinia.

Next up were the dive-bombers, six Breda 88s. They came on the scene some eight minutes after the Capronis. Again, the British fleet put up effective flak and drove the Bredas away with no damage done. The three anti-aircraft cruisers, *Sirius, Charybdis* and *Phoebe* were deadly accurate, each claiming an Italian bomber shot down. The three survivors fled the scene of battle like dogs with tails between their legs.

Nine Savoia Marchetti 84 bombers carrying torpedoes came two minutes later. While the British flak guns had to be re-trained to low altitude to counter the wave skipping planes the results were much the same. The Italians launched their torpedoes from too great a distance, scored no hits and lost one of their aircraft. This last air attack did accomplish one thing for the Italians. In avoiding the torpedoes the British formation lost its cohesion and order. As the Italian torpedo bombers fled, Force H was scattered about the sea.

Lt. Commander Roland Webster, Gunnery Officer of the Anti-Aircraft Cruiser *HMS Sirius* was pleased with the ship's performance against the Italian air attack. Webster and his four-man team had been closed up at air-action stations in the Number one Radar Office since dawn. The Number one Radar Office was in the aft superstructure, just forward of 'X' turret and almost immediately beneath the aft gun director housing. The office was a small, rectangular cabin connected directly to the radar receivers spinning atop the foremast above the bridge and the mainmast atop the aft superstructure. A bank of radar display tubes rested on a heavy steel table along one wall. From the radar office the ship's guns could be commanded under radar control. There were four duplicate cabins aboard ship. If the main office were damaged control of the guns could be taken over by any of the other three Radar Offices, manned during action stations with alternate crews.

The Italian attack was detected at a range of 23 miles, leaving plenty of time for *Sirius* to alert the rest of the fleet and to train out all her armament. The attack was poorly coordinated, allowing Webster to concentrate all his guns on each attacking force in turn. *Sirius* and the other ships in the force put up a terrific barrage the Italians showed little willingness to confront.

In the turrets and gun tubs the gun crews were cleaning up their spent shell cases and deriding the competence of the Italians. In the magazines men were shuffling ammunition, moving fragmentation shells into racks closer to the hoists to the guns above. On the bridge Captain Brooking and the helmsman were striving to resume *Sirius'* place in formation. The entire fleet was in disarray as the battlecruiser, five cruisers and the oiler had all been forced to alter course to avoid torpedo tracks. Flags and signals flew from the yardarm of the flagship *Renown* ordering each of the ships to shape course back into formation. After about ten minutes the seven heavy ships were coming back together with *Sirius* leading *Evening Dale* and *Kenya* in the port column and *Phoebe* in front of *Renown*, *Nigeria* and *Charybdis* to starboard. The escort destroyers formed a fluid circle about the heavy ships.

Webster allowed his mind to drift away as the routine of the ship was restored and his well-trained gun crews made everything ready to repel further attacks. Always his mind returned to his wife Althea. The Webster's were Londoners, solid upper-middle class residents of Kensington Gardens adjacent to the Hyde Park district of England's Capitol. Roland was the son of the Director General of a large import-export firm with thousands of employees in the London area, mainly in the docks of the East End. He'd attended the best public schools and it was widely expected he would follow in his father's footsteps in business.

Webster met Althea Spencer at a New Year's Eve celebration December 31, 1937 at the very swank Dorchester Hotel. Her father was one of London's most renowned Doctors and humanitarians and a Dean at the Royal College of Surgeons. A mix-up in the seating arrangements placed the two families together at the same table, though they'd never met. The two mothers got along well enough, though the Doctor and Roland's father had little in common, but Roland, then twenty-four was captivated by Althea's soft brown curls and long fluttering eyelashes over hazel eyes.

"My name is Roland," he introduced himself when the orchestra took a break.

"Hello, Rollie," she smiled, tipping her head to one side in a way that stole his breath. "I'm Althea."

As a boy Roland had fought many times with his schoolmates over being called 'Rollie', often coming to the verge of expulsion over his brawling, but when Althea called him Rollie his pulse quickened and his palms got sweaty. They danced the night away until at midnight, as the Dorchester orchestra played Auld Lang Sine he kissed her, quickly, discretely and without a hint of complaint from her.

Shortly after midnight the Maitre d' Hotel approached the table with a telephone for the Doctor. It was a call from Hospital. There'd been an accident and he was needed to perform emergency surgery. Roland volunteered to drive Doctor Spencer in his automobile, an offer the Doctor gratefully accepted. He also asked if Roland would be so kind as to then deliver Althea and her mother to their home in Marylebone near Marble Arch.

The courtship was short, both families realizing the two were made for each other. Roland proposed to Althea that February over a late dinner at the Savoy Grill. By June of 1938 they were married, taking as their honeymoon a steamship cruise to South Africa, then an overland trip to Rhodesia where they joined a safari. Althea proved as good a shot as Roland, though only on inanimate targets; she always seemed to miss the easiest of shots when the game was afoot.

On return to London they moved into a spacious and elegant flat in the West End. As war clouds gathered over Europe the couple went about their lives together. They gave hardly a thought to what was going on in the outside world. Roland assumed more responsibilities at his father's firm while Althea sought fulfillment in volunteer work.

Webster was a worldly man and he'd known other women, but on their wedding night he found in Althea sexuality he'd never known before. The honeymoon seemed to never end. They made love in the mornings before he left for work and he often found her waiting for him in the evening when he returned. Sometimes by late afternoon he could no longer concentrate on his work. Then he would make excuses to his staff and leave work early to be with her. He knew there was no other woman on the planet for him. For all their lovemaking they looked forward hopefully to Althea becoming pregnant, but each month passed without success. Each month they shrugged and laughed and kept trying.

Then came that awful night in September 1939. They sat holding hands, listening on the wireless to Neville Chamberlain's heartbroken explanation to the British people that they were once again at war.

It came as no surprise when Roland was activated from the London Division of the Royal Navy Volunteer Reserve that yuletide. He left the couple's flat three days before Christmas to report for training to *HMS President* at her permanent mooring at King's Reach London down from Blackfriars Bridge. They'd both cried as he stepped into the taxi and pulled away from the curb.

He specialized in gunnery. The training was accelerated and the debacle in France in the spring of 1940 led to his posting to a naval flak battery near Dover in June where he expected his men and guns to face the German Invasion force everyone knew was building across the channel. Despite the emergency he had frequent leave and he visited Althea in London as often as he could. Every parting was worse than the last.

At first, he feared for her, living in the capital with massive Luftwaffe air raids expected at any time, but through July and August he'd witnessed far more aerial action at Dover than was seen over the Capitol as the RAF and Luftwaffe fought the Battle of Britain over East Anglia, The Downs and the English Channel.

Then as summer turned to autumn the Luftwaffe changed tactics and London became the target of a furious onslaught. At first the bombing was mainly restricted to the East End and the docks where London's poorest bore the brunt of the suffering, but in November bombs fell in the fashionable West End, democratizing 'The Blitz'.

Despite his pleading and the availability of splendid country estates of both families Althea refused to evacuate, insisting on remaining in London. She assisted at her father's hospital for a time, but she found her element as a volunteer in the Housewives Service, a part of the Women's Voluntary Service (WVS). She drove a pumper truck for the Auxiliary Fire Service, one of over 4,000 London women to do so during The First Blitz. She performed innumerable other duties as well, passing out blankets at air raid shelters, fitting gas masks at distribution stations and filing records for the ARP, the Air Raid Precautions organization.

On the night of December 29-30, 1940, a Sunday, she was serving tea and scones to firemen and rescue workers when the most devastating raid to date took place. That night London came very close to catastrophe. Hundreds of small fires merged in two great conflagrations, each over a half-mile on a side that threatened to join in the center of the city and would have done so but for the courage of the cities firemen.

Althea and the other women set up their refreshment operation in front of a poulterers shop in Pimlico. They served hundreds of exhausted firemen and rescue workers and were just preparing to move to a new location when a stick of bombs shattered the block, collapsing the four-story façade into the street.

Roland was left in a hell of suspense and tension for two days as Althea was initially listed as missing. When her body was at last pulled from the rubble and identified by her parents he was granted an emergency leave and raced home for the memorial service.

On return to Dover he filed a request for sea duty, but before it was granted he was posted for an extended training run at the Royal Navy's gunnery school at Whale Island, Portsmouth where Roland excelled at both theoretical and practical courses. He had a single-mindedness to his studies that few of the other students could match. He graduated near the top of his class with an exceptional recommendation from his instructors.

He was first posted to *HMS Druid,* a wood-hulled minesweeper working the cold and dangerous waters of the channel during the bitter spring of 1941.The Luftwaffe delighted in harassing the under-gunned 'sweeps' and he'd seen plenty of action, with *Druid's* pitiful few machine guns claiming several kills.

In January 1942 *Druid* was sent to dry-dock for a refit and Roland was reassigned to *Sirius,* then nearing completion at the Portsmouth Yard, seeing her through her fitting out and sea trials. But through all the months at sea or ashore his yearning for Althea haunted his waking moments. Only action and endless hours of hard exercises and gunnery drills gave him any peace from his remorse. Consequently his gun crews were among the most highly trained in the Royal Navy.

"Sir! Radar contact, bearing zero-four-two, range sixteen miles," his senior rating, amn named Jones reported, snapping Webster from his reverie. Jones' flat, sullen features belied a quick and lively mind, and he'd become one of Webster's most trusted operators on the radar apparatus. Webster spun around from the porthole. He'd been watching the ships come back into formation, and trying to get a breath of fresh air at the same time.

"Sixteen miles!" he exploded. "How did they get so close before we detected them?"

"They're at low altitude, Sir," Jones replied, his eyes glued to his screen. "They're climbing now to gain altitude for the attack."

Webster snatched up his headset and put it over his ears. There was already conversation on the tactical circuit. "Bridge, Radar plot," he heard. "Air contact, bearing zero-four-two, range sixteen miles." Webster grunted in satisfaction that the enemy formation was detected just as quickly in the alternate radar office. His crew was indeed well trained.

"Radar plot, bridge. Confirm contact."

"In-bound aircraft, bearing zero-four-two, range down to fourteen miles," the first voice said. Webster recognized it as belonging to Lt. Kerry, in charge in the alternate radar plot. "They're coming in low, bridge, we only just detected them," Kerry finished somewhat lamely.

The reply was a laconic, "Acknowledged."

Webster threw the switch to communicate with his guns.

"All batteries, enemy air-attack approaching from the northeast.

Main batteries, load with H.E., prepare for independent firing."

Jones spoke again. "Range nine miles, bearing still zero-four-two, target is splitting into two groups, designate upper group as 'D' for Dog, lower group as 'E' for Echo."

Jones was one of two radar operators in the office, seated at a low table in front of the display screens, headset clamped to his ears, telephone voice tube hung on cords about his neck. The two radar receivers each fed their signal to two display screens in each of the four radar offices to assure a failure in one screen wouldn't blind the ship at a critical moment. A young, but talented rating named Meese manned the other console.

"Target Dog altitude 6,000 feet," Jones sang out. "Range five miles, bearing shifting to zero-nine-zero. They're going to come from dead ahead. Target Echo altitude 2,000 feet, range four miles, bearing changing to zero-zero-zero. They're coming in on the beam. They're splitting up, different altitudes and angle of attack."

"Bloody Germans," said Webster. He and his crew recognized the characteristic discipline and coordination of a German air attack. They'd seen enough of them in the four months since joining the Mediterranean fleet. *HMS Sirius* was a new ship, having been completed and entered service just that year, but Mediterranean service was very busy and she'd seen action many times already. Now they waited as the two groups of attacking aircraft approached from different altitudes and direction in order to split the defensive fire of the British ships.

A lookout's observation came over the ship's circuit. "Destroyers making smoke."

In the engine rooms of the fleet's destroyers, stokers dampened the flow of air to the boilers and added small amounts of cold, un-atomized oil to the fuel flow. Dense clouds of black smoke billowed from the destroyers' funnels, spreading over the sea, in theory masking the ships from view from the sky. The sound of 4.7-inch guns popping a mile to port came to Webster's ears through the open portal. He reached over and swung it shut, securing it with the latch.

"A, B and Q turrets, engage target Dog," Webster ordered. "X and Y engage target Echo. Main batteries under radar direction."

The ship's three forward turrets were 'A', 'B' and 'Q'. 'A' turret was foremost, closest to the bow, 'B' turret behind 'A' and

'Q' turret just forward of the bridge. 'X' and 'Y' turrets were mounted on the cruiser's stern. By Royal Navy tradition one turret was manned by Royal Marines. Aboard *Sirius* they manned 'X' turret. The guns in the forward turrets elevated to 65 degrees while the after turrets trained out to point abeam of the ship at 30 degrees elevation. Webster watched the blips on the radar screens crawl closer to the center, closer to the ship.

"FIRE!" he shouted.

The crash of *Sirius'* ten-gun main battery rocked the ship. The Radar Office trembled at the shock transmitted through the ship's superstructure. In the turrets the crews worked to quickly reload the rapid-fire guns as the shell hoists hummed up from the magazines deep inside the armored hull of the ship. The guns crashed again and again, up to six times a minute.

"They're concentrating on *Renown!*" shouted Jones. "Target Dog is passing over us now at 6,000 feet. Target Echo is losing altitude. Those will be torpedo bombers! They're dropping down for their attack."

"Secondary batteries, FIRE!" shouted Webster. The sharp popping and cracking of the smaller flak guns contributed to the din as the 20mm and 40mm guns opened up. He jumped to the rear of the office and looked out the observation slit at *Renown* a half mile behind and the cruiser *Kenya* another half mile back. Every gun was blazing, even the 15-inch rifles of the battlecruiser's main armament. These were directed against the torpedo bombers approaching from the north and were used to throw waterspouts up in the path of the wave-hopping aircraft. Through the smoke and haze he watched as *Renown* took a sharp turn to starboard. The ponderous bulk of the ship heeled over as her angle through the water slowly changed. Within seconds a pair of heavy bombs flashed through his view and splashed into the water two cables to port of *Renown*.

"Good-O!" shouted Webster.

The crash of guns reached a new ear-splitting crescendo. Webster strained to see through the rear observation slit. The sea was covered in the smoke screen laid down by the destroyer escorts in an effort to hide the fleet from the Luftwaffe bombers, but it also prevented the ship's gunners from visually targeting the attacking aircraft. All fire was radar directed now.

Webster turned back to the radar screens. The 360° sweep of the radar antenna was shown on the round screens as a green line radiating from the center and sweeping clockwise around the screen face. The tiny pinpoints that denoted individual aircraft were multiplying to the north in the direction from which the wave hopping torpedo bombers were approaching. As he watched several of the foremost pinpoints disappeared as they closed towards the center. These were aircraft dropping into the sea, hit by the wall of flak thrown up by the fleet.

Suddenly *Sirius* heeled to port as Captain Brooking ordered violent evasive action. Webster steadied himself on the back of Jones' chair. He looked at Jones' screen. Two pinpoints had worked themselves inside the range where the 5.25-inch guns lost effectiveness, the shells no longer having enough time to arm themselves before passing the target by. Both targets were to port and aft of *Sirius*. Jones threw a switch, shifting the fire of the after 40mm and 20mm guns against these two targets, but Webster knew it was too late to prevent them from dropping their torpedoes. Both targets were within 1,000 yards of their intended victims, the battlecruiser and cruiser behind *Sirius* in column.

Webster jumped back to the aft observation slit. Smoke from the guns and the destroyer screen lay thick over the water, born in great gusts across the stern of *Sirius,* obscuring his view of the ships behind them. He squinted in the gray murk, trying desperately to discern what was happening. Then, out of the smoke and haze he glimpsed *Renown,* turned hard a-port, swinging her great bows ponderously round in evasive action.

The 15-inch rifles in the battlecruiser's main turrets were silent now with the enemy torpedo bombers too close to target with the main guns. Her secondary armament crackled all up and down what he could see through the smoke screen of her port side, red hot tracer lashing the sky in streams of lead, hung like strings of Christmas lights across the water. In the distance the shells threw up spouts of water as they struck the sea. Even in broad daylight the gunfire put up by the battlecruiser was dazzling.

*Renown* continued to swing to port, her bows turning so slowly, overcoming the momentum that carried her forward, dragging her round to port. To Webster it seemed she must surely have dodged the torpedo fired at her when the bomber burst through a wall of smoke and into his vision. It raced across the water at a height of just forty feet, tipping from one wing to another as the pilot fought to dodge the flak fire directed against him. The HE 111 bomber lifted its nose and roared across the bows of *Renown*, its nose, belly and waist gunners spraying the ship's decks as it passed, disappearing into a bank of smoke as quickly as it had appeared. Webster was just about to turn back to the radar screens when the torpedo struck, hitting its target just aft of the bridge on the port side. A huge fountain of water, dwarfing those of the flak shells blasted into the air. From the other ships in the fleet the waterspout against *Renown's* side seemed to rocket into the sky, reaching to the very tops of the battlecruiser's masts and spreading a shroud of mist and spray that completely obscured the great ship.

The curtain of water seemed to hang, impossibly suspended over the battlecruiser, hiding her from view. Webster watched, hardly daring to breathe until the cascade fell back into the sea and on the decks of *Renown*. The deluge was strong enough to wash several men overboard and to inundate the flak gun tubs on the port side of the superstructure. Their fire went out like a spent match. As the haze and mist cleared he watched for an indication of the damage the ship had suffered, but to all outward appearances she shook off the torpedo like a dog shaking itself dry. The torpedo struck in a place where he knew an armored band of steel belted *Renown* to some feet below the waterline. In places this armored belt was as much as six inches thick.

He said a quick prayer for the big ship then turned back to the radar screens. The two pinpoints that had slipped in to launch their torpedoes from close range were both moving off, though as he watched one of them flickered and disappeared, one more German bomber that would not reach home. The fury of gunfire slackened and fell in intensity as well. The crisis was passed. For the first time he noticed the stink of cordite that permeated the office from the guns on deck. The room was now blazing hot and the sweat ran from Webster and his men.

"Is everyone all right?" he asked over the fading sounds of the barrage.

His crew all reported they were unhurt. He pulled a small wooden cask from the corner of the room and took a long draught of water. It was warm, but sweet, rinsing away the taste of burnt powder and fear. He passed the cask around to the others.

"Keep your focus," he warned the men. "Just like Jerry to try to sneak a lone raider in amongst when he thinks our guard is down."

He turned again to the aft observation slit. An eerie silence descended on *Sirius*, broken only by sounds wholly natural to her crew, so natural as to be ignored; the soft swish of water down the ship's side, the low hum of the forced air blowers sucking huge drafts of air down to the boilers below the waterline and by a quiet rattle and clank as a spent shell casing near one of the turrets rolled about in the scuppers.

The smoke was clearing in the stiff southerly breeze and he could now see *Renown* clearly. She appeared unharmed and seemed to be having no difficulty in maintaining her course and speed. No list was evident. He sighed in relief. The courage of the German aviators in pressing home their attack was a wonder to him. Force H and the escorts had thrown a veritable blizzard of high explosive and solid shot into the sky, yet two of the German torpedo bomber pilots and at least one of the dive-bombers had pressed in to attack at close range. He shook his head in amazement.

The smoke was clearing rapidly, blown apart and away on the southerly breeze. *Renown* was coming back to starboard, rejoining her position in the formation. A gust blew away the last of the smoke lingering about her superstructure. Webster frowned. A pall of black, oily smoke rose into the sky from behind *Renown.* He peered through the murk, trying to see the source of the smoke. Finally as the battlecruiser resumed her position in column *HMS Kenya* sailed into view.

"SEND A SIGNAL!" shouted the *Staffelkäpitan* into the interphone. His Heinkel 111 torpedo bomber shuddered and lurched. The squadron commander fought the control column as it was nearly torn from his grasp. Wind roared through the shattered glass nose dome. "Give our position! Report one battleship, one heavy cruiser hit!" The twin-engine bomber bucked again, smoke pouring from its port engine. "Tell them we are bailing out! And hurry! I can't hold it for long."

Torpedo bomber squadron 100 limped home for Sardinia. Eleven HE 111's, each carrying two 21-inch torpedoes had attacked Force H at 6°, 48' east, 37°, 6' north. They'd scored just one hit, against the port side of *Renown*. Only seven of the bombers would reach home and each of these carried wounded or dead airmen.

Bomber squadron 250 faired better on casualties. All of its fourteen planes returned to base though four were damaged. It had scored one hit and several near misses. The German attack force had been lucky, catching Force H while it was separated from the aircraft carrier *Furious* and before its complement of fighter aircraft was airborne. One of Bomber 250's Ju 88s hit *Kenya* with an aerial bomb directly between the funnels on the seaplane deck, penetrating two decks before exploding in a paint locker, just aft of the officer's wardroom, the Action Station of the Surgeon Commander and most of his medical staff. The bulkhead between the compartments was torn open and blazing paint sprayed into the wardroom. The Surgeon Commander and his staff were wiped out in a blowtorch of flame that spread into the junior officer's quarters and the wireless office in the superstructure where it raged out of control, sparing only the Junior Medical Officer and one pharmacist. Their action station was in the Engineer's flat well aft. For several moments after the bomb struck, the ship was also out of control, the bridge watch all thrown from their feet and momentarily stunned. The XO in the emergency steering compartment was thrown against a bulkhead and suffered a broken collarbone.

The bridge watch collected themselves and took back control of the ship, but for a critical minute and a half she held a steady course, providing a nearly perfect target for the German torpedo bombers. Two aircraft launched a total of four torpedoes against her and it was only through a combination of extraordinary luck and superb seamanship that Captain Russell and the bridge watch were able to collect their wits and to conn the ship, combing the tracks of the torpedoes and evading them.

*HMS Kenya* was still in mortal danger however from the fire raging in her superstructure. As the fire spread the Captain was nearly forced to abandon the conn, until he turned the ship's head into the wind to carry the flames aft and away from the bridge. *Kenya's* damage control parties fought the blaze from for'ard, pouring seawater onto the flames, but when the fire was finally extinguished the Captain and crew knew it was because the fire had burned itself out, consuming all the fuel in the after superstructure, leaving it a charred hulk. *Kenya* was left with no wireless communication, no Doctor or sick bay and over seventy dead and injured.

At Decimomanu airfield near Cagliari, Sardinia the *Staffelkäpitan's* signal set off a furious round of activity. Every attack aircraft on the base, German and Italian alike was prepared for action. At Decimomanu the Luftwaffe and Regia Marina had assembled a powerful force of bombers, fighters and maritime patrol aircraft. The two air forces had some 200 combat aircraft on hand in anticipation of Operation Herkules.

The Luftwaffe Geschwader, or air-wing, held over 100 aircraft of four distinct types. Three squadrons were of torpedo bombers, totaling thirty-six HE 111s. One of these squadrons had already attacked Force H with eleven aircraft, scoring the hit on the battlecruiser *Renown.* The second squadron's thirteen bombers sat on the field, torpedoes slung under wing, fueled and ready for flight. The third squadron's twelve HE 111's were in the hangars being worked on by the ground crew. Fuel was being pumped, machine guns loaded with ammunition. The deadly 21-inch torpedoes were being towed on bomb trolleys from their underground depot at the far north side of the field. They would be loaded last. Both squadrons were to attack before sunset.

The three torpedo squadrons on Sardinia were among the most experienced at maritime strike flying in the Luftwaffe and represented fully one third of the torpedo bombers in the entire German Air Force at the time. Even so, less than a third of the aircrew including pilots had ever flown a mission in which a torpedo was dropped at a live target.

JU 88 bombers comprised two more squadrons, one of thirteen, the other fourteen aircraft. The larger of these had also already attacked Force H, scoring the hit on the cruiser *Kenya.* The second squadron was sitting on the field, ready to take to the air. This squadron shifted from Catania Airfield on Sicily on June 23rd, shortly after the decision to implement Herkules was made in Berlin. It had been bombing the Maltese airfields and its only experience attacking shipping was against vessels at anchor in Malta's Grand Harbor.

Two squadrons of JU 87 Stuka dive bombers totaling twenty-one aircraft rounded out the bomber force. Rugged and dependable, but slow and with a range of just over 650 kilometers the Stuka seemed a less than ideal maritime strike aircraft, yet the gull-winged bomber already held a fearsome reputation in the Mediterranean, doing cruel damage to the Royal Navy, first at Crete then in a series of Malta relief convoys. But Force H was still at the extreme limit of the Stuka's range when the signal reached Decimomanu. The JU 87's would have to wait for their crack at the British until the fleet moved closer.

The final two squadrons of Luftwaffe aircraft were Messerschmidt Bf 109e fighters comprising 10 Jagdstaffel and 66 Jagdstaffel or 'hunter' squadrons. The twenty-eight 'Emils' had a normal maximum range of 725 kilometers, but special new equipment was available to the fighter squadrons. In very limited supply, fuel drop tanks had reached Sardinia. Carried under the fuselage these tanks held enough fuel to extend the plane's range to 1,050 kilometers, but the air drag they presented in flight cut the fighters performance drastically, so the tanks had to be dropped from the aircraft before combat. Only seventeen of these fuel drop tanks were available at Decimomanu.

At 1200 hours the second Luftwaffe strike against Force H began to take off. First off were thirteen HE 111's followed by twelve of the JU 88's of 73 Staffel. The thirteenth aircraft in the squadron was grounded at the last minute by mechanical failure. Last off the ground were fourteen Bf 109e Emil fighters. Three of these carried a drop tank. The entire force set course to the southwest to intercept the British fleet.

Moments later another flight of fighters began to leave Decimomanu. The other fourteen Bf 109s roared off the field in pairs and threes. These set course to the south and southeast and were quickly lost to sight.

"How long till *Furious* rejoins?" asked Admiral Burrough.

"Another twenty minutes, Sir," his Flag Secretary, Lt. Harris replied. The two men stood on the port bridge wing of *Renown*, watching the plume of smoke rising high into the sky from the stricken cruiser, *HMS Kenya.*

"Find out how soon she can launch fighter cover and anti sub patrol," commanded Burrough, "and get a damage report from *Kenya.*"

Harris went off to carry out his orders.

"Admiral Burrough?"

The Admiral turned and found Commander Oats, the Intelligence Officer waiting expectantly. "Yes, Oats?"

"Sir, the German torpedo bombers are a bit of a surprise. We've known for some months the Germans were developing such aircraft based on the He 111 bomber and that they've been working them up to operational training levels from several bases in the Baltic." Oats shook his head. "But their presence here is a complete surprise. I have no way of knowing if we've seen the whole force or if there are more of them."

"Thank you, Oats," replied the Admiral. "Something tells me we've not seen the last of them, though." Captain Daniel stepped out on the bridge wing and silently handed the Admiral a clipboard. Burrough scanned it quickly.

"Some good news, at least Captain," he said appreciatively to Daniel. "With no worse than minor flooding and no reduction in speed I should say *Renown* is very fortunate to have taken that torpedo so well."

"Yes, Admiral," replied Daniel. "The torpedo blister lived up to its design. It appears to have absorbed almost all the energy of the explosion." The two men turned their attention aft and wondered how badly *Kenya* was hurt.

The pall of black, oily smoke followed *Sirius* as she and the other ships of Force H forged their way steadily eastward. Ten minutes after the last of the German bombers fled the area *Sirius'* radar detected the arrival of fighter aircraft from *Furious.*

"A bit late, chums," Commander Webster noted under his breath.

By 1230 that afternoon *Furious* and her three surviving destroyer escorts steamed up over the western horizon and the fleet was reformed with *Sirius* leading *Renown* and *Kenya,* still smoldering, in the port column and *Phoebe* ahead of *Charybdis* and *Furious* in the starboard column with *Nigeria* bringing up the rear. *Evening Dale* sailed alone between the two columns. *Kenya* trailed a pall of smoke but the flames that had flared high into the sky were diminished. Still, the column of smoke would serve as a beacon to guide any U-boat or enemy aircraft to Force H. Three Fairey Fulmar fighters were in the air ready to defend against air attack and two Swordfish 'Stringbags' patrolled the perimeter of the fleet, guarding against submarine attack.

In the radar office minutes seemed to stretch for hours. Webster's chin rested on his chest and he began to doze off. Althea often came to him as he drifted off to sleep. "Silly Rollie," she said. "You can't sleep now!" He snapped his head up, rubbing his eyes and brushing sweat from his brow. He looked around the office and saw his men were in no better shape. He pressed the switch to activate his telephone connection. He called to request fresh water be brought to the Radar Office.

"Open all the portals!" Webster commanded.

The ratings at the radar displays looked at one another in confusion. It was against regulations to open the portals while the ship was closed up at action stations.

"Open the scuttles now!" Webster repeated.

The ratings jumped up and flipped open portholes down each side of the office. Air moved through the opened potholes, ventilating the office, taking the temperature down ten degrees in a few moments. Webster took in grateful gulps of fresh air, then looked at each of his men in turn. All were showing signs of recovering their wits, though Jones was still flushed. A loud rap came from the office door. It swung open and a cask appeared on the shoulder of a brawny seaman.

"You ordered fresh water, Sir?" the seaman asked him. The water cask was passed around the Radar Office. Jones took a deep draft on his turn then each of the men soaked his collar.

All over *HMS Sirius* men coped with the heat as best they could. Those on open decks, in the flak gun tubs and in lookout positions at least enjoyed the benefit of the wind, but those closed up at action stations, in the turrets and most especially in the engineering spaces suffered cruelly from one of the hottest days of the summer. The Black Watch, as the engine room crews were known, labored in temperatures of 130° F. Conditions were the same on the other ships of the fleet. Men struggled to stay alert and ready for the attacks they knew must still come. Spent shell casings were stowed and the guns cleaned and below decks in the magazines shells and powder charges were shifted to racks closest to the hoists. When all was in readiness there was nothing else to do but wait.

Webster looked at his watch. 1240 local time. Over an hour since the last attack.

"Radar contact, bearing zero-three-eight, range twenty-two miles, six-thousand feet," Jones called out. Jones pointed to a large bright blip on the screen as Webster leaned over his shoulder.

"Bridge, radar!" Webster spoke into his telephone.

"Radar, bridge."

"Bridge, we're tracking an aerial target to the northeast, bearing zero-three-eight, range twenty-two miles."

"Range still twenty-two miles, target bearing now zero-three-five, altitude steady at six-thousand feet," Jones said. "Target course two-seven-five."

"They're moving into position for a beam attack," said Webster. He stepped over to the ports and shut them as he spoke into his telephone set. "Main batteries, train to port, A, B and Q turrets slave to the forward radar director, X and Y to the aft director."

"Target range twenty miles, bearing zero-three four, shifting course to one-eight-five."

"They're moving in for the attack," said Webster. "Secondary batteries," he spoke into the phone again, "keep to your zones."

"There's the fighter patrol moving to intercept," said Jones, pointing to his screen. Webster watched a much smaller blip move on an intersecting angle to the enemy blip. He knew there were only three fighters airborne, outdated, slow Fairey Fulmars. Others would be scrambling from the flight deck of the carrier to form a second echelon to shield the fleet from attack. Webster flipped a switch on the console and the Tannoy speaker above the radar screens scratched to life. The speaker cut in the radio-telephone conversation of the fighter patrol pilots.

"-any fighters. Cut straight in for the bombers," a voice said. Static skipped and sparked through the conversation. The roar of the fighter's engine could be heard in the background.

"Go to port, Green-two," said another voice, "I'll take the one to starboard."

"Roger-o!"

"They're breaking off!" shouted the first voice.

"Bloody Eye-ties. No stomach for the business!"

Jones pointed at his screen. "The target is separating, Sir."

The Tannoy squawked again. "You're on him, don't let him

shake you, Green-one!"

A new voice came over the air. "Let them go, Green-one. Return to station, return to station." Webster and his men knew this was the air controller aboard the carrier.

"You've hit him Green-one!" one of the pilots shouted. "Stay on him, you've got him!"

"Green-one, break-off and return to station immediately!" the air controller shouted.

Jones pointed at the screen. The blips were all at the far edge of the set's range, passing off the edge of the screen.

"Green-one!" shouted the controller. "Return to station. That is an order! Acknowledge, Green-one!"

"Green-one, acknowledged," came the reply at last. The pilot's voice conveyed his disappointment clearly, in spite of the static in the transmission. "Returning to station."

Webster realized he'd been hunched over the back of Jones' chair, staring at the screen, listening to the radio drama over the Tannoy. He stood and stretched his spine, then lifted his arms over his head. He was about to offer Jones a brief spell from the radar screen when the rating jumped in his chair.

"Commander!" he shouted. "New target, bearing one-zero-zero! Range is thirteen miles, course two-eight-zero, altitude 3,000 feet! They've slipped under our screen again!"

For a moment Webster's tongue was thick in his mouth, and his mind could force no words from his lips. He stared at the new blip on the screen, just to starboard of dead ahead of the fleet, growing in size as he watched. At last he snapped out of his shock.

"Bridge, radar!"

"We know, radar! *Phoebe* has just signaled!"

Webster quickly regained his composure.

"Forward turrets, train in, elevation thirty degrees!"

On bearing one-one-zero the enemy aircraft were just to starboard of dead ahead and approaching fast.

"Two more aircraft airborne from *Furious,*" announced Jones.

"Bridge, radar," said Webster into his telephone. "We won't get much aerial cover. Just five fighters airborne from the carrier so far." He switched the Tannoy speaker back to the gunnery circuit to monitor the talk among the lookouts.

"Bearing one-zero-five, range eight miles, course two-eight-zero, altitude steady," Jones kept the reports coming.

A moment later the distant bark of flak guns heralded the beginning of the attack. The Tribal class destroyers leading the fleet were first to bring the aircraft under fire at a range of five miles. Aboard *Sirius* the crew waited tensely for the enemy flight to come into range.

Webster checked over Jones' shoulder at the radar plot. The attacking aircraft were spreading out in a giant fan to the east, dividing the fire of the fleet, and approaching in an arc from the port beam around to starboard.

Webster flipped a switch on the console and spoke into the phone again.

"Main battery train out to starboard, accept radar direction." To Jones he added, "Slave A, B and Q to the forward radar director, X and Y to the aft director. Select a primary target for each director."

Jones controlled the forward director, while the other rating, Meese controlled the aft radar director. They each focused their radar direction controls onto an individual aircraft target.

"Coming into range now," Jones observed calmly.

"Main battery, FIRE!" shouted Webster. The deck lurched beneath his feet as all six of *Sirius*' forward main guns belched fire and steel together.

"Range four miles!" shouted Jones over the crash of guns. "Targets are separating altitude! Looks like about a dozen dive bombers climbing for altitude, the same number dropping down for torpedo attack! Bearing now one-seven-zero, range three miles!"

"Put the secondary batteries on local control!" ordered Webster.

The gunnery officer stepped to the port bulkhead and lifted his binoculars from their cradle. Hanging them about his neck he spied out the port. A pall of smoke hung over *Sirius* and the other ships in the fleet, both from a fresh smoke screen being laid by the destroyers and the cordite from the guns. The staccato chatter of smaller automatic weapons joined the crash of heavier guns rising to an incredible din. Puffs of smoke were bursting about the fleet, hanging in the sky like great, obscene, black cotton balls. Commands and warnings crackled from the Tannoy as lookouts and gunners struggled to target the attacking planes.

"Swing right twenty-degrees, elevation thirty!"

"Come up dammit, come up! You're below him!"

"Lead the target!"

Webster peered through the smoke trying to spot any of the aircraft through the murk. The bark of guns was deafening, forcing the men in the office to shout over the din.

"Range one mile!" shouted Jones.

"Aft target hit!" added Meese. "Shifting target!"

"Secondary battery, fire at will!" the Commander shouted.

Webster strained to see through the smoke and haze, but at first could discern no targets. Then, bursting from the cloud of smoke less than a mile to starboard and slightly aft a twin-engine bomber broke into view forty feet above the wave tops. It tipped down on its starboard wing, then straightened, dancing through shell bursts and streams of brightly glowing tracer shells. Still it came on, growing in his glasses till it filled his vision.

Almost he imagined he could see the pilot behind the glass nose dome, laboring to hold the aircraft on target. His drew his breath in a gasp as he saw the heads of the two torpedoes, one slung under each wing between the engine and the fuselage.

He dropped the binoculars and watched the bomber, a Heinkel 111 rush towards the fleet. At less than one thousand yards the first of the two torpedoes dropped clear, followed a split second later by the other. They splashed into the water, plunging he knew to a depth of at least fifty feet before their internal fathometers brought them back towards the surface to run at a pre-set depth.

Freed of its load at last the Heinkel dove for the deck seeming to fairly skip across the wave tops, speeding to escape the curtain of fire and death it had flown into. Without the weight and drag of the torpedoes the bomber accelerated and was much more agile. It roared past *Phoebe* and towards *Sirius* as if on a collision course, bent on suicide. At the last possible second its nose lifted and it roared directly across the cruiser's stern, streams of fire following it every inch of the way. Adding injury to insult *Sirius* was struck in her upper works by automatic flak cannon fire from both *Phoebe* and *Renown*, shells intended for the bomber, leaving glowing red holes punched in the thin steel of the superstructure. The plane roared away to port and astern, its belly and waist gunners spraying *Sirius* as it passed. A bullet ricocheted off the armored sides of 'X' turret and banged into the bulkhead outside Webster's port; bent and flattened it dropped with a clatter to the deck outside the scuttle.

Webster was no longer watching the bomber though. His gaze was riveted on *Sirius'* sister ship as *Phoebe* went hard over on her starboard side, turning into the course of the torpedoes to "comb the tracks".

Perhaps, had there been only one torpedo to avoid she would have turned clear, but the attack was delivered with such skill and daring and at such close range there was no time to dodge both torpedoes. The first fish passed just ahead of the cruiser's bow, but the second caught her amidships and beneath the keel. The explosion seemed to lift her 5,400 tons clear of the sea. Water rocketed out horizontally from both sides of *Phoebe*, momentarily blotting her from the view of men aboard *Sirius*.

For a moment even the guns fell silent as though holding their breath along with their masters, waiting to see what had befallen the cruiser. The water fell back into the sea and a fine mist slowly settled as *Sirius* continued on her way. Once again Webster found himself staring, trying to pierce through the cloud of spray and smoke.

At last *Phoebe's* bow emerged. The fog and spray fell back as a curtain on some monstrous stage on the Strand, revealing the ship from bow to stern. Webster's heart skipped. *Phoebe's* back was broken, bent in the middle like a giant flattened letter 'V'. Her screws still raced, propelling her forward, pushing the open wound in her belly deeper into the water. A sudden rumble in her bowels announced the explosion of her boilers as cold seawater burst into the engineering spaces. Her two funnels belched a cloud of smoke and steam; scalding seawater fell back onto her decks.

As she fell astern Webster watched in horror as the stricken cruiser rolled onto her starboard side and settled on her beam end into the sea. Men jumped from her decks into the water and swam for their lives. No order to abandon ship was given; none was needed. They leapt from the gun tubs, from their lookout posts, from the bridge wings tossing away signal flags and clip boards, binoculars and tin hats. Many had the misfortune to abandon ship over the starboard side and found themselves fighting to get clear of the superstructure as it fell into the sea. Even as catastrophe befell *HMS Phoebe* the German attack was pressed home against Force H. Webster had no more time to watch *Phoebe* go down. He snapped back to his duty at a shout from Jones.

"Here come the dive bombers!"

"What bearing?" Webster shouted back.

"They're spread across the whole compass to starboard!" An edge of panic crept into Jones' voice.

Webster stepped across the room and put a hand on Jones' shoulder. In as calm a voice as he could manage and still be heard he sought to steady the man's nerves. "Select a target Jones," he said, "and slave A, B and Q turrets to your director."

Jones nodded and taking a deep breath he did as he was ordered, his training and the many hours of drill and practice helping to steady him.

*Sirius'* guns continued their banging, the main batteries now elevated nearly to the vertical to counter the dive-bombers hurtling down on the fleet. Over the din and crash of guns Webster heard a sudden wild cheer from the gunners and loaders on deck, as if the home team had netted a goal in the final seconds of a scoreless match. He looked out through the starboard observation slit in time to see a Ju 88 trailing smoke and flame plunge into the sea less than a cable's length away.

The deck heeled under his feet and he knew Captain Brooking had ordered evasive steering to avoid attack. He braced himself against a steel cross member in the bulkhead and looked out on the decks on the starboard side of the ship's superstructure. Directly beneath him the starboard twin 2-pounder pom-pom gun hammered away at a target high in the sky on the starboard quarter.

Webster twisted his head to look out and up through the port, but his angle of view was impossible and he could see nothing. Looking back at the pom-pom he could see its angle of elevation slowly drop as its target descended, the distinctive sound that gave the pom-pom its nickname never wavering as its crew hustled to feed four shell clips to the guns. He looked again and this time the bomber was in sight a mile to starboard and falling in a steep dive towards *Renown*. Aboard the battlecruiser every gun but the giant 15-inch main battery was firing at the plane. A burst of flame and smoke spouted from the Ju 88's port engine, but the cheer died in Webster's throat as three heavy bombs detached from the plane and plunged towards the sea, just before the aircraft disintegrated in a flash of flame and debris.

Slack-jawed he watched as the bombs descended, as if in slow motion. They pitched down in a line that straddled *Renown's* bows, the first plunging into the sea to starboard and the third to port, but the second struck her in front of her forward turret, crashing through the thin deck plates beyond the breakwater. The force of the explosion rocked the great ship.

Webster held his breath and squinted his eyes nearly shut. He knew the magazine that fed shells and powder charges to 'A' turret, the battlecruiser's forward main battery was just aft of the explosion. An armored belt of steel protected the forward magazine as well as the barbette, the great tubular support structure on which the massive weight of the turret was supported and turned. The belt began just in front of the turret and extended down both sides of the ship to just aft of the bridge wings. Another smaller belt protected the magazine for the after main battery. But *Renown's* armor was of a different design than other British capital ships. The battlecruiser design, tested in the First World War, sought to combine the firepower of the battleship with the speed of the cruiser. *Renown* satisfied these goals. Her six fifteen-inch MKI rifles were the most powerful and accurate in the British arsenal and her Brown-Curtis direct drive turbines pushed her across the seas at a top speed of 29 knots. But something was sacrificed to achieve such speed without losing firepower and that something was armored protection. Full battleships sported up to fourteen inches of armor about their magazines, but *Renown* carried only nine inches. If the blast penetrated the armored belt and touched off the ammunition stored in the magazine the resultant explosion could devastate not only *Renown,* but also the other ships nearby, including *Sirius.*

A flat, muffled *WUMPH* sound came across the water to his ears, not the cataclysmic blast of extinction he feared. After a moment he dared to open his eyes again. Black, oily smoke was billowing from the battlecruiser's bows and sweeping aft down her decks, but there was neither indication of a list nor a slackening of her speed.

He turned back to the radar plots. Jones pointed to several small blips on the screen. After a moment it became evident they were on convergent courses to the north.

"The last of the bombers are pulling off, Sir," he said to

Webster. He shifted to point at another, smaller blip. "These are the three fighters that were off chasing the Italians. They're in a good position to pick off any cripples headed back for base." Jones pointed to a last blip on the screen. "These are five fighters *Furious* has scrambled to meet the attack. They're moving in behind the Jerries too. Should be able to clean up the leavings, Sir."

The guns had all fallen silent aboard *Sirius*. The only sound of firing came from a destroyer on the port bow, delivering a few parting shots at the fleeing Germans. With his ears still ringing from the barrage Webster switched the Tannoy back to the radio-telephone circuit to listen in on the fighter pilots again.

"-position."

"On his tail now, but still out of range. Few more seconds and I'll have him."

"Describe your target Red-one!" This would be the air controller aboard the carrier again. The air staff wanted to inventory the planes and types in the attack and judge how many were destroyed, damaged or had escaped from the action.

"Target is a Ju 88. He's trailing smoke from his port engine and appears to be having trouble keeping the aircraft in straight flight. I'm a thousand yards behind him closing fast."

Webster watched the screen over Jones' shoulder as he listened to the fighter pilots move in to destroy as many as possible of the fleeing Germans. The blips on the screen were all coming together to the north or port of the fleet at a range of about twelve miles. The German bombers had all dived to low altitude to gain speed and escape the British fleet as quickly as possible. At these low altitudes they were already nearing the limits of *Sirius'* radar. They'd soon pass from its arc of detection entirely. The green line radiating from the center of the display swept round the screen, high lighting the positions of the various aircraft on each circuit, the British aircraft in two groups closing on the cluster of returns for the German planes.

"Range down to three hundred yards," said Red-One.

"Sir!" Jones exclaimed.

"I see it Jones!" answered Webster.

"Bridge, Radar plot!" shouted the voice of Lt. Kerry. Without waiting for the customary acknowledgement he went on. "Fresh radar contact to the northeast. The German bombers have a fighter escort picking them up for the return home. The escort is above our fighters. They've got to be warned!"

*HMS Nigeria* was equipped as a fighter direction ship, with both the radar and the specialized wireless equipment to manage and direct fighter aircraft in combat. *Sirius'* radar, though powerful was not equipped with the latest friend-or-foe identification apparatus to allow it to distinguish individual aircraft in a melee. Further, her radio/telephone gear was not tuned to the frequency to allow her to communicate directly with the pilots in the air.

"On him now!" shouted the voice of Red-One. "Scratch one Ju 88!" he exclaimed.

"Red and Green flight leaders!" shouted the air controller from *Nigeria*. "Radar plots show probable German fighters closing in on you from the northeast, bearing zero-three-five!"

"What's their Angels?" shouted back Red-one. The air controller had failed to pass along the German fighters' altitude.

"Eight thousand feet, range three miles from you," answered the controller.

"Don't see anything yet," said Red-One.

"Don't mix with the Messerschmitts," answered the controller. "Get back on station now."

Another voice broke in on the circuit.

"Bandit diving on your tail, Green-Three!"

"Break left, Green-Three, break left!"

Jones traced his finger on the screen where the drama was playing out in flashes of green.

"I can't shake him!"

"BREAK LEFT!"

"GET HIM OFF –." The pilot's frantic cry for help was interrupted by the sound of shattering glass and the hammer blows of cannon shells striking his cockpit.

Webster stood and slapped his palm in helpless frustration. He turned to move to the port observation slit intending to use his binoculars to try to see the aircraft, even though he knew they were too distant to be seen, but he stopped short. His men were staring at the Tannoy, listening to the drama being played out in the air, not keeping their watch. He turned back to the console and threw the switch on the speaker, breaking off the radio/telephone chatter of the pilots and cutting back in on the ship's tactical telephone circuit.

"Get back to your screens," Webster told his men softly.

The unexpected appearance of the Bf 109 fighters spelled real trouble for the eight Fulmar pilots from *Furious*. Their obsolete carrier based planes were much slower and less maneuverable than the German machines and they fell easy victim to the hungry wolves from Sardinia, three of whom had arrived with plenty of fuel for combat, courtesy of the drop tanks they had carried from Decimomanu. Only two Fulmars returned to *Furious,* both damaged.

The survivors of the second German air attack against Force H limped home. Thirteen He 111 torpedo bombers attacked the British fleet, scoring just one hit, but a crucial one against *HMS Phoebe,* at a cost to their number of seven bombers shot down and the other six all damaged, though incredibly the plane that had sunk *Phoebe* had only minor damage from shrapnel, its glass nose dome smashed, and minor injuries among the crew. The Ju 88's suffered heavily as well. Of fourteen to attack the British fleet only nine reached Sardinia. Two of these cracked up on landing, though their crews were saved. The Messerschmitt Bf 109s escaped the action unscathed, though one was lost as it ran out of fuel three miles out to sea short of the airfield at Decimomanu. An Italian Navy air-sea rescue boat saved the pilot.

The Luftwaffe command considered this attack less than fully successful. On the debit side, fourteen of twenty-seven bombers in the attack force were lost with most of their crews while only the one torpedo hit on a British cruiser appeared on the credit side. The bomb hit on *Renown* was not seen by any of the surviving crews. In addition, the command was unaware that the cruiser was sunk. The crew of the He 111 that delivered the strike was certain she'd been hit, but they passed into a smoke screen before the torpedo actually struck and did not see the mortal blow delivered to *Phoebe.*

At this time The Luftwaffe on Sardinia believed the British force to be composed of five cruisers, one of which was likely damaged to an unknown extent, an undamaged battleship, an aircraft carrier and eight to twelve destroyers.

Results of the first two attacks were flashed to higher

commands, first in Sicily, then on to Rome and Berlin. An addendum to the message moments later detailed Luftwaffe losses in the attacks.

Billy Wilson checked his compass. His course held steady at dead east, bearing zero-nine-zero. He checked his watch and his chart. Another thirty minutes till his next course change. He would turn southeast to course one-two-zero, skirting across the mouth of the Gulf of Tunis for fifteen minutes, then after passing Cape Bon turn due south on one-eight-zero staying clear of Pantelleria Island before turning east again for the final run to Malta. During his transit of the Sicilian Narrows he would stay as close to the Tunisian coastline as he possibly could without arousing action from the French air force. Throughout the entire flight all Spitfires were to maintain strict radio silence until they were within sight of the island. Fighter control at Malta would transmit a homing beacon for them to navigate the last twenty miles or so to Hal Far Airfield.

Billy checked his wingman. The other Spitfire bobbed off his starboard wingtip a comfortable forty yards away, close enough to maintain easy contact, but not so close as to require exhausting concentration to avoid collision.

He waved at the other pilot who responded with a thumbs-up. Billy smiled thinly and checked his watch again. Twenty minutes to the course change. He flashed five fingers four times to his wingman, then made a veering motion with his hand. Another thumbs-up acknowledged his signal.

Billy checked his fuel gauge. Fuel consumption was well within his safety margin. Barring any misfortune they would have plenty of fuel to reach Malta. He looked down to starboard. Barely discernible through the haze lay Jalitah Island. It was the first of his visual checkpoints and it confirmed his navigation was spot on.

He marked his chart with the sighting then scanned the horizon ahead and to the sides, hoping to catch a glimpse of other Spitfires, but there were none to be seen. He settled back in his seat and thought of his friend Bryan. His mind drifted back to the time Bryan and he had spent together with Gwen Summers.

He'd met Bryan shortly after joining the RAF at the start of the Battle of Britain in the summer of 1940. They were assigned to the same training establishment at Glamorgan in Scotland where they'd gone through their Elementary Flight Training. Billy quickly recognized in Bryan the sort of chap everyone loved. Bryan was full of life and fun and also quick with a quip or joke, but he was far from the best pilot in their class. Still, he wasn't the worst and Britain was desperate for pilots. Bryan's flying, combined with a fair amount of help from Billy on the classroom part of their training and a measure of natural charm were just enough to see him through. By the spring of 1941 they were posted to an operational squadron flying Hurricanes on patrol over the Bristol Channel near Cardiff and Swansea. The Luftwaffe by this time largely restricted its actions in the area to nighttime raids of the seaports and an occasional lone bomber attack against the airfields or seaports and the two pilots saw little action.

One weekend in November he and Bryan got leave from their training program and decided to visit the ancient resort town of Bath, near Bristol. They borrowed the car of the wing's Chaplain and set off from the airfield. The autumn weather had been sparkling clear and brisk all week, but on the Saturday morning that they set out low, scudding clouds and a freshening wind foretold rain. They were on the road for less than an hour when the rain came, heavy and pounding with gusting winds. Bryan was driving with Billy navigating down a narrow county road when they came upon the tiny village of Scrapton.

"Bryan, this Scrapton place is not on my map," Billy complained. "We'd best stop and get directions."

Aside from two-dozen small cottages there was a small inn named The Ram's Gate, a Church of England with rectory and a stable. A shingle hung over the stable advertised "Veterinary Services".

Bryan and Billy parked in the lane in front of The Ram's Gate and made a dash for the door, pulling their collars up around their ears. Four small tables clustered about a cold, stone fireplace and five stools at the bar were all empty of patrons. A sputtering lamp gave dim illumination. A lad of about fourteen years was mopping the floor behind the bar.

"Excuse me," said Billy cheerfully. "My friend and I are a bit turned round. Could you tell us if we're on the right road for Bath?"

The lad looked at them stupidly, with his jaw hanging slack. At first Billy flattered himself that the boy was in awe of seeing two pilots in uniform, but soon he realized the boy was slow.

He spoke again, more softly and slowly.

"Is your mum or dad here, son?" he asked gently.

The boy carefully set the mop against the bar and exited through the back door without a word. Bryan and Billy looked at each other and shook their heads in sadness at the boy's condition. They studied the room while they waited. Ancient, hand-hewn beams in the ceiling and walls had absorbed the pipe and fireplace smoke of generations. No two chairs or stools were quite alike and all seemed ancient beyond years. A darts board hung to one side of the fireplace; a set of three yellow-shafted darts tightly grouped in the bull showed how the last game had ended.

"Yes, Sirs," came a man's voice behind them. "How can I help you two gentlemen this morning?"

Bryan and Billy turned to greet a short, barrel-chested man in a dirty undershirt. The man smiled solicitously, revealing more gap than teeth in his mouth. He scratched the gray stubble of a three-day beard.

"Er, thank you," Billy said. "We're set out for Bath and I'm afraid we're a bit turned round. Are we on the right road?"

"Oh, yes, Sir," said the man, "you're on the right road a'right. Just you be keeping to the main road you're on till you come to a marker, oh about five mile down yonder and it'll direct you just fine." The man paused. "Leastwise, if'n they haven't changed the road since I was last in Bath that is."

"Er, when were you last in Bath?" asked Bryan.

"Oh, let me see now, Sir," the man said, rubbing his stubble again. "I was married there in 19 and 24," he concluded after a moment.

"Thank you very much," said Billy. "Good day."

"Good day to you, Sirs," said the man and stood to watch them leave.

When they got back in the car the two friends sat and looked at each other.

"I don't know whether to laugh or cry," said Bryan finally.

Billy chuckled and shook his head.

"Count life's blessings everyday, Bryan," he replied. "Let's get moving."

This time Billy drove as Bryan navigated. They moved on out of the village of Scrapton, continuing on the 'main road' anticipating the marker that would direct them on the path to Bath. The rain was heavier than ever and the wind blew the last of the autumn leaves down from the great trees, oaks, elms and chestnuts that lined either side of the road, plastering them to the windscreen. Just a few minutes after leaving Scrapton the wipers were unable to keep up.

Suddenly Billy cried out and swerved off the road, jamming on the brake. The car jolted and bounced, coming to rest in a small turnout in front of a farm gate.

"What is it, Billy?" cried Bryan.

Billy didn't answer, but jumped out of the car. Bryan followed him back down the road in the direction from which they'd come. Billy was kneeling in the road with his back to Bryan. Rain pelted against their hats and macks and stung their cheeks. Bryan knelt beside Billy.

"You've hit a dog, Billy!" he exclaimed.

"Thank you, Bryan," Billy said, flashing anger. "I didn't know what it was."

"Sorry, Billy," said Bryan, defensively. "I didn't mean anything by it." Changing tone he asked, "Is it dead?"

"No, he's not dead," replied Billy, softening. "But he's badly hurt."

The dog was a collie and was breathing very slowly and shallowly. Billy petted the collie's head gently. It moved slightly and opened one eye to look at him. It was soaked and began to gently shiver.

"What are we going to do?" Bryan asked.

"We'll take him back to the village," answered Billy. "You remember the sign over the stable? There's a veterinarian. Perhaps he can help the dog."

"There's some newspaper in the back seat," said Bryan. "Let me spread it and we'll put him in the car."

The two men got the car turned around and were back in the village in less than ten minutes. Billy parked the car in front of the stable and they both got out. The stable door was ajar slightly and they went in, stamping their feet and shaking out their coats of the rain. The inside was dark and cold and smelled of animals.

"Halloo!" Bryan called out.

A rustling and snorting of ponies and the bleeting of a pen full of sheep was his only answer.

"Careful, Bryan," said Billy. "Softly. We don't need a stampede in here."

Their eyes began to adjust to the gloom. Billy pointed at a door that led off the sidewall of the stable. He walked over and knocked on the door. After a moment he heard footsteps on the other side. Bryan joined him just as the door opened.

Bright light spilled into the stable and a wave of warmth washed over Bryan and Billy. A wonderful rich smell of cooking wafted out the door and the two friends gasped, but not at the smell of food. The girl who stood in the door looking at them was the most beautiful either had ever seen. They judged her about twenty, with long, flowing blond curls, sparkling blue eyes and flawless, translucent skin. She was slim and tall, willowy even, and dressed in a simple plaid skirt and crème colored fleece sweater that fit tight across her bosom. The sleeves were pulled up to her elbows. Her fingers were long and delicate with short clipped nails. A wisp of curl fell down over her forehead.

"Hello," she said. "How can I help you?" She smiled and her beautiful face became radiant. The light behind her in the kitchen lit her hair in a golden halo. Ever afterward remembering that moment Billy hung his head and laughed. She wasn't really an angel, but memory of that moment always made him think of the pictures of the Saints in his boyhood Bible.

"Can I help you?" she repeated, laughing now.

"Excuse me, Miss," Bryan said, recovering his wits first, sweeping his hat off his head and returning the girl's smile, but briefly, sadly. "I'm afraid there's been an accident."

Her smile was replaced with a look of concern.

"Is someone hurt?" she asked. "Do you need a Doctor?"

Billy's heart skipped at her lovely face showing worry.

"No, thank you, Miss," Bryan told her. "We're fine, but we need to talk to the Veterinarian quickly. You see, there's a little dog been hurt, awfully hurt, and we're not sure if he can be saved."

"Oh, no!" she cried. "Where is he?"

"He's outside in our car, Miss," Bryan answered. "Should we bring him in?"

"No, don't move him!" she said. "I'll get my father."

She turned and ran from the kitchen.

Billy turned and marveled at his friend. He'd seen Bryan 'operate' with the ladies before, but it never failed to amaze him how quick he was when talking to a girl. Often diffident and unsure in the air, Bryan came into his element when dealing with women. Billy on the other hand was still tongue tied when the girl came back with her father, the veterinarian.

They brought the dog into the house to a small surgery off the kitchen. The girl's father examined him and found he had a broken right foreleg and was in shock. He shooed the pilots out of the surgery, inviting them to a spot of tea in the kitchen. The girl poured their cups, then hurried back to assist her father.

Bryan and Billy conversed softly in the kitchen waiting for the verdict.

"I tell you, Billy," Bryan said. "She's the one!"

"Come on, Bryan!" scoffed Billy. "You don't even know her name!"

"That doesn't matter now, Billy. I'm going to marry that girl!"

The memory faded from Billy as he raced through the sky over the central Mediterranean. He sighed and checked his watch. Five more minutes to the course change. He checked his wingman again. He was still there, a little more distant perhaps, but still bobbing up and down in the cross current of air from the south. Billy flashed him five fingers and the veering hand signal. Once again his reply was a 'thumbs up'.

Billy's mind drifted away again. He and Bryan spent every free moment that winter and spring just passed with Gwen Summers, the daughter of the country veterinarian from Scrapton.

The two pilots never made it to Bath that first weekend, staying in a room above the Ram's Gate until they were told the dog would survive, but on other occasions the three of them visited the ancient city, touring the Roman ruins there, and once they'd taken the famous baths, though in separate men's and women's pools. They called themselves the Three Musketeers; hardly original, but it seemed fitting. Billy and Bryan found themselves growing apart, but Gwen was the glue that still held them together, until one day Billy realized she was also the reason he and his friend were estranged. Billy knew that he too loved Gwen Summers, but that he could never tell her so.

For her part Gwen was smitten by Bryan and his sophisticated, big-city ways. When he invited her down to London for a weekend she accepted, over the objections of her widowed father. Weekends to London became a common thing, with Bryan begging leave at every chance. Billy started to skip the trips to London when Bryan and Gwen began to spend most of their time locked away in a hotel room.

Then came that Sunday night in May. Bryan was overdue at the station. Billy feared a car crash or some other accident, but the explanation was much more mundane. Bryan trailed in very early Monday morning, with a flight scheduled at first light. He crept into their quarters and slid into his cot still fully dressed. Billy had to rouse him a short two hours later to get ready to fly.

Bryan was pouring a quick cup of coffee when he broke the news.

"We're married, Billy," he said simply between gulps.

"Who's married?" Billy had laughed. "You can't be married. You've got to have Nesbith's permission to marry, you know that." But even as he said it he knew in his heart that Bryan was telling the truth.

From that day forward the argument never ceased. Billy urged Bryan to confess to their squadron leader, Commander Nesbith. Bryan procrastinated, always finding some way to delay and stall. It went on that way right through the time they received their orders to report for embarkation at Plymouth and the argument continued after they boarded *Furious* at Gibraltar.

Billy flashed on the image of Bryan's Spitfire dropping off the end of the carrier's flight deck. He jammed his palms into his eyes and screwed them shut, only just managing to block out the scene. He rubbed his face to restore his concentration.

With a start he realized his wingman had pulled ahead of him and was wagging his wings up and down. Billy stared at the other pilot who held his left wrist up and tapped his watch face with his other hand. Billy snapped his own watch up. Three minutes past time to change course! He looked across at the other pilot and nodded his head vigorously, giving the signal to veer off to the southeast. He boosted the throttles to regain his lead position as the two planes banked to starboard. He quickly ran the math to estimate how far out of position they'd flown while he was gathering wool. At a little under four miles per minute for three minutes they'd gone about eleven miles too far to the east before turning to the southeast. He checked his compass and made a quick adjustment to his course, coming to one-five-five degrees. He checked his wingman and was relieved that he seemed to understand the maneuver and was following along. Billy rubbed his face again and shook his head from side to side. He'd made a potentially fatal error that he could not afford to repeat and he vowed not to let himself drift away again.

The minutes flowed on and Billy busied himself checking his instruments, compass and fuel gauges and in going over his calculations on the course change. He confirmed that his little detour had taken them about eleven miles too far east. To make their next landfall at Cape Bon, Tunisia they had to cut back almost straight south. They would make up about a third of the lost time, but would still fall about two minutes off their original pace. He double checked his fuel gauge and calculated he still had fuel to spare to reach Malta.

They flew at 20,000 feet at a ground speed of 210 miles per hour to optimize fuel consumption. The minutes passed in the steady hum of the Spitfire's Rolls-Royce Merlin engine. The sky was a washed out blue with haze hanging over the sea, obscuring the details of tide and waves. Billy squinted against the hazy sunshine to the southeast. There! What was it? A thin, flat, white line stood out against the murky haze some miles away. Slowly, it resolved in his vision till he knew it was a vapor trail, moisture condensed on an aircraft wing or body then whipped away behind in the slipstream. Black specks grew in his vision till he could count three aircraft. He estimated their course and speed as closely matching his own and concluded they must be Spitfires from *Furious* on the way to Malta. His detour had allowed the three fighters in the group behind him to catch him up and pass. They were now a few miles ahead of him and his wingman.

The fighters grew larger as he angled towards them, but he realized he was behind them and would remain there unless he sped up to overtake them. He thought it over a minute and resolved to catch up and join the other fighters. Better a group of five together than he and his wingman alone. He turned and waved to his wingman, signaling to him his intention to catch up the other fighters. Once again his wingman gave him the thumbs up in acknowledgement.

Billy pushed the throttles forward and began to make up the distance. It occurred to him to not come up from behind too quickly. Nothing can give a fighter pilot a start like having another craft suddenly appear on his tail. He toyed with the idea of keying his radio-telephone a couple quick clicks to draw attention, but decided against it. It could as easily draw the attention of German or Italian listeners as much as his fellow RAF pilots. He decided to pull off to port a bit and approach from the side. He signaled to his wingman and began a quick bank to port.

Something flashed in the corner of Billy's eye. He looked back towards the other Spitfires and at first saw nothing. He was just about to look away when the flash came again above and behind the Spitfires. He stared into the haze and then he saw them. More vapor trails.

His heart fell and he cried out, "Behind you!" but of course his fellow pilots couldn't hear him. Four Bf 109 Messerschmitts were diving on the three Spitfires, coming down on their blind spots directly behind and above the tail.

Billy reacted instinctively, snapping back to starboard and ramming the throttle forward to its stops. His Spitfire bucked and threw him back against his seat with the acceleration. He flashed in front of his wingman, climbing for altitude, his engine screaming at full power. He ate the distance quickly, but not as fast as the German 109s. They were at full power too and they were diving on the clay pigeons sailing along serenely before them.

Billy cursed and keyed his radio-telephone.

"SPITFIRES!" he screamed. "DIVE! Bandits on your tails!"

The three Spitfires wobbled in their flight as though the pilots were stunned out of lethargy. The center and port fighters in the British flight veered and dove and three of the German fighters followed, but the pilot of the starboard machine was not as quick. He hung in his position an instant longer before he began his dive. The lead Bf 109 showed the telltale puffs of gun smoke erupting from its wings as its machine guns and cannon fired. Tracer shells flashed through the sky. The tardy Spitfire's cockpit exploded in a shower of glass and flame that trailed away behind the fighter. It held its flight for only a moment before flipping over on its back and spiraling down to the sea below.

Billy gritted his teeth in frustration. A low growl escaped him as he tried to ram the throttles through their stops. He was still a mile away from the Bf 109 that had shot down his squadron mate. The Messerschmitt glided out of its dive, its pilot looking for his comrades and not yet aware of Billy climbing up from beneath him.

"Come on, come on," he muttered under his breath. "Hold on."

The belly of the Messerschmitt filled his gun sights and he squeezed the trigger on the stick. Smoke and flame burst from the underside of the German fighter. It spun away to starboard diving for the deck, but still under control.

Billy considered following it, but knew his fuel situation didn't allow it. He might still have to fight again as he approached Hal Far or worse, stooge about to the south of the island waiting to slip between German raids in order to land. The wounded Bf 109 would have to count as a probable.

It finally occurred to Billy to look behind him. His wingman was there holding position, keeping Billy's tail clean. He gave Billy another of his thumbs up signals. Billy waved back. He turned and tried to determine the fate of the two Spitfires that had dived away from the German ambush, but the other aircraft were lost somewhere to the south in the haze and he couldn't spot them. He considered searching for them to the south, but he had to husband his own fuel. He couldn't afford any diversions. Anyway, the visibility was so poor he might come within just a few miles of his squadron mates and never see them in the haze. He signaled his wingman to resume their course.

Tense and alert now, Billy kept a constant watch to all sides and behind. Anywhere four Messerschmitts could prowl others might be near as well. They'd continued for only a few minutes when three specks appeared in the distance in front of them, climbing to meet them. Billy knew immediately these could not be British machines. None of the Spitfires from *Furious* would be on the reverse course from Malta and no fighter based on the island would have come this far out to meet the reinforcements. They had to be enemy, either Italian or more Germans.

Billy calculated his options quickly. He could try to avoid the enemy planes, skirting around them to port or starboard, but he abandoned this strategy even as it formed in his mind. The enemy had as surely seen him as he'd seen them and would simply adjust their courses to head him off. His next inclination was to fight it out, but he knew the odds were against him and even should they survive the encounter they could ill afford the fuel it would consume. They couldn't turn round and go back the way they'd come.

He made his decision and signaled his wingman. He wished for just a moment that Bryan was there, but he ruthlessly suppressed the thought. He had no time for wishes. Billy and his wingman tipped the noses of their fighters over and dove, throttles forward to the stops again, straight for the enemy aircraft. The five aircraft hurtled towards each other at a combined speed of over 600 knots. At those speeds the enemy planes were a blur to Billy but they looked like more Bf 109s.

As the planes came within a half-mile the Germans began to spread their formation, giving themselves room to maneuver and avoid head-on collision, exactly what Billy was counting on. As the range closed Billy squeezed the trigger on the control stick. His Spitfire's guns coughed and spat hot lead. Almost immediately the Germans returned fire, but they were already veering away to avoid collision and their aim was wide.

Billy and his wingman blazed through the Germans and past them, holding their dive and course, giving the Germans no opening to engage or divert them. Billy craned his neck and looked for the Germans. They were circling in a tight turn coming back to follow the impertinent Brits, but they'd lost too much space and Billy knew they couldn't catch him if he held his speed. His altimeter showed he'd dropped from 20,000 feet to 11,000 feet already. He looked behind him again. The Germans were still there, now matching his speed and dive. He looked over at his wingman. He was right with him, but Billy thought he could see fluid trailing from the other Spitfire's port wing.

He checked his altimeter again. Down to 5,000 feet. He craned around and the Germans were still there, perhaps a little more distant, but still in the dive about a mile or a little more behind him. 3,500 feet. If the Germans followed him right down on the deck it could be trouble. He'd have to pull out of his dive before them, losing speed while they held theirs, leaving him and his wingman exposed to attack from above and with no room to maneuver below them.

The dive continued; his altimeter showed 2,000 feet. He looked back over his shoulder again. The Bf 109s were still there following them right down to the deck. His engine screamed in torture as the dive took the Spitfire over 400 knots. He had to do something to shake the Germans, fast. He risked taking one hand from the stick and waved at his wingman, signaling to him to veer off and split up. A quick nod was his only reply and the other Spit banked away to starboard. Billy hauled his stick to port. The two Spitfires split away in nearly opposite directions, Billy to the east, his Wingman to the southwest.

He looked back again. The maneuver had worked! The Germans were momentarily confused as to which plane to follow. After several seconds of indecision one of the Germans came after Billy, the other two after his wingman, but they'd lost precious time in the pursuit. By the time the lone German was back on Billy's trail he had opened a good three miles between himself and the Bf 109. With only a single German to contend with Billy again considered offering combat, but he knew that even a successful dogfight would cost him too much fuel to safely reach Malta. Already he was pushing the safety margin to its limit.

At 1,000 feet Billy flattened out his dive, but kept the throttles pushed forward despite the fuel this consumed. He looked back again and saw the German machine arcing away to starboard, giving up the chase as hopeless. Billy eased the throttles back to the Spitfire's optimum cruising speed for low altitude. He breathed a sigh of relief. He assessed his position. He was now completely alone with no idea where his wingman was or even if he had survived the encounter with the Germans.

He was also unsure of his exact position. He estimated himself to be somewhere to the east-north-east of Cape Bon, but was unsure of how far east. It was a critical question. He knew he needed to turn south to fly around the Italian held Island of Pantelleria, and he did this now, taking a dead south heading one-eight-zero for the time being. But if he was too far east he also needed to cut back to the west to avoid coming too close to the enemy island. On the other hand, if he weren't as far east as he feared and he cut back to the west he would use precious fuel unnecessarily in lengthening his flight. In the end he elected to hold his straight south course and play it by ear. He stayed low, dropping gradually to 500 feet, reasoning that if he were approaching Pantelleria he could hide better from any radar device the enemy might have in operation there if he remained down on the deck. In any case, climbing to altitude at this stage of the flight might use almost as much fuel as it saved.

The minutes crept by uneventfully, but he was too keyed up to relax again, and mercifully thoughts of Bryan were banished. He stayed alert, watching for any sign of aircraft or for a hint of land either to his east, the port side, or dead ahead, straight south. This leg of his flight was scheduled to last less than twenty minutes, covering only sixty to seventy miles before he turned to the east for Malta. Unless he picked up a sighting of Pantelleria he would have to guess when to turn east for his destination.

When after twenty minutes he had not sighted Pantelleria he made the assumption that he was south and west of the Italian island and he banked over to port for the final and potentially most dangerous leg of his flight. If his navigation was close to accurate he should be within forty to forty-five minutes of Malta. He decided to aim for a point he guessed was somewhat to the south of his destination. That way if he didn't come directly upon the island he would at least know which way to turn. It could only lie to the north.

He checked his compass, coming to course one-zero-five, a little south of east. He knew it was too soon, but he turned on his radio receiver anyway; it was pre-tuned to the frequency of the Malta beacon. He listened carefully, but the telltale signal wasn't there. He scanned the sky in all directions, looking for any sign of enemy aircraft. The sky was clear. He sat back in his seat and checked his fuel gauges. He had enough fuel to reach Malta, if he was anywhere near where he thought he was, but his margin was much lower than planned when he'd taken off from *Furious* at 0832 hours that morning. He checked his watch. 1024. Not quite two hours in the air.

This was the longest flight he'd ever made; the few combat sorties he'd flown from air stations in the south of England were much briefer, out over the channel and back. Once, he'd flown as far as German occupied France, covering a force of Blenheims as they returned from a raid against Cherbourg. That flight took over an hour.

He squirmed uncomfortably in his seat. He needed to urinate. Billy had heard plenty of horror stories about pilots who got distracted by physical discomfort of this sort and fell prey to enemy fighters and he was determined not to become the subject of such a tail himself. He forced his full bladder from his thoughts and concentrated on the flying tasks before him.

Once more he scanned in all directions. Still no other aircraft. 1044 hours. Perhaps only twenty minutes to landfall. Still no homing beacon. He checked his fuel gauges. They showed less than fifteen percent of his fuel remaining. If he was very careful he could remain in the air for perhaps another thirty minutes.

The Merlin engine droned on and Billy's tension rose as the minutes and his fuel slipped away. He tried to resist looking at his watch, but now found himself marking nearly every minute of the flight.

At 1104 hours he deemed he should be directly south of Malta, yet there was no sign of the island and his wireless set still had not detected the homing beacon. He checked his fuel gauges. They showed about seven percent fuel remaining.

It was time to turn north. He banked slowly to port, scanning the horizon as he did. No sign of land or other aircraft did he see, but at less than 1,000 feet he knew his perspective was limited as was the range at which he could detect the homing beacon. He checked his compass as he turned, swinging right through heading zero-zero-zero all the way round to three-four-five, before easing back to starboard and settling on due north. Not a peep from the wireless.

After five minutes on his northerly course he began to question his own judgment. He frantically reviewed every course adjustment and every aspect of the dead reckoning he'd done from the moment he'd lost his concentration and missed the course change north of Tunisia. He could find no potential error that put him more than twenty miles off course. Nonetheless, the last thing he wanted was to find land only to have it be enemy territory on Sicily.

"Steady Billy," he murmured to himself. "Think it through. Where have you gone wrong?"

He'd just come to the decision to turn round and go south when something caught his eye, just for an instant on the northern horizon. He strained to see, but whatever it was had disappeared. Billy decided to climb to see if he could spot it again. For a long moment the propeller hub of his Spitfire blocked his view as he gained 500 feet in altitude. As he leveled off he strained again to see anything but hazy blue sky to the north. He scanned from dead ahead then around to the west slowly, then back to dead ahead and slowly to the east. Nothing. He sat back and rubbed his dry, tired eyes. He blinked and scratched under his flight cap and started to turn round.

Suddenly, he saw it again. Excitement rose in him as he recognized what he'd failed to identify the first time. A puff of back smoke hung just above the horizon. A moment later another joined it and as he flew further north more and more came into view. He was seeing an anti-aircraft barrage from afar. It had to be Malta!

Doubt crept back and his excitement eased off a bit. If it was Malta why was there no homing beacon? He checked his instruments. His gauges showed he was nearly out of fuel. Whatever was ahead of him he had no choice now, but to pray that a friendly welcome on British territory awaited him.

He turned a page on his knee notepad and double-checked the contact frequency. That morning during the briefing aboard *Furious* Commander Nesbith had admonished them to establish contact with fighter control at Hal Far before attempting to land, else the gunners on the ground might assume them to be enemy and shoot them from the sky. He flipped the switch to activate his transmitter.

"Malta, fighter control," he called. "Malta, fighter control, this is Gamecock two-two, repeat, Gamecock two-two, over."

Each of the thirty-six aircraft flown from *Furious* that morning had a unique call sign that was transmitted in code to Malta before they'd ever left Gibraltar. Bryan's had been Lambswool two-four.

"Gamecock two-two, this is Mother Roost," came the crackling reply almost instantly. Billy sighed in relief.

"Mother Roost, Gamecock two-two," he answered. "I'm low on fuel. Request immediate landing instructions."

Six or seven puffs of smoke burst in a group over what he could now see was land ahead.

"Negative Gamecock two-two," the air controller answered him. "There's a raid underway. The field is currently U/S. Orbit to the south. We expect the field to be clear in twenty, repeat two-zero minutes."

Billy's stomach turned in a tight knot. The airfield was unserviceable! He looked at his fuel gauges. They all read empty. He had only minutes to stay in the air.

"Mother Roost, this is Gamecock two-two declaring a fuel emergency. Estimate three minutes flying time remaining." A long pause stretched till Billy was near to a scream before Mother Roost answered.

"Gamecock two-two, acknowledged. Make your approach low and fast from the southeast. Line up on the eastern edge of the strip. It's a little cleaner. You'll get just one chance at landing, Gamecock. We'll try to keep the Messerschmitts off you while you land. Good luck."

Billy didn't bother to acknowledge. The hundred foot tall white limestone bluff he'd been told to expect at the south end of Hal Far field was clearly in view, waves crashing against its base. The runway came into view. Fires burned on both sides of the strip with black, oily smoke gusting away to the north. Blackened craters lay everywhere, including on the strip itself. Billy adjusted to line up on the east side of the landing strip, as instructed, though he couldn't see a bit of difference between the east and west sides. The whole runway looked U/S to him.

He eased the throttle back as he approached land and stole a glance into the sky around the airfield. There did not appear to be any German fighters waiting to pounce on him. The end of the runway literally ran right off the island over the bluff and out to sea. He came over land at a height of about fifty feet and quickly eased down toward the runway. He was just about to set down when a massive crater loomed ahead of him. He lifted the nose and hurdled over the fire-scorched pit, settling back down to ground beyond the crater. The strip was very rough, strewn with large lumps of earth and loose rock. It took all his concentration and strength to hold the Spit on the runway.

The Spitfire slowed as he rolled down the strip. Smoke drifted across the runway from a fire burning to his left. He spared a quick glance at the flames as he passed. A single engine aircraft burned out of control in a revetment two hundred yards away. A figure dashed out of the ditch on the side of the runway and stood ahead of him in the middle of the strip waving his arms frantically.

The man directed Billy to veer off the strip onto a taxiway to starboard. In less than a minute his Spitfire was parked in a revetment two hundred yards east of the runway, its propeller slowly spinning to a stop. A tan colored camouflage net hung over the revetment. Ground crewmen rushed to the plane, lifting its tail plane from the ground and manually walking the Spitfire around till it faced back out onto the field. An army Corporal leapt onto the wing and pulled back Billy's canopy.

"Out you come, Sir," the army man said. "Step lively now, we've a fresh pilot ready to step aboard."

Billy unsnapped his harness and climbed stiffly from the cockpit.

"I imagine you 'ave to wee, Sir," said the Corporal as he helped Billy down from the wing. "There's a convenience right over there, Sir." The Corporal pointed to an old fuel tin by one wall of the revetment. "Before you go, Sir," he caught Billy's arm. "What is the condition of your aircraft?"

Billy pulled the goggles from his head, rubbing the creases they'd pressed into his face.

"She's absolutely 'bingo' fuel and I estimate I used about half my ammunition," he answered. "Otherwise, she spun like a top the whole way through. Absolutely top notch."

"Thank you, Sir," said the Corporal, releasing his arm. "As soon as you're done you're asked to report to the operations center." He pointed to a low, sandbagged bunker a hundred yards away. A Bofors gun barked nearby followed quickly by two others. The tonk-tonk-tonk of the Bofors' was quickly joined by the louder crack of the heavy 3.7-inch flak guns. Looking up in the sky Billy saw black specks at hi-altitude over the field.

When Billy finished at the fuel tin he started off for the ops center, but hadn't gone but a few feet when a RAF officer intercepted him.

"Gamecock twenty-two?" he asked him.

"Yes, Sir, Flying Sergeant Billy Wilson, Sir."

"Group-Captain Reed," the man replied. "What time did you leave *Furious* this morning?" he asked Billy as they moved towards the ops center again.

Billy stopped and leaned down to unsnap his note pad from his knee. He referred to page one as he resumed walking.

"I was off at 0832 hours this morning, Sir," he answered.

"I see," said Reed. "Er, you were in Commander Nesbith's trio then?"

"Oh, no, Sir," Billy laughed. "Commander Nesbith was first off the deck, around 0815 hours I should say." He stopped suddenly and looked at Reed. "Has Commander Nesbith arrived, Sir?"

Reed ignored the question.

"Which trio were you in then, Flying Sergeant?" he asked instead.

"Well, Sir," Billy replied. "I was flying leader for trio eight, number twenty-two off the deck."

"You were twenty-second off the deck this morning?" pressed Reed.

"Yes, Sir," answered Billy.

"What happened to the other two of your trio?"

Billy started to speak, but choked up unexpectedly. He cleared his throat and began again.

"One crashed on take-off, Sir," he answered slowly. "I became separated from the other near Cape Bon when we were jumped by Messerschmitts. I'm not sure what happened to him."

"You were twenty-second off the deck this morning?" repeated Reed.

"Yes, Sir," Billy answered again. "Sir, how many have landed so far."

Reed looked at him a long moment. Bombs crashed down on the north end of the field.

"You're the first, Flying Sergeant Wilson. You're the first."

Kenneth reported back just after dawn to the Duty Officer in the mess at Hal Far with his right arm in a sling. Cuts and bruises on his face and hands attested to the trouble he'd found.

"What happened, Wiltshire?" asked the Navy man.

Kenneth told the story of the explosion that destroyed the seaplane at Kalafrana and how it had wreaked havoc on the people on the ramp.

"Have that arm looked at by the surgeon," the Duty Officer ordered. Kenneth was sure the officer thought he was a malingerer, faking an injury or that perhaps he had hurt himself to avoid combat.

Kenneth made the long trek to the station infirmary in the cavern at the southwest side of the field, his right arm hanging limply in its sling. Searing pain flashed through his shoulder each time he tried to lift the arm. Small arms fire crackled away to the north, closer than ever it seemed to him. He checked in at the hospital then waited for hours to see a Doctor. Wounded poured in to the hospital and the galleries delved from solid limestone were crowded. Injured men had filled all the available beds and lay on blankets stretched on the cold floor of the caverns. A very tired Doctor at last found a moment to examine Kenneth's arm. A Maltese nurse hovered nearby to assist.

"Hold on now, Wiltshire," he said. "This won't hurt a bit." With that he took Kenneth's injured arm by the wrist, lifted it straight out to his side, pulled and twisted. Kenneth had some idea what was coming, having seen the same procedure used on the separated shoulder of a farm hand at home in South Dakota, but he still yelped in pain as his shoulder was popped back in its socket. The nurse helped him into a sling.

"Just keep the arm immobilized. In a week or two you'll be fine," the doctor told Kenneth.

Kenneth left the hospital to deliver his medical orders to the Duty Officer at the mess. He was torn between his desire to get into the air to hit back at the Germans and the numbness in his useless arm. The officer glared at him and shook his head.

"Very well, Wiltshire," he said. "You're off the flying list." The officer made a check mark on a sheet of paper. "It might interest you to know that we're expecting thirty-six Spitfires delivered today," he went on. "We're going to need every pilot to get them back in the air. Now get on down to the Kalafrana air raid shelter.

Extra pilots are to be evacuated if possible."

Kenneth left the mess, but he didn't go to the air raid shelter. He walked with his head down towards the air operations bunker. The bunker was a sandbag affair, dug deep with just a few feet above ground level. Its roof was covered with limestone gravel and dust to blend it into the surrounding terrain when viewed from the air. He entered the bunker and mingled with other pilots and aircrew there, Navy and RAF alike, over a hundred men in total. Cigarette smoke hung thick against the low ceiling and a quiet buzz of conversation filled the bunker's main chamber, but he was in no frame of mind for conversation or the kind of hi-spirits that young pilots engage in, even at desperate moments. The bunker was dim and cool and had a strange, stale odor.

The mood among the Royal Navy staff in the bunker was tense and expectant. Off-duty flyers and ground officers alike lounged about, smoking and conversing in undertones. They seemed to be watching a door in the rear of the bunker. Against one wall of the bunker Kenneth spied steam swirling up from a large kettle on a table. He wound his way through the crowded bunker to the teakettle, careful not to bump his injured arm. He chose from an eclectic selection of mis-matched cups, all chipped and cracked and poured a spot of tea. It was weak, made with tealeaves already used too often, and for the thousandth time on Malta he wished for a cup of strong, black American coffee. Kenneth closed his eyes and sagged against the sandbag wall of the bunker, rolling his neck and letting his mind wander. A moment later he caught himself just as he was about to drop the cup and fall asleep on his feet. He shook his head, blinked his eyes and carried the cup to a table in the center of the room. Several navy pilots were at the table talking quietly among themselves.

"Mind if I join you?" Kenneth asked.

The navy men gestured for Kenneth to sit.

"Does anyone have any news?" Kenneth asked after sipping his tea.

"The German have taken Luqa this morning," one of the Navy pilots said. "They're massing near Safi for an attack on Hal Far."

"Bloody hell," groaned Kenneth.

"That may not be the worst of it," the Navy man continued. "Word has it the Germans have cleared Ta Qali and are landing transports, delivering troops by the hundreds."

"What, if anything are we doing about it all?" asked Kenneth.

The Navy pilot pointed to the door at the rear of the bunker. "We're expecting some word on reinforcements. The fleet is said to be flying in a squadron of Spitfires this afternoon."

"The duty officer told me the same thing," Kenneth said. "Thirty-six Spitfires some time later today."

The airmen chatted aimlessly among themselves, sipping their weak tea and marking time, but always watching the door at the rear of the bunker. The Navy men explained to Kenneth that the door led to the air station's wireless office. From time to time the door opened and a messenger or orderly entered or left. Each time the door opened the pilots' conversation ceased as they watched for some hint that the Spitfires were in-bound.

At 1105 hours an air-raid siren began to sound and a few moments later Kenneth heard the bark and chatter of flak guns followed by the thud of heavy bombs crashing down on the airfield. Dust and dirt filtered from the roof of the bunker, but the pilots went on with nonchalant conversation, covering their teacups with their hands to keep the dust out.

A few minutes after the raid began the door to the wireless office opened and a messenger ran out. He dashed through the bunker and out the exit. A Navy Lt. Commander followed the orderly out the wireless office door. He stood on a bench and surveyed the room. Conversation died away to an eerie silence punctuated by a crescendo of flak and exploding bombs outside the bunker.

"I am Lt. Commander Morgan," he said. "RAF pilots Hathaway, Reynolds, Graves and Walsh come forward please!"

Benches scraped as the four named pilots stood and made their way through the crowded bunker to the officer.

"For the rest of you," the Navy officer continued, "please remain to-hand. We've just gotten a communication from the first of a flight of Spitfires that flew off the decks of *HMS Furious* this morning. They'll begin landing in a few moments."

A cheer erupted among the pilots in the room. Kenneth winced when the Navy pilot beside him slapped his shoulder. The Navy officer went on, raising his voice to be heard above the celebration.

"As the fighters land they're to be refueled and if necessary re-armed then gotten back into the air immediately with a fresh pilot to hit the Germans. We're expecting up to thirty-six Spitfires this afternoon, so you RAF chaps are going to be busy. I'll be calling you in groups of four or five as the aircraft approach." He stepped down from the bench and led the four RAF pilots away.

Now the pilots in the room resumed their conversation, but at a much more energetic level. It took a moment for Kenneth to realize the flak guns were silent. No more bombs exploded on the field.

The entrance door to the bunker opened and a voice shouted, "There's a Spitfire over the threshold!"

Pilots stampeded to the door, bursting out into the hazy sunlight of a warm Maltese afternoon. Shielding their eyes against the glare they cheered lustily as a Spitfire touched on the runway, bounced once over a crater and settled back down to earth. Kenneth and the other pilots remained outside the bunker watching for the arrival of more Spitfires. In just about ten minutes the first Spitfire was airborne again, taking off to the south along with the two Spitfires that had been pushed down the Safi Strip that morning, racing into the sky and climbing for altitude. Army crews worked feverishly on the runway, filling in craters, removing debris and smoothing the landing surface as best they could.

Kenneth checked his watch. 1135 hours. Twenty minutes since the first Spitfire landed and there was still no sign of any others. Kenneth reflected on his own experience flying into Malta earlier that spring. On that day Ta Qali and Luqa were beehives of activity as his flight descended on the two fields, thirty-three aircraft touching down in just over forty minutes. The pilots around him were quiet again as realization dawned on them that something had gone wrong to delay or prevent the arrival of more Spitfires.

At 1140 hours the air-raid sirens began to sound again. The pilots shuffled back into the bunker. Their unease grew when no other Spitfires followed the first onto the ground. By 1300 hours unease grew to something very like despair. They began to trickle away to their billets even before the air raid sirens sounded again at 1320.

>>>>>>>>>>>>

The Axis consolidation of Luqa airfield continued the afternoon and into the evening of June 27th. Pockets of resistance were systematically wiped out. The wounded of both sides were retrieved from the field and taken to aid stations where German doctors and corpsmen worked with the help of British prisoners to save as many lives as possible. The scene at the aid stations was ghastly with bodies of the dead stacked up in heaps. At every aid station other piles grew as well, legs to the left, arms to the right.

Throughout the day the sound of heavy guns away to the north came to the men at Luqa at irregular intervals. To the Axis forces the sound was cheering; the Italian Navy was active and the scheduled landings on the island's northern shore were taking place. To the British forces the sound of the guns spelled disaster.

Late in the afternoon Italian paratroopers of the Folgore Division cautiously approached the station armory at the southwest end of the field. The heavy steel blast doors at the cavern entrance were closed tight, locked from the inside. A squad of Italian engineers crept up to the door and began placing explosive demolition charges to seal the entrance. Kuno watched through his binoculars from a distance of over a kilometer. He and Captain Thaler were hunkered down in a bomb crater on the east side of the main runway. Kuno could lift his glasses just high enough to see over the crown of the strip. Axis activity on the west side of the main runway at Luqa was almost completely shut down as the dangerous task of sealing the armory entrance was tackled.

The Italians worked quickly and efficiently, led by a young Lieutenant; no wasted motion or time. Kuno admired the young officer's professionalism and the quiet way he went about leading his men, giving orders without any shouting or arm waving, kneeling to help when a specific task needed an extra hand. He lowered his glasses and spoke to Thaler.

"Very un-Italian, this Italian," he said.

"A good officer," Thaler agreed.

Kuno started to ask if Thaler knew the Lieutenant's name, but he never had the chance. A volcanic explosion obliterated the limestone bluff into which the armory was delved, wiping out the party of Italian engineers in a flash. Huge limestone boulders were hurled high in the air. Kuno and Thaler fell to their faces and curled into fetal positions, hugging the inside of the bomb crater. Secondary explosions shook the ground beneath them as bombs and other munitions stored by the British in the caverns of the armory cooked off. Luqa was the RAF bomber station and hundreds of heavy, high explosive bombs were cached there since before the war. The chain reaction of massive explosions continued for many minutes as one gallery of the armory after another was breached. The noise was ear shattering. Stones rained down all about the field and several came within meters of Kuno and Thaler in the crater. Both men and hundreds of others at Luqa cringed and tried to burrow into the earth. Finally the pace of explosions began to slacken and Kuno dared to lift his head again. An enormous cloud of gray and black dust and smoke spiraled upward, completely obscuring the site of the armory. An occasional explosion lit the smoke and dust like lightning inside a storm cloud. Kuno and Thaler rose to their feet and surveyed the field. Men were picking themselves up all over Luqa, congratulating each other on being alive.

"We must return to the HQ," Kuno said, "and make a report to Colonel August on this."

"What of the attack against the last airfield?" asked Thaler.

"I don't see how it can come any earlier than tomorrow morning," Kuno replied as the men climbed out of the crater and began their trek to the headquarters of the 23rd Regiment. "Units are all mixed up and jumbled. It will take the rest of the day to sort them out."

"Have we the strength for the attack?" Thaler wondered.

"Good question," said Kuno. "We need further reinforcement before we can take Hal Far."

Kuno detailed his orders to Thaler as they walked. Thaler was to set about reorganizing the Regiment, consolidating survivors into five units of about company strength and to inventory the available ammunition, weapons and supplies, making a list of anything in short supply so that an air drop could be arranged.

"It is good to see you safe, Major," Sgt. Tondok greeted them as they arrived at the HQ, a sandbag bunker taken over from the British at the north end of the field.

"Thank you, Sergeant," replied Kuno. "Please put through a call to Colonel August."

"Yes, Sir," said the Sgt. "The Colonel has already called several times looking for you." A moment later Tondok handed Kuno the field phone.

"Major Schacht here!" he spoke into the phone.

"SCHACHT!" shouted the unmistakable aristocratic voice of the Baron von der Heydte. "That was a hell of a bang your Italians triggered. Are you safe?"

"Yes, Colonel," Kuno smiled. "I am quite well."

"Good, good. Listen Schacht, when can you expect to attack the last airfield?"

Kuno repeated his words to Thaler with no hesitation. "Not possible before morning tomorrow, Colonel. Troops are scattered and low on ammunition. Also, I feel it would be unwise to attack without local communication between the Air Force and ourselves. Our strength is dangerously low. We'll have to rely on close air support to overcome the British. They are sure to make their last stand a desperate one."

"Very well, Schacht," the Baron answered after a moment. "In that event I want you to return here before sunset. We'll plan the attack while your team packs up its wireless gear for the move south."

>>>>>>>>>>>>

The Wehrmacht high command gathered at the Fuhrer's bunker beneath the Reich Chancellery in Berlin to track progress of Operation Hercules. In the early morning hours of June 26th Reich Marshall Göring and the Fuhrer joined Admiral Raeder and Field Marshals Keitel and Halder to receive the initial reports of the airborne landings. The news that the first landings had taken place on schedule and without unexpected problems led to a burst of euphoria and to effusive praise from the Fuhrer to his officers. However as the morning hours crept on the news was not so promising. Word that contact could not be established with the landing force at two of the three airfields cast a pall of gloom over the assembled senior officers and the Fuhrer. Hitler railed against Admiral Raeder, blaming him as the architect of the operation and its primary proponent for convincing the Fuhrer to go ahead with it in spite of his own misgivings.

Initially Raeder counseled patience. An operation of this complexity would of course see unexpected challenges, but the officers and men were of the highest caliber. He was confident they would adjust to the situation and prevail. But as the early morning wore on towards the dawn the news from Malta was dominated by reports of heavy fighting and stiffer resistance than anticipated. Hitler's fury grew and Raeder wisely kept silent.

Not until the morning of the 27th when word at last reached Berlin that the high ground at Mdina had been taken and that Luqa airfield was being attacked did the mood begin to swing again. Now the Fuhrer lavished praise on the paratroopers and their ability to crush the British resistance. As the day progressed it became apparent that the Luftwaffe had almost complete mastery of the skies over Malta. The Fuhrer felt confident enough to take a mid-afternoon nap. He slept from three in the afternoon till almost seven that evening.

Shortly after his sleep began the command bunker received a report from Sicily that the British had somehow received reinforcement Spitfire fighters. These were the sixteen fighters that survived the flight from *HMS Eagle* on the 25th. The high command dreaded the prospect of informing the Fuhrer of the fighters' arrival. Their relief was palpable when the Kriegsmarine forwarded the signal from Franz Popitz and U-212 announcing the sinking of a Royal Navy aircraft carrier forty hours earlier. Thus, when the Fuhrer awakened and entered the bunker for an update he was given the news of the carrier's destruction, before he was told of the Spitfires. And so it went into the evening of the 27th. News of fresh victories was offset with, if not defeats, then mounting reports of fierce resistance on the island and of the Royal Navy's response to the invasion. Elation alternated with concern.

When the disappointing results of the second air attack against the British fleet reached Berlin the Fuhrer's nerves reached their highest pitch. He stormed and raged about the conference room at the incompetence of both the Italian and German air forces.

"Reich Marshal Göring!" he roared. "You are to order an all-out effort from the Luftwaffe on Sardinia! Every available aircraft is to attack the British fleet immediately!"

The Reich Marshal clicked his heels and shouted, "YES, My Fuhrer!"

"I will accept no excuses and no apologies!" Hitler went on. "Every aircraft must attack and press in against the British! They must not reach Malta!"

At Decimomanu the signal from Luftwaffe HQ in Berlin to mount an all-out attack came as preparations were already under way to do exactly that. Estimates of the British Fleet's course and speed placed it nearing the approaches to the Skerki Bank around 2050 hours, about forty minutes before sunset. The decision was made to attack the British as they neared Skerki. The shallow waters to their south would limit the Royal Navy's maneuverability, making the fleet more vulnerable, especially to torpedo attack.

The available aircraft largely dictated the plan of attack. Just 12 undamaged He 111 torpedo bombers remained on the field. By contrast there were nineteen Ju 88s and twenty-four Ju 87 Stukas on the field along with over twenty Bf 109s available as escorts.

The Heinkels were the most effective aircraft against shipping but were too few to strike a devastating blow on their own. The Ju 88s were not designed as dive-bombers and the results of the first two attacks seemed to bear out that they were ineffective in the role, at least against warships. The Stukas on the other hand were widely respected by friend and foe alike, though in truth they were reaching the stage they would soon be seen as obsolete, vulnerable to fighter attack due to their slow speed.

The plan that developed sought to maximize the attributes of each type of aircraft. The Ju 88s would attack from medium height, in long gliding approaches while the Stukas' would bomb from high altitude and the Heinkels would approach at wave top height to deliver their torpedoes. In this way the three bomber types would force the British to divide their flak fire from the wave tops to directly overhead.

Finally, the plan called for an all out effort against the airplane carrier and the battleship. All other targets were to be ignored. The aircraft would begin taking off at 1945 hours.

"BRIDGE!" Lt. Peter Walker shouted into the interphone. "Can you hear me?"

"YES!" *Renown's* Executive Officer shouted back. "I hear you! What is the situation?"

"It's bad, bridge, very bad!" Peter shouted back. He held the phone receiver to his ear with one hand, covering his other ear with the other hand. "The fire is right up against the armored belt. There's no room aft of the fire to get at it. We can't get past it to get forward of it. The only place to fight it from is directly above, from the weather deck where the bomb penetrated!"

"Where are you now, Walker?" the XO asked.

"I'm forward in 'A' shell room, right in front of 'A' turret's barbette!" shouted Peter. "I have a thermometer against the bulkhead here. It reads 135° Fahrenheit and it's climbing! The fire is right on the other side of the armored belt. I can hear it! The belt is too hot to touch. I estimate the temperature on the other side of the belt at 1,000 degrees!"

The magazines and shell rooms were the most sheltered and quiet places in the ship and in tropical waters were usually the coolest as well, with air conditioning and humidity controls to protect the tons of powder and shells kept there. Conversation in the magazines of a warship is usually muted as though men fear a loud noise or unguarded remark could upset the delicate chemistry of the ammunition, causing its fickle nature to turn against the crew. Muted conversation was out of the question now however. Despite nine inches of steel separating the magazine from the fire the roar of the conflagration, though muffled somewhat, came through the armored belt nonetheless.

Reggie looked about him. Shells for the 15-inch guns were stored in this part of the magazine, stood upright four deep on racks, their snub noses gleaming dully in the dim light of the compartment. Aisles radiated like spokes of a wheel from the base of the barbette of the turret above. The next room over contained the cotton swathed bundles of gunpowder used to propel the mighty shells on their way from the muzzles of the big guns. The cotton was specially treated flash fabric, designed to burn completely and instantly with no ash remainder when the gun was fired. A smoldering spark left in the gun barrel after firing could prove disastrous when the next round was loaded. A spark in the magazine could devastate the entire ship if it came into contact with one of those bundles. So, too could the heat radiating from the forward bulkhead.

"Are the sprinklers damaged?" shouted the XO from the bridge.

"No! Not that I can tell!" Walker looked at the thermometer on the wall. "And if it keeps getting hotter here we're going to find out soon! Fifteen more degrees and the sprinklers will come on. The cooling system is already on maximum."

He and the XO both paused. They knew that if the sprinklers went on the magazine would be safe from explosion, but also that the ammunition would be ruined. With the fire extinguished ammunition could be transferred from magazines further aft, but only with extraordinary effort and care. Otherwise, without ammunition 'A' turret would be useless.

"Get your damage control teams on deck, Walker!" said the XO. "We've got to put out that fire!"

"Yes, Sir!"

Walker hung the brass phone back on its cradle. All instruments and tools in the magazine were brass to avoid the risk of a spark being struck. He glanced back up at the thermometer. 137°. Reggie turned and ran for the ladder to escape the magazine, passing through the anti-flash curtains that hung at intervals in the chamber. He passed the central hub of the barbette and the great hydraulic hoists that lifted the shells and powder charges up to the guns.

He came to the armored escape trunk, the cylindrical steel tube used by the magazine's crew to enter and exit in an emergency. He climbed into the trunk and closed the lower hatch behind him. The trunk was pressurized to always force air out of the trunk, away from the powder and shells as a precaution against a spark or flame entering the magazine. He clambered up the ladder and engaged the interlock mechanism at the top hatch. It prevented the upper and lower hatches being both opened at the same time. He emerged between decks next to the cylindrical barbette. One more passage way and ladder and he was on the weather deck, emerging on the starboard side of 'A' turret.

Black, sooty smoke billowed along the deck making him cough and splutter. The deck presented a scene of pandemonium to the amateur eye. Men ran back and forth amid much shouting and gesturing, hauling hoses and extinguishers to the fire. Others manned the mains, hydrants and valves that supplied water for the hoses. The roar of the fire was much more pronounced in the open than it was in the magazine. Looking forward Peter saw flames leaping up from the deck, blowing across the deck to port.

Against the starboard side of 'A' turret stood a rack on wheels, holding gas masks, tanks of bottled oxygen and asbestos fire suits. Walker ran to the rack and started climbing into his fire suit. In less than a minute he was testing the valve that fed oxygen from the tank on his back to the respirator covering his face. The suit was bulky and cumbersome and the hood muffled sound. Thick asbestos mittens covered his hands.

He started moving forward to the edge of the bomb hole. Gusts of wind tore gaps in the screen of smoke pouring from the hole, exposing sheets of angry red and orange flame. Here and there Walker saw flame tinged in blue and white, nearly translucent. Oil or chemicals were feeding the flame. Other men in asbestos suits manned three-inch fire hoses, pouring water down on the fire. Massive pumps below decks sucked huge drafts of seawater from the ocean to feed the fire hoses. Three or four men held each three-inch hose, the man at the end fighting to control the high pressure nozzle and keep the stream of water directed down into the hole.

As Walker toddled towards the fire he found the deck ripped and bent, jagged edges twisted upwards by the force of the blast. With the smoke and flame billowing from the wound it was difficult for him to assess the size of the opening, but his sense was that it was smaller than he'd expected, perhaps only ten to twelve feet in diameter. Paradoxically, this was not a good thing. A smaller hole on deck meant that the bomb had penetrated several decks before exploding and that most of the bomb blast's energy was spent inside the ship.

Walker reached the front of one of the hose lines and leaned forward to try to catch a glimpse down into the hole. Flame and smoke obscured his view completely and the heat of the fire began to transmit to his body, even through the asbestos suit. He leaned out a little further trying to determine how deep the wound extended. For just an instant the flames swirled clear and the smoke parted. He gasped involuntarily. The bomb had penetrated at least three decks. Steel deck and bulkhead plates glowed white hot in the inferno. The roar and crackle of the fire was deafening, even inside his asbestos hood.

The flames and smoke swirled back and obliterated his view, but the glimpse he'd caught was enough to tell him the situation was very serious. Unable to reach the fire below decks they would have to fight it from above, pouring water down the hole onto the flames, controlling the fire until it burned itself out. Meantime they had to cool the armored belt before the heat it was radiating set off the fire sprinklers in the magazine, or worse if the sprinklers failed, ignited the powder charges just a few feet from the blaze.

He stepped back from the hole, turned and patted the lead fireman on the shoulder intending to demonstrate with hand signals and gestures the need to direct the play of water against the steel belt below, but the deck rumbled beneath his feet. He flinched away from the fire just as an explosion launched a huge ball of flame from the wound in the deck like the eruption of some primal volcano.

The blast hurled Walker and the men of his fire fighting teams off their feet. Peter landed face down on the deck with the breath knocked out of him. He pushed himself onto his knees, gasping for air. The asbestos hood and glass faceplate restricted his vision so that he had to turn his whole body to see anything to either side. He turned to one side to see if any of his crew was injured. A sharp pain in his left side made him gasp as he turned. He struggled to his feet, clutching his left arm against his side.

All about him men were picking themselves up off the deck, amid burning patches scattered around the deck and on 'A' turret's glacis face. Something hit Reggie in the legs below the knees, nearly dropping him to the deck again. He turned and looked down. The fire hoses were whipping across the deck, water spraying everywhere but down the hole. Men began to control the hoses, laying their bodies across them, pinning them to the deck until others arrived to help, but one hose was still completely out of control. Its brass nozzle flashed across the deck, smacking a man on the knee, felling him like an oak struck by lightning. The nozzle reversed course, flying under pressure against the turret with a clang as clear as a Sunday church bell. One of the damage control team jumped on the hose and held it down while others worked their way forward to the nozzle. Walker moved back to the edge of the bomb hole where the first of the hoses was back in use spraying the fire. He put his hand on the shoulder of the front man. They pressed their faceplates together to talk.

"We've got to cool the armored belt!" shouted Walker. The

man's face was only inches from his own and it felt strange to shout. He pointed under his feet. "The magazine is getting too hot!"

The man didn't try to answer, but nodded and dragged the hose around to the side of the hole, the other men now on the hose following his lead. Walker quickly gestured for the other hose teams to follow suit, then moved to examine one of the flaming patches on deck. He discovered the fire was being fed by paint stored in the forepeak in the bows. The explosion had most likely been from tins of paint cooking off in the heat.

Clouds of steam poured up from the hole as water from the hoses found the hot spots. The damage party began to gain the upper hand on the fire. The volume of smoke diminished steadily and soon the flames were no longer leaping up above the deck. The fire crews were able to move right to the edge of the hole and play their streams of water directly on the sources of the blaze.

As the fire came under control Peter backed away from the hole and gingerly began peeling out of the fire suit. He was drenched in sweat. His left side ached and he couldn't lift his left arm more than a few inches from his side without stabbing pain.

His path to the bridge to report was slow and pain filled. He went out of his way to avoid vertical ladders; even so climbing the four decks to the bridge exhausted him.

"Ah, Walker," said the XO. "There you are! What is the situation?"

"The fire is nearly out, Sir," he began, struggling for breath. "The forepeak is ruined along with the paint and chain lockers and the forward electrical stores room. The starboard anchors are both gone, and all three for'ard capstans have been unseated." He paused for breath. "We can drop the port anchor but I'm afraid we'll not be able to recover it until we've been in a shipyard for repairs."

"Good show, Walker." The XO looked him up and down. Reggie's uniform was soiled with soot and sweat. Grease was smeared across his forehead and one cheek. "And do get yourself cleaned up won't you? An officer should present a more tidy appearance don't you think?"

In the chartroom behind *Renown's* bridge Lt. Harris handed Admiral Burrough a clipboard.

"Damage reports, Sir," he said.

The Admiral scanned the top sheet then flipped through several more pages.

"Not as bad as I'd feared," he remarked, handing the clipboard back to Harris. "*Phoebe* lost. *Kenya* badly damaged, but still able to maintain speed."

"Yes, and for all the smoke and fire *Renown's* fighting power and speed are not affected either," said Captain Daniel proudly.

"We must expect the Germans to have saved their worst for us as we approach Skerki," Commander Oats said, tracing his finger across the chart. Admiral Burrough, Flag Secretary Harris and Captain Daniel, commander of *Renown* were together with Oats in the flagship's chartroom, plotting the fleet's course for the upcoming hours before darkness.

"What does that mean exactly, Oats?" asked Burrough.

"I should think they'll hit us with everything they have available as we approach the narrows, Sir," answered Oats. "They'll attack from the north to try to drive us into the shallows. They'll throw everything they have on Sardinia against us, perhaps adding flights from Sicily as well."

Burrough only nodded thoughtfully.

As the sun passed its zenith then began to drop in the western sky the heat of the day built until many men of Force H felt on the verge of heat exhaustion. Even those in open positions, the lookouts and gun crews in open gun tubs suffered. During the early afternoon watch the wind generated by the ships' movement felt more like the blast from an oven. As the dogwatch went on the men also looked forward to relief from 'Action Stations, Air Attack'. After sundown the threat from the air would be gone, as axis attack aircraft of the time had no surface search radar equipment. The danger from the sky would of course be replaced by a redoubled danger from beneath the surface.

StaffelKäpitan Heinrich Trott checked his wingman. The other Stuka lay just off his port wing bobbing gently in the crosswind. He looked back to his instrument panel. Altimeter: 2,000 meters. Compass bearing: one-seven-five degrees. Chronometer: 2105 hours. He scanned the surface of the sea. A huge spreading plume of black smoke hung to the south. At its top the plume was miles wide. Heinrich pressed the button on his throat microphone cutting in the short-range radio-telephone.

"Turn to starboard to course two-seven-zero on my mark," he said. " Five, four, three, two, one, mark!"

Lt. Commander Webster, Gunnery Officer of *HMS Sirius* watched *Renown* as the fire was fought, with the battlecruiser standing away from the other ships about a mile to the south to battle the fire. The plume of smoke from the blaze stood two miles high in a towering column that spread as it rose. At its top it was blown flat by some racing current of air in the upper atmosphere. The smoke was as good as a radio beacon to home enemy submarines and aircraft against Force H.

All through the afternoon Webster braced for renewed air attacks, keeping his men at the highest pitch, ready to direct fire against attacking aircraft. But the radar screens remained empty of all but their own patrolling fighters and swordfish aircraft. Occasionally, at the very edges of the radar screen a blip appeared briefly and then faded. Never there long enough to bring the fighters in against it, it reappeared at intervals, always in some fresh direction, then slipped away again as the Axis scout plane kept a respectful distance.

But in the late afternoon, when at last the smoke from the fire aboard *Renown* first diminished, and then ceased Webster breathed a heavy sigh of relief. Almost it began to seem that Force H would escape further attention from the Luftwaffe. Perhaps the German Air Force on Sardinia had already made its best effort.

"Aerial contact, bearing one-eight-three," Jones called. "Range, twenty-two miles."

"What about fighter cover?" asked Webster.

"Four airborne," answered Jones.

Webster flipped a switch and spoke into his phone.

"Bridge, Radar," he said.

"Radar, bridge," came the reply.

"Radar plot shows aircraft inbound," said Webster. "They've worked around to the south on bearing one-eight-three."

"Get ready, Guns," said the XO, using the ubiquitous nickname of Gunnery Officers throughout the Royal Navy. "Jerry is going to give us another go it seems."

"Range down to eighteen miles," said Jones. "The target is spreading out. Looks like a large flight, at least twenty aircraft.

They're holding altitude at 6,000 feet."

"Dive bombers then," answered Webster. He passed his hand over his eyes and tried to think.

'My God,' he thought to himself, 'I'm tired.'

He looked down at Jones' screen. It took a moment to recognize what was out of place.

"What's this return here?" he asked Jones, pointing at a blip to the northwest.

"That's the fighter patrol," answered the rating with a sidelong glance at Meese, "from the carrier."

"Well, keep track of him Jones," replied Webster. "We'd like to not shoot down one of our own."

"Yes, Sir," Jones answered. "Range now down to five miles. The destroyers in the starboard screen will start firing soon."

Right on cue Webster heard the distant, muffled crack of 4.7-inch guns.

"Sir!" shouted Jones. "Fresh contact, bearing zero-zero-zero, range thirteen miles."

"Bloody Germans!" cursed Webster. "Alert the port secondary battery!"

"Sir, they'll be approaching from both north and south simultaneously," Jones pointed out. "They'll divide our fire."

"Slave the port battery to the aft director," said Webster. "Slave all the main turrets to the forward director."

The blips crept closer to the center of the screen. From outside the radar office the sound of other ships firing intensified, but Webster held back the fire of *Sirius* until the bombers were well with range. At every gun aboard the cruiser the gun crews waited for the order to fire. As the lead bombers pass inside the three-mile range Webster finally spoke.

"Main batteries SHOOT!"

Even as he finished the command the ten 5.25-inch main guns began to fire, shaking the cruiser from stem to stern and in every compartment. Every man aboard at every action station, even those deep below the waterline in the engineering spaces knew the battle was rejoined as the shock of firing the guns transmitted to the hull. Seconds later the lighter flak guns, 40mm Bofors and 20mm pom-poms joined in. The din was horrendous as once more the men of *Sirius* and Force H fought for their lives.

In the skies above the fleet StaffelKapitän Heinrich Trott pulled his flight goggles down over his eyes. The bombers had broken through the thin screen of British fighter cover, the swarming Bf 109 fighters giving the British pilots all they could handle. Now he pressed the radio-telephone pad on his throat.

"All aircraft, focus on the heavy ships in the center of the formation," he said. "Ignore the destroyers in the screen."

The first puffy black bursts of flak began to appear, still some hundreds of meters distant, but that would not last long, Trott knew. He banked sharply to port for ten seconds then came back on course. Seconds later shells began bursting in his original flight path. He dove, banking again to port, changing both altitude and bearing this time to complicate the aim of the British gunners. Again the flak bursts filled the sky on his original course.

He was passing over the outer screen of destroyers now, less than a mile from the heavy ships. The flak guns were once again zeroing in on him. One last time he jinked, this time to starboard for a quick five count then dove. The ruse worked again with the British shells finding only empty sky. He held the dive. The view through his windscreen was spectacularly beautiful. The setting sun cast its rays across the sea. White wave tops alternated with darkened, cobalt troughs. Into his vision swam the wide, flat deck of the airplane carrier, its wake trailing away behind in a wide serpentine sweep as the carrier twisted and turned below him. An airplane moved down the forward deck towards take-off. A line of four fighter aircraft sat on the rear deck waiting a chance to launch.

The flak finally began to catch up to him, the first bursts wide of the mark and too low, but rapidly adjusting to his course. Too late now to change course or take evasive action; he had to hold the dive on target. The Stuka's sirens began to scream as his speed built up in the dive. He centered the bomb aim sight on the aircraft on the forward deck and squeezed his trigger. The Stuka's machine guns bucked and spat, spraying hot lead at the deck below.

Streams of glowing red tracers whipped past his windshield as a blizzard of flak fire rose from the carrier. The Stuka shuddered and jolted as shrapnel found its way into the wing roots, then past. Heinrich Trott held the dive. A black cloud spread across his vision as a shell burst directly in front of the plane's nose. The windscreen starred and he was slammed in the shoulder; blood splattered the inside of the cockpit. He knew he was injured, but he felt no pain, only a cold determination.

The Stuka burst through the flak into the open. The carrier shifted course and was swerving out of the bomb aim sight. His left arm was useless, but he gripped the stick tighter with his right hand and hauled the Stuka back on target. Shells were bursting all about him again, but the flight deck grew in his vision. Wind was blasting at the damaged windscreen, whistling through the splinter hole, breaking bits and pieces of glass away and throwing them in his face.

The carrier filled his vision; he was dead center above the flight deck. He released his grip on the stick and quickly toggled the bomb release switch then hauled back desperately on the stick with all the strength he could muster in his one good arm. He kicked the air brake pedal and the Stuka, lightened by release of the three bombs started to swing out of its dive.

The scream of the sirens slowly fell off as the water rushed up to meet him. Trott pressed himself into his seat back, hauling on the stick with everything he had. The water raced past beneath him, now too fast and close for him to distinguish one wave top from the next. The horizon came up into his view as the Stuka's dive finally flattened and the plane came into level flight barely twenty meters above the surface of the sea. Heinrich braced the stick with his knee and gripped his throat microphone pad.

"Hans!" he cried excitedly. "Hans, did we hit her?"

No reply came from the back seat.

"Hans!" he shouted.

Heinrich craned around to look behind him. His shoulder gave him a sharp stab of pain as he twisted. Hans was slumped over his navigation table, motionless. Heinrich turned back around and examined his instrument panel. The altimeter and fuel gauge were smashed, but the compass was functional and showed him on a northerly bearing. He knew his fuel supply was adequate, unless the tanks were punctured. He looked out on the sea. Rank upon rank of wave tops spread before him to the north. He settled in for the long flight home.

Lt. Commander Webster directed the guns of *HMS Sirius* against this last air attack of the day. The German bombers ignored *Sirius* and concentrated the fury of their attack against *Renown* and the carrier, *HMS Furious,* with the dive-bombers attacking from the south and east, He 111 torpedo bombers from the north.

The Fairey Fulmar fighter planes airborne when the Germans attacked waded in against the dive bombers, striking two of them from the air and disrupting the attacks of two others before they were swept aside by the Bf 109s. The other Stukas bored in against the fleet's southern flank.

"Shift target!" shouted Webster. "Bring the aft batteries to bear on this one!" He laid his finger on a blip on Meese's' screen, a dive-bomber on the starboard beam.

Deep within the ship, in the transmitting station the banks of mechanical computation devices whirred and chirped as they calculated all the variables that went into aiming the main batteries. Speed, course, range and altitude of the target were fed from the radar aerials and speed, range and course of *Sirius* herself went into the strange devices along with temperature, humidity and a dozen other variables, even the angles at which the ship heeled over on the waves. Finished target solutions came out and were fed to the guns.

Every ten seconds each of the 5.25-inch main batteries fired, overlaying the tonk-tonk-tonk of the 40mm Bofors and the pom-pom-pom of the 20mm guns. For the third time that day *Sirius* spit fire into the sky in defense of Force H and once again her aim was true.

The dive-bomber Webster pointed to dove on *Renown,* targeting the battleship from out of the hazy glare cast by the setting sun. As it approached its bomb release it was caught square by a 5.25-inch shell from *Sirius'* 'X' turret; shattered by the direct hit it plunged in pieces into the sea between the columns of the fleet, a pool of flaming petrol marking its grave. As the attack from the south reached its full fury the secondary guns to port began to bark. The torpedo bombers were within range.

At the sound of the port guns Webster moved to that side of the radar office, looking out the observation slit there, but little could be seen through the smoke and haze but the flash of tracers arcing out flat across the sea. He jumped back to the radar screens.

What he saw made him gasp. The attacks of the dive and torpedo bombers were perfectly coordinated, striking the opposite flanks of Force H simultaneously. A powerful force of dive bombers was attacking from the south, to starboard while torpedo bombers attacked from the north, to port, effectively dividing the anti-aircraft gunfire of the fleet.

As he watched the radar screen it showed two of the bombers to port veering off at an angle to attack *Sirius*, perhaps mistaking her in the smoke for one of her larger consorts.

"Port forward quarter to fire on the easterly target, port aft quarter on the westerly target," he ordered calmly, then listened as the ratings relayed his commands.

He stepped back to the port observation slit. Tracers arced out in furious streams like long, sinewy fingers feeling about blindly for the bombers, skipping over and past, around and about them as the planes swerved and ducked to avoid the flak. With his trained eye Webster could distinguish the fire of each gun. The forward two-pounder pom-pom found the range on the more easterly of the two bombers, raking its nose with shells from the quadruple barreled flak gun, shattering the He 111's cockpit in a shower of flames. The nose lifted briefly and the pom-pom's shells walked down the belly of the bomber before its nose tipped back down and it plunged into the sea with a splash. A brief cheer erupted on deck among the gunners and spotters before attention turned quickly to the other threat.

The second bomber seemed to lead a charmed life, side slipping or diving to avoid the fire pouring from the guns of *Sirius*. Once the first bomber was down the fire of the forward guns shifted to the remaining plane, focusing upon it the full fury of the cruiser's port guns. Flames burst from the port engine of the Heinkel, yet still it came on. At a range of 800 yards the two torpedoes it carried were released, plunging into the sea just as the bomber's luck finally ran out. The port engine exploded, severing the wing from the fuselage, sending the bomber into a flat spin across the sea.

The deck heeled under Webster's feet as *Sirius* took evasive action. Webster staggered back before regaining his balance. He jumped back to the observation slit, scanning the waves, looking for the tracks of the torpedoes, but he'd lost their bearing and couldn't find them. He counted down the seconds, bracing for an explosion.

The crackle of automatic cannon fire continued and finally

Webster decided the torpedoes had missed their mark. *Sirius* remained a lucky ship. The cruiser came back on an even keel and Webster stepped to the starboard observation slit, lifting his binoculars to scan Force H. *Charybdis* held station at the head of the starboard column with *Kenya* and *Evening Dale* loosely in line behind. A fire burned on the aft deck of the oiler, with black, oily smoke billowing away to port. Webster could see a team of firefighting crewmen attacking the blaze. He stepped to the aft observation slit and peered out. The smoke from the fire aboard the oiler lay across the sea behind *Sirius*. In the murky light he strained to see the battlecruiser and carrier astern. He waited, breath held, for a glimpse of the ships. Finally as his lungs felt about to burst the bows of *Renown* crashed through the smoke barrier and into view. He exhaled in a burst of relief as the entire ship emerged from the smoke with no new damage evident.

He turned back to the radar consoles.

"Target report!" he barked.

"All targets withdrawing, Sir," said Jones.

Webster stood behind the radar consoles and checked the screens.

"Cease fire, all batteries," he ordered.

Jones repeated the order and the bark and crackle of gunfire slowly died away till the only sound was the distant popping of the smaller guns in the destroyer screen. After a moment even these died away, leaving a silence broken only by the ringing in the ears of the men of Force H. All across the fleet men slumped in stunned silence at their action stations, dazed, looking skyward for any hint the attack would be resumed. Even in engineering spaces deep below the waterline British seamen stared at the deck plates above their heads, praying the concussion of the flak guns firing would not continue.

"ALL GUNS-," Webster choked himself off, realizing he was still shouting. With a conscious effort to control his voice he tried again.

"All guns report," he ordered, in a nearly normal voice.

Once again Jones repeated the order and the condition reports began coming back almost at once. All guns reported ammunition at hand very low, but aside from a handful of minor injuries among the gun crews all were ready for action.

"Radar, Bridge," came over the Tannoy.

Webster switched the circuit to his own headset and responded.

"Bridge, Radar," he responded. "All targets out of range and retiring, all guns report shell stocks low, but otherwise ready for action."

"Radar, Bridge. Acknowledged," came the reply. "We'll be standing down from Action Stations, Air Attack in a few moments."

"Bridge, Radar, Aye," he replied.

Webster put his hand on Jones' shoulder.

"Come on, Jones," he said. "You're relieved."

Jones peeled his telephone headset off, laying it on the console in front of him, but for a moment he just sat there, staring at the radar screen, finally standing slowly.

Webster started to speak to him again, but was interrupted.

"C'or, Blimey!" exclaimed the observer at the aft slit. "Oh, Sir," he said. "It's *Furious,* Sir!"

Webster jumped to the slit and gasped.

"Open the portholes!" he ordered.

As the scuttles came open fresh air gusted through the radar office, but this did nothing for the crewmen there. Their attention was riveted on the spectacle astern. It was indeed *HMS Furious.* The carrier was emerging from the bank of smoke from the burning oiler, but was itself ablaze, the fire back-lighting *Renown.* Flames swept across the flight deck, fanned from the starboard-side island to port in flying gusts of fire by the *Sirocco* south wind. Great, angry black billows of smoke poured away to port.

A group of men were trapped by the flames on the flight deck forward of the island. A gust threw a great sheet of flame forward, catching a number of the men clustered at the end of the flight deck. As Webster and his men in the radar office of *Sirius* watched in horror tiny candles of flame ran helter-skelter about the distant flight deck of *Furious.* Other men tried to beat out the flames, but the wind gusted again and threw another sheet of fire at them. Burning men began leaping from the flight deck into the sea, sixty feet below. Others leapt from the flight deck into the deep shadows of the gun deck forward.

The great ship was racked by a series of explosions on her hanger deck. Bright flashes and flames erupted from her sides, pouring into the sea. Aviation fuel tanks ruptured and began spilling their contents over both sides like some monstrous lava flow from hell. Blazing fuel covered the sea to port and starboard.

"Good God!" said Webster, almost inaudibly.

*Furious* slewed round to port, her steering out of control. Whether the navigating watch was dead or the steering gear destroyed was impossible to tell. As the carrier presented her starboard beam to them the men of *Sirius* saw Fairey Fulmar fighters parked on the rear of the flight deck hurled into the air as another string of explosions tore at *Furious'* innards. Ordnance was exploding now, bombs, torpedoes and depth charges aboard aircraft or waiting to be loaded, stored for ready use on or near the hanger deck.

Two 500-kilogram bombs, dropped by StaffelKäpitan Trott from his lead Stuka, had struck *Furious*, penetrating the flight deck just a few yards apart on the starboard side near the carrier's island. Passing through the armored flight deck they exploded on the hanger deck below amongst the ship's air operations crew as they worked to ready various aircraft. These included a pair of Fairey Swordfish bi-planes loaded with depth charges and intended for anti-submarine patrol over the fleet after moonrise that night. The hanger deck was an instant conflagration as aircraft fuel tanks ruptured and exploded. When the depth charges aboard the two Swordfish exploded the ship's fate was sealed as the high-octane fuel tanks below the hanger were first punctured, then exploded. Hundreds died in the first minutes after the bomb hits. The only hope of saving the ship was to turn her to port in a great sweeping arc to her reciprocal course of due west so that the south wind would carry the flames over the starboard side, allowing her damage control teams to fight the blaze, but the entire sailing watch in 'Pip', the starboard navigating position was wiped out, including Captain Bulteel and the Coxs'n. With no one at the helm *Furious* continued on her easterly course for some minutes before the set of the sea slewed her round to due north.

By then, it was too late. Her fate was much the same as of the four Japanese aircraft carriers sunk by the Americans earlier that month at Midway. No order came to abandon ship. Afire through the whole 540-feet length of her hangar deck, wracked by exploding ordnance and fuel, her crew abandoned her spontaneously.

Aboard *HMS Renown* Admiral Burrough watched *Furious* burn and knew she was lost. Even more, he knew that without air cover his already slim chance to reach Malta and affect the outcome of the battle there was now nearly zero. The battlecruiser and the four cruisers *Sirius, Kenya, Nigeria* and *Charybdis* would be exposed without air cover for the next day's wave of air attacks if Force H ventured closer to Malta and the German airfields on Sicily.

While Burrough considered it folly to proceed without air cover he deemed it necessary to seek permission to retire. He therefore composed a signal detailing the damage and expected loss of *Furious* and the reasons he proposed that Force H be withdrawn to Gibraltar, saving the remaining warships from further enemy air attack. Routed to the Admiralty in London it read:

*Secret. Most Immediate.*

*Regret to inform their Lordships of the impending loss of HMS Furious, struck by two or more armor penetrating aerial bombs at 2127 hours this date. Rescue of Furious' crew currently under way. In light of loss of air cover, loss of anti-aircraft cruiser HMS Phoebe and of damage to HMS Renown, HMS Kenya and HMS Evening Dale propose to retire westward for home station to avoid further losses to ships and crews. In this commands opinion pressing on to 'X' ( Malta ) will expose balance of Force H to unacceptable risk of further air attack. Will hold position as Furious crew is recovered pending reply.*

Considerable time was taken to encode the lengthy message and it was not transmitted until 2148 hours. When the expected acknowledgement from London did not come back the message was repeated at 2218 hours, London acknowledging receipt at 2225.

Meanwhile, the Tribal Class destroyers were set to the task of rescuing as many of the carrier's crew as might be brought away safely. It was a delicate operation. As her engine rooms were abandoned *Furious* lost way and settled beams on to the set of the sea with her bow pointed due east. She held an even keel. It was impossible for the destroyers to approach her from the north as the fire was still being driven over the ship's side by the south wind. But from the south the approach was almost as dangerous, with fifteen-foot seas crashing against the great vertical flanks of the carrier. Ultimately the destroyers settled in ahead and astern of *Furious,* launching small boats to pick up swimming survivors. A fortunate few were actually rescued unharmed and feet dry as they climbed down scrambling nets from the bows of the burning ship directly into the rescue boats.

First Sea Lord Admiral Sir Dudley Pound was working alone in his office overlooking Horse Guards Parade in the Admiralty building. The sun, still up in London's summer evening sky lit the parade ground outside his window. The blackout curtains were pulled back, flooding his office with natural light.

Pound was an experienced naval officer with many years of command at sea behind him. He'd been the Royal Navy's Mediterranean Fleet commander before relinquishing the command to Admiral Andrew Brown Cunningham to take up his new duties as First Sea Lord. Despite this there were instances of friction between Pound and his subordinate fleet commanders.

Cunningham for one had often felt that Pound was too distant from the realities of the war at sea in the Mediterranean. ABC, as Cunningham was ubiquitously known, especially felt that Pound didn't fully appreciate the importance of naval air power in the theater and that the Mediterranean was starved of modern fighters for fleet coverage and air defense. ABC was uncharacteristically bitter over the evacuation of Crete, feeling that just a few squadrons of Spitfires could have saved the island and dramatically reduced the Royal Navy's losses during the German airborne invasion the year before.

Pound has suffered the criticism of history, both for his actions during the invasion of Malta and for the events just days later in the first week of July surrounding the Arctic convoy PQ 17 and the Battle of the Norwegian Sea. There can be no doubt that long days at his desk in London and the stress of his office were starting to take their toll on Admiral Pound though it would be some months before the brain tumor that eventually claimed his life was diagnosed. It cannot be known today how much affect if any his undiagnosed illness was having on Pound in the spring and summer of 1942.

A discrete knock at his door interrupted his concentration.

"Yes, enter," he called. The door opened and a Lt. Commander of the Admiral's staff approached the great oaken desk.

"Two signals for you, Sir," the officer said, handing Pound two envelopes and a clipboard.

Pound signed the receipt for each signal and dismissed the Commander before tearing the envelopes open. The first he opened was from Admiral Burrough, in command of Force H. It announced the imminent loss of *HMS Furious* and Burrough's desire to retreat in the face of the enemies overwhelming air superiority. Pound groaned aloud. *Furious* was the second carrier lost that week in the western Mediterranean trying to relieve Malta and was all but the last fleet carrier available in the west. Only *HMS Victorious* remained west of Suez and she was committed to the covering force for convoy PQ17, bound for the north Russian ports of Archangel and Murmansk. She was anchored at that moment at Scapa Flow in Scotland's Orkney Islands and was much too far away to aid Force H or Malta.

Pound massaged his temples for a moment, pondering his reply to Force H. He concurred at that moment fully with the opinion of Admiral Burrough. To continue on to Malta without air cover would invite the complete destruction of Force H by air attack.

He glanced at the other envelope. It was marked **ULTRA-SECRET** and **URGENT.** With a sigh he tore open the envelope and read the contents. His heart leapt. The signal was from Station 'X', the super-secret British code-breaking unit at Bletcheley Park outside London and it provided the details of a fresh wireless intercept from the Italian Air Force, the Regia Aeronautica at Decimomanu air station, Sardinia to Commando Supremo, the Italian High Command, in Rome. This was the signal sent by the Italians earlier that afternoon and it was a most unusual signal as it detailed actions undertaken not by their own, but by the GERMAN Air Force operating from the same airfield. The signal reported that the Germans were uncertain of the success of their attacks, claiming several torpedo and bomb hits against British warships, but without consequent claims of sinkings. The signal went on to describe losses suffered by the Luftwaffe as very heavy. After three attacks against the British Fleet moving towards the Sicilian Narrows the Germans had lost seventeen He 111 torpedo bombers, twelve Ju 88's and twelve Ju 87 Stuka's. Four Bf 109 fighters had also been lost. The Italians reported a further toll of twenty-seven bombers of their own lost or damaged. The signal added that the

Germans had a total of only sixteen air-worthy bombers left on Sardinia with no torpedo bombers available for further strikes. The tone of the message was more than a little petty, as the Italians seemed to be gloating over the losses suffered by their ally, with so little apparent result. It concluded that local Italian commanders deemed the British Fleet too powerful to attack again until the British force had been reduced by submarine or surface ship action.

To Pound the intercept completely altered his view of the strategic situation in the central Mediterranean Sea. With only sixteen bombers capable of flight and most importantly with none of the highly dangerous torpedo equipped He 111's the Germans on Sardinia no longer posed an undue hazard to Force H. Even without air cover the remaining ships should be able to cope with all the Germans had left to throw at them. The Italian Air Force had as much as conceded the passage of Force H, at least until it was significantly reduced.

Pound snatched up his pen and signal pad, scribbling his reply to Burrough. When he'd completed it he pressed the button under his desk summoning his aide.

Admiral William Burrough paced the flag plot aboard *HMS Renown* impatiently.

It was over an hour since his message to the Admiralty in London was sent a second time. Since then *Renown* and his remaining cruisers, *Sirius, Charybdis, Nigeria* and the damaged *Kenya* and the fleet oiler *HMS Evening Dale* had pulled away from the burning hulk of the aircraft carrier *HMS Furious*. Accompanied by a screen of destroyers to protect against submarine attack the big ships had pulled away to the west while Burrough waited for confirmation of his plan to withdraw. That he would receive such confirmation he had no doubt. The condition of his ships and the lack of air cover made proceeding on to Malta out of the question. Indeed, if he had not received a reply by the time rescue operations on *Furious* concluded he was prepared to act on his own initiative, using the coming hours of darkness to cover his escape to the west. He already had the signal prepared ordering the fleet to set course due west.

'What the devil is keeping their Lordships in London?' he wondered. 'Did they have to be dragged from bed, or from the buffet at the Savoy?'

"Admiral Burrough," his flag officer, Lt. Harris spoke, breaking in on his less than charitable thoughts about his superiors. "Signal, Sir."

Burrough spun on his heel, taking the signal pad from Harris. He scanned the message flimsy briefly, then read through it again carefully.

Watching Burrough, Lt. Harris marveled at the Admiral's self control.

Burrough turned to Harris.

"You've read this of course?" he asked.

"Yes, Sir," replied Harris softly.

Burrough lifted the flimsy and read from it aloud.

*"Force H need not concern himself with the possible loss of ships due to air attack. Proceed to 'X' as planned."*

"A bit bloody terse, isn't it, Sir," asked Harris.

"Yes, it is," answered Burrough, "but clear enough for all that. We're to go on to Malta and the devil with the losses we may suffer on the way."

Harris reached for the flimsy and Burrough handed it to him.

"This bit that you '...need not concern yourself with the loss of ships due to air attack.'" Harris said. "That's what they told Cunningham at Crete isn't it."

"Just so," said Burrough, "and it was a bloody slaughter then." He paused and gazed down at the chart table. "Only worse this time," he continued softly. "At least at Crete Cunningham could withdraw out of air range for most of the day; try to dash in at night and evacuate the troops." He straightened. "Here, there's nowhere for us to hide."

"It'd be one thing if the message included some word on air cover coming from Suez, or confirming that the aircraft flown off *Furious* this morning were prepared to support us from Malta," said Harris. "But this-," he paused and shook his head. "It's as if they've weighed the situation and decided Force H is expendable."

Burrough looked at Harris angrily. "What ever made you think we're not?" he asked.

>>>>>>>>>>>>

Maggie spent the day of the 27th confined in the air raid shelter east of Hal Far airfield. She'd awakened there in a cot, with her friend Elizabeth looking at her with deep concern.

"Good to see you again, Maggie," Liz said softly. "How do you feel?"

"Groggy again," Maggie said. Her voice was thin and weak. "And my head hurts. What happened?"

"What do you remember?" Liz asked.

Maggie closed her eyes and thought for a moment.

"We were waiting to board the seaplane," she said. "Down at the docks at Kalafrana." She paused. "I don't remember any more." She opened her eyes. "What happened?" she repeated.

"There was an explosion," Liz replied. "Chappie thinks the seaplane touched off a mine in the water."

"Oh, God," groaned Maggie. "Some of the team was already aboard weren't they?"

"Yes, Maggie," Liz replied. She hesitated a moment. "Gabrielle is gone Maggie. So is Simon."

Tears welled up in Maggie's eyes. "That poor boy," she sobbed. "That poor, sad boy. Who else?" she asked.

Liz ran down the list of those killed at Kalafrana.

"Nearly half the team," Maggie cried. "What about Chappie?"

"He's all right," Liz answered. "He's working on our next move, what we're going to do next. There's rumor of another try tonight."

Maggie's heart skipped a beat as memory returned.

"Oh, Liz," she gasped. "Kenneth was with me! What about Kenneth."

"It's all right, Maggie," Liz said to her. "Kenneth is fine. He hurt his arm or his shoulder, but he's fine."

"Where is he, Liz?" Maggie insisted. "I want to see him."

"He's reported back to the airbase, Maggie," Liz chided her gently. "Don't worry. He's fine."

Maggie slumped back on her cot, exhausted by fear and sadness. Eventually she slept again. She awakened in the late afternoon. Her head was still splitting, but another pain took her attention. She was hungry. Once again Liz helped her eat.

Kenneth stayed at the air operations bunker at Hal Far for several more hours, hoping for the arrival of more Spitfires or of cheering news, but neither came. The one pilot who'd flown in from Furious was debriefed for over an hour by the station commander before being released to mingle with the airmen in the air ops bunker. Kenneth joined a crowd that gathered around the new man.

The navy pilots from Hal Far questioned the RAF pilot at great length about the situation with the fleet, but as Kenneth expected the Air Force pilot had very little news of note to offer other than the general composition of the fleet, describing it as a battleship, five cruisers and a gaggle of destroyers in addition to the carrier *Furious,* and the time and position from which they'd flown off the carrier that morning.

Kenneth listened with rapt attention to the tale of the sole RAF pilot to arrive, like himself a flying Sergeant. His name was Wilson. His description of his encounter with the Messerschmitts near Cape Bon and of the last, tense moments of his flight as his fuel dropped to zero kept all his listeners enthralled.

Wilson had many questions of his own about the ground situation on Malta and on the prospects of repelling the German led invasion, but the 'Old Malta Hands' as Kenneth thought of himself and the others had no good news to offer on this account either. Billy also asked about the planes and pilots who had flown in two days earlier from *HMS Eagle.* The news here was bleak as well. Sixteen Spitfires had actually landed safely on the afternoon of the 25th, but several were destroyed on the ground during intense Luftwaffe air raids and most of the remainder were shot down in action against the massive sweeps of Me 109s down from Sicily that same afternoon. When none of the four Spitfires flown in from *Furious* returned safely from their first sorties against the German invasion force it was the last straw for many of the pilots at Hal Far. They sank into a dispirited state.

Kenneth couldn't stop worrying about Maggie. He wondered if her injuries had worsened as a result of the explosion at Kalafrana the night before or if there was another effort under way to evacuate her team. Kenneth still had little idea as to the nature of Maggie's work on Malta, but he knew it was secret and she'd impressed upon him the danger she would be in should the Germans capture her.

Late in the afternoon he resolved to take some fresh air.

Leaving the bunker he walked towards the east gate of the station, in the direction of Kalafrana and the shelter where he'd left Maggie. The sound of small arms fire to the north continued and in the distance he could see Junkers transports circling away to the west from Ta Qali. He spent several minutes observing them and concluded they were taking off from his airfield. The Germans had managed to clear at least part of the runway and make it serviceable. He suspected this meant hundreds of air-landed infantry were arriving every hour to reinforce the German paratroops already on the island.

Away to the north came the sounds of a heavy artillery bombardment. He hoped this meant the Royal Malta Artillery was firing on the German airhead at Ta Qali, but as the Junkers continued their flights he suspected this was not the explanation. Luftwaffe fighters continued to orbit Hal Far, careful to stay outside the range of the still formidable flak defenses on the airfield. The drone of German aircraft overhead was a constant reminder of Malta's plight.

Hundreds of men were in evidence above ground at Hal Far, manning the flak guns or digging trenches, filling sandbags or otherwise engaged in strengthening the field's defenses. To the north of the small strip he saw hundreds of men digging in along the length of a low ridge that ran across the island in an east-west direction.

As Kenneth approached a 40mm Bofors flak gun in a sandbagged pit, he pulled his last pack of smokes from his pocket. Looking inside he saw there were just four cigarettes left. Kenneth didn't smoke before coming to Malta and was still not a heavy smoker, but now he lit one and continued on. The crew of the flak gun, lounging about the pit, but remaining alert to man the gun at an instant's notice, was adorned in the soft outback hat and kangaroo emblem of colonial forces.

'Aussies,' Kenneth snorted to himself.

"Here, Mate!" shouted one of the Australians. "Give us a fag!"

Kenneth laughed and shrugged. "Here you go friend!" He tossed the pack with his three remaining cigarettes to the Aussie gunner. "Keep 'em!"

"I always did say you Yanks was alright," the Aussie thanked him.

Kenneth moved on. His arm started to throb and his thoughts kept coming back to Maggie. He couldn't shake a terrible feeling of worry for her. He continued walking as he smoked until he reached the station's eastern gate. As he approached the guard station there he saw that the road was barricaded with huge limestone blocks and strung with barbed wire. To either side of the gate Royal Marines were dug in among the boulders and brush, situated to cover the approach to the Air Station.

Kenneth spoke to the tough looking Marine Sergeant at the guard station.

"I'm going to visit the air-raid shelter down the road, Sarge'," he said. "You won't have me shot if I come back after dusk will you?"

"Sorry, Sergeant," the Marine answered stiffly, with a significant look at Kenneth's RAF wings. "No one is to leave the station without orders." He held up his hand to cut-off Kenneth's objection. "No exceptions. Now be a good little pilot, won't you? We're busy here. Someone has to defend the place don't we?"

Kenneth shook his head, but said nothing. As wrong as it was he understood the Marine's bitterness. The RAF had let Malta and its defenders down. He turned on his heel and began the trek back to the ops bunker. He hadn't gone far when the air-raid sirens began to wail. At first he was inclined to ignore them and keep walking, but when the flak guns started to fire he found a slit trench and jumped into it, cradling his arm to protect it. Soldiers, sailors and marines sheltered with him in the trench.

"Blimey!" quipped a young private of the Devon Regiment, affecting a cockney sneer. "We've got real inter-service 'armony 'ere, 'aven't we?"

A moment later the flak picked up in intensity. A Marine pointed to the east and shouted, "There they are, the sods!"

Kenneth and the others in the trench turned and watched a trio of Stuka dive bombers approaching the field in a line with about a half mile between the planes, just enough separation to divide the fire of the flak gunners. The first Stuka dropped its load of bombs across the northern end of the field, hitting trenches and other defense work there. The second Stuka followed close behind. Both winged away unscathed. The third Stuka was not so fortunate. The gunners found the right altitude and a shell burst just meters below the engine of the bomber. Fire erupted from the engine cowling and the Stuka staggered in mid-flight. With flames streaming down the fuselage the dive-bomber plunged into a rocky limestone outcrop on the east side of the field.

The men in the trench let loose a furious cheer, tossing hats in the air and pounding one another on the back. Kenneth winced in pain at every touch, but cheered with the rest of them. Moments later the all-clear sounded and he was on his way again. As he approached the air-ops bunker he patted his pockets, looking for his cigarettes until he remembered he'd given the last of them away to the flak gunners near the eastern gate. A group of pilots was lounging outside the entrance to the bunker. Kenneth walked up to them hoping to bum a smoke.

"Anyone have a –,". An ear-shattering blast interrupted him and he dove for cover beside the bunker, the other pilots huddled beside him. The force of the blast shook the ground beneath them. Sand and gravel spilled down the sides of the bunker onto their heads. Explosions continued in a steady string for minutes before beginning to die down.

"Good God!" one of the Navy pilots exclaimed when he finally dared to lift his head. "What the bloody hell was that?"

"Has to have been an ammunition dump, hasn't it?" another of the Navy men replied dryly. "Or maybe even the station armory at Luqa." He reached nonchalantly inside his jacket and pulled out a packet of smokes. He tapped one out and put it to his lips, but his hand shook when he tried to light it. Despite themselves the pilots all laughed.

Later, inside the bunker Kenneth was sipping tea and chatting quietly with the other aircrew when an announcement was made.

"Can I have your attention please!" shouted the same Navy officer, Commander Morgan, who'd earlier told them of the arrival of the Spitfires from *Furious*. The airmen quickly settled down in an expectant silence.

"Thank you!" the officer continued. "Pending the arrival of additional aircraft all unassigned aircrew are to report for other duties as follows. Fleet Air Arm and RAF non-pilots are to report to the Station infirmary on the west side of the field. You'll work with the local Maltese in assisting the medical staff with wounded. Return to your billets and take all your kit with you. You're going to be busy and won't have a chance to come back for anything you've forgotten. FAA and RAF pilots will remain here until further notice. That is all."

The officer turned and went back into the wireless office, leaving the airmen to wonder at the implications of their change in status. There were a good many long faces and sad farewells as pilots and aircrew said their good-byes. Most assumed they would never see one another again.

Over an hour after the last of the airmen left to clear out their rooms the officer returned to the bunker and called the pilots to attention again. The main chamber felt deserted to Kenneth at that point. Over seventy airmen had gone, leaving about fifty FAA and RAF pilots behind, including the four new arrivals from *Furious*. The Navy officer mounted a stool and called the pilots to gather round.

"I've to begin by assuring that all non-pilots have left the room," he said, surveying the men in front of him. The pilots all looked at one another.

"Nothing but pilots here, Sir," a Navy Lt. finally answered.

"Right then," said Commander Morgan. "I've first to swear all of you to secrecy on what I'm about to tell you." He gave the assembled pilots a very stern glare. The pilots nodded their heads and responded with a chorus of 'Yes, Sir's.

"It's about why you've been separated from your aircrew," Morgan went on. The pilots looked at one another with raised eyebrows.

"The decision has been taken to begin an evacuation of the island," said Morgan, "but the numbers that can be gotten away are quite small. This is no Dunkirk and no bloody Crete either. We shall be fortunate to evacuate a few hundred all told. Naturally, there is a priority list and quite frankly you pilots are higher on the list than other aircrew." He paused for a moment and shrugged before continuing. "Or for that matter, desk officers." The pilots all knew he was referring to himself. "You're to bring the absolute minimum of kit, just what you can carry on your person, no bags or luggage of any kind. Be at the east gate by 2300 hours. From there you'll be led to a point of embarkation for the evacuation."

Morgan pointed behind Kenneth to a Navy pilot who had raised his hand.

The pilot stood and spoke. "Are we to go out by air or sea, Sir?"

"I don't have any information on the means of transport off the island," said Morgan. "You'll just have to play it by ear."

Kenneth arrived at the east gate of Hal Far Air Station at 2240 hours. He was not however the first pilot there. More than two-dozen of the airmen were already waiting when he arrived, standing in little groups in the moonlight. Kenneth recognized the new arrival standing off to one side alone.

"My name's Wiltshire," he introduced himself, extending his hand. "Kenneth Wiltshire."

"Billy Wilson," the new man responded, shaking hands. "Canadian?" he asked.

Kenneth put his head back and laughed. "No," he said, "But an understandable mistake I s'pose. American."

"Oh," said Billy. "Sorry."

"Well, your Maltese vacation's been cut short hasn't it?" Kenneth changed the subject.

"I'll say!" snorted Billy. He pulled a pack of cigarettes out and lit one up. "Barely twelve hours and off again. At least I hope so!"

Kenneth gave a meaningful look at Billy's cigarette.

"I say!" Billy exclaimed. "I've no manners! Here! Have a smoke!"

"Thanks," Kenneth said, looking at the pack. American made Chesterfield's, 'Not a cough in a carload' printed across the pack. "You know," he began, "before I came here I never smoked." Kenneth accepted a light and took a long, deep drag. "You might want to keep those to yourself," he added quietly. "Otherwise you won't have them for long."

Away to the north a machine gun chattered nervously. A flurry of small arms fire followed, lasting several minutes before dieing away to an occasional rifle shot. The two Spitfire pilots went on smoking and chatting quietly in the dark. As the appointed hour approached more pilots arrived at the east gate until Kenneth estimated there were between sixty and eighty men there, milling about uncertainly in the dark. An airplane buzzed high overhead putting a temporary end to all conversation as the pilots nervously watched the sky. The plane droned off to the north. Kenneth held his watch up to the light of the moon. 2320 hours and there was still no sign or word of anyone to give the pilots their orders or directions.

"Running late, are we?" observed Billy.

"Yes," Kenneth replied. "I suppose someone should approach the Marines on guard at the gate, but I've already tangled with them today. I'm afraid I'd only get their peckers up."

"Best to wait a bit, then," said Billy, uncertainly. "Perhaps one of the others…."

"Yes, perhaps," Kenneth answered.

"How do you suppose they plan to take us off?" Billy asked. "They can't plan to fly us out can they?"

"I shouldn't think so," answered Kenneth. "They tried that last night." He quickly told the story of the Sunderland destroyed at Kalafrana the night before, leaving out details concerning Maggie and her secret work or of his relationship to her. "If they're to get anyone away at all it has to be by small boat or perhaps submarine," he concluded.

The two pilots went on talking quietly about inconsequential matters of home and family, but Kenneth checked his watch every minute or so. He'd resolved to approach the Marine on guard if nothing had happened by 2340. Just as his self-imposed deadline approached he heard the voice of Commander Morgan.

"All pilots gather round, please," Morgan ordered, calling out over the murmured conversations. Kenneth and Billy moved quickly to the guard station, kneeling in the dirt in front of Morgan. The Commander stood on a stack of sandbags. Morgan wasted no further time. Even as the pilots gathered round he began.

"You pilots are to be evacuated by submarine from Kalafrana during the remaining hours of darkness." He began. "The first stage is to get you to an air raid shelter midway to Kalafrana. There you'll be sorted into two groups of about forty men each. The two groups will then move down to the RN seaplane base at Kalafrana for embarkation. Are there any questions?"

"What about transport to the shelter and Kalafrana, Commander?" a pilot with an Irish accent asked.

"There's no transport to be spared at the moment," Morgan answered. "It's shank's Mare for you lot!"

The pilots broke out in a polite laugh. Shank's Mare. They would walk.

"Right then!" said Morgan. "Your guide is from the Royal

Marine detachment. Corporal Hartley-," gesturing into the sandbag
pit at a Marine non-com standing there at parade rest, "-knows the
way in the dark and best yet he knows the passwords, so you won't
get shot by our own lads along the way." Morgan paused a
moment, then as he jumped down added, "Good luck!"

Immediately the pilots began talking among themselves again
and milling about.

"Come on," said Kenneth to Billy. "Stay with me." He circled
round to the front of the machine gun pit and approached Corporal
Hartley.

"Here, Corp'!" he said. "I've been to that air raid bunker
myself several times in the past two days. How 'bout my chum and
I lend a hand in guiding the party."

Hartley glared at Kenneth in the moonlight, assessing his
Sergeant's stripes, then his pilot's wings.

"You've been there, 'ave you Sergeant?" he asked. "Tell me
about the way."

Kenneth turned and gestured down the Kalafrana Road. "The
tricky part is making the turn off the road," he said. "It's to the
right about half a mile and if you don't know what you're looking
for you can walk right past it and never know it. Once you're off
the main road the track leads through a field of boulders and scrub
till you come to one really big boulder. Go round the back side of
it to the left and the shelter is at the far side of the clearing."

"All right, Sergeant," the Marine answered, convinced Kenneth
knew the way. "You take charge of the RAF lot and stay close.
Everybody on the 'ole bleedin' island is trigger 'appy tonight.
They'd as soon shoot a pack of pilots as say 'Bob's your uncle'.
Password tonight is Werewolf and the countersign is Webley
Station. Got it? Lot's of 'W's for German tongues to trip
theirselves over."

Kenneth turned and shouted above the din. "RAF to me!" He
turned to Billy. "Help me get 'em lined up 'toot sweet' Billy. Pair
'em up, then let's get a head count and be on our way." He didn't
tell Billy the real reason he was so anxious to get to the shelter
quickly.

Within minutes Kenneth and Billy were leading thirty-three
RAF pilots in addition to themselves through the gate and down
the Kalafrana Road. With frequent admonitions against straggling

he set a brisk pace. The moon provided plenty of light to see their way and in little over a half hour Kenneth led his group to the turn-off in the road.

"Halt! Who goes?" came the challenge out of the dark bushes to the side of the road. The snap of a rifle bolt being drawn back sent a quick chill down his spine.

"Werewolf!" he said, taking pains to pronounce the 'W's clearly.

"Webley Station," came the reply. "Come forward, state your name and your business."

Kenneth held his hands out from his hips as best his injured shoulder would allow and approached the bushes. "Flying Sgt. Wiltshire," he began. "I'm leading this group of RAF pilots to the air raid shelter off the road here."

"We was expecting a Marine guide," growled the voice.

"He's behind this first group," Kenneth explained. "I'm about the only RAF man that's been to the shelter. I volunteered to help guide."

"All right then," said the voice. "Move on down the path and don't anyone go wandering about in the bush, not even for a 'wee' if'n you're not to be shot. You'll be challenged again at the shelter."

"Right-o!" acknowledged Kenneth. He turned to the pilots and repeated the instructions to stay on the path and added his own to stay together. The group moved off again, down the narrow lane to the right of the road. Kenneth slowed the pace here as he didn't want to risk getting turned about in the boulders and straying from the path, but he had no trouble identifying the large boulder standing out above the brush that marked the front entrance to the shelter. He passed the challenge of the guard there and moved on across the clearing. He and Billy counted the pilots off and found all accounted for. He checked his watch. 0035.

"There's someone I want to look for," Kenneth told Billy. "Stay here and meet the Corp' when he brings the Navy lot in will you?" Without waiting for a reply he turned and ducked past a guard and through the blackout curtains into the shelter. The main room was dimly lit by several kerosene lanterns hung from the low ceiling and was very crowded. Hope filled his heart as he saw several women in the group, but as his eyes adjusted to the dim light and he scanned the room he saw neither Maggie nor any of the other familiar members of her unit. He turned a full circle looking for anyone he recognized, but there was no one. He started to move to the back of the shelter for a closer look, but an Army Captain with a clipboard stepped up to him.

"What are you about, then?" asked the Captain in a pronounced Sandhurst drawl.

Kenneth snapped to attention. "Flying Sergeant Wiltshire, Sir," he said. "I've just led a group of RAF fliers down from Hal Far for evacuation."

"Have a list, do you, er, Wiltshire?"

"No, Sir," Kenneth answered. "Its an ad hoc group thrown together at the last minute."

"Ad hoc, you say?" said the Captain. "Well, that may be the RAF modus operandi as it were, but NOT the Army's I can assure you!" the Captain chuckled at his own wit. "Put together a list with name, rank and service number, Wiltshire, then check back in with me. That is all." The Captain turned and sauntered away.

Kenneth closed his eyes and counted to three then set about begging a sheet of paper and inquiring after Maggie and her unit. He couldn't have named the 'Y' Service had he known the name himself and he got a number of blank looks as well as several extra sheets of paper before one of the women he'd noticed when he first entered the shelter recognized his description of Maggie.

The woman was an English Civilian, middle aged with wisps of graying hair at the temples and Kenneth wondered briefly to himself what she was still doing on Malta after all those long months of siege.

"Oh, yes," she said. "I remember the poor, young dear. Head all swathed in bandages, hardly moved about at all and when she did it was as though she had a dreadful headache."

"When did you last see her, Ma'am?" Kenneth asked respectfully.

"Oh, well, it hasn't been very long at all," the woman said. "Not a half hour ago I should say the young girl and her party were summoned to board lorries for the trip to Kalafrana. I must say there was rather a to-do about getting them out first, ahead of everyone else," she sniffed haughtily.

"Thank you Ma'am," Kenneth bowed slightly and backed

away. He was torn between the anguish of having missed her by such a short time and the hope he felt at knowing Maggie was on her way to Kalafrana again. He stepped back outside the shelter and busied himself making the list of RAF pilots the Army Captain demanded. He went man-to-man getting the required details and was grateful for Billy's help in keeping the pilots in a tight group. In the meantime Corporal Hartley delivered the group of Royal Navy fliers. They were milling about outside the shelter with no apparent aim or direction.

"Pardon me, Sir," Kenneth coughed and stepped forward with the list, offering it to the Captain. "The RAF list you asked for, Sir."

The Captain peered at the list for a moment. "How many total did you say Wiltshire?"

"Thirty-five, Sir."

"Order this list by rank now, will you Wiltshire? I'll be about. See me when you're done."

Kenneth gritted his teeth, but sat down at a table and rewrote the list, placing the officers at the top followed by the Sergeant Pilots, including himself and Billy Wilson.
Once again he approached the Captain to deliver his list.

"What about all these Royal Navy Chaps, Wiltshire?" the Captain asked him. "They came in with you didn't they?"

"No, Sir!" Kenneth answered quickly. "There's a RN officer has their roster, Sir. Shall I get him for you, Captain?"

"Yes, please do."

Kenneth went back outside, determined to find an officer among the Navy pilots to deal with the Army Captain. He was moving among the Navy flyers in the clearing looking for an officer when a lorry with hooded headlamps lumbered round the large boulder and into the clearing. It stopped with a squeal of tortured brakes on the gravel under the cover of the camouflage nets. Another followed it a moment later. The drivers left the engines running. The Army Captain came out of the shelter with his clipboard in hand, spoke briefly to one of the drivers then went back in the shelter. Kenneth stepped onto the running board of the first lorry and spoke with the driver, an Army Sgt.

"Have you delivered a mixed party of men and women to Kalafrana tonight, Sarge? He asked.

"'Oo wants to know," asked the Sgt. suspiciously.

"Lord Haw-Haw," Kenneth answered sarcastically in spite of himself.

"Oh, that's 'ow it is, is it?" replied the driver. "Well, your lordship, you'd 'ave better sources of information than me now wouldn't you."

"Ah, now Sarge," Kenneth pleaded. "I've got a bird with that group and I'm worried about her, see?"

"Well, that's something else again," said the Sergeant, brightening. "Which one was she, chum? That little blonde bit or the raven 'aired one?"

"The one I'm looking for has her head all wrapped in bandages," Kenneth said dryly.

"Oh, that one," said the driver, disappointed. "The raven was 'elping her. Yeah, delivered that lot on the first trip, about forty minutes ago. I think they was still waitin' on the apron when I dropped the last load."

Kenneth checked his watch as he dropped down off the running board. 0055 hours, June 28th.

The Army Captain emerged from the shelter leading a group that included the woman Kenneth had talked to earlier. They began to load into the lorries. High overhead a Luftwaffe plane droned past.

>>>>>>>>>>>>>

The swish of surf against the concrete apron and an occasional scuff of a shoe on a loose stone were the only sounds to be heard. Maggie clung tightly to Elizabeth's arm as the 'Y' Service team survivors made their way down the concrete apron to the water's edge. They'd waited over two hours since arriving at the seaplane base. Now two rubber dinghies bobbed against the seaplane ramp. Black clad sailors knelt in the water, holding the boats steady against the gentle waves inside the breakwater at Kalafrana. Out on the bay a squat, dark shape sat low in the water. Moonlight glistened off the dripping wet skin of the submarine.

Section Chief Chapman moved quietly amongst his team, helping to calm nerves stretched taut with tension. Not a member of the team had forgotten the sudden death that had visited

Kalafrana the night before. Blackened, twisted struts and frames still poked from the water where the Sunderland flying boat had burned.

"Holding up are you, Maggie?" he asked softly when he came to her in line.

"Liz is holding me up, Chappie," Maggie answered with a quiet smile. "I'll be fine."

"I'm going to have you put aboard first thing," Chappie told her, "with the other injured. That way the crew can place you out of the way and in a bed."

"I'm sorry for all the bother, Chappie," she replied sheepishly.

"Nonsense!" he scoffed. "Now come along. The sailors are waiting."

Maggie said nothing, but looked back over her shoulder towards the road to Hal Far Air Station. The buzz of an airplane engine drifted to her ears.

Chappie murmured in her ear. "The best thing you can do for him now is to get away safely yourself," he said. "Now come along."

Elizabeth and Maggie were helped into one of the dinghies along with Esther Woldridge. A splinter had caught Esther in the arm when the time bomb exploded under the Sunderland flying boat the night before. Her arm hung in a sling, but the wound didn't seem to have dampened her irrepressible spirit.

"I can't wait for a big, juicy beefsteak!" she exclaimed, rather louder than suited the sailors rowing the dinghy. One of them shushed her.

"Of course," she went on, just a little quieter, "one can't have a beefsteak without a gin and tonic to wash it down!"

The soft splash of oars was her only answer.

"I do hope we get posted home, or at least get home leave," she went on. "What about you Maggie? Wouldn't you like to see your Mum and Dad after this lot?"

"Yes, Esther," Maggie whispered. "Of course I would." But Maggie wasn't thinking of her parents. Tears were quietly streaming down her cheeks.

The boat bumped up against the rounded pressure hull of the submarine. Maggie's feet barely touched the sides of the sub as she was lifted out of the dinghy and onto the deck. Esther was right behind.

"OOH!" Esther squealed. "Watch the hands, laddie," she scolded one of the sailors.

"Silence on deck!" boomed a voice from atop the conning tower. Esther finally kept her tongue in check and was quiet.

Maggie and Esther were led to a hatch in the narrow, flat deck in front of the conning tower. Deck hands helped Maggie onto the top rungs of the ladder below the hatch. An instant later she felt her feet gripped from below and she was lowered into the submarine. It was a sensation much like going down in a lift. When her feet finally landed on a deck she was hustled quickly to a small, curtained off partition and bundled into a tiny bunk.

"Stay here please, Miss," said a kindly sailor. "It's going to be a mite crowded soon and we can't have you underfoot."

Kenneth chafed at the slow pace the lorry made on its way down the hill to Kalafrana. He could have walked it faster. In fact, he had tried to convince the Army Captain that he should lead the RAF pilots to Kalafrana on foot, arguing that the two lorries were insufficient to move all the evacuees in a timely fashion. But the Army Captain didn't go for it.

"Good to see you thinking on your feet, Wiltshire," he said in that drawl so maddening to Kenneth, "but the fact is the ramp at Kalafrana is already dangerously overcrowded as it is. Getting you and your pilots down there early won't get one more person off the island tonight. Relax and wait your turn for the lorries."

His turn had come, along with his RAF brethren at 0230 hours. At least he'd managed to get his group in ahead of the Navy pilots. They still waited at the shelter. Kenneth and Billy leapt into the cab of the lorry along with the driver and as they crested the last hill before Kalafrana they were treated to the same beautiful view of the bay Kenneth had seen the night before.

"Look there!" exclaimed Billy. He was sitting in the middle between Kenneth and the driver. He pointed out through the windshield at the harbor entrance between Delimara Point and the Kalafrana breakwater. The low, dark silhouette of a submarine slid through the moonlit waters, slipping out to sea. Even as they watched it the sub slid smoothly beneath the waves, barely a ripple marking its passing.

"Have we missed it?" asked Billy.

"Relax chum," said the driver. "Look right down below us, just past the 'angar."

Billy and Kenneth squinted to see. For a moment they could see nothing but a pool of inky black water past the hangar, but in a few seconds two shapes emerged in the gloom. Two more submarines sat in the bay, nearly invisible in spite of the moonlight. Eventually Kenneth's sharp eyes spied several smaller shapes moving on the water between the apron and the subs, rubber rafts carrying evacuees to the submarines. The driver shifted gears and the lorry eased on down the hill, pulling into the built up area behind the waterfront and the seaplane hangar.

Kenneth jumped from the cab and was off like a shot for the ramp, dodging through the rubble of the waterfront buildings. At the top of the concrete seaplane ramp a Military Policeman stopped him. A queue of over fifty people waited their turn to be rowed out to one of the waiting submarines.

"Hold up there you," snarled the MP. "You don't think for a minute you're going to jump this queue do you?"

"No, Sir," Kenneth answered, breathlessly. "I can see there's an orderly queue here. I'm looking for someone whom I hope is near the front of the queue, if she hasn't been evacuated already."

"A girl, hm?" The M.P. nodded sagely. "Not many women here now. There was a group earlier. Couple of nice lookers too. Describe her to me, son. Maybe I've seen her."

An air raid siren began its mournful wail. Cries of alarm went up from the queue on the ramp.

"There!" shouted a man on the apron. "Over Delimara!"

A flak gun on the quay down the shoreline started to bark, strobe flashes illuminating the water. Others joined in, but over the crack of the guns Kenneth could still hear the scream of aero engines in a dive. The crowd on the queue stood as if rooted in place, staring into the sky across the harbor.

"Clear the ramp!" he shouted. "Get off the ramp! Get to cover!"

The M.P. blew his whistle. The shrill blast electrified the crowd into panicked action. Too late. The diving Stukas fired their nose and wing mounted cannon and machine guns, raking shells through the shallows in front of the seaplane ramp, violent fountains of water erupting into the air. The shells walked up onto the ramp, cutting into the crowd packed there, tossing bodies and parts about like straw before the wind. Kenneth and the M.P. ducked back into the cover of the hangar. From their hands and knees they watched as the crowd scrambled to escape the attack. Through the chaos he watched one of the two submarines moving slowly towards the breakwater, crewmen scrambling across its deck, all but diving headfirst down its hatches.

Then came the bombs. Six heavy bombs, 500-kilos each plunged down in a string in the shallow water with the last on the concrete seaplane ramp. Kenneth fell flat to his face and covered his head with his good arm, curling into a fetal position beside the M.P. One shattering roar after another walked up the ramp towards the hangar entrance, hurling football sized chunks of smashed and jagged concrete like missiles. Flame from the blasts swept into the hangar over the backs of Kenneth and the M.P., singing their hair and blackening their uniforms.

Kenneth lay stunned on the floor of the hangar, ears ringing, in a state of semi shock. When at last he dared to move he looked out over a scene straight from hell. Bodies were scattered all over the ramp. One of the bombs had hit squarely in the middle of the ramp and left a smoking, blackened crater. Huge cracks and fractures radiated out from the crater and seawater was already starting to trickle into it.

He remembered the M.P. he'd been talking to and rolled over to check on him. The M.P. was slowly recovering his wits as well. He struggled to his knees and looked at Kenneth. The two men were kneeling, their faces just inches apart. The policeman's forehead was soot blackened, his eyebrows and hair smoldering. His eyes were wide with fright. Somehow this struck Kenneth as intensely funny and he started to laugh. Soon the M.P. was laughing too. Their mirth grew, each man's hysteria fed by the other's, until Kenneth felt his sides must burst. Finally he began to gain control of himself.

"What the hell's so funny?" he asked, still chuckling.

The M.P. wiped his eyes and sat up. "You should see your face," he answered. "Your hair and eyebrows are all smoking!"

Kenneth dissolved in another hysterical fit of laughter and the M.P. was infected again. They leaned on each other, laughing as they struggled to their feet.

"So are yours!" Kenneth sputtered.

The M.P. turned and surveyed the carnage, finally shaking himself of the fit that had seized him.

"Good Lord!" he exclaimed, sadness and sorrow coming over his face.

A flaming patch on the water's surface lit the ramp area in an eerie, spectral orange glow. Beyond the fire the conning tower of a submarine protruded from the water, cocked over at a crazy angle. Men were struggling over the side and into the water from the sub. As Kenneth watched the conning tower lurched over to an even more extreme angle in the water as the fractured hull beneath settled into the silt on the bottom of the harbor. Kenneth looked for any sign of the other sub, the one he'd seen moving towards the breakwater at the moment of the Stukas' attack, but there was no evidence of it. Whether it now lay on the bottom, a tomb for its crew and passengers or had made its escape in time he could not say.

On the ramp the cries of terribly wounded, burned victims had begun. Kenneth and the M.P. moved to begin helping wherever, however they could. A moment later the RAF pilots were there with them. They'd witnessed the bombing from behind the hangar and rushed forward to help the wounded. Kenneth was kneeling over a badly burned man when he felt a hand on his shoulder. He looked up and found Billy Wilson looking down at him.

"Come on Kenneth," Billy said gently. "Let's get you to the medics."

"I'm fine," he answered. "It's this man needs help."

"He's beyond help, Kenneth," Billy said. "Right now you've got to take care of yourself. Come along."

Kenneth allowed himself to be led away from the seaplane ramp at Kalafrana. For the second night in a row he'd witnessed disaster there. On this night it spelled the end of official efforts to evacuate Malta.

Maggie lay in the Captain's bunk, listening as the rest of the 'Y' Service team and seemingly dozens more were brought aboard. The curtain to the Captain's cubicle was left open, affording her a narrow view of the passageway outside as evacuees were packed aboard the sub. Soon the crew was forced to step over or to squeeze past the passengers as every nook and cranny of the sub was jammed with refugees. After nearly a half-hour of loading it seemed the crew was satisfied that no more could be brought aboard and she heard the hatches slammed shut and the diesel engines burst to life.

Within minutes she felt the sensation of movement and a gentle rocking as the sub began to slip out of the harbor. The steady pulse of the diesel engines rose to a heavy throb then quieted and the rocking motion stopped. She guessed this meant the boat had submerged. *HMS Undefeated* glided on, away from Malta, away from Kenneth.

In the ten days that followed Maggie's escape from Malta the submarine made a slow and agonizing passage westward the one thousand miles to Gibraltar. Forced to submerge before dawn each day, the hours of daylight dragged on for the crew and passengers of *Undefeated*. By late each afternoon the air in the boat became foul and fetid, drenched with the smells of bilge water, diesel fuel, sweat and fear. With forty extra persons embarked the oxygen levels fell to the point that all aboard were panting for breath by the time the boat surfaced and the hatches were cracked at dusk.

The suffering intensified when one of the two diesel motors that drove the boat on the surface packed up on the second night of the return to Gibraltar. Laboring along on one engine *Undefeated* was held to a top speed of just six knots on the surface for the nine hours of darkness each night, and no more than two knots while submerged during the day. Progress through the central sea was held to less than a hundred miles in each twenty-four hours. Not until the boat was west of 3° East longitude, roughly due north of Algiers, did her captain deem it safe to surface during daylight hours, and then only for an hour or so around mid-day to freshen the air and charge his batteries.

Maggie lay in the captain's bunk for the entire journey, enduring agonizing headaches compounded by oxygen deprivation. She ate very little and slept as much as possible, especially during the day, and the crew, taking pity on her did everything possible to make her comfortable, but she still found herself with long hours of boredom every day. Unavoidably these were filled with worry and uncertainty about Kenneth. Was he a POW? Was he even alive? With nowhere else to go her mind took her to every dreadful possibility she could imagine.

By the time word spread through the crew and passengers that they were only a day away from reaching safety at Gibraltar a new worry resolved in her mind. She was always very regular and no matter how many times she calculated and rationalized the delay, she knew she was a week late for her menstrual cycle. She didn't need a doctor to tell her she was carrying Kenneth's child.

"SCHACHT!"

Kuno smiled at the familiar voice of Colonel August. Shielding his eyes against the glare of the setting sun he gazed up at the ramparts of the ancient fortress of Mdina. He returned the Colonel's wave and tapped the driver on the shoulder.

"Stop here," he ordered.

The Kubelwagen staff car lurched to a halt and Kuno climbed out of the back seat. The car was a surprise. He'd been about to begin the long trek on foot back to Mdina when the car's horn sounded up the road from the 23rd Regiment's HQ at Luqa. It was leading a small convoy of two light trucks. Lt. Steup leapt from the rear of the vehicle and Kuno saw the car was loaded with cable reels and field telephone sets. The trucks carried most of his regimental communications section and their wireless gear.

With a bow and flourish Steup presented the car to Kuno. "Compliments of the Baron," he explained. "He is anxious for you to report to him at Mdina at the double! I am to remain here and establish local communication with the Air Force."

Kuno did his best not to show it, but he was grateful for the transportation. Thrice wounded since landing by glider two nights previously he was worried about his own stamina for the nearly five kilometer walk back to Mdina. With the car and despite the deplorable condition of the Maltese roads the journey took little more than a half hour. Along the way he saw hundreds of fresh German and Italian infantry streaming down from Ta Qali to Luqa. These men were regular army infantry, not elite paratroopers. A steady stream of Ju 52 transport aircraft roared overhead. It was quickly apparent that the runway at Ta Qali was cleared and the transports were landing there, disgorging their passengers and taking off again for the return trip to Sicily.

When the car reached the southern fringes of Ta Qali these facts were confirmed. The field was abuzz with activity. All fires on the field were extinguished, the runway was clear and the west side of it was in operation. Craters were filled and the strip smoothed for take-off and landing operations. On the eastern side of the runway gangs of Italian soldiers worked to make the field fully operational. A number of light vehicles, some retrieved from wrecked gliders, others liberated from their British owners were in use carrying ammunition and other supplies away from the transports on the landing zone, returning with wounded to be evacuated by air. Along with the wounded the Messerschmitt pilot, Heinz Sauckel returned to Sicily aboard one of the first flights out of Ta Qali. In the days following the invasion German propaganda made full use of Sauckel's exploits, dubbing him the "Ace of Malta". The handsome young man's face appeared in newsreels and printed media for weeks after the battle.

Two light tracked vehicles, known as Bren Gun Carriers to their former British owners were towing wrecked gliders away from the runway. Fresh defensive works and trenches were dug around the southern perimeter of the field and several large open-air tents were set up on the southeast corner of the field. Anchored by the derelict hulks of the British tanks knocked out the day before the tents were in use as field hospital and open-air morgue.

Kuno checked his watch as he bounded up the stone steps of the battlement to Colonel August's HQ. 1913 hours, June 27th. Kuno saluted with his bandaged right hand to the trooper on guard at the base of the watchtower and began the climb up the stone stairs. The HQ was nearly as busy as the airfield. Luftwaffe staff officers with clean-shaven faces and neatly pressed uniforms scurried about on administrative errands. Signs in German had appeared on many doors designating one military bureaucracy or other. Kuno found the Baron on the top floor of the tower. He was looking out through one of the embrasures in the stonework, using his field glasses to scan the airfield.

"So good to see you Schacht!" the Baron exclaimed. "No further injuries since last we met I take it?"

"I am quite well Baron, thank you," answered Kuno, returning the warm smile. "And yourself, Sir?"

Colonel August snorted. "After Crete and the first hours of this little skirmish I have concluded I am quite immune," he laughed. "Come, let's sit and have a bite of food, then you can update me on the situation to the south."

The two officers dined in the turret of the tower on a simple meal of brown bread and salted pork, washed down with a pot of captured British tea. The turret offered a nearly 360° panoramic view of the island. To the east on Ta Qali field air transport operations continued at an almost constant pace. Kuno counted forty landings and as many take-offs in a one hour period. Each incoming plane disgorged a load of infantry or many heavy boxes and crates of weapons and supplies. Each outgoing flight carried wounded Germans or British prisoners back to Sicily.

To the south of Ta Qali men and material continued to flow towards the remaining pocket of stiff British resistance at Hal Far airfield. From time to time the breeze carried the sounds of small arms fire, never quite letting up entirely as the troops of the expanding Axis airhead probed the British defenses. Smoke curled from several places, but primarily from the still smoldering ruins of the Luqa Station Armory, destroyed by the British earlier in the day. To the north too, fires burned and smoke billowed skyward. Colonel August told him that the Italian amphibious landing at Qawra was firmly ashore after meeting initial resistance much stiffer than anticipated. From time to time the sound of naval artillery battering the British defenses could be heard.

"By this evening I expect a link-up with our armored force," the Colonel told Kuno. "I plan to pass our panzers directly through to Luqa for tomorrow's attack on Hal Far."

Only to the west was the view serene and quiet. Three kilometers of broken heights separated Mdina from the sea. Glimpsing the tranquil blues of sea and sky Kuno could almost forget the horrors and death of the past two days. Their meal complete Kuno apprised Colonel August of the situation at Luqa. The two officers huddled over a map of the island.

"We hold almost the entire airfield," Kuno reported. "Only the extreme southern end of the main runway is not yet secured. British snipers are active on the west side of the field, but they are being dug out one-by-one so that by tomorrow morning we shall be able to develop our attack fully with no interference from that quarter. East of the field the resistance is of small, disorganized units and has not presented any great difficulty."

"So far, so good," murmured Colonel August.

Kuno tapped the map at the south end of the Luqa runway.

"Here is where the problem will be," he said, shaking his head. "The British have withdrawn in surprisingly good order to prepared positions in an arc from the ridge lines on the west to St. George's Bay on the east. It is apparent they have planned this line for a final stand for some time." He shrugged his shoulders. "Nonetheless," he went on, "with coordinated air and panzer support the outcome should not be in doubt, so long as reinforcements continue to arrive in the numbers I have seen this afternoon."

Colonel August nodded his head thoughtfully. "Once Hal Far is taken it only remains to see if the British will contest the urban areas around the harbors on the eastern shore."

"Do you think they will, Colonel?" asked Kuno, his brows lowered in worry.

"Madness to do so, of course," said the Baron, "at least from a strictly military viewpoint, but these British…" he shook his head again. "They can be very stubborn in defending lost causes. They were so on Crete."

Kuno shook his head. "Street fighting is not pleasant," he remarked.

The Baron didn't answer, just nodded his head. After a moment he changed the topic.

"I want you back at Luqa before first light," he said. "You'll retain command of the 23rd for now, and keep it in reserve for the assault. Not much fighting punch left in the regiment I imagine."

"It's down to less than one third strength at this point," Kuno concurred, "though the men hope to find many of their comrades from the first drop held captive at Hal Far."

"In any case," the Colonel went on, "your primary duty tomorrow will be to coordinate air support for the attack. It's why we brought you after all," he laughed.

"I must thank you someday," smiled Kuno.

"Get yourself some sleep, Kuno," the Colonel ordered, turning serious again. "You're going to need it tomorrow. I'll have you wakened in time."

When he did waken it was from a variation of the same dream. Somehow he always found himself attending the funeral of his two sons, Rolf and Edmund. This time they were being buried beside the runway at Ta Qali, in the shadow of one of the tanks he'd knocked out the day before with the PAK gun. Colonel August officiated the funeral on a gray and dreary day. Hundreds of paratroopers stood at attention, or so he thought, but just before waking he realized they too were all dead. Wooden crosses propped them up in standing positions.

Kuno rubbed his eyes and scratched the stubble of his beard. He checked his watch. 0230. Somewhat earlier than he'd expected. The trooper who had wakened him stood back respectfully for a moment then spoke.

"Colonel August requests you join him in the turret immediately, Major," he said.

"Yes of course," Kuno replied, swinging his feet stiffly off the cot and onto the floor, wincing as the stitches in his chest pulled. Moments later he climbed the spiral stone staircase to the top of the tower. As he emerged into the center of the turret strange, orange flashes of light came through several embrasures on one side. Colonel August leaned against one of these embrasures looking out into the night.

"Ah, Kuno," he said quietly. "Sorry to waken you early, but I saw your sleep was restless." A faraway look crossed the Colonel's face. He shrugged. "I too, dream."

"Quite all right, Colonel," said Kuno wondering at the strange mood the Baron displayed. He stepped over to the open embrasure. "What are the lights from, Sir?"

"Thought you would want to see this," the Baron replied, beckoning Kuno to the opening. "Not a common thing for a soldier to see."

Kuno stepped to the window, peering out into the darkness. He was disoriented from the climb up the spiral staircase and at first wasn't sure which direction he was looking.

"This is the northwest?" he asked after a moment.

"Indeed," replied the Colonel. A flurry of flashes erupted from the far distance. "Out over the sea. There is a naval battle underway there," he said, nodding out the window. "For several minutes now."

The sky was dark for a moment then another flurry lit the sky.

"The British," breathed Kuno, a sudden chill dread running down his spine.

"Yes, and presumably our Italian allies as well," answered the

Colonel. "Doesn't give me a warm feeling."

Kuno said nothing, but remembered the young Italian engineer at Luqa the afternoon before. A series of heavy flashes rolled one after the other in succession. Kuno counted six in all. Seconds later they were answered by nine more from a slightly different bearing.

"How far distant?" he asked the Colonel.

"I can't be sure," Colonel August shook his head. "Well over the horizon certainly."

The two officers stood in silence, watching the ebb and flow of the fireworks display. Several minutes after Kuno joined the Colonel in the turret the brightest flash yet lit the horizon. It flared up, flickered, died down a little and then rose in brilliance for several seconds, holding its intensity, dominating all the lesser flashes that surrounded it. Finally it subsided, but there seemed to remain a long-lasting glow at the point of its origin.

"Someone has scored a hit," observed Colonel August.

"But who?" asked Kuno rhetorically.

The distant exchange of gunfire continued unabated, each sequence of flashes representing a salvo from the guns of one side or the other.

"What is the plan should the British win this sea battle?" asked Kuno. This time he turned to Colonel August and waited for an answer.

The Baron shrugged. "It will fall to the Air Force to stop them," he said. "The bombers will have to be diverted from tomorrow's attack on Hal Far against any British ships which survive this." He nodded his head to the northwest as a string of flashes signaled a broadside being fired.

Kuno opened his mouth to respond, but just then a stupendous flash lit the western horizon like the sun risen in the west, holding its brilliance for long seconds before subsiding. Both men watched, slack-jawed at the spectacle. Many seconds after the flash a rumble as of distant thunder came to the turret.

"Damn!" the Baron issued an uncharacteristic oath. "I wasn't counting. Were you?" he asked Kuno.

"No," replied Kuno. "I never considered we would hear anything at these distances."

The exchange of flashes continued, but there were no more dramatic explosions.

Colonel August glanced at his watch. "It is getting late," he announced. "I think it would be best if you got started towards Luqa soon." He nodded out the window. "This may be wearing on nerves there."

"Yes, Sir," said Kuno.

Giussepe Gianaclis remained on the bridge of *Muzio Attendolo* through the morning hours. Three times the cruiser and her sister ship *Raimondo Montecuccoli* stood in with the battleship *Vittorio Venetto* to bombard the Maltese shoreline. The three heavy ships waited for the smoke to clear and for circling spotter aircraft of the Italian air force to report which targets needed to be attacked again, then resumed the bombardment.

Giussepe checked his watch. 1245 hours. He leaned out over the port bridge wing and watched the landing force move into position. The landing fleet was a motley assortment of all sorts of craft. At its core were twenty modern tank lighters with shallow bottoms and bow ramps that would drop down on the beach to disgorge the tanks aboard. The entire fleet of ferryboats from the Straight of Messina was requisitioned for the operation. They would go in first, driving themselves up on the beach to land infantry. A dozen small merchant steamers stood ready, loaded with men to transfer in small boats to the ferries. Fifteen destroyers and torpedo boats screened the entire force. In all over nine thousand men and forty tanks waited offshore for the order to land.

The first of the ferries to head for shore passed the *Muzio*. At its top speed it barely made eight knots and its progress towards shore was agonizingly slow. Giussepe could see the infantrymen crouched in the bows, taking what cover they could from the thin iron shell of the ferry. *Muzio's* gunnery officer, Commander Marco Spoleto moved quietly to stand beside him, his headset still clamped to his ears, wires trailing back to the center of the bridge. The two officers stood in silence watching the ferry make its painstaking way the five kilometers in to the beach. As it reached a point three kilometers offshore the next ferryboat moved in to follow it. The Italian plan called for the infantry to land first, secure a beachhead and then for engineers to follow with steel and wooden mats to put down on the sand of the beach for the German tanks to cross. Without the aid of the mats it was feared the tanks would bog down in the soft sands and loose shale of the beaches. The first ferry was within two kilometers of shore with no opposition yet seen.

Giussepe turned to the gunnery officer.

"So far, so good, Marco," he said. "You and your guns have done a good job silencing the shore batteries."

Marco shook his head. "It's too easy," he replied. "Those guns were set in many meters of concrete and stone. I don't believe we have destroyed them all."

At that moment, as if to make a prophet of him a waterspout erupted in the sea 300 meters to starboard of the lead ferryboat, hurling water thirty meters in the air. A second later the sound of the explosion carried across the water to them.

"SHIT!" exclaimed Spoleto. He flipped a switch on his headset and shouted into the telephone mouthpiece suspended under his chin. "Give me a spotting report!" He turned and ran back to the center of the bridge.

Giussepe watched the ferry as it turned to starboard, altering its course as it continued on at full speed. Less than a minute later another waterspout erupted, near the ferries original course and less than 100 meters to port. Spray and mist descended against the side of the ferry, but it continued on unscathed, turning again, this time to port to throw off the aim of the shore battery. Another interminable minute passed. The ferry was less than a thousand meters from shore. Giussepe heard the soft whirr of *Muzio's* main turrets turning atop the barbettes and of the guns elevating to fire. A third shell screamed down on the ferry, this time nearly under her bows. The ferry reared up and smacked back down on the sea. He snatched his binoculars to his eyes. The bows were drenched by the waterspout falling back on the ferry. Men lay sprawled about on deck, wounded or dead.

*Muzio's* forward turret spoke, the center gun firing a single shell, ranging for the enemy shore battery. He lifted his glasses to the land, but could not find the fall of the shot. High atop *Muzio's* mainmast he knew spotters for the gunners were observing the shot. On the bridge he heard 'Guns' speak again.

"Up two hundred, left one hundred and fire for effect!" he shouted.

Another brief whirr and then the cruiser let fly with a full broadside. Too late, for just as the ship rocked back from the recoil another shell plunged down on the ferry, this time striking it near the funnel, exploding among the men packed on the second passenger deck. Giussepe was appalled at the carnage. Bodies were flung overboard by the explosion like so much confetti at a holiday parade. As the smoke from the explosion cleared away he could see men writhing in agony on the upper deck. For all its awful effect the men aboard the ferry were actually lucky. Had the shell plunged to the lower deck before exploding its toll would have been much higher. As it was, the ferry continued on its way pushing in for the last few hundred meters to the beach.

Smaller explosions from light mortars started spouting in the water near it and through the binoculars he could see lines of splashes from machine gun and small arms fire as the ferry grounded on the shore.

Men began to tumble over her bows into the shallow surf. Many fell in the water and did not get up, but others forced their way ashore, stumbling across the sand, firing their weapons. *Muzio's* guns spoke again, just as *Raimondo* also fired. Their combined broadsides fell just inland of the stone sea wall and the road atop it that ran along the coast fifty meters from the high water mark. Smoke drifted down on the beach, obscuring the scene. The second ferry closed on the beach without being fired upon, ducking into the cloud of smoke like a virgin grateful to hide her skirts from the town cad.

The Gunnery Officer rejoined Giussepe as a third ferry disappeared in the smoke that still lingered from the last broadside. Now the ferries began running into the beach in pairs rather than singly. The two officers watched, confidence growing as the first pair moved in on the beach. The first ferry ashore, though damaged, completed disgorging its passengers and backed away from the beach. It was returning with several dozen wounded aboard and for its next load of passengers and was passing to port of the inbound pair when the British fired again. This time a trio of heavy shells slammed into the sea just inshore of the inbound pair. Both were drenched with water and riddled with shell fragments.

Spoleto spun away with a curse and began the process of retargeting his guns on the new threat. Before any of the three heavy ships could return fire the British fired another salvo. This time a shell scored a direct hit on one of the ferries, setting it afire and stopping its engine immediately. It started to settle by the bow and very soon men were diving from it into the water. The outbound ferry spun hard over and set about rescue efforts. It in turn was bracketed by a third salvo from the British shore battery. Finally *Muzio, Raimondo* and *Vittorio Venetto* all fired. After several more salvos and further damage to the landing ferries the British guns were silenced.

So it went through the early afternoon; a cat and mouse game in which the British held their fire until the Italian landing craft reached points that were pre-registered for accurate fire. Troops did manage to trickle ashore, but losses mounted as the day wore on and with each landing craft damaged the speed with which the force could be put ashore was reduced. By late afternoon it became doubtful whether the entire force could even be landed by nightfall.

Giussepe took a quick meal in his cabin at 1700 hours and returned to the bridge in time to witness yet another bombardment of a British shore installation. His friend the Gunnery Officer Marco Spoleto was still on the bridge, directing *Muzio's* fire. When Marco saw Giussepe he arched his eyebrows significantly and nodded to the bridge wing. Giussepe waited a moment then joined him.

"It's building to a disaster Giussepe," murmured Marco discretely, careful to not be overheard. "We don't have half the force ashore. We're hours behind schedule."

"The British guns are the cause of the delay?"

"Yes," replied Marco. "That and over-optimism on the part of our own planners. I don't think we could have kept the schedule even if the landings were unopposed."

"What news do we have of the troops ashore?" asked Giussepe.

"I haven't had time to stay on top of that," answered Marco, "but the last I heard they are having a rough time. They keep calling for the tanks to be landed, but against these shore batteries…" He left the thought unfinished, shaking his head. Giussepe leaned in close. "There are rumors of a British fleet approaching, Marco," he murmured.

Marco glanced around discretely. "I think they are true, Giussepe," he murmured back. "There have been several wireless communications delivered to the Captain." He hooked his head back to the center of the bridge. Marco looked at Giussepe. "Have you had any sleep?" he asked.

"Not since yesterday morning," replied Giussepe.

"Better get yourself some rest, Giussepe. I have a feeling your services will be required tonight."

"What about you, Marco?" Giussepe asked.

Marco snorted. "There may be nothing for me to do!" he laughed. "We've already expended nearly a quarter of our 6-inch ammunition."

The Italian landing was indeed in difficulty. While nearly three thousand men were ashore as dusk approached this was only half the planned number and none of the tanks or other vehicles had yet even attempted a landing. The little fleet of ferryboats suffered greatly. Three were sunk and three others suffered such damage that they were withdrawn from the landing operations. Ashore, the troops were less than a kilometer inland from the landing zones south and east of Ghallis Point along the coast road towards Floriana and Valletta and were meeting heavy resistance. They were reliant on the guns of the ships offshore to crush pockets of British resistance.

The moon rose at Malta the afternoon of June 27, 1942 at 1730 hours, almost two hours before sunset and by the time the sun's last light was fading the moon was shining across the sea and illuminating the landing beaches enough that operations could continue, though at a slower pace.

For their part, the British were in desperate straits themselves. The troops defending the northern beaches could expect no help from the regiments garrisoned on the three airfields and if the Italians managed to land a sufficient force to press inland and link up with the German and Italian airborne troops already at Ta Qali and Luqa, the battle for Malta might be as good as lost.

The initial bombardment had silenced a number of shore batteries and every time any of the surviving guns fired against the invaders the ships offshore brought heavy fire down on the British guns. The men of the Royal Malta Artillery Regiment suffered terribly. Recruited from the Crown Colony of Malta the troops were defending their native soil, or rock as the case might be. They were determined and wily. They held their fire until they were sure of their targets, then rained steel and ruin down on the Italian landing force until the heavy guns of the ships offshore sniffed out the location of the battery and destroyed it. In nearly every case the Maltese served their guns to the end. One-by-one these batteries were found and snuffed out in a painstaking and deadly game of cat-and-mouse.

The British mounted several counterattacks as well, but each time they concentrated enough infantry to drive the Italians back a rain of steel poured in from the ships offshore and slowly the Italian toehold grew. British infantry adopted tactics that would become all too familiar to Japanese troops defending their island empire later in the war. They kept in close contact, often within grenade toss range of the Italian lines; too close for the heavy guns offshore to fire on them. Hand-to-hand combat became frequent after sunset.

As the evening wore on the tide of battle started to tip away from the defenders. After 2100 hours fire from the shore batteries ceased. There were no more British guns in range to fire against the ferryboats bringing troops ashore and the Italians began landing the tanks. The first two lighters reached shore at 2135. Their bows splashed down in the surf. Engineers scrambled ashore with steel and wood landing mats. Each lighter disgorged two tanks by 2200 hours. Others followed and by 2300 twelve tanks were ashore. The tanks were part of a special German armored unit equipped with vehicles captured from the Soviets on the eastern front. The Russian model T-26 tanks weighed ten and a half tons and were armed with a 45mm main gun and two machine guns. They moved off the beach and up onto the coast road to support the infantry already ashore.

Later that night they were followed by heavier tanks, also captured by the Germans on the Eastern Front. The Soviet KV II tank was massive, weighing over 53 tons and stood 12 feet tall. Its turret housed a powerful 152mm howitzer. Slow and cumbersome the KV II had proved ill-suited for the fluid style of warfare in Russia and it had not yet been used in its design role of bunker buster. The ten KV II tanks the Germans landed on Malta would.

Awakening to a rough shaking Giussepe sat bolt upright in near panic.

"What is it?" he demanded.

The young seaman who had wakened him backed up and hung his head.

"I am sorry, Sir," he said. "I knocked many times, but did not hear your answer."

Giussepe looked at his alarm clock as he swung his feet off the bunk onto the deck. 2320. He had slept almost four hours. He listened to the sounds of the ship. The deck vibrated with a soft hum beneath his feet. He estimated the engines were running half ahead. No shouts or cries betrayed imminent action. The ship had a gentle roll. It was almost as if *Muzio* was on a peacetime cruise. Giussepe looked at the young seaman.

"What is it?" he asked again.

"Captain's compliments, Sir," the young man said. "You are asked to come to the bridge immediately."

"Very well," replied Giussepe. He'd slept fully clothed and needed only to tighten his tie and slip on his uniform jacket and cap as they left his tiny cabin. Giussepe wended his way through crowded passageways and up two decks to the bridge, entering through the chart house. The bridge was blacked out; only a meager glow from the binnacle and compass platform provided any man-made light, but the full moon bathed the superstructure of the ship. The officers and ratings were outlined against the windows. Captain Digiacoma sat in his chair at the center of the bridge apparently asleep. Giussepe approached and cleared his throat quietly.

"Ah, Gianaclis," said the Captain. "Thank you for coming so quickly." The Captain slid down from his chair and walked back into the charthouse. He snapped on the red battle lantern over the chart table. The red light illuminated the table yet preserved the night vision of the bridge watch. Giussepe followed the Captain into the charthouse, stealing a glance at the table before the Captain turned and spoke again.

"We have received a communication from Commando Supremo," he began. "They expect a large British fleet to force the Straights of Sicily shortly, around midnight. Our torpedo boat flotilla is ordered to attack them and bar passage, but Rome expects some of the British will get through." He pointed to the chart. "Their objective is obvious," he continued. "They must fight their way through to Malta and shell our positions ashore." He shrugged. "Our goal is also obvious. We must stop them. Admiral Iachino expects *Muzio* to lead the way."

"Does the Admiral wish to pass north of Malta or to the south?" asked Giussepe.

Captain Digiacoma smiled. "You tell me Giussepe."

Gianaclis leaned over the chart.

"The British will want the straightest line to the island," he said, "to arrive before dawn if possible. After dawn they will be more vulnerable to air attack. They want to shell the island during the hours of darkness." He stabbed down on the chart to the southwest of Malta. "Somewhere here where all three airfields lie within range of their guns."

"Very good, so far," said Digiacoma. "North or south, Giussepe?"

"North."

"Why?"

"Two reasons. If we go south we must pass down the east coast of the island. Whatever fast attack boats the British have available will be based at Valletta and we'd be vulnerable to them as well as in danger of the minefields along the east coast. If we go north around the island we are closer to our own air cover on Sicily."

The Captain nodded his head. "And your second reason?"

"The British must approach from the northwest. Our straightest course to cut them off is to the north."

"Chart the course, Giussepe. North."

A short time later moonlight dappled the surface of the sea behind *Muzio*, the wave tops sparkling like gems on a black velvet background. The south wind had moderated and gentle, five-foot seas washed under and past the Italian cruiser and the fleet she led. Behind *Muzio Attendolo* sailed *Raimondo Montecuccoli* and behind her the great battleship *Vittorio Venetto*, her 15-inch guns trained in. Nine destroyers ringed the heavy ships providing anti-submarine protection.

All twelve ships of the fleet were darkened, not even their navigating lights were on. Not that they were needed. The moon reached its fullest phase the night of June 27-28, 1942 and the sky to the northwest of Malta was clear of clouds or fog. Giussepe looked out over the bridge wing of the *Muzio* and smiled. A spirit of anticipation seized him and he sensed the same feeling among the other officers and crew of his ship. They were sailing to meet the British Royal Navy in battle and for once they did so with confidence. Captain Digiacoma addressed the ship's company just after 0100 hours the morning of the 28th, alerting them that a British fleet was passing the Skerki Bank and was headed for Malta to intervene against the invasion. It was the job of the Regia Marina to stop them and stop them they would, he assured the men. A great cheer went up from every deck of the cruiser, from every turret and magazine, from every gun tub and every space where men were closed up at action stations. These men, these inheritors of a tradition of inferiority to the British Royal Navy, burdened with the stigma of Cape Matapan, Taranto and a dozen other lesser defeats at the hands of the British were determined that this time, at Malta, the British would not pass.

On the bridge the Captain spoke quietly, confidently as *Muzio* raced at over thirty knots to the west.

"Activate the 'Gufo'," he ordered.

High atop the foremast and the mainmast the German supplied 'Owl' hummed to life.

>>>>>>>>>>>>>

At last Webster had a chance to sleep, though not in the comfort of his cot in the small cabin he shared with another officer aboard *HMS Sirius*. Webster was on the bridge, just below his Surface Action Station in the main Gunnery Control Tower above and behind the bridge. He sat on the deck in a corner, his head lolled over, seemingly fast asleep, but always his mind was tracking what went on around him.

After the final air attack of June 27th his anti-aircraft gun crews were stood down from first degree of readiness and the men in the main turrets and magazines were relieved. The decks were swept of spent shell casings and the guns were cleaned. The crews in the radar plots were replaced. Much of the ship's company stood down from the highest state of alert, though the guns and lookout positions would be continually manned for as long as the ship remained in hostile waters; indeed, even when in a friendly port the watch was never completely relaxed.

As soon as Action Stations were reduced to Second Degree of Readiness the Paymaster Commander and his galley staff swung into action. Oil fuel lines to the stoves had been drained before the ship left Gibraltar to reduce risk of fire, but live steam piped up from the engine room boilers was applied to great vats in the galley, heating fifty gallons of soup and ten gallons each of tea and hot cocoa. Piles of bully beef sandwiches were made and stacked on trays for distribution to the crew. When all was ready the Paymaster Commander was given permission by the Bridge and the 'Bosun's plaintive Cornish voice piped over the Tannoy, "Cooks to the galley."

One might think it was rather late to summon the cooks to the galley, as the evening meal was already prepared, but over the centuries the Royal Navy had developed some curious customs, seemingly designed to confuse the landsman. In RN parlance the 'cooks' were not the men who prepared the meals, but rather were those tasked with the responsibility of picking the food up from the galley and delivering it throughout the ship. From every gun tub and turret, magazine, boiler room, radar office and damage control station, from the bridge, the torpedo launchers, sick bay and after steering position, one man left his station, went to the galley and brought the food back to his mates, balancing trays of sandwiches atop stacks of enameled iron soup bowls and cocoa mugs. Through long practice the 'cooks' timed their movements so that only a small percentage were away from their posts at any given moment, and the Paymaster Commander's galley staff arranged the food so that each cook found trays with exactly the right number of servings for his station. To the men of *Sirius* and the other ships of Force H the meal served that evening revived and refreshed them till, almost, they could forget the trauma of the day, almost put aside the death and destruction they'd witnessed.

As the evening meal concluded and trays and cups were returned to the galley the soft sounds of a mouth organ came from the port side, below the bridge and aft. One of the crew of the 40mm Bofors gun there, a young lad named Carmichael was gifted with the instrument and on many nights at sea he played his harmonica, helping the men within earshot, including those on the bridge to smile or laugh for a few minutes. Usually he played light and jaunty tunes and Webster often found himself tapping his foot or gently slapping his thigh in time with the music. Other men often sang to accompany the young man's play, but tonight Carmichael's mood was reflected in the rest of the ship's company. No jaunty ditty, no toe-tapping dance tune did he play.

Carmichael played The White Cliffs of Dover, slowly and sweetly, drawing out each note. The decks of *Sirius* fell silent. Only the rhythmic swish of the sea and an occasional softly murmured command intruded on the music. In his mind Webster was suddenly back at Dover, commanding his battery of flak guns, dreaming of his next leave with Althea. The silence lasted many minutes after Carmichael finished the tune and he did not play another.

With the passing of daylight the threat of air attack was removed, at least until the moon rose higher in the sky, but the danger was far from over. With darkness, or what passed for it on those moonlit nights at the end of June, submarines now posed an increased risk to Force H as it continued its plodding way to the east towards Malta. The operators in the Asdic cabinets behind the bridge of each cruiser and destroyer in the fleet intensified their concentration, listening with straining ears for the slightest sound coming from their headphones, the least signal or hint of a submerged threat.

The British fleet continued its transit to the Skerki Bank in the first hour of darkness at 2230 hours, Admiral Burrough having chosen the northern route over the southern. It afforded him more room to maneuver and as he approached the Sicilian Narrows his meteorological officer told him conditions were right for fog and low clouds. Burrough felt the northern channel gave him a chance to slip past enemy forces into the open waters between Sicily and Tunisia. The northern channel also gave him the chance of bringing the 15-inch guns of *Renown* to bear against the German lodgment on Malta by first light of June 28th.

As the British fleet neared the Skerki Bank Admiral Burrough formed his surviving heavy ships into a single column to pass through the narrow, deep-water channel. *HMS Sirius* led off with the damaged *HMS Kenya* right behind. *Renown* was next, followed by *HMS Charybdis, HMS Evening Dale* and *HMS*

*Nigeria* bringing up the rear. The destroyers were spread ahead and to the sides of the heavy ships, the fast and modern Tribal Class destroyers *Eskimo, Sikh* and *Tartar* forming a shield to the front, with the World War I era destroyers *Westcott, Vansittart, Wishart, Verdun* and *Wanderer* to the north and *Venomous, Laforey, Vanquisher* and *Wolsey* to the south. All twelve destroyers refueled from the oiler *Evening Dale* before reaching Skerki. As it approached the Skerki Bank the entire fleet was making 19 knots, the best speed of the slowest ship, *Evening Dale*.

>>>>>>>>>>>>

The crash of waves against the bowsprit alternated with the roar of the main induction vents as *RM Perla* forced her way through gentle seas to the southwest. Occasionally as she met a wave a sheet of water was flung back against the conning tower and the men on watch, drenching them anew, momentarily drowning out the noise of the induction vents sucking drafts of air into the boat to feed the diesels.

Lt. Renaldo Cosani scanned the horizon to the south, looking for a telltale splash of wake, a silhouette, anything to betray the presence of enemy warships, but the sea was an inky black barely distinguishable from the sky. The full moon was well up in the eastern sky, but the haze of the day had turned to low, scudding clouds over the surface of the sea and visibility was variable. Now and then the clouds parted and gave a clear, moonlit view, but mostly he could see no further than a mile or so. The clouds thickened and settled into a low fog as the evening wore on. He checked his watch by the hooded lamp on the binnacle. 2253 hours. If the British Royal Navy were to make a run past the Skerki Bank it would have to be during the upcoming hours of relative darkness. The British would not wait till daylight. He reached down and flipped open the cover on the voice tube.

"Bridge to Conn," he said.

"Conn to Bridge, aye?" came the immediate response from his Executive Officer Luigi Mortobello.

"Come left to course one-three-five," he ordered. "Time for our southeast leg."

"Left to one-three-five, aye," answered Mortobello.

Cosani resumed his surveillance of the sea as the boat swung to the south then continued on to her southeasterly heading. Cosani set out a patrol pattern to the north and a few miles to the west of the Skerki Bank in a box five miles on a side. Shaped like a diamond with its four tips on the four points of the compass the course took thirty minutes to a side at ten knots. They'd been on station for nearly three hours.

Cosani began to reconsider the chance that the British might have taken their heavy ships south of the Bank, close in to the Tunisian shoreline. Such a course held the advantage of being further from all Axis air and naval bases and also held an element of surprise. The British might take that course, in spite of its dangers. They had done so before when only merchant ships escorted by destroyers and light cruisers were to pass. But for heavy ships like battleships and airplane carriers the south course was fraught with hazards. The deep channel was much narrower to the south of Skerki, at one point just four miles wide and in any case would be patrolled by Italian surface torpedo boats so there was no chance of slipping through undetected. To pass through this narrow channel at night would be very difficult, but to do so before the moon was high enough to light the passage would be almost impossible.

Cosani lowered the glasses and shook his head. If the British had chosen the south channel it made no difference to his immediate plans. He couldn't reach a position to attack them in the south channel anyway, so all he could do was trust his luck that the British had done the sensible thing and chosen the northern passage where the channel was wide enough to permit a column of heavy ships to pass with escort vessels to either side.

He leaned down to the voice tube again.

"Bridge to Conn," he said. "Is there anything on the sound detection apparatus?"

"Conn to Bridge," Luigi replied. "Negative. Quiet on all bearings."

"Acknowledged," he answered, closing the cover on the tube.

He resumed his search of the seas taking his time to go round the compass completely. He started to lower the glasses, but hesitated, scanning back across a sector to the southwest he'd just completed. He saw nothing but more clouds and the inky blackness to the west where the moon had not yet lit the sea, relieved here and there by a star breaking through a gap in the clouds. Once again he started to lower the glasses, but stopped. He understood now what had drawn his attention back and he focused on an area of especially dense fog, low on the water. Just then *Perla* shuddered and lurched and a blast of water was flung in his face as the submarine plowed into a heavy wave.

Coughing and spluttering he lowered the binoculars and reached for the voice tube.

"Bridge to Conn," he gasped out.

"Conn to Bridge, aye?" answered Mortobello, his voice showing concern for the Captain.

"I'm all right, Luigi," he answered. "Come right to one-five-zero. Mark the log with the time. Contact with heavy ships, bearing one-nine-five. We're going to maneuver ahead of the British for a shot on their port beam."

"Aye, Captain!" replied the XO excitedly.

"Dive the boat!" ordered Cosani. "Dive the boat!"

Bridge lookouts tumbled down the conning tower trunk while the boat slid beneath the waves.

Cosani was last down the trunk, slamming the hatch down behind him. The Chief Petty Officer of the boat jumped up the ladder and dogged the hatch closed. Cosani wiped his face on a towel and strode to the conning table where the XO joined him.

"Come left to one-three-five immediately," he snapped.

"What did you see, Captain?" asked Mortobello.

"The British fleet is here, Luigi!" exclaimed Cosani. "Right on schedule! At least four heavy ships in column with destroyers forming an escort in front and on either side." He threw the towel in a corner before going on. "I almost missed them Luigi," he said. "Just a dark outline against a fog bank." He pointed at the chart pinned to the table. "I'm going to maneuver in front of the British, slip inside the destroyer screen and attack the heavies!" He stabbed his finger down on the chart. "Make ready all tubes and torpedoes," he ordered.

"Yes, Sir!" snapped Mortobello.

"Up periscope."

Cosani pressed his face to the eyepiece as the tube slid up from the well.

"These swells will mask our approach," he said. "Luigi take a bearing. Mark!"

"One-nine-five," answered the XO.

"Down scope."

Cosani jumped excitedly to the chart table as the periscope returned to its well.

"The British are hugging the shoal line here," he said, using a pencil to point at the northern edge of the Skerki Bank. "They are moving at around 20 knots to the northeast. We'll be in position to attack in about twelve minutes."

"Can you distinguish the ship types?" asked Mortobello.

"Not yet, not for sure," said the Captain. "But at least four heavy ships surrounded by destroyers."

In the next minutes Cosani took several periscope sightings as *RM Perla* held her course. As the British drew closer the composition of their fleet became clearer.

"Two cruisers in the lead," he described his view through the periscope. "Battleship in the next position, with a heavy cruiser, maybe another battleship bringing up the rear." He adjusted the periscope angle slightly. "Down scope. The second battleship might be an airplane carrier. Luigi, start a stopwatch. Count down one minute."

A minute later the XO said, "Mark!"

"Up scope!" Cosani knelt to the eyepiece and rode it up, twisting the handles back and forth. "Down scope! Stop engines!" he shouted before the tube was even fully extended. "Destroyer approaching fast. He should pass directly above us. When he does we'll wait a moment, then I'll pop the scope for another look. It will be our final firing bearing, Luigi. Be ready."

Seconds later the hushed crew listened, barely daring to breathe as the destroyer's screws thrashed the water over their heads. Cosani stood in the control room as the sound of the screws approached, waiting for the 'ping' of active sonar. If the British used it here they couldn't fail to detect the *Perla*. The screws reached what seemed a thunderous crescendo to the crew, but the ping never came and the destroyer passed on. The Captain waited until the sound of the destroyer was nearly gone before speaking.

"Start engines," he said calmly. "Up periscope."

Once again he rode the periscope up as its hydraulic ram lifted it from its well.

"I see tracer shells over the water to the south of the fleet," he said.

Commander Oats shifted nervously from foot to foot on the starboard bridge wing of *Renown*. Reports from the screening destroyers indicated fast moving surface radar contacts away to the south. Admiral Burrough stood at the rail, scanning the sea through his binoculars. Intermittent banks of fog and low cloud scudded across the surface; a major break for the British. With clear skies the light of the full moon would have bathed the fleet, exposing it once again to possible air attack.

Yet the fog was a two-edged sword. The Motor Torpedo Boats speeding about in the fog to the south of the fleet were much too quick to target with radar directed fire. At least four MTBs were darting in and out of the fog, playing hide and seek with the destroyer screen, probing for a chance to slip inside the screen and deliver their deadly cargo of torpedoes against the battleship or cruisers.

The forward gun mount of a destroyer in the starboard screen fired, illuminating the night in a strobe light flash. Within seconds the destroyer's secondary armament joined in, lashing the sea with 20mm and machine gun fire. The pop and crackle of automatic cannon fire carried across the water. Tracer shells whipped the sea, ricocheted from the wave tops and tumbled away into the night. The destroyer's 20-inch searchlight clicked on, stabbing its beam through the dark, flashing it back and forth, probing like a finger in the dark for its quarry, the Axis MTB. A thin stream of tracer shells came back out of the fog and played across the destroyer's hull and superstructure, bounding away at crazy angles with tumbling shells whirring and whistling in their disrupted flight. A bright white flash silhouetted the destroyer as the searchlight was hit and exploded, but away in the fog a fire burned and the destroyer maintained its fusillade, battering the MTB to pieces. It drifted clear of the fog, stopped dead in the water, blazing from stem to stern and down by the bows. Oats watched, fascinated as the torpedo boat slid beneath the waves. The gunners on the destroyer kept pouring fire into the spot, even after the boat was gone. Finally their fire stopped and the sea was quiet and serene again. He was nearly blinded as his eyes struggled to re-adjust to the near darkness.

"Round one to us," said Admiral Burrough.

At that instant a brilliant orange flash split the night, lighting the surface of the sea like day. It held and grew in intensity and Oats felt heat from it even though it came from the other side of the ship. Admiral Burrough and his staff rushed across the bridge to the starboard wing as the fireball roared into the sky and died. To port, the oiler *Evening Dale* sailing in the middle of the column of heavy ships seemed to stagger from the impact of the torpedo hit in her port bows; slewing briefly to port she struggled to right herself and shouldered into the next sea.

Oats stared at the oiler, willing her to survive the blast. A second flash erupted, this time near her stern, again on the port side. The flame didn't reach as far into the sky this time, but the stern seemed to lift from the sea and water rocketed out from under it into the sky. The oiler lost way immediately, her propeller shafts snapped by the force of the second blast.

"Oh, God," groaned Oats, leaning over the rail and watching *Evening Dale* fall off on her port side, losing speed.

"She's badly hurt!" exclaimed Lt. Harris.

No sooner were the words out of his mouth than disaster deepened for Force H. The third and fourth torpedoes in *Perla's* spread of four fish passed behind *Evening Dale*. The third shot missed entirely, but the fourth fish veered off course due to a faulty gyro and by twist of fate found *HMS Nigeria* sailing in column 500 yards behind the oiler. The torpedo exploded amidships under *Nigeria's* keel, opening both her engine rooms to the sea. Cold seawater flooded the compartments and in seconds reached her boilers. They exploded one after the other sending plumes of flames roaring up through the smoke stacks and into the night sky. *Nigeria* lost all electrical power and forward propulsion and immediately began to settle on an even keel. Within a minute her freeboard was gone and waves were crashing over her starboard rail as she wallowed in the troughs between waves.

"Signal the cruisers to hold their speed," snapped Burrough. "We daren't stop here. The E-boats will pick us all off one-by-one. Signal *Wolsey* to stand-by *Nigeria*; *Verdun* and *Vanquisher* to stand-by *Evening Dale*."

"The tanker might be saved," objected Harris, looking back

towards the stricken oiler "She's not afire."

"Certainly," replied Burrough. "If we had time to rig a proper tow-line and if we weren't a thousand miles from the nearest friendly port. But we can't leave her and we can't tow her to Malta, Jim. If she can't keep up her crew will have to be taken off and we'll have to finish her ourselves."

To the north one of the destroyers in the port screen laid a pattern of depth charges over the suspected position of the enemy sub. Cosani and his crew had heard the report of three torpedo detonations through the thin hull of *RM Perla,* and enjoyed a brief celebration before they grabbed hold to weather the expected storm of depth charges. Fountains of water, yellow tinged from the chemicals in the explosives, were launched in the air. The low rumble of exploding depth charges echoed across the sea, but there was no time for a concerted counter-attack against the enemy submarine. After dropping just twelve charges the destroyer hurried to catch up to the rest of the fleet.

As the fleet swept east the men of Force H struggled to remain alert. Roland Webster swayed on his feet and nearly toppled over. He caught himself and snapped back upright. He was nearly asleep on his feet. The rest he'd gotten, curled in a ball in the corner of the radar office was all too brief. After less than an hour he was awakened, summoned to the bridge to control his guns in the action expected that evening.

A flare exploded dead ahead of *Sirius*, lighting the sea like the noonday sun. In spite of himself he looked up and stared for a second directly at the star shell floating down under a small drogue parachute. He snapped his eyes away, but not before the flaming image was burned into his retinas.

"Secondary batteries be alert!" he shouted into his telephone. "They're counting on the distraction."

The port bridge wing lookout shouted. "Target bearing zero-nine-zero, fast boat!"

Webster ran to the port wing, scanning the sea. *HMS Venomous* was astern to port, charging forward with a bone in her teeth, hurling a great bow wave off to either side. Her forward 4.7-inch gun mount barked, firing a lightning streak off into the night to the north. Streams of slower tracers arced and weaved from her light guns at the target away in the dark outside the pool of light thrown by the star shell. Aboard *Sirius* the star shell cast the bridge and the men there in stark relief. Shadows danced back and forth at the back of the open bridge as the shell swung to and fro under its drogue parachute and sank toward the sea.    The night went dark as the star shell fell into the water. *Venomous* snapped on her port searchlight. Its beam probed out over the sea, poking and prodding among the banks of fog as its operators searched for the enemy boat.

Webster watched tensely, willing the searchlight to find the enemy MTB. *Sirius'* main guns and her port side secondary batteries were all trained out to the north, sweeping back and forth as though sniffing for the torpedo boat. Suddenly the light jerked, abeam of the destroyer, sweeping across the enemy boat and on into the darkness beyond, then quickly snapping back and latching onto the boat. Webster stiffened. The white, red and black German Naval Ensign snapped in the breeze from the sternpost of the E-boat. The E-boat fairly leapt forward as its engines were slammed to full throttle. Within seconds its bow was lifted out of the water and it was flying at over forty knots, fairly skipping across the surface of the sea, dodging in and out of the searchlight's beam. Shells from *Venomous* and *Sirius* flew out into the night, but the E-boat's speed was deceptive and the gunners trailed their target. Tracers and heavy shells flashed across the sea, bouncing off the wave tops and tumbling away into the darkness like flat stones skipped on a quiet mill pond. .

The German's were firing back, using green tracers to distinguish their own fire. At a thousand yards the 20mm Oerlikon mounted on its bow banged away at *Venomous*, raking her port side, pounding across the bridge and feeling for the searchlight. A glowing shell ricocheted away from the destroyer's superstructure and tumbled toward *Sirius*, whirring through the night. Webster heard it smack something solid above his head.

Finally the British gunners started to find the range. The Germans on the Oerlikon gun were swept away in a hail of 20mm shells from *Venomous*. Shells slammed into the open bridge, splintering the windscreen, sawing down the mast. The German Ensign fluttered away to the water. Water cascaded back on the boat from near misses.

"YES!" shouted Webster. He twisted and turned, willing the

destruction of the German fast boat.

A puff of smoke erupted on the port side rail of the E-boat and for an instant he thought a heavy shell had found the enemy, but the puff was repeated on the starboard side and this time he saw the sleek form of the torpedo as it leapt from its launch tube and slid into the water. As soon as its deadly 'fish' were launched the E-boat went hard over to port and began to dodge away veering to either side at irregular intervals. Shells smacked the water all around it; geysers of spray drenched the decks as it fled. Webster heard Captain Brooking barking out commands.

"All ahead, port!" he shouted over the frenzy of firing guns. "All back starboard!"

The engine enunciator rang as the commands were acknowledged in the engine room deep in the bowels of the ship.

"Put your helm hard to starboard!" the Captain shouted. The coxs'n at the helm spun the wheel and pressed against it, holding the rudder over. The deck heeled and Webster braced himself against the rail as *Sirius* leaned into the turn.

He tried to follow the torpedoes, but they'd disappeared in the dark sea. He stared at what he estimated their track should be, wide-eyed trying to find them. And then he had them, the thin phosphorescent streaks of bubbles trickling to the surface giving them away. Both torpedoes were on course for *Sirius*, they couldn't miss.

"Port batteries, fire into the water!" he shouted into his phone set, but he knew chances were next to nil of detonating either torpedo, the film directors at Sheperton Studios notwithstanding. Only in the cinema did the sharp-eyed young gunner take cool aim, fire and hit the detonator on the head of the torpedo. The automatic cannon of the port battery lashed the sea with shells as the torpedoes closed in. The cruiser was turning oh, so slowly and the torpedoes were coming so fast. His heart sank as he realized there was no way they could miss. His eyes were riveted on the tracks.

At three hundred yards the torpedoes were only seconds away and the length of the cruiser's port side still lay exposed. A gray wall plunged across his line of sight. Startled, he blinked and looked up. *Venomous* had continued her charge at full speed and had drawn abeam of *Sirius*. Webster gasped as the destroyer's intention came clear to him. *Venomous'* bows lifted on a wave, then plunged down as she rolled over the wave, passing directly in front of the torpedoes just one hundred yards off the port beam of *Sirius*.

The two torpedoes detonated almost simultaneously against the port side of the World War I era destroyer with a force that threw Webster and those around him on the bridge wing down on their backsides and with a flash that lit the night again like day. A deafening roar drowned all other sound. He scrambled back to his feet and leaned out over the rail in time to see *Venomous* still on the rise, split in half between the bridge and her forward funnel. The front half of the ship reared up and plunged back down, the bows knifing into the next swell. With engines still racing the after portion of the ship surged forward, driving its open wound into the sea, her lateral bulkheads collapsing with a sound like shattering glass that carried across the wave tops. Within seconds the stern of the destroyer drove itself beneath the waves; only boiling water as trapped air escaped remained to mark its passage. The fore part of the ship bobbed like a cork with the bow pressed down in the water.

Incredibly, as *Sirius* continued her turn to starboard away from the calamity that had befallen *Venomous* a ragged cheer erupted from the bridge and superstructure of the destroyer. Webster fought the lump that suddenly filled his throat, and his voice failed him.

From the center of the bridge Captain Brooking calmly issued his orders to bring the ship back on course.

"Half ahead both," he said. "Put your helm amidships."

Webster found his voice at last, calmed by the Captain's display of cool. "All guns remain alert," he said. "Don't watch the destroyer, keep your eyes on your sectors." He forced himself to look away from *Venomous* and walked to the center of the bridge, trailing the wires of his telephone headset behind him. The bridge watch of the cruiser settled in to quietly do their jobs. When conversation was required it was conducted in undertones and murmurs.

Force H struggled to leave the Skerki Bank and its torment behind. Shortly after the loss of *Venomous* the enemy torpedo boats broke contact and dropped behind the British fleet. Webster thought it strange the enemy would let them go so easily.

<<<<<<<<<<<<<<<<<<<<<<<<<<<<<<<<<<<<<<<<<<<<<<<

As Force H left the shallows of the Skerki bank behind and glided on through the eerie, moonlit fog a stupendous explosion rocked *HMS Tartar*, one of the modern Tribal Class destroyers leading the fleet. Webster was on the starboard bridge wing of *Sirius* searching the sea to the south with his binoculars when the mine went off against the destroyer's starboard side. Over a mile away, *Tartar* heeled over to port, thrown off course by the force of the blast. She rocked back to starboard and just kept right on going, rolling over on her starboard beam and settling directly into the sea.

In the column behind *Tartar* the bridge watch of *HMS Charybdis* reacted frantically, throwing the cruiser into a tight turn to port to avoid the foundered destroyer, scraping past less than a half cable's length from the upturned hull. *Kenya* followed the AA cruiser past the site of the sinking and though none could stop to rescue any survivors the rails of both cruisers were lined with seamen who threw life vests and rafts to the few men who'd managed to get overboard before the destroyer turned turtle.

The shock of *Tartar's* sinking had barely registered when the destroyer flotilla leader, *Laforey* was mined. Away to port of the main body of the fleet *Laforey* was chasing a possible submarine contact on ASDIC when she touched off a mine under her stern. Her commander, Captain (D) Hutton, the man in charge of the destroyer force signaled to the flagship that *Laforey* was completely disabled, her propellers and much of her stern blown off by the explosion, but that she was otherwise seaworthy. He recommended that torpedoes sink his ship after survivors were away in the ship's boats. *HMS Vansittart* carried out this dreadful duty then hurried to catch up to the fleet, leaving many of *Laforey's* survivors adrift. Many tense minutes followed as the fleet sailed on, seamen and officers alike waiting for the crash of another mine exploding. Leaving Skerki behind, Force H sailed into the open waters of the Strait of Sicily, just hours from Malta.

As the shock and adrenaline rush of combat wore off Webster found he was more bloody tired than he'd ever been before. The temptation to close his eyes and let go even for just a few minutes was nearly overwhelming. For once thoughts of Althea didn't cross his mind; only the desire to sleep. The only thing that stopped him from curling up on the spot was the knowledge that if he did nod off it wouldn't be for just a few minutes. If ever he fell asleep he knew nothing could waken him again for hours.

He looked at his watch. 0216 hours. Twenty-two hours straight at action stations. Webster knew the crew of *Sirius* was in no better shape than he was. All were desperately tired, but that might not have been the worst of it. Many of the men were in a state very near to shock. They'd witnessed one hard blow after another delivered by the enemy against Force H. The spectacle of burning men leaping from the flight deck of *Furious* the afternoon before or of the pitifull few survivors of *Tartar* struggling in the water as the remaining ships of the fleet sailed past the sinking destroyer were forever etched in horror in minds too tired to cope or to understand.

Now with *Sirius* in the lead Force H was just hours from its goal, the purpose, the justification for so much death and suffering. No longer slowed by the oiler, *Evening Dale* the fleet surged forward at its top speed of 29 knots, racing towards it destination, Malta, ninety-five miles to the southeast, just beyond the horizon. By dawn that morning, the 28th of June the fleet would be in position to bombard the German airhead on the island and perhaps to turn the tide of battle back in favor of the British garrison.

"Commander Webster report to the number one Radar Office," the Tannoy speaker scratched behind him on the bridge. "Repeat, Commander Webster report to the number one Radar Office."

It took Webster a moment to realize the summons was for him. He picked up the telephone on the port bridge wing and requested the switchboard operator put him through to the Radar Office.

"Commander Webster here," he said after the connection was made. "Is that you Jones?"

"Yes, Sir," Jones replied. "Sorry to bother you, Sir, but the forward radar suite is acting up. Losing signal intermittently. Getting worse steadily. Just about all packed up now."

"Have you run your checks?" asked Webster.

"Yes, Sir. Everything checks out fine here in the office. It all points to a problem with the transmitter."

"Very well, Jones," he said. "Meet me at the foremast. We'll have to climb up the lattice to see what's the problem. Bring the keys to the electrical panel."

In less than a minute Jones met Webster at the base of the foremast between the bridge deck and the forward funnel. The night air was cool and sweet as *Sirius* knifed through calm seas at 29 knots.

Webster watched carefully as Jones locked down the heavy levers on the massive 500 amperes circuit breakers that protected the radar transmitter/receiver atop the mast. With the circuit broken the aerial slowly spun to a stop. Webster notified the bridge by telephone that the main radar was temporarily disabled.

"All right, Jones," he said. "Up you go. Start with the transformer box, then go on to the aerial itself."

Jones shinnied up the lattice mast to the box that stepped the electrical voltage down for the motor that drove the aerial and for the signal generator. Swaying gently back and forth forty feet above the deck Jones reached up to open the box, but he paused and reached around, running his hand over the side panel.

"Oil dripping here, Sir," he shouted down to Webster.

He unlatched the access panel and shined a hooded penlight into the box, then reached around first one, then the other side of the box. He slammed the access panel shut and shinnied back down the mast.

"The transformer is shot, Sir," he told Webster. Jones pulled a rag from his pocket and started wiping thick, viscous oil from his hands.

"The reservoir has sprung a leak?"

"No, Sir," Jones smiled. "It's been shot. 20mm I should say. The hole to port is about this big," he said holding his thumb and forefinger together in a circle. "The shell passed clean through the transformer, punctured the reservoir and went out the starboard side about this big." He held the thumbs and forefingers of both hands together forming a circle about six inches in diameter. "The reservoir is completely empty and the inside of the box is a hash. I'm amazed the aerial has been working at all."

Webster's mind went back to the battle with the Axis MTBs at Skerki when he'd heard a shell slam into something solid high in the superstructure. He massaged his temples, trying to think past the fog that clouded his brain. It was at least a three-hour job to replace the transformer.

His head snapped up and his eyes went wide as the action stations alarm sounded. The action stations alarm was designed to shock a man, no matter how tired, into instant motion and it worked well. Jones and Webster and hundreds of others aboard *Sirius* and the other ships of the fleet were galvanized into action. Jones spun and dashed away for his post in the number one radar office forward of the armored barbette of 'X' turret while Webster scrambled up the ladder to the bridge deck above.

Aboard *Muzio Attendolo* Webster's counterpart, Commander (Guns) Marco Spoleto sat in his gunnery control tower watching the electronic arm sweep around the display screen of the 'Owl', so nick-named by the Italians for its ability to see in the dark. Marco's eyes went wide and a smile lit his face. He activated his telephone connection, first to the bridge.

"Enemy contact bearing two-seven-five, range twenty-six miles," he alerted Captain Digiacoma. "We're closing on the enemy at a combined speed of sixty knots."

"Acknowledged, Spoleto!" the Captain replied. "I will turn to port to bear all guns. Commence firing as soon as they are in range."

Marco spoke next to his gun Captains in the four turrets of the cruiser's main battery. "All guns accept direction from the Owl," he ordered.

*Muzio* began to heel over in the turn to port. Green lights on his master control panel indicated all four main turrets were under radar direction and ready to fire. Marco stared intently at the radar screen. Unconsciously he raised his arm slowly over his head in anticipation. The minutes dragged slowly on as the electronic arm swept the screen, drawing the British closer with each turn, closer to the twelve-mile mark that would put them in range of his main battery.

"FIRE!" he shouted. *Muzio* lurched from the recoil of her eight 6-inch guns firing in salvo. Through the armored decks and bulkheads the roar of the guns was muffled, but still powerful. Seconds later he heard the mighty roar of *Vittorio Venetto's* nine 15-inch rifles.

He counted off the seconds for the shells to reach their targets.

"Maintop, report!" Marco shouted into the phone.

"Short five-hundred, adjust left three-hundred," came the excited reply. Marco supervised adjustments to the control panel, as one by one the eight green lights came on telling him the guns were reloaded and ready to go.

"Fire!" he shouted, even as the last green light flickered on. Once again the ship lurched and the muffled roar of the guns reverberated in the radar office. He waited tensely for the observer in the maintop to spot the fall of shot.

"ON TARGET! ON TARGET!" came the near hysterical shout. "We've straddled the lead ship! Commander! The British still have not fired!"

No manual adjustment necessary this time, just wait for the eight lights.

"FIRE!" he shouted again.

Marco closed his eyes and counted off the seconds till the shells would strike.

"HIT!" screamed the observer. "A HIT! She's on fire in the bows!"

"FIRE!"

Jones was below the mid-ship port pom-pom when the first salvo fell ahead of *Sirius*. He skidded to a stop and turned to see the last three waterspouts of the eight shot salvo. The light of the full moon was sufficient for him to note the water was yellow-tinged from the chemicals in the explosives. At the same moment he heard the scream of heavy caliber shells curving directly over *Sirius,* roaring like trains racing through the underground in London. Instinctively he ducked, then was on the way again as the heavy shells landed in the sea to port of *Renown*, 800 yards behind *Sirius* in column.

The cruiser heeled to starboard, away from the shell splashes just as Webster reached the bridge deck. He blessed the endless hours of drill and practice he'd put his gun crews to as he saw the muzzles of 'X' and 'Y' turrets train out to port.

Webster reached the gunnery tower hatchway and yanked back the clips that secured the door. He turned and looked out to sea as the hatch swung open. He heard the screech of in-coming shells just before the tearing, rending crash above and behind him. Shells splashed into the sea to port and starboard. Extraordinary gunnery for the second salvo, but he wasn't admiring the enemy shooting. His heart fell to his stomach as he watched the mainmast, severed thirty feet above deck, tip and fall, crashing down across the midships port pom-pom gun tub. Twisting and convulsing of its own weight the mast bent and buckled across the gun tub, mangling the up-turned barrels like string and crumpling the thin armored sides of the tub, crushing the gun crew, before smashing down on the port torpedo station. Webster sagged against the hatchway. A rock fell into the pit of his stomach and his knees went weak. With the loss of the mainmast both radar arrays were out of action. *Sirius* was blind.

He felt a hand under his arm and he staggered backward as his heels caught the ledge at the base of the hatch. *Sirius* was rocked as a 6-inch shell slammed home and exploded somewhere forward. Splinters from the blast peppered the armored shell of the FDR. Other shells of the salvo landed in the sea to either side of the ship. Webster staggered to his feet and stumbled into the Fire Direction Room nodding a thanks to the rating who had dragged him through the hatch before the shell hit. The FDR was his post for surface action stations and he quickly scanned the director control panel. None of the green lights for the ten guns of his main battery were lit. He snatched up the telephone set and jammed it down over his ears.

"VISUAL TARGETING! VISUAL TARGETING!" he shouted. "Radar direction is out!" He would have to rely on direction given to the guns by his observers stationed at the highest points in the ship's superstructure. Equipped with optical range finders they would pass elevation and bearing commands to the gunners. Slower and more cumbersome, and worst yet, at night less accurate than radar direction it was all *Sirius* had left.

WHAM! Webster was thrown from his feet, slamming painfully against the bulkhead. WHAM! The ship was rocked again by yet a third hit. Webster struggled back to his feet, settling the telephone set on his head. The deck lurched under him as he regained his bearings. *Sirius* was finally hitting back.

Admiral Burrough ran from the charthouse of *Renown* as the action station gong sounded throughout the great battlecruiser. He glanced around the blacked-out bridge. Spying Captain Daniel on the port bridge wing he hurried over. Flag Secretary Lt. Harris and

Intelligence Officer Commander Oats were right behind. The Admiral reached the Captain's side as the first salvo of heavy shells crashed down to port. The massive, twin turrets forward of the bridge were only just beginning to train out, bringing the muzzles of the 15-inch guns to bear in the general direction of the gun flashes to the east. The Captain lowered his binoculars and snatched up the telephone set on the bulkhead.

"Radar Office, Bridge!" he shouted. "Have you got the range?"

"Bridge, Radar Office. Just picking them up now. We'll have a solution in a moment."

"Commence firing as soon as you're ready," the Captain ordered and slammed the phone down in its cradle just as the scream of shells signaled an in-coming salvo. Heavy shells plunged into the sea in a line 400 yards to port.

"Damned fine shooting!" exclaimed Burrough. Flashes erupted on the eastern horizon.

"Put your helm to starboard," the Captain called to the helmsman. *Renown* heeled into the turn, but her enormous bulk was slow to turn and her momentum at 29 knots was huge. She'd barely begun to alter course when the second salvo fell. Four heavy shells fell in a line amidships and to port with the fourth shell landing close aboard and spraying water along the lower weather decks. The fifth shell passed between the foremast and the mainmast; it and the final four shells splashed down to starboard.

"Come on, come on," growled the Captain. He reached for the telephone, but just then *Renown*'s guns fired a broadside, each of the six guns of the main battery hurling a two-ton shell across the sea. The great guns sagged down to their reload elevations.

"Steady amidships," the Captain called his command to the helmsman. He and the Admiral snatched their binoculars up to watch the fall of shot, but despite the bright moonlight and powerful glasses they couldn't get a clear picture of the enemy ships at that range of almost thirteen miles. A round of flashes lit the eastern horizon. *Renown*'s port side battery of 4.5-inch guns spoke for the first time, though still beyond range.

"Make a signal for the destroyers," Admiral Burrough ordered. "Attack with torpedoes."

The third enemy salvo crashed down. *Renown* rocked as a shell landed squarely amidships, plunging through the deck plate and exploding below the port side eight-barreled 2-pdr pom-pom gun just aft of the for'ard funnel. The officers on the port bridge wing all cringed away from the heat of the fireball that rocketed skyward. The superstructure in the area and the funnel were riddled with shrapnel and the three lifeboats there were smashed to flaming matchsticks in their davits. Secondary explosions followed as the ready 2-pounder ammunition cooked off. The gun crew was wiped out by the blast and the blizzard of razor sharp shrapnel that accompanied it. As the smoke cleared blood flowed from the scuppers at the base of the gun tub.

"Third salvo on target!" exclaimed Jim Harris.

"Only one conclusion possible," shouted Oats above the din. "The Italians are firing by radar!"

*Renown's* guns began to elevate. Reloaded, they were ready to fire. The six 15-inch MK I guns fired in salvo, one barrel after another belching smoke and fire. The last gun of the after turret had just fired when the Italian's found the range again.

The first shell plunged down between two of the dual purpose, twin 4.5-inch gun turrets on the port side, exploding two decks down, between the barbettes of the turrets and atop the 9-inch thick armor plate protecting the 4.5-inch magazines. Once again flame roared into the night sky, but the armor belt held. Tortured steel, superheated in a flash to 500 degrees, buckled, but refused to part. The forward 4.5-inch turret was seared by the blast, its ring twisted and buckled so that the turret could no longer train, its gun crew killed instantly. Number two turret was lifted from its ring and tipped like so much laundry from atop its barbette. It toppled aft, crashing down on number three turret. All six guns of the port secondary battery were silenced.

A second shell struck at the base of the mainmast atop the after superstructure. The blast ripped down and through the enlisted mess deck, largely empty with all hands at action stations, starting a raging fire that fed on the hammocks and personal possessions of the men. The electrical circuits to the mainmast radar transmitter were cut. A third shell landed on the fantail, penetrated the weather deck and plunged down and through the ship's starboard side into the sea without exploding.

Aboard both *Renown* and *Sirius* most officers and men on deck were busy dealing with the shock and damage to their own ships and so didn't see *Kenya* and *Charybdis* join the action. The two ships hurled the full weight of their combined broadsides at the targets that only now were appearing at the edges of their own radar screens.

*Renown's* main battery fired then drooped back to horizontal to reload. Another set of heavy flashes to the east showed the Italians had fired again while the battlecruiser's guns hung slack. In the turrets the heavy steel shells were loaded and rammed into the breeches, followed by the cotton bags of gunpowder to propel the shells. But the Italians had found the range and were not about to let *Renown* loose. Another salvo screamed down on the battlecruiser. Two hits this time, the most damaging yet. The first fell at the base of the funnel abaft the bridge, shattering the smoke stack at deck level, leaving it with a gaping ten-foot hole in its side. The great boilers in the for'ard engine room deep below the waterline lost the draught from the funnel. Without proper draught the oxygen sucked into the combustion chambers fell by half and the ship began to lose way almost immediately. The second shell slammed home atop 'A' turret, plunging through its thick roof armor plate and exploding within the turret, extinguishing the crews serving the two guns. Blowout panels and hatches in the turret allowed most of the force of the explosion to vent outside and flash curtains and panels stopped the blast from reaching directly into the powder magazine or shell room below, saving the ship from an annihilating detonation, but six great bales of cotton bound cordite gun powder just hoisted into the turret exploded too, sending the first fireball seen by Kuno Schacht and Colonel August on Malta into the sky. Flaming wreckage spewed from the bulged out sides and top of the turret, fouling the guns of 'B' turret just aft. Damage control teams would have to clear the wreckage before the guns of 'B' turret could be fired again. The officers on the bridge wing raised their heads above the thin armored rail and gazed down on the devastation. 'A' turret burned merrily with its armored sides already glowing a dull red.

"Bear away to starboard!" ordered Burrough. "Signal the cruisers!"

"Hard to starboard! Flank speed! Make smoke!" shouted the Captain. His orders were acknowledged from the bridge, but the great ship slowed and her turn was very sluggish. Her aft turret belched fire, but its two shots seemed pathetically weak to watchers on both sides of the battle.

But Marco Spoleto was beginning to worry. After the first three or four salvos from *Muzio's* guns the British began to shoot back. Wild at first, but quickly adjusting for bearing and range the enemy fire bracketed *Muzio* on the last salvo. The volume of fire falling on the Italian fleet was increasing steadily. In fact, the three British cruisers carried a total of thirty guns in their main batteries, ten 5.25-inch guns on *Sirius*, eight 4.5-inch on *Charybdis*, twelve 6-inch guns on *Kenya*. Even discounting *Sirius* due to her loss of radar control the guns of the British cruisers outnumbered their Italian opponents twenty to sixteen. Of course, Spoleto wasn't privy to these exact numbers, nor to *Sirius'* loss of radar, but it was becoming apparent that the weight of British fire would tell against the Italians in a prolonged action.

*Raimondo Montecuccoli* was banging away at the two smaller targets bringing up the rear of the British battle squadron, while *Muzio's* target, the lead ship, turned away to the south after being hit at least six times according to his observers. Both she and the enemy battleship were making smoke and withdrawing southward at a range of just over eleven miles.

"Shift target," Marco ordered. "Concentrate on the third ship in column."

His guns shifted bearing and the green lights on his panel indicated all eight guns were ready.

"FIRE!" he ordered. The ship rocked from the recoil of the guns then came a sudden, different jolt. Marco knew *Muzio* had been hit. A 5.25-inch shell from *Sirius* exploded on the bow of the cruiser, forward of the breakwater. It wrecked a chain locker, but did little other damage of immediate consequence. The danger was that the British finally had the range. Digiacoma threw the ship hard to port, away from the British, opening the range.

As the two groups of heavy ships drew apart their lesser companions were charging headlong together. The destroyers of the British fleet led by *HMS Eskimo* went to flank speed on receipt of Admiral Burrough's order to launch a torpedo attack. On the Italian side the nine destroyers under Admiral Iachino led by *RM Granatiere* were deployed in a screen ahead of *Vittorio Venetto* and the two cruisers. The Italian destroyers were not radar equipped, but with clear skies and the full moon shining on the sea the lack of radar became less important, especially as the range shortened. At four miles the British opened fire with their 4.7-inch main guns. The Italians followed suit, then executed a turn to port, laying a smoke screen as they did. The British picked up the turn on radar and launched a volley of torpedoes at a range of three miles. The Italians were blinded by their own smoke screen and didn't detect the torpedoes.

Peter Walker and his damage control team were in action again aboard *Renown*, frantically tearing at the wreckage that had fouled the guns of 'B' turret. As the battlecruiser made its turn to starboard they levered the twisted and blackened junk overboard. In some cases the steel was still glowing hot, sizzling briefly as it struck the water. By the time *Renown* circled round, re-crossing her own course 'B' turret was tracking and elevating freely. Burrough brought his fleet into position for the starboard 4.5-inch battery of the battlecruiser to bear on the enemy. He'd also re-ordered his line of battle, putting *Charybdis* in the van with *Kenya* close behind. Blinded *Sirius* brought up the rear behind *Renown*.

The Italian destroyer screen had meanwhile suffered its first loss. *RM Cesare* was struck in the stern by a 21-inch torpedo. Her engine room flooding she drifted to a stop. Her crew lined her rails and cheered as the balance of the Italian destroyer force rushed by.

*Vittorio Venetto* and the Italian cruisers were busy as well. As the range to the British heavies widened Commander Spoleto spoke again with his Captain.

"Bridge, Radar."

"Yes, Spoleto?" answered Captain Digiacoma.

"The British destroyers are closing on us at flank speed," he told the Captain. "I recommend we shift targets to the destroyers."

"Agreed!" shouted the Captain. "Don't let them within torpedo range!"

Marco singled out two targets in the approaching destroyer force, assigning one to the forward guns and the second to the aft turrets. With the range down to five miles it was practically point blank for *Muzio's* main battery. The guns were trained out to starboard and on a flat trajectory.

"FIRE!"

Flame belched from the cruiser's guns, the shells' arcs nearly flat as they raced out over the sea.

"Down eight-hundred, left one-hundred," the observer in the maintop called adjustments to the aim.

Now the British destroyers found themselves in trouble as the two Italian cruisers and the starboard secondary battery of *Vittorio* found their range. *Eskimo*, still at flank speed, led a turn to port to escape the 6-inch guns of the Italian fleet. Not quickly enough. The radar directed fire of the Italians was spot on. *Muzio* hammered *Sikh* with three hits from her forward battery. The first shell went home in the destroyer's sides just above the port waterline, gutting the stoker's mess deck. The second struck the torpedo shop, wrecking the launchers and wiping out the crew of torpedo men there as they worked to reload and the third hit exploded directly on the bridge, sparing only one member of the bridge watch, a young signalman blown back down through the charthouse hatch. The Engineering Officer deep in the engine room knew what had happened when his urgent calls to the bridge went unanswered. He rushed to the emergency steering position on the poop deck and took control of the ship, steering her away to the south, on fire, but her engines and main battery intact.

*Vanquisher* suffered the full attention of *Raimondo Montecuccoli*, taking two hits, one destroying the radar office, killing the staff there, the second plunging into the sickbay and the adjacent wardroom where over thirty wounded survivors of other lost ships were crowded in for treatment. They and the destroyer's tiny medical staff were wiped out in the blast. *Vittorio* targeted *Wishart*. To observers on the other destroyers she seemed nearly swamped by waterspouts as six-inch shells fell close aboard. Most naval shells are fused to not explode on impact with the sea, but the shell that landed just feet from *Wishart's* port bow did explode, springing her bow plates and admitting many tons of sea water. Her bows peppered with splinters *Wishart* turned at reduced speed and followed *Sikh* away to the south.

To this point in the battle neither side had landed a crushing blow, though the weight of damage inflicted favored the Italians, with *Sirius'* gunnery crippled by the loss of her radar, the destruction of 'A' turret and the port secondary battery aboard *Renown* and three destroyers out of action against the one shell hit on *Muzio* and the torpedo hit against *Cesare*. Now the two fleets approached each other like two wary boxers who'd already taken the other's measure, each grimly determined to hammer the other down.

Burrough maneuvered Force H into position to fire to starboard bringing *Renown's* starboard secondary battery into the fight, largely negating the loss of the port secondary battery. For his part Iachino preferred to keep the British at long range. He'd already proven his Owl radar was at least as effective as the British equipment and he didn't want to expose his heavy ships to another torpedo attack from the British destroyers.

Iachino also labored at a profound psychological disadvantage that of all those involved in the battle only Burrough fully appreciated. The Italian navy had operated since the outbreak of the war on the "Fleet in Being" strategy under which they dared not risk their very limited supply of capital ships in action. So long as the mere threat of Italian battleships remained the British were forced to maintain strong forces as a counter to them. Should the Italians lose *Vittorio Venetto* the British might enjoy a freer hand in future naval operations in the Mediterranean. His tactics in the battle were guided by an abundance of caution.

Not so Burrough. He'd already rolled the dice against all odds by his very presence near Malta with his remaining heavy ships. He had nothing to lose from bold action. He determined to press his luck.

"Signal to fleet," he ordered from the starboard bridge wing of *Renown*. "Steer course one-one-five, match the flagship's speed." He turned to Captain Daniel and Commander Oats and explained his orders. "If the Eye-ties are going to draw away from us we may as well drive them ahead of us to Malta. Every mile we can make before dawn gives us a better chance at reaching the island and carrying out our mission."

"Yes, I see," said Captain Daniel, "but if they choose to shadow us from port my secondary battery is useless."

"He won't go to port," Burrough shook his head. He'd already personalized the battle as a contest between himself and his counterpart in command of the Italian fleet.

"Everything for him rides on stopping us reaching Malta. If I get past him to starboard I'll throw the destroyers back at him to slow him while I make a dash for the island. He knows that. He'll stay ahead of us and to the south, to starboard, to block our path. Order the guns to hold fire until either the enemy fires or the range has closed to give our cruisers a shot."

Daniel relayed the order, then came back and stood next to Burrough.

"Damage reports coming in now," he said quietly, holding a sheaf of papers. "'A' turret is wrecked. 'B' turret is cleared and back in commission. Its being put through its paces now to assure it trains and elevates properly. Our own speed is held to no more than eighteen knots until the damage parties can seal off the hole in the for'ard funnel. Estimates are it'll take an hour or more. Admiral, we're in no condition to make a dash for Malta."

"But he doesn't know that," said Burrough, nodding his head towards the distant enemy.

Marco Spoleto watched the British fleet move at the edge of his radar screen. He'd reported the enemy's change of course and bearing straight for Malta to the Captain. Now *Muzio* and the other Italian ships seemed content to watch the British from extreme range. One thing puzzled him. *Muzio* was outside the range of her own guns, but well within range of the enemy battleship. Why hadn't the British fired to force her further away? He checked his watch. He was astonished that only nineteen minutes had elapsed since *Muzio* had fired the battle's first shots.

The telephone rang. It was the bridge relaying the order from the flagship to the Italian destroyers to launch a torpedo attack. At the same time he felt a surge from his cruiser's engines. *Muzio* was picking up speed again. Seconds ticked by and the radar plot showed him that *Muzio* and the other two heavies were moving to take position directly in the path of the British fleet while staying at extreme range. The answer hit him as he watched the blips of the Italian destroyers crawl across the screen. He activated his telephone headset.

"Bridge, Radar, let me speak with the Captain."

"Captain here. What is it Spoleto?"

"Captain, I believe the British must have sustained damage to the main guns of the battleship. Either they are out of action or have been damaged. Perhaps their radar is down. They don't fire so as not to reveal the damage."

Captain Digiacoma paused then said, "Stay ready Marco." The

connection went dead.

Marco chafed at the inaction. He bit his nails in nervous tension. The phone rang.

"Spoleto," the Captain said. "We're going to move in for the attack behind our destroyers. We are to engage the lead cruiser. Fire when in range. Good shooting!"

"Yes, Sir!"

Marco felt the ship heel over to starboard as she moved round. The maneuver brought all eight guns of her main battery to bear and within seconds she was closing the range, drawing close to the point where her fire could be effective. An enormous CLANG sounded against the hull followed by the noise of an explosion nearby. The British had opened fire first, outside the range of the cruisers. A 15-inch shell from *Renown* struck the sea just forty meters to port, a football-sized chunk of shrapnel striking *Muzio* just above the waterline beside 'A' turret. *Muzio* sailed on, her engines geared up to her top speed of 37 knots. Once again he held his hand in the air in anticipation. The lead British ship crept into his guns' range.

"FIRE!" he shouted. The deck lurched beneath him as all eight guns fired in turn.

At almost the same instant eight miles away the gunnery officer of *HMS Kenya* held his hand up.

"SHOOT!" he shouted. The six guns of *Kenya's* forward turrets fired, but the after battery could not bear on the target. They were screened by the cruiser's own superstructure.

An instant later *Vittorio* and *Renown* rejoined the action, firing at each other. As *Muzio* continued her turn she traded fire with *Kenya* behind *Charybdis* in the van of the British force. Both ships nearly disappeared from view in a hail of shells, waterspouts drenching the weather decks. On the third exchange of salvos the British scored, hitting *Muzio* on the fantail. Damage was minimal, though the emergency steering position was wrecked. On his fourth salvo Marco returned the favor in spades. A 6-inch shell crashed down on *Kenya* abaft the bridge, just where the German bomb had fallen the day before. It plunged past the wreckage of the floatplane and through fire blackened, heat twisted deck plates, striking the 4-inch armor over the top of the magazines. The initial explosion was not spectacular, bulging out the already twisted decks and bulkheads amidships and sending a flickering tongue of flame as from a candle into the night sky. But a spark or flame penetrated the aft magazine, setting off first the cotton swathed bundles of gun powder, then the store of 6-inch shells. The secondary explosion was literally shattering, lifting the after turrets from their mounts and hurling them over *Kenya's* port side. The force of the blast crumpled bulkheads adjacent to the magazine. Searing flame roared into the engineering spaces and through the crew accommodations. A shaft of fire rocketed straight into the sky from the after portion of the ship. An instant later the forward magazine detonated as well in a second titanic blast, rending the cruiser stem from stern and driving her hull deep into the water. The fireball rose hundreds of feet into the air.

"Hard a-starboard," yelled Captain Daniel aboard *Renown* as he cringed away from the heat of the explosion. The shattered hulk of the cruiser lay directly in his ship's path. The men on the bridge all dove for cover as a rain of steel hurtled down on the battlecruiser. A twisted, mangled section of railing smashed against the armored box of the wheelhouse. A hail of deadly shrapnel swept all exposed surfaces of the ship forward of the bridge superstructure, slashing down any man in its path.

Men on deck of the Italian ships stared in awestruck horror at the spectacle. Few had ever seen a major magazine explosion before. The sound of the blast took many seconds to reach across the intervening miles to the Italian ships. A ragged cheer rose, but few took it up. Most understood that hundreds of men had just died.

Oddly, the destruction of *Kenya* and the sudden change of course it caused may have saved *Renown*. An entire salvo from *Vittorio Venetto* plunged down on the battlecruiser's original course. Now *Renown* turned to port and struck back; 'X' turret aft joined 'B' turret and the starboard 4.5-inch guns and belched flame. Seconds later observers in her maintops reported two or three hits on the Italian battleship.

Admiral Burrough watched the battle from the bridge of *Renown*.

"Order the destroyers to attack with torpedoes again!" he commanded. Lt. Harris started to turn away to carry out the order, but Burrough stopped him. "Jim," he said. "Order *Sirius* to join them."

Harris opened his mouth to question the order, but a stern look from Burrough stopped him. "Yes, Sir," he said.

Moments later *Sirius* swept past *Renown*, 1,000 yards away on her port beam. The cruiser accelerated to her maximum speed of 33 knots to catch-up the destroyers who were already on their way to the attack, a creaming wave falling from her bows. ·

As *Sirius* raced past *Renown* on her way to join the fleet's destroyers Webster was coaching his gun crews and spotters. With her radar eyes blinded *Sirius* was dependant upon optical observation of the target and of the fall of her own shot. The optical range finders were located atop the fore and aft superstructures. Observers determined the range by focusing the widely spaced lenses of the binocular devices on the target. At the bottom of the stereo view was the focal range in tiny white characters. In theory they were as accurate as radar at any visible distance, but at night, even under conditions of full moon it was difficult for the observer to be sure the range finder was properly focused. The range provided to the guns in calculating elevation had constantly to be adjusted as the relative position of the ships changed making accurate, sustained gunnery almost impossible for Webster to achieve without radar guidance.

Between salvos of his own guns the sound of the popping of the British destroyers' guns came to him. The range to the enemy was closing. Already the Italian destroyers were within 5,000 yards and waterspouts were popping up about *Sirius* as the Italian shells felt for her.

Webster peered through his periscope sight in the FDR. The British destroyers were spread in an arc in front of *Sirius*, with *Eskimo* in the center 500 yards directly in front of the cruiser.

"FDR, bridge. FDR, bridge," came over his phone set.

"Bridge, FDR," Webster responded.

"Shift your fire, Webster!" the Captain shouted. "Concentrate on the destroyers in the center! We've got to clear the way for our torpedoes!"

Webster acknowledged the order and set about redirecting his guns. In seconds the three forward turrets were trained in, pointing almost directly over the bows and on flat trajectories. ·

"FIRE!" he shouted. The deck lurched under his feet as the six guns in the forward turrets spit hi-explosive shells at nearly point-blank range. Results were almost instant. At close range and bright moonlight the optical range finders were as effective as radar direction. A pair of hits in her bows rocked *RM Quintino*. Ablaze, she turned away, her forward gun mount smashed.

*Sirius* fired again targeting *Ascari*, hitting the Italian destroyer's superstructure. She remained on course only because most of the watch on her shattered bridge was dead. *Sirius* kept up her fire, pumping salvos of 5.25-inch shells from her six forward guns at the destroyers in the center of the Italian line. The Italians veered away, maneuvering at high speed to avoid the deadly barrage. The British destroyers charged into the gap, hoping to close the range and deliver a fusillade of torpedoes against the Italian cruisers and battleship.

Following *Kenya's* destruction Spoleto shifted *Muzio's* fire, directing his forward guns against the charging British destroyers while the aft battery concentrated on the cruiser following them in support. Post-battle reconstruction of the two ships' logs reveals the two cruisers were only 6,000 yards apart at this point in the battle, *Muzio* broadside to the British, but *Sirius* presenting only the narrower aspect of her bows as a target.

Marco's first salvo from the forward guns scored a single, devastating hit against *HMS Westcott*, entering the superstructure just below the destroyer's bridge, plunging through her wardroom and the thin armor plate protecting the engineering space, before exploding in the engine room. The blast wiped out the engine room crew and snuffed the fires in the boilers; shrapnel shattered the steam lines. Sparks and flame poured from her two funnels and the ship rapidly lost way.

Meanwhile the first rounds from the aft guns splashed down aft of the British cruiser and Marco brought the elevation on the guns down to nearly flat trajectory, confident his second salvo would strike home, but fate took a hand at this point. The electrical circuit board for the motors driving 'X' turret shorted, overwhelmed by the voltage coursing through it. 'X' turret would no longer train, leaving only the twin 6-inch guns of 'Y' turret to target the British cruiser.

Meanwhile four British destroyers had shortened the range sufficiently to launch their torpedoes. Responding to a signal flag from *Eskimo* they executed a quick turn to port and each launched three torpedoes over their starboard rails. Just as *Muzio* zeroed in on *Sirius* Captain Digiacoma threw his ship into a hard turn to starboard, towards the British to comb the tracks of the British torpedoes. 'Y' turret was blocked from firing by *Muzio's* own superstructure.

*Sirius* now turned to starboard, bringing her aft turrets to bear. All ten of her 5.25-inch guns targeted *Muzio*. With the range down to 4,500 yards it was impossible to miss. The Italian cruiser was hammered by five hits, raking her bows and forward superstructure. One shell smashed through the splinter shield at the base of the bridge, and furrowed the deck before skipping away, up through the deck above, tumbling off into the night without exploding. Two shells penetrated the bows and exploded in the capstan flats. The port anchor slipped and ran out to its stops before parting its chain and was lost. The breakwater forward of 'B' turret absorbed the blast of the fourth shell. The final hit struck high above the bridge, wrecking the forward range finder.

All told *Muzio* had been very lucky, but Captain Digiacoma was unnerved, especially by the shell that passed through his bridge less than three meters from where he stood and he ordered a hard turn back to port, away from the British. The maneuver probably saved his ship. The next salvo from *Sirius* screamed past to starboard, on *Muzio's* original course, just one shell finding its mark, passing down the length of the starboard rail and exploding on the fantail. *Muzio* continued her turn through 180°, settling on a course of zero-seven-five. With fires burning both fore and aft she raced away from the battle. In frustration Marco Spoleto continued to direct the fire of her 'Y' turret against the British cruiser.

The British torpedo attack achieved results too. *Vittorio Venetto* was slow to turn and was hit in the starboard bows by a 21-inch 'fish', probably from *Eskimo*. Several small compartments flooded and her speed was reduced as damage control parties raced to shore up injured bulkheads. She slewed round to starboard and took on a five-degree list, but her main and secondary batteries kept up their fire. Ignoring the British destroyers and the cruiser behind them the Italian battleship continued trading salvos with her British counterpart.

Incredibly, *Renown* had suffered seven hits from heavy caliber shells and thirteen more from 6-inch shot, but the armor over her magazines had held. Nonetheless, her fighting power was cut substantially, with one main turret out of action forward and extensive damage to her superstructure and secondary batteries and one of her two radar aerials still without power. Her Captain maneuvered her like a sport car turning her to port just enough to let the after turret bear and shoot, then back on his easterly course while the aft guns were reloaded, then turn to port again to repeat the process. Her four remaining 15-inch guns gave a very good account of themselves, trading shot for shot against *Venetto's* nine heavy guns. At 11,000 yards *Renown* found the mark scoring three hits in two quick salvos. One shell struck the glacis plate of *Venetto's* forward 15-inch turret. The concussion jammed the elevation gears. Down to six guns in her main battery and with a growing list *Venetto* also turned away and began to flee the battle.

The Italian battleship had a parting sting to deliver however. As the range widened she flung one last salvo from her after turret at *Renown*. The first shell was short, landing just under the battlecruiser's bows, puncturing the bow-plates with shrapnel. The other two shells both struck home, one plunging down on the fantail above the rudder. The third shell landed at the base of the forward superstructure below the bridge. The blast hurled every man on the bridge off his feet. Fires started in the junior officer's quarters and quickly spread. Within seconds flames were licking the rails of the exposed port bridge wing.

Admiral Burrough picked himself up slowly, cradling his left elbow in his right hand. His Flag Secretary, Lt. Harris was unconscious, his breathing short and shallow. He'd struck his head on the railing. Commander Oats struggled to his feet, physically unharmed, but dazed.

As the Italian fleet withdrew Force H staggered on towards Malta at reduced speed. The moral ascendancy of the Royal Navy over the Italians had asserted itself again, as at Matapan, Sirte and a dozen other engagements, but the margin was narrower in the Naval Battle of Malta; narrower and paid for at greater cost than ever before.

<<<<<<<<<<<<<<

Kenneth stared blankly out over the now peaceful waters of Marsaxlokk Bay. Oil from the sunken submarine's ruptured fuel tanks had burned on the surface of the water for several minutes, but wave action thinned the oil and now the fire was out. Moonlight was again the only illumination in the blacked out harbor. The dozens of seriously wounded had been evacuated from the ramp at Kalafrana, taken inland to the Air Station infirmary at Hal Far or to the civilian hospital at Birzebbuga up harbor. The dead were laid out in a makeshift morgue in the seaplane hangar.

Most of the Navy and RAF pilots who'd hoped for evacuation had begun the long trudge back uphill to Hal Far. Many expected to be assigned to a rifle company for the last ditch defense of the Naval Air Station. It was over an hour since the bombing of the sub. The seaplane ramp and quayside were nearly deserted.

Kenneth sat on the stone quay near the wrecked hangar and smashed ramp of the seaplane base, staring out over the water of the bay to the darkened Delimara Lighthouse on the far shore. He couldn't stop his mind from wondering if Maggie was dead, or worse, if she were suffocating, trapped in the iron coffin of a sunken submarine just a few yards away. He'd managed to find several of the crew of the sub that lay partially submerged a hundred yards from shore. To a man they insisted no women were aboard when they were bombed, but that didn't account for the other sub he'd glimpsed, the one making for the breakwater just before the German attack struck. He had no way to know if it survived the attack or even if Maggie was aboard it. The M.P. with whom he'd sheltered in the hangar wasn't sure which sub the young woman with bandaged head had boarded. After several minutes staring out over the water Kenneth heard someone sit down beside him. He turned and smiled at Billy, the RAF pilot who'd flown in that afternoon from *HMS Furious*.

"Nice mess we're in, hmm Billy?' he said softly.

"A real sticky-wicket," Billy agreed.

The two sat in companionable silence for several minutes, listening to the soft lapping of waves against the base of the stone quay. In the distance the faint sounds of small arms fire drifted to them from Hal Far.

"How are you still in the RAF, Kenneth?" asked Billy. "Why haven't you transferred to your own Air Force by now?"

Kenneth smiled. "I put in for a transfer right after Pearl Harbor," he explained, "but it hadn't come through yet this past winter when they came around asking for volunteers for the Med. I had to withdraw the request to be allowed out here."

"Be careful what you wish for!" Billy snorted.

Kenneth shook his head. "No regrets, Billy," he said, thinking again of Maggie.

Billy was silent a moment. "Well," he said finally, "it looks like our best bet now is a POW camp. If we're lucky."

"I suppose we should make our way back to the airfield," Kenneth offered after several minutes. "They'll be needing every man."

"A real fight to the finish you think?" Billy asked.

"Without air cover I don't imagine the field can be held," shrugged Kenneth. "The Germans will pour troops in by air at Ta Qali and maybe at Luqa too until they overwhelm us with sheer numbers."

Billy climbed to his feet. "Well," he said. "We'd best get back up that hill before daylight."

"Yes, I suppose you're right," Kenneth agreed, but he didn't move to join Billy. He was peering out over the moon dappled waters with increased intensity.

"What is it Kenneth?" asked Billy, turning in the direction of Kenneth's gaze. "Is there something out there?"

"Yes, I think so," replied Kenneth. "There," he said, pointing up the coast. "Close in-shore. A boat of some kind."

At first Billy saw nothing, but then the dim outline of a small craft emerged from the shadows. It was slowly and quietly moving toward them in the shadows along the quay a couple hundred yards north of where they sat watching. As it came closer its form became clearer.

"Its one of the air-sea rescue launches," Kenneth said as the boat came within forty yards of them. It passed them quietly about twenty yards from shore and continued on its silent way till it drew abreast of the sunken sub. It then turned out into the bay and pulled in close to the tilted conning tower of the sub.

"What do you suppose that's all about?" wondered Billy.

"Let's walk back down to the ramp and find out," Kenneth suggested.

The two strolled down the deserted quay towards the launch. They were in no hurry, just curious about the odd behavior of the launch. They stopped and watched as they drew adjacent to the sunken sub. The launch was in close to the tilted conning tower. There were about a dozen men on the boat dressed in a motley mix of uniforms and civilian rags. Two men scrambled onto the conning tower of the sub and climbed down the still open hatch, emerging a moment later soaking wet. Snatches of conversation drifted across the water, but the two pilots could make nothing of what they heard except that there seemed to be an argument underway.

Finally Kenneth could bare his curiosity no longer and he called out to the men on the launch and sub. "Ahoy, the rescue launch," he called through cupped hands, trying his best to sound nautical. "If you're looking for survivors they've all been taken off."

The argument on the conning tower stopped as the men there noticed Kenneth and Billy for the first time.

"We're not looking for survivors," an English voice called back from the shadows on the conning tower. "Now bugger off!"

Kenneth and Billy looked and each other and shrugged. They turned and began to carefully pick their way through the rubble away from the ramp. The men on the conning tower and the launch resumed their argument. Kenneth had gone just a few steps when a raised voice carried across the water to his ears.

"… not enough fuel I tell you, dammit!"

Kenneth spun on his heel and walked back to the dockside.

"Are you looking for fuel?" he called back across the water.

Once more the argument ceased and the men turned their attention back to him.

"What if we are?" asked the same man who'd answered before. "You have some up your sleeve, maybe?" Derisive laughter erupted from the men still aboard the launch.

"Depends on what kind of fuel you need," Kenneth replied. "And on what you need it for."

"We're going to drink it," replied the man on the sub. "Have one bloody big piss-up!"

"I bet not," answered Kenneth. "I bet you need it for the launch. What does it take, diesel or petrol?"

"What bloody difference does it make?" snarled the man. "You haven't got any of either."

"But I know where to get some," answered Kenneth coyly. "Plenty of either in fact, not ten minutes from here."

The men on the sub and the launch began talking to one another again in undertones Kenneth couldn't hear.

Billy tugged on Kenneth's sleeve and whispered to him. "These chaps don't seem right, Kenneth. I bet they don't have orders."

"No, they don't," Kenneth agreed. "I bet they stole the launch too."

"Then what are you doing?" Billy pressed. "You're going to get us in trouble."

"You still have your side-arm, Billy?" Kenneth asked.

The man on the sub spoke before Billy could reply.

"All right then, mate," he said in a smooth and agreeable tone of voice. "Where's this fuel of yours? We're on the King's business and don't have time for games!"

"Bollocks!" Kenneth growled back. "You're not on the King's business. You're out to save your own hides. You're going to try to escape the island with the launch and you need extra fuel to try it!"

Silence from the boat. Finally the man spoke again. "You're a smart one a'right," he said. "Now, so what if we don't fancy spending the war in a POW camp in the Reich? It's our duty to escape!"

"Right you are!" agreed Kenneth. "Ours too. We're going with you."

"You don't sound like seamen to me," growled the man.

"No, we're pilots," acknowledged Kenneth.

"There'll be no passengers on this trip! Every man must do his share."

"Our share is coming up with the fuel," argued Kenneth.

The men on the launch debated amongst themselves again. Kenneth and Billy heard the apparent leader say, "What difference does two more make?"

"Where is this fuel?" the man demanded finally. "The sun'll rise in another hour and a half. We've to be away by then if we're to have a chance of being missed by the bloody Luftwaffe!"

"We'll have to show you," answered Kenneth. "How much do you figure to need?"

"At least two hundred gallons of diesel."

"Two hundred gallons!" exclaimed Kenneth. "Good Lord!"

"Have you been wasting my time?" the man barked.

"No, the fuel is there," said Kenneth. "At least it was two hours ago. But we can't carry that much. We'd never get it moved in time. We need transport." He stroked his chin in thought a moment, though of course he already had the answer.

"I can arrange transport too," he called across the water. "But you'll have to come ashore. We'll need help in loading the fuel tins."

Some more argument aboard the launch, then it moved slowly towards the quay. A rope came flying out of the darkness. Billy caught it and wrapped it loosely around a cleat on the quay. As the launch bumped roughly against the stone quay a barrage of profanity erupted from the man Kenneth had talked to. The man leaped onto the quay, untied the rope from the cleat and re-tightened it in a neat, clean knot. Kenneth studied him carefully in the dim moonlight. Over six feet tall and muscularly built he was dressed as an ordinary seaman, but his bearing was that of an officer if not an aristocrat. Keen eyes peered from beneath jet-black brows and rather longish hair.

"All right, pilot," he addressed Kenneth. "Where's this fuel?"

"Do we have a bargain?" Kenneth asked. "The two of us go with you?"

"You don't even know where we're going," observed the man.

"Nor your name," parried Kenneth.

The man shifted his gaze back and forth between Billy and Kenneth, sizing them up.

"Commander Smith, R.N., at your service," he said at last.

"Smith, eh?" said Billy.

Smith ignored him. "Where's this fuel?" he repeated.

"The deal?" Kenneth pressed.

"Yes, yes, the two of you go with us," said Smith impatiently. "That is, if we don't waste what's left of the night debating the point."

"The fuel is up the hill, partway to Hal Far," Kenneth said. "There's an air raid shelter off the road and a fuel depot with tins of diesel and kerosene."

"I know that shelter," Smith said. "It's a long hike uphill from here with a Navy checkpoint between us."

"Not much of a problem for a Navy Commander," Billy piped in.

Smith smiled for the first time, revealing strong, white and even teeth. "The Navy and I may be, er, not on speaking terms just now."

"We can get past the checkpoint and the guards," said Kenneth "They know me well and I have the password and countersign for the night."

"And they're just going to turn over the fuel stock to you, eh?"

Kenneth looked at his shoes. "I, uh, haven't quite figured that out yet," he admitted.

"Never mind," said Smith. "Get me through the checkpoints, I'll handle the guards."

"There's to be no one killed or hurt!" Kenneth exclaimed as the thought occurred to him for the first time.

"No, of course not!" assured Smith with a frown. "Let's get started." He made a quick hand signal and two more men from the launch leapt onto the quay. To Kenneth they each looked like lesser versions of Smith, tall, well built and stern.

The five men began picking their way through the rubble of the smashed wharf buildings, working their way back to the cleared road behind the hangar. From there they made their way up the slope to the Hal Far road and on toward the turn at the top of the hill.

"Maybe you'd better give me the password and countersign now," said Smith, "in case something happens to you."

Kenneth laughed. "Just be sure nothing happens to me."

"What kind of transport do you have in mind?" pressed Smith.

Kenneth thought a moment then shrugged. "There's an old Model T lorry at the shelter," he said. "We called it a pick-up back home in the States. It has a small cargo bed. We should be able to load it with enough fuel." He left unspoken his prayer that the Model T was still there.

The five men picked their way through the rubble of the wharf area, making their way to the Kalafrana Road and began the climb up the hill. Commander Smith, or whatever his name really was, set a rapid pace and soon Billy and Kenneth were forced to trot to keep up with Smith and his men. There was no conversation. The two pilots, each young and fit were breathing heavily as they reached the crown of the hill and came to the first guard checkpoint.

"Halt! Who goes?" came the challenge from the shadows at the side of the road.

"Werewolf," said Kenneth slowly and clearly.

"Webley Station," replied a Marine Corporal stepping out of the gloom. "State your business."

Kenneth started to answer, but Smith cut him off.

"We're bound for the fuel supply at the Kalafrana air raid shelter, Corporal," Smith said, adopting the same Sandhurst drawl that had so irritated Kenneth earlier that morning. "Wounded can't be moved without it."

The Corporal, conditioned by years of service to respond to that voice snapped to attention. "Very well, Sir!" he barked in his best parade ground manner.

"Carry on, Corporal!" said Smith as he moved on up the road.

"We'll see if that works at the shelter," Kenneth murmured to Billy under his breath.

Presently they came to the turnoff to the shelter. Challenged again by the guards, this time Smith gave the password and did all the talking. It dawned on Kenneth as they made their way down the track that he and Billy were no longer needed. Smith had both the location of the fuel and the password and countersign for the night.

As they rounded the boulder and entered the clearing Kenneth crossed his fingers that the Model T was still there. He was relieved when the dark shape of the truck materialized in the gloom under the camouflage nets. As they approached the stacked tins of fuel they were challenged once again.

"Halt, who goes there?"

"Werewolf," snapped Smith, then without waiting for the countersign reply began issuing orders to Kenneth, Billy and the roughnecks with him. "Load this lorry with forty tins of petrol," Smith directed still affecting the drawl. "I'll be in the bunker finding the C.O.," he snapped.

"Uh, Pardon me, Sir," one of the guards stammered. "None of this fuel is to be taken wi'fout written orders."

"That's why I'm getting the C.O., Private, "Smith explained patiently as though to a child. "I shan't be long. Assist these men in loading the lorry," he said with a wave of his hand. "The wounded have been waiting for medical attention too long as it is."

"Yes, Sir," said the Private uncertainly.

He turned back to the Model T and found Smith's men already loading it. Kenneth nudged Billy in the ribs and stepped under the net; lifting a five-gallon tin he carried it to the truck and into the cargo bed. After a moment the Private slung his rifle and turned to help. The five of them worked steadily and within moments loaded over forty tins of fuel, stacking the last of them precariously atop the others. As if on cue, Smith stepped from the bunker with the Army Captain in tow.

"Right!" he snapped. "Everything in order?" he demanded imperiously.

The guard answered smartly. "All loaded, Sir, just as you ordered."

"Right!" Smith snapped again. "Sergeant Pilot," he said, pointing at Kenneth. "You'll ride with me. You other men will ride on the running boards."

Kenneth ran around the other side of the truck and climbed in. Within seconds the Model T was coughing and spluttering away from the shelter, Billy and the two roughnecks hanging on to any purchase they could find.

"Thank you, Captain, carry on," Smith waved absently as the Model T jolted around the large boulder and up the path to the Kalafrana Road. It was soon evident though that the truck was overloaded; it was barely able to crawl up the slight incline.

"You three hop down and push!" Smith barked to Billy and the others. "Not you Pilot," he said to Kenneth. "You stay here. You'd be no good pushing with that shoulder anyway."

Kenneth stared at Smith. He'd never mentioned his own injury.

Lightened of 400 pounds and with the three men behind pushing it the old truck labored up to the crown of the hill barely at walking speed. They passed the guards in the shadows at the intersection and jolted up onto the main road. As the road eased downhill the truck started to pick up speed.

"All right you three, jump aboard," Smith ordered. Kenneth noted the Sandhurst drawl was gone, replaced by Smith's only ordinary imperiousness.

"Well, Pilot," he said as the truck lurched down the hill.

"Now's your last, best chance to bugger off. I don't think you're up to what we're about to try."

"What exactly are you about to try?" Kenneth asked. "Where are we going?"

Smith took his eyes off the road and glanced at Kenneth.

"East," he finally said.

"East is a big place," Kenneth noted dryly.

Smith laughed. "Yes, it is," he agreed. "All right," he relented after a moment's thought. "If it isn't already, Alexandria will likely be abandoned within a few days. With the airfields in the Western Desert in German hands the base will be unlivable. Same may be true of Port Said. We may have to go as far east as Haifa to find safe harbor. Over 1100 miles at eight to ten knots. Say five, maybe six days. That's if the engine doesn't pack it in, we don't run into a storm, etc. We've to pass through bomb alley between Crete and Libya to boot. I make our chances about one in ten."

Kenneth sat back and thought a moment. "What do you make our chances if we stay?"

Smith shrugged. "Pretty decent actually. We'd lie low till the fighting ends, then surrender to the Jerries and spend the duration in a nice, cozy POW camp."

"Doesn't appeal," said Kenneth.

Smith looked at him again. "Nor to me," he said, "But at least you'd be alive."

Kenneth's mind turned to Maggie and the brief weeks they'd known each other. He was suddenly filled with a certainty that she was alive and had escaped the island. The thought of spending the war locked away from her, not even able to communicate was just too much.

"I like east," he said.

Smith nodded his head. "Can you speak for your friend?"

"Yes, I can," Kenneth answered without hesitation.

"All right then, Pilot. Here are the ground rules. You'll both follow my orders without hesitation or question. If I order you overboard you'll jump. Understand?"

Kenneth nodded. "Yes, I understand."

"Yes, what?" Smith demanded.

"Yes, Sir," Kenneth replied as the truck ground to a halt behind the smashed seaplane hangar at the Kalafrana ramp.

Smith leapt out of the cab and reached into the cargo bed, hefting two tins off the top of the pile like they were nothing.

"Load up you Pilots," he ordered, setting off with his two silent companions in tow.

"Yes, Sir," Kenneth answered. He lifted a tin out of the back of the truck with his left hand and set off towards the harbor launch. Billy followed behind carrying two tins.

"I overheard your little chat, Kenneth," Billy said as they picked their way back through the rubble-strewn alley to the wharf.

"Are you in?" Kenneth asked.

"In for a penny, in for a pound," laughed Billy. "You're right. I don't fancy myself a POW either."

After they delivered the first load of fuel they returned with the rest of Smith's men to the Model T. In three round trips all the fuel was aboard the launch. As Force H approached Malta from the northwest the rescue launch put out from Marsaxlokk Bay, skirting close inshore to Delimara point then plowing on to the southeast. Within minutes of clearing the harbor breakwater it was bouncing through six foot swells. Smith and his men rode the chop well, but Kenneth and Billy started to feel seasick almost immediately.

"This is going to be a long trip, Billy," Kenneth groaned as the two pilots hung over the rail.

>>>>>>>>>>>>>>>

At Comiso a stream of bomb trolleys made their way in the pre-dawn gloom from the northern extremity of the strip towards the rows of aircraft lined up along the runways. Aircrew were beginning to board their craft, going through pre-flight inspection routines in preparation for the morning's operations. Fuel bowsers worked their way down the lines, topping up wing tanks. Armorers fed belts of machine gun and cannon ammunition to the guns. These preparations went on through the night.

News of the sea battle to the northwest of Malta was slow to reach the Luftwaffe on Sicily. Admiral Iachino was busy assessing the damage done to his ships as he withdrew from battle and was in no hurry to inform Rome of his failure to stop the British fleet's passage. Commando Supremo in its turn was in no hurry to pass the news along to their German allies. By the time word that the British had defeated the Italians at sea reached the Sicilian airfields the first glow of daylight was illuminating the eastern sky.

Dawn found the air wing staff officers in the operations center reviewing the sequence of flight operations for the assault on Hal Far. The initial air attacks were to be carried out by three waves of aircraft, Ju 87 Stukas and Ju 88 bombers almost exclusively. Only a handful of fighter aircraft would be launched to provide cover. It was a certainty that the British had no more fighter aircraft of their own to attack the bombers.

Each wave would comprise over fifty bombers. The first wave would attack the pre-arranged coordinates fed from the ground forces on Malta through the flight controller, 'blue-two-one' then orbiting over the heart of the island. The second wave was to follow-up with attacks on specific targets missed in the first wave. The third wave was to be held in reserve, available to hit unexpected points of resistance during the ground assault on Hal Far. The bombers were laden with a mixture of mostly light bombs of 500 kilos or less, though a few were armed with larger 1000 kilo bombs for breaking open bunkers and other hardened defenses. There was not a single torpedo or armor piercing bomb on any plane on the field.

At Catania airfield the eastern horizon was tinged with the first hint of the dawn still to come. Flares lit the flight line as a Ju 88 roared down the runway and into the air. Tipping over on its starboard wing it turned and climbed away to the southwest, rising to meet the first rays of the sun peeking over the rim of the world, finding the light at 2,500 meters altitude. Skirting to the west of Malta its crew waited impatiently for the surface to be illuminated. They'd been told that a major sea battle had been fought between the British and Italian navies to the west of the island. Intercepted wireless traffic between the Italian fleet and the Italian Naval HQ, however was inconclusive. The Germans hadn't broken the code of their ally and repeated requests for information went unanswered by Rome. The JU 88 was dispatched so the Germans could find out for themselves the outcome of the battle.

At 0540 they flew over the Italian fleet. A battleship and two cruisers screened by seven destroyers were steaming slowly to the northeast. Fires burned on the three heavy ships and columns of smoke rose into the sky. The battleship in particular appeared wounded, with a plume of leaking fuel oil evident on the water behind her. The Ju 88 continued on, following the sheen of oil to the southwest.

It took only minutes to find the British. First a small ship appeared, a destroyer, followed less than a minute later by five more destroyers and three heavier ships. To the crew aboard the German bomber the British ships appeared unscathed. No smoke billowed from fires and no oil trailed away on the surface of the sea.

The Ju 88 carried no bombs. It was flying fast and light for reconnaissance only. Its duty was to find the British fleet and report its position, staying over the fleet to the limits of the bomber's fuel. Its pilot maintained a respectful distance, out of range of the flak guns on the ships below.

"They're British all right," the pilot said after several minutes scrutinizing the ships through his binoculars. "Make a signal," he ordered, looking over his shoulder to his navigator/wireless operator. "'One battleship, two cruisers, six other ships, course one-zero-zero, speed twenty-five knots, thirty miles from Malta.' Add our position and send it right away."

He settled back to relax and to wait. There would be quite a show once the bombers from Sicily arrived. They were little more than twenty minutes flying time away. He expected a short wait.

"Navigator to pilot," he heard in his headset.

"Yes, what is it?"

"I have not received an acknowledgement to my signal from Sicily."

"Have you checked the receiver?" the pilot demanded. A cool shiver ran down his spine.

"The receiver is functioning properly," the navigator replied. "I am listening in on any number of tactical signals from the airfield to other units, including the flight controller over the island."

"Send the signal again," commanded the pilot.

"I have sent it three times so far, but no acknowledgement from Catania."

"What are you saying, dammit?" demanded the pilot. "Was your signal transmitted or not?"

"I am afraid the transmitter is malfunctioning," answered the navigator. "We are scheduled to make a status signal right now. If Catania does not receive this signal they will begin calling for us. We'll know for sure within five minutes."

With a worried sigh the pilot sat back again, but now the minutes seemed to drag forever. Meanwhile the British fleet crept two miles closer to Malta.

"Navigator to pilot."

"Yes, do you have a reply?"

"No. I have resent the sighting report. Catania is calling us asking for a report. I can hear them clearly, but it is plain they have not received our signal."

He'd been expecting this answer and the pilot had already determined his course of action. He threw the Ju 88 over in a tight banking turn to the northeast, back toward Sicily. They'd have to deliver their sighting report in person.

The first light of dawn on June 28, 1942 found Major Kuno Schacht at the command post of the 23rd Parachute Regiment at Luqa airfield. He and the balance of his communications squad and Colonel August with his regimental command staff had traveled by the light of the moon from Mdina, once more using the limited supply of motor transport available to the Germans on Malta, passing through bomb-shattered towns and villages. On the journey they saw hundreds of fresh Italian infantry. Air landed that night at Ta Qali with the runways lit by burning fuel drums the Italians were on the way south to join the planned assault on Hal Far field.

Thousands of mainly Italian troops poured onto the island during the night through the airhead at Ta Qali and more arrived every hour. With the coming of daylight the rate of reinforcement was expected to accelerate. Already over thirty thousand Axis troops delivered by sea and air were on the island.

With the support of the Fuhrer in Berlin who fended off Italian claims to lead the force on the island Colonel August retained de facto command of the airborne invasion and had reestablished his HQ at Luqa, the better to control the coming attack. He directed the bulk of the new arrivals to the south, towards Luqa airfield to participate in the assault against Hal Far scheduled for 1000 hours the morning of the 28th, less than five hours away.

Throughout the night just passed the crackle of small arms fire barely slackened as the British and Axis forces maintained close contact with one another. Kuno and Colonel August surveyed the field through their binoculars as light from the rising sun spread over Malta.

"When will your communications with the Luftwaffe be established?" asked the Baron von der Heydte.

"According to Steup we've had intermittent contact for some time, Colonel," Kuno answered. "The Air Force has promised to have a controller airborne over the island by dawn. Assuming there are no hitches we should be in contact with him shortly."

"Good, good," responded the Colonel. "See to it personally, Kuno. We must have air support if the final assault is not to be a bloodbath. I must see to the disposition of the Italians."

"Not a comfortable feeling to have the attack so dependent upon them," observed Kuno wryly.

"Yes, I know," said August, "but our own units are too worn down from two days of continuous fighting. They haven't the strength left to lead the assault. I'm going to hold our paratroopers in reserve. Regular German and Italian infantry with support from the panzers will lead the assault with the Italian paras following in close reserve. I'll throw our men in wherever a breakthrough is achieved."

"I haven't seen the tanks yet," observed Kuno.

"They are struggling down narrow tracks north of Ta Qali," the Baron replied. "The same thing which delayed the British in hitting us with their tanks delays us in bringing our armor to bear."

"What are to be your lines of attack?" asked Kuno.

Colonel August lowered his glasses and pointed. "I'm going to demonstrate at the west side of the field as though mounting a direct assault there. But the main force is going to hit hard directly to the south against the airfield perimeter. The flatter ground gives me a better chance to bring the panzers into action. We'll hit them from two sides."

Kuno nodded his head in understanding. "Then the air attack must come in front of the demonstration to the west and also directly to the south?"

"At first, yes," agreed August. "But be sure there are sufficient aircraft held back to follow-up the initial attack as well."

Colonel August left to see to the Italians while Kuno became engrossed in managing the details of his communications center. His team occupied a below ground level bunker that had been the

Air Station Operations Center at Luqa field. It abutted a rocky shelf to the west of the runway. From the front entrance it commanded a view of the entire airfield.

The Bunker's British occupants had abandoned it in rather a hurry and it was largely intact, though the British had planned the details of its demolition months in advance. British engineers destroyed nearly everything else of value on the field as the German assault swept south from Ta Qali, but a stick of Luftwaffe bombs severed the fuses for the Operations Center's demolition charges. Paratrooper engineers cleared the bunker of its explosives that morning, making it ready for use as combined command post and communications center.

The British had removed or destroyed their own wireless apparatus before abandoning the bunker, along with anything else of direct military value, but they'd left hundreds of yards of cable and phone line behind. Sgt. Tondok nearly squealed with delight and drafted a squad of German infantry to harvest the bounty. Dozens of filing cabinets stuffed with personnel files, maintenance logs and other documents were left behind as well. These would provide grist for Axis intelligence specialists and translators if the island could be secured. For now Kuno ordered them shoved into a dark corner. As the finishing touches were put on the communications setup Kuno lingered behind Lt. Steup, looming over his shoulder, impatiently waiting for contact with the Luftwaffe air controller to be established. He checked his watch. 0615 hours.

Without ceremony Steup depressed the send key and transmitted the regiment's code name. The response was as immediate as it was gratifying.

"Greetings, Malta!" crackled from the speakers. "Designate this contact Blue-Two-One, repeat, Blue-Two-One."

"Greetings, Blue-Two-One!" responded Steup cheerily. He turned to Kuno, smiling and flashed thumbs up. Kuno returned a thin smile and nodded once to acknowledge the speedy contact.

Steup got down to business. "Blue-Two-One, are you ready for targeting coordinates?"

"Affirmative!" came the reply. "The bombers are stacked up at Sicily waiting for the launch order."

As Steup began relaying the target sequence for the coming

attack Kuno went to inform Colonel August of the reestablished wireless link. He found the Colonel on the roof of the bunker, kneeling inside a ring of sandbags the British had used as a machine gun nest and observation post.

"Ah, Schacht!" exclaimed the Baron. "I trust you have good news?"

"Yes, Colonel," said Kuno. "Contact with the air force is established. Steup is feeding them the coordinates for the attack right now."

"Good, good." The Baron pointed off to the southwest. The newly risen sun illuminated the crowns of the ridgeline there. "The English have been busy," he said. "See there." He handed Kuno his binoculars. "They have reinforced their lines."

Kuno peered through the glasses a moment before handing them back to Colonel August.

"Yes," he said. "I count at least a dozen embrasures for light field pieces. They'll have our forces under direct fire when the attack starts."

"You'll have to take care of that, Kuno," said the Baron. "Each of those guns must be dug out by bombing attack."

"Costly to the Air Force," Kuno observed. He winced as the stitches in his chest pulled. "The flak guns on Hal Far will give our flyers a very rough time."

The colonel nodded his head. "I hope Malta is worth it," he said. "Personally, I wouldn't give a penny for the whole damn place."

A burst of machine gun fire rattled to the south, disturbing the morning stillness. A flurry of sub-machine gun and rifle fire joined in and lasted several minutes before tapering off to an occasional shot.

"Everyone is nervous," commented the Colonel.

"Does the attack remain on schedule?" asked Kuno.

"Yes," said Colonel August, turning to Kuno with a stern look. "1000 hours we attack!"

Kuno stood to go, but at that moment the sound of a distant explosion boomed over the field. Colonel August jumped to his feet and the two men turned in the direction from which the blast had come, to the north.

"What the devil?" exclaimed August. The two men stood rooted in place trying to see or hear the source of the explosion.

A half-minute after the first, four more blasts reverberated across the island.

"That's heavy artillery!" exclaimed Kuno. "On Ta Qali!"


Harold Burrough sat in the Admiral's chair on the bridge of *Renown*, leaning uncomfortably away from his injured left arm, nervously watching the chronometer on the bulkhead above the helm.

Throughout the fleet men sat slumped at their action stations as the sun rose that morning, June 28, 1942. For over twenty-four hours the men of Force H had manned their guns and hoists, engine spaces and radar offices, exposed lookout platforms and their damage control stations. Fed bully-beef sandwiches and cold tea at action stations they'd tried to sleep, for the most part unsuccessfully, at their posts. The last full measure of exhaustion was upon them. But now sleep was out of the question. The alarm for dawn action stations sounded, but was not necessary. Every man aboard every ship was already closed up, had been closed up all through the long night, through the running battle with the Italian fleet and on until the dawn. To many in Force H it seemed a false dawn, for it did not bring hope, but rather the certainty of death and defeat.

Daylight in enemy waters under enemy skies meant the Luftwaffe would come to pay its traditional dawn visit. Without air cover and with such damage to the ships of the fleet an air attack in strength by the Germans could only mean the end of Force H. And slowed by the Italian battle fleet and the damage done to the flagship Force H was still forty miles from Malta.

Damage control teams worked feverishly, beginning even before the battle with the Regia Marina was finished, before the Italians scurried away to the north. Aboard *Renown* they first fought the fires started in the superstructure by the Italians' final shots. For a time these fires threatened to drive Admiral Burrough, Captain Daniel and their staffs from the bridge, but Lt. Peter Walker and his damage parties were up to the task again. For the second time in two days they fought a major fire aboard the battlecruiser. First they checked the fire then beat it back upon itself, extinguishing the flames in little over an hour. Despite his cracked ribs Walker donned his protective suit and led his men to the heart of the blaze. By 0415 the fire was out.

But their work was not done. Even before the flames were extinguished Walker pulled men off the fire line and put them to work patching the gaping wound in *Renown's* forward funnel. The ragged edges of the damage were hammered down with huge sledges and thin sheets of tin siding were welded over the wound. As the last hole was patched the great boilers of the forward engine room regained their draft and the Flagship of Force H gained way. With a gathering bow wave she sped up till she attained 28 knots, near her former top speed.

Commander Roland Webster paced the bridge as *HMS Sirius* raced east to meet the dawn. Damage parties were busy aboard the cruiser as well, extinguishing fires and shoring up weakened bulkheads. There was no time to repair either radar aerial however. Webster felt out of place. He belonged in his radar office, prepared to direct his guns against the air attacks he felt certain were only minutes away, but with both radar aerials out of action the radar office was useless. He listened intently to the short-range radio net from the other ships in the fleet, relying upon the still functioning radars aboard *Sirius'* sister ship, *Charybdis* and the battlecruiser *Renown* for early warning of approaching aircraft.

Dawn was a very dangerous time. Should the Germans attack directly from the east the rising sun would blind his spotters and gunners. As the pre-dawn glow brightened the horizon Webster spoke with his gun captains via interphone, warning them to stay alert.

A feeling of tense expectancy filled the men of Force H as the sun's blazing orb rose above the eastern horizon. The sky was clear, with no hint of cloud or fog or even the characteristic mid-summer haze to provide even a modest cover for the ships. It would be a fine, hot day.

Admiral Burrough moved to the chart house behind *Renown's* bridge to study a map of Malta. Commander Oats and Captain Daniel stood with him. The Flag Secretary, Lt. Harris was below in sickbay, clinging to life with a serious concussion. The Admiral's left arm was in a sling. He'd fractured it above the elbow when he was thrown from his feet by the final hit from the Italian battleship.

"We can be absolutely no further than eighteen miles from target to be in range of the main battery," observed Captain Daniel.

Burrough nodded his head and pointed to the map.

"Yes," he agreed, "and with the primary targets Ta Qali and Luqa between three and five miles inland we've to close to within thirteen miles of the western shore to be in range."

"How close do the cruisers have to be?" asked Oats.

"Too close," answered Burrough. "I won't take *Renown* in that close and I don't want to separate us from the cruisers' flak guns. We'll stay together. The cruisers and destroyers will provide anti-aircraft defense for *Renown* while our big guns hit the German landing zones."

"We'll have to break radio silence soon," said Daniel. "We've to connect to observers ashore. We won't be able to see the fall of our own shot."

Burrough rubbed his forehead. The pain in his arm and exhaustion were combining to give him a massive headache.

"Yes, of course you're right," he said at last. "We're just over an hour from being in range. Go ahead and establish contact now. It will probably take that long to get patched in to the observers."

Captain Daniel nodded his head and left the charthouse through the aft hatchway. He would deliver the order to the W/T office himself.

Oats stared intently at Burrough.

"Perhaps you should get some rest, Admiral," he said, "before we reach the island."

Burrough looked at him and smiled.

"An hours sleep wouldn't help me now, Oats," he answered. "Besides…" he began. "Well, anyway," he continued. "I'm sorry I got you into this Oats. Should've left you at Gib."

Oats feigned surprise. "I wouldn't have missed it, Admiral," he exclaimed.

"See if you can get me some tea, will you Oats?"

Aboard *Sirius*, Commander Webster worked each of his gun crews through a few elementary drills, more to keep them active and alert than because they needed any practice. He found himself curiously refreshed by the dawn, even though it presaged air attack and the prospect of death. Once *Renown's* funncl was repaired and the fleet increased speed hope stirred in him that they might reach

Malta in time to tip the scales back from defeat.

Word spread quickly to the lower decks that Force H would be in range of Malta in little over an hour. Men sat silently at their posts, without even the usual banter and complaining that made life tolerable for the average seamen of the Royal Navy.

The sea was calm and the only breeze came from the passage of the ships over the surface. On every ship in the fleet men braced themselves at the highest possible vantage points and scanned the sky for approaching aircraft. Aboard *Charybdis* and *Renown* the radar aerials spun relentlessly atop the fore and mainmasts, the unblinking eyes searching the skies for signs of approaching danger. The three remaining heavy ships of Force H and their scant escort of destroyers were running flat out to the southeast, towards Malta and every two minutes brought them another nautical mile closer to the island.

Shortly after sunrise radar detected a lone aircraft approaching the fleet from the northeast, the direction of the enemy airfields on Sicily. The lone snoop shadowed the fleet for some minutes, but then to the surprise of every officer it fled back the way it had come and the radar screens remained mysteriously clear.

At 0610 hours commands were quietly issued. Deep in the ship men in the magazines and shell rooms began the process of preparing ammunition to be hoisted to the guns. At 0615 hours the four 15-inch Mk I guns in the two surviving turrets trained out to port and elevated. Pre-loaded they were ready to fire and awaited only the final command. At 0620 *Renown* began her turn to starboard, bringing her parallel to the coastline. She reduced speed to steady the gun platform.

Burrough sat upright in his chair, ignoring the pain of his broken arm. He caught Captain Daniel's eye. "You may fire when ready, Captain," he said with a surprising calmness. Through all the dangers and difficulties they'd endured, for all the damage and loss suffered by the ships and men of Force H, *Renown* stood within reach of her mighty guns of accomplishing the mission she'd set out upon.

Captain Daniel turned and took two steps to the observation slits in the center of his armored bridge. "Commence firing," he ordered.

One gun of 'B' turret forward spoke; a flash of flame, a smoke ring and the first shell was on its way. Captain Daniel had arranged for the wireless conversation between the spotters on Malta and *Renown's* gunnery officer to be heard over the Tannoy speakers on the bridge. At a range approaching fourteen miles it took over forty seconds for the shell to reach its destination.

"Down 1000, right 200," the observer spoke slowly and clearly, enunciating every word. "You are long for Ta Qali runway." The gun barrels twitched in minute adjustment.

"SHOOT!" The Gunnery Officer commanded, his voice overloud and tinny sounding in the speakers.

The deck lurched as the guns of 'B' turret fired in rapid order. A second later the twin guns of 'X' turret aft followed suit. Four shells weighing nearly a ton each hurtled out across the sea towards Malta. As the crews in the hoists and turrets worked to reload the guns the bridge watch stood silent.

"Down 100 and fire for effect!" said the observer.

The Captain arched an eyebrow at Admiral Burrough as the gun barrels were adjusted just the least bit.

"SHOOT!"

Once the order to fire for effect was given the guns were loaded and fired as quickly as possible without waiting for further adjustment from the forward observer.

"On target, on target!" the observer shouted. "FIRE FOR EFFECT!" His voice bordered on frantic.

"What is it? What's wrong?" asked Oats in confusion.

"SHOOT!"

The four guns fired again in succession. Admiral Burrough waited till they were done before leaning over. He spoke from the corner of his mouth. "Malta doesn't realize we have only four guns in operation," he said. "They think we're continuing to fire ranging shots when we should be bringing our whole main battery to bear."

"Why don't we just tell him?" asked Oats.

"If the Germans are listening better to keep them in the dark," Burrough replied patiently. "Though in truth they are probably quicker on the uptake than our observer friend. In any case, it shan't be long before we shift our fire to Luqa. We need to crater the runway at Ta Qali to interrupt take-offs and landings. We're on target now. Four guns will take longer than six, but we'll wreck the runway for the rest of the day at least."

The mighty guns continued their work, pounding the runway at Ta Qali as *Renown* slowly cruised down the coastline.

"Coming within range of Luqa," noted Daniel.

"Continue to fire on Ta Qali," said Burrough. "Say five more salvos. We've got to put the runway completely out of commission. We may not have the chance to switch our fire back again."

Daniel said nothing, but nodded his acknowledgement. They continued to pour steel onto Ta Qali, each gun rising and firing about every thirty seconds.

The Tannoy squawked to life. "Bridge, Radar.

Captain Daniel answered the call himself.

"Radar, bridge. What have you got?"

"Aerial contact, Bridge. Bearing zero-six-five, range twenty-two miles, at 9,000 feet. It's a large flight, Captain. Looks like over fifty aircraft."

Burrough leaned down from his chair. "Go ahead and switch your fire now, Captain. Time to hit Luqa while we can."

Again Daniel merely nodded as he relayed the order to his gunnery officer.

Three Ju 52's landed at Ta Qali just minutes after dawn. They'd taken off from Comiso in the pre-dawn darkness; laden with critically needed ammunition they came to rest at the south end of the runway where Italian infantry formed human chains to unload the heavy crates and boxes. Dozens of wounded were laid out on stretchers next to the runway. Attended by medical orderlies and corpsmen they waited their turn to be loaded aboard the transports for evacuation back to Sicily.

As the last of the Auntie Jus came to rest the first ranging shot from *Renown* screeched across the field and landed 1000 yards to the east of the runway's mid-point. Men all over Ta Qali field, German and Italian alike stopped in their labors and stared dumbfounded at the explosion. Seconds passed before they began scrambling for cover. On the runway a cry of consternation arose from the Italian infantry, but their officers cursed and berated them back in to line to continue the unloading.

The next shots came in a salvo just one hundred yards off the runway, four heavy rounds still to the east, but shifted to the south end of the field. The Italians broke and ran for cover. Nothing their officers did could stop them.

The first Junkers was almost emptied of cargo; its pilot fired up its three engines in quick succession and began taxiing onto the strip. Without waiting for any ground control or clearance he shoved the throttles full forward to their stops. As the loadmaster tossed the last boxes of his cargo out the door and with motors thundering the transport slowly gathered speed and rolled up the runway to the north just as the third salvo bore down on the field. The four hi-explosive shells straddled the runway. One of them plunged down among the wounded waiting for evacuation. Plumes of smoke and dust enveloped the Junkers in its takeoff run, peppering it with grit and gravel. As its pilot struggled to retain control it lifted off the strip, winging away to the north, leaving its two fellows to their fates. As it cleared the ridgeline at the north of the field the next salvo fell.

At Luqa, Kuno and the Baron dashed down to the communications center inside the bunker. Kuno shouted to Steup as they raced across the room.

"Get me Ta Qali on the field phone!"

Steup spun in his seat and snatched a phone from one of the dozen or more cradles that lined a shelf on the wall.

"Ta Qali? This is Luqa!" Kuno shouted. "Do you hear me?"

"Luqa! Luqa!" came the shouted reply. "We are under fire here! Heavy guns from the west have the runway zeroed in. They've already destroyed two transports on the runway. Further landings are impossible until the guns are silenced!"

The runway and adjacent areas were abandoned as the shelling continued. Men all over the field raced for cover, taking shelter in the many dugouts, bunkers, trenches and bomb craters on the field. It became evident very quickly however that the shelling was specifically targeting the runway itself, not the broader area around the strip. While the two Junkers transports caught on the ground were quickly destroyed along with much of the most recently arrived supplies, casualties were amazingly low. Aside from the deaths of many of the wounded caught beside the runway waiting for evacuation only a few dozen were killed or injured.

After less than twenty minutes the shelling suddenly ceased. Germans and Italians alike paused to survey the runway. As smoke and dust slowly cleared away the two burning transports seemed to be the only damage done, but as the gentle south wind cleared the field the true scope of the destruction became apparent. The runway was heavily cratered with nearly sixty large caliber shell hits directly on the strip. No section of runway was ignored. The British had methodically worked the barrage from the south end of the runway to the north, leaving dozens of craters, some as large as forty feet in diameter and ten feet deep. It might be days before Ta Qali was serviceable again. Yet the British had not had time to zero in on any other valuable targets at Ta Qali. To the east of the runway the German tank force landed the day before by the Italian Navy was making its way south, headed for Luqa Airfield and the expected attack against Hal Far. The panzers sped up to clear the field and were left unscathed by the bombardment.

The start of the shelling galvanized Kuno Schacht and Colonel August into action at Luqa. It was immediately evident to both men that the barrage must be coming from the sea and that Ta Qali was only the first target. The British would soon shift their fire to Luqa. Colonel August and his command team scrambled to disperse the Italian and German troops massed on the field for the scheduled attack on Hal Far. If the troops were not under cover before the bombardment of Luqa began there would be a slaughter.

Kuno leapt from the field phone to the wireless set and snatched the headset from Steup as soon he heard the news from Ta Qali. "Blue-two-one, blue-two-one," he called. "Come in please!"

"This is blue-two-one, Malta," the reply was instant. "What the hell is happening down there?"

"The airfield at Ta Qali is being shelled," shouted Kuno, dropping any pretense or formality. "It has to be naval artillery. The British are shelling us from the sea to the west. We need immediate air attack with all available aircraft if we are to save the invasion!"

<<<<<<<<<<<

"Signal from Flagship, Sir."

Aboard *Sirius* Captain Brooking turned and addressed the young signalman. "Read it, Marsh!" he commanded.

"Assume line ahead formation astern flagship. Prepare for air attack," Marsh replied.

"Come left ten, Helm."

*Sirius* eased in 600 yards behind the Flagship, sliding over her wake as *Renown's* main battery fired. The battlecruiser's barrage lifted momentarily as the great guns were re-targeted, shifting from the runway at Ta Qali to the Axis positions at Luqa. Now they thundered out again.

"Webster!" the Captain snapped. "Ready your guns. Jerry is finally on to us."

Commander Webster smiled. "Tumbled to us, has he, Sir? Wonder what tipped him?"

A chuckle went round the bridge. Captain Brooking smiled thinly. Webster was at his post on the bridge, the better to direct his guns in the anti-aircraft role with the coming of daylight. Webster had spoken quietly with the Captain before dawn. Ammunition for the 5.25-inch guns was seriously depleted. Of acute concern was the inventory of HE anti-aircraft shells. The air attacks of the previous day had bitten deeply into the main magazines.

"Main and secondary batteries, prepare for air attack," Webster said, toggling the switch on his telephone headset. "We'll get our initial bearings from the Flagship, but then we'll be on our own, visual targeting. Independent fire for all guns."

*Renown* fired again targeting Luqa with a full salvo as the German air attack approached.

"Aircraft bearing zero-four-five!" the port bridge wing lookout shouted.

"Main battery track the lead aircraft and wait for the order to fire," Webster said into his telephone. A mile astern of *Sirius* the tribal Class destroyer, *HMS Sikh* opened fire, her six 4.7-inch guns and two 4-inch guns popping away. The destroyer's bridge was blackened and twisted from the 6-inch shell that had struck her hours before and the ship was still being conned by her Chief Engineer from the emergency steering position. To watchers aboard *Sirius* the destroyer's fire seemed puny and pathetic against the mass of bombers approaching the fleet.

Webster waited tensely as the Germans flew into range. He gasped as the scale of the attack became evident. The sky seemed filled with enemy bombers.

"Main battery, fire!" Webster shouted into the phone set. His gunners anticipated the order and the five twin turrets barked out together. Once more *Sirius* fought for her life. *Sirius'* gun crews served their weapons frantically, feeding ammunition of all calibers, firing as rapidly as possible at the enemy aircraft. The crack of the heavier flak guns of the fleet intermingled with the rattle of the smaller caliber 20mm, 2-pdr pom-poms, Oerlikons and 40mm bofors. Above all these the 15-inch main guns of *Renown* sounded out nearly twice a minute as the battlecruiser strove to maintain the bombardment of Luqa in spite of the air attack.

This German attack was unlike any other the fleet had seen. Poorly coordinated, the Germans flung themselves at the British ships with undeniable bravery, but the pilots and their crews had planned a much more familiar mission, attacking ground targets. Not until they were airborne did most learn they were to attack ships at sea. In any event very few of these pilots had any prior experience on shipping strikes. One aspect only of the German attack reflected discipline and coordination. Every bomber bored in on the three heavy ships. The destroyers in the screen were completely ignored.

Yet the attack was massive and its very lack of coordination made the British task of defending against it difficult as aircraft dove on the fleet from every angle and direction. As the Germans pressed in to attack the British Force H came to full speed again.

"'A', 'B' and 'Q' turret," shouted Webster, "target: three Stukas bearing zero-nine-zero, 4,000 feet at eleven o'clock!"

The electrically driven turrets swung out with barrels pointed to port and nearly vertical. The six guns popped away in rapid-fire mode. Puffs of fluffy, black cotton candy erupted in the sky overhead. The Stuka pilots were bunched too tightly together, making a single, large target much easier to hit. *Sirius* knocked two from the sky before ever they could release their bombs. The third Stuka, riddled by shrapnel from near misses, hurtled down, diving on *Renown's* port side against the mangled wreckage of her port secondary armament. The battlecruiser's lighter flak guns joined in against the remaining Stuka, which made no effort to evade the deadly fire pouring into it. The bomber crashed into the sea a cables length from *Renown's* port side.

As the Stuka slammed into the sea a Ju 88 dove out of the sun, angling for *Sirius*. The radar directed guns of *Charybdis* and the remaining flak guns on *Renown* had all they could handle on their own and could do nothing to help blinded *Sirius*. With no radar direction of her own, *Sirius'* gunners were dependant on visual targeting. The Ju 88 came from a perfect angle of attack and wasn't seen until too late to stop. A stick of six 500-kilo bombs tumbled from the bomber as it pulled up out of a shallow dive. At the last instant Captain Brooking recognized the danger.

"Hard a-starboard!" he shouted.

Webster stared in horror as the bombs wobbled out of the belly of the German bomber before stabilizing in their flight and plunging towards *Sirius*. Almost it seemed that they were aimed directly at him, that some malevolent intelligence guided the bombs in their descent to seek out and find him personally. He ducked down behind the splinter shield and clasped his hands above his head, waiting for the blast to rip apart the bridge.

The cruiser rocked as the bombs crashed down in a hell of noise. Webster screamed in fury and fear as the cacophony of explosions went on and on. He was slammed flat to the deck by the concussion and bounced up and down on the hard steel plates. Something punched him hard in the sole of his left foot and he drew his knees up tight against his chest. A sudden deluge of seawater descended upon the bridge, drenching him, leaving him spluttering and choking for breath.

As the water flowed away to the scuppers Webster slowly crawled to his knees. From all fours he looked about the bridge. Water was still cascading down onto the bridge from the range finder tower above it. Others of the bridge watch were slowly regaining their wits as well. Captain Brooking staggered to his feet and leaned over the voice tube, gasping out an order. Webster reached up to grasp the rail and pulled himself to his feet. The thin steel splinter shield below the rail was perforated like a cheese grater with dozens of holes, some as big as a fist punched through it and with jagged, razor sharp edges. He staggered to his feet, but immediately fell back to his knees. He looked down at his left foot. A jagged hunk of blackened, charred steel was stuck in the sole of his shoe. He reached down and tugged at the metal and his shoe came off in his hand. He stared at the sole of his foot where the sock had been torn and punctured by the shrapnel, but there was no blood. Amazingly he was uninjured. He stood holding the shoe and the piece of metal and assessed the ship.

The six bombs from the Ju 88 fell close aboard the port side of the cruiser, exploding on impact with the water, peppering the ship with shrapnel, springing open a series of hull plates and deluging the weather decks. The port side flak guns fell silent as their crews clung to rails and stanchions to keep from being swept overboard.

At almost the same moment that *Sirius* turned to starboard Captain Daniel was forced to turn *Renown* to port to avoid a Stuka attack. The two ships were suddenly separated by over 1,000 yards limiting the support they could lend each other. It was a momentary advantage that airmen trained in anti-shipping attacks would have seized, but it almost slipped away from the inexperienced Germans.

Only the almost accidentally timed attack of a trio of Ju 88's took advantage of the sudden vulnerability of *Renown*. Stooping in a shallow dive from the east they came at *Renown's* port side. With three guns of her port secondary battery out of commission and the midships pom-pom smashed by an Italian 15-inch shell the flak fire they met, though still formidable was weaker than it should have been. Instinctively the three pilots spread out with the left most bomber targeting the bows, the center plane diving amidships and the Ju 88 on the right aimed at the stern of the battlecruiser.

"Hard a-port!" shouted Captain Daniel, turning the ship into the attack.

*Renown's* for'ard port pom-pom banged away. A scratch crew manned the octuple mounting since the rain of steel that slashed across the decks when *Kenya* exploded had slaughtered the regular gun team the night before. The loaders struggled to establish the rhythm of movement while the gunners and spotters were out of synch with one another. Nonetheless, the eight-barreled gun put up a terrific barrage of lead directed at the center Ju 88. The pom-pom was a notoriously inaccurate weapon in World War II, relying on volume of fire rather than any degree of precision for its effectiveness, but for close-in defense its blanket coverage could be quite daunting to an attacking aircrew.

With grim determination the British matelots served their weapon. Streams of tracers arced out from the gun, black puffs erupted all about the German bomber, but still it came on. Machine gun fire from the plane started to pepper *Renown's* decks near the pom-pom and one of the loaders fell, hit by a random bullet.

At 400 yards range the pom-pom fire was as concentrated as it got and the bomber looming up before the gunners seemed huge and impossible to miss. 2-pdr shells walked from the wings directly into the glass nose dome of the bomber. They shattered the glass and shredded the cockpit. Out of control the bomber nosed over and started to turn to port into a flat spin, still headed straight for the pom-pom. Its fuel tanks burst and exploded; chunks of wings and airframe spun away in all directions. As the flaming wreck plunged toward *Renown* the pom-pom crew dove for cover; all of them that is but the gunner. He held his weapons on target, firing steadily as each gun ran out of ammunition. The twisted, flaming wreckage of the Ju 88 slammed into *Renown's* aircraft hangar behind the aft funnel. Its bomb load exploded on impact, shattering the hangar and toppling the seaplane crane. Fire rapidly took hold.

The Ju 88 diving on the stern never delivered its bombs. The octuple pom-pom mounted atop the aft superstructure splashed it into the sea 400 yards to port. Forward, the last of the trio of Ju 88's roared over the battlecruiser's bows, dropping a string of bombs perpendicular to her course. A 500-kilo bomb crashed through the deck just feet from the hole left by the bomb hit suffered the afternoon before. Blast and fire weakened decks and bulkheads crumpled under the force of the explosion. Plates were sprung open in the bows, but with all flammable material in the area already burned away there was no fire. Heavy flooding began in the capstan engine flat, cable locker and other forward compartments and was aggravated by the ship's high speed, but the Captain didn't dare order speed reduced. Peter Walker's damage parties raced to shore up bulkheads and to limit the flooding as best they could.

*Renown* plowed on, her 15-inch guns maintaining their fire throughout her hi-speed maneuvers, fighting off one bombing attack after another. The fire in the aircraft hangar spread to the aft superstructure, fed by lubricants and fuels for the spotter airplanes. Once more a tremendous column of black smoke rose from the ship. It blanketed the fantail and temporarily drove the crew from the aft pom-pom position. Smelling blood the Luftwaffe bored in for the kill.

At Luqa, Kuno and his team abandoned their bunker, believing it would be a prime target for the British shelling. They had time to take only a small, short-range transmitter/receiver in order to remain in contact with blue-two-one. Running hunched over they dashed for a trench line two hundred meters south of the bunker even as the first shells fell on Luqa field. The Baron and his command staff were right behind.

Colonel August leaned close to Kuno and shouted in his ear to be heard over the crash of a salvo of four shells at the south end of the runway.

"This has the makings of a bloody disaster Schacht!" he shouted. "What has your Air Force controller to say?"

Kuno waited for the din to die down before answering. "He assures me every aircraft of our first attack wave has been re-directed to attack the British ships. He has no explanation for how the British got within range without being detected, but obviously the Italian Navy lived up to its reputation," he concluded sourly.

August sat back on his haunches contemplating the situation. Another salvo fell on the field, this time well to the east of the runway and clear of any troop concentrations. To Kuno it seemed the British fire was random or at least poorly directed. He had no way of knowing how much the Luftwaffe attacks against Force H were at that very moment disrupting accurate gunnery of the British.

The Colonel leaned forward again. "The attack is postponed," he said. "Even if the bombardment ends right now we won't have the Luftwaffe support we require." He paused for a moment before going on. "You've got to get the word out Kuno."

"Right," Kuno replied. "And that means going back into the bunker to use the field phone connections."

"Don't take too long," August laughed, slapping him on the back. "I'm going to need you later!"

The bridge of *Sirius* fell silent as the last of the German bombers retreated to the northeast. For over a half hour they dogged Force H, attacking from all angles and directions, at times swamping the defenses of the fleet. Force H gave a good account of itself with eighteen German bombers confirmed destroyed and many others presumed damaged as they fled the scene.

The stink of cordite drifted through the bridge of the cruiser as the bridge watch stood mute and dumb, stunned by the continuous crash of guns and bombs, exhausted by endless hours at action stations. Webster sagged against the port wing bulkhead, still gripping the telephone mouthpiece hung about his neck, his ears ringing. For once, thoughts of Althea did not intrude; they couldn't. His mind was numb.

A cloud of smoke hung over the water in every direction, but was especially thick forward where a black, oily column boiled into the sky amidships of *Renown*. Angry, orange and red tongues of flame leapt up through the smoke, towering above the mainmast. The flagship slowed and turned onto an easterly bearing, allowing the light morning breeze to blow smoke and fire over the port side, away from the fire fighting crews who were already at work. 'B' turret was still firing, hurling shells down on Luqa field, but 'X' turret aft of the fire could not be brought to bear. Only the two guns forward were active against the German airhead.

Webster and the others on the bridge stood horrified by the spectacle of the flagship burning. Captain Brooking broke the spell.

"Lookouts mind your sectors!" he snapped. "Guns! Report!"

Webster jerked his eyes away from the flagship and queried his gun captains. Moments later he broke the news to the Captain.

"Ready ammunition is nearly exhausted at all guns," he said.

"Well, get the crews on it!" barked Brooking. "We can't let Jerry hit us with our pants down!"

Webster moved closer to the Captain. In an undertone he went on. "That's not all, Sir," he said. "The forward magazine is almost exhausted of high angle ammunition."

"How much left?" demanded the Captain.

"We'll be firing armor piercing if there's another attack," Webster admitted.

"Signal from Flagship, Sir!" the starboard bridge lookout shouted.

The Captain left Webster and joined the lookout. "Read it!" he commanded.

"Fires out of control, can you assist?" the man said.

"By God, that we CAN do!" said Brooking. "Get the port watch fire fighting teams on deck," he ordered. "Get the hoses and extinguishers out!"

Striding to the helm he began the process of conning the ship in close to *Renown*. Coming close aboard a damaged ship at sea is always delicate, but when the damaged ship is ablaze the danger is magnified. It was impossible to approach *Renown* on her port side; flames fed by the stock of aviation fuel kept under the hangar were being fanned to her port along with dense, choking smoke. The exposed metal of the hangar was glowing red and had burned through in several places. *Sirius* slid smoothly down the starboard side of the flagship, wooden fenders draped over her port side to cushion her against the towering hull of the battlecruiser.

The heat from the fire was fierce, the bridge watch all cringing away as they passed *Renown's* aircraft hangar. Paint in the superstructure of *Sirius* began to bubble and smolder from the intense heat. The crackle and roar of the fire made conversation almost impossible. Orders had to be shouted to be heard. Fire fighting teams dressed in asbestos suits were already stretching hoses and manning the pumps and valves while *Sirius'* own portside flak guns were all abandoned due to the heat. Water began arcing up from a dozen nozzles across the gap between the two ships. Clouds of steam were added to the smoke and flame.

With just enough thrust from their propellers to maintain steerage the two ships sailed slowly together, the two crews battling the blaze aboard the flagship. *Renown's* 'B' turret fired steadily, but slowing from its earlier pace. The gun crews were tiring.

The set of the sea was from the south and while gentle it was still strong enough to push *Sirius* down on her larger consort. The two ships lurched against one another in spite of Captain Brooking's best efforts to keep the cruiser apart. Each time *Sirius* rolled into *Renown* there was a sickening crash with a dull thump that resounded through every plate and bulkhead of the ship. The battlecruiser's armored sides were thick enough to withstand this treatment for some time, but the smaller cruiser and her thin hull plates were not so tough. Soon the port side hull above the waterline was creased and dented amidships from the repeated impacts. Combined with the damage done by the stick of bombs earlier *Sirius* was soon leaking from a dozen points.

After what seemed an agonizing eternity to Webster the flames aboard the flagship began to subside and the dense column of smoke began to thin.

"The bridge, *Sirius*!" The shouted greeting carried across from the bridge of *Renown*.

Captain Brooking stepped out on the port bridge wing. Shielding his eyes against the sun he looked up at the larger ship's bridge. He was shocked to see Burrough there with his arm in a sling.

"Hello, Admiral!" he replied. "Beautiful morning isn't it?"

"Good-o, Brooking!" replied Burrough. "Captain Daniel tells me the fire is just about under control. He expresses his thanks, but wishes you would stop scratching his paint!"

*Renown's* forward battery fired again, momentarily interrupting the conversation.

Brooking cupped his hands and shouted, "My forward magazines have exhausted their A.A. ammunition. We'll be using armor piercing in the next air attack."

"Understood!" shouted Burrough. "We're about ready to get underway. We'll turn to the south to bring both turrets to bear." He turned away for a moment as *Renown's* X.O. spoke quickly to him. When he turned back concern was written on Burrough's face. "Let's move Brooking!" he shouted. "Radar reports a large return to the northeast. We have less than five minutes!"

As the two ships pulled apart and came up to speed they turned together to the south. *Renown* resumed firing from her aft turret even as feverish preparations for the anticipated action continued. Ammunition lockers were restocked at all the flak guns and aboard *Sirius* a human chain moved flak ammunition from the aft to the forward magazine. For the exhausted seamen it was backbreaking labor, carrying the heavy shells down narrow passages and through numerous watertight doors and bulkheads. They succeeded in shifting just eighteen shells.

"Signal from *Charybdis*, Sir!"

"Read it!" snapped Brooking.

"*Charybdis* says, 'Second air contact, bearing two-seven-five, range twenty-three miles. Looks like a one-two punch'."

"Two-seven-five!" exclaimed Webster. "Due west!"

Brooking turned to him and smiled. "The German gentlemen of Sardinia want in on the kill, Guns," he said. But he was only half right. The enemy planes did originate on Sardinia, but they weren't German. The Italian Air Force had finally concluded that if they were to be in on the kill they couldn't wait any longer to join the attack.

Captain Brooking shaped the course of his cruiser to fall in behind the flagship at a distance of 600 yards, close enough for the two ships to provide mutual support, but not so close as to limit his maneuverability in the coming action. *Renown, Sirius* and *Charybdis* were now on a southeasterly course, skirting the western shore of the island at a range of eleven miles. *Renown* resumed her bombardment of Luqa, the guns of 'B' and 'X' turrets trained out to port and firing regularly again.

"Good Lord!" exclaimed Webster under his breath. He lowered his binoculars a moment and wiped the lenses free of dirt and blemish. He was staggered by the array of aircraft about to pounce on Force H. From the northeast and the west two immense flights of enemy aircraft were bearing down on the fleet. Somewhere deep inside, his professional detachment forced him to admire how the Germans had coordinated the two attacks. They could not possibly have been better timed to swamp the flak defenses of the British ships. Over fifty bombers approached at high altitude from the northeast, strung out in a stream of 'v' shaped flights, three to five bombers each. To the west at least as many more were approaching at low and middle altitudes and spreading to north and south to envelope Force H. The two attacking forces would arrive at precisely the same moment, covering the sky in nearly a 360° arc with only the southeast sector clear of enemy bombers.

As the enemy planes closed in the guns of the fleet tracked round to target them. Desperately the destroyers raced to and fro laying down a smoke screen, hoping against hope to hide the fleet, to cover it and prevent accurate bombing, but Webster knew the smoke was a two-edged sword to *Sirius*. With her radar suite disabled the cruiser would have to target the enemy visually. The smoke screen would hide the hunters as well as the prey.

"Signal from flagship!" shouted the young signalman. "Maneuver independently."

"Very well," murmured Captain Brooking as if to himself.

"Ring up emergency revolutions!" he commanded.

"Emergency speed, aye!" The engine room enunciator rang back in acknowledgement of the command.

"Helm!" the Captain barked. "On my signal come hard to port."

"Aye, hard-aport," answered the helmsman crisply.

The pop-pop-pop of the destroyers' 4-inch guns was followed almost immediately by the crackle of their smaller caliber flak.

"Forward main battery track the northern target," Webster spoke into his telephone on the gunnery circuit. "Aft main battery, track the western group. Hold your fire for close in shooting and make every shell count!"

Webster shifted his binoculars back and forth from one group of bombers to the other. The western group, coming in low over the water flitted in and out of view, hidden one moment by the smokescreen laid down by the destroyers, flashing into view the next while the first aircraft of the northern force angled over in their dives. *Charybdis* and *Renown* opened up, almost together, their combined flak guns peppering the sky high above with black, angry blossoms of flame and smoke.

Webster withheld *Sirius'* fire. Without radar direction and with stocks of high-explosive ammunition desperately low he would wait for the enemy to come to nearly point-blank range before firing.

"Forward batteries, target three dive-bombers red sector, eleven o'clock!" he said calmly into his telephone. The six 5.25-inch guns swung out and up to port, sniffing the air for their prey. "SHOOT!" he shouted.

'Crack-crack, crack-crack, crack-crack,' the six guns barked out one after the other. Once again the stink of cordite invaded the bridge as deadly black flowers blossomed high in the sky above the fleet. From aft he heard the guns of 'X' and 'Y' turrets open up as well, but he had no time for them as his attention was riveted on the threat from the north.

"HARD A-PORT!" shouted Captain Brooking.

"Hard a-port, Aye!"

The ship heeled over in its turn just as the forward battery spat again. The three Stukas tipped over in their dives and plummeted towards *Sirius*; already their sirens could be heard screaming over the crash and crackle of the flak guns. A shell burst directly under the nose of the lead Stuka. It staggered, flames streaming from the engine housing and it tipped over on its starboard wing, breaking to pieces as it began to spin. The other two Stukas veered away, the pilots unnerved by the destruction of their leader. At 3,000 feet they released their bombs which plunged into the sea to starboard, well wide of *Sirius*.

"Torpedo in the water!" The shout came from the lookout on the starboard bridge wing. "Green two-zero, green two-zero!"

Webster spun about. The young lookout was jumping up and down pointing out over the bridge wing. "THERE! THERE!" he shouted.

The mid-ships pom-pom was hammering away at the enemy torpedo bomber flitting in and out of the smoke screen as it wheeled away after dropping its deadly fish. As it tipped up on its starboard wing Webster recognized it as an Italian Savoia.

"Bloody Eye-ties," he growled. Into his phone circuit he commanded, "Starboard secondary, shift targets, shift targets! Dive bomber, green forty at thirty degrees!" he shouted.

The bridge was bedlam now as the Captain shouted his commands in conning the ship and lookouts on either bridge wing called out warnings of approaching aircraft. The crash and pop of the guns, the roar of aircraft passing close overhead and the rolling thunder of exploding bombs were deafening.

"Hard to port!" shouted the Captain, now standing directly behind the Coxswain at the wheel and once more the cruiser heeled over sharply, turning away from the track of the torpedo. The Italian bomber disappeared back into the smoke screen, apparently untouched.

Webster pressed his hands to his earphones, trying to block out everything else and to hear the chatter on his gunnery phone net.

"Forward batteries report high-angle ammunition exhausted, Captain," he shouted to Brooking. "They're switching to A. P. now!" A curt nod was his only acknowledgement.

He turned to the starboard bridge wing to check on the dive-bomber coming from that direction when he was slammed from behind, thrown headlong from his feet. He rolled into the corner of the bridge, the wind knocked from him, gasping for air. A Ju 88, hidden from view by the smoke screen had dropped a 1,000 kilo bomb close aboard the port side of the ship, just abeam of the bridge. It exploded in the water less than twenty yards from the ship's side. The blast seemed to heave *Sirius* out of the water and back down with a jarring crash that stressed every rivet and welded joint in her frame. Shrapnel sliced through the air, ricocheting off the armored decks and sides of the ship. An immense fountain of water sprang up and fell back down on her decks, sweeping the crews of the starboard secondary batteries off their feet. As if some giant had blown out a match the guns fell silent. To add further injury the tail gunner of the bomber hammered away with his twin 7.62 mm machine guns as the bomber roared overhead. The bullets cut like a scythe across the starboard bridge wing, cutting down the young signalman and the lookouts there.

Webster pulled himself cautiously to his knees, gripping the bridge wing rail. Smoke drifted across the bridge and over the continued din of crashing guns and exploding bombs he could hear the cries and moans of injured men. He tried to stand but a weight held his lower legs pinned to the decks. He looked down and saw the explanation for how he'd been knocked down. The young signalman from the bridge wing saw the Ju 88 at the last moment and threw himself against Webster's back, bowling him over, saving his life. A bright stain spread between the shoulder blades where a cannon shell had snuffed out the boy's life.

Webster gently disengaged himself before standing upright and turning back to the center of the bridge. Captain Brooking was also regaining his feet, but his face and white tropical shirt were covered in blood. His cap was gone and his hair was wild and disheveled.

"Captain, Sir!" exclaimed Webster, shocked at the Captain's appearance. "You're injured, Sir!"

Captain Brooking looked at him, but only shook his head and reached to take hold of the wheel, steadying the helm and bringing the ship back under control. Only then did Webster notice the Cox's'n, still on the deck, his face torn apart by a six-inch piece of smoldering shrapnel imbedded where his nose had been. He looked away quickly and fought his gorge. The blood on the Captain was not his own, but that of the Cox's'n, dead at his feet.

"See to your guns, Webster!" shouted Brooking. "Get them back in action!"

Webster stripped the phone set from his head and dashed out

the port bridge wing and down the ladder there to the gun deck below, stopping first at the twin 40mm Bofors gun immediately aft of the bridge. Smoke drifted like the thickest London fog across the decks and the sea just a few feet away was nearly hidden from his view. The drenched crewmen of the gun were picking themselves up from the deck, coughing and spluttering. The gun tub still had not completely drained of water. He reached into the tub and hauled the pointer to his feet, manhandling him back into the gunner's chair.

"Get this gun back in action!" he shouted. "Move!" and then he was gone, leaping over the rail and down to the deck below where the mid-ships octuple pom-poms were also still silent.

The mainmast had been cut away and heaved over the side and the pom-pom barrels replaced, but the gun tub was still bent and misshapen from the crushing impact it had suffered the night before when the mast collapsed on it. Here, closer to the bomb blast he found the crew in much worse condition than those of the Bofors gun a deck higher. The pom-pom crew were drenched as well, but also stunned by the concussion of the blast. Every man had blood trickling from his nose or ears or both. Several were unconscious and one loader was draped across the gate of the tub. He'd caught the full blast in the back and though untouched by shrapnel he was assuredly dead. None of this crew would be back in operation anytime soon.

Webster reached down in the tub and stripped the phone set from the head of the crew's spotter. Whether the man was alive or dead he could not tell.

"Get the alternate crew to the mid-ships port pom-pom," he commanded. "Send a first aid team as well." With that he slammed the phones down and moved on to the aft Bofors. Here he found the team well on its way to recovery. The aimer was already seated in his chair and was training his guns back out to sea. The loaders and spotters were on their feet as well and ammunition was coming up to the tub from the magazine below.

Webster took a moment to scan the sea and sky. The smoke screen was thinning out some or perhaps the ship had simply entered a clear patch. The smoke parted and *Renown* appeared suddenly over a half-mile to port. He gasped. The battlecruiser was afire again, this time with smoke billowing from her hull abaft the superstructure. She was turned on her beams and seemed to be wallowing from one set of the sea to the next with no evidence she was underway. Her main batteries were silent and so far as he could tell so too were her anti-aircraft guns. He thought he detected a list to starboard, but couldn't be certain that it wasn't just the deck tipping towards him as waves passed under her hull.

In an instant the smoke screen closed down again and *Renown* was gone from his sight, but he was certain the great ship was mortally wounded. He hurried back towards the bridge. The alternate crew was at the mid-ships pom-pom, helping the first aid team clear the original crew from the tub and getting the guns ready for action again. He noticed now that several of the barrels were bent and the men were working quickly and skillfully to swap them out.

As he reached the bridge wing he paused a moment to catch his breath and to try to pierce the smoke screen again in the direction he'd seen *Renown*, but she was completely screened from view. He noticed though that the pace and fury of the battle seemed to have diminished.

Captain Brooking turned to him as he came on the bridge. "Well?" he asked simply.

"The port secondaries will all be back in action in a few minutes, Sir," he said as he picked his phone headset back up. A senior quartermaster now held the wheel and the coxs'n's body had been removed. The bridge deck had been hosed down and the blood washed away, but the Captain was still a frightful site, covered in blood and as he looked closer Webster realized bits of flesh and bone were stuck to the Captain's shirt.

Webster moved closer to the Captain and in an undertone he asked, "Have you had word from *Renown*, Sir?"

"No, nothing from the flagship since the smokescreen went up," the Captain answered, looking searchingly in Webster's eyes.

"The smokescreen parted for a moment while I was aft," he replied. "I got a clear view of her. She's stopped, dead in the water, beam on to the seas and burning like a torch."

Kuno popped his head out the bunker door and listened. The concussion of the heavy shells had stopped and the smoke and dust of the barrage were just starting to clear. An eerie silence lay across Luqa field. Even the omni-present small arms fire had sputtered out as if soldiers of both sides had called an armistice. The silence left a strange ringing in his ears.

Here and there around the field he saw heads popping up from bunkers and trenches like some colony of rodents warily emerging after the passage of a hawk. A few fires burned, mainly among the wreckage and litter of the few German gliders not already destroyed by the British before evacuating the airfield. There was little enough else left above ground to burn.

"Schacht!" The now familiar shout carried to his ears. He stepped out of the bunker into the open and scanned about for the Baron, spying him finally coming towards the communications bunker from the direction of the runway.

"Here Baron!" Kuno waved his right hand over his head.

Colonel August paused at the bunker entrance to catch his breath, turning and looking over the airfield as he did so. He swept his hand in a half circle to the south.

"We need to check our communications and get a strength return from every battalion on the field," he said. "I also want to hear from the Air Force. Is the shelling ended for good or is this just a reprieve?"

"Already under way, Colonel," answered Kuno. "Our communications have done surprisingly well under the shelling. One phone line to the southwest is out of commission, but I have a team on the way to find the break and splice it. So far, the various units are reporting only light casualties here at Luqa."

"What about Ta Qali?" asked the Baron.

"Casualties are also surprisingly light at Ta Qali," said Kuno. "But the real damage there is to the airstrip. I've spoken to the commander of the Luftwaffe engineer detachment. He says it will be at least tomorrow before aircraft can land there again." Kuno laughed. "He says that's if he can work the Italian troops like dogs for two days."

August smiled. "I have no compunction about that!" he said. "But if it is going to be two days before air landings can resume I may choose to bring the Italians down here for the fight."

Kuno frowned. "We already have nearly a thousand wounded awaiting evacuation," he said. "If the assault on Hal Far goes forward there will be hundreds more. Many will die for lack of medical care."

"The attack on Hal Far depends largely on the Air Force and upon whether the shelling is really ended," replied August. "Tell your engineer to work the Italians for now, but be prepared to send them south on short notice. And get in touch with the Air Force! Find out what strength they have to attack Hal Far today and how soon!"

"Yes, Sir!" snapped Kuno. He spun on his heel and ducked back inside the bunker. His communication platoon was nearly all present along with a number of paratroopers drafted as runners and orderlies. Once again Tondok and Steup controlled the wireless, while Corporal Weiss and the other enlisted men managed the field phones. Corporal Weiss stood and handed him a handwritten sheet of paper.

"Here are the strength returns from the different units on the field, Major," he snapped. "Only the Italian Folgore Regiment has not reported yet. We've located the break in the phone line and are repairing it now. We should have the Folgore returns within a few moments."

"Thank you, Weiss," Kuno said. He signaled for one of the paratroopers at the door. "Take this to Colonel August immediately," he commanded the man.

He turned towards the wireless just as Lt. Steup peeled the headphones off and stood.

"Are you in contact with the Air Force, Steup?" Kuno demanded.

"Yes, Sir!" replied Steup.

"Well, what have they to say?" asked Kuno impatiently.

"They have delivered two heavy attacks against British surface fleet units west of the island," Steup said. "They claim to have scored many hits on three heavy ships, but the flight commander insists they must be attacked yet again to remove the danger completely. The third attack wave is getting ready to launch from Sicily right now."

"What forces have they available for close support here?"

"At the moment we are limited to a fighter patrol, Sir."

Kuno shook his head and checked his watch. Still only 0815 hours, but so long as any doubt remained that the shelling might resume or the Air Force was unable to provide air support the attack against Hal Far could not proceed. He turned to summon another orderly, but Corporal Weiss interrupted him.

"Major, there is further word from Ta Qali," he said.

"Yes, what is it, Weiss," Kuno growled.

"Ta Qali reports twenty-one of our panzers have passed the south end of the field and are on their way here."

"I must find the Colonel," said Kuno.


As the destroyer smoke screen slowly cleared the damage to *Renown* became evident. Fires raged out of control in her after hull, a towering column of black, oily smoke rose into the sky and she lay stopped in the water, her engines snuffed out. Less than ten minutes after the last bomber fled, leaving only a single aircraft hovering outside flak range, flags ran up on the battlecruiser announcing the decision to abandon her and requesting *Sirius* and *Charybdis* to come along side to take off survivors.

"Make a signal to the flagship," said Captain Brooking. "My port side plates are sprung, will come along your port side."

A moment later the signal was acknowledged.

"All right, every one lively now," snapped Brooking. The blood and gore on his shirt had started to dry and harden, which somehow made it even more ghastly. "We haven't much time before the bombers return to finish the job. We've to get alongside, take off the crew and get away again before then else we'll be a sitting duck."

In a series of clipped commands Brooking conned the ship up from behind the battlecruiser, crossing her wake and sliding along her port rail, putting *Sirius'* mostly undamaged starboard side next to *Renown,* moving past the blaze at her stern, coming alongside amidships. At the same time *Charybdis* pulled up to the starboard side of the battlecruiser.

The heat from the flames was not as intense as Webster might have expected. Unlike the earlier blaze this was still largely a between decks fire and had not yet erupted out onto the open weather decks. Spots in the after superstructure glowed red from the heat of the flame within and damage control parties were playing water from their three-inch hoses on the hot spots, but there was no effort or plan to extinguish the fires, only to keep them at bay while the ship was evacuated. *Renown's* after engine rooms were torn apart by a 500-kilo bomb dropped straight down the after smokestack, igniting the fires and sealing the great ship's fate. Unable to propel herself and with her main electrical circuits destroyed, unable even to train her guns she was a giant rendered impotent.

*Renown's* rails were already crowded with crew waiting to be taken off, but there was no sign of panic. Officers and the senior chiefs kept order and assured no one was left behind. Fenders were thrown over the sides of both ships and as *Sirius* rose on each wave her decks were nearly flush with *Renown's*. With each set of waves dozens of men made the leap between the ships. Wounded were handed as gently as could be from one ship to the other, whenever the waves brought the two ships especially close. From time to time the ships crashed together, splintering the fenders and denting *Sirius'* sides. On such occasions some of the most amazing transfers took place, with seamen literally stepping from one ship to the other with as little fuss as stepping off a train at Victoria Station.

Webster watched the operation nervously from the bridge of *Sirius*. He could see the masts and upper superstructure of *Charybdis* bobbing up and down on the other side of the battlecruiser, but could see little of the evacuation on that side. The transfer, especially of the wounded seemed to take forever and there were hundreds still aboard *Renown*. With every passing minute the danger of renewed air attack grew.

Captain Brooking came up behind him. "Get down there and lend a hand, Guns," he ordered calmly. "See if you can speed things up any. Pull men from the port watch to help the starboard side if needed. We've got to get away from here!"

"Yes, Sir!" Webster replied. Once more he stripped off his headset and left the bridge, this time out the starboard side wing and down the ladder to the mid-ships deck. Now he was looking up to the decks of *Renown*, the battlecruiser's big bluff side towering over him at one moment, drawing almost even the next as the two ships bobbed side by side on the waves. There was little he found he could do to help or hurry the operation. Teams of seamen lined the rails of *Sirius*, grabbing the evacuees from *Renown* as they leapt between ships, dozens every minute. Most were quickly and efficiently directed out of the way, while the wounded were gently, even tenderly carried below decks by seamen and stokers who'd seen little enough tenderness in their own lives. Webster marveled that such men came from the slums and tenements of the cities, wondered for the thousandth time how Britain came to have them.

He watched as a group of four stokers, distinguished by their soot begrimed faces and clothes stepped over *Renown's* rail. They stood facing outboard, gripping the rail behind their backs and with their heels barely in the scuppers as *Sirius* rose to meet them. They timed it perfectly and the four together stepped aboard *Sirius* with a nonchalance that brought a thunderous cheer from watchers on both ships.

One of the men bowed low, then reached in his pocket. Fishing up a coin he pressed it into the hands of a young lad of *Sirius'* starboard watch.

"Table for four, my good man," he deadpanned in a high twit accent that carried the length of the mid-ships deck. Webster had to laugh with the others who witnessed the tableau. The four were led away from the rail to make room for the next arrivals.

The evacuation was going smoothly, all too smoothly so perhaps the tragedy was inevitable, but as *Sirius* rose on a wave a row of men aboard *Renown* prepared to jump. They'd gauged the two ships' motion carefully and timed their leaps to land on the smaller cruiser just as her decks reached their highest point. A group of ten men leapt almost together, but just as they were committed to the jump some fluke of the sea, perhaps a cross set of waves conspired to cut-off *Sirius'* rise by at least five feet. Worse, she tipped to port, away from *Renown* and the gap between the two ships suddenly and unexpectedly grew to almost fifteen feet.

With startled cries the jumpers lunged for *Sirius* and the hands waiting to pull them to safety. Four of them made the jump cleanly if narrowly, landing with their feet barely on deck and two others were grabbed about the arms and shoulders and hauled aboard after smacking knees and thighs painfully against the ship's side, but the last four were not so fortunate. They slipped through the grasp of the men at the rail and plunged into the water between the ships.

Webster and many others jumped to the rail and stared down at the floundering sailors. One bobbed back up, sputtering and coughing and looked directly in Webster's eyes for an instant before turning to look at the solid steel sides of the canyon he had fallen into.

"Get lines to those men!" shouted Captain Brooking from the bridge rail where he'd witnessed the accident.

Even before he'd shouted the command, ropes were flying down to the men in the water. Dozens of strong arms stood ready to heave as soon as the swimmers grasped the ropes. But there was no time. As if with some sort of vicious malice and in compensation of the set of waves that had thrown the two ships so suddenly apart the sea just as suddenly brought them back together again, crashing *Sirius* against the side of the larger ship in a grinding collision that smashed the remnants of the fenders and sent a teeth jarring groan through the cruiser's decks and plates. She seemed to hang there, suspended, pressed against *Renown's* side by an invisible hand determined to rub right through her thin skin.

No one aboard *Renown* seized this perfect opportunity to step across to *Sirius*. All stood transfixed, dreading and yet knowing what would be revealed when the two ships parted.

Finally, after a breathless age *Sirius* wallowed away from *Renown*. Webster closed his eyes and turned away from the obscene froth on the surface, all that remained of the four men so alive just seconds earlier.

"Move lively now!" The shout came from behind and above him. Webster turned and marveled at the calm of Captain Brooking, focused on the lives that might yet be saved, ruthlessly pushing aside thoughts of those for whom no hope remained.

On the next wave set the jumpers resumed and Webster could see that many fewer were waiting to make the leap. Mostly only officers remained with the few seamen of the damage parties still fighting the fires from above decks. Looking up to the port side bridge wing of *Renown* he saw the bridge watch finally making its way down the ladders to the 'tween decks area. The signalmen and lookouts led the way followed by the junior officers of the watch.

From the mainyard he saw the Admiral's flag lowered and hastily stowed. He realized Admiral Burrough and his party was going aboard *Charybdis*. With her radar suite intact she made a much more suitable flagship than did *Sirius*.

There were still a dozen or so men of the damage parties waiting at *Renown's* rail when a tumult of shouting erupted from

*Charybdis* followed almost immediately by her Action Stations Alarm. Webster felt the engines begin to beat beneath his feet and *Sirius* began to inch away from *Renown*.

"Come on you lot!" Webster shouted at the men still aboard the battlecruiser. "Jump for your lives!"

The last men waiting to abandon ship made running starts and one after another they hurdled the gap as *Sirius* pulled away. Several of them landed awkwardly, twisting knees and ankles, but all were aboard before Captain Brooking shaped his course to take the two ships apart. As the gap between the ships widened flames at last broke out on deck from the ventilator hoods on the battlecruiser.

"Commander Webster to the bridge, please," the Tannoy squawked.

When he arrived Webster found *Sirius'* bridge watch standing silent, as though struck dumb by what they had seen. None could blame them if this were true. For nearly thirty hours the men had stood to action stations without a break and in that time they had witnessed death and destruction to last any man a lifetime. Ship after ship of Force H and its escort was sunk or damaged, battered by U-boats, the guns of the Italian fleet and most especially by a continuous rain of bombs and torpedoes dropped from the sky. Now the two surviving cruisers stood by as one of the destroyers prepared what for many was to be the crowning indignity, the most awful loss of them all. *HMS Eskimo* was to sink the flagship *HMS Renown* with torpedoes.

*Sirius* and *Charybdis* and each of the remaining destroyers including *Eskimo* were crowded, no, were jammed with survivors of other ships. Over 500 survivors from the battlecruiser's complement of 1200 filled every nook and space below decks of *Sirius*. Her sickbay overflowed to the wardroom and overflowed again to the mess decks and to the ordinary seamen's berthing compartments with her own wounded and the wounded from *Renown* and her Surgeon Commander had his hands more than full.

Still among the survivors were many who, though exhausted, were uninjured and who volunteered to serve the cruiser that had rescued them. They filled out the flak gun crews and damage parties, served as added lookouts on the weather decks and as stokers in the engine rooms. Below decks nearly a hundred of them formed a human chain and began the process once more of shifting a few of the remaining HE shells from aft to forward magazines.

*Sirius* and *Charybdis* moved away a mile to the south of *Renown* as soon as the last of her crew were taken off. The battlecruiser continued to wallow, slowly settling on her port beam and dead in the water as the fires aboard caught hold. From near the stern to just forward of the shattered 'A' turret angry tongues of red and orange were breaking through the base of the clouds of boiling, black smoke that once again towered into the sky.

Captain Brooking watched the battlecruiser die from the port bridge wing of *Sirius*. Several of the doomed ship's crew took places on the bridge as lookouts. Tears streamed down the chubby cheeks of one young rating. Webster judged his age at no more than eighteen, perhaps only sixteen.

"How long did you serve aboard *Renown*, son?" asked Webster.

The young boy sniffed and wiped his sleeve across his nose and eyes.

"I joined in January, Sir," he said, stifling a sob. He gave Webster a sidewise glance. "I'm sorry, Sir," he said. "I haven't cried since me mum passed."

"All right," said Webster gently. "But dry your eyes now. You've a job to do."

"Yes, Sir!" the boy snapped. He wiped his eyes again and made a great show of focusing on his sector.

Webster moved away from the boy a few feet and watched as *Eskimo* made her run to launch her torpedoes. She approached the stricken heavy ship from the south at a leisurely fifteen-knot speed. Turning to starboard as the range closed to under 1000 yards her 21-inch torpedo launchers mounted just behind the aft smokestack swung out over the port side. A puff of steam erupted from the launcher and the first of the torpedoes was ejected over the side. It was quickly followed by three more as *Eskimo* emptied all four launchers into the sea. The destroyer continued her turn to starboard as the deadly fish sped towards their target. Captain Brooking came and stood beside him as Webster watched the dreadful tableau.

"Pray God, *Eskimo* makes it a clean business," murmured Brooking under his breath.

"Yes, Sir," Webster nodded. "Nothing worse than having to go back and hit her again."

At that moment the first of the torpedoes struck *Renown*. A great waterspout shot into the sky against her stern, towering over the after turret and superstructure. It was followed a brief second later by the sound of the explosion reverberating across the sea. The spout had not settled when the second fish struck. One after another all four torpedoes slammed into *Renown*, spread evenly down her starboard side. As the waterspouts settled back the tons of seawater momentarily quenched the fires and the curtain of smoke and haze parted to give a clear view of the battlecruiser. Tiredly she hung for a moment, poised between life and death, then with increasing speed she rolled, beam on to her starboard side, settling lower in the water as thousands of tons of seawater flooded her compartments. The tall superstructure smacked flat against the sea as she fell over on her side and for a moment slowed her death. But nothing could stop it now. She resumed her roll, exposing the hole in her port side torpedo blister from the hit she'd taken from the HE 111 only the day before, and then her barnacle encrusted bottom rolled into view, glistening in the morning light, as rivers of water flowed off her. She settled straight down in the water and then was gone, the last sight of her the flat rudder and four great screws, stilled now for the last time as she began her final journey, to lie forever on the bottom of the sea.

The bridge of *Sirius* was silent, save for the muffled sobs from the boy.

"Signal from *Charybdis*, Sir," said Marsh, the signalman softly.

Brooking turned to him, but said nothing, waiting expectantly.

"A single word, Sir," the signalman said. "Ammunition."

Brooking turned to Webster. "What is the state of the ammunition supply, Guns?" he asked.

"The main battery has no more than five rounds per gun of HE, Sir," reported Webster. "We're shifting thirty rounds from aft to forward now. The secondary batteries are a little better off, but not much. Another all-out attack and we'll be scraping the bottom of the barrel on all anti-aircraft shells."

Brooking nodded thoughtfully and turned back to the signalman. "Signal the flagship," he said. "A.A. nearly exhausted. A.P. plentiful." He turned back to Webster. "For all the good

Armor Piercing will do us now."

A moment later the new flagship replied. "Load with A.P. for parting gesture," the signalman read the flickering Aldis lamp. "Shape course southeast for Alex."

"Acknowledge," ordered Brooking. He turned to Webster. "That's it then," he said. "We'll swing round the island to the southeast and target the southernmost German positions with armor piercing as we go by."

"Then run all out for Alexandria," observed Webster, an empty feeling in the pit of his stomach.

"Not much else can be done now," replied the Captain. Once again Webster marveled at his cool. "As he said," Brooking went on, nodding across the water to *Charybdis,* "shelling Jerry with armor piercing is little more than a gesture. *Charybdis* and the destroyers must be equally short of H.E. We'll need every round of it if we're to reach safety."

The battered remnants of Force H staggered south and east along the Maltese coastline on a course to bring the 5.25-inch guns of *Sirius* and the 4.5-inch guns of *Charybdis* in range of Luqa field. Leading the reduced fleet was *HMS Eskimo*, with *Wanderer* and *Verdun* to port and starboard and *Charybdis* and *Sirius* in line behind. *Wolsey* and *Vansittart* took up position on the flanks with *Vanquisher, Wishart* and *Sikh* bringing up the rear. These last three along with *Sirius* all showed clear evidence of the damage they had sustained, with burnt and twisted superstructures, holed and dented hulls and in the case of *Wishart,* a thin sheen of oil trailing away behind her.

Aboard *Sirius* the Navigator poked his head out the charthouse door. "We'll be in range of Luqa airfield in two minutes, Sir," he reported to the Captain.

"Very well," replied Captain Brooking. To Webster he said, "Be ready, Guns. We'll want to pour it on in rapid-fire mode for as long as possible. I suspect we shan't be able to turn about for another go."

"All guns report ready and loaded with armor piercing, Sir," answered Webster.

"Signal from Flagship!" shouted the young signalman. "Commence firing when in range. Good shooting."

Turning again to Webster Brooking said, "Give them all the

licks you can, Guns. You won't have but a few minutes in range."

"Yes, Sir!"

Webster pulled his headset down around his ears and spoke. "Main batteries, maximum elevation to port and shoot!"

The ten guns of the main armament barked out in salvo, the right hand gun of each turret firing, followed a second later by the left hand gun. By the time the last gun fired the first was ready to shoot again as the armor piercing shells were lifted up out of the magazines and into the turrets.

Webster flipped a switch and he was tuned to the circuit carrying the voice of the artillery observer ashore on Malta. He waited for the report on his shots. After what seemed an eternity, but was really only thirty seconds he heard the observer.

"You're short of the field," the man intoned. "Up one thousand and fire for effect."

Webster turned to the Captain. "We're at maximum elevation and still short of the target a thousand yards, Sir," he said. "Can we move any closer?"

Before Brooking could reply the bridge signalman interjected. "Signal from *Charybdis*, Sir. Many aircraft, bearing zero-zero-zero, range twenty-two miles."

"Damn!" spat Brooking. "Come left twenty degrees, make speed thirty knots." He turned again to Webster. "You'll have about four minutes to target Luqa before you have to shift targets to repel this air attack. Make it count!"

Webster merely nodded his head. He was in direct contact now with the forward observer on Malta.

"I tell you we have exhausted our hi-explosive shells," he insisted in exasperation. "We have nothing but armor piercing left. We'll be firing those against the next air attack."

He listened intently a moment.

"We didn't come all the way from Gibraltar with no H.E.," he fairly shouted into the phone. "We've expended it against air attacks."

He paused again. A smile lit his face. "A bunker you say? That's the kind of target worthy of armor piercing. We'll be in range in a moment."

It didn't take long after *Renown's* last shells struck at Luqa field for the sound of small arms fire to resume its crackle and pop. Likewise, the Axis and Allied forces both resumed their preparations for what both sides expected would be the final battle for Malta.

British troops were busy stocking forward trenches, foxholes and bunkers with ammunition and with enjoying the first full ration they had been issued in months, Lord Gort and the regimental commanders agreeing the men needed their full strength to stand any chance against the upcoming attack. British snipers were also active, making it difficult and occasionally costly to their enemies to prepare themselves for the anticipated attack.

On Hal Far itself the RAF and Fleet Air Arm aircrew worked side by side with the ground troops, stripping machine guns and 20mm cannon from the many derelict aircraft on the base. These were rushed forward and sited to cover the northern approaches to the field.

For the Axis, the small number of vehicles in their possession were kept fully employed bringing ammunition, rations and weapons forward to the troops, German and Italian alike, preparing for the assault against Hal Far. The return trips were used to haul the many wounded, including British troops, back to the airhead at Ta Qali where the main aid stations were established and hope of eventual evacuation lay.

The delay in launching the attack did have benefits for the invaders. Six heavy mortars were finally retrieved from wrecked gliders at Ta Qali and brought forward with a stock of ammunition to Luqa. German troops were busy digging these guns in and preparing the ammunition for use.

With the damage to the runway at Ta Qali the stream of reinforcements onto the island dried up almost completely with only the trickle of troops still coming ashore from the Italian beachhead in the north, pushing slowly down the coast road towards the Capitol, Valletta.

Re-supply operations also slowed dramatically. With the runway at Ta Qali out of commission and the strips at Luqa subject to direct fire from the British the Germans were unable to land aircraft anywhere on the island. The German and Italian Air Forces were forced back to parachute drops and then of only the most critically needed supplies. The stock of parachutes on Sicily was almost exhausted.

For once, Kuno and his team were nearly idle. Aside from a modest fighter patrol over the island the air force was completely occupied in flying against the British fleet and the supply operation ran smoothly, if slowly. Kuno and his men remained in the former British air operations bunker, monitoring reports from the Luftwaffe on the state of the Royal Navy fleet. Both front and rear doors of the bunker were propped open to admit fresh air into the stale smelling interior.

Of all the members of the team only Sgt. Tondok had yet to show any ill effects of sleeplessness over the past three nights and Kuno detailed men off in pairs to catch some rest. Several of the enlisted men lounged near the field phones, ready to receive or relay any messages. Kuno himself spelled Lt. Steup on the main radio. Within minutes Steup was asleep, curled up in a corner of the bunker, snoring.

Kuno sat back, alternating between listening in on the Luftwaffe bomber circuit and tuning the receiver dial slowly back and forth, listening for any other signals of interest. He stopped for several minutes and listened in as the third wave of bombers started to take off from the Sicilian airfields and began their flight to once again attack the British fleet, then moved on, spinning the dial up and down the range of frequencies.

His hand froze on the dial as an English voice came through his headset, speaking as clearly as though he were in the next room. Kuno's knowledge of English was very limited, restricted mainly to a few words of conversational English and those he'd picked up in the soldiering trade. He knew for instance the English word for panzer was 'tank' and that this word had other meanings in English, but he was not able to follow the conversation until he heard the words "hi-explosive". His ears picked up at this and he listened intently, trying to make any sense of the gibberish on the airwaves.

No adjustment of the receiver was necessary; he could hear the conversation plainly, but could understand very little of it, other than the tone of the speech was heated or angry. A moment later he heard and understood the words 'armor piercing', but his blood ran cold at the word 'bunker'. Suddenly he understood the whole conversation as though it was spoken in German. He turned and stripped the earphones from his head. "TONDOK!" he shouted.

Webster waited tensely as the range to Luqa closed. The guns were all set, ready to lash out at the bunker commandeered by the Germans at Luqa. The forward observer fed the coordinates of the bunker to Webster, but these provided only a starting point for finding the target. *Sirius* herself couldn't be sure enough of her own precise position to fire blind. He would fire ranging shots starting with 'A' turret forward until he was on target, then fire the full weight of the cruisers main battery in rapid-fire mode.

"Should be in range again now, Sir," the navigator called from the chart house.

Webster stepped to the port bridge wing rail and lifted his binoculars to view the island, shimmering behind the morning heat waves. Tall, barren cliffs fell straight to the sea, blocking any view he might have had of the airfields or the fall of his shots, but he held the glasses anyway as he gave the command to open fire.

"TONDOK!" Kuno bellowed again, but for once the tough Sergeant didn't appear as if by magic at his side. The enlisted men near the field phones leapt to their feet as soon as Kuno began shouting, and Lt. Steup and the other sleepers were groggily coming round.

"Steup!" Kuno yelled. "Close up the bunker. NOW STEUP! We're about to be shelled! Alert any men within earshot outside as well!"

Lt. Steup stumbled to the front entrance. He pulled the door shut and stacked a pile of sandbags against it to hold it closed. One of the enlisted men did the same at the rear door. Kuno turned his attention to the field phones.

"Start alerting the regiments," he ordered. "Tell them we can expect to be shelled concentrating here at the north end of the field at any minute! FAST!" he snarled.

The young signalmen jumped to the phones; cranking the chargers they were quickly spreading the word. Steup stumbled back to the main radio and Kuno.

"Should we evacuate, Major?" he asked, stifling a yawn and rubbing his eyes.

"No time, Steup," said Kuno. "We're going to be shelled right here at the bunker with armor penetrating shells and it will begin any time."

Steup frowned and looked at Kuno quizzically.

"I'm not losing my marbles, Steup. I intercepted the conversation between a forward spotter and a British warship."

At that moment the first shell from *Sirius'* forward 'A' turret slammed to earth. The explosion was muted and distant, more felt than heard.

"Take shelter everyone," Kuno ordered. The men scrambled to comply. Kuno sat down beside the file cabinets in the corner of the bunker and waited. It was not a long wait.

"Up 800, left 400."

Webster relayed the instructions to his fire directors. Minute adjustments in the elevation and bearing of the guns in 'A' turret were made. The second gun fired then drooped back down to the reload position. He listened intently and smiled when the observer spoke next.

"Up 100, right 50 and fire for effect," he ordered. "All main guns fire for effect!"

'B' turret fired first, then 'Q', 'X' and 'Y' turrets in sequence before coming back to
'A'. A full ten-gun salvo hurtled through the clear morning sky towards Malta. Seconds later the eight 4.5 inch guns of *Charybdis* 500 yards to port and closer to the island followed suit.

The resumption of shelling on Luqa sent hundreds of German and Italian troops scurrying for cover again, Colonel August among them. He found shelter in an abandoned air raid shelter to the west side of the field just as the first full salvo bore down on the command bunker. Raising his head just above the lip of his bunker he watched as the eighteen rounds slammed to earth around the north end of the field and realized immediately the British were not firing hi-explosive shells. There was no blast above ground. Each hit dug deep into the earth before exploding. It threw lumps of earth and shattered limestone in a short diameter around a small crater, but did little damage. The Baron knew that with such ordnance only a direct hit on a specific target could be effective. As the second salvo tore into the earth in an even tighter group to the north end of the field he knew immediately what that target was.

Kuno and his communications team pressed themselves flat to the floor of their bunker, taking what shelter they could behind or beneath furnishings. The first shells seemed muted and distant, but each subsequent round seemed to step closer to them till each successive hit shook more dirt and dust from the low ceiling. The eighteen guns firing in sequence were enough to maintain a nearly continuous rate of fire, a shell landing every two seconds.

Kuno pulled a wad of bandage from his first aid kit and pressed it over his mouth and nose. He peered through the choking dust, trying to see each of his men, but only Steup was visible, curled up in the corner with his arms drawn over his head. Steup was slowly pounding his fists against the sandbags of the bunker wall. Kuno knew the man was on the verge of panic.

The shells walked closer and closer until a shell slammed into the ground at the base of the rear door to the bunker, flinging the door off its hinges into the room. Steup lifted his face to the ceiling and let loose an animal howl. Still screaming he leapt to his feet and started to run towards the open door, trying madly to escape. Kuno swung out his boot, catching Steup on the shin of his right leg as he passed. Steup dropped in his tracks and Kuno was on top of him in an instant, pinning him to the floor.

A second shell slammed into the bunker, this one over the central arch of the roof support beam, crashing through the beam and burying itself deep under the floor before exploding. Kuno's ears ached from the concussion. The bunker was rocked by yet another direct hit; sand began to pour down on him as the ceiling started to collapse.

The frustration and helplessness and the mounting terror were becoming unbearable till even Kuno began to wish for a clean end to it, for one shell to burst down upon their heads and extinguish them. He was struck in the small of the back by the dead weight of a pile of sand bags, knocking the wind out of him, leaving him with bright spots dancing before his eyes. He swam at the edge of consciousness with the roar of collapsing timbers and falling sandbags in his ears.

After an eternity of agony he was able to gasp for breath again and was surprised to find he was not completely smothered, though the air was thick with limestone dust and grit. He levered himself up on his knees; his broken hand and the stitches in his chest made him yelp in pain. The lantern had fallen from its hook on the ceiling, but was still on, casting a pale glow through the ruins of the dusty bunker. Peering through the gloom Kuno could see other signs of movement as his men stirred and struggled upright.

Beneath him he felt Steup move. Kuno rolled off the Lt. and sat up. He assessed the situation. The roof of the bunker had collapsed in several places, but surprisingly there was still room to stand. He reached over and gingerly lifted the lamp from the floor and lifted it to peer about the room, turning first to the radio apparatus. Another surprise; the dials and circuits all were still glowing.

He shook his head to clear the ringing in his ears and only then did he realize the shelling had ceased. He paused to listen intently, but his ears were still filled with non-descript noise. He swung the lantern around the room. The front door was partially obstructed by a pile of sandbags that had fallen against it, but appeared intact. The rear door entrance was completely buried.

He felt a tug on his sleeve and he turned to see Steup sitting up also and apparently speaking to him, but the words were merely faint gibberish.

"Get a grip on yourself, Steup!" he growled, but his own voice sounded as if he were underwater.

The two men leaned against one another as they stood and stared about the room.

Steup stepped away and over a table collapsed under the weight of dozens of sandbags. He stooped and helped one of the enlisted men to his feet. As the others slowly recovered Kuno did a quick headcount. All the men in the bunker appeared to have suffered minor injuries at worst. Only Sgt. Tondok remained unaccounted for.

"Check the radio, Steup," said Kuno. His voice was still strange, but was coming back to him. He turned to the door. Picking his way over the rubble and ruin of the room he began pulling sandbags away from the door. Several of the enlisted men joined him and together they cleared away the opening. The door was twisted in its frame and finally had to be kicked down from within, an act that brought more sandbags down from the ceiling, but when the door finally gave way a burst of bright morning sunshine stung their eyes. Kuno breathed deeply of the relatively fresh air that flowed in the bunker entrance. He stepped outside. Several groups of German troopers were rushing towards the bunker to assist. The now familiar white limestone dust of Malta drifted away to the north on the morning breeze and the ground surrounding the shelter showed mute evidence of the bombardment with dozens of pockmark shell holes in sight.

Kuno stepped back in the bunker and picked his way over to Steup at the radio. Steup was seated on a pile of sandbags with the headphones on, twirling the receiver dials.

"Come in, Blue-two-one," he said into the transmitter. He looked up as Kuno approached. "Nothing, Sir," he said, shaking his head. "The equipment all checks out, but I can't raise a signal at all."

"It must be the aerial," Kuno said. "Get the men to work finding it and repairing any damage. We MUST re-establish contact."

"Yes, Sir."

Kuno worked his way back outside where he found the haze clearing away until he could see the south end of the field again. A motorcycle with sidecar was racing up the runway towards him. The staccato chatter of small arms fire once again carried to him on the south wind.

"SCHACHT!"

Kuno waved to the passenger in the sidecar. Before the machine rolled to a stop the Baron stood and leapt out of the seat. He trotted the last few yards to Kuno and stood before him, smiling and shaking his head.

"You and I are of a kind, Schacht," he said. "More lives than a cat!" he patted Kuno's shoulder raising a cloud of dust.

"Perhaps, Baron," said Kuno dourly, "but Malta is using up my lives too quickly."

Colonel August appraised Kuno. His uniform was torn at the knees, cut from wrist to shoulder on his left arm and pinned back together, and slashed across the breast. Bloodstains soaked the uniform in a dozen different places and the stains had reacted by absorbing dirt and dust in muddy-looking patches. Kuno's dark beard which had required him to shave twice a day to be presentable in Berlin, now showed nearly three days growth. His face was smeared with dirt and a patina of dust covered him head to foot. All together he was perfectly filthy.

"By God," said the Baron, shaking his head again. "You're a soldier all right."

"What damage did the shelling do?" Kuno asked, changing the

subject.

"None, other than here at your bunker," August replied. "It was very specifically targeted to take you out. Odd the British didn't use hi-explosive shells," the Colonel mused. "In any case, what is the status of your communication equipment? Shot I suppose?"

"That's the good news," said Kuno. "I believe the only real damage is likely to the aerial. We can fix or replace it with relative ease. Steup is working on it now."

"Why do you suppose they stopped, the British?" asked the Baron.

Kuno shook his head.

"See to your men, Kuno," the Baron said. "Then get us back in communications with the air force. Find out when they will be done fooling around with the Royal Navy."

*Sirius* heeled over in a tight, hi-speed turn to starboard. The crash of the rapid-fire flak guns and the stink of cordite again filled her bridge as the third Luftwaffe air attack of the morning bore down against the pitiful few survivors of Force H. Webster braced himself against the turn, gripping the bent and twisted bridge wing rail with one hand, his telephone mouthpiece with the other.

The third air attack of the morning was in full swing with a force of Ju 88 and Stuka bombers attacking the survivors of Force H. *Sirius* and *Charybdis* had broken off their bombardment of the German positions at Luqa field at the last possible moment as enemy aircraft drew near and the whole fleet ran engines to maximum speed, complicating the task of the German bombers.

The crack and pop of the fleet's flak defenses roared out against the attackers, but to Webster's trained eye the fire was well below its peak efficiency. The men were exhausted. Gunners stared over open sites with sleep deprived, dazed expressions; loaders stumbled from ammunition racks to the guns, barely able to keep their feet.

Webster leaned out over the rail and watched the portside amidships Bofors gun crew at work. The aimer was tracking a Ju 88 as it skipped across the water towards *Charybdis,* two cable lengths away to port. The twin-barreled guns banged away in their rhythmic way, but the guns didn't track smoothly. The barrels lurched up and down almost drunkenly and the shells weren't on target as they had been the day before. The Ju 88 flew on, releasing its three bombs at close range across *Charybdis'* course. The second bomb plunged down under the cruiser's bows, riddling the thin steel bow plates with splinters and fragments.

Webster became aware that the Bofors fire had stopped. He looked down to see what had happened. For a long moment he could see no reason the gun had ceased fire, yet there was something odd about the scene in the gun tub, something he couldn't put his finger on. He passed a hand across his tired eyes, then with a grim set of his jaw forced himself to concentrate.

Ignoring the crackle and snap of other guns and even the roar of diving aero engines he stared at the Bofors and its crew. And then he had it. It was so obvious a child should have seen it, so obvious that a child would have seen it, but he was as exhausted as the crew and it took too long to spot the problem. The young loader, on the gun's left side, the stoker Carmichael who used to play the mouth organ - 'My God, was that just last night?' wondered Webster to himself, - had placed a clip of four 40mm rounds into the loading slot backwards. He stared at the clip, uncomprehending, uncaring as to why the rounds weren't being fed into the gun. On the right side of the gun the other loader stood and stared, holding his own four round clip, waiting for the boy to correct his mistake and reverse the shells, but he said nothing. Indeed no member of the gun crew said anything, not even the aimer; they all stared stupidly into space unable to summon the will or energy to fix the problem.

Webster cursed and stripping the headphones off he launched himself down the bridge wing ladder to the gun platform. He vaulted the armored shell of the tub and shouldered the boy aside, lifting the shells and turning them right. The clip slipped into place and the first of the shells dropped into the gun's chamber. The other loader snapped out of his trance and loaded the right side gun.

Webster turned and found the boy, seated against the inside wall of the tub, sobbing, with his head in his hands. He reached down and lifted the loader to his feet, hauling him up roughly by the shirt front, meaning to slap some sense into him, but one look into the boy's miserable, exhausted eyes stopped him. He patted the boy on the shoulder and led him to the ammunition hoist, guided his hands into the box to lift out a fresh clip, then turned him back to the gun.

He leaned close and spoke into the boy's ear to be heard above the din of the battle still raging all around.

"*Sirius* needs you now Carmichael!" he said firmly, but somehow kindly. "Your friends in the engine room need you to stay awake, son. You won't let them down again will you?"

The boy looked at him then passed his sleeve across his eyes. "No, Sir!" he said, a look of defiance replacing the stupid lethargy.

"Good lad!" Webster said, then turned to leave. He vaulted back over the gun tub's railing and headed back to the bridge. The Bofors began banging away again behind him. But he knew his intervention gave only a temporary boost to Carmichael and to the other men in the gun crew. The last full measure of mind-numbing, soul-wrenching exhaustion was on the men of the cruiser. Over thirty straight hours at action stations had taken a toll that a few well-chosen words appealing to the comradeship of the crew could not overcome for long. Yet that very comradeship was all the men of *Sirius* and the other ships of Force H had left. No high-minded appeal to King and Country or to the ideals of democracy could keep these men in the fight. Only their sense of obligation to their friends and shipmates would serve them now.

Webster paused at the base of the ladder up to the bridge, holding himself up on the ladder rails. He was as tired as Carmichael and he knew it. He closed his eyes for a moment and imagined letting go, just slipping off into blessed sleep. He snapped his eyes open when he realized he was swaying, nearly asleep on his feet. He started up the bridge ladder, though it seemed as likely that he could climb Olympus at that moment. One foot after the other he worked his way back to the bridge wing, stooped and retrieved his headphones.

He was about to put the phones back on his head when the faint but clear sound a Stuka siren pierced his exhaustion and snapped his head up. He scanned the sky, looking up into the sun and through the dense clouds of thick, black smoke once again blanketing the fleet as a screen. At first he saw nothing, only the blinding glare of the sun in his eyes and he silently cursed the damaged radar aerials that blinded his guns in these conditions. Suddenly though he realized that one of the black spots that swam before his eyes wasn't moving randomly in circles as the others were, but was moving in a purposeful line towards him and the ship. He forced himself to focus, just as the Stuka opened up with its 20mm cannon.

The shells sprayed into the sea just off the port rail, but the pilot quickly corrected his aim and walked the stream of shells right in amidships, hammering first through the midships pom-pom gun tub in a shower of sparks and ricochets that wiped out the gun crew and pounded the barrels and mounting of the gun into so much scrap iron, then moved forward, feeling its way to the 40mm Bofors gun mount he'd just left.

The bofors crew reacted and the twin guns started to spit out return fire, banging away directly into the sun as the Stuka's siren grew louder and louder. But there wasn't time enough to bring the guns on target, to feel for the Stuka and to bring it down or drive it off. 20mm shells walked their way through the Bofors crew, quickly, more quickly than the pom-pom, but the effects were no less devastating to the Bofors crew. They were cut down as by a scythe, in an explosion of blood and gore.

The Stuka siren was all Webster could hear now, drowning out all other sounds of battle. And then he saw the bombs, nose down, with their yellow-fused tips clearly visible as they descended through the smoke screen and angled like thrown darts for their bulls-eye. At the last possible moment Captain Brooking threw the ship hard over to port, and Webster nearly lost his footing, but he couldn't take his eyes off those three yellow-tipped bombs falling in a tight cluster that it seemed could hardly miss. He threw himself down behind what was left of the bridge wing splinter shield and rolled into a fetal position with his hands over his head and his knees pressed up nearly to his chin as the bombs plunged into the ship.

The deck bucked and heaved beneath him and he was bounced up and down, hard and in quick succession by the explosions and he immediately felt intense heat against his back from the first bomb. One-two-three shattering roars pounded him as the three bombs went off in quick succession. The first bomb plunged through the scuppers on the narrow catwalk aft of the forward funnel and into the stoker's mess, starting a fire there and in the adjacent galley.

The second bomb struck the hull of the ship just above the

waterline, plunged through and exploded in the 20mm ammunition magazine, setting off the small stock of shells that still remained there. Had there been a full outfit of ammunition in the magazine no doubt the devastation would have been much worse, but it was bad enough as it was, leaving a fifteen feet long gash down the side of the ship to just above the waterline, as if some monstrous opener had pried open a tin of peaches.

The third bomb exploded on impact just five feet off the port side in the water just abeam Webster on the bridge wing. It sprayed bomb fragments all along the port side, punching holes from the waterline all the way up to the trunk of the forward funnel and springing open the few undamaged plates in the port side forward to the anchor chain locker. The port side anchor chain itself was severed and the anchor splashed down, plunging straight to the bottom, a short five feet length of chain trailing behind.

A drenching wave of water fell back against the ship's side and for once the waterspout was a blessing, as it quenched a number of incipient fires and even dampened the blaze that sprang up immediately in the galley.

Webster uncurled himself carefully, sputtering and coughing, wiping the seawater from his eyes. His cap was lost, washed away by the wave and he was drenched from head to foot. He got to his knees and turned to lift his eyes above the splinter shield, but there was little enough of it left; just a shattered, twisted wreck punched full of jagged holes remained. He had no idea how he had escaped the splinters and bomb fragments that ripped through the shield and onto the bridge, but it was clear others were not as fortunate. Captain Brooking was still on his feet, conning the ship through yet another hi-speed turn and the quartermaster at the wheel was in control, but on the far side of the bridge a pair of bodies were sprawled out across the deck in unmistakable postures of death. Looking closer he realized the dead were the young signalman, Marsh and the boy from *Renown* whose name he did not even know.

On his own side of the bridge the signalman and both lookouts were still down. One of the lookouts clutched his shoulder and cried out in pain as blood poured through his fingers. The other two lay still.

Webster staggered to his feet, resting his hand on a thin section of railing that had survived the blasts. He yanked his hand back in pain. The railing was still hot from the bomb blast and energy of the fragments. He looked down and over the side and could see the torn and buckled plates of the ship's hull, jagged pieces of steel projecting out from the ships fresh wounds.

His gaze carried back to the Bofors gun platform just aft of the bridge. The guns themselves still pointed to the sky, but the crew had been wiped out. Men and parts of men lay in torn and bloody heaps with the gun aimer slumped across the mounting. It was impossible in most cases to tell which arms and legs belonged to which bodies. Further aft the pom-pom gun tub was just as grisly, with blood flowing out the scuppers and over the side of the ship.

A movement caught his eye. Something stirred on the Bofors gun platform inside the gun tub. A man heaved himself to his knees, shrugging off the ghastly remains of one or more of his fellows, then staggered to his feet. His back was to Webster as he leaned drunkenly for a moment against the railing, then, as Webster watched dumbfounded the man reached into the ammunition box on the side of the gun tub and pulled out two clips of ammunition. Turning he stumbled over the dead and loaded one of the clips to the left side gun, then felt his way around to the right side and loaded the other clip. The man was drenched and blood flowed freely from a nasty gash above his temple, but when he wiped the blood and seawater from his face Webster recognized young Carmichael, the man he'd spoken to just moments before.

Carmichael staggered to the gunner's chair and gently, tenderly even lowered the aimer to the deck, then sat himself down and peered through the gun sights. He wiped the blood from his face again and smoothed his wet hair back over his head, then settled himself into the chair and rested his hands on the trigger grips, peering intently through the sights.

Webster turned and looked out over the port side and gasped. A Ju 88 was in its final run against the ship. All up and down the port side of *Sirius* her anti-aircraft fire sputtered out like a spent candle, crews either killed and wounded by the Stuka bombs or washed away from their guns by the deluge that followed the third bomb's explosion. The Ju 88 attack was unopposed. Only Carmichael at the Bofors gun was in position to hit back. Webster turned back to Carmichael and opened his mouth to shout at him, to order him to shoot, but no words would come. He was still gasping for air himself.

"Why don't you shoot?" he breathed out, barely more than a whisper. Carmichael waited. The German began firing his twin 7.92mm forward mounted machine guns. Not as formidable as the Stuka's 20mm cannon they still sprayed lead across the port side of the ship, driving what few men remained there under cover.

The Ju 88 closed to point blank range before Carmichael fired, bang-bang, bang-bang, bang-bang, bang-bang. Eight quick shots and the Bofors guns were out of ammunition, but eight shots were all he needed. Carmichael's aim was true, the shells streaming into the nose of the bomber, shattering the cockpit and killing the crew less than a hundred yards from the side of the ship. The plane nosed up and incredibly flew on, roaring over *Sirius* at masthead height, its bombs still held in the bomb bay. The hand that would have released them was stilled. The Ju 88 nosed over two hundred yards to starboard and crashed into the sea.

Webster stared back at Carmichael, slumped back in the aimers chair of the Bofors gun, the glazed stare once more his only outward expression.

"Come left ten," Captain Brooking said from the center of the bridge. "Shape your course to stay with *Charybdis*."

*Sirius'* guns fell silent and as he looked about the bridge Webster realized that the flak fire of the fleet was slowly petering out till finally only a single automatic gun on a destroyer somewhere to starboard was firing and then finally it was silent too.

The captain picked up the telephone beside the binnacle and spoke. "Damage parties report!" he ordered. "Starboard side damage watch lend a hand to port side."

All through the action black oily smoke had flowed across the ship, but now *Sirius* broke clear as the south wind and her own momentum blew away the smoke of explosions and the screen laid down by the destroyers. *Charybdis* came into clear view on the port quarter. Smoke poured from her fantail and Webster could see men in firefighting suits attacking a blaze that raged there, flames leaping forty feet above deck.

A blinker flashed from *Charybdis'* bridge.

The young boy at Webster's feet struggled to his knees. Still gripping the wound in his shoulder he read the blinking Aldis lamp.

"Signal, Sir," gasped the young rating to the captain. "Withdraw at best speed, course southeast."

Brooking nodded.

"Both ahead full," he said. "Steer course one-three-five."

*Sirius* followed *Charybdis* away from Malta, beginning the long and dangerous journey to Alexandria, Egypt. The two cruisers and their retinue of destroyer escorts maintained high speed through the daylight hours of the 28th, putting many miles between them and the Luftwaffe bases on Sicily. As darkness fell that night the fleet slowed to a sustainable twenty knots. Exhausted crews finally had a chance to grab a few hours sleep.

Daybreak on the 29th found the remnants of the fleet passing through the narrow sea between the German held Greek island of Crete to the north and the Libyan bulge of Cyrenaica to the south. Once more the ships increased speed. Over a dozen German airbases lay within range of their course, but incredibly through the daylight hours no air attacks materialized.

In the early morning hours of June 30th the shattered remnants of Force H limped into Port Said, the northern terminus of the Suez Canal, the great naval base at Alexandria having been already abandoned by the Royal Navy. Wounded and survivors of other ships were passed ashore and fuel was taken aboard, but no time was given even for ammunitioning before the two damaged cruisers entered the Suez Canal. Roland Webster had time once again to dream of Althea as *Sirius* and *Charybdis* began the long journey for Durban, South Africa and a dry dock for repairs. Neither would arrive, but that tale is told in The Gates of Victory, sequel to this story.
>>>>>>>>>>>>>>>>

Ghostly shapes flitted through the murk lying like a blanket over the ground. One moment nothing could be seen but smoke and dust, then for a few fleeting seconds a group of men passed within a few yards and then were gone, always in the same direction and always without a word; only the clank or rattle of equipment, the scrunch of boots on gravel and the hoarse panting and coughing of men exerting themselves in the choking, suffocating cloud broke the silence.

Within yards of his position Kuno knew hundreds of men were sheltered in trenches and dugouts and among the field of tumbled boulders just to the west of the airfield boundaries. But he could see none of them. The men of the 23rd Regiment over whom he'd been given command and who now waited as the reserve force for the attack were completely hidden by the dust.

The British naval bombardment of the German positions on Ta Qali and Luqa airfields that morning was short, but devastating, closing down the airstrip at Ta Qali, preventing further reinforcements being landed. Worse, the Luftwaffe suffered serious losses in driving the British fleet away from the island. It took through the afternoon for the air force to gather its strength to bomb the British positions at Hal Far.

The time was 1930 hours, almost two hours till darkness. Or rather it should have been two hours till darkness. The sun was still high in the western sky, on its way towards sunset admittedly, but far from the horizon. Bright sunlight should still have prevailed across Luqa and Hal Far airfields, but did not. Instead a gray and shapeless blanket covered the southern part of Malta, blocking out the sun till it was just a vague, half-forgotten thing, its light a diffuse and barely perceived glow. Many who turned to the sky looking for the sun that day would never see it again.

The Royal Navy Air Station at Hal Far stood defiantly against the Axis invasion. Invested to the west and north there was still a tenuous connection via the Kalafrana Road to the built up snipers made the journey between the two remaining pockets of resistance a very dicey proposition for the British.

The Luftwaffe bombardment of the British defensive positions was just concluded. The sound of aero engines retreating to the north faded and then was gone, leaving behind a muffled silence and towering columns of smoke and limestone dust that merged as one and flattened across the ground, held to earth by the faintest hint of a south breeze. Under its cover German and Italian troops moved up to their start points.

Kuno stood outside his communication bunker, a kerchief tied round his neck and covering his nose and mouth and like every paratrooper on the field, German or Italian he had put his goggles on for the first time since he had landed over two days previously.

Even so, the smoke found its way into his lungs, the dust under the goggles and into his eyes. He wondered how the regular infantry, not equipped with goggles, were coping.

Away to his left he could occasionally hear a gear grinding, the roar of an engine suddenly revved too high or the rattle of treads as the German panzer detachment moved slowly down the runway towards Hal Far. In the near darkness these sounds had an eerie, spectral quality as though some ghost was wandering about in the neglected garden of a fog bound English manor house, rattling the chains that bound the forlorn spirit to earth.

The sound of small arms fire died away till there was almost none to be heard save for the occasional crack of a rifle or short burst of an automatic weapon. Even these few sounds of firing were curiously muffled by the blanket of smoke and dust.

Kuno imagined the scene on the front lines. British troops who survived the Luftwaffe bombing were emerging from their dugouts to this gray and shapeless world, occupying their trenches and strong points, scrambling to their guns, hoping to find them intact. Disoriented and uncertain, coughing and choking on the dust, dazed from the bombardment they crouched, straining to pierce the thick curtain of dust left by the bombs, trembling with the after effects of the adrenaline pumped into their blood streams as they hunkered in their shelters.

German and Italian troops surged forward, the veterans among them joining their officers and non-coms in urging the others to quicken their pace. They knew the smoke screen was an extra benefit of the bombing that must be taken advantage of and that could not be counted upon to last. Soon they would make first contact with the British and the battle would be joined.

As though on cue a machine gun barked out, the slow, throaty chug of a Vickers. It was followed by a flurry of rifle fire and then the short, sharp bursts of MP 40 Schmeisser machine pistols and the crack of stick grenades. The sounds of grenades were a good sign. They told Kuno the Axis troops had gotten very close to the British front lines before being detected.

Almost immediately the volume of small arms fire increased to a deafening din that even the cloud of smoke could no longer stifle, though it was still difficult to discern the direction from which any given sound came. Now and then the crack of light field guns was heard. Obviously the Luftwaffe had not silenced every gun in the British perimeter. Kuno presumed the British were firing blind onto pre-registered coordinates in hopes of catching German and Italian troops in the open. With a clear field of fire those guns could have had a devastating affect against the attackers, but under the current visibility he doubted they were effective at all.

He turned and walked through the gap in the sandbags – it could hardly be called a door anymore – into the enclosure that had been the British Air Ops bunker at Luqa. He strode purposefully to the tables set up in the lee of one wall and which held the wireless apparatus upon which the invasion still depended for contact with the outside world and the bank of field telephones that connected the bunker to all the various units, German and Italian then on the battlefield.

Lt. Steup sat at the wireless console, headphones clamped down over his ears, eyes closed as he listened to some erratic or barely audible transmission. Sgt. Tondok and several enlisted men, including two Italians who spoke German, sat in front of the field telephones, waiting for a ring. Tondok turned to Kuno.

"All assault units report reaching their jump-off positions, Major," said Tondok. "Nothing yet since the attack began."

Kuno nodded his head and stared at the field phones. Boots crunched on gravel behind him. Colonel August stood beside him, hands folded behind his back. The two men stood together in silence, staring at the phones, feeling the mounting worry and uncertainty. The smoke and dust were still so thick that nothing of the developing attack could be seen. They were entirely dependant on reports from the front lines being phoned in to the HQ.

Kuno drew a deep breath and turned to speak, to say anything to break the unbearable tension, but one of the phones rang first.

One of the Italians reached to pick it up.

"Allo?" he spoke into the mouthpiece. "Allo?"

The man squinted his eyes shut and pressed a finger in his other ear, straining to hear the report. After a moment he spoke again, babbling on for many seconds in Italian before listening again. He turned to Colonel August and Kuno still holding the phone to his ear.

"Colonel, Augusto," he began in heavily accented German. "Folgore say the fighting is-a very heavy, however they have broken into the first line of-a the British trenches and are-a flanking out the defenders."

The Colonel nodded his head and speaking slowly and clearly he asked, "What about the smoke? Is it clearing away yet?"

The Italian listened intently, watching August's lip as he spoke. He paused a moment, looking at the ceiling as he translated the questions in his own mind, then nodded and spoke into the telephone again before turning back to the Colonel.

"Colonel Augusto," he began again. "Folgore say the dust is-a clearing slowly. Folgore say can see about-a fifty meters, no more."

August nodded again. "Very good!" he said. "Order Folgore to press the attack forward aggressively." The Italian thought for a moment then spoke into the phone.

Kuno looked up over his head as a patch of blue sky shined through before the murky dust and smoke closed down again. Still, the air was noticeably clearer, with patches of brightness where the sun struggled to break through.

Within minutes reports came in from each of the major units in the assault's first wave. Heavy resistance and casualties were reported, but progress was being made all across the front lines as the British fought doggedly, then fell back in good order from one defensive position to another. Kuno and Colonel August stepped back near the front entrance of the bunker, looking out towards the south.

"I don't like it," said Colonel August. "The British are yielding ground too easily. They have some trick up their sleeves."

Kuno remained silent waiting for the Baron to think through the dilemma. The crack and rattle of small arms fire intensified, rising to a crescendo where all the firing blended into one long drawn out sound like fabric being ripped along a hemline. August listened to the sound for a long moment before making his decision.

Turning to Kuno he said, "Order the panzers forward. They are to prepare to punch through the British defenses then flank the rest of the line moving to the west. They must be ready to attack at a moment's notice! I want to wrap this thing up tonight." He turned and looked up into the sky. "There's no telling what tomorrow may bring," he concluded.

Kuno snapped to attention. "Yes, Sir," he said crisply and spun on his heel back to the wireless table.

As the sky cleared reports continued to pour back into the HQ. As before, the British contested every trench and dugout, making the German and Italian attackers pay dearly for every yard of ground gained, but when a position became untenable the British abandoned it, falling back in good order, taking their weapons and wounded with them. The battle for Hal Far was shaping up as a very bloody affair.

At their positions overlooking the Safi Strip British gunners waited expectantly. They'd been crouched down behind the gun shields for over an hour, ever since they'd emerged from their air raid shelters and taken up position with their camouflaged guns. Their legs were stiff and cramped, but the sound of small arms fire continued to move ever closer and none dared to stand and stretch. They were dug in along a line that ran just below the crest of the second low ridge separating Luqa and Hal Far fields and on either side of the Safi Strip. Cut and graded with backbreaking manual labor by Malta's garrison the gravel taxiway snaked around a limestone quarry at the southern edge of Luqa field through low hills and fields of tumbled boulders to the north edge of Hal Far. The British used it to transfer aircraft back and forth between the two airfields, especially when winter rains made the unimproved strip at Hal Far unserviceable. Now it was the only flat ground on the north side of the field the enemy could use to bring tanks to bear on the battle.

Automatic weapons rattled with a sudden increase in intensity. A moment later British infantry came scrambling back toward the guns, some men helping the wounded, others conducting a disciplined and orderly rear guard defense. Those not wounded dropped into trenches and foxholes prepared for them for exactly this moment. The last of the infantry streamed back, a few felled by enemy fire as they ran zigzagging back and forth. The dense clouds of smoke and dust raised by the Luftwaffe's bombing at the start of the attack began to dissipate, but the air was still foul with the stench of burning and death. The gunners pressed themselves lower behind their shields and waited.

They hadn't long to wait. At first a few dim figures could be discerned moving slowly out of the dust; crouched low and alert they ran from rock to rock, dropping prone every few feet to cover each other. These Italian paratroopers had learned the hard way not to rush forward too rashly against the British infantry positions. They were angry and frustrated at the losses they had suffered and at the way the British seemed to melt away from them just as they were about to be cornered.

Now the Italians came on slowly, creeping towards the British positions carefully, trying to pierce the lingering haze that hung in the early evening air. The British held their fire. For the first time since the attack began an hour earlier the sound of small arms fire was not continuous, just a rifle shot here, a short machine gun burst there. The Italians were tempted to believe the British were broken, but their hard won experience told them this battle would not be so easy.

Hundreds of Italians were now in evidence, some as few as thirty yards from the foremost British positions; so close were they in fact that the men of Devonshire could hear the Italians talking amongst themselves and while they couldn't understand the words they clearly understood the tone of the conversations. The Italians were filled with doubt about pressing on.

But after several minutes of indecision whistles blew up and down the Italian line and men crept reluctantly forward till the closest of them was just ten yards from the ingeniously hidden Devons. These British had endured short rations on Malta for months, done backbreaking labor keeping the air field at Hal Far in working order, they'd every one of them suffered amoebic dysentery, the dreaded Malta Dog, at least once. There'd been no mail for months nor did they know when or if their outgoing mail would ever be delivered. They'd cursed the Italian Air Force for keeping them awake at night and cursed the Germans for the relentless bombing they'd suffered during the day. They were lean and wiry and despite the short rations they had confidence in their inner core of strength; it had been tested often enough that they knew it wouldn't fail them lightly. Most of all though they were tired of being pushed around and they weren't going to take it lying down. With a cold fury they waited for the Italians.

At last, after holding his nerves together for too long one of the Italians could take no more. He fired his rifle blindly ahead, just to see what he could scare up. The result was more than he bargained for. Hundreds of Devons popped up from their hidey-holes and camouflage and let loose with a furious barrage of rifle and machine gun fire. The nervous Italian was cut down in the very first burst by a dozen different shots and dozens of his comrades quickly followed suit, till every exposed Italian was cut down or driven back under cover and the only movement before the Devons was the pitiful writhing of the wounded.

A hoarse cheer rang out from the British lines as their fire sputtered out. The Axis attack in the north was stopped in its tracks as the Italians fell back to their start point, the dry streambed of the Wied il-Qoton.

Kuno and Colonel August waited nervously for further reports to trickle in. The initial messages of hard fighting but steady progress were followed quickly by complaints of stiffening resistance. By the time word came that the Italian paras were stopped at the north end of Hal Far both men knew the assault was not going to be a walk in the park. Neither of them had ever expected it would be.

"Order the 293rd Infantry in to stiffen the Italians," the Baron told Kuno. The 293rd was a regular German Army regiment. "They and the Italians are to attack again. We must drive the entrenched British infantry from the northern entrance to the field in order to set our panzers free on the flat ground at Hal Far!"

By 2000 hours the second assault on Hal Far was under way, led this time by the fresh Germans of the 293rd Infantry Regiment, landed by air at Ta Qali during the night just passed. Like so many units in the German Army the men of the 293rd were mainly conscripts with a leavening of veteran NCOs and officers to hold their spirit together.

The Germans passed through the ranks of the shaken Italians and took their places at the start point. At long last the heavy mortars delivered in the gliders of the first wave two nights before were put to use. Brought south to Hal Far they now targeted the Devons in a ten-minute barrage that concentrated on the areas immediately adjacent to the Safi Strip. The final five rounds fired from each tube were smoke shells.

The German infantry crept forward the final few yards as the last of the mortar shells pounded down in front of them. Smoke and dust once again blanketed the area around the Safi Strip. Seconds after the last smoke round landed the leaders of the assault blew their whistles. The German infantrymen leapt to their feet and charged through the gritty, choking cloud.

British machine guns barked, fired blindly along pre-sited axes. Men cried out and fell to the ground, but the assault wave continued, picking up speed like a wave crashing against a beach. With a roar the Germans fell upon the British positions, firing at point-blank range and jumping into foxholes and trenches.

Up and down the ridge across a four hundred meter front the assault became a vicious and brutal hand-to-hand nightmare. Knives flashed and rifle butts rose and fell as hundreds of individual battles to the death were fought. The assault powered inexorably forward, the German troops possessed of a sudden blood lust to kill. The British fell back to the top of the last ridge separating the attackers from pouring down upon the airfield.

Here, Lord Gort held his reserves. Eight hundred men of the Devonshire Regiment waited, held in check by their officers, their long tradition of discipline keeping them from racing forward prematurely. The Devons waited until they could hear the labored panting of the Germans as they scrambled up the short slopes of the ridge. With a cry the British troops sprang up on their firing steps and poured a fusillade of fire down on the Germans. Caught in the open, unable to take any shelter from the murderous fire the German assault wavered and then collapsed, the survivors racing back the way they'd come, helping their wounded where possible, leaving them behind in most cases. As dusk gave way to night a terrific cheer erupted from the British lines. The Germans were pursued by taunts and insults as they fled.

Kuno and Colonel August waited impatiently for reports to come back from the attack, the Baron studying a map of the island spread out on a table. Soon after the first call from the front line it was evident that the second attack against Hal Far had failed also.

"We must break this line of resistance!" snarled the Baron, pounding a fist into the open palm of his other hand. "Schacht! Get the Air Force on the wireless," he ordered.
"Request a concentrated attack. Every available bomber is to hit the British forward lines. They are to concentrate the attack within two hundred meters of this roadway." He stabbed his finger down on the map, tracing the Safi Strip.

Kuno spun about and relayed the orders to Steup, who had

maintained contact with the Air Force throughout the day and into the night. Within minutes he had the reply from the Luftwaffe controller, circling above the island.

"The Air Force says they have eleven Stuka and three Ju 88 bombers available within fifteen minutes," he reported to Colonel August. "Or if you wish to wait one hour they can attack with twenty-one Stukas and nine Ju 88's, Sir."

"My God!" exclaimed the Colonel. "Is that all that remains of the hundreds of bombers we began this operation with?"

"Attacking a fleet at sea is apparently a costly endeavor," remarked Kuno softly.

The Baron looked sharply at him for a moment, then softened. "Yes, of course you're right, Kuno," he said. "Our flyers have suffered their share today, too." He turned away a moment, stroking the stubble on his chin.

Kuno and Steup waited in respectful silence and for once Kuno did not know what choice he would make if the decision were his. Finally Colonel August turned back to them. From the set of his jaw it was clear he'd made up his mind.

"We'll wait one hour for the heavier attack," he declared. "Steup, you are to coordinate the time and signal flares between the fly-boys and the front lines." He looked at his watch. "It is now 2208 hours," he went on. "Schedule the attack at 2315. That should give you ample time to sort out the details."

"Yes, Colonel!" snapped Steup. The Lt. turned back to his wireless and conveyed the decision to the Air Force. Meanwhile, the Baron turned to Kuno.

"Schacht, I want you to marshal the 23rd Regiment," he ordered. "Get them in position to follow right behind the Italians once the bombers have cleared a gap." He put his hand on Kuno's shoulder. "We must punch through the British defenses. If this thing drags on much longer there's no telling what the British may have up their sleeves. I want to wrap up Hal Far by tomorrow morning then we can turn our attention to the ports and the urban areas surrounding them. You understand?"

"Yes, Baron, perfectly," replied Kuno, a smile playing across his face.

The Baron von der Heydte returned the expression. "What's to smile about?" he asked.

"Something General Lorzer said," Kuno replied. "About telling my grandchildren about my experiences with the Luftwaffe."

"God willing we'll both bounce our grandchildren on our knees," answered the Baron.

Kuno set out immediately to round up his command. The 23$^{rd}$ Regiment was well under one third its original strength by this stage of the invasion, but its men had been held in reserve now for over twenty-four hours and were as well rested as any Axis unit then on the island. During the day Captain Thaler saw to it that the men were fed, minor wounds were tended and that every man carried a full load of ammunition and supplies. Canteens were filled from a well at the south end of Luqa field and the men were allowed to sleep when they could find peace between shelling and bombardments. Thaler kept the men close to hand near the abandoned British bunker appropriated by Kuno as his communications shelter.

Within minutes they were moving off in groups of twenty to thirty towards the south end of Luqa field. There they skirted the limestone quarry and the broken remains of a Wellington bomber that had skidded off the end of the runway and crashed into the quarry months earlier, abandoned by the RAF. They moved cautiously down the Safi strip till they found the crowded battalion aid stations set up by the Italians to treat their wounded. Kuno was there to greet each group and he ordered them off the road and to scramble up the slopes of the first ridge line, stopping before they reached the peak, hunkering down in trenches and bunkers left behind by their former British occupants.

Small arms fire was steady and regular, with occasional flurries, but with nowhere near the intensity of the earlier battles. For the moment the British seemed content to sit back and wait for the Germans to make the next move. As Captain Thaler ushered the last of the Regiment up the escarpment to their positions, Kuno checked his watch. 2255; twenty minutes to wait for the air attack. He moved off the road into the angle of a crumbled rock wall where the nearest field telephone was setup.

"Connect me to headquarters!" he ordered the operator.

Within a minute he was talking with Tondok.

"All is in order here, Tondok," he said. "Tell the Colonel we await his order to attack."

"Yes, Major," replied Tondok. "Hold for the Colonel, please."

A moment later the unmistakable voice of the aristocrat turned paratrooper came over the line.

"Schacht," he said. "Good luck to you again. I don't want to visit Calypso's Cave without you!"

Kuno smiled. "Thank you Baron," he said. "I wouldn't miss it."

"Good, good," the Baron replied before hanging up the phone.

Kuno turned and trudged up the slope, shedding the sling from his left arm as he climbed. He flexed the muscles of his hand and forearm, wincing as pain from the wound in his bicep flared. He ruthlessly pushed the pain aside and unsnapped the cover of his holster, making sure he could draw the pistol with ease. His broken right hand was useless, but he found that the pain in his left arm was tolerable. He stuffed the sling in a pocket of his jump suit to retrieve later. He found Captain Thaler where the taxiway cut through the ridge, just a few yards off the road.

"The men are all in position, Major," Thaler reported. "What are our orders?"

Kuno checked his watch again. 2309. "We're to stand fast for another six minutes. The Air Force is scheduled to deliver a heavy attack against the British. We should see a series of red flares at 2315. That is the signal for the bombing to begin. Thereafter we are to wait for the order to join the assault."

Thaler nodded and started to speak, but at that moment a mortar round thumped down behind them along the road. Kuno and Thaler knelt down quickly. A group of Italian medical corpsmen just had time to scramble off the road and to hide behind some loose boulders before a short, sharp barrage of ten more rounds slammed down, working its way north up the road.

Thaler waited a moment before picking himself up. "Ten minutes ago those would have hurt us badly," he observed.

"Yes," replied Kuno. "The British are obviously suspicious of this delay. Best get to your men, Thaler. It won't be long now."

As Thaler turned and made his way off the road a faint noise came to Kuno's ears. He felt almost as much as heard the sound of aero engines approaching. Turning to the north he scanned the sky, but though the moon was well above the eastern horizon and the sky was brightly lit it took him long moments to locate the source.

Finally, he glimpsed a glint of moonlight reflected from a

wingtip or glass canopy and then the shapes of the aircraft, barely darker than the clear night sky behind them. He counted fifteen aircraft, though he assumed others were outside his vision, and though difficult to estimate especially at night, he guessed they were around 2,000 meters altitude. Five neat 'vees' of three aircraft each skirted to the west side of the island as they began their approach, both to prevent the still formidable flak batteries around Grand Harbor from reaching out for them and to avoid being backlit by the moon rising in the east.

His attention came back to earth as a series of red flares arced out towards the British lines to mark the targets. Kuno couldn't see them, but he knew that great, colored panels of fabric were stretched out on the ground for the pilots to differentiate friendly positions.

Engine notes rising, the first three bombers tipped over in their dives. Bright flashes from the direction of Hal Far erupted followed immediately by the sharp crack of heavy flak guns firing less than a kilometer away. A dozen searchlight beams snapped on and probed the sky like alien fingers, feeling for the thin skin of the bombers, seeking to crush them in beams of dazzling light as great ugly splotches of smoke and fragments burst around the Stukas.

Suddenly, one of the searchlight beams passed over then snapped back onto the middle of the three bombers. The Stuka wavered in its flight, the pilot blinded by the intolerable glare of the lamp. Other beams joined till the Stuka was held in a cross fire of light, soon followed by a blizzard of tracer shells as the lighter guns, the 40mm Bofors on the field joined the barrage. The other two Stukas veered away from their companion, putting distance between themselves and their unfortunate leader.

A bright flash burst close aboard the lamp lit Stuka and it staggered in its plunge, tipping first one way, then another, then corkscrewing round in an uncontrolled spin, plunging to earth within the British lines, but hundreds of meters off its target and without ever having released its bombs. An enormous explosion lit the sky and rumbled the ground beneath Kuno's feet. The other bombers succeeded in dropping their bombs, but nowhere near the intended targets. Cursing, he turned and ran for the field telephone.

Lord Gort stood outside his HQ on Hal Far field, watching the German bombing attack develop. When the searchlights snapped on and singled out the Stuka dive-bomber he smiled in anticipation and when the Stuka slammed to earth just off the north end of the field's main runway a cheer erupted from the British defenders, clearly heard after the din of the explosion died away. He turned his attention from the burning wreckage and watched for the next German planes to attack.

The searchlights probed the night sky, feeling for their next set of victims. Companion radar apparatus controlled each of the lamps, giving them the uncanny accuracy that dazzled the German pilots in the first attack. Gort waited expectantly for a repeat performance, but the Germans were slow to oblige. It seemed the bomber pilots were not willing to attack against the spotlight beams.

"Perhaps Jerry has no stomach for it," Gort remarked to himself.

WHAM-WHAM-WHAM-WHAM-WHAM-WHAM.

Six sudden blasts rocked the west end of the field near the positions of two of the searchlights. Just seconds later they were followed by six more, closer still. Shrapnel from the blasts shattered the glass lens over one of the lights. It flared in sudden incandescence then died to a feeble glow. The operators of both lights scrambled for the safety of nearby slit trenches.

"Douse the lights!" Gort turned and shouted into his HQ.

The lights were already winking out over the field as their crews recognized the danger, but the German mortars had the range on the first pair now and they hammered three more volleys of 120mm shells down on the lamps. Both were turned into smoldering heaps of tin.

So began a deadly, three-way game of cat-and-mouse between the bombers on the one hand and the searchlight and flak batteries on the other, with the German mortars playing a Devils hand in the mix. Each time a bomber dove on its targets one or more of the lights would snap on, trying to pin the bomber like a fly on flypaper, highlighting it for the aim of the flak gunners.

The moment a searchlight snapped on the German mortars would shift target to it, groping in the dark and with only indirect observation to confirm the fall of the shells. The first round of this game went to the British with one Stuka knocked down and the other two knocked off their aim, but the second round went to the

Germans as two more Stukas dove on the Safi Strip, laying six heavy bombs down on target among the British positions on the ridge, winging away safely to the west and then the north for their return home to Sicily.

The British searchlight crews were wily though. For the next attack a searchlight on the east side of the air field snapped on, probing for the German bombers, but then, just as the first mortar shells were in the air, this light snapped off and another from across the field took up the challenge. It was able to snap on and quickly acquire one of two diving Stukas before the German mortars could shift their aim, holding the bomber long enough to let the flak gunners send it limping away, smoke trailing from its engine, its bombs wide of the mark.

Now the Germans tried their hand at a decoy. Another pair of Stukas began their dives, but veered away without dropping their bombs as soon as the lights began to close in on them. The mortars found and destroyed another searchlight while a trio of Ju 88's swept in at low altitude, skipping over the tops of the broken ground to the west of the field, roaring directly over the front-line defenses of the British and pounding the Safi Strip target. Streams of tracers trailed after the bombers, but they all escaped without evident harm.

And so it went, with the British desperately fighting to stave off the attacks of the bombers, the Germans determined to press the attacks home, and with the mortars picking off the searchlights one-by-one. Attrition slowly told for the Germans until finally every searchlight on the airfield was destroyed or damaged and knocked out of commission, but the British tactic achieved much for the defenders. The Germans were unable to deliver a concentrated attack and a great many of theirs bombs went astray. In addition, the timing of the attack plan was thrown off. Kuno and Colonel August had hoped for the air attack to be delivered in a span of some twenty minutes, but in the event it took nearly an hour for the last of the aircraft to drop its bombs. With three bombers shot down and several others damaged the last of the German aircraft escaped to the north at 0010 hours the morning of June 29th, 1942. The invasion of Malta was in its fourth day and the issue still hung in the balance.

As the smoke from the final bombing runs drifted across the

battlefield the Italian and German infantry, already blooded on the Safi Strip formed up for another try. Kuno observed these men closely as they moved up for the attack. He was heartened to see a steely gleam in their eyes as they moved off into the moonlit night towards the British lines.

Moments later the sound of small arms fire began to pick up. Kuno nodded to the field phone operator who put the call through to the HQ.

"Major Schacht here, let me speak to the Colonel," he said tersely.

"Schacht!" The Colonel's voice responded after the slightest delay. "Has the assault begun?" Kuno cupped his broken right hand over one ear and strained to hear the Colonel over the sound of firing.

"Yes, Colonel it has," answered Kuno, raising his voice to near a shout. "And as I'm sure you can hear the British still have plenty of fight left in them."

"I'm sending the panzers south, Kuno," replied August. "This attack must succeed!"

Kuno made his way back up the slope of the ridge. He found Captain Thaler where he'd left him, peering over the top of the ridge with binoculars.

"Not much to be seen I'm afraid, Sir," said Thaler, handing the glasses to Kuno. "Dust and smoke are obscuring most of the action."

Kuno took the glasses gingerly, wincing as he lifted them to his eyes with his left hand, struggling to focus the lenses without using his right hand. After a moment he gave up, handing them back to Thaler silently. He listened to the sounds of battle and strained for any sign of a runner or messenger, but there was nothing. He checked his watch.

Up and down the ridgeline German paratroopers lined the crest, crouched down to avoid the occasional stray bullet that smacked a rock or passed over their heads. To a man they were filthy dirty and unshaved since leaving Sicily. Many showed evidence of minor wounds, with bandages and slings in evidence on several men nearby, though in truth he knew few of them could match his own disheveled appearance. He scratched the stubble of his beard.

"Get the men ready, Thaler," he ordered. "Be prepared to move out on two minutes notice."

"Yes, Sir!" snapped Thaler. He scrambled away to inform battalion and company commanders.

Kuno turned his ear to the battle raging just a few hundred meters away, but almost completely obscured from view. Rifle and machine pistol fire predominated, with the odd grenade explosion. Now and then, at the very edge of hearing amidst the din he thought he could detect a human voice, crying out in pain or anger. Absent now was the sound of machine guns for either side. The fighting, he knew was at close quarters, perhaps in many instances hand-to-hand.

He checked his watch nervously. The assault had been underway for twenty minutes. By now there should have been runners reporting back from the action, but he'd received no word of any. The firing continued unabated; if anything the fight sounded fiercer now than when it was first launched. He made his decision.

"Thaler!" he shouted. "Two minutes! We move out in two minutes!"

Thaler waved an acknowledgement and turned to shout the word down the line. Kuno bent his ear to the battle again, worried now that he may have waited too long, that already the tide of battle had turned back against the attackers and the moment the 23rd Regiment could tip the scales was past.

As if to confirm his worst fears the heavy bark of a Vickers machine gun started up followed by a flurry of rifle fire. Kuno turned first to his left. Using hand signals he gave signs ordering a forward advance at double speed. Turning to his right he repeated the motion then waved the whole force forward. The paratroopers of the 23rd Regiment leapt up on the crest of the ridge and began pouring down the opposite slope.

As he ran down the slope Kuno drew his whistle from the tattered and torn remains of his tunic and clamped it between his teeth, then double-checked his holster, assuring free access to his pistol. Once he slipped and instinctively put his right hand out to brace his fall, yelping in pain as the broken bones in his hand ground together. But then he was up and moving again, keeping pace about twenty meters behind the lead troopers. Soon they were passing the bodies of dead German and Italian infantry, left where they had fallen in the first assaults.

As he ran he tried vainly to pierce the suffocating clouds of limestone dust that blanketed the battlefield again. The moon was almost directly overhead and its glow suffused the dust with a strange, orange glow, like a harbor light shining through a thick sea fog. Even on the steppes of Russia Kuno had not seen such thick, persistent dust. He couldn't see much more than twenty meters in front of him and the lead troopers were just dim shapes making it difficult to keep contact with them. He quickened his pace to close the gap.

He looked down at his feet as he stepped through an area filled with small boulders and stones in the narrow gully between the two slopes. When he looked up several of the men in front had dropped to their knees and drawn their weapons up. Breathlessly, he dropped to one knee and drew his pistol. His whistle was still clamped fiercely between his front teeth. With every breath he exhaled a tiny chirp escaped it.

Suddenly, out of the murk a man stumbled towards the paratroopers, staggering from exertion. Kuno lifted his pistol, prepared to fire, but the man passed through the front rank of paratroopers and none of them fired. A second later Kuno saw the man wore the uniform of a German Army private. He was clutching his right arm. Kuno stood and moved to block the man's path.

"HALT!" he ordered.

The private skidded to a stop in front of him, his eyes wide with fear, panting like a horse run near to death. He sank to his knees and bowed his head, gasping for air. Kuno saw blood trickling through the fingers clutched over a wound in his bicep.

Kuno gave the private a few seconds to catch his breath before speaking again.

"Look at me!" he commanded. The private snapped his head up and looked Kuno in the eyes. Discipline and training were still strong in him.

"What is happening in the attack?" he demanded. He glanced around. More paratroopers came to a stop, bunched up near the private, eavesdropping in effect. He waved them away and they moved slowly off a few meters. The private was finally able to blurt out a few words as he gasped for air.

"We hold," he gasped, "the top of the ridge." He shook his head. "But the Tommies have counterattacked."

Kuno didn't wait to hear any more. Putting the whistle to his lips he blew three short, sharp blasts, then signaled the advance to continue at the double. As the paratroopers scrambled to their feet he hauled the young private to his feet.

"Get back to the start point!" he ordered. "Tell them Major Schacht orders the panzers forward!" He made the young man repeat his instructions then propelled him back towards Luqa with a hearty shove, before turning and racing up the next slope. Already the leading troopers were out of his sight in the smoke and dust.

Midway up the slope they began passing abandoned British positions. Bodies of both sides lay scattered everywhere in grotesque postures of death. Kuno stepped around two men locked in a death embrace, the German's hands wrapped round the Englander's throat, a knife twisted in the German's stomach still held in an iron grip by his opponent. Here and there a wounded man groaned, but there was no time to stop to tend the fallen.

Rifle fire intensified to his front and now he could hear voices as well, shouted curses in English and German and Italian, caught in brief snatches in lulls in the firing. The battle might be only yards away and still he could see nothing.

A Schmeisser fired, its short burst like tearing fabric. A second later another fired and this time Kuno saw the muzzle flash. Then more shapes were rushing at him out of the murk; three men rushing down the hill. He lifted his pistol, but strained to identify the uniform before firing. One of the men solved the dilemma for him by firing his rifle and felling one of the paratroopers a few meters in front of him. He aimed, but before he could fire other paratroopers cut all three Englishmen down with bursts of machine pistol fire.

Not breaking his stride he continued on up the hill, gasping for air now; his lungs felt like he was being suffocated. Spots danced before his eyes as oxygen deprivation began to hit. Another shape plunged towards him, thrusting a bayonet tipped rifle in front. Once again Kuno raised his pistol to fire and once again others beat him to it, cutting the Englander down in a hail of fire.

He forced himself forward, pumping his leaden legs with every ounce of reserve energy he had. And then he was atop the ridge, stumbling toward a line of sandbags at the rim of a trench. Bullets kicked the dirt around his feet and a buzzing sound raced past his left ear. He charged forward, past a burnt and blackened 2-pounder anti-tank gun sitting at the edge of a bomb crater, its carriage and one iron wheel smashed and the gun tipped over on its top.

He tumbled into the trench, landing painfully in the bottom atop a dead body, of which army he could not see. He struggled to his knees and then to his feet sucking the foul, dusty air into his lungs in great whooping gasps. Up and down the trench he saw a mixed bag of German and Italian infantry and German paratroopers lining the trench, firing over the rim into the darkness on the other side. One of the Italians suddenly cried out and sagged back to the bottom of the trench, dropping his rifle and clutching at his chest.

Kuno staggered to the trench rim and heaved himself up on the firing step. Poking his head above the rim he was startled by the appearance less than a meter away of a British soldier, bayonet pointed straight at his face. He ducked to one side as the Tommy lunged at him. The bayonet passed him by and the Tommy staggered to his knees, thrown off balance when he missed with his thrust. Kuno could hear the Englander gasping for air as frantically as he was. He pressed the muzzle of his pistol to the man's temple and fired. The soldier's momentum carried his lifeless body on into the trench.

He turned his gaze back out over the rim of the trench, down the hill towards where he knew Hal Far field lay, but he still couldn't see more than a few meters through the impenetrable limestone dust. More ghostly shapes raced towards the trench, even as the last of the paratroopers tumbled into it behind him. A whistle blew to his front and as though sprung from the very soil of Malta British soldiers materialized in front of him, charging with bayonets lowered. There was no time to prepare, no time to plan a proper defense or to establish a reserve force behind the trench to react to any British breakthroughs. All he could do now was fight for his own life and pray.

Kuno held his fire, letting the Schmeissers of his paratroopers tear into the English ranks, cutting men down in wide swaths. This was the kind of action that made the Schmeisser a deadly weapon; close range against packed ranks. He'd seen its murderous effects before, on the steppes of Russia, but here at Malta where so many German troopers carried it the impact of the MP 40 was incredible. Without armor support to suppress the German fire the English Tommies charged into the hail of lead and were mowed down in scores.

German troopers fired till they'd exhausted their magazines, then quickly swapped in a new one and continued. Still the British came on in a suicidal frenzy. Not even on the Eastern Front where the Russians held so little regard for their own lives had Kuno seen such determination in a frontal assault.

Slowly but inexorably the British worked their way closer and closer to the trench line. It was now clear to Kuno that had his own force arrived just moments later they'd have found the tables turned, with the British in possession of the trench and he and his men would have been on the receiving end of this fire.

A pair of shapes charged out of the mist directly towards him, firing their rifles from the hip as they ran. The paratrooper next to Kuno was caught while changing magazines and was struck in the throat by a bullet. He fell to the floor of the trench with an awful, gurgling cry. He lay there, thrashing and gasping, clutching his hands to his throat. Kuno lifted his pistol and fired, but his aim with his left hand was off and the two men kept coming at him. They'd spotted him now and were firing at him as well. He took a deep breath and held it before squeezing off the next round. One of the Englishmen staggered backwards, spun and fell on his face, but the other kept coming. Kuno adjusted his aim and fired again, hitting the man in the abdomen. Pain and anguish erupted on his face, but anger and determination were still there and he kept coming. Kuno fired again and the man fell face first into the dirt on the very rim of the trench, his wide, staring eyes now lifeless.

Kuno raised his head to look just over the man's body. He became aware that the volume of Machine Pistol fire was slackening; whether due to casualties or a shortage of ammunition he did not know. Still the British came on in ones and twos and small groups, probing for any point of weakness where they could retake a portion of the trench and then spread out through it. For the first time he began to consider the possibility of giving ground, of leaving the trench and retreating back the way they'd come.

With a shout a large group of ten or more Englanders charged the trench. Spread out over a ten-meter front they fired at anything that moved at the rim. With a bloodcurdling cry they surged forward. Luck was with them. Either all the nearby Schmeissers had exhausted their ammunition or were caught at the moment of exchanging magazines. Kuno was the only one to return fire, dropping two of the men with five shots. The others plunged into the trench leaping down literally atop several German defenders, knocking them to the floor of the trench.

Before they had a chance to finish off the Germans a trio of Italian infantry charged at them, swinging their rifle butts as clubs, striking one of the British a killing blow to the head and dropping another to the ground in agony with a blow to the stomach. The few seconds of reprieve gave Kuno the chance to eject his magazine and replace it with a fresh one, his weakened left arm trembling with the effort. He slammed the magazine home by striking it against his own helmet and fired into the mass of British in front of him. In seconds they were in a heap on the floor of the trench, their feet and legs all tangled together as they drew away from his pistol. One only had the presence of mind to take aim at him. From less than a meter away Kuno realized the man couldn't miss him, the bullet couldn't possibly go astray. He swung his pistol to fire, but knew that he was too late; the Tommy already had him dead to rights.

With a snarl the Tommy pulled the trigger. The hammer fell with a click on an empty chamber. The man looked down at the rifle that had betrayed him, then back up, wide-eyed just as Kuno fired and dropped him in his tracks. Other paratroopers had rallied to the short, sharp fight and were finishing off the Englishmen now. Kuno looked for the Italians. One lay dead, his face shot away. The second Eye-tie, a lieutenant knelt over the third, applying a battle dressing to a gaping bayonet wound in the man's shoulder. Kuno caught the Italian's eye and gave a quick nod of appreciation.

He stepped back to the trench rim and peered over the top. For the moment at least there were no more British in sight. The sound of firing died to an occasional rifle shot or short burst of Schmeisser fire. He wondered if the attack were finally broken or if it was just a lull before one more renewed effort, one last surge was made. Looking up and down the trench he saw Germans and

Italians alike treating the wounded and stripping the dead of weapons and ammunition. He knew each of his men had started the assault with at least four spare magazines. It was a measure of the battle's intensity that it seemed they'd just about used all their ammunition.

Kuno replaced his spent pistol magazine with a fresh one, noting he had just two left. He moved his two remaining spares into the front pocket of his tunic the better to reach them in a hurry. Then he rummaged among the dead nearby, coming up with a heavy revolver from a dead Tommy officer. It was a Navy Colt and was attached to the man's kit belt by a thick cord tied to a ring on the pistol butt. He drew his knife from its sheath and severed the cord. He ransacked the man's pockets, finding ten rounds. He checked the cylinder. Empty. He ejected the used shell casings and reloaded, putting the extra rounds in his pocket next to the spare magazines. He dug further among the dead and came up with a bayonet and a fragmentation grenade. He sank the bayonet into the wall of the trench to keep it handy, then painstakingly threaded the ring of the grenade onto a tab on his tunic so he could pull the grenade free and arm it with one hand.

His immediate needs met, he turned to the situation at hand. To call it desperate was an understatement. His force had only just repulsed a determined British counterattack and now was critically low on ammunition. Casualties were heavy, though not nearly so bad as they would have been had the British held the trench. For their part the British had suffered terribly. Heaps of dead and wounded lay in front of the trench and even in it. It was a ghastly scene, like some painting of a Napoleonic battlefield or a photograph of the trenches of the First World War. Kuno found small solace in the realization that only an even more desperate plight than his had led these British to such an attack in the face of the withering fire they'd met. He prayed that the British had had enough.

He detailed off two men to go back the way they'd come and return with as much ammunition as they could carry, then he set off down the trench in the direction he hoped to find Thaler. Along the way he paused to give encouragement to German and Italian alike. For once Germany's allies impressed him. He knew that if he should live to be a hundred he would never forget the three

Italians who jumped into the middle of ten Englanders, buying him the precious seconds to reload.

As he moved along the trench he found very few officers alive and uninjured. The price of leadership was high, he thought, yet he did not dwell on his own longevity or luck, he simply accepted it, in the quiet, but unshakable belief that despite the deadly perils he continued to face he would come through this battle safely.

He had only gone about fifty meters when he saw Thaler moving towards him in the trench. Thaler paused to pat a wounded man on the thigh and Kuno watched the Captain as he moved through his men. Thaler had an easy way with the men and Kuno could see he was well liked and respected by them. Kuno sat down to wait for Thaler to come to him.

"Good to see you alive, Major!" Thaler exclaimed with a smile.

"And you, Captain," Kuno replied. "We hold the ridge to the east to about two hundred meters past the taxi strip. How far to the right do our lines extend?"

Thaler turned and nodded towards the west. "We hold the crest of the ridge for about five hundred meters in that direction," he said. "But our right flank is in thin air right now. No contact at all with any of our forces to the west. If the British figure that out...."

"We'll be in a pretty pickle," Kuno finished the thought.

"I agree!" said Thaler heartily. "Most of the men have less than a full magazine of ammunition left. They are scrounging among the dead and wounded, even the Tommies for anything with which to repel another counterattack." A bullet thumped into the dirt above their heads and both men settled lower in the trench without interrupting the conversation. "Anyway," Thaler continued, "I don't believe we have the strength left to force our way onto the airfield alone."

Kuno nodded his head. "How many men left fit to fight Thaler?" he asked.

"From this end I've counted forty dead and seventy-four wounded," Thaler replied, nodding back down the trench in the direction from which he'd come. "Not many more than a few dozen of our own or Italian infantry left either." He paused a moment and shook his head. "The Italians acquitted themselves quite well," he said in wonder.

"Magnificently!" Kuno agreed.

"Anyway," Thaler went on, "I've sent men back for more ammunition, but whether they get back before the British attack again…." He let the sentence trail off.

"All right," said Kuno. "You go back to the right, I'll anchor the left and we'll see what fate brings us. No matter what we can't let this ridge line go back to the British," he said sternly. "It's already cost too much."

An explosion rocked the hillside, followed quickly by four more. Thaler ducked down next to Kuno before poking his head over the rim again.

"Light mortars," he said. "The British are getting the kitchen sink ready for us."

Kuno heaved himself to his feet. Crouching low he started back the way he'd come, stepping over and around the dead and wounded.

"Keep your head down Thaler," he shouted back over his shoulder.

As he returned to his position in the trench overlooking the Safi Strip the mortar barrage intensified. He estimated the British had twenty to thirty light mortars in the 50mm range in action. Soon they were on target, dropping the shells all along the crest of the ridge, making any movement out of the trench nearly impossible. Even lifting his head above the rim to assess the prospects of another British counterattack was difficult and when he did the cursed limestone dust the barrage was kicking up once again defeated his view.

A new note in the symphony of death came to his ears. Heavy explosions on Hal Far.

The German 120mm mortars were responding to the British barrage, poking blindly about hoping more to disrupt enemy movements than to actually knock out the British mortars. Still the barrage against the trench lessened somewhat and he was thankful for that, but occasionally a round landed directly in the trench and this meant further casualties among the surviving Germans and Italians.

A series of mortar rounds landed nearby and Kuno flattened himself to the trench floor. When they'd passed he sat up and realized the barrage had stopped. The German mortars still thumped down to the south, but the British shelling had ceased.

"Get ready!" Kuno shouted. "Get ready!"

The men he'd sent for ammunition chose this moment to make their final dash to safety. Scrambling on cut hands and bloodied knees they tumbled into the trench landing with thuds on its rocky bottom. Each man's pockets were laden with spare magazines, but just as important they had brought an MG 34 and three boxes of machine gun ammunition back with them. Both were winded from the long climb with their heavy load, but Kuno gave them no time to rest, quickly relieving them of the ammunition which was hurriedly distributed then sighting them with the machine gun at a bend in the trench where they would be able to fire effectively both to the left and right.

A voice shouted in English and rifle fire began to pepper the rim of the trench. Kuno drew his pistol and peeked over the edge. Still nothing could be seen through the smoke and dust, but he ducked back down quickly anyway as bullets were thudding into the earth all around him. He checked the men near him. They were all ready, German and Italian alike, hunkered down against the front wall of the trench, biding the moment to rise up and fire. From the volume of fire coming at them they all realized the British were counter-attacking in strength. Few had any illusions that they'd be able to hold.

Sporadic fire broke out as the Germans spotted the first targets coming at them out of the murk. But another sound was there as well, faint at first, almost a whisper of sound that he couldn't be sure he'd really heard, but then growing in strength until he was quite certain. He turned and looked back to the north, down on the taxiway between the two airfields. He strained to see through the dust and then a quirk of breeze lifted the dust for just a moment and he saw them. Just as quickly the dust settled once again, but the glimpse he'd had was enough.

Turning back to his men in the trench he shouted to them. "PANZERS! Our panzers have come!"

The word passed like an electric current down the trench. PANZERS! The Germans and their Italian allies were suddenly filled with hope. They turned with a new determination to meet the counterattack.

Kuno thought about the glimpse he'd had of the monstrous panzers. The Safi Strip was about thirty meters wide to accommodate the wingspans of the various aircraft the British shuttled between Luqa and Hal Far fields, but it was strewn with limestone boulders and pocked by bomb craters that the tanks had to skirt carefully to avoid throwing a track. German infantry was moving up cautiously along with the tanks, but were still over two hundred meters away.

The newly arrived MG 34 spat a short burst and then another. A moment later it was followed by a fusillade of rifle fire and a hoarse cheer as the British began their charge. Kuno peeked over the rim of the trench and gasped. Hundreds of British were racing towards them through the thinning haze. Ghostly shapes flitted and ducked into and out of bands of moonlight tinted smoke and dust in a surreal scene straight from Dante's view of Hell. The ridge crest and slope, absolutely devoid of any sign of vegetation or animal life might have been the surface inside some volcanic crater with sulfur vents spewing a foul and deadly miasma of poison gases that stopped men in their tracks and sent them tumbling to the ground writhing in agony or to lay still, never to move again.

Once more he withheld his own fire, knowing that this fight was going to come to him and that he'd need his few bullets at short range. He turned and gave one last look towards the tanks. The dust was definitely thinning, borne away on a breeze from the south, but while he could clearly hear the panzers now, even above the escalating firing, he couldn't see them. He estimated they might be less than a hundred meters away.

With a start he remembered his whistle. Pulling it from his tunic he began to blow into it, three quick chirps followed by three longer ones, over and over. The British to his front took note and veered towards the source of the sound, choosing it as their focal point. The MG 34 burped out a long stream of fire, cutting down a group of Tommies who made the mistake of bunching up.

With the British a mere fifteen meters from the crest of the ridge they lobbed a volley of hand grenades up at the German positions. A few sailed over the trench and a very few expertly pitched fell right in the trench, but most fell short and rolled or bounced towards the trench line. One rolled straight towards Kuno's face as he peered over the rim. Instinctively he reached out with his left hand and swatted it back the way it had come. He ducked back quickly just as the grenades started to go off.

WHAP, THUMP, CRACK. The fragmentation grenades exploded with a different sound depending on where they ended up, muffled in the trench or on the flat ground to either side. Dirt and gravel rained down on him at the bottom of the trench, his hands over his head.

Even before the last grenade exploded he was back on his feet. He knew the British were charging in right behind the grenades, using them to cover the last few desperate meters of ground. He pulled the grenade off his tunic, counted three and flipped it over the rim of the trench, letting it roll down the hill in front of him. It went off with a sharp crack just four or five meters away. Amidst the crack of its explosion he heard several men cry in pain.

Kuno jumped onto the firing step and leveled his pistol over the trench rim, firing at the shadowy shapes that filled his view. Few others of his men reacted as quickly and their fire seemed pitifully weak; certainly it was not enough to stop the British wave about to engulf them.

He dropped the whistle from his teeth and emptied his clip at the charging British. He knew he had no time to reload. Instead he dropped the Walther and dragged the Navy Colt from his waistband. It was heavy and unwieldy, especially as he was forced to fire it left handed. It kicked like a horse when he fired it, but with his first shot it knocked a Tommy backward off his feet. He took slow, deliberate aim at the groin of a charging soldier and fired again. The muzzle kicked up; blood burst from the man's chest, just below the throat.

He fell back against the wall of the trench and fired almost straight up at an Englishman as he dropped into the trench. The Tommy fell against him with a scream that faded slowly as they were both brought to the ground.

As he fell under the Tommy's weight he heard the sound of a heavy tank gun, followed swiftly by two more and then the sharp bursts of machine guns. He heaved the dead man away and struggled to stand as the 152mm howitzers of the KV II tanks fired at point blank range at the stone and cement road block the British defended across the Safi Strip. Jumping back on the firing he step he lifted the Colt over the rim and was surprised to see the British fleeing back down the hill away from the crest and the fire of the tanks. He held his fire, watching them flee pell-mell, back into the mist that still clung to the hillside in spite of the freshening breeze. Suddenly a gust of wind shredded the smoke and dust before him, lifting it like a curtain and there, twenty meters away stood a British officer, arms wind-milling above his head, rallying the troops. Already several had stopped their retreat and were slowly working their way back up the hill.

Kuno stared at the officer in his braided cap with the red band. Obviously this was a senior officer, perhaps even of field rank. He was also the oldest man Kuno had ever seen on a battlefield and he held great respect with his men for though they had been running for their lives a short moment before, now they were standing their ground and turning back to resume the attack. Others were coming up the hill behind them.

Kuno lifted the Colt, took aim as best he could manage and fired. The heavy pistol jerked up with the recoil. Nothing! He'd missed. Using the heel of his right palm he cocked the hammer back on the Colt again, and lifted it above the rim. He took a deep breath and held it before firing. Another miss! Once more he cocked the pistol and lifted it to aim. He had only one round left and he knew he'd never be able to load it again quickly enough. Just as he was about to fire several British troops passed in front of his line of fire, blocking the target. In frustration he lowered the pistol and looked first to his right and then his left. The nearest German troops to him on either side were oblivious to the man standing so few yards away, rallying the British to another attack. He lifted the pistol and waited, hoping the soldiers would move out of his line of fire.

One of the men stumbled to the ground and another leaned down to help him up, but the officer had moved several feet up the hill. Kuno shifted his aim and slowly squeezed down on the trigger. Out of the corner of his eye he saw another man moving into his line of fire, but he ignored him and gently squeezed off the shot, just as the soldier passed in front of him. Furious, he ducked to one side the better to see the British officer, but now he was nowhere to be seen. Kuno sidestepped down the trench, ignoring everything, but a burning need to know the fate of the officer. A thin curtain of dust slipped across his view again, but just as quickly was gone on the strengthening breeze. He strained to see.

There! A knot of British soldiers was kneeling on the ground.

Two had slung their rifles and were lifting a prone figure between them. The incipient rally sputtered and faded as the Tommies lost heart.

Kuno ran down the trench to the nearest German trooper still firing. He patted the man on the shoulder and pointed at the group of British now carrying the figure down the hill.

"Stop those men!" Kuno shouted.

The trooper nodded and aimed his Schmeisser, cutting loose a long burst, moving his fire back and forth in a short arc, ripping into the British. Two of the bearers and several other men fell. The others dropped their load and stumbled away a few yards before inching their way back.

"I am out of ammunition!" the paratrooper shouted at him.

"SHIT!" Kuno cursed and cast about for any sort of weapon. He reached to the bottom of the trench and lifted a British Lee-Enfield .303 rifle of the sort carried by British soldiers since the First World War. "Try this!" he shouted, shoving the rifle at the paratrooper.

The man hefted the unfamiliar weapon, nestling it tentatively in the crook of his shoulder. He took slow, deliberate aim and squeezed the trigger. At twenty meters he could hardly miss. Another of the British cried out, spun and fell to the ground. The others had had enough. They turned and fled.

Kuno took the time to reload the Navy Colt before struggling up over the trench rim. Moving cautiously he prodded each still form on the ground before him. He found several wounded among the British and he carefully moved any weapon out of reach of these before moving on.

Since spotting the officer he'd ignored all else, but now as he inched his way toward the elderly Englander the other sights and sounds of the battlefield intruded back on his consciousness. The crack of tank guns was steady and regular and seemed to be coming from the front to his left along with the chatter of machine guns. The sound of small arms diminished almost to silence; the only sounds were the moaning and crying of the wounded writhing in pain along the slope up to the crest. A young English soldier was sobbing piteously, crying "Mummy, Mummy," over and over.

Kuno approached the officer and now could see the General's stars on his lapel. He poked and prodded each of the men fallen nearby before approaching the General, first feeling for a pulse. Finding none he poked the body to provoke any reaction, but there was none. Kuno tucked the Colt into his waistband, careful to set the safety first and then knelt beside the dead British General. There was a neat hole in the center of his chest just below the sternum. A thin trickle of blood soaked the uniform there and Kuno saw the shot had been immediately fatal. He rifled through the man's trouser pockets first, rolling the body to either side to get into the hip pockets, coming up with a small stash of personal items, a comb, nail clippers, tobacco pipe and a book of matches then moving on to his tunic, checking the outside pockets. Nothing. He reached inside the tunic to check the shirt pockets passing his hand over the wound in the chest, presumably from the Colt now tucked in Kuno's jumpsuit. The shirt pockets were empty.

He was about to give up when he thought to check the tunic for inside pockets. There were two, one inside each lapel. The left side contained a paybook with a photo of its owner. Holding it to the dead man's face the likeness was unmistakable. He read the name and it was familiar to him, but he could not say why. Next he checked the right pocket where he found several sets of folded papers.

He unfolded them carefully, pausing to scan each before looking at the next. There were two letters in the little pile of documents. One was sealed and addressed as though it had yet to be delivered. The other was held in a torn and stained envelope. The paper was embossed with a coat-of-arms and the handwriting was vaguely feminine. Kuno stuffed the letter back in its envelope quickly with the uncomfortable feeling of being a voyeur, even though he neither read nor spoke English and he could make no sense of the letter.

He moved on to the next set of papers. These were immediately of more interest to him as they were obviously message flimsies, though he was unable to tell if they had been received or sent by the man whose body he'd found them on. Picking one of the messages he scanned down the page. Other than the date of June 23, 1942 he was again unable to translate and was about to refold the flimsy when something caught his eye. The name Rommel jumped off the page at him, in any language the same. He read the message carefully and as best he could phonetically. He recognized a few words such as the English word for gasoline and the name of the country Egypt, but little else. He folded the page carefully and went on to the second flimsy.

This message was also dated June 23, 1942 and bore the same address as the first. Kuno scanned it slowly. Midway down the page he gasped; a chill ran up his spine and his scalp tingled. Eyes widened in shock, he examined the word very carefully, holding the flimsy up to catch the moonlight. He stared at the word, so close in English to its spelling in German. He wondered if it could just be a coincidence, if somehow this similar word in English had a meaning entirely different than the name in German. Each letter of every word was printed in block, capital letters and it was impossible to say if the word was a name or not.

He studied this flimsy carefully, but could make almost nothing else of it, but as he refolded the message the certainty grew in his mind. Finally he folded all the papers together inside the pages of the paybook and tucked them into his inside tunic pocket. He turned around slowly until he found what he was looking for, one of many British rifles nearby, this one with its bayonet still affixed. He stood and planted the rifle in the ground next to the dead General, then knelt, removed the man's cap and placed it over the rifle butt. He wanted the body marked for a more thorough search later.

"Major Schacht!" Kuno turned around looking for the source of the call. "Major Schacht!"

A young Army Lieutenant stood at the crest of the ridge looking down into the trench, his Schmeisser cradled in his right arm.

"Here," responded Kuno, but his voice was just a croak. He hadn't realized how dry his throat was. He paused and unsnapped his canteen, taking his time to unscrew the cap and take a long swallow. The water was brackish and warm, drawn from the well near Luqa that morning and Kuno didn't know it then, but he was in for a case of the Malta Dog because of it. He screwed the cap back on and waved the canteen over his head.

"Here!" he shouted.

The Lieutenant spun about and scanned down the hill till his eyes fell on Kuno waving his arm. The young officer hopped over the trench and ran down to meet him.

"Colonel August sent me to locate you, Sir," he explained. "I am to tell you that our tanks have broken through and are on the flat ground of the airfield now. Colonel August requests you accompany me to meet him, Sir."

Kuno nodded his head.

"Of course, let's go."

The Lieutenant turned and led the way off the ridge, down and to the left towards the Safi Strip. The breeze had freshened considerably now and was blowing the dust and smoke from the battlefield. The south wind carried with it the smell of the sea and a hint of moisture. Tank guns continued to fire to the south, as did small arms and the occasional mortar, but these sounds were diminishing and seemed more distant. The fight was moving further away.

Kuno paused a moment and closed his eyes. He was dead tired and his body ached in a dozen different places. A cool breeze brushed his face. He opened his eyes and looked up at the sky. The clouds of dust that had enveloped him it seemed for hours were finally dissipating, torn apart and blown away on the freshening south wind. The moon shone through gaps and here and there stars twinkled in the sky. Coming back to earth he gazed out to the south. The wide expanse of Hal Far field lay before him. Squat dark shapes moved slowly about the field like monstrous turtles come ashore from the sea. Now and then one stopped and fired and the sound of small arms fire continued, but behind the tanks hundreds of German and Italian infantry and paratroopers were spreading out, clearing every trench and dugout of resistance. Already a long line of prisoners was being formed up and moved out at the northwest corner of the field.

Kuno shook his head. Just a half-hour earlier he'd been fighting for his life and had the British forced him off the crest of the ridge they might yet have defeated the invasion. He'd lost count of how many times the Axis had courted disaster in the four days since launching Operation Herkules. He looked down the hill. The young Lieutenant was standing a few meters away, watching him, waiting patiently. Kuno turned one last time to survey the crest of the hill. Axis troops were beginning to move among the bodies, seeking any wounded to aid. He shook his head again and picked his way over the bodies and around the stones down the hill.

<<<<<<<<<<<<<<<<<<<<<<<<<<<<

It was a fine, sunny morning with the kind of amazing clear blue skies that only a Mediterranean summer can bring. The smell of dust borne up on the south wind from the Sahara brought the promise of a hot afternoon. To the east Marsaxlokk Bay sparkled in the morning light with wind-tossed whitecaps pushed north past the breakwater by the gusting wind. The Khaimsin had returned to Malta. Behind him, to the south tendrils of black, oily smoke were scattered by the freshening wind.

A long column of dusty, forlorn prisoners marched slowly at the side of the road. They were headed north towards Grand Harbor for eventual evacuation. The Italian guards watched casually, rifles slung. Where after all could an escaped prisoner go on Malta?

The road cut inland as it passed Birzebbuga, leaving the waters of Marsaxlokk Bay behind. The Kubelwagen crept around obstacles in the road, the tumbled down wall of a house here, a bomb crater there, but the passengers didn't mind. They continued their journey in pleasant and companionable silence, enjoying these few moments of relative peace after the last four days of combat hell. Not until they came to a point in the road affording them a view straight up Grand Harbor to the sea did either man speak.

"Halt here a moment, driver," Colonel August said softly, as though he regretted the sound of his own voice.

The two officers stepped down out of the open-topped Kubelwagen and strode to the side of the road. For an instant they appreciated the inherent beauty of the harbor, with the limestone battlements towering above the quays, but then the reality of the war intruded. The harbor was An ugly, rainbow sheen of fuel oil covered the water in a greasy coat and everywhere they looked the waterline was fouled with a filthy black smear. Flotsam bobbed all over the harbor. Smashed docks and piers completed a picture of devastation. The only sign of life in the harbor came from a small, wooden torpedo boat. Flying the Italian flag it crept slowly across the harbor, taut wires stretched from its gunwales out into the water. The process of clearing the harbor for use had begun.

Sweeping it clear of mines was the first step.

Kuno and Colonel August looked at one another and returned to the car with not a word spoken. They continued their journey from Hal Far to Valletta. When they'd set out around mid-morning after a shave and a chance to wash up, a bit of sightseeing seemed just the thing, but now Kuno regretted it. Everywhere they went the natural and man-made beauty of the island was spoiled by war. Quaint villages were now filled with shabby hovels; picturesque waterfronts were polluted sewers.

They moved on into the built up areas at the base of the harbor, around a corner and into the city of Floriana, suburb of Valletta. Nearly every building lay in a shattered heap of crushed limestone blocks and splintered timbers. The cleared path in the road narrowed and narrowed further until finally the driver was forced to stop. The car could go no further.

"Perhaps the old town is in better shape," said Colonel August hopefully.

Kuno nodded and they dismounted again. German Military Police, Chaindogs as they were known in the service, moved through the streets, looking for any British service men that had so far eluded captivity. A squad of Italian soldiers stripped to bare chests had conscripted about a dozen male civilians to the task of clearing rubble from the street. The Maltese moved in a desultory fashion, surly and recalcitrant.

"Wait here for us," Colonel August instructed the driver. He and Kuno moved off down the street picking their way on a narrow, cleared footpath, at points not wide enough for them to walk side by side.

"This city is quite historic," Colonel August pointed out. "It was built by the leader of the Knights of Malta, a chap named Valette following the siege by the Turks centuries ago. All of Christendom hailed Malta for turning back the Islamic horde."

"A shame it had to be treated this way now," answered Kuno.

August sighed. "Yes, this war is a great pity."

"It was forced upon us," Kuno objected.

August laughed, short and humorless. "Oh, yes! I agree," he said. "Germany had no choice. If we are ever to prosper and breathe free we must fight." He stepped over a large stone that had rolled into the path. "Still, I wish that places like this could be spared. Not everything of the Old Order should be swept away. There is a place for antiquity."

Kuno looked at August, startled. These were very nearly his own words to himself prior to the assault on the heights at Mdina on the first day of the invasion.

Before he could say anything the drone of aero engines came to them on the hot south wind. They stopped and turned, looking to the south and west, finding the source of the sound. A flight of three Ju 52 transport aircraft circled the field at Ta Qali, swooping down low for a look at the runway. The "Auntie Jus" filed off to the north then settled in one by one to land on the field, dropping out of sight behind the ruined urban landscape.

"The runway is back in operation," observed Kuno.

"Yes, and a good thing too," responded the Colonel. "Over four thousand wounded await evacuation and that's just our own men and the Italians. There's no tally yet on prisoners needing medical attention."

"Do we have a count on our casualties?" Kuno asked.

August shrugged. "Preliminary numbers show the second division has lost over four thousand dead or missing, though I expect some of those may turn up yet. We freed a number of our men from a cavern to the west of Hal Far. They are mostly from the failed drops on Hal Far and Luqa." He shrugged again. "I have no idea how dearly the Italians paid for their amphibious landing on the island, of the losses in men and machines by the Air Force, or the Italian bloody navy," he said, bitterness creeping into his voice. "Surely thousands more all told."

"I hope Malta is worth it," said Kuno quietly.

"You will know soon enough, Kuno," replied the Colonel. "I have received your orders. Field Marshall Rommel is anxious for you to join him in Libya. He's asked that you be forwarded to him immediately." August turned to him and smiled. "A transport is due to pick you up this afternoon. It carries your own Army uniform and personal effects down from Sicily, then it's off to Benghazi for you!"

"A bit presumptuous of them don't you think?" snickered Kuno. "After this lot to just assume I'm even still alive!"

August laughed and slapped him on the back. "You're just like me Schacht! Indestructible!" The two men laughed together.

"I told my wife I was bound for a nice, safe staff job," Kuno observed wryly. "I haven't decided yet how to tell her about this detour."

The Colonel smiled and shook his head. "Rommel has a reputation of leading from the front, you know Kuno."

"Yes," he replied. "I expect there will be plenty of action in North Africa."

"Especially now," August agreed, nodding his head. "With Malta in our hands I'm told the next series of convoys are already forming to carry supplies and reinforcements to Rommel's army. I expect the new Field Marshall will be anxious to renew his offensive."

"On to Suez," said Kuno.

"And beyond," said the Colonel. "Rommel's strategic goal must be the oilfields of the Persian Gulf. If all goes well you have some very exotic travels ahead of you, Schacht."

The two men continued on down the path in silence, Kuno lost in thought about the strange wonders of the Arab world. They came at last to the Great Ditch, the ancient defense work that cut across the peninsula, separating the capitol city of Valletta from Floriana. They crossed through King's Gate and on into the old city, working their way down through bomb blasted streets, picking their way through the rubble till they came to a large open square. Several large craters made the square all but impassable and heaps of rubble on all sides seemed ready to collapse. Incredibly, a large stone statue on a pedestal on the far side of the square seemed untouched. Kuno and Colonel August stared at it for several minutes before either recognized the figure.

"I believe that must be Queen Victoria," said the Baron at last.

"Amazing!" said Kuno. "She appears unscratched in the midst of all this." He waved his bandaged hand at the destruction everywhere.

The two officers turned and went down a side street, making their way to Lascaris Bastion and the crenellated battlement that overlooked Grand Harbor. German intelligence knew that Malta's Military HQ was below Lascaris and a team of Chaindogs had taken possession of the site. Smoke drifted up from the mouth of an entrance cut into the living rock of the peninsula. British demolition parties had obviously done their work here.

The two officers who had become close friends in the short time they had known one another gazed out over the harbor, but once again they found it to be a filthy eyesore and they turned away.

"I have something for you Kuno," said August as they moved back up the spine of the peninsula the way they'd come. Kuno arched his eyebrow quizzically, but said nothing. August stopped and reached in his pocket.

"I received permission for this from Berlin this morning," the Colonel continued. "I am proud to present you with the Luftwaffe Ground Assault Badge." He reached up to Kuno's lapel and pinned the medal above his breast, then stepped back and snapped a salute. Kuno came to attention and solemnly returned the salute, suppressing a grimace at the pain in his broken right hand.

"So far as I know Kuno you are the only officer in the entire Army who has received this medal."

"Thank you, Colonel!" Kuno exclaimed. "This is a great honor!"

The Baron checked his watch. "Come," he said. "I am expected to meet a flight of dignitaries from Rome within the hour at Ta Qali. After that we should just have time to visit Calypso's cave before your flight is due to arrive."

The two men walked quickly back up the street to King's Gate, then across the Great Ditch, leaving Valletta behind. They turned the corner to the street where they'd left the car. Two hundreds meters away the driver was sitting on the boot making faces for three young Maltese children. The Italian work gang and their Maltese conscripts had moved on, as had the German Chaindogs. So far as Kuno could see they had done little but shift some rubble from one side of the street to the other. Besides themselves, the driver and the children the street was deserted.

Kuno started at the sound of shifting rocks amongst the ruins to his right. Instinctively he reached for his pistol, but the Walther was gone, left behind in the trench at Hal Far. The bulky Navy Colt was stuffed into his holster in its place. He rested his left hand on it as they walked towards the car.

"Relax Schacht!" chided the Baron.

Still a hundred meters to the car Kuno heard more noise among the ruins to their right. As they passed the remains of the Malta Telephone Exchange his nerves were a-tingle. A shiver ran down his spine. Suddenly out of the ruined doorway a shape detached itself from the other shadows. It jumped out into the street in front of them. Kuno yanked on the Navy Colt, but it was wedged into the holster made for a much smaller gun and it stuck. The young British soldier lifted his arm.

"GORDON!" he shouted and fired, just as the Colt finally came free.

Arthur Arbottle was nearly buried alive in the first moments of the attack. When the telephone exchange was bombed he and his friend Gordon were trapped in the doorway across the street, hemmed in by the moronic oafs he'd bumped into on return from his trip to Zita at Dolly's whorehouse in The Gut. What remained of the building collapsed on them all, as luck would have it with Arthur on the bottom of the pile. He lost consciousness amid the falling stone and timbers.

He awakened in total darkness barely able to move at all. One of the oafs lay across his body making it difficult even to breathe. It was a wonder he had not suffocated while unconscious. He squirmed and struggled but found that only his right hand and forearm had much freedom of movement at all. He'd shouted for help, but none came, probably because all the debris around him muffled his cries.

Shaking the oaf made no difference and it finally dawned on Arthur that the oaf was in fact dead. Only then did he remember that Gordon was with him. He called out to Gordon, but got no reply. Eventually he decided that Gordon too was dead and that he was the only one alive in the heap of bodies. Slowly, using only his right hand at first he began to shift debris. After hours of gasping labor he was finally able to ease the crushing weight across his chest and stomach and breathe a little easier.

Thirst began to torment him, especially as his fingernails could just reach what felt like a canteen clipped to the oaf's belt. He cried and screamed and shouted, and though he often heard the sounds of battle raging on the island he was never heard, or at least no one responded to his cries. In despair he slept.

He awakened as if from a bad dream, but the waking was worse. He now had a raging thirst and was still pinned almost motionless under the oaf and the collapsed building. He realized he was losing the feeling in his legs and was not sure if he was even able to still wiggle his toes.

The thought of paralysis energized Arthur. Working once again with just his right arm he dug steadily and relentlessly, clawing at the rubble till his fingertips were bloody and he'd lost most of his fingernails, but at long last he was able to shift his body under the oaf and to give his left arm some freedom. His throat choked with dust and in advanced stages of dehydration he slept again. He didn't know the time, but the invasion had been under way for nearly thirty-six hours when he awakened for the third time in an agony of thirst. He remembered the canteen of the oaf and he worked for over an hour to get his body in position to reach it. When he finally unclipped it, it contained just a few ounces of water, but they were heaven sent to Arthur and gave him the stamina to continue digging.

Finally, after more than two days pinned beneath the oaf's body in total darkness he was able to wriggle free, only to discover that he was still trapped. A heavy beam had fallen across a large pile of limestone blocks, supporting a triangular chamber barely three feet tall at its tip and five wide at the base. When he'd managed to restore the circulation to his legs he set about digging himself out of his mausoleum. He found that a breath of fresh air came to him from one side of the beam, so he started there, working in complete darkness, pulling out small chunks of debris at first and wedging aside larger pieces with a splinter of wooden beam. Working his way straight up he was soon inside a narrow chimney of rubble. Each piece he pulled free above his head he wiggled past his body and dropped at his feet like a mole tunneling the earth.

Throughout his ordeal he heard sounds of the battle raging over his head, but of course he had no idea where exactly the fighting was, much less who was winning. Oddly enough at this point he had just two thoughts that kept him digging. First, someone had to survive so Gordon's family would know what happened to him, and second to rejoin his unit, the Devons and to kill some of the Germans who'd done this to his friend.

His thirst returned, but there was no more water, only more stone to move. After burrowing through twelve feet of rubble he broke through to a hazy night sky with the full moon just past its zenith above. At the same moment that Kuno Schacht walked down the slope of the ridge to Hal Far airfield, Arthur Arbottle crawled free of the ruins and tumbled down to what was left of the street, adding to his collection of bruises.

The streets of Floriana were completely deserted. By this point the British had rounded up all their men and moved them out to Hal Far. Had Arthur moved up the peninsula toward Valletta he would have come to the Army guard station at King's Gate, not yet abandoned, but he moved back through Floriana in the general direction of the airfields. The few Maltese civilians left in the city at the start of the invasion had fled, or taken refuge in the deepest air raid shelters. If not for the sounds of the last stand at Hal Far field Arthur might have thought himself the last man on earth.

Crazed by thirst he began searching for water, staggering or crawling from one building to the next, searching for any moisture. He caught a cockroach and chewed it down, less out of hunger than thirst, but the bile taste only made him thirstier. By this time Arthur was quite insane. He didn't know why he took the pistol from the body of the M. P. down the block from the telephone exchange, but somehow in the back of his mind he still had one coherent thought; vengeance for Gordon.

Shortly after dawn Arthur found water. A few cupfuls had dripped from a broken pipe and collected in a basin in the lavatory of one of the ruined buildings. Stale and brackish and tasting of limestone Arthur drank it all, then leaned back to rest.

He awakened next to the sound of children laughing. He crawled to the edge of the rubble and peered out. After so long in darkness the morning sunlight was nearly blinding to him, but shading his eyes and looking up the street he saw a German sitting on the boot of a car, making faces at three Maltese children. He never wondered at how children could still find it within them to laugh after all that had befallen them. He only saw the German and the chance for revenge. He clutched the pistol and quietly began to crawl closer.

He'd gotten within fifty yards of the German when he heard voices down the street. Craning his neck over the rubble he saw two other men coming towards him at a brisk pace. He realized he needn't move other than to conceal himself and that they would come to him. He crouched in the shadows of the doorway and waited. He could still hear the sound of footsteps, but the conversation had ceased. In an agony of suspense he couldn't contain his impatience. He shifted to peer through a crack in the ruined entryway, setting loose a small torrent of pebbles by accident. He froze then heard a short laugh and a few words that he couldn't understand.

Judging the time was right he jumped out of the doorway with an incoherent cry. He could see now that they were officers! A worthy target. Lifting the pistol he pointed it at the Germans and shouted the one thing that came to mind.

"GORDON!"

He squeezed the trigger, once, twice, three times, barely able to aim at all and then one of the Germans had drawn his revolver and was firing it.

Kuno ducked the instant he saw the pistol come up in the young soldier's hand. Still struggling to draw the heavy Colt revolver with his left hand he dropped to one knee while the Tommy fired his pistol. The Colt finally came free and he leveled it with his left hand and fired. At a distance of just a few meters his aim was true and the young man fell back, the pistol clattering away from him among the rubble.

Colonel August also ducked when the Tommy fired, or so Kuno thought. Now the Baron lay flat on the ground, his face pressed into the street, his skin already an ashen white to match the limestone dust.

Kuno quickly felt over the Baron's back, searching for a wound. He finally found it down low on the left side below the kidney. An exit wound, it trickled blood. He gently rolled the Baron over on his back. The entry wound had already bled copiously, soaking the Baron's tunic and trouser tops. Kuno gripped his right sleeve with his left hand and yanked it down, tearing the sleeve from the tunic. He rolled it into a tight, hard mass and stuffed it directly into the wound, then rolled the Baron over again. He pulled his sling from his tunic pocket and stuffed the exit wound in the Baron's back with it. The driver came running as soon as he heard the shots. He skidded to a stop and knelt beside Kuno.

"Help me get him to the car!" Kuno ordered, "Quickly!"

The two men hefted the baron between them and hauled him the fifty meters to the Kubelwagen, Kuno's broken right hand howling in pain to protest the abuse. They gently laid the Baron von der Heydte in the back seat of the car and Kuno crawled in beside him.

"Ta Qali!" he shouted. "Hurry! We must get him to the aid station there."

The driver backed the car out of the street at breakneck speed, bouncing over rubble and debris until he came to a wide clearing where he could turn around. From there the drive to Ta Qali was made on the very edge of disaster. Twice the car skidded in loose gravel, coming within inches of careening off the road and into the ditch. Any time the driver could free a hand from the steering wheel he leaned it on the car horn, clearing the increasingly busy road in front of him. Axis troops and British prisoners alike leapt clear of the car's path.

Kuno kept watch on the plugs he'd forced into the two wounds to stem the Baron's bleeding. Both were sodden and beginning to drip within minutes. Amazingly, Colonel August regained consciousness as they approached the airfield. He seemed to be trying to speak and Kuno leaned close to his lips to hear.

"Of what do you dream, Kuno?" the Baron asked in the barest whisper.

Kuno sat back in confusion for a moment, then connected the question to the Baron's remarks when he'd wakened Kuno from his sleep that night at Mdina.

He leaned down close to the Baron. "I see my boys, Friedrich," he said, using the Baron's name for the first time. "I see them in uniform being buried."

"I too dream, Kuno. I dream of the bull."

Kuno shook his head. The bull. What could that mean? He dismissed it as the ravings of a gravely wounded man, but the Baron went on.

"You asked me about Crete, Kuno," the Baron whispered. "I dream of the Minotaur. He and I are trapped in the maze and he is pursuing me."

Once again, Kuno was confused. Crete? The Minotaur? The Maze? What was the Baron trying to tell him? Somewhere in the back of his mind swam a connection to ancient Greek mythology, but he couldn't put the pieces together.

"Save your strength Friedrich," said Kuno softly, stroking the injured man's hand. "We're almost to the surgeon. Hang on!"

The car careened around a corner and then bumped up onto the flat surface of the runway at Ta Qali. Kuno became aware that men were shouting at them as they raced past, but his eyes were riveted on the Colonel. He was plainly fading. Loss of blood had weakened him to the point he could no longer speak, but his eyes remained open and his hand was responsive to Kuno.

Once again the horn was blaring as the Kubelwagen hurtled off the runway, fishtailing in loose gravel before skidding to a sideways stop in front of the main surgical tent. The door of the car flew open and medical orderlies were there, pulling Kuno gently but firmly aside and lifting the Baron onto a stretcher. He was carried to a Doctor in blood stained apron standing near the entrance flap smoking a cigarette. The Doctor threw the butt down and quickly examined the Colonel.

"Take him inside immediately!" he ordered. "My table!"

Kuno reached out and gripped the Doctor's arm.

"Doctor, will he live?" he demanded.

"Not if you don't let go of me!" snarled the surgeon. He yanked his arm free and ran into the tent.

Kuno sat down on the running board of the car and held his face in his hands. The tragic, stupid waste of the Baron being killed now with the invasion won staggered him. He sat with his head in his hands for many minutes, caught in a fog of despair and anguish, his professional detachment shattered.

Finally he began to reawaken to events surrounding him. After the first flight of Ju 52s he and the Baron had seen from Valletta others had followed. Once again a steady stream of aircraft were landing on the field. Food and medical supplies were quickly off-loaded and the transports were turned around, each carrying a dozen or more critically wounded back to Sicily. Hundreds waited their turn, laid out on stretchers beside the runway, tormented by the mounting heat.

Kuno stood and surveyed the field. He realized he was standing just fifty meters from the bunker from which he'd commanded the anti-tank gun on the first day of the attack. Turning full circle he saw the tank that had crashed across his trench line that first morning. It stood now as the anchor for the southwest corner of the medical tent. Beside the tent a long line of German infantry and paratroopers mingled, waiting their turns for a mess kit of stew at a field kitchen. He suddenly realized he hadn't eaten in over a day, but somehow he still was not hungry.

To the north he saw a jumble of wrecked gliders, pushed and piled into a heap to clear the runway. To the west lay the heights at Mdina, gaping, jagged holes blasted in the ramparts of the ancient fortress and from the south the smell of smoke drifted up from Hal Far.

His attention returned to the Medical tent. How long had the Baron been in surgery? Kuno checked his watch and tried to calculate, but the best he could do was to estimate he'd brought Colonel August in about forty-five minutes earlier. He paced up and down impatiently.

"Major?"

Kuno looked up to find the blood stained Doctor staring at him.

"Are you all right, Major?" the Doctor asked. "Are you wounded?"

"My wounds have been treated, Doctor," Kuno replied. "What is the condition of the Colonel?"

The Doctor shook his head. "Colonel August's condition is critical. The bullet passed cleanly through him, but it has hit a kidney. In addition the Colonel has lost a lot of blood." The Doctor shrugged. "I've done everything I can for him here. I've stopped the bleeding and given him an emergency transfusion, but he needs more surgery if he is to live. I've placed him at the front of the line for immediate air evacuation."

"Can I see him?" Kuno demanded. "Is he conscious?"

"You can see him for a few moments if you hurry to the runway," the Doctor replied, "but he is heavily drugged. He may remain unconscious for several days."

"Thank you, Doctor!" Kuno exclaimed. Turning away he hurried around the tent towards the runway.

"Major, Schacht!"

Hearing his name he drew up short. Looking around he found the Baron's driver chasing after him.

"Yes?" he answered. "What is it? Quickly!"

"Sir, the Baron was scheduled to meet a group of dignitaries from Rome in just a few minutes," the driver reminded him "What am I to tell them?"

"Dignitaries?" asked Kuno angrily. "Dignitaries? You mean

men that don't fight and bleed and die?"

The driver just stood in front of him, turning his cap over nervously in his hands, a pained expression on his face.

Somehow then the anger drained from Kuno. He just felt incredibly tired.

"I will meet the dignitaries," he said "I will make the Baron's excuses for him."

"I'm sorry, Sir," the man whined, "but the plane has already landed." He pointed out to the runway where an Italian transport aircraft, painted in glaring white with the red emblem of the Regia Aeronautica was taxiing to a stop.

"We'd better hurry," Kuno said bitterly. "We mustn't keep the dignitaries waiting."

Kuno returned to the car with the driver. He sat in the front seat and closed his eyes briefly during the short trip to the Italian transport. When the car came to a stop he had to force them open again. He stepped out of the car, just as the exit door of the transport opened and the steps folded down. First out of the aircraft was a mustachioed Italian General in resplendent white uniform. A chest full of medals and ribbons and shoulders heavy with gold braid glittered in the bright morning sunlight. The General paused on the top step and surveyed the field. He frowned a moment then continued down the steps. He was followed by five other Italians of lesser rank, but barely fewer decorations before four German officers stepped from the plane. Last out were a pair of lowly privates, one each Italian and German. These hurried out in front of the General as though to clear his path as Kuno strode forward.

Kuno came to attention before the Italian General and introduced himself.

"I am Major Kuno Schacht of the German Army," he said formally. "I welcome you to Malta, Sir".

The General surveyed Kuno's dirty, torn uniform with obvious distaste. The Italian private turned to the General and chattered away translating Kuno's words. To Kuno it seemed the private spoke a long time for such a brief introduction. The General spoke, his eyes fixed imperiously on Kuno. When he finished the private bowed obsequiously to the General before turning to Kuno and translating.

"General-e Bastico asks a-where is Colonel Augusto? General-e

Bastico was expecting to be a-met by the senior German officer."

"Please tell the General that Colonel August has been wounded," Kuno replied, gritting his teeth. "He is already on his way back to Sicily for emergency treatment."

The private translated this exchange to Bastico. The General sniffed and pointed to the Kubelwagen as he spoke again.

"General-e Bastico asks is this his transportation?" the private translated. Then in an undertone he added, "General-e Bastico was expecting a reception with a-full military honors."

Kuno nearly laughed aloud, but controlled himself and replied, "Please make my apologies to General Bastico. At this time there are no military bands on Malta to provide the honors as befit his rank. Yes, this car is for his use. I am sorry that the limousines have not yet arrived from Sicily."

The private thought this reply over for a minute before translating back to the General. Kuno was quite certain the translation was not verbatim. He also noted the hint of smiles exchanged among the German officers from the plane who stood to one side observing the conversation. Finally the General spoke again.

"We will take this car to the headquarters of the Italian landing force," the private said.

Kuno softened a moment. "You will find many acts of bravery have been performed by Italian soldiers here," he said with sincerity. He turned and pointed to the Baron's driver. "This man can be your guide," he concluded with a bow to the General. Straightening up he snapped a salute that the Italian returned in a careless gesture. The General stalked off to the car, followed by his retinue. Kuno wondered without really caring one way or another if the General would notice the sticky pool of the Baron's blood in the back seat. A brief argument broke out among the Italians as they decided who would ride and who would walk.

Kuno turned to the German officers, looking at them in detail for the first time. They were a Luftwaffe Major, two army Captains wearing medical insignia and a Kriegsmarine Lieutenant.

"Gentlemen," he said. "Malta is at your disposal. I do not know what specific plans Colonel August had in greeting you. What are your expectations?"

"I am Major Galt here to begin the survey of the airfields," the airman replied. "Lieutenant Sickel is here for the harbors," he said, pointing at the Navy Officer. He paused and looked at the Army officers. "Captains Trowitz and Pfeifer are Doctors," he concluded.

Kuno turned to the Doctors. "Your services are sorely needed, Gentlemen," he said. "The aid station is just a few hundred meters to our south." The two medical men nodded and hurried back to the transport where they began directing the offloading of medical supplies.

"You can arrange transport to the harbors down near the aid station, Lieutenant," he said to the Navy man. "That's where you will be most likely to commandeer a car. And Major," he went on, "I assume you would wish to establish yourself here at Ta Qali as the only field currently in operation?"

"Yes, Major Schacht, that is correct."

"I am to board a flight for Africa soon and I must locate the ground control staff. Would you care to accompany me?"

"That would be most appreciated! Thank you Major!"

Kuno and the Luftwaffe Major began walking back towards the main runway where a Ju 52 was warming up its motors for takeoff. The two men walked in silence until the plane was off the ground and the roar of its engines had faded away to the north.

"This place has the stink of death," said the airman, wrinkling his nose. "My immediate impression is that the invasion had a very rough time."

"Rough is right!" exclaimed Kuno. "We're very lucky the British are not shepherding the whole invasion force into POW cages right now."

Galt looked at him. "What went wrong? Faulty planning? Was the drop off target?"

"No, no," said Kuno. "The operation was meticulously planned and every drop was right on target, at least here at Ta Qali."

"Then did we underestimate the British force?" pressed Galt.

"In a way," answered Kuno. "We underestimated their intelligence. They were ready and waiting for us."

Galt stopped in his tracks and stared as Kuno went on a pace or two before turning round, a curious look on his face.

"Of course, the British would have noted the build-up of gliders and transports on Sicily," said Galt.

"No doubt," said Kuno. "But this was different. In the very first minutes of the landings I noted whole platoons and companies of British soldiers in full kit." He shook his head. "The British knew this invasion was coming within a day or two. They definitely had advance warning."

Galt began walking again slowly.

"Major Schacht," he said after a moment. "Your impressions are very troubling. Would you say they were shared by Colonel August?"

"Absolutely!" snorted Kuno. "We discussed it several times."

Galt wore a thoughtful expression. "We'll have to look into the possibility of a spy," he said, almost to himself.

Something in the way Galt spoke pricked Kuno's attention. He looked at Galt carefully for the first time.

"You don't wear flier's wings, Major," he observed. "What part of the Luftwaffe do you belong to?"

Galt smiled thinly. "You are most observant Schacht!" he laughed. "My uniform is a ruse. I am in the Nachrichtendienst, here to establish a signals security center."

Kuno drew in his breath. The Nachrichtendienst! Military intelligence responsible for assessing enemy intentions and capabilities as well as for operational and signals security within the German Armed Forces.

"Major Galt," he said. "I wish to emphasize to you my conviction on this! The British absolutely knew we were coming. They responded within minutes to our landings where we expected at least an hour to gather ourselves on the ground. They very nearly destroyed the landing before the second drop could arrive. Only timely and accurate bombing by our planes saved the situation."

"I see," said Galt. "Operational security will bear investigation. I assure you we will look into this thoroughly."

The two men continued on their way. As they approached the runway Kuno let out a startled cry.

"Do you speak or read English, Galt?" he demanded.

"Yes, I am fluent in English," Galt answered.

Kuno stopped and reached into his pocket.

"What do you make of these documents?" he asked. He handed over the folded message flimsies, letters and paybook he had taken the night before.

Galt looked at the two envelopes quickly.

"Where did you get these?" he demanded.

"I killed a British General last night," Kuno replied. "I took these from his body."

Galt held up the open envelope.

"This is a letter to Lord Gort, the British Governor-General of the island," he said. "It appears to be from Lady Gort. This other is a return letter from him to her." He smiled. "A pity it will never be delivered," he said.

Galt turned his attention to the message flimsies, unfolding the first carefully. Kuno watched Galt, waiting expectantly. The contents of the message rocked Galt. Color drained from his face and his jaw hung slack. He stared at the message reading and re-reading it as if in disbelief.

In an agony of suspense Kuno blurted out, "Tell me, Galt, what does it say?"

Galt held the message up and Kuno noted the Intelligence officer's hand shook.

Finally, in a small voice Galt responded. "This is a message from the British high command addressed to Lord Gort," he began. "It announces the fall of Tobruk last week to the Afrika Korps."

"There's more to it than that, Galt," Kuno prodded. "What is it?"

Galt pointed into the middle paragraph of the message.

"This text here," he said, his voice still small and weak, "purports to be a translation of the text of a message General Rommel sent to OKW after Tobruk was taken."

"Surely such a message would have been encoded?" asked Kuno.

"Yes, surely," murmured Galt.

"Look at the other message, Galt," Kuno urged. "I noticed something in it that may be important also. See?" he asked, pointing at the word he'd recognized when he first looked at the note the night before. "Hercules! In English, spelled with a 'C' instead of a 'K', but it's the same word isn't it?"

"Yes," said Galt, "it is."

"The British even had the name of the operation didn't they?" asked Kuno.

"Yes," said Galt in shock. "They did."

Kuno boarded his flight at Ta Qali shortly after 1200 hours the afternoon of June 29th 1942, having never made it to Calypso's Cave, nor learned any more of the Baron von der Heydte's condition. The other passengers had flown down with the transport from Sicily and were all officers assigned to the German Military mission to North Africa. They stared curiously at the bedraggled paratrooper in torn jump tunic, but he turned aside their conversational gambits politely, but firmly. He watched the island of Malta recede behind them and then sat back on the uncomfortable bench seat. He felt he should try to eat something, and the other passengers offered him food, but being airborne again had his stomach tightening in knots and he declined the food.

He settled back to make the best of an uncomfortable two and a half hour flight to Benghazi. He slept and dreamed. For once his dream didn't involve the funeral of his boys and for this he was grateful, even as the dream unfolded, but soon his heart was racing and a cold fear gripped his heart. He was lost at night in a wilderness of tumbled boulders and scattered scrub brush. He wandered about, but everywhere he went he had the dread feeling that he'd seen it all and been there before. Soon he became aware of a presence away in the darkness. He was being stalked, but he could never catch a glimpse of his pursuer. He only knew that something horrible, something he could not quite identify was out there in the dark and it was looking for him.

Kuno's fellow passengers became alarmed as he first cried out in his sleep then broke out in a profuse sweat halfway to Benghazi. None were Doctors or medical corpsmen and there was nothing they could do for him, but wait for aid in Libya. The pilot of the Ju 52 radioed ahead that there was a medical emergency aboard and a Doctor and ambulance were waiting as the flight descended on the runway. Kuno was placed in a stretcher and carried to the ambulance, then taken to hospital where he lay unconscious for a day as the medical team fought to keep fluids in him. He had contracted the dreaded Malta Dog, amoebic dysentery and he was by no means the only Axis serviceman to suffer its effects as a reminder of his time on Malta. Hundreds of men were laid low by it and several deaths are recorded. By the time he was recovered enough to leave hospital and assume his duties as liaison officer to the Air Force events in the desert were shaping toward another climactic clash, on land, sea and air as Field Marshall Rommel and the Afrika Korp sought to conquer the British 8th Army, the Nile Delta and the Suez Canal.

This will be the tale told in *Operation Aida, The Gates of Victory.*

59604789R00410

Made in the USA
Lexington, KY
10 January 2017